Speak Right On

Mary E. Neighbour

Speak Right On
Dred Scott   A Novel

The Toby Press

First Edition 2006

The Toby Press LLC

POB 8531, New Milford, CT 06776-8531, USA

& POB 2455, London WIA 5WY, England

www.tobypress.com

ISBN 1 59264 144 X, *hardcover*

A CIP catalogue record for this title is
available from the British Library

Typeset in Garamond by Jerusalem Typesetting

Printed and bound in the United States by
Thomson-Shore Inc., Michigan

Contents

For Andrew
who reveals the signals in the noise

For I have neither wit, nor words, nor worth,
Action, nor utterance, nor the power of speech,
To stir men's blood. I only speak right on.
I tell you that which you yourselves do know.

William Shakespeare:
Mark Antony in Julius Caesar, *Act 3; sc. 2*

Prologue

Papa's grave is unmarked. Nor does Mother Earth reveal his burial site; she has leveled the barrow, reasserting her natural figure. I point to the tangled grass of Lot 177 and appeal to my son, "Harry, will you remember this is where your grandfather is buried?" That I alone can find this spot weighs on me, and the grievous reality galls my sensibilities that, even in death, the white man splinters our family.

Taylor Blow arranged to have my father reinterred here at Calvary after the Wesleyan Cemetery was abandoned. Defeated in my efforts to oppose his decision, I have similarly been powerless to secure additional family plots here. I am not even permitted to erect a headstone; that requires Taylor Blow's sanction, and I am too grudging to bring myself to petition him anew.

The first time we buried Papa, before the War, we had a headstone: "He who has done his best for his own time, has lived for all times." Mama and Eliza were still alive. I was thirteen, dazed by all that was occurring. Papa's body had been laid out before the hearth for two days, and wafts of camphor and ammonia coiled down my throat to nest like restless snakes in my stomach. Mama kept the windows and door open for me, but that September was particularly

I

cold and the constant hearth fire added its smoke to the miasma. Often the cross-currents caused the flames to jump about crazily, and I dreamed each night that the fire broke free and flames engulfed us all. At the funeral, a crush of strangers attended, many declaring what a great man my father was. The crowds and the words confused me; I couldn't recognize Papa in their midst. My confusion numbed me, and I didn't cry. To this day it torments me that I did not properly say goodbye.

Taylor Blow was there, tears on his cheeks as he eulogized Papa with that passage from *Julius Caesar*. In casting Papa as Mark Antony, did he see himself as Caesar—the good friend, wronged and martyred? What irony.

I should not be unkind. Were it not for Taylor Blow I would not be educated, I would not be free. Even the War would not have freed me, for without Taylor Blow helping my father get his plea to the Supreme Court, there likely would never have been a Civil War or Emancipation. I should be grateful, but Taylor Blow once owned my father. Taylor Blow, a Southern sympathizer, whom my father embraced as a friend, well-nigh as tenderly as kin. Taylor Blow, a white man, who continued to exercise ownership even after death so that my father lies buried alone here at Calvary and will remain separated from his family, despite having fought so hard to keep us all together.

My heart entombs this unforgiving resentment, and I try to leave no marker. I would not have my son's dreams haunted by my rancor. He is only eight; there are forces aplenty in this world that would snatch his innocence too soon. I wish my father were here to tell Harry how it was. Papa would have been able to tell a story, showing Harry the goodness that Papa believed in, which escapes me.

On our walk home, Harry and I pass a small group protesting the flattening of Big Mound. It is the last of many ancient burial sites in St. Louis. Some whites join the Indians, but of course to no avail. A long procession of wagons carts away the earth, and the resurrected artifacts are cremated in a great bonfire. Gusts from the river skitter the ashes along the ground and through the air. I breathe in something so foul it causes my gorge to rise—probably just fish rot from the wharves, yet I sense it is more: the stink has become memory, never to be eradicated, forever recalling death, decay, and feckless outrage. In a hundred years, who will remember why St. Louis is called "Mound City"? Will those Indian children be able to sustain a tradition of honoring their ancestors? The dead must make way for the living, I understand that, but must we erase their legacies?

At home, Harry helps me uncrate my dead sister's possessions. I have missed her so much that I have yet to open these boxes. I am looking for her interviews with my father. Before Papa died, he let Eliza write down all the stories he could tell: of his Gran, of the warrior women, of his life in slavery, and of his struggle to free his family. With care I root through dresses, blankets, a seeming library of books. Lingering over her collection of pressed flowers and their lost bouquet, I beseech her: Eliza, dear sister, child of the river, I pray you have kept those treasured stories safe.

At first, I am able to locate only the picture of him. After the Supreme Court decision, newsmen swarmed like gnats, and one made a daguerreotype of Papa's image. He is posed formally, he appears little and old, yet the picture captures a beloved expression: his relaxed lips smiling, his flared eyes pushing up his eyebrows and creasing his forehead. It is a good likeness. He doesn't look like a slave; not sullen, not guarded, not angry, not even sad. He looks like he has something to say.

Next I find Papa's polished clacking bones and old Joe's carved age-stick together in an antique cigar humidor. The bones have cracked and yellowed, looking like wood; the age-stick has hardened and whitened, looking like bone. Harry wants to know what these things were used for.

I place the bones on either side of my middle finger and tattle a simple rhythm. Their chatter is surprisingly high-pitched, and a little hollow. "These are musical," I say, "and this—" I pick up the age-stick with my free hand. It is quite beautiful; crude and complex, elusive and evocative. It is history. Testimony. A summons. Wielding it, I feel a childish thrill of wonder and joy, as if I had been handed the dawn and told to fashion the day. "This," I continue, passing it

3

along to Harry, "is an age-stick. Slaves used to make them, each one telling the story of a life." Harry fingers the notches on the age-stick, squinches his eyes in puzzlement.

"There's a story for both of these keepsakes," I say. "If I can only find the pages my sister wrote."

As I rummage, Harry tosses the age-stick back into the box. He has grown disinterested in what he cannot understand. He asks, "Is it true Grandpa started the War?"

The question cuts me. So much was lost during the War. "Some say so," I answer.

"Because he killed white people?"

Imagining the schoolyard boasts that gave rise to such an idea, I hug him around the waist and draw him close. "No, Grandpa's weapons were words. His strength was his stories." At that moment I spy a leather portfolio with the brittle pages—those that survived the War, at any rate—that hold Papa's stories. The first thing I pull from the portfolio is a handbill from 1854, printed on a half-sheet of thick stock. I read aloud to Harry:

> *I thought it hard that white men should draw a line of their own on the face of the earth and on one side of which a black man was to become no man at all, and never say a word to the black man about it until they got him on that side of the line....*

"These are your grandfather's words," I tell him. I don't recognize this pamphlet, but I do recognize Papa's sentiment, and the long-legged sentences he often used—although the printer obviously citified Papa's country grammar. I flip the card over:

> *There is not a drop of the white man's blood in my veins. My ancestors were free people of Africa....*

"That means your ancestors, Harry, were free people of Africa too. Some were warriors and some—like your grandfather—were storytellers, called griots. While some people do regard your grandfather as a warrior of sorts, mostly he carried on the griot tradition." I shake the pages of the portfolio. "These are all his stories."

"Grandpa read these to you when you were little?"

"Griots don't read their stories; they tell them out loud, they perform them. In winter, Papa might tell his tales by the fire, as you and I sit now. But the cold had to be very intense to send him indoors. He preferred to be outdoors, usually on the porch. That's where I remember him best, with the sky turning twilit behind him." I pull Harry onto my lap, thankful he doesn't protest he is too big.

"In those days we lived down on the alley behind 11th Street, in a small, wooden shanty tucked behind the big houses where the white people lived. Dozens of those two-room, one-door boxes lined dank, mud-rutted backstreets that were less thoroughfares for traffic than an organized grid of open trenches for raw sewage. Go ahead, crinkle your nose, but truth to tell the sewage was just a lazy trace smell beneath homier odors of hay, manure, trashpit fires, and the simmering chicken stock vapors from Mama's cooking fire in the dooryard. Oh yes, in those days we typically had our cooking fires outdoors.

"The worst thing about the heavy air was how it labored Papa's breathing. His words were clear enough, weighted with the confidence of an old man looking back, yet they were frizzed by the consumption that would soon claim him. In the last few years, his voice became like custard: whipped full of air, with a slight crust.

"He often told his tales just before first dark, when the dust and the smells of the day sank into the earth. Mama'd bring out tea and set beside Papa. That porch barely accommodated the three hickory rockers Papa had made, so I often sat on the woodplank floor, leaning against Eliza's knees. Overhead a canvas awning stretched from the soffit to two sycamore saplings in the yard, but the low, setting rays stubbornly slanted in beneath the canvas.

"Papa always began a story the same way, the way his griot ancestors once did: he drew a deep breath and puffed twice, 'uh-uh.' His eyes widened and roamed out to the horizon and back again to us. His arm beckoned, as though to a friend approaching from the distance. He would chant, 'A story, a story! Let it go, let it come.'

"Eliza or I would give back the ritual response: 'Good! Let us be off!'

"Then Papa began, emphasizing the old Virginia dialect, a drawl that never hurried his story. He stood and moved about, acting out the parts. Given how cramped we all were, it's a good thing your Grandpa was small, graceful too. When he moved, it was a force like fire: fluid and captivating, even when he was old.

"Eventually, of course, he got too sick to stand. Then he let his hands perform. Papa's fingers rapped smartly on the arm of his rocker, setting a rhythm to his tale. Or his palms brushed together, bouncing up and down on his thigh in a more complex beat, a percussion exotic and intricate, his hands blurring like hummingbird wings."

"Show me, Mama. Tell me one of Grandpa's tales."

Suddenly I feel closer to my father than I have for a decade. I stand before our hearthfire and in my best imitation, attempt to echo Papa's husky drawl and relaxed parlance. My fingers snap to the tempo of a tale he had repeated many times. I puff twice, "Uh-uh. A story, a story! Let it go, let it come."

Harry, remembering, urges, "Let us be off!"

I begin: "At the beginning of the world, god set down two satchels. The white man come along, opened the one, and claimed the paper and pencil. The black man come along, opened the other, and brung up the hoe and reed flute.

"Some say this explain why the black man be slave to the white man, but I say all it explain is the white man and his books." My palms rustle in a brief pat-a-cake. "White folk treasure they books, sure 'nough."

Harry cocks an ear toward me. "That's it?"

"This story is done, but it's just the first link in a long line of stories—another is waiting patiently for its turn." I pick up the portfolio and pass it to Harry. "Do you want to try reading one?"

Chapter one

Upriver, Downriver

I love a good story, always did, but I don't care so much about books. That's a difference you find with black folk. White children, see, grow up hearing the same story told over and over again the same way. Whether it be a fairytale or a history lesson, each time the book be opened, it be the same old story. Whilst black children grow hearing the story told different all the time. My kin never trucked in no books. Tales was all told out loud, the African way. All the village folk'd gather round the great fire whilst somebody would stand—couldn't tell a story proper without moving to it. A story's got to sway and mark time. Later another somebody'd get up and tell—perform—the same story, yet tell it different, in a contest to see who could give it over best.

My Gran used to tell a story each and every night but she never told one the same way twice, and she'd all the time have that knack for knowing the right time to tell which one. That's the knowing of the griot, and Gran passed it down to me. You'll never get that from no book. Gran's story ability come from her papa, a trader up and down a big old river in Africa. He done learned the different tongues of the people along the way, and he picked up stories from this village

7

and that. He used to say a story's got two sides to it: a upriver side and a downriver side. Upriver he heared the stories, and as he traveled and thought through them, the meaning took hold. Downriver he told them, quilted-like with things he hisself knowed.

This here's my downriver story. I don't expect there's many more upriver ones left for me. But that's how it should be. This here will be a upriver story for my two gals, till they start telling they own downriver tales. Sure 'nough, the griot blood runs in they veins, too.

Very respected folk, them griots, 'cause they told the tales and kept the history, both. The stories are the history. Like the satchels tale—puts me in mind of the dream my Gran used to tell, a dream what come to her the day 'fore I got born. She dreamed of Nana-Buluku, the one god, setting down two satchels. Gran, 'course, knowed this part of her dream to be the old folktale. But her dream moved on beyond that. She next seed a small child, what she understood to be her as yet unborn grandchild—me. I go to one satchel and pull out the hoe and the reed flute. I begin to play that flute so beautiful it conjures the great serpent Da, what done helped Nana-Buluku to create all the world and everything in it. That's why rivers and mountains go all twisty, 'cause of the way Da slithered along. Then, once the world got filled with trees and rivers and mountains and critters and people, it become so heavy that Nana-Buluku told Da to coil up beneath the world, so as to keep it from toppling over.

But in Gran's dream, there's Da, come forth to the sound of my flute—and sure 'nough, don't the earth begin to jiggle and shake? Even I's scared. I stop my flute playing and call, "Go back, Da, go back." But Da does not go back.

"It is the wish of Nana-Buluku that you play your flute for all the world to hear," he says, "and if the world trembles and rolls, that too is the wish of Nana-Buluku."

Then Da puts me on his back and carries me away.

8

Chapter two

Warrier Women

I ain't boasting. Gran told that story about me and Da to help keep me rooted. Us black folk been sent, summoned, and scattered about the world, disallowed to grow roots. Ain't I been took all over this country—from V'ginia to Alabama to Missouri, on up to Wisconsin Territory and all the way down to the Texas border—without no choice about the going? But each time I get yanked up, I recollect Gran's dream, and each time I know how Gran is my root, and I's her branch.

That's what it means to have kin, and even iffen I never got as good as Gran at storytelling, I got a bit of the griot in me. I got the stories, upriver-n-downriver, of them trader men what roamed where they liked. And I got the blood and bone of them warrior women, too, what stood strong against hunters on two feet and four. That's right: womenfolk amongst my kin was warriors.

Often as a boy I'd pester Gran for them tales. "Come up to my hug," she'd say, and I'd curl up betwixt her lap and her hug, resting my head on her breast, feeling the stories come outten her, with her soft cinnamon smell wrapped round me. I must've asked Gran for one in particular more'n a hundred times: tell me, Gran, tell about

Nyota's rising up. Not always would she tell that story, but in telling it she wagged her finger in my face: "Mind you listen good, Dred. Listen inside. Our kin be talking to us."

My kin was Fon people, come from a place called Dahomey, back there along the River Mono, back where they was free. They lived where the womenfolk trained to fight as soldiers to protect the village. Wearing horns on they heads, they carried machetes, sling-shots, and bows with poisoned arrows. They carved pictures of big old bull elephants on they shields, signifying they would trample the enemy. They had spies, too, and most times learned iffen another village was stretching eyes at them. They'd go and attack first, beating the breath outten everybody they found. Even the men of other villages feared to face them.

Gran's gran was such a soldier. Nyota, which means warrior, was knowed for her killing aim with the slingshot. Along with her two sisters she fought many battles, fought deadly. She had a pink-moon scar under her chin where the enemy one time tried to take her head off, 'cept Nyota got the enemy's head off first.

'Course, by the time Gran knowed her, Nyota's a grandmother and not out in the jungle no more. She's still mighty, but mostly she stays in the village as a guard. Till one day Nyota and her village was attacked when they wasn't expecting it, overrun by the Oyo people, and all my kin what was there that day was made slaves: old Nyota and her daughter, Njeri, and Njeri's daughter, Sanjo, which was Gran's name when she was a girl.

Gran was only about five then, and she didn't know she was a Oyo slave. The worst of it was how she missed her father, spent every hour watching for him to appear and take her home. Other than that, her days was much the same, working alongside her mother. Only they wasn't tending they own house now. She and Njeri was put to work for some white missionaries and traders. Mostly they tended the house and garden of a priest, a white man what learned Gran Bible stories. She liked them Bible stories 'cause it put a light on why the white people acted how they did.

By the time Gran was hardly ten, though, she and the rest of my kin got sold again, this time to slave traders. They was led with hundreds of other Africans to a prison fort on the coast. Marched for weeks. Once there, in crowd and filth and hunger, they waited. Likely they never knowed what they was waiting for, nor what was waiting for them. Still, Nyota knowed these changes meant trouble. A warrior to the end, she tried to free everybody. She led a escape, and it were so smart. Stripped of slingshot, stripped of poisoned spear, stripped of machete, she armed them people with all they had left: theyselves.

⁂

The slave fort was a stoneblock, medieval structure with turrets and thick wooden gates secured by an iron beam that locked in place. An infernal clamor echoed along its chambers and walls, but the noise wasn't from the hundreds of slaves—they huddled scared and silent in dungeon chambers. The racket came from the regiments of guards who drilled, caroused drunkenly, shouted orders, and cursed the sun and the slaves.

A bored guard slouched at his post with another sentry, monitoring a long tunnel of cells. Beneath the din of regular slave business, they heard a cushioned, heavy vibration, a single thump. Chasing down the noise one said, "Sounds like a body hurled across a cell," then immediately realized there was no room in any of the pens to throw a body. The slave ships were overdue, the fort was packed beyond capacity. After inspecting several stalls that showed no sign of disturbance, they paused outside Nyota's cage, surprised by the peculiar arrangement of the slaves inside. In parade formation, the slaves stood shoulder to shoulder, wall to wall, ten rows deep. These were mostly women, the so-called Amazons. The sentries had been warned to take special precautions with them.

Nyota stood alone, facing her brigade, her back to the guards and the metal bars. She was a rhinoceros of a woman: a hulking, muscular torso, stubby limbs, a wrestler's neck and shoulders. The guards shouted at her, but she didn't turn. One poked a musket muzzle into her back, and she yodeled a single ululation, not in pain or in protest but in command. Her troops roared and stomped their feet.

A tremor ran up from the packed-earth floor, and the guards

readied their rifles. Nyota whipped around, gracefully pivoting on one foot, and with another command a hundred grimacing grotesques confronted the captors. Each slave's face contorted into bizarre leers and snarls; tongues slithered out from between bared teeth. The guards fumbled backwards. Then, as if faced with nothing more than a child's prank, they returned to their post, laughing half-heartedly. They continued to ignore subsequent protests, believing the thumps and grunts were just slave antics. Not even the officers suspected the true nature of those military exercises, even when slaves in other cages began adopting the ritual, even when it expanded to include the chanting: a monotonous, dull, low chorus answering the simple, contrapuntal rhythm of Nyota's calls, while the stomps beat furiously underneath the cyclic phrase.

For a week the feverish rite infected more and more slaves, but the symptoms of this strange frenzy were suffered by the guards. Many grew irritable, haunted by headaches and nightmares, yet they lived with it because nothing deterred the bizarre behavior. Not a dousing, that left the slaves to shiver through the night. Not withheld rations. Not beatings—though they were loath to give beatings; they understood the risk of a battle with such a mob.

Finally, one night when the temperature had dropped and the air was still, when the waters of the Endless Lake lay calm and the owl's cry carried for miles, in the midnight lull when the prison hubbub subsided, Nyota led the revolt. Thousands of captives within the prison began humming, following the rhythm she set with her hands. They punctuated the drone with stomps, and throughout the small hours their whomps and howls intensified.

Guards felt their blood seethe; sight flickered; ears popped. The earth began to tremble and roll. Dust cascaded from beams into chinks that blossomed in the hard, mud floor. Cups on tables and whips on the wall skittered and swayed. Mortar cracked and wood creaked. Insects and lizards scurried from crevices. Rats decamped and even some of the patrol deserted as the violence of the tremors rose with the volume of the chants.

Too late, an officer understood the noise was a weapon. He alerted the Major that the entire prison could crumble if they didn't stop the infernal bawling and bumping. The Major scoffed, until a door to a pen finally burst at the hinge from the buzzing pressure. He gave the command to use muskets, lashes, and ropes to subdue the rush of loosed slaves.

⁂

Nyota's call to rise up might've become a victory song iffen the chanting and stomping done lasted longer. That whole prison might've crumbled like a sugar cube in her fist. But it weren't to be. After a few of the cage doors loosed, slaves begun running and shouting, breaking the vibration and so giving up the only weapon they had.

You ever think of your voice as a weapon? Not many people do. I think of it, often. Like each time I went up to that courthouse, I went to sign my mark on another piece of paper holding my words—words that maybe was gonna get me freedom.

Sometimes, though, I would see them slave auctions on the courthouse steps. Nnn, nnn, nnn! The same place what can tell me I's free is the same place what rips apart family after family. I seed the chained coffles being dragged from the courthouse to the docks. Seed the fathers' shoulders humped in shame. Seed how fear and unknowing whittled the faces of the young'ns into death-masks. I felt something animal-like scramble up my throat when I thought of my own two gals being sold away. I ain't a fighting man, but I think it's the blood of my warrior kin, pumping to the rhythm of Nyota's rebellion.

Chapter three

Middle Passage

Nyota never made it outten the prison. She got killed in the uprising, leaving her daugher, Njeri, alone and wondering how to protect her three children. Yes, three: there was my Gran, called Sanjo. Then there was the twins, two baby boys what Njeri done birthed back in Oyo. They was all left to make that terrible middle passage alone. Well, theyselves and about four hundred other slaves, but they was alone all the same.

You ever hear tell of that middle passage journey? You done read about it, but see, I heared the rememory direct from somebody what endured the not-knowing and the being stripped naked. Endured the terrible certainty that nary a thing be in your control; you can't even control what spills out your body, and whether or not you lie there itching in it for days and weeks—till you be wrapped in your own dung, pus, and vomit like a second skin so thick you stop being able to know the difference betwixt the little varmints hopping and crawling over you and the itch and twitch of your own skin breaking out in rash from all that filth. No, you only can know for sure when the rats crawl on you, 'cause they got heft, 'cause they the only thing getting fatter day by day. That's all the knowing you got: the rats and the crazed itching. Everything else is why.

Gran didn't ask why, but her mama did. Njeri asked why, never stopped. Her whys crashed through her thoughts the way the surf claws at the sand, slipping back away. It never takes hold, yet it changes the shape of the sand. The crashing waves of why done changed Njeri's mind and the shape of her soul. Which explains Gran wagging her finger in my face when she done told the rest of the story about our kin. "This ain't like my other stories," she'd say. "Them other stories I tell the way I stack wood on a fire: to make the fire blaze and throw out heat. But this part about the middle passage be more like a flooding rain: you got to stand solid to get through this kind of story."

᠈ᠷ

To tell the story of her mother's transfiguration, Gran altered her voice to sound like her mother: each utterance like swallowed sand, soft and so dry it caused a pain just to come up the throat. Gran performed; she was a griot. She swayed from the waist like someone on a boat, like someone praying.

Njeri prayed to Bon Dieu, a Christian god varnished over an African god. She had stopped praying to the familiar Ioa, spirits that the white priest called "saints." Although the white priest said that the Ioa saints knew everything, could be everywhere, Njeri believed none of them had left the shore. Only Bon Dieu was left. Or so she hoped. So she prayed. And in all her prayers, Njeri asked: Why?

On her back on a splintery wooden plank less than three-feet wide, she prayed. Her legs, shackled, could move but a little. The twins, one at each armpit, fear-clutched her breasts if they were awake. It used to hurt, but now they slept most of the time; when the ship rolled she had to pinch their naked skin to keep them from falling to the filthy floor. Beside her, facing in the opposite direction, Sanjo was laid out. On Njeri's other side, another slave woman's feet defined the limit of her world, which kept shrinking and shrinking.

She barely cared anymore. Her life was an education in how to do without. Only in her dreams did she revisit all that she had lost, like the fragrant herb garden she tended as a girl; the hut she slept in with her sisters; Bogi, her dog; the boy with the triangle scar on his cheek and the reed whistle he made her. In her dreams she revisited the rich legends of her people that she had been schooled in, replaced now by a white god and a blue woman and their thin son dripping red blood on a wood plank.

Njeri had learned, as well, to do without her husband—whom she never saw again after the Oyo captured all the women. He didn't even visit her dreams, and that made her so lonely. She had learned to live without the hope that he might someday find and rescue them; that he, like her father, might still be traveling the trade routes, up and down that wagging tongue of a river that also she could do without. She long ago put away those things of her past and learned to live without them.

Each day, Njeri's world shrank a little more, and she learned to do without things that once had seemed essential in her life: walking freely, breathing deeply, speaking her thoughts, and eating, too, for days at a time. She could do without all of that, and she did. In fact, Njeri learned that she could even do without her mother. In the weeks since her mother had died, she learned to do without talking to Nyota, or asking her advice, or even remembering her.

Yet she could not do without Bon Dieu. She could not do without asking why. "Why" festered like the blisters that laced her back and buttocks, and she questioned Bon Dieu all her waking hours and even in her sleep.

"Are you listening, Bon Dieu?" she asked, trapped within the house that floats, thinking: So many cry out to you that I am not surprised you do not hear me.

Her cries were just whispers now, anyway. The whites gave the Africans no water to slake their thirst, no food to fill their bellies, no air to breathe in that swilling pissoir. Her twins, at either breast, eventually gave up. They and Sanjo rarely woke anymore, and Njeri gave thanks to Bon Dieu for at least sending her children sleep.

Such a great honor, she felt, that Bon Dieu had given her twins like Mawu and Lisa, the sacred twins of Nana-Buluku! When her twins were born, she thought all those fires she had lit to the

Blessed Mary must have pleased her. Mary probably spoke favorably to Bon Dieu, so that he sent Njeri twins. When they were born she thought, surely, he meant to show her life could feel like a gift again. That maybe her family would be whole again, living all together again. Or at the very least, their master, father to the twins, might act more kindly.

Instead, he sold them all to the whites.

Instead, her mother died in that fort.

Instead, her milk dried up, and the cries of misery from her babies racked her. She saw them slip from bad to worse to wretchedness. Njeri's anguish became constant.

Silently she prayed to be like the Holy Mother, to accept Bon Dieu's will, but she failed to understand how. She prayed: How, Bon Dieu? Don't you want to see them comforted? You could bear to see men nail your son to wooden boards, but I cannot bear much more of my babies' misery.

Each day there was less and less that she could do for them. She weakened. She was nearly as helpless as they. Their hunger inflated her own. Her belly swelled from a glut of hunger. Of the little bit of mash slopped out, she gave most of it to her twins, though it wasn't enough. In between feedings she offered her fingers for them to gnaw on, but they were not fooled. Oh, and their crying! She could not bear their crying—finally just whimpering. She cried into their crying mouths to replenish their water, until she dried up completely—a dry flake in a floating wooden house, surrounded by water. Deliriously she thought: "You have a sense of humor, Bon Dieu."

Finally she was totally dry. No sweat, no tears, no milk, not even urine. She had nothing left to offer her children. She was barely even a woman anymore. After the birth of the twins, the blood from her womb never flowed again. Although she found that she could still bleed—in a hazy desperation she punctured each index finger with splinters from those planks they called beds, and she poked her bleeding fingers into their mouths for them to suck on. This need to do something for them, to mother them, drove her senseless.

She swooned.

When she awakened, Sanjo was gone.

In her panic, she remembered she had a heart. She had forgotten it; Sanjo's absence resuscitated it. It beat now in slow, rough, irregular thumps, like a distracted woman beating a rug. Her thoughts raced, trying to understand. This was not the regular time that the slaves were brought on deck in small groups, to be doused with sea water and made to hop and shake in a parody of dancing. Yet it also was not night, the time when the whites snatched up one or two for their foul appetites. And surely Sanjo had not escaped. Had spirits come to save her? Had Bon Dieu answered her?

Sanjo's absence left a gaping hole beside Njeri, a dense shadow eclipsing all else, as big outside her body as the swollen hunger that filled her body. For the first time she noticed how big the belly of the ship was. All that time on the water, she had only noticed before how crowded, how suffocatingly stacked all the bodies were. Now she felt isolated, abandoned in a big, black pit.

With her loneliness came fear. Then came shame, because she understood this was a test; Bon Dieu was challenging her to feel like a mother again, like her own mother would feel: fierce and protective. Instead Njeri felt like a child, alone and scared. She felt not a mother, not a person, just a small, dark, shivery thing, a thin cobweb stretched to its breaking between fear and shame. She hung that way a long, long time.

When Sanjo finally was returned from above, Njeri became a person again, a mother ready to defend. As the sailors chained her daughter down, Njeri tried to spit on the one nearest, but she was sapless. He took no notice and absent-mindedly mumbled that word the whites said when someone sneezed.

Then they were gone—they spent as little time as possible down there, holding their breath like men diving under water.

With Sanjo filling the emptiness beside her, Njeri's heart beat rhythmically again, then faltered as she watched a single tear trickle down her daughter's cheek. She thought: Precious water, gone to waste.

"Where have they taken you, daughter?" she asked. But Sanjo did not reply. Sanjo trembled as though cold, and Njeri feared they had raped her. She was barely ten, but those whites had done it to younger than she. "What have they done to you, child?" Like Bon Dieu, Sanjo did not answer.

Like me, Njeri thought, my daughter can make sense of nothing. Will I ever know what happened? Will I ever understand what is happening? Bon Dieu! I beseech you!

Njeri imagined her wooden rosary, imagined her fingers fretting each bead. She recited the prayers like an incantation, till at last her daughter's trembling ceased and Sanjo returned to sleep. Then Njeri decided to check.

Blessed Mother, she prayed, you who watched your child suffer too, guide my fingers. Let me not wake my child when I check. Let me not add to her fears but let me find solace for my own. Please, Blessed Mother, please let Sanjo still be whole.

Njeri stroked Sanjo: her hand, her thigh, and it was like stroking herself. Njeri too felt soothed. Still, she must continue. She had to know. So much she did not know but this she could. Her world had not shrunk so much that she could not hold on to the importance of her daughter's virginity. Gently, gradually as she stroked, she eased one finger inside, then deeper: Sanjo was whole. Njeri was so relieved she could have wept. If she could have wept.

If I could, she thought, I would weep that you have pushed me this far, Bon Dieu, because you give me no food, no water, no answers, no comfort, nothing to ease the misery of my babies, and yet on the heels of relief you send me jealousy.

Njeri could not deny it. Lodged in her breast, a bonfire of resentment cauterized her ravaged heart. Feeling the heat rise to her neck, she thought: If they did not take Sanjo to do it, then maybe they gave her something—some water, some food, some attention that she could later use to her advantage. Our advantage.

And she felt greedy, greedy and jealous like no mother ever can be. Flames of need and shame stormed her face and stoked her thoughts: This is what you give me, Bon Dieu! Begrudging my own daughter—this is how far you've pushed me! Why, why? Where is the good in this? My children are not like your son. He was the salvation of many; my children will just die and be lost, with no one but me to mourn. Where is the good in making them suffer? My heart is closed to this awful thing. Back in Oyo, the priest said all women should take their example from Mary—well, Bon Dieu, how did she feel when she learned her son would be sacrificed? How did she accept your will? Tell me how to do it and I will at least try. The priest said that you keep the good close to you and send the evil into a pit of fire. You have sent me and Sanjo and the twins into this pit of watery filth. What does that mean? What are you saying? I confess I am no fit mother. I repent these wicked thoughts. I am ashamed I failed this test. But these tiny babies, what could they have done to deserve this? Oh, what and why and how? Bon Dieu! Your silence wastes me.

Questioning the god of the men who chained her, Njeri fell asleep. And while the floating house, the slave ship, carried them farther from the Gold Coast of Africa and closer to the Virginia shores, across the Endless Lake, Njeri dreamed her last dream: of her mother, Nyota. Of a full, round moon dazzling a sky as black as a beetle back.

The moon gave birth to Nyota, and she floated through a moist, night-fragrant sky. Her dark silhouette approached, becoming more familiar, and Njeri's breath quickened in her sleep. Nyota, scarred and sinewy, emerged from the moon with her machete in her left hand. Yet she was not dressed for battle. A maidenhair vine girded Nyota's waist. The great muscles of her thighs were defined by a thin, dark blue robe that blended with the midnight sky, so it appeared to Njeri that her mother was the sky. Njeri breathed her mother. That familiar, ocher-earth scent filled her lungs and fed her belly.

Nyota reached out to Njeri, palm downward, and in her dream Njeri stretched for that beloved hand but never touched. With her stretching, not-touching fingers and her believing, unweaning heart, Njeri finally wept, wet and succulent dream tears.

Nyota lifted her hand: wait. Hovering above the Endless Lake, she slowly waved her palm, upward-facing, across the moonlit water. The moon shone brilliantly behind her head, casting her face in shadow, illuminating that beautiful, burnished palm, glinting off the machete she now extended to her daughter. "You cannot come with me yet, daughter. First send the little ones."

Njeri awoke with the love of the Blessed Mary in her heart and the vision of her own mother before her eyes. She prayed: Bon Dieu, I thank you. I understand.

I will do as you bid.

Because they are so good, only the good for them. Only the best for them because they are goodness itself. No more crying. No more hunger. No more fear. No more questions. All will be calm and bright. My children will have this Endless Lake, tender and silent, warmed from the sun and calmed by the moon. Because they are so good.

And I, like Mary, will be your obedient bride. I will do as you bid.

࿊

Gran done finished the story in her own voice, 'cause this last part be *her* story. It brings to a end Nyota's tale and Njeri's too, and begins the upriver tale of Sanjo, by her lonesome. In the downriver telling, Gran painted the picture of the rocking, creaking boat, the slick deck as sailors hurled buckets of water over the unchained slaves, the so-called dancing. This was the last day she ever seed her mother alive. Njeri was hopping, holding the twins, trying not to slip and fall, then she stood still, seeing her chance to follow her dream. She did not ask "why"—she acted.

"Over the side of the ship went both twins at once," Gran told, "swift and soft as fish in a creek. Think back, Dred, to when you was a little boy playing—how difficult it was to catch the fish as they glimmered by? So it was difficult for me to catch those babies. I was not standing in the right spot. Only did I catch the look of surprise on they matching faces."

Gran fell silent, her eyes soft and smeary, her mouth pulling down in sorrow with the rememory. Sink or float, I don't know what them babies did. Sanjo stopped watching them. She looked to her mother, expecting to see fright, but Njeri was calm, with a smile such as she used to smile when kissing her young'ns each night before sleep. She reached for Sanjo, saying, "Let us follow, daughter. Let us go with the twins to Nyota." But a sailor swooped down and grabbed

Sanjo away. Njeri had only seconds left to finish her promise to Bon Dieu. She crossed her hands over her heart, as if to hold it in, and with one leg over the side of the ship and a look what hurt Sanjo's eyes like sunlight, she called, "Follow me, daughter," and dropped into the water.

I asked Gran once if she wanted to follow. I think that was the onliest time I was ever scared to ask Gran a question. She answered me true, though. "Did I want to go?" she repeated. "I ain't sure. The choice was gone 'fore I knowed what I wanted. The choice did not come again."

Enduring the rest of that journey, the sailors kept Sanjo chained in the ship's belly. No more did they bring her up on the deck with other slaves to dance. Even though that dancing used to make Gran feel like the frog hopping from the fire, still she done looked forward to it 'cause it felt so good to move her limbs, to have the stench that clung to her skin thinned by the salt water.

She stayed chained to her stink and her sores for the rest of the passage, not knowing betwixt sleeping or dreaming or waking. Ate no food but didn't die, so likely the journey ended soon after. Two men slaves carried her from that suffocating pit; she had no strength nor the wits for walking on her own.

Only years later did her gumption return. She waked to find herself no longer a child. She was tall, full-figured, strong-muscled: drifting along now in a sea of cotton. Plucking the soft, white balls from the prickly shells, she seed her fingers be long, tough, callused. The names of the slaves what worked beside her she knowed. English she knowed. At the end of the day she returned to a cabin where she ate and slept beside a man she knowed to be her husband, even if she couldn't recollect ever meeting him. And when he put a boy in her arms, she knowed this was Jacob, though she couldn't recollect birthing him.

From that day her life became clear to her, but she never recollected not the smallest moment from all them years betwixt the ship and the day she worked in the cotton field. Not then and not never. Them moments done seeped through her and run off, like water through parched soil.

23

Gran ended her tale there. It were an ending I didn't like. It were hard for me to understand, 'specially as a boy. "Couldn't Njeri gone and killed them sailors," I asked, "instead of her babies? Couldn't she fight, like Nyota? You, too. Ain't we got the blood of them warrior women?"

Gran reached out to hold my face betwixt her two palms. I felt the roughness of her skin and the gentling of her answer. I was a man before I understood it.

She said, "Njeri, my mother's name, means 'warrior's daughter.' Her way was not the warrior's way. She was only the daughter of a warrior.

"No warrior, either, am I. I am Sanjo. My name means 'heed the past.'"

Chapter four

Totem

Y ou might say her name be the onliest thing survived that middle passage with Gran. One of her names, anyhow. Africans, see, get different names: a couple at birth that stay secret, then a couple more as they grows, at this stage and that. Gran gave me two African names when I was born, but they ain't for no book. I can say the name she gave me when I come to my manhood, though: Nyasanu, man among men.

'Course, a slave gets the whip for calling they own babies any name other'n what the master gived them, so we didn't much use the African names. I knowed her name was Sanjo, but I called her Gran, same as everybody else on the plantation. Fact, as a young'n I'd hear somebody say, "it's a gran' day," and I'd think they meant it belonged to my Gran. Which made all kinds of sense, 'cause she could possess the day in a way to make it her own. She used to say, "Just get outten my way," and everybody, including Master Peter, let her get on with what she be doing. We maybe didn't own nary a thing—our clothes or a bowl or even a crust of bread—but Gran surely could possess. I confess, she did possess.

That's a thing most slaves give up, but not Gran. She possessed power, much as the sun itself. She possessed backbone, like an ox. And didn't she know just about everything worth knowing? All that she knowed, all that she could do, that's what she owned. That was hers. Kept it inside her, doled it out, found some more and never runned out.

My Gran was grand, sure 'nough. Nobody disrespected her, not even the Master. White or black, people outside the house what come to visit always called her Josie Scott, both names, and you know you never hear slaves called by they last names. Just they first. Only Gran got that respect.

Anyways, here's what I's saying about names: in Africa Gran's name was Sanjo, but in V'ginia her slave name was Josie Scott. Even Gran had to live with a slave name. Then on top of that, everybody on the plantation and all those what knowed her personal-like, called her Gran. Sanjo, Josie Scott, Gran: three names for one mighty big woman.

Why Scott? Well, 'cause Gran belonged to old Richard Blow, Master Peter's papa. And before that, when she was a young gal—a towel what be spun, as they say, 'fore becoming a towel what be woven—she belonged to Richard Blow's wife, a Scott.

So I's called Scott 'cause Gran was called Scott and 'cause my papa, Jacob Scott, though I never knowed him, was her son. And I's called Dred after Missus Blow's grandpapa, Etheldred. For me, they shortened it to just Dred. That there's the first story about my name, what I heared from Master Peter as I growed. That's the one he minted and stamped. But there be a much better one—one that ain't so much about a name as about how I come to lose my mama and papa.

That's the third story, though. First I got to tell you the second story about my name.

I didn't start out the slave of Master Peter. Fact is I got myself birthed on his papa's farm. Seems I arrived about six weeks too early and smack dab in the middle of such a tribulation that old Richard Blow didn't get around to naming me. So Gran took to calling her new grandbaby Hundred, seeing as I's born on the first day of the first month of the new 1800s. You got slaves named for days and you got slaves named for months, but I's the onliest one I know what's named for a whole century! Anyways, Gran said she was sore disconsolated at the time, and Hundred sounded to her like a promise.

The name stuck, but later when I got old enough to talk, which was quicker'n most, I couldn't wrap my tongue all the way round Hundred, though I was real good at that 'dred part, so I was always called Dred. By then I was on Master Peter's farm (which had a name itself: Zephyr), and they let Gran go on calling me Dred but said it was after old Etheldred.

'Course, there be a good many jokes about my name meaning something to fear, which I guess is funny 'cause I always been so small. But it does have a dark side to it, and that brings me now to the whole story, the one Gran wouldn't tell me till I was full-growed, a man of thirty year. This last version is the one that still skitters through my dreams at night.

As I say, I entered this world at a time of powerful commotion, six weeks early, which always occasions worriment. Next thing to happen, my poor mama died 'fore I reached the end of my first holler. Bless her soul, she was better off. Better off than Gran, left to face the two men what thought they was my papa: Gran's own son, Jacob, and their master, old Richard Blow. And each of them men wanting to kill the other, with only one of them having the power to do it.

Let me tell you about old Richard Blow: he was one of them early Americans, a different sort of master than the "gentleman-farmer" sons he raised. That earlier bunch had no time to be posh. They put up they noses at "Continental" comforts. They was too isolated to mingle in society. They had dirt under they fingernails and laughed at any man what didn't. Them early Americans fought the British for independence, then set about claiming and taming the land. They carved out large tracts, pulling down trees from the sky and hoisting up boulders outten the earth. They flooded where it were dry and dammed where it were swampy. Be it land, family, or slave, they bent all to they own will. They said they did it all for family, but it were the land that fixed they choices. The land ruled everything. And Richard Blow worked his slaves from the time they could stand to the time they couldn't.

They was drove hard, yet they was a different kind of slave, just as he was a different kind of master. Them slaves had know-how. On them olden farms, slaves was apprenticed in any trade necessary to keep the farm going: as smithies, tanners, weavers, carpenters. That was the whole world, right there on the plantation, for master and slave. And iffen there come a season of bad worms, every man, woman, and child, free or slave, went out to the fields to pluck them critters offen the t'bacca leaves.

Times was hard, tight, and controlled, but with a sort of balance, too, even iffen it weren't fair. Richard Blow'd whip a boy, son or slave, what rode a plow horse in from the fields 'stead of leading it in. His missus'd stay up at night to nurse a child with the flux, black or white. Slaves often ate almost as good as the master, and when they ate in the fields, they ate together. Saturday night frolics was enjoyed by all together, and nobody missed church meeting on Sunday. Richard Blow ate slept, prayed, and worked right alongside his slaves, with everybody living and everything happening—birth, sickness, and death—under one roof. Richard Blow considered hisself the father of all his children and all his slaves.

By'n'by, Richard Blow become rich enough to claim and tame more land, claim and tame more Africans. Cabins got built for the new slaves. Birth, sickness, and death now happened under different roofs, and Richard Blow—being a settle-aged man what made the earth yield to him and now knowing that soon he must yield to it—seed a sly advantage in them separate roofs.

That's what caused the commotion on the day I got born: old Richard Blow figured hisself to be my papa. 'Cept I was no lighter then than I is now. When he seed how very black and runty I be, he begun to doubt actually being my papa as much as whether he want to claim me. So when he seed Jacob hanging nervous-like by the birthing cabin, well, he begun to feel like the rabbit what raced the turtle and lost.

⁂

Dred's mother, Jenny, was a new African on Richard Blow's plantation two years before Dred was born. Gran could always spot the recent Africans, wasted from that journey across the water, and she saw Jenny that first day she arrived, roped to a dozen other women, a splintery twig tied in a bundle of stouter women.

Nearly a year passed before Gran saw Jenny again. She was running sure-footed but scared across the tobacco rows, leaping over spring's first leaves, bounding from row to row on a zig-zag course. Later, when Gran knew Jenny better, she learned that Jenny's spirit was the springbuck; that Jenny's people say that the lion's stride is long, but the path is beaten by many springbuck.

The sun was setting while Jenny ran from the lion, clutching up her sap-colored, sackcloth dress, bare-foot and bare-headed, racing toward the sun as if to catch it before it set, or else to sink along with it. She ran from Richard Blow as he leisurely jogged on a barrel-chested roan, stalking his prey along an intercepting course at the edge of the fields. He waited for her to clear the tobacco rows before charging, not wanting to trample or bruise those tender leaves. He was a man who enjoyed the chase, with little doubt about the outcome. Until Jenny veered toward the big house. Anticipation turned to vinegar at the prospect of being seen by his wife from an upstairs window, much as Gran watched from the kitchen, where she prepared dough for the next day's bread.

But Gran didn't see the Master catch Jenny. She turned her back to the window and breathed in the promise of clean, white flour, her turning away made easier because she didn't know Jenny yet, only that Jenny had been on the farm about a year, mistress of the old springhouse.

Many plantations have a springhouse; many plantations have masters like old Richard Blow; many women have been subjected to both. The Blow springhouse was a stone shed isolated beyond the fields. A creek once ran under it, so it had been used to keep the butter and milk cool. But old Richard Blow dammed the river and dried up the creek. Then the only thing cooled there was his own lust.

As soon as Jenny arrived on the plantation, she became his prisoner there. She was taken to that springhouse as a recent import, chucked into the gloom and yelled at, though she understood not a word. Yet she understood the clank of that familiar chain-rattle, key-scratching sound; it told her she would be alone for a while.

She listened hard: ears, nose, and fingertips all together aquiver. Birds and insects, her heart thudding. As the light shifted, crickets. A small creature scurried along the dry creek bed. Nothing more.

In the fading light her heart slowed. Muscles, knotted for months in sickness and strain, loosened in small jerks. First between her shoulder blades, then her legs, her hands, finally in her stomach. My body is going back to its old shape, she thought, like it was before the boat. Like it was back in Wambu.

She stopped herself from remembering home, concentrating instead on her prison, its walls of strange, green stone, the peaked roof's splintery planks, the knifeblades of light. Only the window without glass was familiar, though this one admitted no light. This one was shuttered and nailed tight.

Jenny knew this was home to no one, yet someone clearly came and went; possibly an angry spirit. The air was thick with a lifeless heat. There was a bucket, holding only the whiff of piddle when she sniffed it. A jug of water, washbasin, and cloth were arranged on a chest of drawers. The water smelled clean and she felt thirsty, but she wouldn't drink it. It might be for the spirits. She knocked on each drawer and heard the hollow emptiness, but the top one contained a swatch of red flannel, and she fell back as if snake-bitten. It was beautiful—the red, the softness—but she wouldn't touch it. That was how she'd been captured. In Wambu, where they never saw flannel, the slave catchers used such bits of cloth to trick the girls into coming near enough to throw a snare around them, trapping them with no more difficulty than netting butterflies.

She turned to the only other furniture in the room. Because of its shape she knew it to be a bed. This one rose up high off the floor on four wooden legs, with several layers of padded materials, topped by a blanket of quilted squares, each a different, faded hue of waste. She wrapped herself in it and rolled across the bed to the wall, pressing her hot cheek against the cool stone, noticing the sparkling chips of mica. Even though the wall was rough and dusty, she nestled into it like her cats that would snuggle into the sleeping cows. Dreamily, she smiled at the thought of home and her throat swelled up. Her tears against the wall loosened finely-layered scabs of mica. Like fish scales, they were damp yet stiff, milky-clear, and through her tears they caught the light and made little prisms. Unlike fish scales they had no smell, and she tried not to but recalled the rotting fish stink of the slave ship. Or was it all those bodies that smelled that way?

She jackknifed upright to a loud rumbling, confused because she hadn't realized she was drifting off. The roll of her empty stomach made her think she was still on the ship. Then the springhouse became real, her muscles knotted again, and the familiar chain-rattle, key-scratching noises told her trouble had returned. It opened the door looking just like old Richard Blow.

❧

Swamp-busted—that's what Gran used to call the sorry souls what had the sorriest work knowed by folk what thought they already knowed the worst of it. Swamp clearing be the meanest work of all. Richard Blow had a small bog at the edge of his land, and he didn't want the land, he wanted the work the land demanded. For any slave too strong-willed to behave as a slave, he learned them they place by putting them to clearing the swamp.

I been used hard, but still I can't make my mind see what don't seem possible: spending your day hitched like a mule to a plow, leather tack round your head and shoulders, cutting furrows under water, pulling against the suck of the muck, not able to stand nor swim, only held in place betwixt the sodbuster, the harness, and the stagnant mud, trying to move forward outten the reach of the mosquitoes overhead and the whip behind.

That's where my mama found herself. So it's a certainty she gived old Richard Blow such a fight in that springhouse he decided to break her. But she wasn't swamp-busted, not according to Gran. Not entirely, leastways, 'cause Gran saw the springbuck that evening, seed my mama's spirit running and leaping through them t'bacca

31

rows. "Some slaves cannot be broke," Gran said. "The master got to choose: kill them or sell them or just keep them as squashed as mortar betwixt bricks."

He treated my mama like mortar. She would've let that swamp kill her 'fore giving in to old Richard Blow, so he brung her out of there. But he didn't want to sell her, neither. He still wanted his way. He arranged for my mama to spend her nights locked and waiting in the springhouse, and by day she was rolling cigars in a shed by the barn, roped to a center post. Richard Blow continued going to the springhouse of nights, and she couldn't stop him, but every chance she got she broke loose. Though she never got far.

Old Richard Blow's scheming was his undoing, howsomever. 'Cause it were whilst she was rolling cigars that my mama met my papa, Jacob Scott. He was the one to bring the cured leaves and haul away the rolled cigars. She choosed Jacob and he choosed her, and they rejoiced when she become pregnant. Gran's heart, though, weeped, 'cause she knowed the trouble it would bring. She knowed Richard Blow believed he still be cock of the walk.

He understood different the day I was born. He took one look at my black face and his own flooded crimson. He stormed from the birthing cabin, and Gran didn't have time to think that were strange, what with Jenny dying and a new baby wailing and her own son, Jacob, sobbing in her lap. With one arm she held me, with the other she comforted her son, till Richard Blow bust through the door, ordering Jacob to stand.

Gran seed the bullwhip in the Master's hand and stood to protect her son. Only 'cause Gran was also protecting me did the old white man manage to pry Jacob away. He pinned Jacob to the wall with three heavy lashes 'fore the rage in Gran's breast broke free. The blood of our warrior kin clawed up her throat and she bellowed. Her voice trumped him. He stopped the thrashing, and Jacob slumped to his knees.

Richard Blow turned on Gran, but he did not raise the whip to her. Even to a man like that, lashing Gran herself were unthinkable. Not 'cause she done been mammy to his children; not cause he felt one lick of sympathy; but 'cause Gran's spirit be the elephant—and when the lion's path and the elephant's cross, it's the lion what yields. Against the elephant, the lion won't use might; it'll use its wits, or attack the young. Richard Blow did both. With one final crack of his whip he walloped the earth and roared, "Quiet!" And even I stopped wailing. Gran said it become so silent she could hear the blood dripping offen my papa's back. The Master turned to Gran with a grin and said, "Fine. I won't beat him, I'll sell him."

Gran begged to keep her son or be sold alongside him. Again the old Master paused. Again he agreed. But still with that awful grin he added, "If I keep Jacob, then I shall have to sell you and the baby. You choose, Josie: who goes, who stays."

Tears froze on her face like wax hardening on a candle stem. She didn't pause. She said, "I won't have no part of your evil. Sell us all, tear us apart; kill us. It's on your soul."

Richard Blow sold Jacob. Right after that he rid hisself of me and Gran, too. "Fear made him give us up," Gran explained. "White folk all the time be fearing poisoning, and everybody knowed I could conjure and cure. Gived more time, I don't know what I might've done. Like before when I was a girl on that boat, the chance was gone before I did choose."

I know full well Gran could've killed Richard Blow iffen she had the mind to. She could've found her chance before we was packed off. Could've conjured the power of them warrior women what come before her—Nyota, fought and killed in battle, killed to protect. Njeri also killed to protect, in her way of seeing things. Drownded herself with her own babies. So it seems the killing stopped with Gran. I done pondered it many a time—did we lose that killing strength when we was took from Africa? Or was it the right and the wrong of it what stopped Gran? 'Cause if Gran went and killed old Richard Blow, it wouldn't be a killing to protect. It would be a killing for revenge.

Still, I ain't certain Gran turned her back to revenge. Maybe she would've done it anyways, iffen old Richard Blow kept us. Instead, he made a present of Gran and me, a wedding present to his son, Peter. And that's why I growed calling Master Peter my master.

So here's the final story about my name, and it makes me unsure whether Gran really did turn her back to revenge. Gran said the whole thing were so dreadful that the name Dred seemed just and proper. "Your name," she told me, "be like my name, a marker for the past."

As I say, I was a growed man when she told me all this, and I looked hard at the whole root and stem of her words. Did she say "marker" like a signpost? Or did she say "marker" like an IOU? I thought back on all she learned me about poisons and curings, wondering iffen Gran all them years felt or maybe hoped or leastways dreamed of a day the Blows would dread the revenge I might one day claim. I thought back, too, on that dream she told of me and Da. Maybe Gran liked something more about that dream, liked linking me to a snake—'cause to Africans, a snake ain't necessarily bad. "A snake," she more'n once told me, "can sneak right up on a lion in its den and kill with a single bite."

I still ain't sure what was in her heart. Could be she did hope I would grow fangs. But the snake ain't my nature. No, I got my mama's nature: the springbuck, small and light. My course is to outrun the lion.

Chapter five

Slavery's Child

White folk typically will say we's born slaves, whereas a black will tell you: "I was born in slavery." There's a world of difference. A child needs training to be a slave—it don't come natural. So when they say we ain't educated, that ain't strictly true, neither. We educated in the peculiar ways of slavery.

Schooling starts early, and the major lesson is work. Babies is took out to the field and set at the end of a t'bacca or cotton row to watch the humped backs of they mothers shuffling from plant to plant. A man once told me he couldn't remember his mama's face, just the shade of sun-faded blue what was wrapped round her head, 'cause that's what he seed all day: the rag, not her face.

It ain't long 'fore somebody puts a broom into the hands of what I likes to call the "wobblers," or shows ten stumpy fingers how to pull a weed up by its roots. Quick learners get rewarded with harder tasks. Slow ones get the switch, and on some plantations they get a whip or a belt. I've seed healed welts on the back of a five-year-old.

I been lucky, myself. My wife sucks her teeth to hear me say that, but I know it: sized next to other slaves, my tribulations come up short. When I was a child I had ring games and word games and spinning tops. I wasn't put in the fields but was with Gran there in the big house. The hardest thing in my young life was small chores in the kitchen—not 'cause Missus Blow set me to work but 'cause Gran never did countenance idleness.

Worst thing slavery done to me was to take my mama and papa, but I didn't appreciate that 'cause I had Gran. She was mother, father, teacher. True to her name, Gran schooled me to heed the past. Her downriver stories of kin, her proverbs, all was to help me see a world other'n the plantation. In Gran's tales, there was possibilities other'n slavery's possibilities.

An early lesson of Gran's was happenstance. She said, "You born into slavery and that's a fact, but it's a fact of happenstance. Onliest reason you got a master is 'cause you come into this world at this place and this time. It ain't 'cause you black, nor small, nor 'cause you done something wrong. It ain't no reason like that. Your kin was free till slavery snatched us. We be like t'bacca: we grow according to the soil, not the seed—and now we's planted in slavery's soil. That's happenstance. But happenstance," she often reminded me, "don't change who you be."

Most her other lessons was protections, things a slave child got to know in order to live amongst white folk. "Don't make white folk nervous," she'd say when I complained about being small, which I did a lot. "Big and strong makes the white folk nervous. Big and black be half of what got your papa sold away. I give thanks every day that some white man ain't likely to look at you and feel threatened by the sheer might of you."

But that didn't turn my sour milk to cheese, 'cause Gran herself was a big woman, and I seed daily how she used her size and her might. Partly she got away with it 'cause she done been Master Peter's mammy, partly 'cause she was just right most the time. So I seed her breaking the rules she laid down for me. Gran should've heeded her own proverb: If you want your children to follow your footsteps, watch where you walk.

That become particular true when it come to Master Peter. She was deep fond of him. She liked that he wasn't like his papa, and she taken a pride in how he turned out. Even when she scolded him, it wasn't with a hard heart. Leastways, not until he begun tippling with some of the local grandees. I was about six when Gran started warning me against him. "Don't be trusting that man, that man's your master." By then it were too late for me to hear. "Master" were just a word, a word what didn't 'count for the sap that run hidden betwixt us. "Master" didn't 'count for how he been raised elbow-to-elbow with his papa's slaves, ate and played right along with them. "Master" didn't 'count for how he was young, fresh-married, with no young'ns of his own when I come into his life. "Master" didn't 'count for how Gran was his mammy, so he felt partial to Gran, and I was Gran's boy, so he felt partial to me, too—even after having children of his own.

I'll say it plain: I loved Master Peter the way a boy loves a papa. He played with me, tickled me, learned me how to use a whittling knife. He provided everything. He was the man with the power: the power to give, to protect, and yes, to punish, though he wasn't never even as hard as Gran. I didn't see his power as power over me. I felt it like any child will feel the strength of a papa: I felt myself inside that power, sheltered by it.

Here's what I be saying: a slave child gets hisself born and iffen he be lucky, iffen he ain't treated like a dog—iffen he's picked up and twirled and grows knowing he got the power to bring a smile to folks—then he gets to feeling he belongs. That's only natural, babies believing they belong in the world they born to.

Not belonging, now that's something else that's got to be learned, and it got to be a hard lesson to overpower the strength of a child what believes different.

❧

On a typical Sunday, after everyone returned from church services, Gran got busy in the kitchen. Peter Blow had recently acquired a stove, a fat, black, iron monstrosity which required constant feeding—a task well-suited to six-year-old Dred. But Dred was feeling dreamy and bone-idle. From the garden, the smell of honeysuckle teased him outside. Knowing Gran would find some task for him, he skirted the outbuildings for cover and made his way to the pasture where the cows grazed. He flopped on his back and the fluttering spring grasses concealed him.

The sky shimmered in heat-streaked blue. Shapes in the drifting clouds flirted with him, and he began spinning tales. The cows ruminated to his chatter. Daisy, one of the gentlest of the herd, chomped closer and closer, until she was munching right next to Dred's ear. Impulsively, Dred scooted between her hoofs, reached up, and squeezed fresh, warm milk into his mouth; a dangerous pleasure, but Dred felt happy and secure. Trouble was something that happened in stories.

A breeze roused him. Dred began to think maybe Uncle Solomon's boy, Sip, would help him fashion a slingshot, and they could hunt squirrels. Hadn't Nyota been an expert with the slingshot? Surely that talent ran in his blood, as strong as the griot's skill. Hurrying toward the quarter along the edge of the tobacco fields, he saw Mary Anne Blow by the granary and set his course on a wide arc to avoid her. Nothing but trouble, that one.

Too late, she saw him and called him over. She was not quite five, but she already understood more about her privileges than Dred did. With increasing frequency she practiced her entitlement over the slaves.

Dred approached skittishly, and his irritation ballooned when he saw her dolls. He hated dolls. She knew this.

"Dred," she said, "I want you to mind Sally and Maggie while I'm busy over here." He followed her pointing finger to a small mound of freshly-turned earth.

"Aw, Mary Anne, they's just cloth and cotton batting, don't need no minding."

"Dred, pay attention to me, now." She mimicked the prickly condescension her mother often used with the slaves. "Pretend like baby Sally is asleep, but baby Maggie's wet and wants her diaper changed."

"I got things to do, Mary Anne. I can't be playing with you now."

"What do you have to do? It's Sunday," she challenged.

"I think I heard Gran calling me."

"You did not. You were way over in the pasture. I'da heard her if she called. Now sit over there and play like you's the mammy and gonna change the baby's diaper."

"I don't want to."

"I say so."

The children squared off, neither sure of the limits of their power.

"Dred! Play like you's the mammy!"

Dred turned toward the house, hoping to see Gran. No one was about.

"Dred! Play like you's the mammy!"

Exasperated, he retorted, "Play like I ain't here."

Mary Anne's lips puckered and her eyes shot fire. He worried what she might do next, but she shifted into a carefree attitude. With mincing steps she returned to the little mound of dirt, picked up a stick, and poked inside the hole.

Dred began to turn away, then looked back, realizing what he had overlooked—the reason Mary Anne was "busy." He added it up: she was digging in the dirt; this digging was more interesting than playing with her precious dolls; and her Sunday morning frippery had been exchanged for play clothes. His whole attitude changed and he slid into the dirt beside her, peeping into the hole. Sure enough, she was nudging a reluctant, fat worm from the crumbling earth, just the kind of worm her papa liked for Sunday fishing down by the creek. Master was going to take them fishing! The prospect of going fishing erased all thought of Sip. A slingshot he could make any day, but fishing—the children were forbidden to play at the creek unless Peter Blow took them, which he sometimes did on Sundays.

"Move over, Mary Anne, and I'll help you dig for more."

She didn't budge.

"I sure do love fishing with my papa," she said.

As if talking to herself, thought Dred.

"And I've got the best worms. I'm going to catch a big one."

Her smile, prim and secretive, gave him pause. She was holding something back. She dangled the squirming worm.

"I'll help, Mary Anne. If he's a real big one, I'll hold the pole while you reel him in."

"Well, guess I'll just have to manage all by myself, Dred Scott," and she turned to look him full in the face, "because I'm going fishing but you're not. Papa's only taking me and Thomas. No slaves."

He longed to punch her. Not too long ago he had, and Gran had whipped him harder than the Missus had. He ran home to Gran and was relieved to see her packing the picnic basket. With a whoop he climbed a chair to peer in the basket and see what goodies they would eat. His smile dimmed as he counted only three sandwiches. "Where's my sandwich?" he asked.

Gran hesitated. "You and me be having our own picnic later, out by the maple."

"Master's going fishing. I want to go fishing."

"You not invited, child."

"But Mary Anne and Thomas are going. I always go when they go."

"Not this time, Dred. Only his own children be going with him this time." She spoke softly, but firmly.

His own children.

Gran continued, trying to brighten the shadow on his face. "You and me's gonna have a special treat—I got johnnycakes on the griddle, just for us. Not for nobody else."

His own children. Dred tried to understand it but couldn't. Lamely, he said, "I's one of his children. When the children go, I go."

"Master Peter got his own children, Dred. That includes Mary Anne and Thomas and baby Elizabeth. It don't include you. You know that."

"But Master lets me ride Gen'ral. He takes me up in the saddle with him and he don't let nobody else on Gen'ral but me. Not even Mary Anne."

"That don't mean you can do everything with him, Dred."

"I tell him stories. When he naps I tell him tales and he says I give him good dreams. He calls me his little griot."

Gran stooped to her knees and ducked her head to look at the child, sorrowful eye to sorrowful eye, letting him read from her eyes what her mouth could not explain.

His eyes filled with tears. She reached out but his little frame would not yield. He wanted no pity. "You don't know! You don't know everything. He calls me 'son'!"

Gran pulled him to her breast. "Child, that don't mean you be kin. It ain't like with Thomas. Master just call any little boy that."

Dred wrenched free. "He don't. Nobody but me and Thomas. I know. You don't know."

Feeling cramped and off-balance, Gran stood abruptly. She didn't want to argue. She winced as he slumped under the weight of this new lesson, his small features screaming defeat and betrayal. With furious rebuke he shook a finger violently at the stove. Too late, she smelled the smoking cakes. "They's burned, they's burned," he screamed. "You ruin everything."

Minutes later, Peter Blow came for the picnic basket. Separating the carefully-folded linen, he peered inside, lifted the top item, and frowned. Carrying the basket to the stove, he shuffled the burnt johnnycakes and selected three of the least burnt. He turned to leave.

"Oh, Gran! I didn't think anyone was here." His own laughter annoyed him. Composing himself, pointedly ignoring how the old woman remained motionless in the corner, he continued, "You forgot to put the cakes in, so I, yes, well, it seems I have everything now." He was on the threshold when he added, without turning around, "You explained it all to Dred?"

Still she said nothing. He turned to look at her, then dropped his eyes and said to the floor, "Fine. I'll be off, then."

When she could no longer hear his steps, she rose and stood at the window. Often while she washed before that window she hummed, releasing the tunes from her childhood like birds from a cage. Her music flew out and settled among the branches of the great maple, and the leaves applauded. Now her heart was silent, struck dumb. Now she silently watched her grandson, striding purposefully toward the stable, where she knew he would confide his sorrows to the horses. His little hands, swinging at his sides, were clenched into fists. Good, she thought, good.

But when Dred returned to the kitchen, fists still clenched, she cupped her two big hands around his little one and saw it was not a fist. His thumb was merely tucked into the palm, with the tiny, half-moon of his thumbnail peeping out between two fingers, and her heart, finding its voice, howled at that moon.

⁂

Surprising how the littlest thing can lead to something stretching through your whole life. Them tucked thumbs led to two things—every time Gran seed them, she added another stone to the rock pile of resentment she be building against Master Peter, so that for all my life, the most friction that sparked betwixt Gran and me was always over him.

The second thing, though, were something good. Gran begun learning me rhythms. She begun patting games with me, and when she told her stories, she urged me to rap out a beat. That's how they done in Africa, she said. Somebody drummed while somebody else told a story. I learned me a whole language: fast and slow, hollow and sharp, muffled and loud. Got so's I wouldn't even know I was tapping till she begun clapping along with me. When I was eight, she made me a fine set of bones. She shaped them and polished them herself. I could rattle them bones along with Uncle Solomon's fiddling. He learned me his fancy rhythms, and we put on quite a show.

Bones or no bones, though, I hammered out a beat on pots, on the tabletop, on my thigh. I couldn't do it round the Missus—drove her to distraction. But Gran never minded and here's why: I couldn't tuck up my thumbs when I was working on a patter.

Sure 'nough, she hated them tucked thumbs worser'n the constant tapping.

Chapter six

In the Big House

Weren't long 'fore I was educated in being educated. Missus was pregnant with her fourth child and was so wore down she convinced Master to hire a governess, more to mind them young'ns than to school them. Mary Anne, the oldest, was only six. Master found a orphan girl from the Catholic place in Lawrenceville, hardly had to pay her. She weren't but a child herself, a fifteen-year-old name of Miss Quinn, and I could see right off she'd never been on a plantation.

Our t'bacca farm was a sight to behold. Zephyr, we called it, a name the Master's daddy gived it. Like a crescent moon, the Nottoway River run down the western boundary of the place, and cupped inside the top of the curve was the big house, facing the water. It were a brick box, but big and roomy, two stories, with four chimney stacks, four chalky columns out front, and windows front and back.

The farm splayed out behind the house like a woman's fancy skirts. The outbuildings boasted a granary, smithy, smokehouse, buttery, summer kitchen, stables, and barns. A corral, grazing pasture, and chicken coop sat in another stretch directly south, and this be where they met the t'bacca fields. The t'bacca barn and warehouse was situated along this same reach of the fields. Kind of a paradise, 'cepting you also got slave cabins mixed in, southeast of the big house, about a dozen cabins lined up like soldiers, two by two, neat and trim like the rest of the place. And betwixt each cabin, all the tidy little truck patches. It was a clean place—no slop near any building. It was all regular tended. One place for dumping slop, one place for burning trash, one place for the compost.

Pretty, too, 'specially when the great garden were abloom. Along the east side of the house running north the great garden burst in midsummer with colorful bean vines, yellow squash, and red tomatoes. The land swelled to a small, rounded hill, rounded like a baby's bottom, with even a slight cleft running along the top. Scuppernong grapes grew aplenty up there, and the entire plantation could be seed from up high there.

When the new teacher arrived at Zephyr, I seed her carriage coming, with her hanging out the window, stretching her eyes over everything, kind of like a insect with its feelers wagging. She were scrawny and dressed all in black, and she carried a great big satchel what tilted her all to one side. I was curious and excited about a new person in the house, but Gran done told me, "A governess is for white folk. This new miss ain't gonna have much to do with you nor me except maybe to keep that Mary Anne outten the way." If that's all it were, that would've been fine with me. But I had a gut feeling it were gonna be a whole lot more'n that, and I sure 'nough was found right.

❧

The Blows were wealthy tobacco growers in 1807, who could well afford the teaching services of an educated orphan. The orphanage's buggy delivered Emily Quinn to the front entrance and departed before she climbed the porch stairs. She was on her own, for the first time feeling doubt cramp her shoulders. Stepping through the open door into a dim interior, she beheld the mistress of the house and her two eldest children lined up regimentally. Mrs. Blow held a baby like a musket on her shoulder. She was an attractive matron, dressed in a modest, gray-blue silk maternity gown. The two children were outfitted more colorfully: red cotton plaid for Mary Anne and royal blue linen for Thomas.

Embarrassed by her dusty, black muslin dress, Emily stammered her name. Then she saw Dred, apart from and behind the others. He wore a mismatched suit of dark gray breeches, white blouse, and a lighter gray jacket. He lacked a vest, but he did have shoes and stockings, and someone had taken pains to make the jacket and trousers, obviously second-hand, fit his small frame in a manner that looked natural. Dred smiled at Emily. It was a simple, friendly child's smile, and it made all the difference.

She regained her composure and realized she was being introduced. "—you shall call her Miss Quinn," Mrs. Blow droned. "She is your new governess." Despite the warmth of the day, Mrs. Blow clutched a shawl tightly about her. She stood ramrod straight and spoke with her chin thrust forward, just like every nun at the orphanage. With each word, her eyes drifted toward the ceiling, then she punctuated each sentence with a sharp, condescending glance down her nose.

"Each morning at eight-thirty," she continued, "Miss Quinn will teach you letters and numbers. Also, manners and customs, with the expectation that you will grow up to be pleasant, intelligent, and well-spoken. As befitting the issue of a gentleman. You will work hard for her so that your father will be proud."

Little Mary Anne scowled. Unsure whether the child's reaction was to herself or to Mrs. Blow's dictum, Emily withdrew a picture book from her satchel.

Mary Anne and Thomas didn't react, but the book acted like sorcery upon Dred, drawing him forward. He stepped up in front of Mary Anne. Emily did know better; slaves were not permitted an education. Yet his interest encouraged her, and as Dred advanced she said, "This book is entitled *Tales from Olden Times*, with wonderful stories, even a talking goose."

Dred's fingers floated toward the book like willow branches lifted on a breeze, but Mary Anne shoved ahead, snatched the book from Emily's hand, and whipped around to face him squarely: "Step back, Dred. This book is not for you."

Mrs. Blow hissed, "Miss Quinn!" and launched into a rant, all about the folly of educating Negroes. For rants, she pinned her gaze squarely on the offender, so that the object of her ire was never in doubt. Now her gaze was fixed on Emily. "Nigras are too slow, Miss Quinn. They lack intelligence. Those who do possess a full share of brain subvert any education given them for the purposes of cunning and treachery. It is a matter of principle. Security. And, I might add, common sense, that you never instruct any of the Nigras as to their letters."

Mary Anne stuck her tongue out at Dred, and to his unguarded face came an appalled look of comprehension. Until that moment the child had not so clearly understood the leprous aspect of his exclusion.

⁂

Missus Blow shot out the room like a spark from the chimney. The rest of us stood looking one t'other, till back flies the Missus all flustrated, saying, "I can't find my paddle. Dred—go cut me a switch. Quickly!"

That cast me down deeper. The switch was surely for me. I went out, cut the limpest switch I could find, and run back with the hope Missus wasn't gonna whisk me in front of Mary Anne, 'cause I hated worser'n the beating the idea of that hellion gloating on me. I gived up the switch. The Missus stood close and leaned down over me, but I knowed better'n to look up at her. I was looking at my shoes when she asked, "Dred, do you know why you're being punished?"

'Fore I could answer, the new lady piped up: "Please, Mrs. Blow, the fault is not his. I'm to blame. I'm heartily sorry. It won't happen again."

Missus carried right on like she never spoken. "Dred, you must be punished for handling that book. You are not to handle books. Unless it is to dust those in the library, and then you are never to open one. Books and Nigras have nothing to do with each other. Do you understand me?" I mumbled into my shoes that I did and braced against the whistle of the switch through air. But next I heared the Missus say, "Miss Quinn, give this boy ten stripes."

46

Sure 'nough I looked up then, to see what this stranger was gonna do. I's lying if steam weren't rising up from her collar. She tried logic: "The boy didn't even touch the book." She tried persuasion: "I understand your anger, but please, I'm the one to blame." Still nothing worked till she gived Missus a outright refusal: "Mrs. Blow, I will not hit that boy."

Emily Quinn saved my behind that day—the Missus forgot all about me and was hot for whisking her instead. Oooh, it were a glad sight for sorry eyes, seeing somebody win in a contest over that woman. Us children, me, the field hands: never did we win with her. Most times even the Master gived in to her. Gran could win sometimes, but never head-on; she had to find roundabout ways.

I heared Missus later with Master Peter, looking to pack Miss Quinn back to the orphanage. He said, "It's your decision, Elizabeth, but you should know I'm much too busy to be finding a replacement in a hurry." What with being pregnant with her fourth child, I reckon the Missus accepted she needed someone to busy them young'ns as much as educate them.

Later when me and Gran talked about it—'course I had to tell her all what happened—I had her splitting her sides over the way Miss Quinn set her spine against the Missus. As I settled on my pallet for sleep, I said, "Looks like we's finally gonna get someone on our side in the big house." But Gran said, "You can only walk around a pepper tree, you can't climb it."

As the years rocked along, howsomever, Gran changed her tune. Miss Quinn was one decent white woman. Her backbone stayed straight and she proved more'n once she were a friend. She was a young woman what slept poorly, and many a night she come down to the kitchen to warm some milk or eat a slice of pie. From the start, she heared me and Gran in our little room off the kitchen, telling stories to each other, and it weren't long 'fore she was whispering to us her own tales. She winked and said, "I won't open a single book, but I'll tell you what's inside as long as we keep it a secret amongst ourselves."

And that's how we did. I learned stories about Greek kings and Napoleon and presidents of the U.S. of A. You could say I got to suck on the marrow without ever cracking a bone.

Chapter seven

Apprentice

I never minded much about the books. I couldn't believe books had anything more to offer than the stories Gran and Emily told. No, the learning I truly hankered after was learning a trade. I was just coming up, going on thirteen, and I wanted to be more than just a house servant. I wanted a skill, something not everybody else could do. I wanted the respect that come with it.

Gran was eager for it, too, though she pulled me down a peg all the time, making sure I didn't forget I was no better'n any of them other slaves what worked the fields. And I did know I was no better'n them, but I also knowed I was better off than them. Working in the big house, we had more of most things: food, clothes, rest. And though I didn't speak it outright 'cause I didn't want to argue with Gran, I also did feel I was favored by the Master, and the proof come with my apprenticeship to Uncle Joe, the blacksmith. I was small and puny—there was other boys more fitted to that labor—but Master done choosed me. "That will be my birthday present to you, Dred. The day you turn thirteen, you will begin an apprenticeship in the smithy."

'Cept the timing were bad with that 18'n12 War. Master Peter left to fight 'fore I turned thirteen, and we all got put under a overseer. Master was grave worried about leaving Zephyr to a overseer—didn't trust a man what didn't own land, what worked just for pay. See, Master Peter was knowed across V'ginia as a crop master. He considered a overseer the kind of help no respecting crop master should ever need. He thought to put Bill in charge of the field hands. He was the lead row man, mostly feared by the others 'cause his anger be as broad as his shoulders.

Missus feared Bill, too, though she wouldn't own up to it. "Am I to consult with a Nigra, then?" Missus said.

She was due any day to birth Patsy, their sixth. A whimperer, that one, whimpering for all the misery that were upon us, I do believe. Missus gave the baby over to the wet-nurse and stayed shut up in her room; Mary Anne took to bossing around the big house; and then poor little Thomas died from the Scarlatina. So I reckon Missus couldn't be running the farm, too, and I reckon Master seed that, so Missus got her overseer. I mark that as the beginning of the time Master runned things less and less, and gived over to Missus more and more. By the time he come back outten that war, about the only thing he was running was running that farm into dust.

Come autumn, Master was atop of Gen'ral and off to the war. Right 'fore he left, he hired Seamus Overton, and I was there when Master gived his parting word to the man. "I do not beat my slaves, and this plantation runs better for it. Situations requiring punishment are to be handled through withheld rations, extra work duties, and, in extreme cases, a single stripe with a horsewhip. No bullwhip will be used on my slaves. Is that clear?"

Overton was a thick man, so may be he only heared part of all that. 'Cause he followed the Master about the bullwhip, but he sure did lay on beatings. With a horsewhip, which is much shorter and lighter than a bullwhip, but Overton didn't mind getting splattered with the blood of them he whipped. "I have a personal relationship with my slave hands," I once heared him joke.

Sunset of the day Master rode off, Overton gathered up all the slaves and introduced hisself. "I be a fair man," he boasted, "but pity help the nigger what shirks his work. And that goes for you wenches, as well." Within two weeks, every slave on the place took his meaning, but "fair" had nothing to do with it. Only "fair" thing about it were Overton didn't want to leave nobody out. Looked like just about everybody would get they turn. The luckiest ones got it in the beginning, when he still kept it to a single strike. Later, you never knowed when he might stop. Later, too, it looked that the lighter heft of the horsewhip sat poorly with him, 'cause he satisfied hisself with a few changes. He frayed the leather, wrapped steel wire round each strand, and strengthened the grip. In short, he fashioned hisself a cat-o'-nine-tails.

That's why we called him Cat Man—'cause his two favorite scourges was the cat-o'-nine-tails and cat claws. Men got the tails, women got the claws. For this he owned a special long, thick glove, went near up to his elbow. He'd snatch one of the barn cats with this glove, rile it yet hold it tight by the scruff of the neck, then drag the scrambling, clawing critter across the bared back of some poor gal what rolled less t'bacca than he figured she ought.

I didn't see the first whipping, though all the slaves was ordered to stand and witness. Gran insisted she needed me with her on another farm, where she was going to midwife. Gran was good with the tricky births, and Missus let her go 'cause Missus done had one or two difficult births herself. But Gran couldn't make up enough excuses to get me away from all the beatings that followed. I'll never forget seeing Bill whipped. Cat Man worked on Bill like a threshing machine, and it took a long time 'fore the craziness left his eyes and he let off flogging.

Long time after that I couldn't close my eyes without hearing Bill screaming. I'd wake up in Gran's arms, her humming and rocking me till my eyes dried, her voice conjuring back sleep. I was nearly thirteen and it shamed me to be crying on a woman's bosom, but I couldn't control what was in my head when I was asleep. I could handle it all right when I was sharp about my wits. Just something about the dreams it gived me, made me shrink back to being a baby.

They was some dark days, sure 'nough, and what I learned be something a heap more dark than the soot from the forge.

❧

"This here stick is whitened and hardened with age, like me," joked Uncle Joe, settling back on the bench, folding and lowering himself like a cog being ratcheted. "Even a blind man can read his age from such a stick."

Dred was itching to learn about the fire and the anvil. His fingers rippled impatiently at his sides, but he held his tongue. As far back as he could recall, the bent old blacksmith had always shown a grandfatherly interest in the daily progress of Dred's life. Of all the slaves, Joe had been the one to visit regularly to check if Dred had provided Gran with enough firewood; to compliment, refuse, and ultimately accept one of Gran's oven-warm delectables; to repay the kindness with his own freshly-caught possums or catfish. Generous Joe, Gran called him.

The day after he turned thirteen, Dred reported to Uncle Joe at the smithy before the rising horn blew, proud of his new calling, his new age, and the new shoes—new to him, at least—given to him by the Missus. With birthdays on his mind he asked, "Uncle Joe, how old is you," unwittingly prompting the old man to take out this strange piece of wood, what he called his age-stick. As they sat together in the smithy, breaking buttered bread Gran had sent along, with the coals in the forge creating a blanket of warmth against the frosty January morning outside, Dred calmed and adjusted to the old man's slower pace.

"Being disallowed to read and write, age-sticks is how the old folk track they birthdays, Dred. Few folk got dates as easy as your'n to count by: for you, iffen you know what year it is, you know how old you is. This be 1813, you's thirteen. Being born in 1800 makes it simple for you. Me now: I can't tell you what year I's born, but I can tell how old I is with this stick. See, this mark here at the top means I's born in watermelon time, and all these slashes underneath it are one for each Christmas after that. Christmas marks the year 'cause the white folk always takes note of Christmas. Then for every ten year, I make a notch like this." He held the stick out to Dred. "See here this first notch? That's when I was ten. Now three slashes after that, and that's when I was as old as you is now."

More slender than the stick they held, the boy's fingers traced the slashes and notches. He could count five notches. These were followed by many smaller slashes. He didn't know the number, but he knew there were many years between the time Joe was thirteen and today. He looked up. "Uncle Joe, you's old!"

"Old as dust. Just remember, though: the older the moon, the brighter it shine."

Dred turned the stick over. "What's these marks on the other side?"

"Each of these reminds me of a special happening. Each is a story, you could say."

"What's this one mean?"

"That's a good one, but work comes first. You work hard and listen to me good, we can finish the day with a story. That a bargain?"

The boy nodded energetically.

"We can begin tonight, iffen you's not too eager to run home and tell Gran all about your first day." He rose and shuffled to the work table, replacing the age-stick in a drawer.

"Uncle Joe, is Gran old, too?"

"A woman like your Gran will never be old. She don't live in natural time."

Something about the way he smiled, and maybe the age Dred now possessed, made the boy think for the first time that Uncle Joe's interest wasn't wholly in himself. Embarrassed, pleased, Dred looked at the fire. We three be like that, he thought: logs, flame, and heat. He hugged Joe, enjoying the way his curved old frame enveloped him.

"Now let's get to work," Uncle Joe said. "Fetch me a hoe to mend."

Along the western wall of the smithy hung all the tools to be repaired; on the eastern wall were all those made or repaired. There were hoes and hammers and plowshares. Beneath these, in half-barrels, were nails and smaller hardware. There was a wide, open space for a horse to be tethered while being shod, where a sway-backed dobbin waited patiently. Joe's work table and bench lined the northern end of the space, and central to all of this was the forge and anvil.

"I's crookeder'n most," said Joe, "'cause I work over this anvil. Being small of stature, you'll likely not get as crooked as me, you won't have to bend so far. You only need to build your muscles. But before I let you anywheres near this anvil, you's got to learn the bellows, learn to regulate your fire so you don't burn up your iron."

Before Dred could tell Uncle Joe he already knew about bellows from stoking Gran's cooking fires, he heard, "What the hell is this boy doing in here?" It was Overton. His sudden presence in the smithy made Dred feel like a runny egg.

Uncle Joe put his arm around Dred's shoulder and slightly shuffled forward. "Boss, this here's Dred, what Marse Peter done instructed 'fore he left to be 'prenticed in the smithy soon's he turned thirteen. And he done turned thirteen yestiddy."

Overton shoved a thumb through his belt loop, and cast about for something else to attack. Uncle Joe's smithy exuded intelligent orderliness: tools hung, hardware sorted and arranged by size, ashes regularly swept, table surface cleared for work. He swaggered over to the barrels, lifted his leg and scraped the muck off his boot onto the lip of the barrel, giving it enough of a shove to tip and spill its contents. "Clean this mess up, boy. And you, old man, see that it stays quiet in here. I'll whip the first one I catch gabbing like a woman."

By the time the mess was cleared, Dred had forgotten Overton's bullying. He was anxious to please and eager to learn, popping questions like fireworks. But Uncle Joe remembered. "Hush, child, don't be bringing that Cat Man prowling back in here. That man capable of going crazy as a wheel off its axle, 'specially 'round black folk what got more know-how than him. You just listen and watch, now, so he can forget about us."

The morning passed without conversation. One by one the broken tools moved from the west wall to hang among the useful tools on the east wall. Dred, learning about fire and wind and the pliability of metal, also absorbed the music of the forge. Forbidden to speak, he tapped and hummed, slapped and drummed. The fire sang soft but crackly. He harmonized with the bellows, and Uncle Joe kept time on the anvil. Tank! Deling-ding! Tank! Deling-ding!

Uncle Joe was finally ready to shoe the dobbin, and Dred, steadying the horse, cooed the sweet music in the old horse's ear. Bending to his work, Joe ventured to talk as he worked. "First and always you want to mind safety. For your horse and for your ownself," he cautioned. "See here: as soon as the nail comes through the hoof, wring it off. Don't leave it sticking out to stab you." He continued to explain each step, and although Dred's restless fingers ceaselessly combed through the horse's mane, he watched each movement, alert and focused.

When the back right shoe was done, the blacksmith said, "Come on back here, son. This horse'll stand steady now. You watch me do this other shoe and learn good, and maybe you can take that rasp and smooth off the clinches."

Smiling at Dred's shiver of excitement, the old man straddled the horse's left leg, bent and lifted the hoof into position between his legs. He frowned at the boy's tapping foot. "Look here: never nail to the inside of this white line where the horse be touchy. Stay clear on the outside of that. And you start the nail off at a pitch, like this, not straight in and not too slanty neither."

Dred leaned in, his hands pattering softly on his thighs, until it wore on the nerves of the old man, who was used to spending his entire day alone. Joe dropped a nail, it glanced off the horse's right leg, and the horse jerked away from his grip.

"Landsakes, Dred, stop twitching! You acting like you got the St. Vitus dance, not to mention you distracting this animal. If you can't hold still, go fetch me more nails."

Mindful of the sharp tips, Dred plucked a half dozen nails from the end barrel and ran back to the old man, who stooped to rest by the forge. The light from the ebbing fire shimmered on his hairless head like a halo. Wearily, he wiped his halo with a rag.

"I vex them in the big house, too, I know it, 'cause I's always playing rhythms. But I can do this, Uncle Joe. I can keep still."

"See that you do. Now, go quieten that horse again. I'll allow this much: you got a way with animals. They like your rhythm even iffen it be a mite much for us people folk. Indeed, I don't believe you'll ever need worry about no nervous nelly flattening your nose."

The horse quieted, the old man got his second wind, and once again the hoof was in place between Uncle Joe's legs. "Good; now bring them nails." Dred held them out on his palm, and as Uncle

Joe looked up from the hoof cradled between his thighs, he shook his head and craned his neck to meet Dred's gaze. Patiently but sternly, he said, "Connect your eyes to your brain, son, and look at the size of these nails. They's much too long!" Again he dropped the hoof, mopped his head, then said, "Come over here and let me learn you the difference betwixt these sizes."

Uncle Joe stood by the row of nails. Each barrel had a number burned into it, Dred now saw: ½, 1, 2, 4. Uncle Joe began his lesson: "All the nails get sorted according to size, and you better not let me catch you mixing them up. Until you learn enough to know a size by eyeballing it, you hold one 'longside another to be sure they belong together, like this. Right?"

"Yes, sir."

"These numbers stand for the different inch sizes." Joe plucked a single nail from the one-inch barrel. "This nail is a inch, one inch, and the number writ on the barrel says '1'—"

Then in stalked the Cat Man. Uncle Joe had one hand on Dred's shoulder while the other pointed. Seeing Overton, seeing him smile and grip his cat-o'-nine-tails, Uncle Joe pulled Dred in close behind him. Taking his time, Cat Man squinted all around the smithy as before, finally resting his eyes on the slaves.

Dred stood still enough, now, and so did Uncle Joe. Rabbit still, thought Dred, and remembered that he forgot his lucky rabbit's foot today. Then he thought: No, I may be rabbit still, but Uncle Joe be ox still. With his hunched back and lowered head, the old man looked ready to charge.

Yet it was Dred who jumped as the cat-o'-nine-tails cracked against the anvil. A spark flew, and Dred realized the overseer platted wire into the cords.

No word had been uttered, no charge had been leveled, but they all knew what the crime was. Dred, young enough to think that there should be reasons that mattered and explanations that should make a difference, broke the silence. "He wasn't learning me nothing, Mister Overton, just showing me the difference betwixt little nails and big nails."

Cat Man shook his cat-o'-nine-tails at Dred and laughed as

the boy cringed. "Don't worry, boy. You ain't gonna meet my cat, not today. But you are, old man. I don't believe you've had the pleasure yet. Come on outside here and get acquainted."

Uncle Joe let go of Dred and shuffled toward the door. His eyes moved left and right around the forge, the eyes of an owner, satisfying himself that all was in order before leaving his shop.

"Move your black arse or I'll introduce you right now!" Uncle Joe's speed didn't change. He didn't say a word. He didn't look at Overton. Dred tried to run to the big house, to Gran, but Overton blocked his path.

"Oh no, boy, I think you better watch. You still owed a lesson for the day, and I'm gonna learn you just how dumb dumb niggers are. Now strip, nigger."

Outside in the weak January sunlight, Dred watched Uncle Joe strip; watched, too, the Cat Man's enjoyment of the humiliation. In stupefied fascination he saw the old man's hairy, bearish body emerge from beneath his clothing, and as he stripped, Dred understood as well the determination in Uncle Joe's pursed lips and jutting jaw. Joe shot that look directly at Dred. Holding the boy's gaze, old Joe began to lengthen, as if he were crooked iron being straightened. His hunch dissolved and his spine flattened. His shoulders squared and his head scraped the sky until it seemed to Dred that the old man became as tall and straight as the tree.

"Hug that tree, nigger."

And while Cat Man engraved Uncle Joe's flat, long back, while the flesh peeled apart to expose the ruddy pulp below, Dred was perplexed by the slowness of everything. He saw a crow on a low branch, frightened by the snap of the whip below, bunch and spring into flight. The branch waved goodbye and a gob of bloody tissue hit the bird's breast before it was gone. He saw how Cat Man's jacket sleeve restricted the full swing of his arm, and he watched Cat Man transfer the whip to his left hand, unbutton the jacket front, and shrug a gnarly right arm out of the sleeve. Then he hefted the handle of the whip once more in his right hand, getting the perfect grip, before raising it up and back. Dred followed the arc of that swing down, no longer seeing Uncle Joe's torn torso; instead before his eyes appeared the image of the old man's age-stick, straight and smooth, carved with the slits and grooves that marked the long line of experiences Uncle Joe had lived.

Uncle Joe was on his knees. His furrowed back left no doubt in Dred's mind that there would never be another notch carved into Uncle Joe's age-stick. He was witnessing murder. Like pistol shots, the whip repeatedly fell. Cat Man continued the flogging even after the old man slumped to the ground, and he never noticed when Dred finally broke and ran.

Dred reached the kitchen and couldn't speak. His face drew Gran to her feet and she said, "Who is it?"

"Generous Joe." Dred crumpled in sobs on the warm hearth, the fire here singing a different song.

Gran threw a few ointments and supplies into a basket and asked, "At the smithy?" Dred nodded. He didn't rise. He could not go back there, and she did not want him to.

Uncle Joe was not yet dead. That night in the blacksmith's cabin, Dred and Gran waited. Joe's back hurt with each breath. Fever trembled him. Dred kept the fire stoked high; cleaned away the dishes from the soup Gran had made; rinsed, rung out, and hung the cooling rags. Finally, there was nothing to do but sit still with Gran and help prepare the next batch of poultices. He relaxed beside her, inhaling her comforting aroma.

"What brings that light to your eyes, child?"

"I's thinking how tall Uncle Joe become." He smiled gently. "Look even now: his feets stick over the pallet."

Gran smiled sadly. "Ain't it a wonder."

The logs sparked once or twice. After a long silence, a fierce burst shot dozens of sparks up the flue. Gran said, "That be all. I reckon he be over now, enjoying his mama's arms round him again."

Dred found himself in Gran's arms, absorbing her cinnamon hug. She rocked him, and when his tears subsided, she crooned, "Dred, honey, out by the tree Generous Joe told me to give you something. He said, 'If I go home tonight, you be sure Dred gets my age-stick. And show him the passing mark.' So here it is, child."

From her apron she produced the stick and a whittling knife and handed them both to Dred. "He wanted you to carve the passing mark. I'll tell you how: right down here, at the end of his experiences, you gonna carve what looks like a snake coiled up. First make a circle, that's right, but don't close it. Now make a extra cut over here for the tail, good; and over on this side make the head with a open mouth, like a open pair of tongs."

"Like it's gonna eat its tail?" Dred asked.

"'Xactly like that. Good, good. Now you keep that in rememory of Generous Joe."

For the second time that day, Dred's slender brown fingers caressed the hardened, whitened wood. Tracing the mysterious markings, he realized he would never hear the stories Uncle Joe would have told. Gran, with arms still wrapped around him, hummed low. "Sing the words, baby," she urged. And while she hummed, he whisper-sang the familiar folk tune:

> *I'm going home, to see my mother*
> *She said she'll meet me when I come.*

A chorus rose from outside the cabin, and Dred knew the others from the quarter had been keeping vigil. They sang strong:

> *I'm only going over Jordan*
> *I'm only going over home.*

Now Gran sang, too, and Dred imagined he even heard Uncle Joe's surprising falsetto, with the ting of the farrier's hammer in it.

Chapter eight

Preacher Boy

I was put to work in the stables after Uncle Joe died. Like he said 'fore he passed on, I was good with animals. So stable boy were fine work, but there weren't no special respect in it, and I was left to wonder on what my manhood was gonna look like.

A boy leaving childhood feels a natural inclination to look up to a man, 'cept who was there? Uncle Joe would've been that man for me; a part of me mourned missing that as much as I mourned the man hisself. Uncle Solomon might've been, 'cept he were away at war with Master. Sam was around a lot, he was the one training me with the horses, but Sam wasn't so much older'n me. He was more like a brother; 'sides, he wasn't a serious fellow.

Then I met Nat Turner. That's right, that Negro what led the insurrection of '31. My childhood friend growed to be the man what killed all them white folk. 'Course, when I first met him, back around 18'n14, Nat was a kind of apprentice preacher in the area. We was probably about the same age, but he always seemed bigger, older. He already had answers when all I had was questions.

Up till then in my life, I believed things was simple: what was good would carry on, and what was bad would pass away. But all that changed with Uncle Joe's death—the bloodthirst I seed, it squeezed my heart. Master being away and just not seeming to care much when he come home on furlough, that put a weight on my mind. Then there was my own body coming up on being a man, things happening I didn't understand, things I felt I should control but didn't know how. I had a swarm of questions.

I didn't question why, like Njeri done. I never did hold with one god like that. Gran done learned me about Fa—what you would call fate. Not a destiny, not a fixed thing. A man moves toward his fate, choice by choice, and he can find it or he can lose it. So I was at the start of understanding that. At the start of moving toward the man I would become and the fate that would be mine. That made me curious, eager, but I never expected no flash of lightning to reveal my fate. Not like Nat did. The spirit of the great white god burned in that boy. Nothing made him happier than to be the instrument of his god, laying down his own will 'fore his god. He called it "faith." I didn't know what to call it, but it fascinated me. It weren't so much that I wanted faith or even missed it in my life; it were more like I just wanted to feel the power and the certainty that Nat felt.

ॐ

Dred, driving the open carriage to church, listened to the Missus and Master arguing. Each time Master Peter returned from the war, there was this arguing. Frequently, as now, it concerned Gran, and Dred strained to catch every word.

"Exempting any slave from Sunday services sets a bad example, Peter. To the field hands as well as to our own children. Gran may be a slave but you cannot overlook that she is also an example to our children. They heed what she does, what she says. You heed what she says." A gust of wind tugged at the brim of Elizabeth Blow's bonnet; she held it firmly in place. "From the day we wed I knew I should have bought my own mammy. One younger. One who wasn't your mammy. One who would listen to me."

"Gran listens to you, Elizabeth."

"Listens and does as she pleases. Because she knows you will excuse her."

"Elizabeth, you are my wife. Gran is a slave. If ever I fail to defer to your judgment in matters of the household, I beg you to correct me."

"So you say. Dred, reign in that team. We're swaying back here like a ship on the high seas!" Speaking as if the boy wasn't present, Elizabeth Blow continued. "I told you he was unfit to handle the phaeton. I cannot understand why Sam doesn't drive us."

Dred had been paying more attention to the argument than to the horses. Slowing them, he felt relieved to see the argument was veering away from Gran, even if that meant his own feet were over the coals. Fortunately, the argument veered again.

Resentment tinged Peter Blow's reply. "Dred would be otherwise engaged and not handling the horses if Overton had been restrained."

"Surely you don't blame me for that! I suppose you think I should have neglected the children, and seen first to the slaves and the crops?"

"No, no, of course not. But you must have observed his tactics. You must have seen he had begun using a whip, against my express order. Dear God, Elizabeth, he killed a man."

She raised her chin. Without blinking or flinching she said, "An old slave died. One with a weak heart. Yes, Overton whipped him. But you weren't there. Neither was I."

Dred was scandalized. I was there, he wanted to scream at her. I seed it all. He felt a bitter despair. Uncle Joe would still be alive if the Master had been home. Dred relived with a gratifying tingle of pleasure the memory of how Master Peter had run off Overton.

The showdown had occurred in the smithy. Dred was loading tools into a crate to be carried to another plantation for mending. Overton was haranguing him, implying that the need to hire a smithy's services was somehow Dred's fault for not having learned the trade before his mentor had been killed.

Intimidated, the boy dropped an armload of tools, and Cat Man promptly blamed him for breaking tools that were already broken. Dred hadn't even known that the Master was due home on furlough, so Peter Blow's sudden appearance in the smithy was like a miracle.

"Three of my best hands," the Master had raged, "You've killed one and run off two others." He was brandishing the cat-o'-nine-tails, and it looked as though the Master would strike the overseer. "And of the slaves that remain—fear and resentment is what I see in faces that used to smile at me. No words can explain the damage you have wrought." Peter Blow dropped his voice to a low menace. "Get off my land and I declare: if sundown catches you anywhere near here, I'll take this whip to you, sir, and we'll determine how fond of it you are."

Dred had never seen the Master so enraged, but it made him look up to Peter Blow even more. Now, carefully keeping the horses at a steady speed, Dred hoped the Master would turn that anger upon his wife.

Instead, Peter Blow adopted a conciliatory tone. He sounded tired. "Elizabeth, you have done an exceptional job running things during my long absence. For these brief furloughs, could we avoid bickering? I concede as your domain the running of the household. However, you must leave charge of the farm and all its offices—including the stables and carriages—to me. Dred has a way with animals, particularly horses. He knows the team and the carriage, too. What he needs to learn is how to transport passengers, and I intend him to be educated in this manner. I prefer Sam drive the children in the barouche. It may be asserted without scruple that, as he's more experienced, the children are safest with him."

They passed the Burton carriage, headed in the opposite direction. The women waved and exchanged greetings, the men tipped their hats. With an arched eyebrow, Elizabeth Blow confided to the breeze, "Well, it appears the Burtons and Gran have something in common. Neither deigns to honor the Sabbath."

"No one can accuse Robert Burton of impiety. It must be Rebecca's health. I understand she has been keeping poorly."

"Not so poorly that she couldn't devour half of Mary Swinton's teacakes on Thursday. She complains bitterly of the heat, but I am not alone in thinking she might find some relief if she didn't burden herself with all that flesh. Ah, we're here, at last."

Dred steered the horses in behind a line of carriages that were discharging passengers. Peter Blow rose to open the carriage door, but Elizabeth stopped him with a gloved hand.

"Let Dred bring us to the door. I don't want to drag my skirts through all this mud."

Peter resumed his seat. "Pull the carriage forward to the pavement, Dred."

Elizabeth continued, "One might think that one of the wealthiest congregations in the county could manage to provide a pavement leading up to the house of God so that worshippers needn't kneel before their Maker with caked mud falling from their clothes."

Dred pulled the carriage forward as others departed, then hopped down to open the door for his master, who corrected him, "See to the Missus, Dred."

The boy ran to the opposite side of the carriage, opened the door, and offered his hand. Elizabeth Blow's hands remained clasped in her lap, her gaze pinned to a cloud. "I prefer to wait for my husband."

He had noticed lately that the Missus avoided touching him or looking at him. Weakly, he wondered whether it was because she had observed the recent, uncontrollable stirrings of his loins. Gran knew, of course; nothing escaped her notice. She knew, too, that he felt anxious about it and merely told him calmly one time, "You'll grow out of it." Uncle Solomon had been there and shot Gran a teasing grin. He ruffled Dred's hair and play-whispered, "You'll grow into it."

Dred now stood self-consciously holding the carriage door while Master Peter helped his wife alight. Sam arrived with the children, and the parents waited on the steps for the family to assemble. Dred and Sam remounted their carriages.

"Sam," called the Missus, "be sure to find some shade for those horses. I don't want them exposed to this sun for the next two hours."

"Yes'm." Sam rotated 360-degrees, surveying the wide-open, shadeless landscape. The church had been erected at the center of an extensive clearing. The nearest copse was a quarter mile distant, adding a half mile to the journey he and Dred would have to make before reaching the tent where the Negro worshippers gathered.

"We could just stay with the horses in the shade," Dred suggested.

"Mmmm-hmmm. Might be we could. Unlessen the Missus catch us. 'Sides, I hears they's a new preacher today, a young Negro, got the spirit something fierce."

"That's Nat Turner."

"You know him?"

"You know him, too. He be the one with Reverend Amos at Uncle Joe's burial."

"Oh, that one. What's Amos doing, learning him to preach?"

"Something like that."

"I hear tell this boy even makes his own spirituals. You know him good?"

"Not really. I just talked with him a spell after Uncle Joe's burial. He's strange in a way, yet something about him struck me awful familiar, too, something I can't make out. I know he got the power of speech, though, sure 'nough."

Wisps of song slipped from the tent as Dred and Sam approached. The reverent tones of "Yonder Comes Day" fluttered into the rousing "Kneebone Bend." The white patroller, hired to ensure sedition was not preached with salvation, slouched outside the tent in a narrow stripe of shade. The congregation slowed and deepened for "Oh Lord, I'm Waiting on You," successfully lulling him to sleep by the time Sam and Dred drew aside the tent flap.

Lined along rows of crude benches sat about sixty slaves. Some of the younger men wore string ties around freshly-washed shirts; a few older men sported cravats. The women had ironed their best aprons and starched the streamers hanging down their backs; several boasted hats with festooned brims, others wore patterned bonnets. Children gleamed from last night's scrubbing and moved stiffly in restrictive Sunday clothes. Sam and Dred slid onto a bench just inside the flap.

All faced the interior of the tent and the unoccupied preacher's platform, an unadorned warehouse pallet. Silence and humidity saturated the air. Drowsiness hung like ether. Bowed heads snapped up suddenly when, from the center of the gathering, a crackling field holler exploded: a lungful of vowels that accordioned from flat to sharp, from low to high, from warning to command.

A burly youth rose to his feet with eyes closed, head bowed. It was Nat Turner. Dred watched expectantly as Nat's arms floated to shoulder height, palms upward. Crisply, in a modulated tone, the boy said, "Brothers, and sisters. Aunts, and uncles. You children and parents: gather together." Backbones slackened by the heat stretched a little straighter. People leaned in toward that voice and held their breath. Flies stopped buzzing.

Into this stillness Nat raised his head, intoning, "Hear me well." With eyes still closed, he commanded, "Open your ears to the word of God and be saved." Gazing all around, easing his huge form gracefully through the crowd, he mounted the preacher's platform. "Open your hearts to the love of Jesus and be free." Half speaking, half singing, he launched into a tuneless, rhythmic recitation, rasping out each syllable as if a saw hewed the words from hardwood:

> *A-ma-*
> *zing Grace.*
> *How sweet*
> *The sound.*
> *That saved*
> *A wretch*
> *Like me.*

The throng took it up, whittled it into melody. Some clapped; some cried out, "Amen, Lord!" or "Bless us, Jesus!" Their harmony became an inspiration reflected in the eyes of the preacher. Nat brought the congregation to their feet with his stare. None could keep their seats, not even Sam, a sometimes-Sunday worshipper. He leaned over and whispered to Dred, "How old he be?"

Dred focused intently on Nat, still trying to pinpoint why he seemed so familiar. "He's my age," he replied.

Though the same age, Nat was already man-sized, his presence authoritative. Yet his voice still occasionally cracked unexpectedly, like Dred's. Again Sam whispered, "I can't figure whether he be a man or a boy."

"Let the sermon determine," whispered Dred.

Nat began his sermon, and the people sat to listen. He could have read from the Bible, but he chose to speak from his heart. "We got business," he said. "We got busy-ness here on this earth, but we also got business, that which God intended for us to accomplish while we walk among men. What is our business? Is mine the same as your'n? How do we discover the divine intention that our Lord God has for us?"

He was silent so long one old man turned to another. "Seems even the preacher boy don't know the answer to that one." But they both attended when Nat continued.

"The sermon today is about young Jesus, a boy of twelve, com-ing on that age when he leaves childish ways behind. That age of thinking on what is his business. Now, back in Nazareth, each year everybody's got to go to town to pay taxes. Jesus, he rides in with his parents and all the neighbors. Takes a few days and some hard-ship, but they get there, they conduct their business, and then head on back home. But don't the family get a day's travel out of town when they see Jesus is missing. Ain't nobody recollects seeing him since they left town.

"All agitated, Mary and Joseph hurry on back to town. Terrible imaginings haunt every step. They're breathless, thinking: 'Why, here we got responsibility for raising the Son of God, and could be he got snatched up into slavery. Maybe some lion dragged him off for dinner! What if we can't never find him? How we going to explain that, come the Judgment Day? The Savior of the world—and we done gone and lost him!'

"They was worked into quite a state when, at long last, they discover Jesus at the church. He's setting there, cool as a spring brook, babbling with the preachers, asking questions and telling them his own thoughts. Soon as she catches sight of him, his mother starts hollering, 'Jesus! Have you lost your wits? What could you be think-ing to put us through such a fright?' She's ready to tan his hide but Joseph, mindful how this be the Son of God and all, stays her hand.

He steps before the boy and says, 'Son, you disobeyed your parents. Explain yourself.'

"And with eyes cloudless as a summer sky, Jesus looks up and says, 'You should know to find me in my father's house. You should know that I be about my father's business.'"

Silence greeted the end of Nat's story instead of the usual "amens" and "praise be's." The congregation was slow to absorb what the young preacher wanted them to understand. All but Dred. He felt the power of the vision offered in the preacher's eyes; it trembled him. It seemed to Dred that the other boy had grown during the sermon, as Uncle Joe had grown out by the tree, as Jesus had grown in the story.

Nat stood on the platform, husky and black, with skin that had the look of good planting soil after a soaking rain. Light played on the sweat in his hair like sunlight on dew in the grass. He glistened. Dred suddenly remembered the stories of the young African prince, the one the old folk said would come one day to break the white man's shackles, the black prince who would gather up his people and fly with them back to Africa. That's why Nat seemed so familiar: in all Dred's imaginings, he had always pictured the young African prince looking just like the preacher boy standing before him.

Abruptly Nat roared, "Are you slaves?" The way he said that word made them feel hot shame on their cheeks. With cooling tenderness, he added: "Care not, for you are children of God. He shall set you free."

One or two muttered, "Amen."

Nat clapped hard and loud, a single beat: "Do you labor as beasts?" Strained silence again, this time tinged with resentment. "Trouble not, for your Father in heaven will grant you strength and patience. Praise His holy name."

"Praise God, praise Jesus."

"Children!" He clapped again. "Are you lonesome? Cry not, for Jesus will suffer the little ones to come unto Him."

"Parents!" Clap. "Do you grieve? Despair not, for Jesus weeps with you. His tears will wash clean your soul."

The clap came again, sounding now like a rifle report. "Do you have faith?" No one answered. He repeated the clap and the question, "Do you have faith?"

"Yes, yes. Praise God, praise Jesus."

"My brothers, if you only have faith, you will want for nothing." Clap. "Sisters, let faith free you." Clap. "Uncles, let faith remove your burdens." Clap. "Aunts, let faith walk with you on the path to the promised land." Clap. "Faith is the business before us all, right here, right now, today." Clap. "Say yes to Jesus."

"Yes, Jesus."

Clap. "Say amen to the ways of the Lord."

"Amen, Lord."

They clapped with him now, certain of his rhythm. "So says Jesus." Some double-clapped. "Such are the ways of a merciful God, your Master in heaven." They had it now, the rhythm, the faith. Several hummed, others stomped.

"Men, come away," urged Nat.

And the men clapped and called, "My Lord, He calls me."

"Women, come away home."

And the women clapped and called, "Come away to Jesus."

"Come away, all. And all will be well for all time, for eternity." This final exhortation was felt rather than heard, as the words of a hymn rose from the congregation. Nat's resonant tenor established the melody, followed closely by the other humming male voices. Softer altos from the grannies gave the refrain, and the clear feminine sopranos carried the words:

> *He calls me by the thunder*
> *The trumpet sounds within my soul*
> *I ain't got long to stay here.*

> *Come away, come away, come away to Jesus*
> *Come away, come away home*
> *I ain't got long to stay here.*

> *Green trees are a-bending*
> *Poor sinner stands a-trembling*

The trumpet sounds within my soul
I ain't got long to stay here.

Come away, come away, come away to Jesus
Come away, come away home
I ain't got long to stay here.

Tombstones are a-bursting
Poor sinner stands a-trembling
The trumpet sounds within my soul
I ain't got long to stay here.

Come away, come away, come away to Jesus
Come away, come away home
I ain't got long to stay here.

Chapter nine

Rites of Passage

Enduring that summer and fall, I seeked Nat out after Sunday camp meetings, and often as we could we shared stories. Gran always told how she knowed I would become a griot 'cause I spoke the African tales 'fore I heared them from her. Seems I was born with them stories in me. And Nat knowed stories as a baby, too, Bible stories. He said he just up and started telling them tales in little baby words. Naturally, his parents and all the slaves found this prodigious and said he must be sent from god as a special voice to speak to the slaves. Even Nat's master done seed him as special and learned him reading and writing and toting figures, which just be an amazement to me, seeing's how Uncle Joe got flayed alive over just knowing about nail sizes.

I was mighty impressed how Nat could read. He read that Bible day and night, knowed every story in there, knowed battles and kings and a thousand different ways of suffering. The tribes of Israel had many tribulations, including slavery in Egypt, and Nat speculated how Africans must be one of them old-time tribes 'cause Egypt, he said, weren't too far from Africa.

'Course, I wasn't just using my ears; my mouth was moving

as fast as his. Fact, we had us a kind of competition. Nat's speciality was the Bible, mine the African tales—and there's a heap of similar stories to both: floods and swarms of locusts, babies what lost they mamas, children like Jesus in a confusion over who be they papa, spirit voices coming from unexpected places like animals or rivers or bushes. We had us a sporting competition.

Thinking I could best him, I told him one day about my kin, about the warrior women, knowing all the while Gran would slap me if she heared how I was using it just to best a friend. But I had a need to impress him, and I considered the warrior women one of my most powerful tales. When I got done telling him of Njeri murdering her babies, I was strutting I was so sure I had him beat. But Nat was just as skeptical about my kin as I was about the great white god.

Nat said, "That's pitiful. All them's burning in the flames of hell now, because God don't abide by murder and suicide."

"That don't figure, Nat," I argued. "What about all them murders in the Bible? God hisself killed a whole mess of people. Even killed his own son, according to you."

"You don't understand. If God tells you to, you gotta do as He say. But you can't just take it into your own head. You got the freedom to choose: you can be His instrument, like a scythe, or you can burn in hell for breaking His commandments."

"Well, if you done listened good, you'd know Njeri believed she heared the commandment of Bon Dieu. So how can you say Njeri wasn't god's instrument?"

"Bon Dieu ain't God."

"Was god to Njeri."

"Ain't the same. Ain't *the* God. 'I am the Lord thy God, thou shalt have no other gods before Me.'"

"Who you to say that old, white-bearded god be any more powerful than anybody else's god? I can say I got better stories'n you but it don't necessarily make it so."

"If you got faith, then you know."

"And if you ain't got faith?"

"Then you burning in the pit of hell come Judgment Day."

"Njeri done got faith. Enough faith to get her nerves together and go and kill her own babies, all on the say-so of god."

"But she believed in a false god. She had the wrong faith."

Well, I never could argue about them Bible tales and win, not with Nat. Not when he pulled that faith card from up his sleeve like a wild joker in Poker. And through all these years since, I never yet did get the faith, nor believe in one god neither. Despite Harriet's good efforts to the contrary. Guess I's just the faithless type, come from a long line of the faithless.

⁂

Dred never knew what strange notion Nat might hatch next, like when Nat decided to eat grasshoppers. Africans, Dred knew, would roast locusts over a fire and eat them. But Dred also knew Nat took no notice of such history. Nat's notion—like all of his notions—came from the Bible.

Dred learned part of the purpose of Nat's strange diet after a prayer meeting. The two boys walked among the long, dry, autumn grasses, examining the ground. Dred said, "Nat, it's too late for grasshoppers."

"I know that. I'm scouting crickets. To practice on."

Squinching up his nose, Dred asked, "You ever tried these grasshoppers before?"

"Not yet. 'Sides, you don't eat them plain, you eat them with honey."

"Too late for honey, too."

"I know that! I got a half barrel of molasses instead."

"Where'd you get that?"

"Took it."

"Stole it? The preacher boy stole molasses?" Dred swatted Nat on the shoulder.

"I got a purpose, God's purpose. You never know what God might ask you to do."

"God asked you to eat grasshoppers? Shoot! Don't go asking me to eat grasshoppers, molasses or no molasses."

75

"I ain't asking you. Neither's God." A flutter of wings set Nat scurrying after a small nest of crickets. Dred didn't even try. Nat returned with two in the palm of his hand.

"Nat, listen: I got a much better idea about how to use that molasses."

"That molasses is mine."

Dred knocked the crickets out of Nat's hands. "Boy, you don't know what you talking about. You making this up as you go along. I tell you what we really ought to do with that molasses: make us some potato liquor."

"I don't drink liquor."

"Why not? Jesus drunk it. 'Sides, I ain't talking about drinking it. We could sell it, make a little pocket change. I heared a traveling show's due in through here next month."

Nat looked up from the grass and rested his gaze in the tree branches, imagining the traveling show. Dred urged him, "I heared Sam telling Bill how to make some. We'll need a sack of potatoes, though. Since you got the molasses, I could sack a sack, so to say."

Nat resumed looking for crickets. "Don't do it. It's not worth it."

Dred squinted at his friend, sizing him up. "You want to be the only one to get away with something. Well, I's just as apt as you."

"I don't want no part in it. Let it be, why don't you?"

They were nearing a stream; the current was strong and noisy. Still arguing, Dred raised his voice, but Nat wasn't listening. With no change in his stride, Nat descended the bank and waded into the creek. Dred watched the brisk water swirl waist-high around Nat.

"Ain't you freezing!"

"I don't feel it. All's I feel is God's presence. You feel Him, Dred? He's here."

"God's in the middle of that creek?"

"I hear Him, clear as I hear you. He's calling to you today, Dred Scott: come be baptized, come be saved by divine grace."

"No thank you, Nat Turner."

"Let's do it, Dred. Baptism, right now, right here. You can ask God's forgiveness."

"Forgiveness for what?"

"That pride, for one thing. Stealing for another."

"You's the one what stole. So far I's just cogitating on it."

"That stealing's on my soul. But I know salvation is my God's great gift. I know I'm assured a place in heaven. But you, you haven't even been baptized. How you going to get any of God's good grace when you haven't even been baptized?"

"For that I got to get creek water up my nose and down my lungs? I'd druther be saved from having to explain to Gran why my toes done dropped off from chilblains."

"Don't you want salvation? To be together with me in heaven on Judgment Day?"

It was not the consequences in heaven, but those right there with Nat that prompted Dred forward. He stepped to the edge of the bank. Nat waved his arms through the water as though hugging the creek, sending ripples that lapped gently over the toes of Dred's shoes. Shoes that would fall apart if soaked. Dred stooped to take them off. Nat waited.

As Dred placed one bare foot into the icy water, Nat retreated into the stream, inviting Dred farther and deeper. But Dred stopped. Abruptly he saw there would be no togetherness, in heaven or on earth. His friend was moving away, toward his own destiny.

Why I parted ways with Nat Turner had nothing to do with the stories we told nor with what god we believed in. What pulled us in different directions were fear. We was both fascinated by it; scared of what we didn't know, scared of what we couldn't control. We was boys coming up, looking to be men, and we had to rassle that devil—fear.

One way we tried was through scary stories. Nat put his britches on when telling them. I maybe had him beat when it come to telling about common people and happenings, but I wasn't even close to Nat on the spooky ones. He told the scariest, and iffen his tale were about a boy, he'd call that boy "Dred," so I got even more scared.

He told one about a boy named Dred on his way to catch

frogs one Sunday, never minding he was supposed to keep the lord's day holy. Nat was big on anything to do with sin and evil. So Dred be humming along when he meets up with Uncle Zeke, who says, "Boy, turn your feet round and come with me to church. It's a sin to be playing 'stead of praying!"

"It may be Sunday, old man, but it ain't the lord's day—this be my day, the one day I get free, and I sure ain't gonna spend it in no hot, stuffy church. I'ma catch me some big fat frogs, and I'ma have a full stomach for one night of the week!"

The old man shakes his righteous head and says, "You best watch out the swamp devil don't get you. Swamp devil only powerful on Sundays, and those who go in there on the Lord's day wind up trading they souls for an afternoon's fun."

Dred laughs at the old man and whistles along on his way. At the marsh, he squats by the side of the water and waits for the frogs to calm to his presence. Soon they start singing to each other and hopping through the muck, and little Dred thinks to hisself: these here frogs are playing, like me. Ain't nothing wrong here!

He bides his time till one fat ol' frog comes close enough for him to jump up and grab it. He falls face-first in the briny water and comes up with a clammy wad of marsh grass 'cross his eyes, but he's got that frog fast by the legs and is right pleased with hisself. He wipes the scum from his face and grins at his captive, its popping eyes and gulping mouth. The more the critter flails, the more puffed-up Dred feels. He wades back to the bank, looking for a rock at the water's edge to bash out the frog's brains. He's almost there when a great big *SUCK* pulls on his foot and trips him up, face-down again into the bog.

The frog gets away, but Dred don't think on that 'cause he's too busy wondering what grabbed his foot. Felt like something alive under the water—not a hand exactly, more like the spiked tongue of a huge, slithering snake, or maybe like the suction cup of a giant leech. Harrowed to the marrow, Dred clambers to the pebbly shore, crawling hand over fist, legs pumping. At a safe distance from the water, he catches his breath and laughs at hisself, till a tingle in his foot reminds him maybe the devil be keeping score here.

Sure 'nough, he got a evil-looking boil rising on his ankle, a stomach-turning greenish color, like the color of the slime on the rocks. Horror hugs his chest as he watches it swell, bigger and bigger. Quickly it's half the size of his foot; then just his toes be visible; now his whole foot be swallowed by the growing blister and it's traveling directly up his shin bone. Everywhere it touches feels on fire, as iffen hot spikes was drove into his flesh and twisted. A putrid smell, like gutted fish innards rotting in the sun, clogs his nose. Dred wants to run but he's stuck, rooted by fear. As the boil bubbles over his knee-cap, oozing yellow bile, creeping closer and closer to his crotch, he commences to scream at the top of his lungs.

Now he be the one with eyes popping and mouth gulping. The stink be so thick he can hardly breathe. The pain be so great he can hardly move. And his fear be so strong he never realize how loud he be screaming till suddenly right before him stands Uncle Zeke.

"Help me! Help me, Uncle Zeke!"

Again the old man shakes his righteous head, more sorrowful this time. Slowly, with his kerchief over his nose, he backs away from the throbbing blob before him. "Ain't no help for you now, boy. You been touched by the swamp devil. Ain't nothing left for me to save."

And the last thing Dred hears, before the stinging pus fills his mouth, his nose, his ears, is the fading sound of Uncle Zeke's voice singing:

Bullfrog jumped in the middle of the spring,
An' I ain't a-gonna weep no more.
He tied his tail to a hick'ry limb,
An' I ain't a-gonna weep no more.

Ooo-wheee, I don't mind saying today that I had the goose flesh standing out on my arms when Nat told that one! And though I never held no truck with god nor Sundays nor holy days neither, I never went catching frogs on a Sunday ever again.

I stayed friends with Nat for two, maybe three year, with more chance to see him once Master come back from the war, 'cause Master got slack on running things and I could get away from Zephyr more. But in all that time I never did get so's I could beat Nat at a scary tale. I never made the little hairs tickle the back of his neck.

I got it into my head one day, though, to scare Nat with a real devil: a dog Bill kept outside his cabin, tied to a tree with a rusty old chain. Only human Devil allowed near him was Bill, and Bill called him Devil 'cause he was a vicious animal, full of a hate what burned in that dog a slow, steady fire.

We stood a ways back from the tree where Devil was chained. He was a brindled mastiff, with eyes the color of tarnished brass. Weighed as much as Bill did. I whispered to Nat, "You get near enough for Devil to sink his teeth in you, ain't no amount of prayer gonna save you." Devil heared his name. Half-opening his dull eyes, he glared at us flat.

"That dog? That dog don't scare me," Nat said.

"Then you don't know what you looking at," I told him.

Nat took one step. Devil's eyes opened full and his ears come forward. Another step, and Devil's lip hitched up, out come a low growl. His ears flattened down. The muscles in his shoulders bunched up, and Nat begun to see what he was facing. He bent to pick up a stick. Devil quick jumped to all fours, exposing his fangs, still growling low—not in alarm but in sheer menace, as if to say, "Come on, I'll mash your flesh like chicken livers and crack your bones for the marrow."

'Cept Nat didn't approach no further. Bill come outten his cabin, meaner'n and madder'n Devil. Bill often put me in mind of a bull with his head lowered, so I generally stayed clear. Iffen I knowed he was home, I never would've brought Nat round.

"You little bastards clear on outta here 'fore I let this chain play out."

We runned and laughed and punched each other on the arm, feeling brave and foolish. I can't rightly say why it should be that children take a specific pleasure in that shivery feeling. Only when we's older do we realize how weak we truly be, and that's what truly be scary.

Nat learned that lesson before me. Right 'fore we stopped

having any connection, I heared how Nat was schooled in his own weakness, when not even the power of his god saved him from the beating he taken.

That were during the time when I didn't see Nat for a whole summer, not even at camp meetings. I finally asked Uncle Amos about him, and he rolled his eyes, clucked his tongue and said, "We was called over to the Burton plantation. Not to bury or wed, but only 'cause Missus Burton taken the notion in her head that when the boys get whipped, it's less bad on her husband if he have a preacher there reading the Bible while the lash falls."

"Nnn-nnn," was all I could say, but I was thinking how Gran always said the white god ain't nothing but a way for white folk to sleep at night.

"I allow it's a crazy notion," Amos went on, "and maybe I should've knowed better'n to bring along Nat. But I figure he got to see it all iffen he expect some day to carry on my duties. So no sooner'n they strap the boy to the wheel, I see Nat's eyes start to jump. Ain't that he never seed no beating before. We see 'em regular on Master Turner's farm. But Nat ain't never seed no beating conducted to the reading of the Bible before. He couldn't abide that.

"I guess I should've kept my eye on the boy, should've recited a passage I knowed by heart 'stead of reading one. Because when I looked up, Nat's lurched out. He's coming up betwixt Mister Burton and the boy what's getting the skin peeled off him. Nat's quivering all over, worser'n the whipped boy, and Mister Burton's a picture of confusion. I hurried over but it were too late. Nat got mighty on Mister Burton, proclaiming fire, brimstone, and damnation! It were terrible. Almighty God, it were terrible."

I could see it clearly. I already knowed how Nat begun to show a partiality for any Bible story with a prophet in it, claiming how the prophets was special people, powerful enough to sit in judgment of the kings. Nat liked that, liked the idea of speaking for god and telling the kings what's right and what's wrong. I seed him clearly, prophetising to the white man with the whip in his hand—might as well command the sea to stop flowing.

"So Nat's confined to the farm for the time being," Amos

continued. "Got hisself shot through the small end of the horn, first, though. Burton beat him, then Master Turner beat him. Beat him till the whip got hot. Now he's just confined."

My stomach boiled; flashes of Uncle Joe tripped before my eyes. Then I seed Nat as he was in the creek, not feeling the cold, and I felt a hope like a prayer that's how he managed with the whipping.

"When you expect him back at camp meetings?" I asked.

"He's got to apologize and take back all that damnation first. And that boy is stubborn. I can't predict when he'll be set loose. Even then, I'll warrant Master Turner won't allow Nat to do no preaching for quite some time."

When I did see Nat again, seems we was just past stemming time 'cause I recollect Master gived me a free day, seeing's how I worked through a number of nights in the warehouse, stripping the leaves. We cured a heap of t'bacca that season, the last year we ever got a good crop outten that soil. Must've rolled double the hogsheads down to the river. So I was pulled off my other duties to work with the hands, stripping them stems 'fore the leaves turned too dry or too damp. Then I got my free day and that's when I seed Nat again, enduring that time of year when the frost comes regular in the mornings, and the smaller runs get choked with all the dead stuff falling from the trees along the banks. That's how Nat seemed: kinda choked up. Wouldn't talk about the Burton trouble.

I shied my mouth, but it set me to thinking he must've apologized in the end. And how could anybody talk about a thing like that? I marked my time with Nat, but we never could get back to that way of speaking easy with each other. I guess I changed, too. My nature begun to lead me, and I was having a time of it just not making a dog of myself with the gals. The more time passed, the less time I gived to thoughts of Nat Turner.

I often think on them days, howsomever; how I explored friendship with Nat, and faith and fear. I look back on it all and see we was just boys, drifting apart as boys do. Boys close to being men, helping each other become men but becoming different sorts of men. Nat and me seed things by different lights. I see us: me barefoot at the creek's edge, him fully clothed, standing solid in the middle of that icy stream, his faith keeping him warm. No way I could ever stand in such water and not feel as though I got ice for bones.

I hope his hard, icy faith protected Nat, the way ice on a fruit crop will sometimes save it from being rotted out by a cold snap. Fear can do that: come up sudden, leave you frozen till it eats you up, like a swamp devil. Nat Turner knowed fear, sure 'nough, had it whipped into his soul, but he let it spur him on. His anger moved him forward, and that icy faith gived him something to walk on, slipping along, maybe, but moving ahead.

I often think on where it led him, and on what he later did. Just before they hanged him he said it were god what directed him to kill the white folk, and I know he believed that. I laugh, 'cause it seems that old, bearded white god is a double-edged sword, with protections for the whites what cut the blacks and other protections for the blacks what cut the whites. Iffen I learned nothing else from Nat Turner, I learned that.

Still, not believing in his god, I look for meaning under a different light. I wonder, after all them years of walking on ice, what happens to such anger and faith? By the time he marched on them white folk, I don't imagine Nat was looking like a African prince no more. No, I imagine him paler and drier, that rich black soil exhausted, all the good nutrients drained. Could be he looked at his soul and seed a pale thing, blanched by the heat of slavery, and he knowed he had to stomp it out, both the cause and the consequence.

But I be spilling about the edges here. Truth is, I can't be sure how much I ever understood about Nat Turner, even when we was boys together. I ain't the sort to be leading no rebellion, so who's to speak on right and wrong? Right comes after the deed gets done, and you set alone with yourself and admit how it feels. In that, I know Nat believed he done the right. He wouldn't risk the fires of hell, otherwise.

So this is how I see Nat Turner in the end: I see him leading them slaves with scythes and axes, off to chop down a mess of white folk, him carrying his fear like a man. Not like a boy—what conjures up a fright and then runs laughing—like a man what alloys anger to his fear and tempers it with his faith in all he holds true. From that he forges hisself a sword and hopes it's strong enough to fight the devil that plagues him.

Chapter ten

Before

From time to time I take out Uncle Joe's age-stick. One side shows a notch for the passing of each year; the other shows the passing of experience, symbols of how he growed. We maybe mark time by birthdays, but we don't grow by them. We grow by the befores and afters, them times when big change rolls over you, when the earth jiggles and shakes. On Joe's stick, carved early on his life, is a flying heart, with a tail like a kite. Not much later is a flat heart, broke in two on the ground.

I was fourteen when my heart first flew from my breast. For a year it soared on the fitful winds of a gal named Lucy, for another year after that it faltered. And soon after I married that gal, made her a part of me, Master Peter smashed us all to pieces.

Master wasn't long home from the 18'n12 war 'fore Missus started pushing for him to get a maidservant for Mary Anne. "Mary Anne's twelve now, she should have her own maid. Little Jane Howley, who isn't half as pretty, got her own maid when she was ten." Comparisons with the Howleys, the Missus well knowed, was guaranteed to spur her husband in the direction she intended. Sure 'nough, the following Saturday night, he crept home long after the embers done cooled in the grate. He come in by the back servants' door, woke Gran, whispering, "I apologize for the lateness of the hour, Gran, but this gal needs a place to sleep. Her name is Lucy, I think, and she is to be trained to help you in the kitchen and to be Miss Mary Anne's maid."

He was carrying a young gal of about fourteen, slung over his shoulder like a sack of flour. He set her down, and even from where I was peeking on, I could see she was far from asleep—just seemed stunned, like a piglet carried in a sack what don't squirm or squeal. Master, on the other hand, be acting somewhat over-large. In his cups.

Frowning, Gran slipped off her shawl and tied it round the gal's shoulders. Something about the young'n made Gran say, "She an island gal?"

"I believe so," said the Master.

Gran wagged her head. "There'll be trouble to bubble now, you mark my words."

"Gran! I hardly expected such silly superstition and bias from you."

"Ain't superstition to know this gal don't speak English. Ain't I right?"

"I suppose. She hasn't spoken a word since I won her."

"Won her?"

I seed him set his backbone straight. He said, "Her native tongue is probably French. She is experienced in picking cotton and will likely be delighted to have housework. Her name is Lucy. I don't think it matters how she comes to be here."

Gran lifted the candle and brought it closer to the girl's face. I could see thoughts shooting behind them eyes, but she didn't look at nobody, didn't even blink.

"She knows nothing about the work you expects her to do," said Gran. "She won't be understanding a thing I tells her to do. And no matter who calls her 'Lucy,' she gonna have to answer to me and to the Missus and to Miss Mary Anne. Was this a bet you won or a bet you lost?"

Master's eyes darted away from the candle and from Gran. "Just do the best you can, Gran. I understand there will be a breaking-in period, during which we will all have to make concessions."

Later, when Gran was snoring and I seed Lucy asleep, too, I crawled over to Lucy's mat and watched her eyes move behind her lids. Her eyes was shaped like young birch leaves, sprouting off the stem of her nose, set wide in her face. I peered close, not blinking, kinda under a spell like when you watch firelight. And though I knowed it to be a trespass, I couldn't help but touch her wild, foreign hair. It fell loose and long, felt just like the long spring grasses down by the creek where I liked to go with the horses and stretch out under the clouds. Oh, I was a goner, right from the start, and I couldn't tell you whether it were her hair or her eyes or her mouth that was most beautiful. She was small, like me, but she was shiny and smooth and perfect, like a doll. Her skin glowed like burnished copper, with nary a hair from her fingertips to her shoulder, smooth and tight and perfect.

I wondered about the island she come from. Iffen she ever seed snow before, iffen she left a family back there. She turned then in her sleep, and my heart about stopped when her night shirt—a big one Gran gived her—didn't turn all the way with her. Then I learned her skin weren't so perfect. I recognized the gnarl of scars from past beatings. My eyes traced a gristly line over her shoulder, and I next learned the pucker of burnt flesh. That poor gal done got branded.

My heart shifted in my chest. I stroked her wild hair. I whispered, "Lucy," and as I done so she opened her eyes right on me. Her eyes traveled from my hand on her hair, up my arm, and locked on my eyes.

"Lucinde," she corrected.

"Lucinde," I murmured. She reached for my wrist. I thought she was annoyed but her touch were light and curious. She put my hand to my own breast, and I understood and said, "Dred."

Gran spent a lot of time showing Lucy how to wash lace and linen, how to powder hair and lace up corsets. Gran was patient with Lucy. Mary Anne was not. That girl started complaining 'fore she even had her eyes open in the morning. By the third day of Lucy's "training," everybody in the big house was a misery. Mary Anne complained to her mama, the Missus complained to the Master, and the Master complained to Gran.

Gran told him outright: "It's like giving a kitten to a two-year-old: somebody's gotta learn the both of them how to treat each other or they's both gonna get mangled."

"The Missus can teach Mary Anne if you can teach Lucy," he said.

"I can learn that gal how to wait hand and foot on Mary Anne and I can keep this kitchen running from dawn till midnight, but I can't do both, not proper."

Took only one more week of everybody squawking 'fore Master decide to call Aunt Hannah in from the fields to help do the cooking. But since nobody liked Aunt Hannah's cooking much as they liked Gran's, the whole plantation still rolled along like a wheel without no axle.

Lucy, though, she played it like a child trundling a hoop with a stick. That gal just wouldn't do more iffen she thought she could get away with less. She bucked routines like a wild colt in its first bridle. Like a horse, too, she showed a equal mixture of startle and startling. Got so's I wouldn't come nigh without whistling, 'cause Lucy lashed out when took by surprise. Yet just as often she brung trouble down on her own head by making other folk jump. She'd jerk out on a impulse, grabbing the cloth on one of the children's dresses to feel its nap, or she'd go poking a finger on someone's arm to see how fat or bony they was. Her ways was strange. She'd talk that French patois that nobody could understand. She'd start laughing for no cause, leaving folk thinking she be laughing at them. She kept everybody off-balance, including Gran, including Master. Everybody but me, that is.

Me—I was having the time of my young life, sure 'nough, 'cause I become Lucy's teacher, too. I understood her best, and she understood me best—or at least let on to, and I didn't care if she be shamming, playing dumb just so's I'd do the chore for her. I loved showing her things, any old thing, like lighting a fire with a flint and piece of cotton. I loved teaching her words and making up games to make the learning more fun. Lucy cottoned to English right quick, and by'n by I was giving her riddles to challenge her. It were a good game, made her think hard, made the work go along faster. First I gived her easy ones, like:

> *Eat 'em hot, eat 'em cold*
> *Eat 'em young, eat 'em old*
> *Eat 'em tender, eat 'em tough*
> *Yet we never get enough.*

Hogs, of course. That were a easy one. Then I gived her harder and harder ones, like:

> *What's slick as a mole,*
> *black as coal,*
> *got a great long tail like a gopher hole?*

She'd work on it through the day, and if evening come and she still couldn't get it, I gived her a clue: "It's something you use every day in the kitchen." And she'd think and show her pretty teeth and think some more. Finally her face lit up bright as the sun, and she flashed them pink gums and shouted: "A skillet!"

She even made up a riddle for me that kept me stumped for the better part of a day:

> *Teeth like a crocodeel*
> *Hide like a eel*
> *Stand solid as a tree*
> *Sing like me.*

I finally figured it out—piano—but it were a good one and I was mighty impressed. Oh, our story them days was having fun and falling in love, when everybody else be complaining about the extra work. Extra, 'cause Master done sold off some slaves so's to buy his-self a race horse. At the same time, he cut back on hiring temporary hands. So all the slaves got extra work. That didn't tighten my reins, though. The more work put on me and Lucy, the more reason to help her and be with her.

Within her first month we done learned her hundreds of words. Words come easy to her, though Missus and Mary Anne never let a day go by without fussing over how stupid she be. "Stupid like a mule," Gran said to me in private, meaning she be just willful, not stupid, and didn't care what name people put to it.

One time Master was called away just as Lucy be serving the dessert. Later when he return to eat his apple crumble, he told Lucy, "Heat this up." She taken the plate to the kitchen and just disappeared. Master waited and waited. Out of patience, he bust into the kitchen, demanding, "Where's my apple crumble!"

Lucy gived her saucy little knee-bend and said, "Master, I do as you say: I eat it up!"

He opened and shut his mouth like a fish gulping air. Only later did he find the words, and it was Gran what took the scolding.

"This gal understand not hardly a word yet," said Gran. "Show her what to do the best I can manage." Which is what she done, but that too become a bed of trouble, 'cause Lucy begun aping Gran's way of doing things. She surely didn't let Gran catch her, but she tried it out on other slaves, standing just like Gran: back straight, arms crossed on her chest, eyes almost closed. Everybody knowed she was being disrespectful and didn't laugh, so she soon gived it up. Not so with her pert little imitation of Mary Anne; that tickled many a funny bone. Lucy mocked that look of Mary Anne's when she was put-out: her jutting chin and the loud sniff of the nose, the little twist of the shoulders. Lucy mimed that pose whenever she and Mary Anne didn't see eye to eye, which were a dozen times a day.

Gran protected and corrected Lucy for a while. After a year done passed and Lucy still be headstrong as ever, Gran tried to warn her about what could happen. One night Gran trucked Lucy on down to Neesy's cabin, to show Lucy the sorry state Neesy be in.

Neesy was a cross-eyed, slow and sullen gal what tended the chickens; kinda gal could rile wilted lettuce. She done gived Master the dopey act once too often, and he turned ugly one day and said, "Neesy, if you act like a heifer, you can be treated like a heifer."

He bred her. That's the awful truth. The first time happened 'fore Lucy arrived at Zephyr, when the farm first started to fail and Master begun drowning his worries in drink. Before he never would've done her that way. After gambling and drink done twisted him, though, you never could be too sure what all he might do. He forced Neesy to sleep in one of the field hand's cabins and warned she better be pregnant by the end of three months, and she was. Later, when that baby been weaned, he sold it.

Gran was scandalized. "This how your papa would've done, and I thought you was better'n that. You call youself a master, you ain't even master of your own weakness. This ain't right, and it sitting over your head like the ax of judgment." He didn't pay her no mind, not like he used to. These days he was tipsy or hung-over most the time, so you couldn't talk to him. Showed no care nor respect for how the farm be run nor for how he treat folks. Even his own family. Little Peter was born and growing; finally Master had another son after his first two boys died, but he just neglected that child. Like maybe he didn't want to care too much. All he cared about was cards, horses, and whisky.

"If a snake will eat its own eggs, what won't it do to a frog?" That's what Gran told Lucy, but that gal was deaf to them African sayings. Anyways, the night Gran marched Lucy down to see Neesy, Neesy done delivered her second IOU baby, so-called 'cause it turns out these babies was traded off as reckoning against Master's gambling debts. But that second baby done come still-born, and that sorry gal was not much alive herself. Just didn't care. Neither Neesy nor the Master seemed to care: Neesy didn't care what the Master heaped on her, and he didn't care what she took. Lucy didn't care about none of it, neither. Gran couldn't make Lucy see how the same thing might happen to her. She didn't drink it in.

Truth be told, I didn't neither, and I spoken English and done lived on that plantation my whole life. Even seeing Uncle Joe beat to death didn't mean in my head that the same thing could happen to me. Gran herself couldn't convince me that something like a cat-o'-nine-tails would ever fall across my own back. Didn't I live my whole life growing up with the Blow children? Didn't I play with them and eat with them? Didn't I sit on Master's knee and give him a riddle or sing him a song? I guess that's how young people do. It's what being young means: you look at the world and see the bad and the ugly, but you make up in your head that, for you, things'll be different. That's how I felt. Because I was young. Because I was in love.

Gran warned me, "You gived your heart too soon." But I told her I gived nothing. My heart gived me no more choice than the ox gives the plowman when it determines to quench its thirst at the creek. My heart went for that long drink of water, dragging me on behind.

❧

Lucy serving as Mary Anne's maid rocked along like a leaky skiff without a rudder. Even after a year had passed, it still took half a day just to dress and groom the young Miss. Something always went awry. Lucy particularly hated touching Mary Anne's dank and slippery hair. The clumps separated disagreeably from the oil of her scalp, and it smelled stale. Pins slid out of place within minutes of being positioned. Combs sagged. The hairdo was invariably lopsided.

"Do it right, Lucy!"

"Pardon?" Lucy feigned wide-eyed innocence.

"You know perfectly well what I'm telling you to do. Do it right!"

With three more pins, Lucy tried to secure a strand in the back, dislodging another that fell behind Mary Anne's left ear. With a sigh, she said, "Pins," and went to the dressing table to collect more. Mary Anne whirled around and the entire pompadour unraveled.

Tearing at her hair, throwing pins and combs on the floor, Mary Anne wailed in a thin, childish pitch, "You useless, incompetent, bungler! Oh, leave those pins alone." She slapped Lucy's hand and more pins bounced on the rug. "I hate you. You're stupid and useless." With a jerk of her shoulders, she turned her back on Lucy, who promptly mimicked her.

Mary Anne caught the mockery in the mirror and advanced aggressively toward the slave. Lucy held her ground with a defiant look. Mary Anne poked a finger into Lucy's shoulder, shoving her backwards, but Lucy immediately took a step forward. She raised her hand but stopped short of returning the blow. Taking advantage of Lucy's hesitation, Mary Anne grabbed a fistful of Lucy's hair and yanked it, eliciting a shriek. At that moment, Elizabeth Blow appeared.

"What is going on?"

"Mother, she's useless and stupid. My hair hasn't been done properly for months."

"Lucy, go help Gran in the kitchen."

When they were alone, Elizabeth Blow gave her full attention to her daughter. No one, not even her husband, called forth such extremes of emotion as her first-born child. Now she struggled to remain calm, understanding her daughter was pitted against a formidable foe, but exasperation frayed the edges of her sympathy. "Mary Anne, your father is unlikely to replace Lucy. You have to set your mind to overcoming these obstacles, and to overcome them without tantrums."

Mary Anne was rubbing lotion into her hands. "Her hair is disgusting, Mother. I just touched it—like grabbing a handful of thorny stems. Why, my palm is nearly scratched."

"Mary Anne! Are you listening to me? I can help you and advise you, but if Lucy is to be your maid, then you must learn how to be a mistress. And you are not behaving like a young mistress."

"And what about Lucy? Her behavior?"

"I will have Gran deal with Lucy."

"Gran won't punish her, not really."

Elizabeth Blow raised an eyebrow in acknowledgement. She paused, then said, "You suggest the punishment. If it's appropriate, I'll see that your father has it carried out."

"Put her in the fields for a week—she'll be begging to come back inside and do things right."

"That's not appropriate to the circumstance. Besides, she'd be too disruptive there, not knowing anything about tobacco. Your father's having a difficult enough time as it is."

"Have her clean all the slop buckets for a week, then."

Elizabeth Blow sighed noisily. "Mary Anne, she already does that for all the females in this house. Who did you think empties them?"

"Oh. I guess I thought Dred still did them all."

"Come sit here with me, my love. Come. Let me explain about being a mistress. You want to be authoritative, but not unduly harsh. You want to devise a punishment equal to the offense. And you want to intervene in a way that is instructive to the slave, so that you won't have to endure the same problems repeatedly. You can't always suc-ceed, goodness knows—they have more ways to thwart good inten-tions than you or I could dream of—yet you must do your best. Now, may I make a suggestion?"

Mary Anne looked expectantly at her mother.

"You and Lucy are having difficulties about your hair, correct?"

"Yes."

"Well, then, it seems to me that Lucy is immoderately vain about her hair, and it also seems to me that her hair is offensively indecorous. Even with a scarf on, it splays out all behind her. Have her hair cropped and order her to wrap her head in a cloth like the older slaves. She'll feel this as a punishment, I assure you, and it will also make her a more seemly servant."

An hour later, Mary Anne appeared in the kitchen. Adopting a tone identical to her mother's, she said, "Gran, I want to speak to you about Lucy."

Gran had expected this—she just hadn't expected it to come from Mary Anne. Bile hung like a fog at the back of her throat.

Mary Anne stood nearly on tiptoe; she chivvied a handker-chief in her hands; yet she managed to confront squarely Gran's silent, stolid, cross-armed stance. "Lucy has been beastly," she proceeded. "She needs to be punished." She paused, expecting Gran to defend the young slave, but Gran said nothing.

"Lucy must learn to do my hair properly. She deliberately messes it up." Gran remained silent. In a final rush of words, Mary Anne concluded her speech. "To punish her, we—I—have decided that her hair should be cut. Cropped to her head. And thinned. It's unsightly, at any rate. And from now on she must wear a head cloth at all times in the house." Not a muscle flinched, not an eye blinked. Gran might have been carved from granite. Mary Anne retreated, still facing her opponent, still on tiptoe.

The following week unfolded as a fractious, covert tug-of-war between mistress and slave. Lucy wore a head cloth, but became increasingly too ill to carry out an instruction; she broke Mary Anne's eyeglasses; frequently she simply could not be found when she was needed.

On Sunday, alone at her dressing table, Mary Anne was sure Lucy had been handling, probably trying on, her jewelry. Stealthily she opened her jewelry box, checked that the pouch she had recently placed there remained closed, then withdrew furtively behind her dressing screen. She had stationed a stool there. She waited patiently.

Within fifteen minutes, Lucy opened the door to the bedroom. "Miss?" Unanswered, Lucy stepped into the room and closed the door behind her. "Miss?"

Believing herself alone, Lucy went to the vanity table, seated herself, and began fingering the items she found there. Her hand moved to the jewelry box and lifted the lid. She tried on a ring and admired it in the mirror. She picked up a bracelet, then noticed the velvet pouch. Eagerly she picked it up, surprised by its heft, and tipped its contents into her hand.

Screeching as a dead garter snake plopped into her hand, Lucy jumped back, and Mary Anne skipped out from behind the screen, scaring her a second time.

"There! That ought to teach you."

Irate, Lucy scooped up the snake and hurled it. "A garter for your dress, Miss."

Now Mary Anne screeched, more in outrage than fear. She lunged at Lucy, and each tried to throw the other to the ground. In the tussle, Lucy's head cloth fell off, simultaneous with Elizabeth Blow appearing in the doorway.

"What on earth is all this yelling?"

They tattled on each other like children, but Mary Anne had the last word, "Look at her hair, Mother. She never cut it! Gran was supposed to cut it and she only braided it. I won't stand for this."

Elizabeth Blow stood heavily in the doorway, pregnant with her eighth child, regarding her daughter ruefully. Her gaze took in the defiant slave, the velvet pouch, and the twisted head cloth and dead snake inert beside each other on the rug. Sternly she said, "Lucy, go to the kitchen and wait for me. Do not leave this house."

Lucy's downcast eyes fixed on the head cloth. She stooped to pick it up as she left.

"Use that cloth to remove the snake," said the Missus.

Grimacing, Lucy scooped up the snake in the cloth and carried it at arm's length.

"And remove my ring from your finger," commanded Mary Anne. Lucy did so, then left the room with the snake.

"This is not working, Mary Anne. With the state of my health I cannot bear this contention. Lucy will be sent to work in the kitchen, and you will have to do without a maid until your father can be persuaded to buy another one. And that may not be soon."

"But Mother, she sneaks in here and tries on my jewelry—"

"I am not addressing Lucy's behavior. I am addressing yours. Lucy has been with us nearly two years now, yet the household remains in upheaval. Everyone has made concessions on your behalf, and I have not seen you show the least sign of appreciation, nor have you seemed to learn the first thing about being a mistress."

"I was only trying to teach her a lesson, teach her to respect my belongings."

"How do I make you understand? You have only taught her to become more unreliable. Nigras have a natural tendency toward deceit, and it is our responsibility, to them and to ourselves, to train them properly, to set an example of virtue by our own behavior. Instead of training Lucy for a position of trust, your example has pushed her further into a position of treachery."

"But it's not my fault."

"I'm sorry, Mary Anne. I know Lucy has been difficult. She came to us with heaven knows what background, with her vicious, foreign ways entrenched. I have tried to counsel you and temper your responses, but you have failed to demonstrate the maturity required of a young mistress."

"All my friends have maids. If I don't have a maid, it will look like we can't afford one. There's already talk about father's financial predicaments."

"That won't work, Mary Anne. I have suffered enough indignities this past year to be impervious to any girlish chatter. I have lived too long with these 'predicaments,' as you call them. Moreover, you are old enough now to know that they are real, to know that your actions, as the eldest, carry more weight than the other children's, and that you are expected by your father and by me to help shoulder some of the burden. Acting as you did today, in a manner we would expect of your four-year-old sister, disappoints us deeply. Now, that's all I'm going to say on the matter. Get yourself ready for church."

❧

Gran wouldn't do it, outright refused to cut Lucy's hair. That about set fire to the Missus, but she couldn't get Master dragged into it. Less'n less he cared about such things. Missus have to have her way, though, so she made Aunt Betty and her girls do it. They dragged Lucy to the stable and used the shears what gets used to trim up the sheep's wool. Aunt Betty's girls had to sit on Lucy to keep her down.

They rassled her down, cussing and screaming—in her island tongue, but I am certain she was cussing. I was working in the stalls, but I knowed there was nothing I could do, not if Master Peter wasn't getting into it. I tried reckoning with Aunt Betty but she said, "I's sorry to do it, but if I don't, then it's my gals get the switch. So what's worse? Cutting hair that don't even hurt, or having these three girls what's innocent of anything get whipped by the Missus?"

There's no answer for questions like that.

'Cept it did hurt. Missus was right about that: it were a punishment that cut deep on Lucy.

Wasn't nothing I wouldn't do for Lucy, but that didn't mean I could change what was happening to her. I slunk away. I's shamed to say it, but I hid, just hunkered down in a stall with Gen'ral, hoping it would get done with. It felt like a year. And I'ma be grateful to the day I die she didn't hold it against me, didn't blame me that I didn't stop them from shearing off her beautiful hair. It were an

97

agony, hearing it going on, the chopping, the scuffling, the rage and defeat in Lucy's voice. Her feathers fell then, sure 'nough.

Halfway through she broke free and they had to chase her some. I heared tussling in the straw on the floor. Finally Lucy's screams died on down to sobs, and beneath that, I heared the creak and crunch of the shears on her hair. Then it were quiet and still. I heared the straw rustling again, then Lucy's cry: "Don't touch it, don't touch it!" She called out for me, "Dred, Dred! Don't let them take it. It's mine. Don't let them take it."

When she called out for me, I went. She didn't want them clearing away her hair, and they left peaceable enough. Oh, my heart hurt to see her there, straw sticking outten her dress and in her hair, what was left of it. They did a rough job. It were all jaggedy. Short. She looked kinda like a porcupine with its quills on end. And all around her on the ground, limp and dead, was that beautiful, wild hair.

I sat next to her, fighting tears back down my throat, trying to match her calm, 'cause she be taking it quiet and hard and dry now. I begun picking up her hair, picking it clean from the straw, but she push my hands so I dropped what I was holding.

"What you do that for?" I asked her.

She took both my hands in hers and placed them on her head, pulled them down so's I stroked her hair, what was left. She let go, and I held her neck, tilted her face to mine, held it close. She smelled like fresh straw. I stroked her hair some more, told her with my hands she was still so beautiful. As I stroked and stroked, she leaned in to me. Our chests touched, and I felt her breasts. A rhythm beat about my head like fluttering bird wings. I stroked her hair, smoothed her brow, traced the line of her jaw, rubbed her lips with my thumb. With my lips. Then we was together on a bed of her hair.

I tasted salt on her cheeks, and her breath smelled like damp tea leaves. I felt a pang pluck my middle like a fiddle string, but it weren't hunger; more like I was hungry all over, a hunger to wrap and hold. My hands had hunger, my eyes, my tongue, the muscles in my arms. My hands and lips knowed what they wanted and how to get it. Lucy was the same. Every part of me, even the hairs on my arms, was straining toward her, reaching up and out to her. I didn't think on nothing. Didn't even think on how I used to wonder about this moment happening for the first time, and would I know how to act, and would I be found wanting.

There was no thinking. No judging. No knowing. Just the flow of what we desired, a desire so strong it carried us both like a current, and us happy to float along. We was one. Then all before what I knowed as love, I now knowed was only the seed of that full flower that blossoms with color and perfume and sweet, silky petals.

"'Fore she left me, she was smiling in them beautiful, birch-leaf eyes. I was on my back in the straw, looking up at her. I drunk in her smile, watched her raise her hand and stroke her head, a question there now where the smile done been. "You don't need hair for your beauty," I whispered. "It's rooted deep down in you. You'll always have it."

When she left, I collected up all that hair. I washed it and dried it careful, and asked Gran for one of her best head cloths. She didn't ask what for, just gived it over. That night I sewed Lucy's hair into that cloth, made a sweet little pillow, and I gived it to her the next day. She reached for it, not understanding, but as soon as she squeezed it she knowed. She kissed me, different from the kissing the day before. That's when Lucy begun learning me a new language: the language of kisses and touches, and all that they can tell.

After all the troublement with Mary Anne, Lucy was sent to be a seamstress 'longside of old Aunt Molly, in a little shed behind the summer kitchen. Lucy might as well been alone in there, though, since Aunt Molly cared about nothing but her quota. Lucy, she cared about her quota, too, but turns out sewing was something that gal had a natural talent for. She was swift and sure with the needle and with the loom.

About that same time I was feeling like I be getting up close to grown, taking on man ways. Loving Lucy sort of made it official, in my mind, leastways. Lucy and me left off playing tag and ring games with the younger children and begun joining in with the older folk, making song, stepping to Uncle Solomon's fiddle. 'Course that was into 18'n17, when there wasn't no Saturday night jigs no more, but the adult folk still gathered when they could, and somebody was sure to get some music going.

That's when I did find the blessing in being small, sure 'nough, 'cause I learned I was good at jigging. Being small was a asset. Sip, now, he was a over-average boy, and about as graceful at a shakedown as a horse what's lost a shoe. Me, though, I could hold a cup of water on my head for a whole tune without spilling nary a drop. The trick is learning to keep all the movement from the hips down, and I got so's my feet flied like tack hammers. Gran laughed at me and said for certain no African spirit showed me that style of dance—Gran danced the way a fish swims, wavy. But I didn't care. Seems my dancing feet was mighty attractive to Lucy. I courted her with rhymes and sparked her with dance.

Weren't all song and dance, though, I admit it; Lucy was like the wind: soothing one day, blusty the next, rousing day after that. Maybe Lucy wasn't right for me, like Gran said. I reckon every time you be tumbled in love, eventually come the time of that first doubt, that first something other than wonderful, that first time you see flaws. Like jigging with a cup of water on your head: you can keep the water from spilling for maybe a whole tune, but sooner or later that water spills.

The drops begun falling from my cup one afternoon up at the scuppernong arbor. Many times Lucy and me sneaked off from work and runned up there to sing and dance, just us two. Sing ourselves breathless, dance ourselves tired, then fall together under the grape vines, feeling the power betwixt us bring back the energy and strength, till that, too, were spent. This particular day, a blistering summer day, we was lazy and quiet. We just returned from a tent meeting and Lucy, with eyes closed, hummed a spiritual whilst I fanned the flies offen her. There were lots, 'cause the grapes was over-ripe; nobody done harvested them since Master had everybody working extra hours just to keep the t'bacca crop straggling on.

I got a pleasure from watching her face, but my arm got tired and I growed restless. "They's too many flies around these grapes," I said. "Let's move over to them pine trees."

Lucy opened one eye. "I like it here."

"That's 'cause I's keeping the flies offen you, gal, but they's driving me to distraction."

"You go, then."

She was in her queenly mood. She liked to fight when she be that way, and I didn't want to fight. I wanted her tongue and fingers and heat-slicked skin. So I didn't change nothing, just continued to fan her.

She rewarded me with half-slit eyes. I knowed that look. I bent over her mouth, bringing my face close to hers, and right 'fore I touched her lips, she closed her eyes again. I hovered over her, the smell of her sweat making me hungry. Sweat slipped from under my arm to my navel, itchy and hot. I wanted to scratch but held off, letting the itching build with the other itching, spurring me on. I brushed my lips against hers.

With a jerk, she shot to her feet and huffed, "Ants. Flies. You. I can't breathe!"

I hardly knowed what course to take. Lucy stomped the ground, then changed again, gived a laugh and twirled round with her arms throwed out, head throwed back. I watched the flash of her teeth go round and round. Stopping just as sudden as she started, she stumbled and laughed. She was right there, but she seemed far from me. I felt she was laughing at me.

Her head cloth done twirled right offen her head. Her hair now was growed long enough to be braided again, in small little stalks round her head. I stood, wanting to bring her back to me, to hold her beauty and breathlessness. But she scamped away. I knowed I was supposed to chase her, but I didn't. I stood under the arbor, holding her head cloth, while she runned toward the pine trees. Halfway there, she walked, oh, and the sway of her hips created a breeze that swelled my heart. I started after her. As I left the arbor, I grabbed a small bunch of grapes. Out in the glare of the sun, kinda without thinking, I wiped the sweat from my neck with her head cloth and for some reason, that recollected Uncle Joe, the way he wiped sweat from his head that day in the forge.

When I reached Lucy in the pine trees, she was sitting with

her back against a tree. I popped a grape in my mouth, didn't chew it. Pressing my lips to hers, I gave her the grape whole. Noisy-like, she sucked it in, bit down and spit it out.

"It's sour!"

She watched me take another grape, chew it like it were Christmas dinner. I handed her another. She took it but spit this one out, too.

"They all sour."

"They good sour."

"Now I's hungry." She was kinda pouting.

"You can have grapes. Lots of grapes. Or you can have me."

Frowning, she reached out, grabbed the head cloth from my hand and fanned herself. We both sat very still. A flock of doves roosted in the shade of the branches, and a few bold ones strutted about the dirt. One found the chewed-up grape, pecked, chased the grape as it flopped around, which attracted two more birds. One spied the other grape. It stepped very near to Lucy. As it darted its beak at the grape, she aptly flinged her head cloth over the bird and pinned down the corners. Under the cloth the bird tried to flap its wings but couldn't.

"Don't," I said. Her lips smiled, but not her eyes. I reached out for the cloth anyways.

"Leave me alone, Dred," she warned.

I stopped. The bird struggled. I recollected Uncle Joe again, feeling confused and ashamed.

Once I learned nature privilege with Lucy, it were clear I left childhood, yet that didn't strictly mean I become a man—I know that every time I remember that dove. I only felt like a man 'cause I had somebody else seeing me that way. Believed I could come into my man so long as Lucy seed me that way. I was looking overmuch through her eyes, not my own.

Now I's a old man. My eyes ain't so sharp. But some things I can see better today than ever when I was a young man. I can see the difference betwixt a young man's fire and a full-growed man's love. A full-growed man wants fire, too, but he values more the durability of his woman. Her courage, her forgiveness, her ability to stay upright when he goes tripping over his own feet. I know I got that with Harriet. She be matching me at every stand. I doubt I would've knowed that with Lucy 'cause with Lucy it were fire and excitement and taking in strange, new things.

Maybe I ain't being fair. Lucy might've growed to quite a woman. Many a time I wondered what would've come of that gal iffen we lived as man and wife. What would've come of us both iffen we done got the chance to go together through all them hard times what followed.

And times was hard, even though I was too much in love to see it.

Chapter eleven

After

Gran seed the hard times upon us. 'Fore everybody else, she seed we was past before and moving swiftly into after. Back in 18'n15, she cautioned Aunty Betty not to let her eldest gal marry, 'cause Master was selling off slaves and not replacing them. Aunt Betty let Franny marry Simon anyways, thought it might be a protection. But anchoring a slave to the farm through marriage only protect the whites, it don't protect the blacks. Within six months, Master sold Simon. That were round the same time Master begun treating Neesy so low. Gran seed that, too, and counseled the young married gals to hold off birthing. Franny listened to her and was mighty thankful once she seed how Master done Simon. Finally Gran seed that good, rich earth itself, parching under the sun, getting near exhausted as the few slaves what remained to work it.

First time ever in my life I heared her talk about running. One of the field hands, a settle-aged man name of Tom, come to Gran, saying he was gonna run. She done what she could to help him, packed him a pouch of curing herbs and some dried meat. That must've been as late as 18'n17. Worried on how low things might get, Gran even talked to me, asking did I want to run with Tom. You could've knocked me down with a feather.

"Run?" I said. "Where? Without you?" I was near struck dumb but she did enough talking for the both of us. She warned me Master was ruining the farm. "Half the cabins be empty now. He's drinking away the farm and gambling away the babies. No telling what he might do next," she said. I argued he wouldn't split her and me up. That just weren't thinkable. 'Sides, I had Lucy to think on. I wouldn't leave her—that weren't thinkable neither.

Then there was one more thing clouding my sight so's I couldn't see what Gran seed. Round this time Master begun training me up in work I dearly loved: he done made me his jockey—not for the official races, 'course, but for the ones the gentlemen put up on they own farms. So I pulled away from Gran, turned blind and deaf to her warnings. It didn't feel like bad times to me. No, it felt like the best of times. I was feeling proud enduring them days, sure 'nough. Even got me a uniform, a sort of poncho to drape over my own clothes. When I was up on top of Blue Streak, wearing my blue and gold colors, I was setting on top of the world.

That were the second blessing I found in being small. I was a sure bet for jockeying. I took to it like a dog after a rabbit. Master learned me the difference in riding a race horse from a field horse, when to hold and when to urge him on, how to eyeball the strengths and weaknesses of the other horses. I loved it all: the speed, the competing—the respect. And I was close to Master Peter again, like the days when he rode with me atop of Gen'ral.

When I was ready for my first race, I was tingly all over in anticipation. I felt we had a good chance to win it. Right 'fore I rode over to the start line, Master gived me to use the most elegant riding crop I ever seed—had genuine gold thread sewed into the grip. Oh, I was so puffed out! I knowed it, then, that I was bound to win that race. I recollects the jump at the start, setting my body in rhythm with Blue Streak, his clean-horse smell, the popping sound of my cape fluttering in the wind we made, and the joy of seeing nothing and nobody in front of me but Blue Streak's pumping head. And when I done it, when I won that race, Master hugged me. I felt just like a boy again, but also like a man. It were a large feeling. He said, "Dred, I can't let you keep this crop now, but I'm going to write it up in my will that when I die, I want you to have this riding crop. It will be yours to remember me by, to remember this triumph."

He gave me that crop, all right—just not the way he said. And when he gave it to me, that's when I waked to how bad times was. I learned they was worser even than what Gran believed.

I don't know iffen I got the breath to talk about it. Some things be past the telling of.

Gran noticed her grandson seemed bigger. The armload of wood he carried to the cooking fire was fatter. His weight as he settled in the chair sounded heftier. His sweat smelled like a man's. She felt both pleased and troubled.

Dred also seemed troubled, couldn't get comfortable in the chair. Sensing he had something to say, she waited while he squirmed and shifted, drummed his fingers, and occasionally muttered to himself. Finally, deliberately, she dropped a copper pot. The clatter snapped him to, and he jumped up to retrieve the pot, then hung it back on its hook.

Still he didn't speak. After some time of silence, she brought the flour bin to the table and said, "This heat's a mess! Missus been whining worser'n the babies, and the air be so damp I can't make decent bread. Nits done got in this flour bin, and when I get enough clean flour to roll, it just clumps. Yestiddy I finally got a loaf baked and it turned moldy by this morning." She sifted through the flour, pinching out the nits, but still he didn't speak. "You put me in mind," she said, "of the farmer man what found a snake hurrying along the road one evening."

Dred smiled wanly. He knew this one. He became still as her story continued.

"'Help me, farmer, sir,' said the snake. 'Help me hide from the men chasing me. They'll chop me up and eat me in their stew if they catches me.'

"Now the farmer just done learned he was gonna get more

money for his harvest than he done expected, so he be feeling generous. He helped that snake by allowing it to crawl down his throat to hide. When two men come along asking about the snake, he smiled and spread out his hands as if to say, no—there's no snake here. And the men hurried on out of sight." Gran pursed her lips together and nodded meaningfully at Dred.

He took her cue and assumed the voice of a farmer man. "'Come out now, snake,' said the farmer. 'Come out and be on your way.'" With a gentle wave of his palm, he gave the story back to her.

"But the snake," Gran continued, "liked his new home and refused to come out. Angry, the farmer hailed a heron what was circling low. Using gestures he made the heron understand his predicament, and the heron winked as if to say, 'Don't worry, I know how to handle such a snake.' And he bid the farmer open his mouth wide, and when the farmer opened his mouth as wide as he could, the heron poked its long bill down the farmer's throat and pulled that ungrateful snake right out and gobbled it down with a satisfying gulp." She didn't even need to look up this time.

Dred assumed the farmer's voice once more. "Which reminded the farmer that he was very hungry, and also late for dinner, but he done disremembered to bring anything for his wife to cook. So he snatched that heron by its silky white throat and said, 'You'll make a very fine supper for me and my wife.'"

Without a pause Gran resumed. "Proudly he turned the heron over to his wife to slaughter and cook, telling her his whole adventure. 'Shame on you,' his wife cried, with her butcher knife raised above the heron's head. 'This helpful creature done you a good turn, and all you think is to cook it for dinner!' And with that she let the bird go free, but as it took wing it spitefully gouged out one of her eyes and flew off into the sky."

Gran finished sifting. Dred moved to her side and picked up a whitened hand from her lap, feeling the silky slide of her powdered skin. With the tablecloth he softly brushed the flour from her fingers to reveal the familiar calluses and wrinkles.

"You kept it short tonight, Gran. I like it when you add links to the whole chain of who done what to who."

"Well, then, here's a ending you ain't heared before."

He looked up at her face. She held his hand in hers now, his unmarred, taut, skin encased in her large, firm flesh. Both were warm and lightly flour-flecked. She said, "When Africans see water flowing uphill, they know someone be repaying a kindness."

Dred frowned and lowered his gaze. "You talking about Lucy, right?"

"No, son. I done made peace in my heart over you and Lucy. That's your affair."

"Who then?"

"Master."

Dred's frown deepened, and he withdrew his hand from hers. "So why isn't he my affair, too?"

"I feel I failed you, Dred. I see you headed down a dangerous path, and I should've done more to guide you."

Somewhat exasperated, he replied, "Gran, I's a man now. You got to allow that I ain't always gonna see things your way. Could be you's right. Could be that being Master's jockey and spending time with him, I's just waiting for water to flow uphill. But I don't see it that way. I don't feel it that way. So for me, it ain't that way."

The last of the flour fell from her fingers as she caressed his face. Pride and sorrow mixed in her voice when she said, "I declare, Dred Scott. I do see the man in you."

He hugged her impulsively, like the boy he so rarely was anymore, with his arms wide and vulnerable around her, and his face buried in her neck. She was surprised, and when his grip relaxed, she pulled back and looked him in the eye. "That's not what's troubling you tonight, is it? You got something else on your heart."

"I need to talk to you, Gran, and you ain't gonna like it all."

"When did that ever stop my ears from listening?"

He took a deep breath and plunged forward. "Gran, just possible I be moving outten the big house."

"What you saying, child?"

"I'ma ask Lucy to marry me, and ask Master for a cabin for us, proper, even iffen it means I got to work the fields."

She pressed her lips together and paused before speaking. "It ain't choosing Lucy what troubles me, Dred. Your heart choosed her and I accept that. But jumping the broom—you not even eighteen yet. She be younger still."

"Young is half the worriment. What with Master selling off Neesy's baby, busting up Franny and Simon, now there's talk that maybe he'll put Franny with Charlie—he's breeding them gals, Gran, and who you think'll be next? I's standing here to say it ain't gonna be Lucy."

"And you think marrying her is gonna save her from that? Marrying Simon didn't help Franny none."

"Master Peter wouldn't do my wife that way."

Gran felt tired and old. It was the same old argument over whether Peter Blow was kind or selfish. If Dred didn't see it by now, how could she change his mind? Ignoring the issue of the Master, she said, "Trying to save somebody ain't a reason to wed. You can't change her fate."

"Maybe it ain't her fate. Maybe I's supposed to do this. And saving her is just one part. I love her. You know I do."

"But do she love you?"

"Gran, you got doubts. I understand that. But you nor nobody knows that gal like I do. We growed something betwixt us and if it ain't love, that don't matter; I still want it."

Gran showed a half-smile and brushed her hands together as though flour clung to them still. Firmly capping the lid back on the flour bin, she carried it over to the cupboard and put it away. With her back still to him so he couldn't read her face, she said, "I's a old woman, now, Dred. You growed up, and I growed old. Guess I don't change as easy as I used to." She felt ready now, able to turn to him and show him the face he needed: a smile full of love and confidence. "You go ask your gal. If she say yes, I'ma make you the finest wedding party this plantation ever seed."

Again he hugged her, this time like a man, with purpose crackling along his spine. Looking up into her face he said, "There's one more thing, and this is for you to choose: if you want, I'ma also ask Master to let you live with us, get somebody else to live in this room and do the first and last chores. Give you a rest. Let you come up to the house after daybreak, come back to the cabin directly after supper. Let you sleep peaceable from dark to dawn. He's got to know you's due it."

Again she caressed his cheek, then pulled him to her breast. "It's gonna be right unnatural here without you, for a certainty. But you do this for me: ask one thing at a time. First ask to jump the broom, then ask after a cabin, then we'll see about me. I can wait."

Dred was apprehensive about asking the Master's permission. He believed his request would be granted, but the stakes were so high. If indeed he was saving Lucy from the fate of being sold or bred, he did not want a direct confrontation with the Master. Despite his bravado with Gran, he knew Master needed to be approached with requests at the right moment. All week the right moment never came. Then Peter Blow left, sailing upriver to sell his hogsheads of tobacco, and another plan formed in Dred's mind.

He spoke to the Missus. He knew her opinion of him was that he had been spoiled, was rambunctious, too forward, so he managed to suggest that being married, having more responsibilities, he would be certain to settle down and become more serious. The bait that proved irresistible, however, was suggesting it might also remove Gran from the house. Elizabeth Blow had been fighting all her married years for control of the big house. Finally she might get it.

Dred and Lucy received Elizabeth Blow's sanction. She even provided a barrel of cider, several pounds of saltpork, and an extra sack of potatoes for the party. Gran felt happy preparing the marriage celebration. All the slaves seemed revived and worked together in a way they hadn't for several years. The women scavenged lace from their own clothes and from scraps around the big house to make one of Lucy's old dresses new and pretty. Aunt Hannah made the bride's laurel crown. Uncle Solomon wove two exquisite rings from reed grasses, then lacquered them.

The party itself was held at sunset, atop the grape arbor hill.

The bride and groom jumped the broom, and since no one could agree who landed first, it was declared that the couple would make decisions equally. Then Gran picked up the broom, swept it behind them, and said, "May all evil be swept behind you." Uncle Solomon took that as a cue to start fiddling, and it quickly appeared that everyone was making up for all the many months since they last frolicked. Dred, when he wasn't dancing with Lucy, clacked the bones. The children sang rhymes and danced ring games. All ate well, and when the party died down and the newlyweds were ready to retire, they found that several of the field hands had decorated one of the empty cabins. Everyone knew only the Master could allot living quarters, but at least the newlyweds had temporary privacy.

For five days the joy of the wedding celebration permeated Zephyr. It felt like old times. Then the Master returned. He arrived back at Zephyr after dusk, already drunk. The trip had been disappointing, the price for his tobacco insultingly low, and his luck at the card table on the boat abysmal.

He sat in his study, shuffling bills and receipts, letters from creditors. Frequently he sipped directly from a whisky bottle. Rising and kicking back his chair, he went to the bookshelf and withdrew a ledger book. Turning to the most recent entries, he studied the names of slaves, their quotas, their actual output. It did nothing to improve his mood. They were all meeting their quotas; it was the land that wasn't producing. As if it were written in ink, he saw he could no longer maintain Zephyr.

He grabbed a scrap of paper and began making rough calculations: what could he expect by selling farm equipment, livestock, this slave or that. Added up, the sum was still unsatisfactory. He recalculated, this time figuring on four of the females being pregnant. That was better, but still insufficient. Rifling through his papers, he finally found the racing circular. He needed a good win. A knock on the door irritated him. He ignored it. Another knock, and he shouted, "Who is it?"

"It's Dred, Master."

With racing on his mind, he suddenly felt anxious. He opened the door. "What is it? Is Blue Streak all right?"

"Fine, Master Peter. Fine."

"Good. What is it then?" He turned his back and reached for the whisky bottle.

Dred edged into the room. "Well, I reckon Missus already done told you I jumped the broom."

Peter Blow froze for a moment, his hand with the bottle raised midway to his mouth. He understood two things, both of which enraged him: Dred was married, and his wife had made a decision that should have been his own. Ignoring Dred's actual question, he said, "When?"

"Last Sat'day."

"Why didn't you wait till I was home?"

Dred, unsure of how to answer, took a deep breath and said, "My nature moved me, Master. 'Fore I do something reckless, I reckoned I best ask permission to jump the broom and do it up right."

Peter Blow took a long draught from the bottle, wiping his mouth with the back of his hand. "Who," he said.

"Lucy." Dred saw, somewhat surprised, that the Master was trying to control a dark anger, and it wasn't just the drink. A wave of anxiety washed over Dred. For the first time it occurred to him that Peter Blow could revoke what the Missus had granted. He realized that's what the Master was thinking: that Dred had come to seek permission for a reality already minted and stamped. Quickly, Dred added, "We been in one of the empty cabins temporary-like, and I come, master, to ask to stay there so we can live proper as married folk. Even iffen I got to work the fields."

Receiving no answer, Dred started to elaborate, but the Master, still with his back to Dred, held up a hand to stop him. In the long silence that ensued, Dred began to sweat. Anger radiated off Peter Blow like a furnace, and that wave of anxiety swelled and sloshed between them.

Finally, Peter Blow said, "I'll arrange everything."

The words did not match the tone. In confusion, Dred remained standing there, searching for a way to clarify the Master's intent. But Peter Blow turned to face him, ordering him to leave, and he did.

Two days went by without another word exchanged between them. Dred hardly saw his master and thought Peter Blow was ignoring the problem. Actually, his master was obsessed with the predicament. One evening Gran heard him berating his wife over the decision to let Dred and Lucy marry, "You have interfered with my plans, Elizabeth. This is a mess, now. A mess I have to clean up."

"I remind you, sir, that you no longer share your plans with me." Her defense was fringed with a tearfulness. "In fact, I have had to take on more and more responsibility, making decisions in your absences, making decisions in the dark. How can I be expected to know your plans when you barely speak to me any more?"

Peter Blow's response was merely the chink of crystal, and Gran knew he was pouring a drink. Elizabeth Blow's tone turned conciliatory. "Peter, I want nothing more than to help you. Tell me what you want and I will fix the mess. I can deal with Dred. Heaven knows I have much less reticence when it comes to Gran and Dred than you."

"My intentions, Elizabeth, had been to breed Lucy, then sell her pregnant, at a higher price. But she and Dred have now been sleeping together for a week—at a minimum. They've been playing house in an empty cabin. How will you fix that?"

"I will simply tell them that their marriage is not valid. They must stop acting like man and wife. Dred will return to Gran, and Lucy will go back living with Aunt Molly. There will be no more cabin. They will be kept apart. Lucy will be paired with whomever you choose, and that buck can do the job of keeping Dred away, rest assured."

With a loud, exasperated sigh, Peter Blow exploded, "Elizabeth, she could be pregnant already. That's the problem. Even if I mate her with one of the field hands—if she becomes pregnant in the next couple of months, I won't be sure who the father is."

"What does it matter who fathers her baby, as long as she becomes pregnant?"

Yelling, he replied, "Do you not see Dred? Our small and puny Dred? Do you not understand that he is the antithesis of a buck? No matter whom she is paired with now, what if she gives birth to a puny baby? I will be held as a cheat, forced to make compensation. So I must either wait several months to be certain she is not pregnant by Dred before breeding her again, or I must sell her for less now, for the price of just herself. And my intention, my plan, was to sell her and a few others quickly. We need the cash."

The argument scuttled off into the tangled undergrowth of money problems and fears of bankruptcy, and ended with Peter Blow's harsh instruction, "Do nothing. I will handle everything that needs to be done." He stormed from the house and rode away, which should have alarmed Gran, but she was too concerned about what her own next action should be. All night long, alone now in her tiny room that recently felt too large, Gran wrestled with what to tell Dred, with speculations about what he might do—what he should do. Maybe he should run. Probably he would if Lucy went with him. She felt certain he would do anything to save Lucy. Yet he was so resistant to hearing anything bad about Peter Blow. What if he refused to believe the Master could be so heartless?

By dawn she had decided she would place the problem before Dred. He was nearly a man now, entitled to find his own solutions. While she prepared breakfast, Gran rehearsed with a heavy heart what she would say to Dred. She was so distracted she failed to see Peter Blow return to the farm looking as though he had been out all night. Not that that would have been so unusual, but she would have taken notice of the two white strangers who accompanied him. She would have noticed the Master send them to the barn while he made his way toward the stable.

Peter Blow found Dred there and gave instructions to ready Blue Streak for a race. Dred was surprised—usually he knew about races in advance and practiced with the horse—but at least the Master was talking to him again, even if he was surly and hung-over. Perhaps if this race went well, he stood a chance of persuading the Master about keeping the cabin. Busy with a strategy to win the Master over, Dred didn't notice where the Master headed as he left the stable: Peter Blow hurried over to the sewing shack.

Readying the horse, Dred was annoyed that Sam was not around to help him. He had the tack and the gear assembled when he noticed Blue Streak had a slight wheeze, and he decided to steam some eucalyptus leaves for the horse to inhale. While he was preparing the infusion, Peter Blow returned, exasperated that Dred was not ready.

"Forget that stuff," he said. "We need to leave right away. Get that horse and gear into the stock cart." Then, with a distinct tone of alarm, the Master quickly asked, "Where is the stock cart?"

Confused by the Master's irritability and now this sudden anxiety over the stock cart, Dred stammered, "I didn't, Sam's not, I, it's still in the barn. I'ma go get it now." He dashed out the door, and Peter Blow's tone, more than his words, arrested him.

"Stop, Dred. No. Don't go to the barn." Peter Blow and Dred studied each other, each trying to read what the other knew. To Dred, Peter Blow looked like a sheep-killing dog: head down, shoulders bunched. In the raw daylight, a fear with no name clutched Dred's heart and he turned and ran toward the barn, his master cursing and yelling behind him for him to stop and obey. He did neither.

First he saw the buckboard, with two mules hitched and Sam up in the driver's seat. The buckboard, used to transport slaves. Next he heard the jangle of iron and knew it was the shackles that were fastened to the body of the buckboard, used to transport recalcitrant slaves. Then he saw Lucy. His wife was shackled and gagged, held to the floor of the buckboard by two unfamiliar white men.

Dred catapulted forward, only to be yanked flat on his back by Peter Blow, who had come up behind him. Ordering Sam to come help, he tussled with Dred until Sam, twice Dred's weight and much bigger, pinned his arms behind him. Hands on his knees, puffing from the exertion, Peter Blow felt an ugly fury. "You go too far, Dred. I have indulged you too long."

Dred was screaming, "Don't do it, Master, don't sell her. She's my wife."

Someone had informed Gran. She approached the barn at full bore. The Master raised his riding crop as if to strike her. "Stay out of this, Gran." Paying no heed, she continued to advance, not pausing until he said, "Stay back or I'll beat Dred."

But Dred broke free and rushed at Peter Blow, tackling him

about the waist. His ferocity was powerful, but Peter Blow beat him back with the riding crop, slashing it across his face and neck, swearing at Sam to regain hold of Dred.

Once more Dred was restrained, blood gushing from his lip and forehead. As Peter Blow warned Sam to control Dred, Gran warned Sam to let him go. "He be a man, now, Sam, and you know a man comes to his day when he don't take the order. Could be this is that day for you, too. You let him go, now."

Frightened, Sam swung his eyes back and forth from Peter Blow to Gran. He maintained a firm grip on Dred. The choice was his. There could be no dodging it.

"Sam, do as I say. You can't afford the consequences should you disobey me."

Sam tightened his grip on Dred, who now flung his legs in the air, hoisting his weight backwards, attempting to throw Sam off balance. Through the blood that gushed and threatened to choke him, he yelled and cried. Peter Blow finally drew a pistol and held it ready at his side. "Stop, Dred, or I'll shoot you. I'll shoot you in the leg and we'll see how you kick up after that."

But Dred continued to struggle and scream, hurling his anger at Peter Blow and proclaiming his determination to Lucy, who seemed dumbstruck by the entire scene. In the stand-off between her grandson and her master, Gran had hurried over to Lucy and whispered urgently. Lucy's eyes raced in a circuit from Gran's face to Dred's to the master's. Gran pleaded with her as Dred continued to flail. Then the girl became very still. She squared her shoulders, grew calm, and nodded. The white man guarding her, as anxious as anyone to see an end to the ordeal, removed Lucy's gag.

When she spoke, her mouth trembled but her voice was steady and clear. "Dred," she called. "Dred," in a soft voice meant to quiet him, and it did. Lucy was crying and hanging her head. "I's glad to go. I ain't never liked it here and don't want to stay no more. I don't want to stay here as your wife. Let me go, Dred. Let me go quiet and fast."

"No!" His refusal erupted from deep within his belly and rumbled like thunder across a vast plain. Peter Blow raised his pistol, aiming at Dred's leg. Sam, also in the line of fire and frightened, loosened his hold on Dred, who managed to get an arm free but couldn't entirely break away.

Gran implored Lucy with a grief-stricken look, and Lucy called out again. She turned her head so Dred would not see in her eyes the light he had created with his gentle and funny manner, his stirring touches and big-hearted acceptance of all her ways. She turned her head but made her voice convincing. "I can't 'bide by you, Dred. You's too small and too soft. I need me a big hunk of a man what's gonna protect me in this world."

Her words cut deeper than Peter Blow's whip. Defeated, ashamed, and heartbroken, Dred crumpled. With a nod from Peter Blow, one white man grabbed the reins and the other stood guard over Lucy, as she was quietly and quickly whisked away.

With stories, you got upriver-n-downriver; with life, you got before-n-after. And I reckon without the before-n-afters, we wouldn't have no stories. But that don't comfort me none. I got pains from them days what lingers. They sear my heart fresh each time they's recollected. Lots of things in life is like that. Lots of things don't pass on into after.

Like when I seed field amputations for the first time. Did you know that after they amputates a man's leg, that man can be looking at the empty space, feeling the stump where flesh ends, and still swear he feel a ache in his ankle? Or like that time in 18'n13, when Scarletina took all them children at Zephyr—not all them passed over. Little Master Thomas was the first, and he passed easy. But later, poor Master Richard what loved playing that piano, after he died Gran and me both seed them keys moving without nobody there to touch them. Then in the quarter, most of them young'ns what caught the fever and died never was seed again, but Aunt Betty's son, Cowboy, what milked the cows—for months after Cowboy died you couldn't get none of them slave children to drink milk 'cause so many told how Cowboy come to them at night iffen they did.

Folks give lots of explanations, but me myself I don't know

why some spirits pass and some linger. I just know it's true. I reckon the world can change a lot quicker'n a man—a man can't always adjust hisself, so sometimes he moves into after, carrying with him the ghost of what was before.

With me, now, it ain't losing Lucy what still haunts me. It's losing Master Peter. See, with Lucy I lost something fresh, something I never knowed before; it ignited like a spark, burned bright, got snuffed out. I missed it, I grieved it, but that's not what messed up my mind. It took losing Master Peter to do that.

Maybe it has to do with what was gived and what was took. With Lucy, I lost what she gived me, yet it were like a seed that growed when I come to love the next time. In a way I still held onto it. But in losing Master, I lost what I had gived him—trust and hope and yearning to be special. Long years of trying to please. And he took that and used it like you'd use a snake in your garden: bash its brains out on a rock, leave the pieces to shrivel in the sun.

Chapter twelve

Alabama Slave

I sunk down in my mind, then. Weakened down. The very thoughts in my head hurt. A part of who I knowed myself to be died.

Master must've done something to my hearing, 'cause sounds was all drownded out by a rushing noise in my ears. I was glad, though, 'cause I kept hearing Lucy yelling how she'd druther be sold than stay and be my wife. I lost a tooth and my lips was swole for a long time, but that was good 'cause my mouth dreamed of kisses that was gone. My eyelids wasn't working neither; they was heavy as headstones. I would've walked around with them shut all the time iffen I could, 'cause I couldn't shut out seeing Lucy everywhere.

That lessened a mite in 18'n18, when Master moved me and Gran and all his property to a small cotton farm in Huntsville, Alabama. Took a riding crop busting open my face to come to know Peter Blow was my master and I was nothing more'n a mule that could talk, property writ down in a white man's book with a price after my name, and a price less than any other man slave 'cause I was such a runt. And after all what happened, Master didn't want to see my hide. So in Alabama, the only duties I had in the new big house was the early-morning chores and the last-at-night chores. In betwixt I worked in the stables with Sam.

I fell down on my work, though, 'cause I just didn't care. Gran covered for me, carrying armloads of wood to the bedrooms and emptying the slop jars. But it were hard on her 'cause her and me wasn't living in the big house no more. We both was put down in the slave quarters, so Gran had all that extra ways to walk, had to wake that much earlier each morning. What with carrying my load, too, she was wearing herself out. That's what started to make me breathe again—seeing that old woman killing herself for my sake.

I finally got on with my work, tried to keep my mind on it, but I still made so many mistakes that Master finally got a young boy up at the house and put me to work in the fields. I didn't care.

In a strange way the cotton fields suited me, suited how low I felt: low as a ant. I was a ant, marching one way, following the ant in front of me, then marching back the same way I come. Nothing had no more meaning than that. Marched along, building something for somebody else till I died. My life didn't matter. My acts didn't matter. And when that don't matter, neither does tomorrow. I stopped dreaming and scheming; stopped feeling the possibilities.

You could say I come to know I was a slave.

ॐ

Dred hunched on a stool with his heels hooked on the lower rung. Through gaps in the rough-hewn cabin walls, he idly observed yellow Alabama dust swirling in sunlight. A tiny movement drew his attention to a crevice where the wall met the dirt floor—mud, actually, at least around the corners of the cabin; there had been a rainy spell. Dred watched a snake's striped head poke into the room, swaying left, swaying right.

When the snake was halfway into the room, Dred leaned forward: "Hungry?" The reptile retreated toward the door, hesitated, slithered toward the fireplace. "Yes, you come see what's in this pot. Come see for your ownself." Dred waited motionless for his prey, knowing it was movement, not sound, that would scare the snake away. The Halloween colors rippled right beneath his left foot, where his toes peeked out from the torn leather of his too-small shoes. "That's right. We'd like to invite you for dinner." As the snake slid past his right foot, Dred swiftly brought the sole of his shoe down behind the unsuspecting head. The victim whipped its body frantically, hissed impotently, and Dred deftly severed the head with a pocket knife. He trudged out of the cabin.

From the well he filled a small gourd, took a sip, and grimaced. Alabama water tasted bitter. Back at the cabin, he kicked the body parts out the door, rinsed and cleaned them, and chopped the body into smaller pieces. Carrying the bits inside, he tossed them into the soup pot and saw, too late, that he had forgotten to discard the head. It floated; its lipless death-grin transfixed his gaze until he imagined he was looking at Lucy's mocking grin, the way she had looked at the grape arbor the day she tormented the dove.

He could not quell the shudder that rippled through his breast, or stop the water from pooling in his eyes. Deliberately, he chose green wood that was still damp to stoke the fire under the pot. As smoke filled the small cabin, he allowed the tears to stream from his smarting eyes; he released the shiver in his breast with a single, coughing sob.

"Landsakes!" Gran had returned. She grabbed tongs and removed the freshly-laid wood chunks to a metal basket. On her way outside with the smoking chunks, she pressed the bellows into Dred's hands, and he began pumping smoke through the door. When she returned, Gran selected seasoned wood to re-stoke the fire, then noticed the head in the soup. Revulsion and despair pinched her nostrils, and she reflected that all Dred's "mistakes" these days had a dark underbelly. She spooned out the head, flung it through the open door, then picked up the bench and carried it outside. She called back, "Best come wait out here till that smoke clears."

Dred followed her outside but remained standing. She looked at him and sighed. Young men, she thought. His bruised heart haunted her.

Returning indoors, she collected a basketful of corn from the root cellar. Settling again on the bench, she began husking. The silken creak of the torn husks seemed loud in the stillness between them. She snapped off the stem with a satisfying crack, placed the cob beside her on the bench, picked up another. Cicadas started whirring in the branches as the sun began to lower. Dred scratched his arm through his sleeve, making a faint crinkling sound.

"The world's a-rustling," Gran murmured.

Dred moseyed over to the bench and shared the husking. He scratched his arm again.

"You still got that rash?"

"Just won't quit."

"It's from working them cotton fields. For certain it's that guano they's using. You ain't 'customed to it."

Her words irritated him more than the rash. "I keep telling you: fieldwork don't much bother me." He would not look at her face. He regretted his rebuke and said, more softly, "It's almost like, out there, there ain't no time. Plowing, hoeing, scraping the cotton, chopping the stalks—I rock along. 'Course, I ain't much good at any of it. They won't let me plow no more, my plow just won't stay in the earth and all I do is make a scratch from one end of the field to the other. I's just plowing air. So they set me to laying down the guano, but it makes me no difference. The other hands sing they songs, I just keep moving along. The sweat rolls offen me, the bugs buzz and hum, I rock along, rock along. I don't mind the toil nor the rash neither."

"Well, it drives me to distraction, seeing you scratch all day— and through the night." She was feeling prickly, too. Between them these days was constant friction. Her nature was not one to relent, but she made an effort for Dred's sake. Softening her tone, she said, "You should try stuffing your mattress with these husks, once we through. These be good, clean leaves. Get rid of that old straw ticking. That could be it, too. Will you do that?"

"I'll try it. But it really don't matter to me whether I scratches or not. I done got used to it already."

There's so much to get used to here, Gran thought. None of it's good, but the worst is this bickering. Sighing again, she renewed her efforts and said, "Settling in ain't come easy. But you know, I begun to feel a mite more at home today when Ephraim—you know that old man what tends the hogs?—he told me a most amazing thing: they got a town south from here called 'Nyota.' What you make of that?"

It worked. A light sparked in his eye as he lifted his head, asking, "They got a town nearby named after your gran?"

"No, I reckon they figure it means something else entirely. But Ephraim say Alabama got a few more towns with African names: Eufaula, Wende, Congo. He don't know what the names mean, 'course. I told him in Dahomey, Nyota means warrior. He say most possible that Africans settle in that area, 'cause he heared how the white people done kept shipping in slaves even after it be outlawed, and somebody raised a ruckus till a bunch of them Africans got to live free on some land they gived them there."

"That right? Free Africans in Alabama?"

"That's what Ephraim say." She didn't believe it herself, but she was happy to let the story feed their conversation.

"You reckon they our kin?"

"Possible. Don't reckon we'll get much chance to meet any, though." She stopped short, thinking how the Master had become too restrictive on this new farm. He wouldn't let them set a toe off the farm, not even for tent meetings. But she voiced none of this. Discussions about the Master would just stir up his pain. She ground her teeth and picked up the last ear of corn. She shucked the leaves, broke off the stem, and sat admiring the yellow corn. "Water may not be as tasty as what we used to," she said, "but at least it's clear of wiggletails, and this corn sure is fine." Reaching down, she flicked a whitish slug from a cob and said, "That worm be the onliest one in the bunch. What say we roast two of these cobs tonight and shell the rest? I'll make some cornbread like we used to do back in Dahomey. In honor of Nyota."

Dred stooped to pick up the basket, then straightened and turned toward the sound of approaching hoof beats. Through the trees, riding bareback on a spotted pony, came young Master Peter. He was not quite eight, but in the face of his father's increasing dereliction, he had grown serious and responsible.

"For sure that baby's fretting again," said Gran.

Peter reined in his pony in front of the cabin. "Dred? It's little Henry again. Been crying all afternoon. Mother wants for you to ride up to the big house with me."

Dred nodded. "Wait just a sec." He carried the basket inside. "It's clear of smoke now, Gran. You eat without me. I'll be back, soon's I can."

Dred stood on the bench, grabbed Peter's arm, and hoisted himself onto the pony. Peter nearly slipped off, but Dred managed to keep them both balanced. "I gotcha. You hold onto Aladdin's mane now, and I'll take the reins." Peter leaned into the pony's neck; Dred leaned in behind him, hugging the younger boy as he took control of the reins. Peter smelled the heat of Dred's sweat under the wood smoke that still clung to his shirt. Dred smelled jerked beef, and his stomach rolled. "What you got in your pocket there?" he asked.

Peter readily withdrew some jerky from his pocket and offered it to Dred, eager to appease the gruffness that had come between them ever since the move. In Virginia, Dred had been the one person he could rely upon for patience and sympathy. Now, Peter never could be sure whether Dred would be his old buddy or another dismissive adult. For good measure, Peter pulled out a second strip and handed it down to Gran. She accepted it smiling, understanding it was the last he had. Then Peter said, "Go fast, Dred. Make Aladdin fly," and the two riders departed in a cloud of yellow dust.

Watching them ride off, Gran lifted a hand to shade her eyes from the setting sun and appeared to be saluting. She smiled sadly, thinking: Little boys. Her heart rode with them.

❧

I called Henry "my little peanut." He come out so wrinkly, and kinda big-headed and chunky-butted. He come into this world just when we all begun the move to Huntsville. Things on the old V'ginia plantation was running downhill like a wagon with no brakes, and all us slaves and most the Blow family, too, was scampering to get out the way of the crash what was coming. Slave or free, we was all harnessed to the same wagon.

More'n a few of us got rolled over. I lost Lucy, 'course, but I wasn't the onliest one hurting. Aunt Betty got both her unmarried gals sold off along with the cow herd. Uncle Solomon, what served Master all through the 18'n12 War and after as his body servant, he lost his boy Sip. Bill was auctioned off, too—though I hear tell he let loose that Devil dog, and I bet it still be ransacking the county, killing chickens and lambs and ripping the throat outten anything stupid enough to let it come near. Then old Aunt Molly, the seamstress, just disappeared. I know she didn't come with us to Alabama, and for a certainty she was too old and broke to sell. She couldn't even recollect the names of her own children. I asked Gran what come of her, but Gran said she didn't know. I ain't sure I believed her.

As for Gran and me, as I done said, Master put us in a chinky old cabin what let in more wind, dust, and rain than it kept out. Done that 'cause Gran wouldn't part her lips to say nary a word to Master Peter. She listened, she got on with what she had to do, but she plain stopped speaking to him, even when he put us outten the big house. The quarters suited me fine, but the change were hard on Gran. Harder still, 'cause we didn't share stories no more. I couldn't— not the telling nor the listening; I just hurt so bad. But it were more than that. Seems we couldn't even talk easy no more. She irritated me so; all I wanted was to keep my distance. I know it hurt her, but I pulled away and kept away as much as I could.

Gran was nursing other hurts, too. All them what got sold was like family. Master done held the auction right there at Zephyr, and that day were the onliest day I ever knowed Gran to stay in her bed and not get up once. After that, Gran walked crookeder, pulled down to one side.

Anyways, little Henry got hisself born in the midst of all that heartache, and he wasn't a pretty baby and he wasn't a quiet baby, neither. He didn't whimper, like little Patsy used to, he cried angry. He come telling the world that things wasn't right, and by gosh he wasn't bound to stay quiet about it! That were the summer of 18'n17, right 'fore we left Zephyr. Mostly I got the duty of quietening Henry. Every night and most the day long, I cradled that little peanut. Missus liked me to take him outside, 'way from the big house, so she could get some peace. This was her eighth child, though only six be living, and she was plumb wore out with all else crumbling round her.

Sad truth is she didn't give that baby her notice, and he knowed it. She'd hold him but never look at him, and he'd reach out to grab her cheek and pull her face to him. But she'd just hand him off to somebody else. Even the other children didn't take to Henry like a natural brother. It were peculiar. Wasn't till Taylor got born and growed, three year later, that my little peanut found hisself a true playmate. Till then, it was him and me.

I couldn't put words to it at the time, but Henry filled a hole in my life, same as I filled a hole in his'n. That little old chap was the onliest creature on this earth what didn't make my aching heart throb worser. And that's all that mattered to me them days: avoiding that ache. Even Gran couldn't do that. She loved me, she tried to comfort me, but she was a part of all what happened. Henry wasn't. He was new-born fresh, and I could be with that baby without rememories burning like vinegar in my wounds.

By the time we settled in Huntsville, Henry was near ready to walk. He already talked some—when he wasn't crying—and he sure 'nough could skedaddle on them little hands and knees. So even after I was off in a cabin with Gran, working the fields like the other slaves, I still rode up to the big house and passed hours there regular-like, on account of Henry. His chief ailment was thin skin. Rashes plagued him like the devil, and all the fancy talcs Missus bought never helped. I had my own medicine for him, a remedy Gran gave me for my own rash: you hunt down the powder-post beetle and collect the sawdust he leave after eating through some wood. It ain't the same as just sawdust; that beetle change it somehow and only that kind of powder act like salve on sore skin. Don't know why it didn't help me, but it worked good for Henry. Got so's just me stepping in the room would quieten that child. I could easy have gived the powder over to somebody at the house—but what fool wouldn't druther play with a baby under a shady tree than pick cotton under the blazing sun?

'Course, I taken heat offen the other slaves. They rightfully resented that a able-bodied hand got to spend half his time playing with a baby. I understand that. But I didn't care about them. I really wasn't much good in the fields, and besides, they was mostly Alabama slaves, I hardly even knowed them or mixed with them. Gran and Henry was all the folks I could fit in my life at that time. That's the unvarnished truth of it.

Well, the seasons rocked along. By'n by, everybody seed we was still rolling downhill, just wasn't so steep a hill this time round. Them Alabama slaves, them what knowed cotton, blamed Master Peter. Said he plowed the land too wet, disturbed them young roots, then starved the stalks by piling wet earth around them. See, the wet earth hardens away from the plant, so the plant can't benefit from the moisture, and later the sun come along and parch them stalks. The field hands all shaked they heads and clucked they tongues and said the only moisture them plants getting be the sweat from they brows. Said they just wasting they labor. Said Master should've waited for the ground to dry. But we had three year running of flooded springs. Master Peter growed impatient and couldn't wait for dry. Dry wasn't coming.

He made a honest show of it, even cleaned up and cut way back on his gambling and drinking, for about a year or so. But no man can control the weather. 'Sides, he wasn't a cotton man, he was a t'bacca man. By the end of the third wet year in Alabama, he done drifted back to gambling and drinking, got hisself bankrupt again, and we was all packing up to move again.

I didn't care. Huntsville meant nothing to me.

꙳

In the turmoil preceding the move from Huntsville, Peter Jr. awoke one morning so early the sun wasn't high enough to cast a shadow. He heard his mother down in the parlor, crying already. His father was snoring down the hall, sleeping one off. He slipped out of bed, taking care not to wake Henry. Barefoot, he tiptoed down the hall, moving with extra caution past Mary Anne's room. If she suspected anything was going on, she would order him back to bed and take charge herself. Though only ten, he felt it was his job, as eldest son, to fix whatever made his mother cry.

He knew little would be accomplished by confronting his mother directly. He needed to reconnoiter. He headed for the back stairway, then heard Gran's monotone humming in the kitchen. Even though she lived in a cabin now, she still prepared the meals each day because his mother, in poor health and pregnant again, relied upon Gran's teas and broths. Peter decided to take the direct route down the front stairway.

He needn't have worried. Elizabeth Blow was so awash in her misery that she was unlikely to notice a horse coming down the stairs. The parlor doors were ajar, and Peter peered around one to see his mother in her dressing gown, collapsed over the piano keys. Though she sat on the stool, she leaned into the piano, resting her head and one arm on keys that had long since stopped resonating. Her other arm stretched out along the keys, her fingers so gently stroking the ivory that they emitted no sound either. The only sound was her crying. She panted heavy, quick, restrained breaths clogged with mucus, reminding him of someone who has run very far. Her posture looked both tender and uncomfortable.

Anxiously, Peter looked around the room. He saw several brandy snifters, mostly empty. The glasses didn't belong here. Every person in the household and most of the guests, too, knew that drinking liquor was relegated to his father's gaming room. That the glasses were in the parlor told the boy that his father had been too drunk to care.

Still, his father's drunkenness had become routine. It could not account for the grief he was witnessing. It seemed to him that someone must have died. His first thought was that it might be a letter announcing the death of his mother's sister, who had been ill recently.

Suddenly Gran was upon him: "Junior, there's none of your business happening down here this morning. Go on and get dressed so's maybe you can make yourself useful."

Peter rose from his crouch and reluctantly trudged toward the stairs. Flinging a look back over his shoulder, he saw his mother had not moved. Neither had Gran. She shooed him up the stairs. After Gran entered the parlor, he sneaked back down a step or two, watched Gran gather up his mother and move her to the settee. Next to Gran, his mother looked like a child. Seeing her so small and vulnerable, he resolved to find out from Gran what the commotion was about. He dressed quickly and went back down to the kitchen.

Yet his talk with Gran left him with more questions than answers. He needed a quiet place to work it all out.

Peter's hiding place was a straggly old fir tree, with venerable ropes of ivy draping its trunk. The branches started above his head but were accessible by climbing the ivy. He was still light enough to manage this. He climbed the branches like a ladder, mounting high to where the long pine needles thinned and the branches began to bend with his weight. Bracing his back against the trunk, wedged in the fork of two limbs, he replayed what Gran had said. The facts were plain, yet what did it all mean? More, what could he do to make his mother stop crying? He climbed down from his perch and went in search of Dred, hoping to find him in a good mood.

Dred was currying old Gen'ral, whose only purpose now was to satisfy the Master's sentimentality. Seeing the troubled look on Peter's face, Dred asked, "What's got you looking so stormy this early in the morning?"

"It's Mother. She's been crying since dawn."

"Your mama cries a lot these days."

"Not like this. She's crying as though someone died. But Gran said it's only because Papa sold off her pianoforte, to settle an IOU—I don't see what's so terrible about that."

Dred rested a hand on top of the boy's head. "You a child still, so it's hard to understand."

"I'm ten," he countered, stepping out from under Dred's hand. "I'm the oldest boy."

Dred cocked his head. "You think you's a little man? Think on it deeper: the world still comes to you, Peter, gives you things. You thirsty, somebody give you fresh milk. You hungry, somebody cook you a meal. You want a pony today, you riding him tomorrow. You got to know it don't stay like that. You want to be a man, well step up and welcome. But know that being a man means things don't always go your way—often you got to go the way of somebody else. Give up something. Make a sacrifice."

Peter's answer was defiant and uncertain. "I do know. Sort of."

Dred softened. "Yeah, I reckon you learning, at that. Anyways, it's the same for women, 'specially mothers. They give up for they children and they give up for they husbands. Your mama, she irascible, sure 'nough, but that's 'cause she done gived up so much to see her family grow right and get them through these hard times."

"But what's all that got to do with the piano?"

"That piano, well, that piano likely the last thing she still hold onto from her own girlhood. The last thing she own that remind her of them carefree days like you still enjoying now in your childhood."

"Kinda like Gen'ral is to Papa?"

"Kinda, but more. Gen'ral was your papa's horse through the war, when your papa was a man already. Gen'ral ain't from his child-hood. Think on Aladdin—imagine you get to be a married man like your papa, with little ones, and Aladdin lives all them years. You gonna grow beyond use of that pony, but you'll still want to keep him, groom him, pass him along to your son. You won't ride him no more, but your son will. Your heart will swell just watching the pleasure your young'ns get from him—in a way that'll mean more'n the pleasure you get riding him yourself."

"It's kinda like how Gran was Papa's mammy and then she was mine?"

Dred worked his jaw and smacked his tongue off the roof of his mouth, tasting acid. Not answering, he picked up the comb and tended the horse's mane while Peter worked to understand the whole situation.

"So the piano is from Mother's childhood?"

Dred nodded wordlessly.

"Well if it's hers, then Papa shouldn't give it away."

"No," Dred said tightly. "What a wife's got, she give it over to her husband when they marries. That's how it be."

"Then he should give away Gen'ral to clear his debts. He shouldn't even be gambling. I heard him tell Mother he would quit."

"That may be. But he can't give Gen'ral away. Gen'ral's too old. Nobody'd want him."

"Then he should give one of the plow mules or one of the field hands. Mother's given up too much."

Dred's eyebrows shot up. He ceased his combing and placed a fist on his hip. "That what you would do, iffen it was up to you—trade off a slave?"

"Well, not you, Dred," Peter said. "But we don't hardly know these field hands. One of them, maybe."

"You know them good enough to know they got family. They got ties here deeper'n you."

Confused and defensive, the boy said, "That's how it is." He kicked at a sack of oats. "You said it yourself. I didn't make up the rules. I just want my mother to stop crying."

Peter Jr. could no longer meet Dred's eye. Dred watched him run from the stable toward the house. He spat on the ground, muttering to Gen'ral one of Gran's proverbs: "If a son carries his father up, the father's loin cloth will cover his face."

Dred used the brush roughly on Gen'ral, and the old horse stamped nervously. "Oh, hush," Dred said disgustedly, though he lightened his strokes. "You got nothing to fear. You nor me: we's too worthless for anybody to bother over."

Elizabeth Blow spent three days and nights in her room, admitting no one but Gran. She did not emerge until the pianoforte had been carted away. On the fourth night, she descended the stairs, ate dinner in silence with her family, then sat in the parlor with her knitting, dully eyeing the empty corner where the piano had stood. Gran entered with a slight rustle of her skirts.

"You want me fix you some baby tea?"

Elizabeth smiled wanly. "Your tea has worked wonders for the first eight births. I suppose we shouldn't break with tradition."

Gran returned to the kitchen. She heard the Master rise from the porch, where he had been smoking a cigar. This house, so much more compact than the Virginia big house, allowed her to hear more than she wanted most times. Now she heard Peter Blow join his wife in the parlor and prepared herself for the tempest that was brewing faster than her tea.

In the parlor, Peter Blow greeted his wife tentatively. She did not return his greeting. She had not spoken to him in four days. But after minutes of silence, she asked him to place more logs on the fire. He did so.

"Elizabeth, I am distressed to have upset you. I apologize."

"I am resolved. Let us speak of it no more."

He nodded, paced the length of the hearth, chin on his breast. She knit a small jacket of white wool.

"For the baby?" he asked.

She caressed her belly. "Yes. A March baby will want plenty of warmth."

"Do you suppose we'll have another boy? To even out the numbers a bit?"

"Gran predicts it will be a boy. But I wouldn't bet on it."

Unsure of how to take that last remark, Peter resumed pacing. Finally he cleared his throat, turned to his wife, and said, "I haven't gambled in a week."

"Five days is not a week."

He sighed.

"And what about drinking?"

"Only at dinner, here at home." He followed her eyes as they darted to the bottles on the liquor cabinet and knew she was gauging their contents. He had taken care to keep the levels buoyed with water. She turned her skeptical gaze to him, searching his eyes for confirmation. Unsure, she dropped her eyes to her work and counted stitches.

"Elizabeth." She didn't look up at him. "Elizabeth, I've received John's response. He writes that it will be well to commence our journey once this crop is in."

She did not speak. He could not read her demeanor and mistook her outward calm for acceptance. Her tears, when they fell, surprised him. He sat by her side and extended an arm about her. "Elizabeth, dear Elizabeth. I will arrange everything. Please, don't despair."

Unyielding, she pulled away to look at him squarely. Anger pinched her lips. "And just what have you arranged for me, Peter?

What is to be my role in the home of your brother where another woman is already the mistress of the house?"

"Charlotte is an angel. She is generous, unaffected. I'm sure the two of you will rekindle the sisterly relationship you have so enjoyed in the past."

"I see. She is the angel—that leaves me to be the fiend, I suppose?"

He stood abruptly. "You are deliberately contrary. That is not my meaning."

"How do I know your meaning? You speak as if we were still intimate. Peter, are you really so blind to how distant we have grown? We hardly speak to each other anymore. You exhibit a growing want of interest regarding my opinions. You make your 'arrangements' without consulting me. You have become so secretive and withdrawn that you are more like a stranger to me than a husband."

"Perhaps if you were less critical and more trusting, I'd be more forthcoming."

"I am the originating cause of all our troubles, aren't I? I've ruined everything. We're lonely and isolated here because I'm too proud to invite our old friends to see us in this degraded state. We're hounded by creditors because my sense of self-respect demands a few civilized amenities about us. You've taken to drinking and gambling because I worry and heckle. I suppose I'm even responsible for the poor cotton yield. Is nothing your responsibility, Peter?"

Gran had entered with the tea tray, but the feuding couple ignored her. She set the tray on a table by the window, nudging aside an exquisite china planter containing a cluster of African violets. The plants were past the season for blooms, but the furry leaves were lustrous and green.

"I have lived up to my responsibilities, Elizabeth. Have you no appreciation for how arduous my task has been? You foster your own disappointment if you fancy that I control the weather or the market price of cotton. There is only so much I can do."

"Yes, you've done your best. And while you dally at the gambling tables doing your best, I remain here at home to give up and give away all that I hold dear. It is unavailing for me to assert that I have given up my relatives, our friends, a fine house, and that I did all that resolutely, because I stand behind you, Peter. That is my role, my responsibility. Even when you took away my pianoforte, my last treasure, even then I said to myself: at least that's all. At least I won't have to suffer the pain and humiliation anymore. There's nothing left to give away now.

"But I was wrong. Now I also have to give up this house that I detest, to go and live off the generosity of relations I barely know. Now you ask me to give up the very role that I sacrificed everything else to hold onto."

"I have made sacrifices, too, Elizabeth. You overlook that."

"Indeed? Oh yes! You've left behind the land you inherited—after you exhausted the soil. You've given up your race horses. You've sacrificed a few antique humidors."

"More: do you forget Solomon?"

Gran, holding a brimming cup and saucer, was about to bring it to her mistress. She halted upon hearing Solomon's name.

"Solomon was dear to me," Peter continued. "More dear than a piano, I assure you. You cannot imagine the bond that develops between those who have been at war together. Solomon was my valet for half my life, and I sacrificed him and didn't replace him."

Suddenly they were both aware of a heat coming from Gran. They watched dumbly as she turned her back to them and poured the contents of the cup into the planter. She picked up the tea tray and left the room.

Elizabeth's lower jaw jutted forward at a deprecating angle. She looked expectantly at her husband. "Well?"

His face was blank. "What is afoot now?" he asked.

"Peter! That was a deliberate insult."

"No, no. I fear Gran is just getting old. She's not what she used to be."

"Of course! Condone her blatant contempt. Make excuses." She rose from the couch and strode to the door. "Grant your old mammy the understanding and sympathy that it obviously pains you to extend to me."

Peter Blow waited to hear the rattle of the bedroom door close upstairs, then walked to the liquor cabinet. He drank directly from the bottle and did not refill it with water.

Chapter thirteen

Lying Shame

By my lights, there's only two things worth telling about them years in Alabama: what happened with Master, and what happened with Gran. I's sorry to say that being a slave, feeling low and shut in, that weren't the worst of things, 'cause I turned feeling low into feeling sorry for myself. That's when I become not just a slave, I become a fool.

Concerning me and Master Peter, what growed betwixt us in them dozen year after Zephyr growed all tangled, like ivy growing on a tree: ivy vine ain't good for the tree, and the tree's only good for the vine so long's the tree's healthy. For them first few years we was in Huntsville, we kept our ways separate. I had little to do with Master. I was in the fields and he was busy failing at cotton and getting back to his ways of gambling. Only he wasn't doing so poorly at the gaming table no more—regular he come home with winnings. One time in 18'n20, right 'fore we left Hunstville, Master got hisself a big windfall and sent the Missus and the girls on a shopping spree. Then he taken his sons, Peter and Henry, off for fun at a traveling show.

He brung me along, too. That was one of the first times he didn't go outten his way to sidestep me. He wanted me to drive, he said, but I knowed it were 'cause he was gonna slink off and gamble. He wanted me there to keep an eye on them boys. I was glad to go, as eager as them young'ns for a day at the fair. I washed me out a shirt the night before, Gran starched a collar for me, and I borrowed a cravat from one of the other hands. It were too big for me and covered most my shirt front, but I felt dandified. It were three year since Lucy, and the thought of her didn't hurt much no more. Truth, I was beginning to stretch my eyes toward the gals, and I felt like the peacock with that orange cravat. Master frown when he seed me, put his hand up 'fore his eyes like the cravat was hurting his eyes, but he didn't say nothing. What'd he care, anyways? Weren't like anybody knowed him. Weren't no woman to hail him and ask after his family. Weren't no man to tip his hat and say, "That's Peter Blow, a crop master if there ever was one."

We was all carrying our hearts lightly that day. We rode in a open carriage, joking and singing along. Master asked me to tell some stories as I drove, and I told one of Nat's old ghost tales. Master was more a papa to his boys that day than I seed him in years, but it only lasted till we got to the fairground. Too soon he was scanning the tents for the card games, plumb deaf to Peter Jr. asking him for money, asking to go see the freaks. His papa finally told him, no, saying it be "ungentlemanly."

That boy didn't really mind, though. He knowed like I did his papa was soon to disappear, and he knowed he could get me to go along and keep a secret. Sure 'nough, that's how it gone. Master finally digged down in his pocket to hand over a fistful of coins to Peter Jr. "Here's a whole dollar," he said, telling him he needn't split the money evenly with little Henry, "but don't be stingy." Them last words did get a rise outten Peter Jr.—all of us knowed, betwixt father and son, which gave little Henry the better care and attention.

Then Master turned to me. He dropped his hand on my shoulder, like he ain't done in a long while. To my surprise it felt good, like times he used to show me how to hold a fishing pole or point out the way a horse walks shows it got a injury on the mend. He gave me a slip of paper, a pass, saying, "These Alabama patrollers are hungry for rewards—just being with the boys might not protect you. Anybody gives you trouble, you show them this paper."

I knowed he was right. Alabama had these paddyrollers what beat and dragged slaves back to they masters, for the bounty. Mostly at night along the roads, so a slave couldn't easy pass from farm to farm. But they'd ride round in the daylight, too, and I heared some low stories, sure 'nough. I was glad to have the paper, and it felt good beyond just having a piece of paper. It sparked in me a old ember that still had some heat. I don't know—a part of my brain said I ought keep up a wall against Master Peter, but there ain't no denying a stronger part of me felt back on the inside, back within his power and protection again.

Then he left us, and we knowed we wouldn't see him till the sun went down, and was just as glad. I rode little Henry along on my shoulders, and Peter Jr. taken me by the hand and dragged me to all the wild animals, the acrobats and clowns, the magic show—oh, we was out of breath! And 'course, we be making frequent stops at the sweets cart. Onliest thing was, they wouldn't let young Peter into the freak tent. We could hear the barker yelling, "See the two-headed calf and the three-eyed pig! You won't believe your eyes! Women will faint at the sight of the real-live ape man, a genuine tribal chief from New Zealand!" But when we got over there, the man said Junior be too young and need his papa with him to get in.

That boy was so downcast. But I had me my own ideas. I crooked my finger. "Look how this tent be sitting right up against them hedges." I led him along the far side of the hedge and found a gap in the thicket. I put Henry in Peter's care and said, "Wait here a sec. Don't let this tyke outten your sight." Then I crawled through the shrub, loosed up a stake from the bottom of the tent, and wiggled back out. Told Junior how to go through, lift the tent, and hunker down till he could slip into the crowd. Only he had to be quick about it, 'cause the sun was going down and I knowed his papa'd be looking for us soon.

So he done it, and I played peekey-boo with Henry whilst we waited, but we waited too long, 'cause it weren't his papa what come along and found us. Circus folk, two horse-riding gals and two boxers, come up on me and Henry. Started giving me a hard time, telling me to move on. 'Course, I couldn't move on without Junior, and I couldn't tell them where Junior be. I hemmed and hawed, but then Junior comes creepy-crawling through the hedge, and it didn't take them boxers long to figure out what we done.

I wasn't scared. They wasn't mean like paddyrollers, just folk what had it hard theyselves, pressing a advantage over somebody they caught lower down. Still, they gived me a hard time. One said I must be one of the freaks, 'cause I's so small. Then one of them horse gals said, no, I was no freak, I was a clown; they started funning me over my cravat. Made me feel ugly and torn betwixt standing up and holding back—they was hard-luck folks, but they was white hard-luck folks. Instead, I pulled out the paper Master gived me, but right off that proved a mistake. Them men couldn't read, and to cover they shame in front of them gals they got heavy on me. One grabbed me up so my feet was dangling, and I don't know what might've happened 'cept Peter Jr. run headlong at the one holding me, charging that boxer with his fists cocked. The big man laughed and tossed me on the dirt and next shoved Peter back on his rump. 'Course, then I had to get up in front of him, and him and the other boxer grabbed hold of me betwixt them, whilst one of the gals pretended like to give me a whipping with a gold sash she took from around her waist.

They wasn't hurting me, just shaming me. At the start, my only thoughts was for the boys. Peter wasn't hurt, but he was red-faced and beginning to look scared. When Henry begun to cry over the ruckus, I seed Peter take that little chap by the arm and pull him close. Then everything went too fast. One boxer kicked my feet out from under me, saying, "Seems we done got ourselves a runaway clown. I'ma return this clown to the ringmaster." And he begun to draggle me through the dirt by my cravat. I kicked and pulled back, and the cloth tore—which was good 'cause it were choking me—but it were like I suddenly become naked. Without that cravat, it were like all them months and years of living the life of a no-'count field hand showed through, and I seed myself in the eyes of them circus women: dirty and useless, not even worth the trouble to poke fun at.

Master Peter come along then, walking fast and yelling. It were plain he was in his cups, so them circus folk slunk off, the men laughing as if to say they wasn't really scared.

I was still on the ground, feeling stupid and shook, recollecting that day when Cat Man blamed me for breaking the tools. Like that day, too, I was grateful Master come along to save me. Kneeling down beside me, Master Peter brushed me off. Gentle-like, he said, "It's over. Nobody's hurt. They're just ignorant circus people who know nothing about nothing." He raised me to my feet, and we both stumbled a mite 'cause he was tipsy. I picked up the torn pieces of the cravat, then threw them down again. But Master went and got them, brushed them off, and tied the two pieces back together. He begun fixing it around my collar so that the torn part wouldn't show. "You know," he said, "I teased you earlier when I saw you wearing this tie, but I couldn't help but wish I had such a cravat myself, for a special occasion."

I knowed Master was just being kind, but his words was like the salve of the powder-post beetle. My skin lost its heat and my breath come regular. I brushed myself off and squared back my shoulders till I happened to look over to Peter Jr. It were plain in his eyes that he knowed, too, his father was lying. Yet around his mouth showed a hurt, and into his eyes come a question as to why his father never spoken to him that soft.

Weren't more'n a week after the traveling show that we all moved sixty miles farther west along the Tennessee River to live with Master's brother, John Blow. Gran and me was in a cabin again, but we both got put to work in the big house this time. Gran didn't run things like she used to—they already had them a woman to run the kitchen—but she helped cook and clean. And me, why, seems Master Peter didn't need to put me outten his sight no more. He surprised everybody by taking me for his valet.

Why did he do that? That's a question I asked myself the very second he first told me, and I asked it over and over many a time during the years we lived with Master's brother. We stayed on John Blow's farm in Florence, Alabama, from 18'n20 to 18'n30, and in them ten year I taken the notion Master wanted sort of to make up for what he done to me back in V'ginia. I said as much to Gran one time, back in them early days in Florence, but she just sucked her teeth and said, "A dirty broom can't sweep clean."

I didn't cross-talk her. I was willing to move along with Master Peter, but Gran wouldn't forgive nor forget. She hated seeing me twining round Master's trunk, and we fussed at each other regular on account of him. All them years of peace betwixt me and Gran, and now there was friction daily. But I was bound not to let her rule me. I was going on twenty-one, feeling it were long overdue that I live according to my own lights. I wanted to be more amongst men and out in the world as much I got the chance to be.

Master be making all that possible, and more. He said, "Dred, I think you'll have some fun coming with me on my trips as my valet. It's better than working in the fields, or around the house, for that matter. But we'll have to spruce you up. I'll pick new clothes, shoes, too, maybe even a horse. Yes, I think my brother would rather lend us a horse than have us take a carriage all the time. Oh, and I think it would be a good idea if you let a moustache grow over your lip."

That startled me, sure 'nough, 'cause neither him nor me never mentioned the bad times. He never done made no mention of the scar he left on me nor on my missing front tooth. When he suggested I grow a moustache, I think I sort of jumped. He seed that and added, "A moustache will make you look older. Many of the places I frequent, and the people I meet, require the look of respectability and responsibility."

I was still enough of a boy not to see that respectability ain't just having manners or looking fine. I wasn't enough of a man yet to see how it's taking responsibility what makes a man a man. You got to step up and be counted enduring the hard times. You got to make reckoning for the times you done wrong. By that light, neither me nor Master Peter was much of a man. We continued to shy our mouths about our past troubles.

Slavery'll do that—for it to run smooth, everybody lies. The slave owner will lie about the wrong he's doing other folk, so naturally he gets to finding it easy to lie about all his doings. And as for the slave, many will trade a comfort for a pain, so naturally a slave can get to lying about all the evil behind them comforts. I become that kind of slave. I went along with Master's lies and his comforts, willing to believe that less bad was the same as good.

So I become the most dudish valet, sure 'nough. Had me a brand new suit and vest, with a hat to match. No more cap, no way, not for me. Had me a cravat, too, and it were all new. First time in my life I wore clothes fresh store-bought. Gran had to stitch them to fit me right, and she frowned the whole time she worked on that suit—but she done it up good. Them clothes fit me like feathers fit a peacock, and I seed the gals turn they heads when I strutted through the quarter.

I was right smart, even smarter than the young masters. 'Course, I weren't spending much time with them anyways. When I become Master Peter's valet, like him I had less'n less to do with the rest of the family. Only for little Henry did I make time. He didn't have his rashes no more, but I made time to play with him and give him some company. He was such a lonely little chap, it plucked my heart strings.

Anyways, I become Master's valet, puffed out my chest in my new clothes, journeyed out with him to other plantations where often we stayed away a whole week. These Alabama slave owners whoop up the merrymaking, sure 'nough. Quadrilles and cotillions, masked balls and galas, parties what lasted for days. Women in they finest frocks, men all dandied, dancing, feasting, picnicking. And always the men would find a quiet place for drinking, smoking, and gambling. Some games went on for days, and if Master was doing well, there was times I didn't sleep for four nights straight. When he slept, I slept. When he ate, I ate. When he drunk, I drunk—just never as much. And when he disappeared into some lady's private bedchamber, I usually found me similar 'commodation in one of the slave cabins. I had me some regular gals through them years, some I was right sweet on, though I never gived my heart over. After Lucy, I kept my heart down in the root cellar, so to speak. But the rest of me—I was living easy and playing in the sunshine. Or so I thought at the time.

Months and years rolled by like that. I growed wild, I don't deny it. I ain't proud of my life enduring that time. Said I was having fun, but many a times I was so drunk I was sick. Said I was a lady's man, but there was getting to be more and more doors that wouldn't open to me 'cause I trod roughshod in my fine new shoes over some gal's tender feelings. Said I was living free, but a few times I got roughed up and rattled by them paddyrollers. I even took to stealing during that time—cigars and extra food and pretty scraps of cloth. I never got found out, but anything I ever stole and tried to give Gran, somehow she knowed and wouldn't take it.

Oh, I was playing the fool, sure 'nough, though when I peered in the looking-glass I seed a dandy. Believed I was having fun and didn't pay no mind to the gray hairs I was putting on my dear Gran's head.

⁂

The woman in the bed next to Dred rolled away from him, leaving one leg draped over his. He let his arm fall over her thigh, and lazily his fingers trailed along her smooth skin, upwards from her knee. Her voice was as soft as a dove's coo when she said, "I like a man what don't hurry before, then lingers after."

Dred, lying on his back, said, "I got nothing but time to give."

"Your master bedded down for the night?" she asked, deaf to his real meaning.

"Snuck off with one of them visiting ladies. A married one, I think."

She snorted. "And they wags they tongues about us!"

They fell silent, each contentedly following their own thoughts into a peaceful sleep, only their limbs still connected to each other. It was much later, when they had rolled apart and slept deeply, separately, vulnerably, that they were jolted awake by the two white men bursting into the cabin.

Dred clutched the raggedy blanket to cover himself and the woman. His heart beat wildly and his head was unclear from sleep and drink, but he rose to his knees to provide her more protection. The first white man yelled, "Goddamn you, Everline! You little whore."

146

It was her master, and he was fumbling with his belt so that Dred couldn't be sure if he intended to whip him or to rape the woman, who was cowering, naked, behind Dred. Then Dred saw the second man was Master Peter. A small bubble of relief popped quickly when he realized the Master was so drunk he had to lean against the door frame to stay on his feet. Dred's heart faltered. He held his breath.

As Evvy's master lurched toward him, comprehension slowly dawned on Peter Blow's face, and he said, "Dred? What are you doing here?"

The other white man had his belt off now, wrapping one end around his fist. He continued to rage, "Evvy, I'll learn you to cavort behind my back. That's not what I put you in this cabin for." With a wail Everline seemed to be attempting to climb the wall behind the bed. Dred put up his arms, knowing it was the worst thing he could do, but his mind seemed to have no control over his body.

"Outta my way, runt. I'll take care of you directly."

He swung his arm back but Peter Blow grabbed it and pulled it down. "Stephen, Stephen, desist. Please, a moment of calm, and I think we can handle this properly." Both men stumbled, unsteady on their feet, but Stephen yielded. Peter Blow continued, "This boy is my valet."

"Yours!"

"Yes." Peter Blow, focused solely on the impending violence, struggled to rise above his drunkenness. "I apologize for this inconvenience and embarrassment to you, but I think I understand and can make things right."

Stephen blinked as he absorbed this information. He held out the belt. "You want to beat him?" he asked.

"No, no, no. Frankly, we may not want to beat them. You see, the problem is partly my own fault."

"You?"

"Yes, you see, I've allowed Dred in the past to seek out his own companions—it's entirely my fault that I didn't restrict him here without first obtaining your permission."

"You allow him to go catting around the slave quarters?"

Peter Blow felt in charge of the situation now, and he worked deftly to bring the other man around. He laughed apologetically, "You see, it's the customs by which I was raised, those old Virginia ways. I'm somewhat old fashioned, Stephen, and I have given Dred to understand that this sort of behavior is not only permissible but desirable."

"Desirable!"

"Yes, antiquated teachings impressed upon me from my earliest years, by my own papa, I fear: he was staunchly opposed to any mixing of the races, yet he wanted his slave crop to be fruitful, so he encouraged his own slaves to plow the fields, so to speak."

All the while Peter Blow was pulling his friend away toward the door, but Stephen abruptly jerked away and halted. "'Opposed to mixing of the races'!" Stephen laughed. "Dash it all—you're practically a Yank, aren't you?" Laughing heartily now at the confusion on Peter Blow's face, he explained, "Why, where do you think we'd be here in the cotton states if we waited for our slaves to build their own numbers! We'd be out there in the fields with them, I can assure you, just to get the crops in!"

Laughing with his host, Peter Blow said, "Precisely, precisely— that's what my father had to do. It was tobacco and not cotton, but for much of his life he was in the fields himself. Such reasoning, if it can be so called, belongs to an age now past and is scarcely comprehensible to a modern man. Truly, those old Virginia ways no longer pass muster!"

The white men were clapping each other on the back. Peter Blow led his host, who had all but forgotten the slaves, out of the cabin. "I'm besotted, anyway," confided Peter Blow. "I merely require a bed to lie down in for sleep."

The drunken voices of their masters passed beyond hearing, but neither slave could settle back in the bed. Evvy went to the small fireplace and began heating water for a toddy. The cups chattered nervously in her grasp. Dred sat on the edge of the bed with his head in his hands. When Evvy brought two toddies and climbed back under the blanket, she motioned for Dred to do likewise. The bed had no headboard but was fitted into a corner of the room. Dred settled his back against the cabin wall and sat upright. Evvy slid over and maneuvered herself between his legs. She nestled into him, sipping her drink.

Finally she broke the silence. "Is Virginia the north?"

"I don't think so. They got plantations and slave owners and slaves. I guess it's just closer to north than here."

"I bet your master be one of them fancified plantation mens, ain't I right? One of them what made the whole country. Probably has him a uniform and medals in his closet."

"He does, but it's from the 18'n12 War, not the Independence War. And he ain't been too fancified, neither, not for some long years now. That's why we's here. Got hisself bankrupted. Nearly got hisself booted out of V'ginia. We's living offen his big brother now."

"Ooooh, and he be out gambling and catting around?"

Dred was quiet.

"Wish I had me a brother like that." A loud guffaw erupted from her, causing her to spill some of her toddy.

"His brother's a real gentleman. Very kind. Shows him respect. Master Peter got nowheres left in this world where he can see respect in the eye of another man. Don't even see it in his own wife's eye, nor in his children's."

She clucked her tongue, imagining how low the mighty have fallen. "You lucky you still with him, then. I knows it well: when the white man go into the gutter, his slaves go south. I been sold four times in my young life, each time farther and farther south." She shifted onto her side and slipped an arm around his back. "So is you one of them special slaves, been with the white man's family for generations, treated 'most like kin?"

"I been with Master Peter my whole life, and my Gran belonged to Master Peter's papa, old Richard Blow. But it weren't how Master Peter said. Old Richard Blow, I mean, weren't like he said. He molested his slave gals. Gran never said so, but I think she even be one of them."

Evvy clucked her tongue again. "Black womens sure be sitting at the bottom of the heap." Resting her head on his chest, with her arm still around his back, she stroked him, then said with surprise, "You ain't never been whipped, is you?"

Dred's tongue ran along the gum where his front tooth used to be. He paused and said, simply, "No."

"And tonight you got your hide saved by your master. Ain't that a turn-around?"

"How about you? You gonna catch it later?"

"Nah, I reckon it's over now. He so drunk, he likely not even remember tonight. And iffen he do remember, I knows just when to mention his missus—that always sends him running with his tail tucked. I be all right." Then her brow crinkled. "Don't know iffen you and me's gonna get any next times, though. Master Steve might move me on outta here. He don't like his gals being with black mens." She giggled. "He think black mens all be better under the blanket than white mens—I guess probably 'cause he think black gals be better'n white ones." She laughed heartily. "I just loves it when white folk envies black folk!"

Dred looked serious and withdrawn. She nudged him. "Don't you?"

"What?"

"Like it when white folk feels that black folk be better'n them?"

His mouth stretched into something between a grimace and grin, and he caressed her hair, tucking her head under his chin so that she couldn't see his expression. "Yes, I do," he admitted. "Even more, I like being better. I been Master's valet now for over five year, and even 'fore that I seed him running hisself down, messing up time after time, and I felt big offen that. There's a part of me enjoyed seeing him fall low—enjoyed it more'n I should, I reckon. It's a low pleasure, a mean enjoyment, but still a pleasure."

Evvy stopped stroking him and stretched her neck to look into his face, grinning mischievously. "My, my. Do the master know his valet ain't his nigger!"

Dred pulled her head back down on his chest and added, "That don't make me feel good no more, though, 'cause no matter how low he falls, I'll always be lower." He grunted and recited, as if to himself, "A snake what swallows a snake will have its victim's tail hanging from its mouth."

Evvy, not listening, continued caressing his smooth back. Dred's hand had begun tracing the curves down her arm, over her belly, around her breasts. He wanted to pay more attention to what his hand was doing, but his thoughts had become turbid, pressing for expression. Out loud he said, "My Gran hates to see me ducking Master's sorry shadow, drinking and loafing with him, taking up his ways. She thinks I want to be like him, but that's not it. Part of me maybe does—or did. Hell, it's just that it's a easy life."

Evvy was kissing his chest, inching up toward his neck and face. She was at his chin when he said, "Gran hates to see me wasting my life, but it ain't like I got much of a life to waste. Might as well just play till the sun goes down."

"Then let's play," she whispered, as her lips finally reached his, and they both shimmied down under the blanket, making love quick and frenzied this time.

In the quiet afterward, before they fell back asleep, Evvy mused, "Still, I never knowed a white man to lie to another white man on behalf of a black man. Never even heared of it. So he must be holding you as something special."

Dred reflected so long before answering that Evvy was snoring lightly when he finally replied, "I used to think so."

Twenty-four hours later, after another long night of carousing, Peter Blow sent Dred home alone. It was close to dawn when Dred approached the cabin, but he was still feeling drunk. Seeing light splay through the chinks of the cabin walls, knowing Gran was awake, Dred stopped outside in the dark, damp night and weighed whether to go back or to go on in. Going back, the Master would surely find a use for him, but it would mean risking an encounter with the patrollers, and he was already lucky not to have been stopped. Master had dismissed him, but had neglected to give him a pass. No, to go back on the roads was too risky.

Steeling himself, he pulled open the rickety door. Her look told him what he already knew: she was not going to hold her tongue any longer. What surprised him was his reaction. Something burly lurched in his breast. Something feral was done with hibernation.

Gran didn't bother with pleasantries. "I bet he didn't even give you a pass." Not answering, Dred shrugged off his jacket and let it fall to the floor. Ignoring this provocation, Gran continued. "But that don't bother you none, does it now?" She sucked her front teeth. "Not much ruffles your feathers no more."

"Only you," he said tightly.

"Don't sass me, Dred. Sassing me won't keep me from saying what's got to be said." She watched him slouch down by the hearth, where dying embers burned slow and cold, offering no light or warmth. He extended his arms anyway and rubbed his hands together. Turning only his head, he looked at her, and the expression on his face took her breath away. He looked wild and fierce. Catching her look of alarm, he turned back to the soot-encrusted fireplace. He felt scared, too. Something had happened to him when he walked through the door, and he struggled to control it. Each held their breath. In the silence an ash-laden, flame-consumed log collapsed with a soft sigh, revealing its glowing interior.

Dred spoke first, in pleading or warning, he didn't know. "Gran, let's not. Not tonight."

He realized that she was sitting with nothing in her lap, nothing to keep her hands busy. He had never seen her sit and do nothing. But he was mistaken, because Gran was very busy. She was thinking about what he said. She was racing to understand what was in the room with them. She was fighting for control of her breathing and her heartbeat. The blood of warrior women beat in her head, and she admitted to herself, for the first time in her life, that her grandmother had scared her as a child. Unleashed, Nyota's intensity and strength had been terrifying.

"I wish I had me a machete," she said, as if to herself. "I got a thick jungle to cut through, and I's somewhat afeared of what be licking its chops in the underbrush."

Dred stood abruptly, turned to her a face of seething anger, and said, "No. No stories, Gran. No proverbs. No Africa. No kin. Talk plain or don't talk at all."

His words acted like flint upon the stone of worry and resentment she had carried in her breast ever since Virginia. "Fine. First thing I got to say is this: you drunk?"

He smirked. They both had seen the Master when the Missus asked the same question of her husband: these days, Peter Blow blithely smoothed his vest, cleared his throat, and plucked his watch from a pocket. Dred pantomimed this and then said what the Master invariably said after examining the watch face, "Not yet."

Gran was on her feet with her hand raised before the smirk had time to fade from his lips. She still towered above him. Her hand wavered in the air as if something held it in check. Then she lowered her arm slowly. Between clenched teeth she said, "You's drunk."

A wave of desperation washed over her, and she clutched him by his shoulders. "Dred, Dred, why you want to be this way? You's headed nowheres with this acting up. You drink and gamble and cat about. Where you think it's gonna get you? I's scared for the consequences even if you ain't. I's scared you's gonna wind up getting beat, or you's gonna make yourself sick, or you's gonna get some gal what you don't even care about with child—a child you can't raise nor protect. Why, you could even get yourself sold away. You ain't around no more to hear what goes on up at the big house, but I's telling you that Mary Anne and Missus sees you as part of the problem. They'd far druther blame you than blame the Master."

He jerked out of her grasp. "Seems fair. You'd far druther blame him than blame me."

"Yes, I would," she retorted, her hands now on her hips. "But you can't tell me I ain't got a right. Landsakes, it don't even make sense. A man what treated you the way Master Peter done, and you follow him like a puppy. Was a time early on after we moved when you wouldn't even look at him. How'd it come to pass that you trying so hard to act like him now? A man what throwed away everything valuable he ever got his hands on: land, money, family. Throwed them all away. And he's gonna throw you away, too, by'n by. Just as he done Solomon. Mark my words."

With each parry they had begun to circle the small cabin like predator and prey, each edging around to find a vulnerable spot. He was trying to find a soft spot to make her retreat. She was trying to find a soft spot to draw near. "It just sticks in your craw, don't it, Gran? That I look up to somebody other'n you. All my life it's been that way. You can't stand for me to love somebody bigger and stronger'n you."

"It ain't that way, you know it ain't. I encouraged you and Joe. I encouraged you and Solomon. With them, you had a chance to grow to equal respect. You ain't never gonna see that happen with Master Peter. He's your master! He owns you. He ain't never gonna have no more respect for you than he got for a good plow horse or a clever dog."

"Do you respect me, Gran? No. You still treating me like the boy you raised. You raised me, you raised him, too—that don't make you know more'n we know. You got no notion what I feel for Master nor what he feel for me. Why, you ain't even spoken to the man in over five year!"

"With good reason. This be a man what sold off your own wife."

"As iffen you ever cared about her."

"I care about everything that happens to you, Dred." Now they stood stock still, face to face. "I care enough," she added, "to be truthful with you, which is more'n anybody can say about Peter Blow."

Until then he had just been snarling; with this, he bared his fangs and sunk them in. "You don't tell truth. You tell stories. Raised me up on stories till I's sick of them. Stories about what's important, right? Stories about being clever, being special, being strong. Well, I's a man now, Gran—a man, not a griot—and I know your stories ain't nothing but lies. Lies! Pretty lies, fanciful lies, lies to help a child sleep at night. I come into my man walking through a forest of lies—that you planted. I hear them crunch under my feet every time I put my foot forward."

His resentment was so strong it threw Gran off balance. She fell into a chair and, biding for time, said, "I don't know what you's saying."

"Don't fret yourself, Gran: it ain't just you. I know everybody lies. I learned from you, first: all them stories about possibilities, telling me I got a tomorrow to look forward to, till I seed that was just a story told to cheer a child. I learned it from Lucy, too. She gived me her love, then couldn't be shed of me fast enough. So why should I expect anything different from Master Peter? Why should I hold it against him that he treated me special, promised me that riding crop, then used it to bust open my face?"

She couldn't follow him; there was so much wrong with what he was saying. Focusing on what was most important, she protested, "It ain't the same. What I tell you and what Master tell you ain't the same at all, and you know it."

"Here's what I know, Gran: the truth don't matter. What you say don't matter. What you believe don't matter. What you do, that's the only thing what matters, and even that don't really matter all that much. That's what I know: whatever a black man does, it don't matter." He leaned over her as she sat, yelling down at her. She did not lift her eyes as he continued. "You want to argue? Say it ain't so? If it be different for you, fine. But I's telling you what come clear to me all them days I picked cotton in the fields, after we first moved to Alabama, after I become a field hand, not suited for work in the field, of no more use than a eight-year-old boy. Know why I didn't sing with them other hands whilst I worked? 'Cause I was working to keep the anger and the shame down, afeared that if I opened my mouth to sing, all that would come up would be a howl. I rolled through them days knowing for cold certain that every low-down, mean word a white man ever spoked about a black man was true about me: I was a lazy, stupid, lying, cheating, worthless animal. That's what was true. And it hit me hard, Gran. Felt like a team of mules done tramped over my body, then dragged the wagon over me too."

Tears were in her voice but not yet in her eyes when she lifted them to his, simply moaning, "Oh, Dred. Dred, Dred."

He flinched and turned his back to her. "Don't! Your pity ain't gonna stop what I got left to say. 'Cause it's you, you I blame. You put blinkers on me like a horse what's jittery. I never deserved that." He whipped around again to fire his accusation. "You raised me believing all them ugly things said about blacks was just the white man's ignorance. That's how you learned me. You raised me up opposite all that, said it'd make a difference in my life to do my work quick and clean, keep my wits sharp, avoid giving a hurt, and never lie about a wrong, even iffen I couldn't always do the right. How many times you tell me: 'Decide for your ownself what's right, then follow your heart.' Ain't that what you said? Always urging me to play it straight, first and last." He was pacing again, unable to hold still.

"And I followed that as a child, Gran, believed what you believed. Till I come into my man and seed how wrong you been all these years. I come to ask myself: why put out all the effort to do good, when the result's likely to be no better than doing evil? Where did all my hard work, smarts, truthing, straight-shooting, and caring ever get me? Nowheres. Got me to where the man I loved like a papa schemed against me, and when I was wise to him he split my face open and knocked out a tooth. Got me to where my wife said to my bust-open face that she didn't want to stay with me. 'I can't 'bide by you, Dred. You's too small and too soft. I'ma find me a big hunk of a man that's gonna protect me in this world.' That was your fault, Gran. You made me soft!"

With pained amazement, Gran realized Dred didn't understand all that had happened that awful day when Lucy was sold. She raised both hands, palms outward, patting the air. Her voice was soft as a cloud. "Lucy didn't mean none of that, Dred! She only said what she did to keep you from getting shot. She seed there was nothing nobody could do for her, and she loved you enough to try and do something good for you before she got sold away."

"More lies? You gonna stand here in my face and throw more lies my way?"

Gran rose from her chair, shaken but determined. "I ain't lying. I know that gal was trying to protect you from Master Peter's pistol, just as sure as I know I's here today trying to protect you from his drag-down ways."

Dred sniffed and his upper lip curled. "Then I must surely be weak and soft, to need all these women in my life protecting me from Master Peter."

She threw her hands up. "I's only trying to make you see he

ain't fit for your love. That a man what owns you can never be trusted. I been trying hard all my life to make you see that."

"Here's what I see, Gran: you was only worried the Master might sell me from you. You didn't trust his power over us. You worried he'd pull us apart, worried so much you figured you better not worry me with it. You tried to hide from me that tomorrow I could wind up in a strange land with strange people." Every time he said 'you' his finger jabbed the air between them. "But look at it through my eyes, Gran: where'd that get me? Got me believing that they wasn't what they actually is: slave owners! And that I wasn't what I actually is: a slave, a piece of their property. You did that! That's how you made me soft!

"And that ain't the end of it. Because buried along with what you tried to hide was also what being a slave means. The lie that hurts me worst of all is you saying how I got some kind of future when I know for a dead certainty I don't." He barked his next sentences to the rhythm of his fist pounding his chest. "I ain't never gonna get free. I ain't never gonna own nothing. And I sure as hell ain't never gonna go down that path again of looking for a wife and children and a tomorrow."

Gran stood clutching her stomach as though nauseated. Her mouth hung slack. She was listening to him, but she was deep within herself, racing again, frantically trying to figure out how they had come to this pass. Weakly she said, "Nobody knows what's in tomorrow. Even if you's a slave for the rest of your days, Dred, maybe tomorrow you might choose a family. Nobody knows."

"That's the first time you ever said right out that I's a slave. The first time in all my years. Finally, you say the truth. I's a slave. We can agree on that. But you's wrong about choosing 'cause I know one thing for certain: being a slave means I ain't got no choice." Dred slumped into a chair. He held his head in his hands and said so low she could hardly hear him, "I learned that just last week. Master got so drunk he didn't know what he was saying. Got to talking about Lucy, which him and me never done. He apologized over Lucy, told me how much it hurt him to do me that way." Dred lifted his head and glared now at Gran. "He told me a nice little story about how he set hisself down that night before he sold her, sat thinking to hisself: I'ma sell Lucy, but should I sell Dred with her or keep Dred with Gran? And he choosed you, Gran. He choosed you for me to stay with. It were his choice, not mine. His to choose who I would stay with and where I would go.

"So iffen I ain't got no choices, then what do I care about tomorrow? My tomorrow does me as much good as the moon in the sky during the daytime—makes not one bittiest bit of difference to how the sun rises and rests. So let me live for today, Gran. Let me live what really is, instead of what you want it to be."

Tears were coursing silently down her cheeks now. "I's sorry. I's so sorry, Dred," she said, "that you see your life that way." She wagged her head mournfully from side to side. "I don't know iffen I got the years left to try to make it right."

He slammed both fists on the table and shot to his feet. "That's what I's saying, Gran! You don't have all the answers! You can't make it right. There's nothing you can do. You got no choice neither. You's just as weak and soft as me. That's been the biggest lie of all!"

She felt punched in the stomach. All the breath and strength had gone out of her. Even her shadow, which had stretched across the rough-planked floor between them, recoiled and cringed. She limped as she moved away from the window, and for the first time ever she seemed smaller than Dred.

He turned and crouched again by the fire, ashamed to see how he had shrunk her.

"I would do anything," she whispered. "Anything to make this a better world than it is, one fitting for you to live in. I thought so long as I was there for you, so long as we was together…." Her words trailed off. Heavily she sank to her mattress and curled into the corner with her back to him. "Maybe when we go over. Maybe with our kin it will all be right again. Maybe there it will be enough for you and me to just be together."

"It will be something," he said dully to the dead fire, "but it won't be enough."

Chapter fourteen

Divided

I'd take it back if I could, all the hurt I gived Gran. Even allowing for afterwards, how some things turned for the better. I cleaned up some, started watching Master Peter with a partial Gran-eye. I stayed his valet but I pulled back from his ways. As for Gran, she begun talking about slavery like she never done before. Stopped giving me fanciful stories and tales and begun giving me real fact. More like history, true stories of what truly happened.

That was when I learned the whole truth about my mama and papa. Learned how old Richard Blow molested my mama and beat my papa. I could hardly believe it, that I growed not knowing that history. "Why you never tell me this before?" I asked her.

She looked sad and sorry, shaked her head and said, "I bargained with the devil." She explained how Peter Blow done promised her he'd sell me off the second I learned about it. He was ashamed of his papa, she said, and didn't want no mention of it never again.

I argued to her how, iffen I done knowed that, I likely never would've felt so open to him. But she stood solid and said, "Dred, I done just had my son sold away from me. Wasn't no way I was gonna risk being the cause of my grandbaby going the same road."

She told me more, too. How the man she lived with, what fathered Jacob, sometimes beat her. She allowed how some slaves would act that way, 'cause it were the one place they could still feel like they have some say—men over women, parents over children. Gran fought back, 'course. Fought back so strong one time she almost sliced his arm off with a carving knife. Made old Richard Blow scared he gonna lose one or t'other, so he separated them. Sold off the man, leaving Gran and Jacob to theyselves.

She told me other slavery stories, too: How Uncle Joe wasn't crooked 'cause of the forge. She showed me the notch on his age-stick what told how, before he come to Zephyr, he once plotted with some other slaves. Gran wasn't sure whether it were to run away or to kill some white man. Anyways, they was found out, and Uncle Joe was hanged from the barn rafters. They tied his hands behind his back and hoisted him up from his wrists. Left him there so long something in his back gived out, and never again could he stand straight. Not till that day with Cat Man.

And she told me what happened to Aunt Molly, what was too old and feeble to come with us from V'ginia. Not many people ever ask what happens to old slaves. Some just get put down, like a animal. But Master Peter, being more feeling and all, he turn his over to some low-life white trash, pay a small fee and don't give it another thought as to how they gets put in some rickety shed till they die, fed on less'n you'd feed a chicken.

That story scared me, 'cause Gran herself be showing her age by then. She had her spells, times when she lived in her childhood. And seeing as how I didn't belong in her childhood, she'd look right at me and not know me. That were hard; ain't no loneliness on earth like standing eye to eye with one you love, and all the love be blanked out. All you see in they eyes is how they don't hold you in no account—don't even know your name.

By'n by I got used to Gran's spells, but when she told how Master Peter done Aunt Molly, it put the chill back in my heart. Gran said Master Peter would never do her that way, seeing as she was his mammy, but I wasn't so certain. That were a change in the weather, sure 'nough: her thinking better of him than me.

Anyways, all them stories Gran told about slavery, bad as they was, worked a kind of cure on me. Seeing what others gone through, I didn't feel so much shame on myself. The feeling sorry for myself lifted. Now in its place come a slow, cold anger. Gived more time, that anger might've built heat, might've helped me move on with my life. But the anger didn't build soon enough. Just as it were getting started, Master moved us all on again. His biggest gamble yet: move to the western frontier to start over. I didn't care about the move, what did I ever care about Alabama? In truth, I was curious about city life and looking forward on going to St. Looey. I just never seed till it were too late how it were gonna change everything.

ᚱ

"Close that door behind you." Elizabeth Blow didn't bother to turn her head to give the command or to see that it was followed. To the others around the dining table she said, "Please, let's continue our meal."

As Gran lumbered back toward the kitchen, her long skirts rustled across the floor. She stumbled slightly. Elizabeth set her fork down and said, "Why is it that you are forever tripping over your skirts? No wonder there are stains everywhere in this house." This elicited a pained look from her husband and embarrassed looks from her in-laws, Amelia and John.

Gran turned then, a gravy boat in one hand, a water goblet in the other. She returned to the dining table, placed the dishes beside her mistress, and gathered her skirts in two fists. "I ain't as big as I was." Still holding her skirts, she rustled out of the room.

Elizabeth's pinched gaze remained fixed on the brown stain beside her plate where Gran a few minutes earlier had spilled the gravy. The worst part, however, was that Gran had insisted on pouring the gravy into her water glass. Into the strained silence, Elizabeth said, "I, too, wish Gran hadn't gotten old. But she is becoming obviously worse. Daily." Peter and John exchanged glances she couldn't read. "Am I the only one who sees her mistakes?" Then, petulantly, "Surely I am not alone in feeling an obligation to our gracious hosts to make our stay here as free from trouble as is feasible."

161

Peter winced at this, as she knew he would. He detested any mention of his dependence upon his brother. He answered his wife with civility, though it was clearly forced. "As you know, Elizabeth," he said, "we may not be imposing upon John and Charlotte much longer." To his brother, he said, "It is a matter much on my mind of late. Elizabeth and I have discussed plans for the future—perhaps, if you are finished, we could discuss this in your study?"

John put a forkful of meat in his mouth, then crossed his knife and fork over the plate. Still chewing, he said, "Dear brother, of course I respect your prerogative to make whatever plans you feel best suit your family, but I trust you know that your presence among us is an inestimable joy." He swallowed his food and continued. "Just look around you: Charlotte and Elizabeth have become close confidants— indeed, at times I only wish I knew the secrets they share! As for me, the chance to work shoulder to shoulder with my younger brother has filled a place in my heart that can be satisfied by nothing else. And your dear children, they have graced this staid old homestead with laughter and life." He was extremely pleased with his magnanimity. Riding the crest of virtue he added, "Why, even Gran's presence, with all its shortfalls, is a nostalgic pleasure that I could not have anticipated. To be sure, her constant mumbling can be disconcerting, but at times I feel as if we were boys again, listening to her stories in the kitchen as we all shelled peas for dinner."

Elizabeth Blow rolled her eyes. "Charlotte, I declare that I have never known gentlemen more indulgent of their mammies than the Blow brothers. Where I was raised, slaves, even beloved mammies, knew their place—or were reminded of it."

John laughed outright, sparing his wife the necessity of responding. "Elizabeth, I am sure your father was correct. Our father, I confess, was a bit of a libertine who could only aspire to gentility through his sons—and we have not always succeeded ourselves. Certainly we are inferior to our good wives!"

Everyone but Elizabeth joined his laughter, though she managed a polite smile. Taking a last gulp of wine, John rose from the table, tugged his vest down over his rotund waistline, and said, "Well, Peter, let's retire to the study then."

In the study, John withdrew a handsomely-carved wooden humidor from a special cabinet. He offered its contents to his brother.

"Why, these are mine," Peter said. "Do you mean to tell me that they are still good, after what? Nearly fifteen years?" He brushed some powdery bloom from the shaft of one cigar and examined it with his nose. Approving, he licked its length, poked it inside his mouth and quickly withdrew it. From his vest he withdrew elegant, small scissors and clipped the end.

"Like Gran," chuckled John, "they've lost a little something in the aging, but thanks to this special cabinet I had made, these cigars have retained their unique flavor." He lit his brother's cigar, then chose one himself and repeated the ritual. Taking his first puff, he said, "You grew a fine tobacco, Peter."

"I appreciate that, John. I have proved an abysmal cotton farmer—and despite your kind words at the table, I haven't been much help to you, either—but I did make a success of tobacco. At least for a while."

"You produced a finer tobacco than father."

"He didn't have the bright leaf. That made all the difference."

"Yes. And it exhausted your soil in the bargain."

"Well, all farming is a gamble. I think it's fair to say I do better at the gaming tables than in the fields. Wouldn't you agree?"

John did not reply but waited for his brother to say what was on his mind.

"John, I feel that I cannot continue to be a burden on you. It weighs heavily on my conscience."

John cleared his throat. "Peter—"

"No, John, do not argue. This isn't easy for me, but I have to admit I haven't been carrying my own weight. You have been most generous. I shall always be in your debt."

"Rubbish. I will not be addressed as one of your gambling acquaintances. Let there be no talk of debt between us."

Peter, irked by his brother's tone, decided to dispense with the parlor-room amenities. "If I were to remain I should feel compelled to stop playing cards, because it's not fair to drag you and Charlotte through the dramas of my winning and losing. Yet I do not intend to give up gambling and do not preach to me."

Matching his brother's candor, John replied with faint sarcasm, "No, no more preaching. I've appreciated the futility of that."

Bristling now, Peter said curtly, "I have a bit of a nest egg now, and I am determined to make my way along a new path."

"And that would be—?"

"You called our father a libertine; I might have said pioneer. He helped fashion those tidewater plantations into a county, helped found the county seat. He made it possible, through his rough ways, for his sons to become gentlemen—as you so rightly pointed out. And I've been thinking I, too, might seek a frontier. I have never been refined enough for the South, I am an inconstant gentleman at best, so why not head west? To St. Louis, at least."

"Really? St. Louis?" John was skeptical.

"Yes. St. Louis," Peter clipped his response.

"I hear life out there displays a want of taste and tact scarcely to be believed," John cautioned. "You remember the Padgets? They went to St. Louis in '20, just about the time you arrived down here. George succumbed to yellow fever and Anna died in childbirth. I have had report from Mark, their eldest, that he has taken responsibility for all seven children, who have become wild—two have married Indians. The best Mark and two of his brothers have managed is to become shop clerks."

"John, I'm not like you. I crave a little wildness. Southern respectability confines me like an ill-fitting jacket. I still have an appetite for new tastes and unfettered choices."

"Our father's blood runs in me, too," John replied. "You know, when you first came here, I was the same age you are now. Ten years ago I had similar cravings myself. A man in his middle years often feels tempted by that siren's call. But consider, brother: what of a man's obligation to the land, to his family, to his progeny? I can tell you without reservation that I am glad I persevered here on the farm. Your own son has been invaluable, and now my grandson is joining me in the fields. That he will inherit all of this, preserve it, grow rich and happy from it—well, Peter, that is one of life's supreme satisfactions."

Peter smiled suddenly, remembering all the times they had quarreled about the differences between them. "Our father's blood runs in each of us, yes. But I think, John, it runs in opposite directions." The tension between them softened, as though masked by the screen of smoke that hung in the air between them. With affection, he said, "Your counsel all the more makes me realize that my mind is quite fixed. I might add that Elizabeth is keen on the idea, too. She has always admired city society, city fashions. St. Louis could satisfy some of her cravings, as well."

John studied his cigar. He recognized in his heart that his attempt to dissuade his brother lacked sincerity. It was time for Peter to move on. Still, he had a duty as the elder brother. "And what about the children?"

"Well, as you say, Peter Jr. has learned a great deal under your tutelage; he demonstrates spirit and capacity. He'll thrive in a city. Perhaps he'll start out as a shop clerk, but I'll wager he'll wind up owning a business. The younger boys are sure to get a quality education there—I understand the Catholics operate marvelous schools, and I'm interested in the discipline they are noted for. Henry is growing quite contrary and rebellious and, of course, Taylor follows right behind him. Those two need a stronger hand than I have been able to apply. As for the girls, well, I can't see that it should matter to them whether they marry doctors and lawyers instead of farmers. Mary Anne, who unfortunately has become pegged as an old maid here, might even have a fresh chance there, perhaps with a widower."

"I see you have thought this through."

"I have given it considerable thought. What nags at me the most is deciding what to take and what to acquire fresh once I'm there. Particularly concerning the slaves. I can't take them all, of course. I'm afraid I will be obliged to sell some."

"Your good wife is correct: you do bear a strong sentimentality toward your slaves."

Smiling ruefully, Peter conceded. "It's true. Yet I do feel it's a pity—this group that came with us this far, they've all been together for so long: through Virginia, then Huntsville, now here. The last of the last, so to speak."

"Those you don't want, I might purchase from you. They have a home here, they have their uses. Have you determined which you will keep?"

"No more than half a dozen, surely. I've thought it should be Hannah and Ruby—at their age they won't fetch much at auction, but I'll still get a good number of years out of them. I may try to run a boarding house, and they could attend the rooms. Also I think Sam and Luke and Dred, because whatever I wind up doing, I'll need a few able-bodied men."

"Not Gran?"

"That question troubled me too, but I have spoken with her and the solution won't be so difficult. You know how Gran can talk around a thing, but she gave me to understand that she herself lacks the conviction that she could survive the journey. I am in full agreement. Besides which, she'd be of little use to me in St. Louis, and I anticipate friction with Elizabeth if I attempt to haul Gran along with us. Elizabeth has been looking forward to being shed of Gran since we wed."

John laughed softly. "It can be that way between wives and mammies. Thankfully, I don't think Charlotte feels that way. I believe she sometimes enjoys the old gal's stories."

"Well, that's precisely what I hoped to hear. You see, John, I think Gran will stay behind and not fuss as long as she believes you won't dump her or send her away, no matter how bad she gets."

John thought about it briefly. "I presume I would not have to purchase her?"

Peter nodded.

"Then we are agreed," John said. "Gran's bouts of senility are getting worse, but I suppose we can just let her card wool or something. She can't do much damage there. I'd be happy to keep her here. Unless she became really demented, of course."

"Of course. Oh, I can't tell you what a weight off my mind that is."

"I'm happy to help—but isn't there another problem? Will Dred go without Gran?"

Peter did not meet his brother's gaze. He frowned at the cigar in his hand and abruptly stubbed it out. "These really aren't very good, John. Let's have one of your fresher cigars."

❧

To this day, leaving Gran in Alabama don't rest easy on my soul. Not that I had much of a choice, noways. Seems like I was about the last to know. By the time I found out, everything was settled, and Gran herself done made up her mind.

'Course, I already knowed we was bound for St. Looey. Master talked about it when the gambling be going on for hours, when he get in his cups. Never entered my mind, though, that he meant to leave Gran behind. And he never let on. He left Gran to make it clear to me.

That day she told me was the longest day of my life. It begun with Gran singing "Many Thousand Gone." That be a slow, mournful tune the cotton pickers singed, usually when they lose someone—when someone go running or go over. I hadn't never heared Gran sing it unlessen we be amongst all the slaves, mourning a passing. But here she be humming it whilst she worked, all morning, all afternoon, and into the evening, over and over. And she was clear in her mind that day, even given her addled ways, so I knowed she was singing her heart's burden. And each time she singed "no more peck of corn for me," it put a chill down my spine. Finally I asked her, my voice kinda harsh 'cause of my nerves: "Gran, why you be singing that over and over?"

She answer me sharp, a warning not to pinch her feathers. "I sing it 'cause I like it." Then she softened and smiled, sly-like, "I particularly like the end." She winked at me and singed it through: "No more mistress call for me, many thousand gone." I chuckled with her, but even to my own ears my laugh sounded flat as cold rain falling on stone.

That night I waked hours after midnight to hear her singing again, humming African this time. I recognized the tune, but long since done disremembered the words. Didn't matter. I knowed the tune right well. The notes started up high and simple and innocent, each next one tripping on down a barren, rocky hill to the bottom,

167

where it become a thick, muddy moan. I sat a bit on my mattress, listening, trying to figure what was going on. Gran broke out of her moan, sung the words, sometimes in African, sometimes in English:

I love Shisha Maley, yes I do
I love my Shisha, yes I do
Mmmmmmmmmm, my love
Mmmmmmmmmmmmmmmm

Of a sudden I knowed that she used to sing that to me as a baby. Knowed it for a certainty. I spoke up. "Tell me, Gran. Lay your burden on me. What is it?"

"How much," she said, as if talking to herself, "how much of a soul be memory?" I wasn't sure whether she was in her right head. She looked all about the room, shuffled on over to the window and looked out. "Sunlight sure be weak today."

A full moon were shining, brightest moon you ever seed, but it weren't no sunlight. I got up and moved her from the window to a chair at our little table. Earlier she been balling up some skeins, and keeping her hands busy always was a good thing for Gran, so I slipped a skein over my wrists, and she begun balling it. "What you saying about your soul, Gran?" I asked.

"When I was young," she went on, "I thought my soul was me, Sanjo." Well, I felt better right there, seeing how she knowed the difference betwixt being old and being young. I felt, too, she knowed me. Wasn't that look of a stranger in her eyes. I relaxed a bit as she continued. "I thought my soul be shaped like a barrel, holding the knowing of all them what I loved and all them what loved me, like a oak barrel that holds the wine and also flavors it. But the older I gets, I see that my soul is crowded with memory, chock full of it, like sediment, 'cept now I's so old there's getting to be more sediment than wine."

"What're you saying, Gran?"

"I's just saying my soul is full of memories. It ain't a bad thing, it's just how I be. I see now that my mama knowed who I was right from the start. Knowed I was all about memory. That's why she named me Sanjo, so I would heed the past, so I would hold onto it and keep it dear, and grow big on it. And I done growed big."

I smiled at her. "You's a big woman, Gran, sure 'nough."

"And all I is and all I ever got in this life, I tried to share with you, Dred. And now comes a time I feel I want to give you my very soul. I want you to take and carry it careful—all that memory, all that past—and hold it dear. It'll make you strong like it done me."

She be talking straight to my heart and my heart understood, true enough; but my head wouldn't allow it. My arms felt heavy from holding up the skein, and my thoughts was confused. "What you talking about?" I kinda snapped at her. "You not making sense."

"I got a lot on my mind, child. I's trying to lay it out for you. Maybe I ain't doing it right, but hold with me now."

She paused from winding up the skein, looked back out the window, and said, "Change be coming, Dred. Change be upon us all, and I been thinking about choices. You recollects the satchels tale? Black man didn't choose the hoe nor the flute, but having got them, well, then he got a choice on what to do with them, see? And that makes all the difference. That's how things change."

"Gran, I's too tired for them old stories. My head hurts. Just tell me plain."

"I's too old for changing the world now," she said, ignoring me. "But maybe you will, maybe you'll be the one to jiggle and shake the world, just like my old dream of you."

My heart were beating fast with the knowledge of what she was laying down before me, but my head still wouldn't allow it. She seed it in my face. She picked up the ball and started winding again. "I been thinking on my mother," she said.

I thought maybe she was gone into the past again, then my heart told me she was telling me a story like she used to, telling me what she wanted me to know, and I listened.

She told me again the story of her mother, throwing them babies offen the slave ship. "But that didn't end it," she said. "No end come with the waters closing over my mother's head, 'cause Njeri lives on in me. And many times I done questioned my mother, like she questioned her Bon Dieu: Why? Why, why? For many years that question troubled my heart, and I accused my mother: You choosed death. You choosed to leave me."

Gran fell silent, then hummed again. I waited this time, not asking her to explain, knowing she would get where she was headed.

"You remember, right 'fore we left V'ginia, that great big storm come inland from the sea? Trees ripped up and cabins flattened, birds throwed down from the sky? And the next day, how calm and beautiful the world was? Shredded bits of life everywhere on the ground, but the earth and sun and sky all in a glory? That's how it was with me when, after much trouble in my heart, I finally seed that my mother had her reasons, even if I didn't like them. Whether I liked it or not, I understood that my mother was more than my mother—she be somebody to herself. She have her own soul, and I was just one part of that, not all of it. And what she did finally, she did for her ownself. Had nothing to do with what I wanted. She choosed what she wanted. Had nothing to do with what I understood. She choosed according to her own lights.

"All them years, that's what made me angry. That's what I couldn't reckon: that for the first time she done something for herself instead of for me. That's when I finally seed that she even believed that what she choosed was best for me, but that it didn't matter if I seed that or not. She was that big. Do you understand, Dred?"

I nodded. I didn't understand, not really; I only knowed I didn't want to understand. I didn't want her to continue.

Then she said it plain. "I ain't going with you to St. Looey."

She might just as well spoke African, for all the sense that made. "'Course you is," I said.

She said nothing. Gran never did waste words trying to convince nobody.

So I rassled this strange thing from a new angle. "So we's staying here?"

"Listen to my words, child. I ain't going with you."

"No. That's foolishness. Who say that?"

"I say."

"Like you and me gets to decide our comings and our goings."

Her brow furrowed. "Don't sass me, not at a time like this."

Then it was me living over my childhood. I felt small and she seemed big again, like she ain't done in a long time. Big and powerful and knowing everything. But she had protected me then, and now she was cutting me, slashing me as if with a knife. "You hurting me, Gran," I said. "This be too hard."

"It's hard, but not too hard. You strong enough for this."

"But why? Why would you stay when I have to go?"

I watched the cinamon-brown of her eyes float behind tears held back. "Finally I gets to choose, Dred. I got the right to choose this time, and I know two things: my job raising you up is done. Took you yelling at me to learn it, but I don't begrudge that. That was my mistake and you was right to make me see you's a man—and I's so proud of the man you become. That's one thing. The other is, like Njeri, I find I ain't inclined to do my living at this late age for nobody but me—nor my dying, neither. 'Cause you know that trip would kill me, child. You know it and I know it. And Dred, I ain't ready to die yet."

"Then I'll stay, too."

She shaked her head sorrowful. "You ain't got the choice this time. Just me. Our roads be parting now, Dred. We traveled side by side a long ways, longer'n most black folk ever gets. Now's the time for you to be on your own road."

The moonlight done moved in through the window, washing over her. Her skin glowed and I heared a loud crack like a lightning strike, but I don't know if it were her heart or mine. And as if there was real lightning, sudden-like all the strife betwixt us from the recent years was shut in the shadows. It felt like all that hurt never happened. We was just as we used to be, and I recollected stories she told, food she cooked, the feel of her hand on my cheek. All the times I runned excited to tell her something. Everything in my life, she shared it; I had no memory where she wasn't a part of the doing or the telling to; for all the stories of my life, I had no story that she wasn't the teller or the listener.

Would anything have meaning without Gran to share it with?

And like the cloud that bursts after the lightening, I cried. Like a baby, with waterfalls of tears and snot and bubbling sobs. I was drowning in understanding. I understood Gran's words, I understood the signs, I understood all the strange hints that had been round me for weeks in the way Master and Missus said things and in what the other slaves didn't say. Gran let me cry in her lap. She was still bigger'n me, no matter how much age done shrunk her. I cried so long I soaked her apron. I felt her cool hands on my head and neck, the heat of her body, her smell of cinamon. I remembered them nights when I had the nightmares about the slaves getting whipped, and how she held me till I slept. I cried, aching to be held that way, forever.

She hummed "Shisha Maley" the whole time, waiting for me to join her. After a long while I did, the African words springing up from I don't know where they done been buried, somewhere deep and long past.

She said, "Before you could even talk, you sang the African songs with me. Seemed you was born with them. Before you could even walk you talked African and as you growed, you told the African tales, even before I told them to you. You was born with them.

"Now I see you growed into a fine man. You a fine, good man, and the best griot I ever knowed, here or in Africa. For thirty year you been telling stories, all kinds, and you gonna keep telling them. You gonna tell rich, downriver stories that speak right on about your life and all what you know and done lived through. Your words, child, will carry your truth. And your truth will carry your love. And your love will be the part of my story that lives on—through all the new people you gonna meet. Through the children I believe you is some-day gonna have. You'll set down with them at night when the sun takes its rest, and you'll tell them about your old Gran. I's going with you in that way, Dred. I'll never leave you that way."

I sat up in my chair and wiped my face on my sleeve. Her good old face was smiling at me, shining with the moon, shining with honesty.

"I believe," she went on, "that you and me been together a long,

long, long-long time. I believe we going to be together a longer time
yet to come. We be like the sun and the moon, what shares the sky at
different times. And our time together up till now's been like them
early mornings, sometimes when the moon stays up late to see the
sun come up, and you see them both, moon and sun, up in the sky
together. Now you's entering your day, child, and the moon will go
away. But it will come back, and so it will go, forever and ever."

I looked up through the window where shifting colors were
changing the night into day. Wisps of lavender clouds edged past
the silvery full moon; in the gray-blue early morning sky, off on
the horizon where the sun was getting ready to rise, a solid bank of
purple storm clouds loomed. I couldn't tell if they was advancing or
retreating.

"The moon's still up, but I don't see the sun," I said.

"Yet you know it's there," she answered.

I felt quieted, empty even of pain, newborn almost, with only
the imprint on my soul of Gran's words. We was quiet together. Gran
was making her choice. All that yelling I done at her about not having choices, finally she was getting hers. That was good, but I also
knowed neither of us wanted to think on those long days we would
face alone.

The skein was balled, and sure 'nough, the reddening sun begun
painting the edge of them storm clouds with a red fringe. The whiten-
ing moon, shimmering pale and fading, waited to say a farewell. But
it were a empty sky. There was no birds flying in that sky. I closed
my eyes and felt there never would be.

"Tell me a story, Gran," I said, with my eyes still closed. "One
you never told before."

She smiled and said, "Wait here." I heared the squeak of the
door to the root cellar. I heared some bumps and scrapes and Gran
humming, this time a sunrise holler. She come back out shaking dust
and grit from a piece of faded, old cloth, a sort of blue sack. She
handed it to me. It seemed very familiar, but I didn't know what it
was.

"That cloth come from a skirt your mama used to wear," said
Gran. "Right after she passed, I be faced with the care of a infant as

well as all my other duties in the house, and one evening I was telling my worries to Generous Joe. Maybe you never knowed he was a mustee. Yes, his mama was Powhatan, and he showed me how the Indians would fashion a pouch for the babies, so the mamas could carry them around and still get they work done. That seemed just what I needed, and Joe showed me how to make one outten one of Jenny's old osnaburg skirts. Then you and me went everywhichwhere together, back to back. I used it till you was a knee-child.

"The women from the quarter clucked they tongues when I'd pass with you on my back. None was bodacious enough to tell me to my face, but they all felt you was too old, at nearly four, to be carried like that. Even if you was as small as a two-year-old.

"I didn't care. I didn't expect others to understand my reasons. I didn't expect nobody else to know the pleasure of carrying you like that, knowing that you could see what I couldn't: I could see what was coming, and you could see what was passed.

"So I kept silent, just passed by them on my way up to the scuppernong arbor. I'd feel the wriggling on my back that told me you was waving to them. And I knowed, in spite of theyselves, they would wave back. Nobody ever could close they heart to you, Dred.

"The view from that grape arbor was my favorite. The whole plantation spilled out like water from a waterfall. I could drink in the long, grassy slope, with patches of cows and horses grazing in the sun; the midsummer great garden, boasting all the colors of plenty; the big house, solid and washed in late-afternoon gold; the river, cheerful this particular day, juggling silvery sun spots on its surface, a few geese marching along the bank. I loved being up there, loved the climb, the setting summer sun, the long, low shadows, the burring of the bees.

"This particular day of which I's speaking, I was singing as I plucked the ripe grapes for Master's wine, and you piped up too now and then, not using the words but keeping the tune and the beat. As we sung along, you gathered up your own little harvest, reaching up a pudgy little arm to grab what dangled down from the overhead trellis. You done become expert at picking the unripe ones, the tart ones. You had a liking for that tang. It were a joke at the big house.

Everybody would watch you bite into a lemon as if it was a juicy peach. Instead of puckering, your cheeks would plump in a smile, and Master would laugh: 'Nothing on this farm gets wasted, not even the sour fruit.' You growed with a appetite for sour: lemons, grapefruit, tart cherries, sour cider. Loved it all, right from the first.

"That day I was feeling your reach and grab as you collected them sour grapes. Oh, we was so fine together, you and me up there. I felt like sparkles of sunlight on water. A song from my child years burst up from my toes, a old African fable sung by a griot, one us children used to dance to. From outten my past I heared the gallop of the ashiko drum, and the echo of the talking drums; the beat of the cowbell, the clack of bones. A flute flitted through like a bird.

"I was dancing. Hips and knees circling, feet side-stepping, my gleaning moved along swift. The basket draped from my neck filled, balancing out the weight of you on my back.

"And you was dancing in your pouch, your little rump rubbing my back, your wiggling feet tapping my butt. You seemed no heavier as a four-year-old than on the first day I ever carried you. Of a sudden, though, all that squirming on my back fell out of rhythm. You no longer danced to the song. And before I knowed it you was gone. No slipping or sliding, no push or pull: the weight of you was simply gone from my back. Turning, I seed you, smiling, dancing, skipping, picking up the song where I broke off, though surely you couldn't have knowed them words—another one of them breakthroughs from the past.

"Neither of us knowed it at the time, but that was the last breakthrough. After that day you no longer told the stories and singed the songs of Africa that no one yet learned you, though all the stories you growed to tell carried the flavor of the past, as if you now was carrying the past in a little sack on your own back, a past that gived the rhythm to your own stories and songs.

"And after that day, you would no longer be carried in a pouch on my back. From that day on, you become a forward-facing child."

Chapter fifteen

Road of Souls

When a tree loses its leaves in the autumn, that's natural, and I reckon a tree don't mind it no more'n I mind it when hairs fall offen my head. But when a spring storm rips the new leaves away, snaps off the branches, I wonder: do that hurt the tree? And after the storm, will that tree feel the other deaths that follow, like how no bird will come nesting?

There's many kinds of death, and I've knowed a number of them. I died a little when Joe was killed; when Lucy got sold; when Master Peter done me so low. But it was when Gran got left behind that I felt like a tree where no bird will nest.

By the time we left Alabama, I was near about as stiff and cold as chopped lumber. Seemed everything was happening to somebody else, not me. I don't recollect loading all our peoples and all our provisions on a boat for a short haul up the Tennessee River, but I know that's how we did. Then we set out in covered wagons and trained across to the Mississippi River, then poled up to St. Looey. Whilst crossing Tennessee, I drove a supply wagon, pulled by a four-up. Master and Missus told me to do this and do that—I did what I could and then didn't give a twig for how it come out.

I don't know how long the journey lasted; never seemed like we made no headway. Got ourselves held back by everything: too much wind, too much sand, too much mud, too much water, too little water. Sometimes, crossing a tributary, everything got so wet we had to stop for a day or two so everything could dry. Unload every sack and box, drape out every stitch of cloth, leave it out for the sun to work on it, then pack it all back up again. Each day passed much like the last. Scenery changed, but it was still all the same: up one hill, down the next; into the woods, outten the woods; rocking across the rivers, bouncing along the trails. Hitching, unhitching. Unloading, reloading.

Change come gradual. I lost all knowing of time 'cepting for sun rise and sun rest. We was like a bunch of terrapins, our wagons like shells, moving old and slow and dull. I seed lots of terrapins on that journey, different sizes and colors but they all goes slow. I watched them critters and I got to wondering if it be pain what sets them to move so slow. Don't it look like it hurts? 'Cause if you ever seed one without its shell, the body looks kinda muscled and fit, so you got to wonder: maybe they move so slow 'cause it hurts, the way it be with old folk.

Which is how I felt: old, bone-aching old, carrying a load what was too much to bear. And like the terrapin, I used that heavy shell to protect me, to hide from folks poking at me. I didn't want no doings with nobody. Being with people hurt. Iffen anybody spoken to me, why then it were like my shell been took off, leaving me all tender underneath. Plain old words done that, just being noticed, 'specially iffen it were somebody showing sympathy. Henry and Taylor, they was just boys but I seed the softness in they eyes. Sam, closest to me in age of all the slaves, he tried funning with me but I couldn't hardly smile. Aunt Hannah tried to mother me, but that was worst of all.

I lingered through my wounds most of that journey west and tried not speaking to nobody, till one night I heared Gran. Her voice come with the wind, favoring me, easing me on, "A snake that swallows a tortoise swallows only shell."

※

The reins were slack in Dred's hands. Each time the wagon jostled over a rock, one or both slipped from his fingers to slap the wooden footboard. Peter Blow, exasperated, had already switched Dred from the horse team to the mule team. The mules barely needed a teamster; they just followed placidly behind the wagon in front of them.

Riding on horseback up and down the string of wagons, the master frowned as he regarded the slave. Everything about Dred drooped: the reins, his hands, his shoulders, his face. The wagon cover had been poorly fastened and also sagged. Crossing a ford yesterday, two barrels of molasses had simply floated away because Dred had lashed them so poorly to the side of the wagon.

Peter Blow didn't mind so much that Dred had to be told everything twice before he seemed to hear a command, nor that commands had to be explicitly spelled out, as if to a child. What he did mind was the growing list of complaints from his wife. There was a fine balance between allowing Dred his mourning and tolerating the nagging from Elizabeth, and that balance was close to being upturned, especially since Mary Anne had begun chiming in. He could freeze his daughter with just a look, but when she went and complained to her mother, he wound up hearing it anyway. That night at dinner, when the camp had been settled and the family sat around the makeshift table, Elizabeth started before the soup was served. "Peter, something has to be done. Another sack of flour has become infested, all because Dred did not close it properly. At this rate, we shall arrive in St. Louis half-starved."

Peter checked his first impulse and managed a courteous reply. "Thank you, Elizabeth, for keeping me apprised." The soup was being ladled out, and no one spoke until Ruby completed the task and returned to the campfire. He hoped that the subject would be dropped, but his wife resumed.

"I think something needs to be done."

"About?"

"Dred, of course. You've been avoiding the obvious: Dred needs to be brought in line. It's as if he thinks he can do as he pleases just because we're no longer on a plantation."

To everyone's surprise, Henry spoke up. Both of his parents

regarded him with raised eyebrows, and he flushed as he came to Dred's defense, but he spoke with an authority beyond his thirteen years. "The point isn't that we're no longer on a plantation—it's that Dred is no longer with Gran. He misses her, isn't that plain? I miss her myself."

While his parents fumbled to find the appropriate response to this unexpected intrusion, Mary Anne joined the fray. "Nobody asked you, you little abolitionist. No doubt you would delight in seeing us all debase ourselves by engaging in sentimental communion with the slaves. In fact, why don't we let them all just do as they please? I'm sure you'd be the first to volunteer to take on extra work because one of them had a headache and didn't feel like working."

"Leaving your grandmother behind is not like having a headache, Mary Anne. And just because I don't embrace every opportunity, as you do, to boss other people around, doesn't make me an abolitionist."

"Enough!" Peter Blow hated this type of dissension. He particularly hated the use of the word "abolition" at the dinner table. With restraint, he asked, "Isn't this journey tedious enough without this bickering during meals? I will handle this situation as I see fit. Elizabeth, you can be sure I will not allow us to starve. We will be able to replace the flour in two days, when we reach Memphis."

Turning to his son next and allowing more of the irritation he felt to flow into his voice, he lectured, "Henry, I, too, miss Gran. She raised me as well, you know. She raised me before she raised Dred, in fact, which is why my father presented her to me and your mother as a wedding gift. But he is an adult now, he doesn't need her as he did then. Few in this life get to hold on to their family forever. Wars, disease, careers—many factors conspire to separate families. Why, I myself no longer have parents or grandparents alive. Now I have parted from my only surviving brother. And a slave, particularly, grows up with the knowledge that economic considerations may prevail over family ties. It's a fact of life by which we all must abide."

When he turned to address Mary Anne, he felt cold, as though commanding a private in the ranks. "Mary Anne, your brother is young and his tender feelings regarding Dred do not make him an abolitionist. You might do well yourself to cultivate sympathetic affections, as behooves a young woman."

Frowning, he addressed his whole family. "As for abolitionists, each of you will be well advised not to toss that word around, especially when we get to St. Louis. I cannot over-emphasize how very different society is there. They have free blacks in the city. They do have slave owners and slaves, but they also have free blacks who own businesses and trades. There is much tension over this issue, and I will not countenance my children, especially my daughters, tossing such inflammatory words about so loosely." He eyed his whole family sternly. "Is that understood?"

"Of course, Peter," said Elizabeth. "However, I must reiterate that we have a problem that is not resolved. Dred's indolence requires discipline."

Elizabeth and Mary Anne both jumped in their seats as Peter Blow slammed his spoon onto the table. In anger he repeated his words. "I will handle this situation as I see fit. I will not allow it to result in any adverse circumstance for my family, nor will I allow my family to harp on it any further. This discussion is over."

He rose and left the table. Mary Anne and Henry glared at each other while their mother's eyes pinched in bitterness. She peered out into the night, over the heads of her children, over the campfire, along the line of wagons until her eyes rested upon Dred. Even though the mule team had been unhitched hours ago, the slave remained slumped on the seat of the wagon, his head thrown back to the sky, his hands dangling between his knees. Through the flames he rippled, but she knew he was sitting quite still, simply staring, just as she was staring. Someone, probably Hannah, had placed a bowl of soup next to him on the driver's seat.

Between mistress and slave, the lambent flames of the campfire lulled her, spirited away her ire, and she slouched uncharacteristically in her chair. She found herself thinking of the day she married Peter Blow. Like Dred, she had been orphaned; her grandparents had raised her. She left them for the first time on her wedding day. Crying and cowering in her room, the only comfort in the world had come from her grandmother, who held her and cooed to her and assured her that all women felt that way before their wedding night.

Her reverie was broken as Dred shifted his position. With a sigh, she straightened her spine, smoothed her skirts, and dipped her spoon into the tepid soup.

Pitching one last scowl at Mary Anne, Henry kicked his chair back and walked in the direction his mother had been gazing. On the far side of the campfire he passed his father, who stood stiffly with his back to the flames. Saying not a word, Henry proceeded to the carriage where Dred sat. He climbed onto the wagon seat beside him and copied Dred's posture: elbows on knees now, upward-tilting chin resting on fists. It was peaceful beside Dred, as though he were cloaked in tranquility and Henry could nestle in under the cloak with him. Even the frogs were silent. Dred's cloak muffled everything but the crackling campfire.

Dred's gaze never left the sky, but he was aware that the boy beside him was bristling. He didn't need to know why, though he liked Henry's ginger, the way he took a stand.

Quite unexpectedly, Henry jumped and uttered, "Hgggeeep." He looked somewhat apologetically over at Dred, who seemed to take no notice. The boy's second hiccup elicited a response—the resonant croak of a bullfrog. Three more times, Henry exchanged hiccups for croaks until Dred said, "I sure hope that mating call works as good on St. Looey gals as it do on Tennessee bullfrogs." Their chuckles started soft and airy—"I'm trying to learn Taylor, so's he can find a girlfriend, too"—and worked up to rippling giggles and belly laughs—"No, you and your brother be too young to go hopping after no frog-legged gals, too young yet to appreciates them"—as they stretched and pulled the joke between them like taffy.

Peter Blow, standing with his back to the fire, felt the wind rise and shift the flames uncomfortably near. He took a step away from the fire but remained facing Dred and Henry together on the wagon. He heard their laughter and noticed how their mirth united them. They leaned into each other. The sing-song of a story being told floated across the night breeze, and he smiled to hear Dred's voice. The slave had barely opened his mouth the whole journey.

He suddenly recalled Dred and Peter Jr. talking excitedly that day at the fairground, nearly ten years ago now. Peter Blow had similarly stood apart on that day, and vividly he recalled the flush of deep embarrassment he had felt for Dred as the circus people ridiculed that shocking orange cravat. He never should have allowed Dred to wear it, especially since he had given Dred charge of his sons.

My sons, he thought with a pang. My defiant and loyal sons— defiant toward me and loyal toward Dred. This time, his flush of embarrassment was for himself.

The soughing wind had made for a restless night. Everyone moved sluggishly after waking, but as they prepared the train for the journey, the wind whittled an edge to everything and urged them along. The campers roused extra energy to keep breakfast fires alight and hats on heads. A clammy breeze helped Mary Anne dress quickly, and for once she didn't keep others waiting. Stronger gusts helped Peter Jr. find his lost pocket watch—it banged against the wheel rim where it had fallen and dangled by its chain. Elizabeth Blow suppressed a satisfied grin watching the ace of spades and a four of diamonds skitter across the campsite and into the brush; there would be no more card games from that deck. The wind-shot grit that made everyone shield their eyes helped scour encrusted porridge from the dishes.

All moved briskly, ready for a day's hard travel. The horses, invigorated, stepped lively into their harnesses. As Dred gathered the reins in his hands, even the mules jigged a little dance. He thought he heard a tune on the wind, and for the first time on the whole, long trip, he hummed. He mounted the wagon and waited for the Master's call: "Let's roll."

⁂

We left our wagons in Memphis, loaded up the flatboats, and poled the rest of the way up to St. Looey, keeping to the muddy waters by the shoreline, outten the strong currents of the middle. Poling upriver on the Mississipp' is slow, hard work, but I learned to like the music of it. The water smacked clear and sad against the boat. The pole swished up outten the water then rasped back down through callused fingers. The boat creaked. Smack-swish-rasp-creak, smack-swish-rasp-creak.

When I rested, oftentimes Henry and Taylor would come by, and with the polers' rhythm behind me, I begun to spin the old African tales. I became a griot again, standing and moving and telling them the way that Gran handed them down to me. We traveled many days like that and finally was just a half-day away from St. Looey when Henry said to me, "Dred, you should write Gran a letter."

What a notion that were! As strange to me as the African way of telling stories was to them boys. Yet the more I thought on it, the more I liked it. White folk with they pencils and papers—seems like some good could come outten that white satchel after all.

St. Louis, Missouri
September 12, 1830

My Dear Gran,

Henry's helping me get this letter to you, doing this writing for me. If my words come strange, it's 'cause I's talking to Henry when I's really thinking of you. Anyways, he says he'll get his cousin, Stuart, to read my words to you in Alabama. I expect if you cook Stuart some of your johnnycakes, he'll do the same for you and you can tell me in a letter how you be. I worry about you and miss you sorely, so it would ease my heart to hear from you.

I got so much to tell you, Gran. All about the trip out west and what city life is like. I got so much to say that Taylor is helping out too, standing by to keep Henry's quill whittled sharp. I wish you could see these boys, Gran. They's become little frontier men.

We's all in St. Looey finally, and it were a long time coming. St. Looey sure 'nough is a interesting place: all hustle, bustle, and noise. Always something going on. Nobody here's too happy, though. Missus Blow, Mary Anne, and little William all taken sick along the way and still ain't up to snuff—Missus say the other

*day, "I wish Gran was here to make me one of her curative teas."
Henry and Taylor takes to city life best.*

*There ain't much I can tell you about the traveling, 'cept it
were long and lonely. It puts a terrible distress behind my words to
tell you this, but nothing felt right without you being a part of it.
From the first as we set out from Alabama, everything was changed.
Everything felt different. My own me felt different. My heart done
told me that you, Gran, was the best part of everything I knowed,
and the west sure is a far piece from where you is at.*

*I don't say this to trouble you. I say it to come close again.
You's all that matters to me, and I left you far behind. Maybe
you was right—that it were too much for you, but my heart don't
believe you was right. My heart still feels troubled by the distance
betwixt us. And I's so far west now that I don't know how things
can ever be made right. I's a slave, and I can't change it to right.
I live with regret for leaving you. I live knowing I ain't never
gonna see you again.*

*That knowing were near impossible to live with on the
journey. I tried going along half dead, but still I dreamed about
you. The dreams was good, but the waking was terrible. I longed
for sleep and dreams, slept all I could, and iffen somebody woked
me whilst I was dreaming of you, Gran, it about killed me.*

*Then I tried facing it, tried recollecting a story what might
explain it to me, to show me the meaning. All them stories you
told where we looked for meaning—I thought certain there must
be one to explain what I be feeling. But I couldn't come up with
one. That's when I realized what be different for me: all the
meaning was gone—gone as all them ancestors and gone as that
homeland I never set foot on. There was no meaning in what was
around me. That's the lowest about being a slave: you get emp-
tied out of meaning and purpose, then filled up with other stuff,
somebody else's other stuff, and all of it got equal weight, equal
value—and that is, no value. Nothing means anything, not even
your lonesome self.*

*Is that how you felt, Gran, on that slave ship after your
mama and the twins went overboard? I think I understand better*

now how you felt, being brung to this strange land and strange language amongst strange people. Uprooted from your home and the people what loved you, the people you knowed and the ancestors what guided your way. That's what it were like for me, Gran, setting out without you: a lonesome, empty journey, full of hungry want.

Gran, out here they got Indians what believe they souls after death go westward to Ke-wa-kun-on, the home after death. To get there, they got to travel west on Che-ba-kun-ah, the road of souls. That's what that journey felt like to me: it felt like the westward road of souls. And I feared that my life would always be just one weary, westward journey along the road of dead souls, searching for home.

I was hauled along. I felt done. I felt small. I felt of no consequence to nobody nowhere. A dead soul. That's how I moved west, Gran, so I can't tell you much about what I seed. I didn't pay it much mind. Mostly I liked the campfires at night. I looked into the flames and recollected the old stories you used to tell me. After awhile, I stopped looking for meaning and just felt the old, familiar pleasure of them tales, and then all day long they kept me company in my head, and I wasn't so lonesome. By'n by it come to be that whenever the wind come at our backs, I thought for certain I heared your voice, telling the tales—the "uh-uh" of your breath as you begun, your whoops and whistles, squeaks and squeals as you moved the story along. I begun to feel you with me as we rolled west.

Remember how Njeri seed Nyota in the moonlight? Well, for me it were the wind that brought you to me, so I had you with me day and night. For me it were hearing you, not seeing you. Well, no: actually, I had to swallow my grin watching how you played havoc with the bonnets and blowed Master's cards into the fire, and I especially 'preciated it when you blowed away them clouds of mosquitoes on the river what clung to us like a lady's veil.

One of the last things you told me, Gran, you said, "Don't give up on our kin. Hold on to believing we'll all be together some day. It's all about that bond, Dred. To be tied and bound to them, *whether it's here or there, now or later. That's how I love you, Dred. You's with me. Always. I's with you. Always."*

I come to the knowing of that truth, Gran, enduring that long journey, learning it from your voice on the wind. I recollect one day in particular, bright and crisp and windy. The sky was clear, not a bird nor a cloud up there 'cept for one patchy ribbon of pure white, snaking betwixt the glare of the sun and the soft, calm frosting of a moon that stayed in the sky the whole day, sharing the sky with the sun just as you said before I left. Later, when the sun set, that thin ribbon of cloud turned pink and then red. I watched it not blinking, till the whole sky melted to purple, with the silver moon shining at its core. I knowed you was up there, with Nyota, Njeri, and them baby twins. And that ribbon of clouds was what held me to you all. That's when I become able to feel again. Able to laugh. Able to look on tomorrow without feeling the life grind outten me. Able to tell a story, glad to have Henry and Taylor there to tell them to.

After that we moseyed along, floated along, farther and farther from you, farther and farther from Africa. But I begun to feel I was carrying you and all our kin with me, 'cause now I was carrying the tales. You and our kin come to life in them tales, and I wasn't so lorn. And I think that must be what you meant me to understand when you told me you was giving me your soul, full up on memory, to help me on my journey.

Did I ever say I was sorry, Gran? I don't believe I did. But I's sorry for all the hurt I gived you. Sorry, and so grateful that I received your good grace on that evening. It come down to me on the wind, filling up my soul. And I understood deep in my soul what you was trying to make me see about staying connected.

Then I knowed something else, too. I knowed you was right that I be strong enough. That I got my own life to lead. That now be the time for me to travel my own road. It were a lesson worth the learning.

It only be a thought in my head right now—I don't quite know how to go about living my own life. Without you, separate from you. I know it's gonna take a heap of living and building.

But I don't feel so small, now that I feel how I got you and our kin with me. I don't know what I'll do here in St. Looey or what will come of me, but I believe I can be the man you seed me to be. I believe I can build a life you would be proud of. I recollect all the good you seed in me, and that's how I's trying to be.

Finally I got the feeling that maybe tomorrow be something worth moving toward. And I got a few other hopes, too. I hope you's comfortable and not ailing. I hope Mr. John kept his promise to you. I hope you maybe find your way some day down to Nyota, that town where maybe you can find some of our kin, tribespeople what will know the proper way to bury you and rest your soul peaceful. Maybe they even know the way back across the ocean.

And I hope you go softly home, and then come on and get me and take me with you, like Nyota took Njeri. I want to go home with you, Gran, to be together some day with you and Nyota and Njeri and the twins. My heart is with you. You are my heart.

Your loving grandson,
Dred

Chapter sixteen

Building

W here Master Peter got it in his head he was fit to run a
boarding house, I don't know. He never knowed nothing about it
'fore we arrived in St. Looey. I think Master had him a deal whereby
he didn't have to pay nothing outright so long's he split his profits.
Something like that, 'cause he surely had no cash for buying nothing,
and there was a heap of repair work. Everything was done on credit,
and it made the Missus moan and shake her head.

   We all got busy right away, settling in and making that boarding house fit for guests, but it be Mr. Nathan Lord, I reckon, what
really run the show. Master Peter hired him 'fore we even got there,
as Mr. Lord was a old hand in the business. A St. Looey native, which
is mighty unusual, seeing as the town itself ain't all that old. That's
one of the strange things about this western frontier: here they call
things old—like a house that's been standing for ten year—that back
in V'ginia we'd call new or young. Being new and all is probably why
frontier folk says so little, too. Back in V'ginia, a man can speak for
five minutes and all he be saying is, "How d'ya do." Here in St. Looey,
folk speaks the least possible, and I learned it were a insult to ask a
man his name 'fore he offered to give it to you.

Anyways, Mr. Lord was a nice man, smart man. Hush-mouthed, generally, but iffen he did part his lips, he said something useful. He told me the most important thing about frontier life I ever heared. He said, "Dred, choose your friends carefully, then hold them close and treat them dear. Fortunes change swiftly out here, and a man needs his friends." Ain't I seed the truth of that?

Mr. Lord said his papa was a trapper, back when St. Looey was just a trading post. And his papa married a Fox woman. You see a lot more of that kind of thing on the frontier. 'Course, lots of white folk still looks at the red man as no better'n the black man, but then again there's them what gets along like neighbors. Me, I's mighty used to the Indians now, but back in 18'n30, a Indian passing in the street with his head feathers and all, well a sight like that could stop me dead in my tracks. Sure, there was Indians in V'ginia and Alabama, too, but they didn't mix all in the towns the way they done in St. Looey. That's the thing about it: in St. Looey, everybody be elbow to elbow with everybody else. A lady in fine lace at the general store could brush shoulders up against the bare arm of a Indian wearing no more'n a vest pulled over his bare chest.

Anyways, after about that first month, we was most settled in, and we begun taking in boarders. Wasn't hard to come by: St. Looey be teeming with trappers and traders, miners and mountain men, immigrants and Indians, mostly all on they way coming through or going out, needing lodgings for a short spell. Master called the place the Jefferson Hotel, and we was soon full up. He done hisself proud, for a turn.

Naturally we had to cook and clean for all them peoples, so most every day me or Sam got sent to the shops for this'n that. Another thing about St. Looey, at least when we first got there, it were easier then for a black man to move around without too much trouble. There were nothing like them paddyrollers in Alabama. I carried a paper all the time, just in case a sheriff or deputy stopped me, but it were rare any other white man challenged my passing.

'Course, that didn't last long. It all changed after my first year there, and it had to do with my old friend, Nat Turner. Everybody felt things change after his uprising, but nobody felt it more'n the black folk. All blacks, no matter slave nor free, begun to be looked at like murderers. Black churches was clamped down, blacks couldn't linger in groups in the town, and the paddyrollers come full force to check on all blacks going to and fro. I even heared that any new free blacks had to get a paper from the courts allowing them to settle in St. Looey.

Howsomever, in them early days I could walk down to the shops without a care 'cept for dodging horses, carriages, vendors' carts, and droves of them long-horned steer being herded through the streets. Why, I even dodged a duel or two. I learned right quick that iffen two white men started hollering one t'other, it's smart to duck behind a corner. Well, I guess I's puffing that up. Them duels was mostly held out on Bloody Island. But it is the truth that every-body white be carrying firearms, and them white men, 'specially the lawyers and politicians, was mighty quick to take a insult.

There was always something going on downtown. I recollect a day I was sent to tote some sacks of cornmeal. I stopped to see why a crowd done gathered, and I joined a large group of folk watching a warehouse get built. Like I say, you see all different types of people together; they ain't separated like in the country. In that crowd was fancy white folk, feathered Indians, slaves dressed in coveralls, shop-keepers in aprons, trappers looking like some kind of skinny bear, and unshaved, gritty deckhands. Then you had the construction workers, what could be white, black, or red, though a white man always be in charge. On this here day, they had one end of the frame already braced up, and men was hoisting the other end up offen the ground. Then another bunch was lifting a crossbeam, with the whole crowd watching to see if they would match all the ends together. It were a thrill, watching the sheer might of them laborers' muscles pulling away, following a plan that some mighty smart man done figured out, a system of ropes and pulleys and braces, for making all them pieces come together. A cheer went up when it worked, and everybody felt they had a part in it.

We all stayed like that, folks talking to the stranger next to them like they was neighbors, till a man rode up on a horse, fast, as like to run down a small bunch of Negroes what was standing together by a puddle. The rider brought the horse up short, it reared and stomped its hooves hard into the mud, like it just had too much gallop yet to stop still. The slaves stood looking up at the rider, wiping mud from they faces, when the rider whisked one of the slaves on the top of his head with the reins, and then they all looked down.

"Get back to work, you lazy niggers. I'm not paying you to stand here loafing. I've got an empty warehouse and a full hold to unload. Get back to work or I'll have you all flogged." He struck another one across the shoulders, and a third slave begun slinking back, come up against the puddle, and hopped across it. I guess that white man thought the man was trying to run, 'cause he plowed his horse through them slaves and grabbed the one that hopped. Leaned down outten his saddle and grabbed that man by his jacket. Then he kicked his heels into the horse, and he dragged that man back through the puddle and along into the crowd. Well, the man couldn't get his feet. He was being drug, and the mud be flying and the crowd be scattering.

A few of the women, white, turned away, clutching each other's hands, and one done got sprayed with mud. They looked to be a family out shopping, with no man to accompany them. A fellow in a light gray vest and tall hat, a Southern-sounding man, scolded the rider. "You sir, conduct your affairs elsewhere. There are ladies present."

The rider let go the slave, and they all run together toward the docks. That white man pulled his horse round, saying directly to the Southerner, "Mind your own business."

"It is my business when a lady needs assistance, and you, sir, are a cause of distress to these good women." He was backed up now by three more well-dressed gentlemen, and they all shooed that rider away, insults being traded back and forth, but no guns drawed.

It done breaked the air of festivity, though. We was no more a group of people all together watching a building go up, we was all separate again. I turned to the Negro beside me. "We best be on about our ways 'fore some white man start giving us trouble, shooing us back to our masters."

Well, this fella stiffens his backbone and says, "I's a free Negro. I don't got to answer to nobody 'cepting myself." He was kinda puffed up in his talk, kinda setting me in my place. But he didn't look no better'n me. Fact is, you can't tell a free Negro from a slave just by the way they's dressed. You see a black man with a silk hat and gloves, and you can spank down money that he's free. But that's the exception. Most don't dress much different'n a slave.

He put his back to me and walked off, when another black man stepped alongside me, hands on his hips, saying about the free Negro, "Thinks he's something better'n the rest of us."

I explained, "He a free Negro."

"So'm I, brother. That don't mean I got to put on airs."

Well, I liked his tone. I answered the man straight. "I ain't never met no free Negro. What is it you do? How do you live?"

He kinda eyed me up and down. "I expect I lives no different'n you," he said, "'cept I keeps all my earnings to myself. As good as I wants to live, that's how hard I works."

I was right curious. "What kinda work you do?"

"All kinds, like you, probably: unloads the ships, cleans offices, drives a dray."

"So you work for the white man too?"

"Yes I do."

"Must feel good, though, not to be beholden. Knowing you's free to just walk away."

He looked out over the ships and across the water, looking far off. Then he snatched his eyes back and looked me right in the eye and said, "I can tell you, brother: I got my freedom papers, but it's a mighty skinny freedom. Ain't none of us truly free."

That man done spoke straight to my heart. His words jumped round in my breast the rest of the day and all the night. There was something new in what he said. Onliest free Negroes I ever heared tell of was supposedly back in the Great Dismal: the maroons, what had a trade in shingles cut from swamp Cyprus. It were even rumored they helped runaways get north, 'cause the white folk'd get lost in the twisty-turny trails of the swampland. But until St. Looey, I never met a free Negro. And the first one I meet, he up and says being free ain't a whole lot different'n being a slave. I believed that, sure 'nough. Made all kinds of sense.

I was still thinking on what that man said the very next day when I got Gran's letter. I recollect it well, 'cause this man's words and Gran's matched up, like the crossbeam and the frame. See, slavery was always opposite to freedom. That's how it always was put up before me and all black folk. But then I got to thinking how the opposite of being a slave don't rest entirely on freedom. It rest inside the man. And that's just about what Gran was telling me.

I was hauling a load of sheets out to Ruby for washing when Mr. Lord brung me a sealed envelope. Soon's I opened it up, there be my old letter, tucked inside a new sheet, what I expected was Gran's letter. Seems my letter traveled all the way to Alabama and come back to me in St. Looey, like a boomerang. That scared me, 'cause I feared maybe she never got it. Maybe something happened to her. My hand shaked when I gived it back to Mr. Lord and asked him to read it to me.

I still carry her letter, a raggedy old piece of paper carried next to my heart. I can't read it, but her words is stamped in my head, and I still like to feel the paper. Sometimes I take it out, hold it close to my nose, and think I can still find a trace of cinnamon there.

Florence, Alabama
January 1, 1831

My Beloved Dred,

Happy birthday, child. I sure did miss spending this special day with you, for the first time in thirty-one year. Know that I was holding you dear in my heart, and I baked you a cake anyways. Me and the rest of the old Virginia hands ate it and wished you great happiness.

I listened with a full heart whilst Stuart read your words. I done asked him to read it over so many times I know it now by heart, like a song. That's why I asked him to send it back to you, 'cause they's such good words and you need that song in your heart as much as me. Sing that song every day, Dred, to your ownself and anybody that'll listen. It's the song of you fully becoming your own man, of you growing into the name I gived you as you growed out of childhood: Nyasanu, man among men.

I know not everything feels right. You writ that your own-self don't feel right. That's 'cause you been through so much, you still catching up with what it all means. But I can see better'n you 'cause I ain't moving so fast. I can see you, clear as iffen you was here. I see you standing inside your own skin now, taking responsibility and thinking things through.

I ain't talking about slavery, you know that. I's talking outside of slavery. Slavery can break a man, but iffen it don't—and I believe now it ain't never gonna break you, Dred—then a man become free inside hisself. He build inside hisself something strong that nothing on this earth can break nor silence—his own story.

As our kin would say: "The sparrow in the hawk's claw cries out not to get free, but to tell others his story."

Our kin knowed that telling your own story is a freedom. It's a freedom what ain't nothing the Master gives you. It ain't a slip of paper nor words writ down in a book. It got nothing to do with the white man's satchel. The kind of freedom I's talking about is in you, Dred. In the way you think. In your way of choosing words. Choosing when to love and when to hate. Choosing the knowing of what's right and not be afraid of calling a wrong a wrong. Living free from doubt and free from shame. Free to know your own mind, free to tell your own story.

Don't fret that you ain't fully catched up yet with yourself. You's headed in the right direction. You'll get there. And when you do, you'll find your words, you'll sing them out—and I'll be singing them, too, here in Alabama and also when I go over. I'll be singing your song till you come home and we can be together again.

So don't worry on me. I's fine. Life ain't hard here at all and I's just waiting to be called home. My days is peaceful. I's peaceful in the knowing that my grandson is Nyasanu, man among men. I's so proud of you.

Your ever-loving Gran.

Chapter seventeen

Dawn's Early Light

The free and the brave," ain't that what the song say? Was round about the time Congress declared that song a anthem that I got Gran's letter and was juggling all these thoughts of freedom—creating my own song, as Gran writ in her letter. My song weren't no anthem, though. I could hum a bit of the tune but I didn't know all the words yet. I sung some bad rhyme 'fore learning how freedom and bravery set together pretty, but they don't set together easy.

The cost of freedom is bravery, and for many folk the price be too high. I don't believe most folk come by it natural. They don't inherit it. Not even Gran, whose gran was a warrior woman. Gran had to build up bravery from a heap of small, bold acts.

That's a lesson never too late for the learning. I learned it in 18'n32, the year of the first bad cholera, when Master Peter died. That year we had such a over-long season of heat, by autumn folk was dropping like the sycamore leaves. All through October you couldn't sleep through the night for the sound of the sawing and hammering of coffins.

Nasty sickness, cholera, though in the early summer when Master took sick, nobody was calling it that yet; the city done seed but a few cases yet. I catched it, too, but was lucky and come through it. I got it just as Master passed on, in June. That were a sad time round the house, 'cause the children were all still feeling sad on the Missus passing, just months before. She never did get strong again after our journey from Alabama. Dropsy taken her.

Death brung the whole Blow family low, but it didn't pull me down so low. Mostly I felt sad that a small boy named Dred wasted so many years yearning after something that never was gonna be, nor ever was. Yes, Master Peter was fond of me—it's just possible I got more heart from that man than his own children done. And I surely done gived him my heart. I can still recall feeling so small beside him, thrilled to feel his power reaching down to cover me. But I also got the knowing of coming to my man, of stepping outside of his power, of looking at him with full-open eyes.

Anyways, Master's passing sure was a hardship on his children. He left a lot of debts. Mary Anne and Peter Jr. taken charge and got theyselves in a big blowout over me. Seems Master went and writ in his will that I should get that fancy riding crop he once prom- ised me. Don't that beat all? Sure 'nough, he writ it down, and Mary Anne was wanting to sell it for cash to pay back on debts, and Peter Jr. was bound and determined to do according to his father's wishes. I was in my sickbed in the basement, right below them. Heared the whole argument. Peter was saying how Master done trained me to be a jockey. How Master and me had a special bond. Well, I hauled myself outten that bed, stood tall as them cramps would let me, and I went up there. Didn't wait to knock, just went in and told them, "Hush your mouths." Peter looked surprised and Mary Anne didn't know whether to listen or to slap me. How I loved throwing that gal off balance! Fore she made up her mind, I got right to my point. "I'ma save you both a lot of trouble if you can be quiet long enough to hear what I's got to say," I told them. "I don't want that crop. Your papa opened up my face with that crop and broke off my front tooth. I don't accept it."

That was it, my first act of freedom. And where the bravery come in weren't in refusing my bequest, it were in speaking right on to the white faces what owned me.

Mary Anne chirped up quick, "Fine," but Peter wanted me to think on it twice.

"You don't have to keep it. You could sell it or do anything else you want with it."

I shaked my head. "I's richer by not owning it," I told him. Then I left. And I imagine they did sell it, 'cause I never seed it nor heared about it again. But I had my say about it, and sure 'nough if there ain't freedom in speaking right on about a wrong.

My first act of freedom didn't ring no bells; nobody took note. In me, though, it struck a deep chord. I liked how it felt, how it sounded, how it fit me. I knowed right then the truth and power of Gran writing about the freedom to know my own mind, the freedom from doubt and shame. And I do believe iffen Gran was around, she would've said, "Sing it out, child. Don't let them fill you up with no thin, blonde ditty. You got your own song, with a African rhythm. You got yourself a anthem."

⁂

Dred, lying in his sickbed, heard the creak of the rickety basement risers but no footfall. He knew it was one or both of the boys. They were the only ones to tread so softly. Henry led, and creeping behind him came Taylor, carrying a small betty-lamp. It shed little light, and Dred felt rather than saw the sadness upon them.

Normally Dred shared a bedroom in the attic of the boarding house with Sam, but since he had taken sick he was isolated in a makeshift basement sickroom. Hannah and Ruby had been tending him during his illness, and he was finally recuperating from what most referred to as "ship fever." Despite rumors of mounting cases throughout the city, few were bold enough to call it by the name all feared: cholera.

He let them get comfortable, each boy settling on either side of his mattress. He propped himself up and asked, "You boys missing your papa?"

Henry cast his eyes to the floor. "I don't know. It's kinda sad everywhere."

"I'm missing you, Dred," said Taylor.

199

Dred smiled and took each boy's hand in his own. "I been missing you, too, though it's right Peter kept you away—no sense having everybody get sick. Since the doc's last visit, though, seems it's all right now for me to have company."

"How're you feeling?"

"I's better. Weak, but over the worst of it." Dred watched the boys exchange glances. Henry was fifteen, a fleshy youth who didn't yet know how to handle his bulk. His boyhood fat was beginning to turn to muscle, though, and it occurred to Dred that Henry would cut an imposing figure as an adult. Taylor, twelve, was scrawny and tended to be overly cautious, although when he knew his mind he could be quite resolute. Dred guessed he would become the sort of man whose quiet reasoning would be heard in a room full of shouting voices.

"You boys ain't my little squirrels no more—you's getting to be almost men." They didn't meet his eyes, and Dred didn't know why. "Still, losing a papa can make you feel just a boy, a lorn, lonesome boy. That's all right. That's how it be even for your older brother."

"It ain't papa. It's you, Dred," Henry blurted.

Henry's words cored through to a cold, hollow spot where Dred felt his own fears churning. His defiance before Mary Anne and Peter remained unpunished, and he still expected retribution. It also seemed inevitable that the Master's death would mean change.

"What you heared?"

"Papa left a lot a debts, you know that as well as anybody, I guess," Henry answered, tentatively.

Taylor spoke up, delivering the bad news. "Mary Anne and Peter have been talking about what's to become of everything, and it looks like they're gonna sell all the slaves."

"They ain't gonna auction us, is they?"

"No, they wouldn't do that," said Henry. "I don't think."

"Anyway," chimed in Taylor, "not to you. Papa already arranged for your sale right before he died."

This alarmed Dred even more. "Who to?"

"Dr. Emerson, the one that took care of mother last year and papa just now."

"I know him. He been good enough to come down here, too. He be the one calling this thing cholera. Gived me a liniment to ease my cramping."

"That's not so bad, then, is it," said Taylor, not convincing even himself. "He seems like a pretty nice man."

Everyone looked glum. Dred still had the hollow feeling of apprehension. He slumped back down on the mattress and couldn't seem to formulate a clear thought. Finally he asked, "What about this place? They gonna keep the boarding house?"

"Nope. Peter doesn't want to give up his pharmacy, so there won't be anybody to manage this place."

"Where you all going to live, then?"

"With Peter, over his shop. They haven't told us yet, but we heard them talking, and it looks like they'll take us out of school, too, so we can help Peter with the business. Charlotte and her new husband will take in William, though, and let him finish his elementary grades. Beth and Patsy will come with us to Peter's, at least until Patsy's wedding next spring."

"What about Mary Anne?"

Henry snorted. "We ought to leave her to fend for herself."

"She'll go to Charlotte's, too," explained Taylor, "but later might move to Patsy's."

Dred, gripped by a viselike cramp, rubbed his stomach. His face was rigid with pain. Taylor jumped up and reached for a pitcher of water. "What can I get you Dred?"

"Don't bother. It ain't that bad. It were worser yesterday. Today it's tolerable. That's the only cramp I had all night, and what I ate and drunk ain't been passing right through me. I been keeping it down. Looks like this nasty sickness ain't gonna carry me away."

"You look kinda caved-in," Taylor said, handing Dred a tin cup of water.

"I ain't well, but I's mending. Gives a man a powerful thirst, though." Dred drank deeply and then relaxed again on the thin mattress. He had grown accustomed to the weak light from the betty-lamp and now could clearly see the distress on the boys' faces. He propped his back against the wall and put an arm around each boy, drawing them to his chest. Henry resisted a bit, and Dred said, "C'mon now, you ain't too big for a little hug." Both boys relaxed comfortably against the slave, and they stayed that way for some minutes. Dred spoke again. "Know what the other stevedores down at the docks calls you two squirrels? 'Dred's boys.' That's how you be called. They know I keep my eye out over you boys."

"Are we going to still be able to see you Dred?" Taylor asked softly. "You think Dr. Emerson will let you still work down at the docks?"

"Nobody can say, son. Nobody but the doc hisself. I think it ain't likely, though." Neither boy raised his head from where it lay on Dred's chest. Dred felt heat emanating from Henry, but Taylor was sniffling. He squeezed the boys' shoulders. "I know it's hard. We all be feeling it hard."

"We can find out wherever you'll be," said Henry, "and we can come visit you sometimes."

"When you reckon all this gonna come about?" Dred asked.

"We're not sure. We heard Peter saying Dr. Emerson himself said you were out of the woods. Sounded like maybe he might come by tomorrow to get you."

"Tomorrow!" Dred sat up straight. The boys did too, looking at him with alarm. Dred's heart, which had been sluggish and weak for several days, now raced. "Tomorrow's too soon, boys."

"That's why we came down tonight."

"We came as soon as we knew ourselves."

Dred threw his legs over the side of the cot and gripped the edge of the mattress. His thoughts were running clear and cold now. He swayed as he stood but kept his balance. The boys stood, too. He placed a hand on each of their shoulders for support. To himself, he said, "I can make it." Dred shuffled a dozen paces toward the stairs, then shuffled back to the bed and eased himself down. "I can make it," he repeated.

"What do you mean, Dred?"

"Boys, I'ma ask something of you that's harder still than what you be facing right now. I'ma ask each of you to think for your ownself, not together, in answering me."

They looked at him expectantly. He patted the mattress beside him, and they joined him again. Then he continued, "Boys, I been thinking on freedom, and I think now is maybe my time. Will you help me get over to Alton?"

"You're gonna run?" Henry sounded admiring and disbelieving.

Taylor shivered. "What's in Alton?"

"I don't rightly know. I only know that they got a lot of abolitionists there. That some slaves made they way across the river to Alton and didn't never get brung back, so I figure they finds a way on through to freedom."

"Sounds awfully risky," Taylor said. "I think you need a better plan than that."

"Ain't got time for no better plan. You say so yourself."

"But what would happen if they caught you?" Henry asked.

"I reckon it'd be rough for a spell. They'd bring me back. I'd be punished. Then Emerson would sell me, most likely. After that, no telling where I could wind up."

Taylor's jaw was set. "I don't think you should do it, Dred," he said. "Not now, when you're so sick. Maybe some other time."

Henry had been thinking. He brought up another concern. "If you ran, Dred, Dr. Emerson would still come after us for his money." Dred nodded, and Henry continued, "Well, Peter doesn't have enough as it is. They could throw him in jail or something."

Henry stood, facing Dred with his shoulders thrown back. Dred raised a hand, palm outward, just as firmly, saying, "Boys, think on this: my whole life I done slaved for your family, long and true and hard. You know that as a fact, and now I's asking you to really think on what that means. I's a man, and I been your slave for all my thirty-two year. If that ain't being in jail, I don't know what is."

"Don't you care what happens to Peter? To us?" Henry challenged.

"You know I do. And I care for you two boys more'n all the rest combined." The brothers read the truth of this in Dred's face. His eyes glistened in the dim light. "I'd surely like to be the one to help you through all the change what's coming up," Dred continued, "but iffen I run or iffen I go to the doc, either way I won't be near. You's gonna have to be the help to each other." Dred now read their faces, seeing in the look they exchanged that they followed his reasoning.

"As for Peter," Dred concluded, "I don't reckon how he would stay in jail. Charlotte's married that fine lawyer, and Patsy's fella's got money, too. They'd get him out, sure 'nough. Yes, it could be rough for a spell, but they would work it out. Folks like you Blows don't get kicked into the gutter. When you stumbles, somebody gives you a hand up. There'll be some bruising, but you'll all get through it, mark my words. Not me, though. It ain't like that for me nor any other slave. Now comes my chance to break out, and I think I should at least try."

Taylor looked firmly at his brother. "Henry, Dred's right. You know he is. And I think we should help him."

Dred, certain now that Henry would help him, was not concerned when Henry remained quiet and began to pace. When Taylor began to speak again, Dred halted him with a hand on his shoulder, saying, "Let Henry do his own thinking. I want each of you boys to make up your own mind. You'd be taking on a big risk, certain to bring down trouble on your heads—trouble you's gonna have to bear alone on your own shoulders."

Finally Henry said, "It'll have to be right away, tomorrow morning, if we do it at all. We'll have to be truant."

Taylor, smiling, shrugged. "They're gonna take us out of school anyway."

"All right," said Henry solemnly. "We'll do it."

"Then there's just one more thing," said Dred. "I want Sam in on our plans. He's the only other one what's ever talked of running, and he can help me along if I feel too weak."

Taylor merely nodded, but Henry sighed. "That'll make it even tougher on Peter, but I guess you're right—we can survive it."

"What do you need us to do?" asked Taylor.

Dred explained how the slaves could best ferry over to Alton if they were in the company of the boys, clearly seen to be their slaves. When challenged for the necessary paperwork to cross, the boys would have to lie and say they didn't know they needed additional papers. They could say they were on an errand for their brother to pick up a druggist's scale, a large and heavy one requiring Dred and Sam to transport it. Once in Alton, the slaves could hide while the boys made enquiries. Dred had heard of a man named Lovejoy who printed an abolitionist paper there. Lovejoy might be able to tell them how to proceed. Whatever happened, Dred promised that he would send the boys back to St. Louis on the evening ferry. Ultimately, he and Sam would strike out on their own, hoping for luck.

Henry looked excited; the adventure began to appeal to him. But Taylor remained apprehensive regarding Dred's strength. "Are you well enough to do this, Dred?"

"I'ma have to be. Ain't no time for getting any better. 'Sides, Sam'll help me along."

The next morning Henry stole some money from Peter's money clip, and the brothers and the runaways made their way to the ferry landing by first light. It was chilly as they set out, and although Dred was no longer feverish, he shivered when the winds blew in off the river. Taylor offered his jacket, but Dred refused. For so long he was the one taking care of them. "This isn't manners, Dred," insisted Taylor. "You're weak and you've got a harsh trip ahead of you. It'll be warm during the day, but you'll want a jacket at night. Take it."

In a single motion, Dred pushed his arms through the sleeves and wrapped his arms around Taylor in a bear hug. Taylor didn't release him until Dred said, "We best get on now."

Before boarding the ferry, Henry spoke to the captain. The others stood at a distance, and Dred and Sam watched anxiously as the boy explained about the missing papers. They exchanged looks of relief when the captain finally accepted the boy's money. Yet as Henry returned to where they stood, the captain followed him. He was a gnarly seaman with a hoarse voice. He was not tall, but stocky and solid. He planted himself before the slaves and eyed them silently. He noticed Dred's jacket, next sizing up the shirt-sleeved Taylor. Finally he said, "Dred, isn't it?"

"Yes sir," Dred responded.

"I seen you working around the docks, is that right?"

"Yes sir, cap'n."

The captain nodded. "You do a right bit of work for such a small fellow."

"Thank you, sir."

"But tell me this: how're you and this big fella here gonna manage to carry something heavy between you?"

Dred looked up into the man's face for the first time, puzzled. "Beg pardon?"

The captain's craggy face broke into a sly grin. "Well, it's kind of like harnessing a hound to a horse, ain't it? You two ain't very well matched. This boy here's gonna be stooped like an old woman by the time you're through." He laughed, but no one else did, and the captain abruptly turned as serious as everyone else. He stood silently looking over the foursome one last time, noting the sickly palor hanging over Dred. Nodding to himself, he turned to board his ferry. As he walked along the dock, he hailed a boy who was loading mining tools for the Illinois salt mines. "Boy," he called. "You know the pharmacy on Fourth and Olive? Run up there and speak to Peter Blow. Tell him the ferry captain wants a letter authorizing these two slaves to cross over."

His back was to the foursome, so he did not see the shock wave that jolted each of them. Sam went rigid but Dred staggered, and Taylor grabbed Dred's sleeve to steady him. As they exchanged alarmed looks, Henry called after the captain with forced authority, "Captain, I assure you, there's no need to hold up your ferry. I am Henry Blow. I work by my brother's side in the pharmacy. You have my word that this trip is necessary, and that these slaves will be at all times within my sight and control."

The captain turned to face Henry, his suspicions now confirmed. He said with sarcasm, "You ain't holding up my ferry, son. I got to wait on the right current for cutting across, anyhow." Dismissively, he turned and boarded his boat.

The four huddled together, whispering fiercely. "That's it," said Dred, watching the young boy sprint across Front Street. "No way we's boarding this ferry. And we can't tarry here long, neither." He looked at Sam. "What you want to do, Sam? Go back or hide out?"

Sam winked with false cheer. "My feets woked up this morning ready to run, and they still ain't had the chance. I guess I still aim to give it to them."

Dred clapped Sam on the back. "Lucas Swamps?"

Sam nodded. "As a start, leastways."

Dred next addressed Henry and Taylor. "I's sorry you boys is gonna catch it now, with not even the certainty of us getting away to lighten your load. But know that we's gonna keep pushing on to freedom. Wish us well."

Taylor looked worried. "Oh Dred, I've got a bad feeling. I think the swamp's the last place you should be. You still look ashy and you're not too steady on your feet."

"Don't you worry. Sam's gonna help me, ain't you, Sam?"

"Yes I is. Don't you worry, little Master. Dred and me's pulled in the same harness many a time, just like you and your brother. We'll get by."

"At least tell us where in the swamp," said Henry. "We can try to come back this evening with blankets and food. We'll have some news, too, about what Peter and the doctor might decide to do."

While the captain was occupied redirecting some roustabouts, the brothers accompanied Dred and Sam to the edge of Lucas Swamps. Before parting, Dred instructed Henry to return to the same spot and proceed inward on a southeasterly course. "We'll be looking out for you, and you be looking out for us. We'll find each other," he said confidently.

"Good luck," said Taylor, hugging Dred about the waist.

"Good luck yourself," Dred responded. "You's gonna need it when you face Peter. You boys think you can handle that without giving us up?"

Henry was full of the energy of rebellion, despite the setback at the ferry. He was very manly when he said, "We can manage it."

The brothers held off returning home as long as possible. In their absence, John Emerson had arrived to collect Dred. Peter Jr. had learned the details of the ferry incident from the captain, but he was as unable to find Henry and Taylor as he was unable to find Dred and Sam. Making excuses, he managed to stall Emerson until the evening.

Finally, the boys returned home and Peter confronted them about the runaway attempt. Of paramount importance to him was settling the debt to Emerson. The doctor unnerved him. Though not much older than Peter, Emerson was a great ox of a man: large and broad with a booming voice and a directness of purpose that recognized no obstacles. Peter wanted only to settle the debt and have no more dealings with the man.

Peter remained resolute in drilling the boys to reveal the slaves' hiding place, though he was not unsympathetic to their motivations. He wheedled, he threatened, and finally he saw that the youths might be manipulated into turning Dred over if he could convince them it was in Dred's best interest. Pressing his advantage by separating the boys and speaking to them individually, Peter argued that Dred's illness was a critical factor requiring the slave's return. He elaborated upon Emerson's obvious benefits as a physician, as well as the doctor's demonstrated past kindness to Dred.

Henry stood equally resolute in defending Dred's escape, but Taylor proved more malleable. Peter finally struck a bargain with Taylor, just as Dr. Emerson returned.

Peter could hardly confess the slave had run away. He made more excuses, but the discussion quickly escalated to an argument. Emerson angrily threatened to file a suit in the civil courts to compel the Blows to either produce the slave or pay him five hundred dollars.

In the midst of this commotion, Henry and Taylor had a chance to conspire. Upon learning that Taylor had struck a bargain, Henry was at first angry, but Taylor defended his position, assuring Henry that he hadn't given up the slaves' hiding place. Deftly Taylor argued the merits of the bargain. "You go to Dred," urged Taylor. "Tell him Peter's bargain and see if he won't come back. I'll stay here and make sure Peter doesn't see that you're gone."

Henry sneaked off, bearing blankets and food, as promised. The swamps were dank and misty, a forbidding place after sunset, but Henry steeled his nerves and thought only of his mission. The incessant whine of mosquitoes and the perpetual struggle to breathe without inhaling them helped to distract him from his fears. Not knowing exactly where he would find the slaves, he cleverly headed in the direction of a pocket of quiet where the frogs weren't singing. He found Dred lying on his side on a swath of tall grasses that Sam had gathered and fashioned into a mat. The air was so warm and the moon so bright they needed no fire. Sam sat with his back against a tree, but rose when he saw Henry approaching. Henry had brought bread and cheese and a flask of water, as well as blankets. Taking the provisions, Sam immediately covered Dred with a blanket.

Dred didn't rise, but Henry was relieved to see he wasn't shivering. He placed a hand on Dred's forehead. "At least your fever hasn't returned," he said.

Dred clasped Henry's hand. "Thank you, Henry. I ain't feeling sick, just tired."

Henry bit his lower lip, then plunged forthrightly into his account of the reckoning with Peter. Dred and Sam exchanged cautious looks as they learned that Peter had spoken to the boys separately. Finally Henry admitted his change of heart. "Dred, Peter convinced Taylor and Taylor convinced me: you're too sick to risk running. You should let the doctor help you and make you well, even though it means staying his slave. I didn't say this to Peter, but it seems to me that once you get well, you can try again. You can wait for a good time and try to run again. Now just isn't the right time. Also, this way Peter will safely collect the money from Emerson, so if you run later it will be Emerson's loss, not Peter's. Anyway, Peter's offering a truce: you and Sam come back now, and there'll be no punishment."

Sam kicked a tree and turned his back. Dred looked solemnly at Henry and said in a low voice, "Henry, your words make me feel sicker'n that cholera done."

Henry responded defensively, "If you had a good chance for freedom, I wouldn't feel this way, but it looks like nothing good will come of this now. It looks like accepting Peter's truce is the best you can hope for right now."

Henry knew he had disappointed Dred, and he fought to hold back tears of confusion and futility. Dejectedly, he said, "I really think this is the best thing, Dred."

Dred said, "I know you's following what you think is best. I

209

don't hold that against you. Everybody's got that right. Me and Sam included. So now I's gonna ask you as a friend to follow your heart and allow me the same. Allow me to figure out what I think's best."

Henry nodded, unsure what was being asked of him.

"You ain't gonna lead them here, is you?" Dred asked.

Henry promised he wouldn't.

"All right, then," said Dred. "Give us some time to think on it. Tell Peter we's swayed, but we ain't made up our minds yet. Find a way to get him to hold off the doctor a mite longer."

Dred and Sam said little after Henry left. They were so quiet the frogs began to thrum around them. Dred broke the silence, saying, "I reckon we's both thinking the same thing: you got to go on without me."

Sam's only response was a pained look.

"What the boy said is true," said Dred. "The risk is bigger now, and I surely is too sick yet. I'd only hold you back, trip you up, weigh you down."

"What will you do?" Sam asked in a hushed tone.

"Don't fret yourself. I might go back now, but I ain't giving up on freedom. I'll find it somehow. You, though, you should try for it now. No sense in both of us going back."

Sam nodded and finally spoke. "Can you find a way to give me time? Can you hold out here a whiles longer, and can we trust Henry?"

"I can hold out, and I trust Henry to do whatever he say. But we don't need to tell him everything. When he come back tomorrow, I'll let on that you's out, trapping or fishing or such. Then when he come the next time, I'll go on back with him. That'll give you nearly two days start. Will that be enough?"

"That'll be plenty, I reckon—so long's they don't track Henry and follow him in here."

Dred chuckled. "Them boys is clever. They'll find ways."

Sam felt embarrassed to be leaving alone, but he sorely wanted to go on. Dred saw his ambivalence and asked, "What're you planning on doing?"

Sam laughed. "Don't got a plan and maybe I don't need one. Our plans ain't come to much, yet."

"You got to try to get across, Sam. Best I can say is to try here in St. Looey what we was gonna try in Alton: go to the abolitionist paper and see iffen they won't help you out."

"I was thinking maybe I'd try one of the free blacks here. Mr. Claymorgan maybe."

"I don't know, I just don't know. He's a mighty impressive black man, sure 'nough. But I see him dealing his business with the white folk. I just don't know. Iffen I was you, I'd try the abolitionists what already taken a stand and already taken some heat on our account."

"Well, I'll do the best I can."

Dred extended his hand. "Help me up. I want to be standing to see you off."

Sam helped Dred up, and the two men hugged briefly. "We been together through a lot," said Dred.

Sam looked at the ground when he replied, and Dred heard the uncertainty in his voice. "Dred, we ain't never spoken on it, but I done you a wrong back in V'ginia, and it's set heavy on me ever since."

"I never blamed you, Sam. We was all in the devil's grasp that day Lucy got sold."

"Well, 'fore it's too late, I reckon I better tell you I's sorry about all that. I wished I had done different."

Dred smiled. "Gran would say, 'You can show a man his brother but you cannot show him his friend.'"

Sam laughed and shook his head. "I never did understand half them African sayings. What's this one mean?"

"Just that a brother you can point to, but a friend—well, you got to seek out and choose your own friends. I's saying you been a friend to me, Sam. I wish you well." Dred took the remainder of the bread and put it in Sam's hand. Sam started to refuse, but Dred insisted, "I can't eat much yet noways, and Henry'll bring more tomorrow. Take it along with you."

Sam took the bread and headed deeper into the swamp. After a few paces he turned around and said, "I wish you was coming with me, but I's certain you's gonna find your way one of these days. I's certain on it."

"I believe you's right: by'n by I'll get another chance. Then maybe we'll meet up again. If not, I'll always be thinking of you, Sam, out in the world, roaming free."

"May it be so."

Dred remained standing until Sam was out of sight. Then he stretched back out on the dried grasses and drew the blanket up to his chin. All the excitement of the run to freedom had drained from him, leaving him empty and exhausted. A heaviness pressed him down. He knew it was partly the sickness, but he imagined it was the weight of slavery constricting his chest. He rubbed his chest with the flat of his hand, trying to erase the feeling. Paper crackled under his vest as he did so, and with a sad grin he extracted the sheet from his vest pocket. He had all but forgotten the parting gift Taylor had shyly given him that morning before leaving for the ferry. Dred unfolded the sheet, a map.

"Is this a map of Alton?" he had asked Taylor.

"No," the boy said, "this is the world. The whole wide world. I wanted you to know the places you've been no matter where else you go." Taylor's finger traced the outline of the United States. "See here: this is America and its territories, and over here, where I marked a circle, this is Virginia."

Dred smiled broadly, shaking his head. "This be a wonder, a pure wonder."

Eagerly, Taylor continued, edging his finger to the left. "Now across here is St. Louis."

"Smack in the middle of everything, ain't it?"

Taylor nodded. Then he dragged his finger across the page, down and over to Africa. "And this is Africa." Again, his finger traced the boundary.

"This whole thing? Why, it's bigger'n the U.S."

Taylor grinned and said, "Now, I didn't know where Dahomey was, so I got my teacher at school to help me. He said it's right in here, along this coastline, extending upriver a ways. He said it's a kingdom."

Dred's finger traced the western coast of Africa. Midway along the coast, where Taylor had made another circle, he rubbed the area back and forth, then drummed a quick rhythm on the page. "It don't seem like much on this here sheet, but look: you could have another Africa in this stretch of water betwixt Africa and America."

"It's a long, long ways," the boy agreed.

"Mmmm-mmmm," said Dred. "My kin come all that way." He was flooded with memories of the stories Gran told about Africa and their kin. "Mmmm-mmmm," he said again. "Kinda makes me feel small and alone." Taylor slipped one hand inside Dred's, and Dred squeezed it, adding, "'Specially now that I's running on farther."

"The teacher said maps show us how we're all connected," Taylor said. "No matter how far you go, you'll always know where we are. We'll be here. We'll be thinking of you."

Dred hugged the boy around the shoulders. "Thank you, Taylor. I'll keep it with me always. Just one last thing: show me Alabama. Show me where Gran is."

Taylor did so, then watched as Dred extracted a burnt stick from the fireplace and rubbed charcoal into the spot where Gran was.

Alone in the swamp, Dred examined the map again, fondly tracing the marks and whispering, "Dahomey. V'ginia. Alabama. St. Looey." He fell asleep, dreaming of the varicolored map and all the places and colors yet to explore. He slept deeply, waking in the morning to find himself remembering the words of the free black man he had met. Dred awoke with the first streaks of daylight and looked up at the sun without squinting, thinking: Sure 'nough, freedom's skinny. Skinny and sickly and weak. But I reckon there may yet be ways to feed it and fatten it and make it grow strong.

Chapter eighteen

Abolitionists and Slave Owners

I look back over my life and I see it like the wedges of a orange, and each slice is like a whole, separate life. One slice was growing up in V'ginia, another was being a slave in Alabama, then there come the time of belonging to Master Doc Emerson. I was mighty trepidacious, thinking on being a slave to some stranger. But it probably were for the best—otherways I'd have to stay and take orders from boys what I myself helped raise up, and it become clear that Peter Jr. didn't have the grit for being Master. He wasn't the kind for bossing slaves. Not me, leastways. He still regarded me as a elder, I could see that plain when I got back from the swamp.

Peter was waiting on me. Worry lined his face more'n anger. He begun complaining how difficult this time were for him, how I be making things worser, how losing Sam was gonna hurt them bad, how he would've thought I'd show more loyalty.

"I's sure sorry to be making your life hard," I told him, pretty sure he knowed I didn't mean it. Henry knowed it. He was there, too, setting over by the window, keeping quiet, till Mary Anne come in the room demanding to know what punishment Peter was gonna give me. Henry started hissing like a teapot, saying how Peter promised I weren't gonna be punished.

I pressed my lips shut and listened to them fuss. Mary Anne wanted blood. Peter warned how whipping me would just shine a bright light on my running, and how they was already breaking the law by not telling the doc I tried to run. Mary Anne still wanted blood. Said they only promised no whipping for me not running—the fact I helped Sam run put another stripe on things. Henry begun yelling, "You promised, you promised you wouldn't whip him. You can't go back on it now."

Peter finally clapped both hands over his ears till everybody stopped flapping they gums. He turned and put it at my feet: "Dred, we desperately need the full price Emerson agreed to, especially now without Sam—and you have to take responsibility for part of that. Now, you will not be punished. But I am asking you to help us hide the fact that you ran."

"You asking me to help sell my ownself," I said.

His eyes stretched wide with surprise. "No, no, of course not. Look, Dred, you know we can't keep you. Of course we would if we could"—Mary Anne snorted but he stared her down, just like his papa used to—"but we can't afford it. That's a fact that can't be changed. I'm just trying to make the best of the facts. Can't you see that I'm trying to help you not get sold south to some horrible cotton plantation?"

For the first time I full understood why Gran hardly never argued: when you see both sides of the wall, all up and down it and along its stretch, with nary a tiny little chink for your breath to pass through, then only a fool will stand bouncing his words against that wall. "I ain't helping you one way or t'other," I said. I even had my arms crossed over my chest, standing with my legs planted apart, just like Gran used to.

Peter was pink and pinched-looking now. His chest heaved when he said, "You wouldn't talk to Papa this way, and I don't think I deserve it, either. It seems we are best rid of you anyway." He marched out stiff, with Mary Anne nearly stepping on his heels, telling him what he ought do next.

Finally it were quiet in the parlor. Henry stood by the window, looking out whilst the tree shadows crept toward the house. I don't know what I was feeling. It weren't all bad. I still had the flavor of winning a argument on my tongue—that's a sour flavor, sure 'nough, but then I always did like the taste of things sour. Yet I begun thinking on the change in front of me, the question of going who knowed where with a new master. It be a whole new slice.

I said nothing, but Henry was a boy what could see how I be thinking. I knowed he compassionated my worriment when he said, "This could be our last day together."

I moved over beside him. Our spirits was hanging heavy as the thick, green broadcloth drapes.

"What do you think it'll be like," Henry went on, "working for a doctor?"

"Don't know. I never knowed a doctor before."

"He's a Yank, you know. From Philadelphia. I heard him tell Peter his mother's an abolitionist. And he's no older'n you, I'd say. Maybe he'll be real easy to work for."

I smiled and hooked a hand on his shoulder. Henry was taller'n me—my head only come up to his shoulder—but he was still a boy.

"I's gonna be all right," I said. I winked and whispered, "'Sides, I come back but I didn't say I wouldn't try to run again."

Now the tree shadows brushed the front steps. The heat from the sun weren't strong enough no more to come in through the glass. Henry played with the tassel of the drapes.

"Dred?" he said, then paused.

He looked kinda nervous. "Go ahead," I said. "Say what you be thinking." I thought he was gonna say something about parting, but he surprised me.

"Dred, if we could keep you, would you still want to run?"

I stood still, feeling a surprising warmth offen that, feeling my heart lift 'cause he wanted to know that. But I didn't know what to say. I done looked at slavery from different angles in my life, but I never before tried explaining it to a boy, a white boy at that. Yet there be Henry, looking at me, with on his face the honest question of wanting to know. Finally I said, "You asking iffen I would stay for you?"

He shrugged, struggling for words. "I mean, is being a slave so bad? You seem happy most the time. You get along so well with everybody. Everybody likes you."

"That's what you see of me, sure 'nough. But you ain't looking at the shadow I carry. I can't choose what work to do. Can't choose who to marry or to have children without fearing they'll be sold away. Can't choose to stay with my Gran. Can't choose where to live."

"Sounds like being a child. I can't choose, either. I didn't choose to come here and go to a Catholic school. I didn't choose to leave it now and go work for Peter. I didn't choose to leave Gran behind. And I don't choose for you to have to go to Dr. Emerson."

"Difference being, Henry, as a child you be receiving the protection your parents gived, with consideration for the time when you will stand on your own. You maybe don't like how they choosed, but all what they choosed was in support of that day when you will become a man. With me, with a slave, the choices ain't a protection, they's a confinement. Ain't nobody planning on a day I'll be standing on my own. No slave owner wants that. No slave will ever get the chance to stand on his own unlessen he steals that chance. No master wants his slave to grow beyond that confinement. His slave's got to grow old and die confined to the same small world the master set down for him."

He still wanted to see it different; I could see that plain on his face. My words was too poor to explain how it feels to be a slave. I tried thinking how else to say it, to lay it out plain as dirt, but all the words in the world seemed just like leafs what falls down—they touches the dirt, but they covers it up, too.

We was standing by the drapes, like I say. These was long and heavy, twice as high as me. And inside, betwixt them and the window, hanged a lace curtain. I reached out and tapped the window pane. "As a slave child, it were like I looked on the world through glass, whilst you white children got to be outside in the grass. I only went out myself when Master or Missus send me."

"But you were out with us, too. You played with us a lot. I remember it."

"I ain't talking now about real grass and real glass—I's trying to answer your question."

"Oh," he said. He stepped closer to the window, pressed his two meaty hands on the glass. Damp finger marks bloomed out round his flesh, and when he dropped his hands, the trace stayed there.

I went on. "I minded being kept behind the glass, but not over-much 'cause I was a child, I had Gran on my side of the glass, and that seemed enough. But it got more tough when I got older 'cause I spent a lot of time at the window, yet I wasn't even allowed to throw it open to breathe in the fresh air. I begun to feel raveled, like a moth what's ready to leave the cocoon, yet my wings was all raveled still."

I pulled Henry back a step from the glass, then reached across him with the lace curtain still in my hand. I pulled it in front of him and wrapped it around him, twirling him into the lace till he tripped on his own feet and giggled.

I paused, leaving him wrapped up in the lace. "I can't lift my arms," he said.

I stepped away to the opposite end of the window. "Come over here," I said. He started shuffling near, then got snagged by the lace and couldn't come no further. He tried to untwirl hisself, but I stopped him. "No, you ain't allowed to turn that way. And iffen you try, you gonna get whipped. And after you's whipped, if you still wants to try, well, we'll likely up and sell you away—no matter you got a family here."

"But I can't really move. I can't be of much use if I can't really move," he said.

"That's all right. You of just as much use as I say you is, and it ain't for you to think on being any more. Now, come on over here like I says."

"But you know I can't. This is as far as I can go."

It come into my mind to make it more real by taunting him on being porky, but I couldn't bring my mouth to move in that direction. Instead, I said, "You's boondoggling boy! Think you can fool me with your lazy, cheating ways? Let's see how far you think you can get with this."

I stepped behind him and grabbed the heavy drape, begun twirling him now inside that one. He disappeared quick.

It were dusk now. No lamp was lit in the parlor yet. The most light come in through the window. I noticed Henry's fingermarks was long faded from the window, and I wondered how much more he would take. "It got pretty dark for me," I said. "Slavery darkened everything. I felt small and low. There come a time when all I wanted was the peace and sleep of the cocoon, but still I had to be a slave and do a slave's work." I seed Henry sway on his feet. "Be still," I said.

"I am. It's just that I can't see anything—it makes it hard to keep my balance."

"No, stay completely still."

"How?"

"You figure it out." I was surprised at how easy it were to keep pushing this thing one more inch. I knowed he wasn't gonna be hurt, and knowed that he knowed it too, but he was beginning to feel uncertain how far this might go. Truth is, I didn't know myself. It become something that were happening to me, too—not like I was making it happen. I was telling a story, but I didn't know the ending.

Henry tried to separate his feet, trying on a wider stand, but he come up short against the cloth and lost his balance, falling into the drape. But because he was wrapped so tight, he didn't hit the ground. He was sorta hanging there at a slant.

"Dred!" he called. "Help me get to my feet."

I said nothing.

"All right, I understand. This is really awful. Will you put me back upright?"

I said nothing.

"Come on now. You know I hate tight spaces. I'm suffocating."

I said nothing.

Next time he spoken, he was angry, with a pinch of scare throwed in. "And it's hot in here. I'm itchy."

I said nothing, but something told me it were enough. When he said, "Please?" I snapped to. I walked over and ended the boy's picklement. Helped him on his feet. Held him firm while I slowly untwirled him. First he come outten the broadcloth, then he come outten the lace. His blond hair was damp, and sweat were atop his lip. He was breathing fast and shallow, and he didn't meet my eyes when he laughed, "Whew! That's a pretty good lesson."

I hooked my hand back on his shoulder and grabbed his chin with my other hand, pulling his face right before mine, wanting him to see the apology there. I said, "I hope that weren't too bad. There just ain't no good answer for the question you asked."

He stepped away from me, and I seed him shiver. I thought he was angry with me. He hanged his head, though, and said, "I feel ashamed."

That surprised me. "You got no cause for shame, son. Nobody would tolerate good what I just done to you."

"No," he said in a small voice. "I mean about asking if being a slave was so bad. I feel ashamed I didn't know."

He lifted my heart again, and I felt a bit of pride in seeing the man he was gonna grow into. I gave him a hug and said, "There's one more thing you'll be needing to know."

He looked a little scared. I shaked my head and smiled, saying, "When I think on running, it ain't 'cause I see myself as a slave—it's 'cause I see myself as a man."

⁂

A soothing, delightful cobweb seemed to envelop Dred. He felt dreamy and didn't know if his eyes were open or closed, though he discerned shadows of varying hues floating across his blurred vision. Gradually the penetrating cold of the ground beneath him caused him to shiver, and from a great distance came an unfamiliar, booming voice calling his name.

"Dred? Dred Scott!"

Someone was lifting him up, helping him to his feet, but his legs wobbled. His vision began to clear but he could make no sense yet of what was happening.

The voice said, "Maybe you're not as recuperated as I thought."

Dred blinked rapidly and saw a braided gold chain and the

checkered silk vest of a man with a very broad chest. He looked higher up, and higher, and higher, finally locating the mouth that spoke to him. He took in a ruddy face, huge teeth, milky blue eyes. He realized this was his new master. John Emerson was saying, "You fainted, Dred. Come sit here. Let your head fall between your knees."

Doing as he was told, Dred took the opportunity to clear his mind and remember what had happened. Two days ago he had ridden from the Jefferson Hotel with John Emerson—Master Doc. As the Master held the reins, the slave sat quietly for the hour-long journey to Jefferson Barracks, the garrison just south of the city.

"I'm a well-respected physician here in St. Louis," John Emerson had said. "It's important to me that everything you do support that." He darted a sideways look at the slave, who said nothing. "I've just received a contract as civilian physician to the garrison, but I will also continue treating private citizens in the city. With me, you'll come in contact with generals and mayors and judges—and their wives and families. I need you to act accordingly." Emerson couldn't read the slave's demeanor. "Your old master, before he died, said you were quick-witted and reliable. Is that so?"

Dred looked at the buggy floor boards, desiring to remain as noncommittal as possible until he had a better grasp of his new situation. "Iffen Master Peter say so," he replied.

"You see, Dred," Emerson resumed, "I don't want you just as a laborer. I'm looking for a fella who can assist me in my practice, help me build a solid reputation. Help me move from a civilian practice to become an Army surgeon. So it's important that I impress the right people. I need someone who can learn the difference between pills and powders. Someone who can drive me to an urgent case in the middle of the night and be sure that I have all my equipment. Someone who can hold a head steady if I have to yank a tooth."

Dred rocked along silently; this was a lecture, not a conversation.

"This means," continued Emerson, "that you will be in situations unlike those you're accustomed to. You may be admitted to private bedchambers. You will be among whites when they are at their weakest and most vulnerable. I need to be able to rely on your discretion and your, uh, well…." He was searching for a word, and Dred's ears perked up. "I'm hoping," said Emerson, "you will be inconspicuous. Almost invisible. The white people I treat shouldn't really be aware that you're in the room. Do you understand?"

Dred groaned inwardly, thinking: what these white folk don't understand! Out loud, he said, "I waited table and cleaned a spill 'fore it ever hit the tablecloth. I tended Master Peter's card games, keeping glasses filled, and walked right behind them gentlemen whilst they was reading they cards. I reckon I know how not to make white folk nervous—that about the first thing I done learned on this earth."

Emerson laughed, and the sight of his big teeth slightly unnerved Dred. "Good, good. That's precisely what I mean. You are quick-witted. You know, I first saw you at one of Peter Blow's card games, and I formed that impression of you immediately. In fact, I believe that was the game when I won you, so to speak. Well, that's beside the point. I know there will be a period of adjustment for you to get used to a new master—I'm just trying to be clear about what I expect. Most importantly, I need to establish with you from the start a relationship of trust and understanding. You do understand, don't you?"

Dred rocked along, patting his thigh, wondering if the man had ever owned a slave before. He would wager he hadn't. He answered only, "Yes, sir."

"So I will treat you fairly, and I expect you to show me the same respect."

"Yes, sir," repeated Dred, thinking: "fairly" on the white man's lips be a word what sounds to a black man's ear more like "at my convenience."

Satisfied, Emerson wrapped up his speech. "I may be the master and you the slave, but that doesn't mean we can't get along. It's my job to handle bodies all day long, and if there's one thing I know, it's that we all bleed red."

He laughed at his joke alone. The mention of handling bodies jarred Dred. Nervously, he asked, "Am I gonna have to touch dead bodies?"

"Well, if I do my job well, not too many." Again Emerson

laughed alone. Then he perceived Dred's unease and asked, "You're not afraid of a corpse, now are you?"

"What's a corpse?"

Emerson flashed his big teeth again. "Dred, there's a lot you can learn if you pay attention, things I'll warrant will be of some interest to you. You'll learn some new skills and some new words, and I'm glad you spoke up and asked what's a corpse. Whenever you don't understand anything, just ask me. Because I can't have you guessing. If I ask you to fetch me asafetida, I don't want you handing me arsenic."

Generous Joe sprung into Dred's memory, and he saw himself at thirteen, with Uncle Joe pointing to the writing on wooden barrels, explaining nail sizes. With a sick feeling in his gut he said, "I don't read."

"I'll show you how to recognize the differences. There's many ways: color, smell, texture. The point is, always ask if you're not sure. Show me the label, and I'll be sure."

Dred nodded, unconvinced. Emerson was blind to his nervousness. He continued, "Anyway, a corpse is just another name for a dead body. That doesn't bother you, does it?" He glanced over and Dred looked away. Dismissively he said, "Well, now, there's nothing to fear. Everybody feels nervous at first. At school, men even fainted. But you soon get used to anything if you're around it enough."

It was two days later that Dred saw his first corpse and, in fact, fainted. As his head cleared and he sat up, he couldn't stop himself from looking again at the form on the table, a white soldier who had died of cholera. The garrison had several cases, and the fatalities were being kept here in what Master Doc referred to as "the dead room." But it wasn't a dead body; it was a corpse: completely naked, dirty gray, and rank. Dred shuddered, and Emerson mistook it for a fever chill. He placed his hand on Dred's forehead, saying, "I don't think you're relapsing, but why don't you just take it easy here."

Dred noticed that his new master's hand remained resting on his shoulder, as he himself had rested his hand on Henry's shoulder just a few days before, except this touch left him uneasy. Emerson's demeanor was unfamiliar and perplexing. As the days with his new master stretched to weeks and then months, Dred struggled to understand what seemed like the Master's generosity: if he ate a meal with Dred, he shared the food equally and always brought the leftovers to the hounds in the kennels; he invited Dred to tell him a story, then told two in return; above all, he encouraged Dred to learn. He tested Dred's memorization of drug names and uses. He demonstrated how to prepare remedies and treatments, then patiently guided Dred's first attempts to apply his new learning. Dred initially feared being educated, but quickly his appetite for new knowledge and skills had him asking for more. Nevertheless, during that whole first year, Dred suspected Master Doc was trying to manipulate him, though he didn't know toward what end.

Emerson, for his part, at first puzzled over the slave's aptitude. Several times he interrogated Dred about his prior training, but Dred only acknowledged that his grandmother had been a "healer." Eventually, however, Emerson grew to rely upon Dred's skills and to enjoy the freedom it provided him to hobnob.

A tentative camaraderie emerged. Gradually Dred formed an understanding of his new master and accepted that Master Doc sincerely wanted there to exist between them not an equality, but a harmony. John Emerson wanted to be liked. Yet Dred found it slightly comical that the large, powerfully-built man rarely noticed when he bumped into others or stepped on someone's foot. He gave little thought to anyone's feelings, including his patients' pain, and seemed to think everyone should jump out of his way. In spite of his desire to fraternize, he often gave offense without knowing why or how. He was bluff, quick to quarrel, and ready to reconcile.

Above all else, Dred observed how desperately his new master wanted to join the Army. John Emerson felt honor-bound to perpetuate a family tradition; unfortunately, he recoiled from the prospect of commanding troops. He didn't want to instill fear or loathing. He knew he could never inflict the harsh disciplines he had seen his father execute: beating men lashed to a wheel, starving them, staking them out for days in the blistering sun. John Emerson was not commander material, and he knew it. He wanted too much to be liked. He wanted to heal. Fortunately, he possessed an innate talent for medicine. He devised new ways to apply old remedies, and his successes were surprising and impressive, if not consistent.

If he became an Army surgeon, he could garner the prestige and privileges of an officer without shouldering more distasteful responsibilities. He could make a name for himself, establish the right connections, and eventually retire from the Army as a relatively young man and resume his second career as a private physician. He could find a wife, start a family, own some land. He could be landed gentry. Gentry—he liked the sound of that.

Passing the examination before the Army Medical Board in 1833, he received his first appointment: assistant surgeon at old Fort Armstrong on Rock Island—an aptly-named, bridgeless, craggy wasteland in the middle of the Mississippi River, some three hundred miles north of St. Louis. It was a disappointing assignment, but Emerson had youthful, high hopes of advancement and more favorable posts.

He and Dred arrived in November at the old Army outpost to find Armstrong hopelessly dilapidated. The gaps in the weather-beaten picket stockade looked like the ebony keys on a piano. Even the roof of the commanding officer's quarters leaked, and the hospital was so filthy that Emerson set up tents to treat the sick. No one bothered to fortify Armstrong because the warring populations of that area had long since been vanquished.

Emerson hated his first taste of Army life on the frontier. Though it was a bustling community—with families, slaves, livestock, a commissary, a school, and a chapel—he had little in common with the officers and less with the troops. He found the enlisted men, in general, to be crude and uneducated, little better than the slaves or Indians. And the officers were typically West Point cadets, rigid and humorless, respecting only the accomplishments of the battlefield. Truthfully, Emerson preferred Dred's company, though he knew it behooved him to socialize with the officers and their wives, and did so.

As the months stretched to years, the doctor felt isolated and trapped. The austere, grand scenery of sky and water did nothing to inspire him beyond prompting the writing each month of a letter to the Surgeon General, requesting reassignment to St. Louis. Emerson wanted society. He wanted the tinkling of women's laughter, not the tinkling of rain water collected in a basin beside his bed.

The three years at Fort Armstrong had quite the opposite effect on Dred, however. He caught on quickly to the mixing of compounds and to matching the name of an illness with its treatment. His curiosity flowed like a waterfall, and Emerson provided the riverbed to guide it. Thinking back on what he had last told Henry, it seemed to Dred that, while he was not free, he had at least moved beyond the glass. He felt a foot taller on the day a patient first requested his own ministrations over the doctor's, and Emerson took no umbrage. He merely nodded approval and said, "Go ahead. You're knowledgeable enough to handle this on your own now."

Emerson was finally reassigned in the spring of 1836, but only because the Army decided to abandon Fort Armstrong. Unfortunately, the reassignment took them deeper into the frontier and further from society. That May, Emerson, Dred, and most of their company under the command of Lt. Colonel Davenport, journeyed to Fort Snelling in the Wisconsin Territory.

&

Strange thing about Master Doc—he was kinder to animals and colored folk than to whites. I seed him a thousand times treating the white folk, giving no more thought to paining his patients than a carpenter worry about the feelings of the wood he's spiking. 'Course, if the patient be rich and powerful, Master Doc be friendly and full of chat and kind words, but only before the doctoring begun. During a treatment, he was all business. He was rough. So it surprised me to see him compassionating with black folk and Indians.

As a instance, when we was still at Jefferson Barracks, they kept there in the prison some of the chiefs from the Black Hawk War, including Black Hawk hisself. They was some sorry-looking fellas, sure 'nough: all thin and wasted, eyes sunk into they heads and ribs jutting out like a farmer's hoe. And never mind how weak they was, the Army latched a ball and chain on each one of them, to keep them from running. Not only was they treated worser'n most slaves I ever seed, the Army let folk come in as if it were the circus. City folk would come down and stretch they eyes like looking at a wild animal in a cage. It were just like a freak show. Well, Master Doc hated that. Complained, hollered, and even writ letters, though nothing ever changed. All he could do was bring them some food sometime, and treat them with powders and such.

He was soft-hearted toward animals, too. Another time, as we was leaving Fort Armstrong, oh, the going was tough! That Mississippi River is a rascal, and it test the best the Army put out there. Worst was when we had to clamber over sandbars and such. We moved in the spring of 18'n36, a wet spring. Come a time once when the bank were so muddy, a young lieutenant couldn't get his horse out. The men in his charge be laughing at him, and he got all flustrated and started thrashing that horse. Poor thing was braying like a mule, its eyes bugging out like a frog, struggling mightily to get away from the man with the whip, but that critter were stuck deep—broke my heart to see a horse treated so low. When Master Doc seed it, he yelled louder'n the horse. He waded right into the muck and pulled that man offen the horse with his two fists. Then he pulled his gun and said, "You hit that animal one more time and I'll shoot you first before I put it out of its misery."

He got me to help him. He knowed by then I was good with horses. I stayed on my mount and took the poor critter's lead, talking to it, trying to soothe it; and Master Doc, he got right down in the mud and pulled up that horse's legs with solid might. He was a over-large man, mighty strong, which a doctor ought to be 'cause he have to be hauling and heaving bodies.

Well, that poor beast come outten the muck all aquivering, seeming half the size it were 'fore it went in the mud, head hanging so low its nose dragged on the ground. Even on solid ground, they couldn't get it to move, it were so shocked and broke. They had to shoot it anyways. "You better never get sick and need my care," Master warned the lieutenant, and I know he meant it.

I should tell about our travel to Fort Snelling. It were quite some journey, with days and days of nothing but prairie, river, and sky. Both the prairie and the sky stretch on forever, without edges. The sky out there is bigger'n the sky anywheres else, yet it's closer, too.

There's all that space yet it kinda hugs you. We was traveling upriver, on the Mississipp', but the strange thing was that the prairie and sky seemed more like water than the river did. On the prairie the high spring grasses ripple like waves, and up above, the lines and lines of clouds washes over you like waves. Was the river that didn't seem like water. River seemed like riding a ornery animal: bumpy, willful, and all the time you be checking its course. I didn't trust that river.

By'n by we finally reached Snelling. Now, that's a impressive sight, coming up the river to see that fort high atop the bluff, them cliffs as white as sugar and the gray stone walls stretching up to the sky. It sits up there right where the Mississipp' and the St. Peter's Rivers join, with a view of everything: both rivers, valley, prairie, and all that sky. You can see clear into tomorrow. There's no sneaking up on Fort Snelling, sure 'nough.

See, all them frontier forts the Army set up so's to control the Indians. By the time I was living there, for the most part the Army was on good terms with the Indians, especially the Sioux. There's more bands and tribes than I can count, but up in Wisconsin Territory you got mainly the Dakota Sioux and the Chippewa, and each hates the other for killing off they kin for generations upon generations. So from time to time you'd get a small band going after revenge on another small band traveling through the countryside. It's like a spark that maybe sets off a big fire, so then they got Major Taliaferro to put out the fire. He be the Indian Agent what lived just outside the fort a ways, and he was a remarkable man. All the Indians called him "Four Hearts," 'cause he so good to one and all—the Sioux, the Chippewa, the whites, and even them French trappers and traders. And anytime the heat rise betwixt this one and that one, well, Major T. stepped right in the middle of it and damped it down—with the Army to back him up, 'cause Major T. was a scrawny sort of fella. Not short, just scrawny. Sickly, too.

Major T. be sick so often, Master Doc and Major T. come to be good friends, which was good for Master Doc 'cause most the Army men was too coarse for him. Major T. was a bookish man, liked to talk for hours round a good fire. That suited me more'n it did Master—he liked the conversation with Major T., but he also was rambunctious and needed to go out with the troops on hunts and excursions. Master Doc be a man to get bored easy, and Army life—iffen there's no wars, leastways—ain't nothing if it ain't boring.

Every day begins with the reveille horn, the flag raising, and the all's-well. The troops run out for roll call, then they do some light work 'fore breakfast, then they do they regular duties. For me and Master Doc, that was bringing any sick to the hospital and tending those what was already there. I kept busy making sure things was cleaned and fires stayed lit, and the best part of my day was when Master would go from cot to cot, talking to the patients and seeing what they needed. I be there right at his elbow. They costive? I got the aloe. They rheumy? I prepare the cups for bleeding, or the leeches if we got them. Pain or fever? Well, I go mix the palliatives, plasters, or pills, as Master tell me. Weren't long 'fore I was so good at the cupping and the plastering that patients asked for me to do the treatment, and Master Doc was fine with that. He knowed he was kind of rough, whereas I could be soft as velvet. 'Course, there be white folk what won't allow a Negro to touch them, but in the Army leastways, I learned that when a man be sick, often that kind of thinking trails behind figuring on how to stop the hurt.

I liked doctoring, sure 'nough. It gived me a great thrill, doing as my mind led me, seeing all I could do by the twist of my own wrist. I was apt and dutiful. I done remembered all what I ever learned from Gran and Master Doc, and I put a careful hand to the healing. Master Doc all the time be saying, "Dred, you amaze me, how quick you catch on." And I just answered him, "I didn't come into this world to rust out."

In some ways, I held the advantage over Master Doc, 'cause my expectations was swelling, whereas Master Doc felt clipped short by fort life. Being a slave and accustomed to slavery ways, I didn't chafe under the Army routines like Master Doc did. He was a man for obeying orders, sure 'nough, but as to the regulations, he seemed to think how the regulations shouldn't always be binding on him, good as they was for lesser folk. He tried the patience of Colonel Davenport and later, Captain Plympton, too. One time, Captain Plympton even throwed Master Doc in jail.

See, Master Doc was the kind of man couldn't take much quiet. If things was too dull, he'd stir them up. And enduring winters up there in Wisconsin Territory, things got as quiet as snowdrop falling atop snowdrop. I should explain about the winters out there, 'cause there ain't nothing like it unlessen you been that far north. Sure, we had summers and winters in V'ginia, in Alabama, in St. Looey: summer heat like them Indian steam baths and pesky mosquitoes; and winter cold that no fire can cut through. We had dry seasons, flood seasons. But none of that was anything to prepare you for what they got up on the frontier. There, the mosquitoes be big as vultures and they swarm like bees. They suck your blood like a leech. Master Doc say iffen a patient need bleeding, he just as well send them out to the marshes in the summertime, 'stead of spending all that time with cupping and such.

The heat run short up there, though. Most the time the weather run from cold to unbearable. Winters be so cold the trees explode like rifle shots from the freezing—and if you ever be caught out on the plains in a snowstorm, you soon afeared the same is gonna happen to your arms and legs. Snowdrifts completely cover a man—fact, Indians will try to shelter in a drift if they get caught out. Not a spring come round that human corpses wasn't found still there when the drifts melted away. The fort always sent out a special detail to collect the sorry souls left this way—mostly Indians but some trappers and travelers, too. Each spring the soldiers set out for miles in every direction, just looking up to the sky, aiming for any spot where the buzzards be circling.

So you can understand that at the fort we was all mighty partial to our fires. When I first come to Snelling, all we had was fireplaces. But by the second winter, a whole boatload of stoves arrived, and it were a bigger event than Christmas. So new they shined, with the only smell of smoke about them being the whiff of sulfur from the forge—they was that new. Officers quarters got them first, then the places like the hospital and the commissary and the chapel, then the barracks. Nobody gived much mind to the slaves, 'course. Nobody, that is, 'cept Master Doc and the Captain.

Captain Plympton got his Jesse a stove but that was the onliest slave, and that was more because Jesse took care of Major's horses and had him a room built 'longside the stables. See, to the Captain, them horses was the chief thing, not Jesse, but Jesse got the benefit anyhows.

Master Doc, though, he learned how there was still a few stoves left at the commissary, and he goes to get one for me. Now, Master Doc was easy on me generally, don't get me wrong, but in this particular happenstance I ain't too sure whether he just wasn't competing with the Captain, figuring that if Captain's slave gets a stove, then the surgeon's slave ought to, too. Master Doc had a mighty high impression of his own importance. So he marched down to the quartermaster.

Quartermaster O'Malley done got his own ideas about how them extra stoves should be used. O'Malley found a use for everything and didn't never let nothing go to waste or not turn a profit. O'Malley had him a sly trade going on with the trappers and probably figured he could get hisself a barrel or two of whisky—which were strictly contraband—in trade for one of them stoves. He was in the commissary, jawing with his clerks on this particular morning.

I knowed Master Doc's aim, and I was keen to have my own stove, so I followed him and looked in through the commissary window. I seed Master enter the commissary, and the quartermaster slipped something out of sight under the counter, quick and light as a thief. Master probably didn't see it, but I did: a flask of whisky. And the sun weren't even up over the watchtower yet.

Master Doc didn't trouble hisself to ask. He just said, "I'm here to requisition a stove."

"Oh, you are, are you?" said O'Malley, with that slow, musical way the Irish got of saying they Rs. A funny thing: lots of the infantry is Irish, and it's right comical when you hears them in council with the Sioux, what speaks they whole language without ever using that sound. Then it's just the opposite with the Winnebagos, what got R-sounds in near about every single word, yet they can't understand the Irish R. So when a Irish soldier tries to talk with the Indians, best thing you can hope for is a full stomach, a comfortable place to set, and a clear view of the charades that is sure to follow. Why, some of them privates is so fresh off the boat they needs a interpreter just to be understood by the whites.

Master Doc, howsomever, understood the quartermaster just fine. Understood the tone as well as the words. Real loud, he cut to the finish line: "Have two privates deliver it to the hospital this afternoon." He turned his back, a smart about-face, and stomped to the door, only to be stopped with his hand on the latch by O'Malley's soft hiss.

"I'll need authorization for that. Doc."

Master Doc did him another about-face, slow-turning this time. Puffed out his chest, tucked his chin down, and growled, "You'll need authorization for that, sir."

I admits I sort of liked the quartermaster: as one short man to another, I admired how he brooked no slight, even iffen he be outranked or outsized. Me, I's sometime intimidated by size. But not O'Malley. He was a scrapper, knotty and small. What he lacked in height he made up for in volume, and his mouth suddenly become a bugle. He begun talking so loud that even iffen I wasn't hiding just outside the window, I would've heared him. Surprised Captain didn't hear him clear over at the HQ.

For a spell it were just a shouting match. Master Doc leaned over the counter and pushed his face nearly touching O'Malley's nose. Both they faces was as red as a cardinal. O'Malley come out from behind the counter and gived Master Doc a shoulder-butt, accidental-on-purpose. Master Doc slapped O'Malley's chest with his gloves, nothing more'n swatting a mosquito, 'cept O'Malley wasn't no mosquito. He was as short on fuse as he was on height, and he swung a hard fist toward Master Doc's middle and missed. Master Doc sidestepped and proceeded to flatten O'Malley with a right cut. Whilst the quartermaster be trying to get up offen the floor, Master Doc shoved him back down with his boot. Master, certainly weighing more'n twice O'Malley, maybe had his doctor's degree framed behind glass and hanged on a wall, but he was no gentleman. He could kick up the dust with the worst of them. Believing the matter to be settled, he stormed out the commissary. Halfway across the parade grounds, though, he stopped short as a shot whistled past his ear. The quartermaster done found his feet and packed him a muzzleloader, aiming on having the last say. That's how mad he was, or how drunk. Hard to tell the difference.

When I seed O'Malley burst outten the door I thought I'd be doctoring the doctor, but no. He was too angry to shoot straight, and Master Doc just stood still in his tracks and turned slow to glare back at the quartermaster, who begun fumbling with the next shot and cursing the old rifle for not firing straight. 'Course, quartermaster wasn't no Captain Scott. Captain Martin Scott was such a dead aim he could've put another hole in the Master's belt and never scratched the man, if he had a mind to. Nothing he ever aimed at lived to tell a tale unlessen he intended to let it go on squawking. But quartermaster plain missed. Not by much, but a miss is as good as a mile, you know. Whilst he was fussing and cussing, Master Doc was taking them big strides, closing ground fast betwixt hisself and the commissary.

Several soldiers by now done come out, and in passing one, Master Doc grabbed the pistol outten the man's holster. He didn't usually carry no firearm hisself, so long as he was inside the fort. So he snagged one as he marched past, and that quartermaster would've been a goner iffen Captain Plympton hadn't also come up on the scene, and he ordered Master Doc to halt.

Like I say, Master Doc obeyed orders. Didn't pay mind to most regulations, but he followed orders. Anyways, from that point it were like two children tattling, and Captain throwed them both in the guardhouse. Master could've easily got hisself outten the jail the same day—all Captain wanted him to do was apologize. But he stayed there three days, refusing to apologize, till Captain had to let him out 'cause the men needed a doctor. And Master Doc knowed that. Knowed he was too valuable to be kept in jail.

Did I get a stove? Well, yes I did. Captain, now, felt bound not to give in to Master, so strictly speaking the stove weren't for me. But Master Doc convinced Captain another stove were needed in the hospital, and soon as he got it, he arranged for me to move from the slave quarters to a little room at the back of the hospital, kinda like the room me and Gran had beside the kitchen in V'ginia.

I was right next to the stove, and it were a great comfort to me in the winters, sure 'nough.

Yet that weren't quite the end of it, neither. Day after I got moved into the hospital back room, some soldier called Master Doc a nigger-lover, and there was a scuffle ending up with Master putting a stitch in the man's eye that he hit! Anyways, there was lingering resentment. For a man what liked to be liked, Master Doc surely could make enemies.

Myself, I wasn't full in the understanding of it. At first I thought Master Doc held colored folk in higher regard than most other slave masters will do; thought maybe his abolitionist mother taught him some kindnesses. It weren't till much later that I come to see how he really regard us as lower, as needing more help. He treated colored folk kinda like some men treats a woman or a child—not expecting too much, holding them to a lower standard. I sees clear now that Master Doc didn't expect so much from me, he just accepted it 'cause it freed him up from doing things hisself. It gived him more room to do the things he wanted to do.

I didn't notice at the time 'cause I was enjoying all that extra room myself. In a way I felt almost free. Working with Master Doc, riding out on them wide-open plains, visiting them Indian villages, trading the know-how of healing, seeing people made well by the doing of my own hands—there was times with Master Doc I'd sometimes forget I was a slave. I was coming up from the bottom then, with room to learn and to grow my skills. I growed confident, and I wanted to test my abilities and to grow everywhichway. The world was bigger somehow, and I become hopeful offen my deeds. I begun to feel the possibilities again. I begun to feel I wanted to share it all with somebody.

That's when I met Harriet Robinson, my compass flower. You don't know the compass flower? It grows wild out on the prairie, a sweet flower with leaves what always point north, so you can always find your direction.

Chapter nineteen

Aurora

Harriet hates for me to swear, but good god a'mighty, I loved that gal from first sight!

I was eighteen when my heart closed up over Lucy, and thirty-six when it opened again to Harriet. She was just seventeen, and it were like she closed the gap of all them years betwixt my being eighteen and being thirty-six. I got the chance to go back and feel eighteen again, to be bursting-glad for the day and soaking-joyful about tomorrow. Those eighteen year melted away like dirty snow, and my heart were under there, thawing, ready to open like a daylily in the midsummer sun. A marvel named Harriet did that.

First time I seed her were the autumn of 18'n36. Master Doc and me wasn't at Fort Snelling but a few months, though we already knowed Major T., the Indian Agent. One day he come to the fort to tell us about a band of Chippewa. He was worried on two counts: they was edging into Sioux trapping lands, and they hadn't never been in this area before. He said, "Doc, I'm sending my Chippewa scout to invite this new band to the council house so's we can settle this trapping issue. But I sure would appreciate you going along to inoculate the bunch of them 'fore they get here." He was well afeared of the smallpox, and not just for hisself. Smallpox already done as much killing in some areas as the wars done.

Master and the Major was talking right there in the hospital, and I was there doing some washing up. Master Doc liked things in the hospital to be clean. "Cleanliness got nothing to do with godliness," he'd say, "but it got a thing or two to do with healthiness."

By'n by Master Doc called me over and explained how we's gonna be traveling out toward the St. Croix River to inoculate them Chippewa. "Load up a mule with supplies," he told me, "and outfit two horses." So I made my way round to the stables, passing Major T.'s buggy along the way. And whooo—setting up top there in the passenger seat was a sight to stop my heart and trip my feet, leaving me weak-kneed, a-wondering who snatched all the air outten my chest. 'Cause there atop the buggy was the prettiest, laughingest gal I ever did see. In her smile was the child she been and the woman she was becoming. She was wearing a bright blue and white apron with a matching bonnet, and she was leaning over to the back of the buggy, tickling two little children there what I knowed to be Major T.'s young'ns. She was facing my way, but only looking at them young'ns, and I think Master Doc called after me three or four times 'fore I found my breath and my feet again, and went about my business.

That were the first time I seed my Harriet. 'Course, she weren't mine yet. I still had to win her, but win her I determined to do. I wouldn't bear no thought on not winning her. The sight of them laughing cheeks puffed up my heart and made it near impossible to wait for another time to visit Major T. to see that face again.

My next chance come not too long after that. It were still autumn, I know, 'cause I recollects she was outside playing in a heap of leaves with the children when me and Master Doc rode up to the Agency one day. We done inoculated near about a hundred Indians, and on our way back to the fort we stopped to tell Major T. all we done. That were my idea. I wanted to get another eyeful of Harriet— and have her take notice of me. So I put it in Master Doc's ear that we could stop off at the Agency, tell Major T. how's we treated three bands, not just one, and probably get us a home-cooked meal.

I knowed that would sway Master Doc. I said life at the fort could be killing dull—but did I mention the food? Oh, eating at the fort were one of the sorriest parts of Army life. Iffen the winter were long and hard, and the supply ships couldn't make it up the river, iffen the men couldn't make it through the drifts to hunt, and the grain supplies wore thin—it just got pitiful. We had a riot one time 'cause the men refused to eat the bread, it got so moldy. Things was different at the Agency, though. Every Indian and every trapper coming through the area stopped there and left a little something, so Mrs. Taliaferro laid a handsome table in any season. Fast as she was gived things, that's how fast she gived them away. Many folks called her Mrs. Four Hearts. It were a known fact: best food to be had for a hundred miles were at the Indian Agency. Later I learned that were mostly thanks to Harriet's cooking, so then I had another reason to chase her!

Anyways, we rode up that day and she be right outdoors there, laughing and playing with three little ones in the afternoon sunshine, jumping and falling down into the biggest pile of leaves you ever did see. Just a mountain of leaves. But still she didn't see me. Master Doc did, though. He seed I was a goner. "Dred," he chid me, "you's too old for that gal." And I said, "No sir, I ain't—round that gal I become just a boy again."

Master Doc sent me to the stables to water and curry the horses. Which I done, and whilst I's there rushing through my chores so I can go kick up a conversation with Harriet, don't Master come through and tell me to bring his bag to the house and help him treat Major T.'s little girl.

Little Amanda was just recuperating from a bout with thrush. All her spots was gone, she was free from fever, and she been eating pretty good. Master Doc check her out and pronounce her over the sickness. "All she need now is to get her strength back," he said—and that's 'xactly what I wanted to hear. She was standing by the window with her pale, little, sad face, watching the rest of the young'ns romping outside with Harriet.

"How about I carry this young'n outside for a last bit of them warm afternoon rays?" I said, and everybody, 'specially little Amanda, seemed to think that were a grand idea. I carried her on my back, she was light as a knapsack. The other young'ns cheered when they seed her, and finally, finally I got Harriet's attention—and it come at me full force. My heart begun a patter as she come close to speak to the child, but I noticed how her eyes was still on me. She come so close I could feel the heat offen her skin. She turned and said to the other young'ns, "Let's build a throne for our little princess." And they did. They all pushed that mountain of leaves to make a throne, and I set Amanda on top, and the other children and Harriet joined hands and danced round in a circle, singing "Johnny Brown."

> *Oh Johnny Brown, Oh Johnny Brown*
> *Oh Johnny Brown, spread your carpet down.*

I lent my voice to the tune and clapped the rhythm while the young'ns skipped in a ring, till Harriet broke the ring and held out her sweet little hand to me. That were all the invitation I needed. I taken her hand—a strong hand but smooth and silky—and I joined them children dancing the ring. We must've singed that song ten times over! Every time the children stopped, I whipped them up into another round. I believe I made up ten new verses, right on the spot. I wouldn't let it end, 'cause I had Harriet's hand in mine. I didn't want it ever to end.

Sure 'nough, I become a starving man, starving for Harriet, and all I got was that one taste 'fore the snows set in. I didn't see her all through that winter, and I ain't ashamed to say I pined for that gal. Urged Master Doc to go visit his good friend Major Talia-ferro—and he wanted to, but it were a hard winter that year. Details what went out frequent got caught in drifts right up to a horse's belly, and the men'd come back with frostbite and snowblindness. So Captain Plympton wouldn't allow nobody outside the fort what didn't need to go.

Finally we got a break from the cold. Gradually the earth softened and begun soaking up all that snow till it were just a thin, wet blanket across the prairie. Wild grasses was stretching up through it, and the air carried warm earth smells. We got a few days of sudden spring, and me and Master Doc rode out by Minnehaha—that's the little falls they got out there, not the great falls of St. Anthony. The Indians call the little one "laughing water," not only 'cause the sound be musical, but also 'cause how it makes you feel. A person can walk along a natural shelf behind the falls, where the sound of the rushing and falling fills you up. It kinda seeps in your ears and sets your blood to pumping with it. Something about it just makes you feel good, makes you want to laugh and dance. It's a beautiful place, and as we rode on past it I recollected Harriet, falling and laughing in the leaves—and I made myself a promise to be behind that falling, laughing water with her one day, soon.

My head were filled with such thoughts, so it ain't no surprise that I didn't see the Indians. But Master Doc didn't neither. We wasn't expecting to come up on no Indians 'cause that land were Dakota Sioux land, and we knowed they was all still in they winter camp over by the lake, fishing, 'cause that be one of the best ways a Indian feed hisself when the snows makes the trapping too hard. 'Course, Master Doc didn't give a hoot about whose trapping ground it were—we wasn't trapping, we was hunting something else altogether: ergot, a kind of mold what grows sometimes on the winter grasses. He collected it for folks like Captain Scott what suffered from headaches so bad they hammered him right down like a floor board.

So I was walking amongst these grasses, spying for the mold—it only grows on the sick grasses. Master Doc was mounted, looking down from his saddle, and neither one of us seed the Indians till we nearly stepped on them. Not Dakota, Chippewa—we didn't know them and they didn't know us. And out there on the plains, well, you couldn't never know about strange Indians. You hear stories that one day a band invite a group of settlers to eat with them, yet on another day they might scalp somebody else, and you never knowed why one and not t'other. Also, Master Doc were in uniform, and the way the Army was out there, you never knowed whether the Indians might have a good knowing of the Army or possibly be keen on revenge.

Anyways, we was facing a score of men, women, and children, a passel of ponies and a pack of rangy dogs. They all was carrying they belongings, moving from they winter spot, looking to choose a new spring camp. So here's all these people and animals, yet they stood still as a fencepost and quieter'n a rock pile. They was waiting just on the other side of a low rise where me and Master Doc was hunting ergot, and when we crested the rise, a small rustle went through the crowd of them, but nobody spoken a word. I couldn't tell iffen there be a chief amongst them. Master Doc raised his hand in greeting, also to show he wasn't gonna reach for his sidearm. I done likewise, 'course I didn't carry no weapon. We was standing nearest what looked to be a family: a man and woman and four young'ns. The littlest of these, a chap no older'n four, I'd say, quick as lightning shot over by Master Doc and placed his little hand flat on Master's foot—Master Doc always did wear the finest boots, had them sent special from the East. That boy squatted down there, patting the thick, shiny leather of his boot.

Well, the mother sucked in her breath and put a step forward, but the father held her back. He didn't move from the spot he was standing on, but his right hand went to his waist and rested on the handle of a knife he had there. I seed it clear, and I believe Master Doc did, too, but he didn't let on. With a speed that were amazing for a man his size, he scooped that boy up and set him high atop his shoulders. The father drawed his knife but now the mother held back the father. She heared the laughter in her boy's whoop and seed that big-tooth smile of Master Doc.

I was mighty impressed by that. All my life I'd been polishing the trick of not making white folk scared, and succeeding mainly 'cause I's small. Yet there be Master Doc, a mountain of man, and he done learned a way to show the might of hisself and not make folk nervous, as iffen he was a bear what come and laid at your feet with its stomach to the sky.

Weren't long 'fore we was swapping with them, the whole time with that little chap up on Master Doc's shoulders. 'Cept for a few Indian words Master Doc knowed, we did all our talking in motions. They come to understand Master were a medicine man, and seems they had a good knowing of white medicine. The father of this little chap had a daughter with scurvy, and he let Master Doc take a look at her. She was as weak all over as the loose teeth in her mouth. Her gums was bloody and there was bruises along her arms and legs. Was our luck that Master Doc be carrying some spignot root with him, and he showed the mother how to make a tea with that, tell her to do it with every meal. Tell her to give it to all the young'ns. Afterwards they tried giving him a nice pipe, but Master Doc showed them the bit of ergot he had, and they was real happy to show us where to find a big patch.

Now, the best part of this whole thing was Master Doc figured we'd better go down to Major T.'s and tell him some strange Chippewa be in the area. Even though they was friendly to us, you never could be sure what might happen iffen they meet up with some Dakota.

I was overjoyed: I was gonna see Harriet again! I was sure 'nough ready. All through them winter weeks, I whittled a necklace for that gal—shaped small, wooden beads and stringed them together with a single, glassy chunk of amber at the center. It were always in my pocket, I polished them beads every chance I got. So whilst Master and Major T. talked inside the Agency, I seeked out Harriet and found her with a washing tub out by the well.

Suddenly I was tongue-tied. I opened my mouth and nothing come out. She giggled and ducked her head. I figured I looked pretty stupid, so I clapped my jaw tight. Then, not even knowing what I was doing, I seed I was holding out the necklace to her.

Her cheeks bunched up like polished chestnuts, and she took the necklace, also not saying nothing. Slipped it over her head and left her hand over her breast, resting on that chunk of amber, and she looked at me with them clear, sparkling eyes. I was about to burst like a butterbean in the hot sun till she turned and ran to the house, leaving me tottering on weakened knees. But she come back out right quick, her smile still bright. She come back to me and reached deep into her apron and pulled out a set of bones—clapping bones, squared off and buffed up. She handed them to me and all she said was, "'Cause you clapped so fine when we sung 'Johnny Brown.'"

I took it as the best kind of sign that Harriet's first gift to me was bones. I can't rightly say what them bones meant to me, 'specially since I done lost the set Gran gave me. I never lost Harriet's, though. I got them bones still. Used to bring them out to beat time for our own little gals as they growed and played they own ring games. And

Harriet's got the necklace still. Keeps it safe put away, says she's gonna give it over to Eliza when Eliza decides to take herself a husband.

Harriet and me started together as a couple right that moment, each of us knowing that the other done spent all them winter weeks thinking on the other. From that moment I begun to think of her as "my Harriet." I courted her throughout the spring, sharing the ways of the griot, telling her all about Gran and a small boy named Dred. She compassionated my worries over Gran. She helped me keep alive the hope that Gran was well—either in Alabama or finally over home, with our kin. I told Harriet about the griots and the warrior women. My Harriet just couldn't get enough of them old African tales. She come from V'ginia, too, but her people had no recollection of Africa. She loved my stories, and I loved holding her in my arms and telling them.

Master Doc and Major T. was right obliging enduring our courting, and the whole fort was helping me out, too, 'cause there was very little sickness that spring, so I had more free time to be riding out to the Agency. I'd help Harriet finish her work and we'd go off picnicking in the fairy circles.

Iffen you never been on the plains, you ain't never seed a fairy circle: a perfect round patch of grass, lush like velvet, soft as a feather bed. Some be no bigger'n a maple trunk, others wide as a house. Nobody knows why they grows that way. Indians say it's 'cause of the rolling of the buffalo what likes to scratch they hides on the ground, but I's happy believing it be fairies. There's magic out there on the plains, sure 'nough. There be playful, happy spirits living in the water and in the earth. And on a rare occasion at night you might catch them fairies floating on air, playing with the lights in the night sky.

I seed them lights for the first time on my wedding night. Master Doc let us camp out by Minnehaha for a couple of days, right after the ceremony, and it were our wedding night when the lights come shimmering in the sky: pale yellow, then green and blue, moving like a curtain in the breeze. So there we was, me and my Harriet, newly wed, stretched out on a prairie circle, with those fairy lights shifting softly over us.

I was holding my Harriet in my arms, our hearts beating the same beat, seemed like the dazzle burst right out of us like shooting stars. All our joy just bust out and floated up there for all the world to see, and the onliest thing that could pull my eyes away from the marvel in the sky was the marvel in my arms, the shifting, curving softness of Harriet, my aurora, pulling me into her light.

My heart fills now, recollecting them days. Her years done doubled since then. She ain't a gal and she don't laugh as often. We been raising up our gals and fighting in the courts. Life has growed more serious. But she still be my Harriet.

My Harriet be quenching rain. She be the rush of the river finding the sea. The purr in a kitten's throat. The prance of a new colt's spindly legs. Harriet be the surprise of a rainbow. The ooze of juice dribbling down my chin from a ripe peach. The knowing that cradles my heart. She be the pop in roasting corn. The flicker in the flame. The weave in the basket. Harriet be the tremble in my voice when I sings a long note. My first sight each day and my last touch 'fore sleep.

Harriet be a story that I never wants to end.

Chapter twenty

Bonded

Harriet and me got us a writ-on-paper, set-down-in-the-books, legal marriage. Most slaves won't get that. Best most slaves gets is the master reading some words and a hop over the broom. Why? 'Cause a master don't want his slaves having nothing official. Them official papers belongs in the white man's satchel, and a black man with papers might get it in his head he's due something. Might start thinking he got a certain right to a bond what shouldn't be broken, and nobody should be selling off his wife and babies.

Sure 'nough that's the thought me and Harriet be thinking when we seed Major T. was gonna give us that legal marriage. See, at the time we wed, Major T. owned Harriet and, like I done said, he was a man of high principle. He also was the official man, the justice of the peace. Believed in official marriage, believed in doing things proper betwixt a man and woman—didn't matter if they was white, black, or Indian. Many white trappers would marry Indian women, and Major T. talked most of them into a legal marriage, just 'cause it were the right and proper thing to do.

So when Harriet accepted me to be her husband, next I gone to Master Doc to ask his permission. He was happy for me, yet he named the problem straight out. "What're you planning on, Dred?" he asked. "You thinking on having an abroad marriage?"

I said no I wasn't. I told him direct I wanted my wife living beside me every day, and I was hoping him and Major T. would strike a deal, that one of them would take both of us.

"I sure am used to you, Dred," he said. "You're my little fella. I wouldn't want to give you up now. Let's go see if Major Taliaferro will sell Harriet."

That's when I learned Major T. taken a particular interest in Harriet's choice of husband. He had a soft spot for her 'cause she done been his babies' nursemaid back in V'ginia, and when they all come to the frontier, she watched over them young'ns careful as iffen they was her own. Lucky for me he liked our match. He seed I was kindly in my dealings and apt in healing. "Let the good doctor and myself discuss the details," he told me. "You help Harriet bring in the washing, and we'll have an answer for you directly."

Harriet was so excited she was dancing. She grabbed my arms and swung me round. "Honeysweet," she said, "I'ma have a dowry to give you, the best dowry you can dream of." I was laughing with her, not knowing yet why till she explained how Major T. long ago promised her that iffen she marry somebody upright, with prospects, that he would free her on her wedding day. Well, I swept that gal up off her feet and twirled her round till we was both dizzy. We was full up on joy and so excited, 'cause even iffen I wasn't free, so long as Harriet was, our children would be free, too.

When we brung in the washing, Missus T. gived us the glad tidings. "We'll miss you, dear," she said to Harriet, and we knowed it were all set for Harriet to be with me at the fort. Since we was all together there, Master Doc said we might as well do the wedding right away. Major T. agreed, but first he had to settle a argument betwixt some settlers and some Indians, something about some stolen livestock. Major T. done a lot of that kind of work, and he were good at it. Even when he knowed the Indians done stole and killed and ate the settlers' stock, he compassionated they hunger and how they hunting grounds was shrinking. Sometimes he would bend his high principles and pretend not to know they stole. Harriet told me there was times he paid settlers outten his own pocket, just to keep the bucket balanced.

By the time Major T. come back, ready to marry us, Missus T. done made the parlor all pretty with summer flowers, and Major T. said the words over us right there at his own hearth. They was words he done read a hundred times—fact, he didn't read them, just recited them. Yet I felt they was fresh writ for us, 'cause it spoken what were in my heart: to stay together and do for each other till the end of our days, no matter sick nor well, no matter rich nor poor, no matter good times nor bad. We swore by that, and Harriet near about cut the flow of blood to my hand, she was squeezing it so tight. Finally we marked our names in Major T.'s official book. I done mine first and I don't write, so I made my x. Harriet, she could read and write some, and she knowed her name, but she marked a x, too. She said she be taking my name, so it should be writ the same.

Missus T. hugged Harriet and gived everybody sweet punch. We clinked our glasses and Major T. wished us happiness and Master Doc wished us health. The young'ns was skipping round, singing a song for us and tossing the flowers. Then Master Doc said, "As a wedding present, I'm giving you two days off to go enjoy a honeymoon. Major Taliaferro will loan the horses, and you can take my camping gear."

He must've seed the surprise on my face, 'cause he laughed and said, "As long as you give me your word to be back in two days—I'll be back here myself then, and we can all return to the fort together."

So that's how Harriet and me got our honeymoon. We played in Minnehaha's laughing waters, and we dreamed beneath them northern lights. Looking up at them breathtaking lights, Harriet said, "Them lights be like our joy today, and that'll fade. But my love for you be like them stars—it will never die out."

We had a magical two days, and then we did return to the fort, stopping at the Agency just long enough to pack up Harriet's few belongings. 'Fore we left the Agency, Harriet spoken up, soft-like. "Should I have a paper about my freedom?" she asked.

Major T. got tight-lipped for a moment, and I seed a flush crawl up his neck and face. We should've knowed right then something smelled like wormy meat, but we was awful confused, by his words and by our sudden tumble from joy to worriment. "I wish I weren't the one to have to explain this to you, Harriet," he begun. "You see, Dr. Emerson and I discussed this—it seems that by marrying a slave, well, that changes things. The, uh, the convention in the territories, this territory—especially when the Army is involved—that is, the way things are typically done…is that when a free woman and a slave man marry, then the woman goes to work for her husband's master. In the Army."

My eyes and my heart was scraping the floor, but Harriet's eyes never quivered. She was trying to read him, trying to understand how this come about, but Major T. was turned to the window and wasn't facing her direct. "Then I's still a slave?" she asked.

"Actually, you'll be a bondswoman." He turned round finally, speaking fast like a boy justifying hisself before the switch falls. "I've already discussed all this with Dr. Emerson—really, he's the one that should be explaining this. Anyway, he will keep you both in bondage for the time being, but he promised me that he will let you buy yourselves out."

I wanted to speak out, to say something to change things back to right. Then with a tone that clutched my heart Harriet asked, "I got to buy my freedom now?"

"Yes, but that's a good thing—this way, Dred also has the hope to be free one day. Dr. Emerson's being very generous," he said. He must've seed plain on our faces we felt no generosity, but he pressed on. "Dr. Emerson will hire you out as servants; you'll work for so much per day, or per week. I'm sure you've seen this sort of thing before. Not everyone can afford to own slaves, so it works to the benefit of all: for those who can't afford a slave, they hire one when needed. There are lots of officers at the fort who don't have slaves, but their wives still need servants. So Dr. Emerson will arrange who you work for, and he'll collect the money, and each week he will set aside a sum that will be payment toward Dred's price."

Major T. still be the onliest one smiling. Harriet and me was grum. Now I did open my mouth to speak, if only to say it weren't right, but Harriet stopped me with a light hand. She moved a step closer to the Major, looking up to his face. "We's gonna work for wages, but the Doctor's gonna keep the money?" she repeated, making sure that's what he meant.

"Look," he said, sounding peeved now, "the most important thing, surely, is that you get to be free some day. Isn't that what you want? Dr. Emerson promised me that you will be allowed to buy your freedom someday, and when you do, you will only have to pay Dred's price. Once you save enough to buy Dred, then he will grant both of you your freedom."

Harriet looked a little brighter, but not much. "And our children?" she asked.

"The same will apply to whatever children you have. At the time Dred's price is attained, you and any children will be free. It's a very good deal. You will all be a family and you will all be free. I secured Dr. Emerson's word on that."

There wasn't nothing else to be said or done. We returned to the fort, and it looked to be that what Major T. said were true, 'cause Master Doc didn't keep me for his assistant much no more. Since there weren't no real fighting betwixt the Army and the Indians, he handled the hospital hisself. I only went with him when he went out to the tribes, inoculating and such. Other times, me and Harriet worked for folks at the fort, mostly the officers and they wives. We never seed no money—he kept our wages—but he said he was regular putting aside a dollar a week toward me paying off my price: fifty cents from Harriet's earnings and fifty cents from mine. He said it'd take about ten year, but then we'd be free. He said.

We said "yes, sir" and "thank you, sir," but alone in our room we was talking it over. I wasn't feeling no more like "almost free"—I was feeling like freedom were a pretty dream and now I was cold awake.

"We could run," I said. "Try for Canada. We as far north now as we likely to get without running on."

Harriet didn't want to run, though. The Indians, the Army, the trappers, and the winters all scared her. 'Sides, I was fast learning my Harriet were a person of high principle, like Major T. She felt beholden to Major T., seeing's how he made a deal with Master Doc. She reckoned I ought to feel some loyalty to Master Doc, as well.

"Master Doc's fine enough for a white man," I said, "but he owns me. And Major T.—well, didn't he go back on a promise he done made you? I already in my life made the mistake of overtrusting a master, I don't want to see you do the same."

Harriet's neck got stiff and she tilted her head. "My life ain't your life. I married you, I joined my life to you, but your mistakes ain't my mistakes. I know Major T. He couldn't help the way things be done in the Army."

It were our first argument. I could see it how she seed it, but I just couldn't feel it the same. In the end, howsomever, I wasn't sure enough about running to keep the argument hot. "Honeycomb," I said, "you may be right. As my Gran would've said, if you abandon your own hill, the next hill you climb is sure to crumble."

⁂

John Emerson knew it was wrong to regard his slave as a companion, yet he had grown accustomed to the daily presence of his "little fella." Now that Dred was bonded out, days at the fort seemed much duller without Dred's banter and his stories, and the doctor looked forward to the times they would still ride out together to an Indian village. The previous week they had stopped off in the village of Kaposia, where the "lithe people" lived under Chief Little Crow. When Dred had asked what "lithe" meant, John Emerson responded, "It's how they move, like everything's a dance."

Dred, thinking of Gran dancing, had nodded and replied, "If the rest of us was birds, I reckon the Dakota would be fish."

They had inoculated two dozen Dakota that day, and Emerson smiled, recalling how he and Dred joined in a game with a gang of boys who were chasing a skunk, pretending it was a wily Chippewa brave. The youngsters had bows and arrows without spear-tips, and when one boy managed to strike the skunk with his blunt arrow, his triumphant crowing turned to a howl of dismay as he took the full brunt of the skunk's countermeasure. Rubbing the boy down with wild sage to help dilute the stink, Dred commented, "You fired on the varmint, son, and the varmint fired back."

Of course, he still saw Dred daily, but the slave now spent most of his hours working for others, and his sparse free time was devoted to his new bride. When Emerson did find himself with Dred, Harriet was usually there, too—and the sight of Dred and Harriet, almost silly in their joy, nettled him. Shouldn't he be happier than his slaves?

The doctor nursed other frustrations, as well. His unremitting requests for transfer were routinely rejected. He began to suspect the Surgeon General harbored a bias against him. He learned through an aide that the S.G. had once said about him, "Men like that are best placed out on the frontier."

Hurt, Emerson puzzled: men like what? Possibly he had offended someone in St. Louis with his concern for Chief Black Hawk and the other Sauk—typically, army officers regarded the Indians as slightly more intelligent than horses, though not as clean or useful. More likely, he reasoned, the S.G. meant he lacked an impressive track record, or didn't have the right connections; but that didn't seem fair. He maintained a good record—not stellar, but steady and positive. So why wasn't he getting promoted? Emerson began to wonder if his prospects would be improved by getting married—it did appear that those advancing most rapidly were married officers.

In October 1837, John Emerson finally received orders to return to Jefferson Barracks. The St. Louis garrison had suddenly lost its surgeon, and Emerson traveled south with high hopes that this temporary assignment might become permanent. He left the Scotts at Fort Snelling to continue hiring out their time, while he looked forward to immersing himself in St. Louis society with the express aim of finding himself a bride.

Yet Emerson was in St. Louis less than a week when he learned that the post had been officially conferred upon a Tennessee doctor, due to arrive at the end of the month. Depressed by the thought of spending another winter in the Wisconsin Territory, he petitioned the Surgeon General in person. At that meeting, his suspicion that the S.G. disliked him was nearly confirmed when the best position he could ultimately obtain—again, temporarily—was to Fort Jesup, Louisiana, along the border with the new Republic of Texas. Santa Ana had been defeated, but the troops stationed to keep the peace were now embattled by malaria, a constant problem for an infantry that was busy clearing logjams and other impediments to navigation on the Sabine River, where the Army aimed both to increase mobility and to decrease the high freighting costs required to supply the fort.

Emerson didn't care whether freighting costs on the river were six cents a pound or two, but he came to be grateful for the increased riverboat traffic because it brought to the lonely frontier outpost Alexander Sanford, a St. Louis iron magnate investigating mining prospects, and his pretty daughter, Eliza Irene—a marriage prospect Emerson decided to mine.

He called her "my little pixy" and strategically commandeered all the free time of the vivacious, Southern belle who seemed younger than her twenty-three years. She responded with giggles to his generous indulgences and coquettishly shimmied like a fish whenever his bearish arm wrapped about her waist or shoulders. Within four months, the two wed, and Emerson immediately summoned Dred and Harriet to Louisiana.

With a deep sense of satisfaction and optimism, the doctor acquainted the slaves with his new bride, stressing that Irene's happiness was now their chief obligation. During Emerson's verbose orientation, Dred remained as silent and wary as he had been that day six years ago when Emerson first introduced himself. Life as Emerson's slave had been better than he might have anticipated back then, yet this new change filled him with foreboding. Missus Irene, Dred was certain, had owned slaves before, and had very fixed ideas about how they should be treated. She queried her husband, right in front of the slaves, as to their fitness. "Are you certain they're healthy? They're awfully small and puny, John. Daddy always looks at their teeth."

John Emerson was oblivious to the silent groundwork being laid between his wife and slaves. To him, groundwork was being laid for his future. He felt he had accomplished a great deal in marrying. Order and opportunity were being harnessed. He and Irene would live the life he felt he was born to lead. When he retired from the Army, he would have connections and a sterling reputation. He would carry on a small, private practice, mostly to sustain important relationships in the community, relationships enriched by his father-in-law's liaisons. He would buy land and build a stately plantation house for Irene, one worthy of the Virginia elegance she had known growing up. Their house would be filled with children, and he would acquire more slaves to work the land. Dred could resume working as his assistant, and Harriet could help Irene run the household. It was a sublimely balanced equation.

Chapter twenty-one

Down South

Harriet and me was down South again, and we knowed it. We steamboated downriver from Snelling, saying farewell to our bright, northern lights. The more south we traveled, the uglier the sky become. That spring of '38 were a mean one, and once we reached the Red River and split off for Natchitoches, we hit storm upon storm. Betwixt the gales and high waters, I was certain we was gonna be pitched into the river.

We finally made it to the fort, howsomever, and if New Orleans be the jewel of Loosiana, Fort Jesup be a hunk of ore. Life there was rough and low, full of folk what'll roll in the dirt laughing at the misery of another creature. Soldiers acting worser'n the bandits they supposed to be keeping from crossing the border. Officers bad as the rest, looking to fill they own pockets. Master Doc, though, ris above that. Possibly 'cause he had his hands too full of doctoring to be meddling with trouble. I went back to assisting him, and I learned our work had little to do with wounds and injuries. Fort Jesup's main malady, worser even than malaria, be the syphilis. Half the soldiers down there got the chancres or the scars from the chancres. Nasty. I seed enough of that specifical sickness to last me a lifetime, though I was only there a few months.

Sure 'nough, it were the end of the honeymoon for me and my Harriet. We got separated down there. I worked in the fort with Master Doc, and Harriet tended our new Missus. They was separate, too, with Master required to stay in the barracks, yet Missus Irene wouldn't even set foot inside the fort. I rarely seed eyeball-to-eyeball with that woman, but this was one time when she had my full understanding, 'cause it were rough living. So she stayed with her in-laws, the Bainbridges, which is how she met Master Doc in the first place.

Harriet heared all about it from the scullery maid: said old Mr. Bainbridge throwed a ball in honor of Missy Irene's sister, what married one of the Bainbridge boys. But Missy Irene, jealous of her sister marrying 'fore her, ruint the party. That gal stirred up a commotion in the pantry, dallying with the surgeon from the fort—sure 'nough, Master Doc! After that, old Mr. Bainbridge and old Mr. Sanford talked in private with the fort commander, and they made it Master Doc's duty to be that gal's constant escort.

Master Doc gived me a slightly different story, saying as how her daddy liked him so much he requested that Master Doc spend all his free time with Missy Irene. But I done seed Master and Mr. Sanford together, and since them two don't have no tender feelings betwixt them, I cleave to Harriet's story. Don't matter, though. Marrying were what Master Doc wanted all along. I's pretty certain he went down there with every notion of getting hitched.

He wasn't married in the same sense as me and Harriet, though. Oh, he got his official paper, all right, but he was as glad to have the paper as to have the wife. He was content to live at the fort whilst his new bride lived at the big house. Not me. I missed Harriet something fierce, 'specially considering on how she be pregnant. Sure 'nough, we was gonna have our first l'il "*hokshiyokope.*" That's the Sioux word for baby—a good word, by my lights, 'cause it's long and complexicated. "Baby" be just too bitsy a word for when it comes to talking about your own first young'n.

Anyways, I felt a powerful need to be by my Harriet's side yet I couldn't—unlessen Master Doc got leave from the fort, which weren't often. So I snuck off when I could, until the summer rolled by and the malaria cases was just a few. I got away more often, and Master Doc knowed iffen I was gone one night, I'd make up the work the next.

At the Bainbridge plantation, Harriet and me shared a pallet in the cabin of a slave family there, god-fearing folk, which Harriet liked, though we didn't get to knowing them too close. I don't mind saying it were like they spoken a different language. I catched on better'n Harriet did—maybe 'cause I recollected some of how Lucy used to talk—so I was all the time translating what they said to Harriet. She never did get the hang of that Creole stuff. First time I snuck off from the fort to see her, I asked her how she be eating, and iffen the baby liked the vittles. "The food's good," she said, patting her tummy, "but don't you go in this river—they eats a lot of 'croffish beast,' what live in the river. Croffish this, croffish that—they eats so much of it, there must be a whole mess of them beasts in there." I didn't know what she be talking about till they offered me some, and then I explained to Harriet how it were just crayfish bisque, and we had us a good laugh together.

It always be hard at first, fitting in with a group of slaves what already works together, and the deeper South you go, the more true that is. Slaves everywheres keeps a delicate balance, and new folk—white or black—upsets that. New folk got to be worked in as slow as adding flour to a sauce, so it don't get lumpy.

Everything was hardest on Harriet, being pregnant: the traveling, being separated, getting used to a new Missus. Missus Irene talked to us like we pieces of furniture with ears and hands. She was young and pretty, but she surely didn't know much about running things. It wasn't that she was stupid, 'cause she wasn't. She just didn't seem to look ahead. She'd go and tell Harriet to iron a dress, then tell her to pack it up, never minding how it were going to need ironing all over again when it were unpacked. Once or twice Harriet spoken up, to say something like, "Iffen you's going to pack this dress, Missus, wouldn't you druther I ironed it fresh when we gets where we going?" Took only one or two slaps 'fore Harriet stopped saying much at all to that woman.

So we was lumps of flour stuck in Missus Irene's sauce. Nothing we could do to make things right or smooth. And she hated seeing Harriet pregnant, though I doubt I'll ever understand why. Seemed like just for spite she'd make Harriet stand in wait—sometimes to hold a light whilst she read, but just as many times Harriet never knowed what she were kept waiting for. Missus make her stand there till her ankles about swole to the size of pumpkins.

You can't know what it feels like to be a man and see your woman abused like that. 'Specially when she carrying your baby. Harriet tried to dodge Missus much as she could, and she found a friend in the scullery maid, Sally. Sally so compassionated Harriet's predicament she took on some of Harriet's chores, just so Harriet could rest. 'Specially toward the end of that summer, when the baby be big and low in Harriet's belly.

Thank goodness the old Surgeon General finally answered Master's letters. Master wrote nearly every week asking for assignment back in St. Looey. He complained up a storm: the malaria was licked; his land up in Iowa were going to wrack and ruin; the weather be bad for his new bride—she needed dry air. His letters was a avalanche, and finally he wore down that Surgeon General. Got orders to move out—'cepting it were only back to Fort Snelling, not St. Looey.

We stayed down there at Fort Jesup just six months, and it were six months too long. Loosiana's damp and its poor effect on Missus Irene come to be the onliest thing me and Harriet liked about the place! Leaving, Harriet said, "I's sure glad to be leaving the South behind." The pity of it were, Irene Emerson carried the South with her.

We all left Natchitoches on the steamboat Gypsey, late in September 18'n38, bound for Fort Snelling. On the way up we docked five days in St. Looey, visiting with old Mr. Sanford. Missus Irene be like a butterfly, flitting from one gathering to the next, drunk with the well-wishing and glad-handing, the presents and the hullabaloo. She was outten the house on so many visits that it were a blessing for Harriet, whose birthing time was coming closer and closer. Finally Missus said a tearful goodbye to her daddy, and we all continued upriver. We got up above where Fort Armstrong used to be when our little Eliza decided to join us.

I'll never forget a single second of that night, starting with the Missus reading her Bible, making my Harriet stand over her with a lamp, snapping at her for swaying even though the whole boat were tipped to and fro like a rocking horse. I knowed my Harriet be feeling mighty low, mighty heavy with the baby, and the best I could do was go to Master—he be playing cards and not much caring about nobody else. I suggested how the time be right for a toddy, knowing how he loved the way Harriet fixed up a toddy. Then I fixed the drinks myself in the galley whilst Harriet sat and rested on her berth. That were good for a short spell, but all too soon Missus had Harriet back holding the lamp, and I swear that woman knowed she was inflicting agony on my Harriet.

It tore at me, seeing my wife used that way—set me back in my mind to the time Lucy was having her hair shorn in the stable, and me hiding there in a stall, hearing her torment. Well, I was a man now, not a boy. I went back to Master Doc to explain how close Harriet be to birthing, how she couldn't be standing for hours, holding Missus's light. It got him all red and bothered—he throwed his cards down and spoken harsh to me—but he went and talked to his wife, telling her I would hold her lamp.

Hours later when I went to bed, Harriet was so miserable she couldn't speak nary a word. Just curled up under her blanket and let me kind of cradle her and rock her and rub her feet in betwixt the pangs. I could feel the baby inside her, restless and ready to take air. A short while 'fore midnight, Harriet begun to moan. My rocking and rubbing wasn't helping no more, and I felt as useless as a water bucket with no bottom. Harriet was sweet, though: many women would just shut out the world, but she held tight to my hand and said, "Dred, this be the time. Our first baby child is ready to come meet you. Don't you be scared now."

Well, I was scared, plenty scared. Seeing the pain on her face, with rememory of all the women I done seed over the years with Master Doc what done died in birthing, with knowing my own mama passed over when I was born. And none of them was delivered on a tossing boat, handled rough by that great Muddy Mississipp'. Sure 'nough, I was plenty scared. At a time like that, I wager any man'd be willing to swap the life of his baby iffen only his wife be all right. I was scared, too, for me—for what this baby was gonna need from me. Was I gonna be enough?

Watching Harriet's pain build, fear and worriment growed in me till she said, "We's gonna need some help, Dred," and I runned to fetch Master Doc. He was still playing cards, but this time there was no harsh words. He was a man born to be a doctor. He be a doctor first 'fore everything else, and I will be grateful even in my grave that he got up as quick as iffen it be his own wife. He tended to my Harriet that night, tended to our little baby, in that cabin that was rocking along the mighty Mississip', and I will never forget that kindness.

Harriet's labor stretched out through sunup. I paced up and down, worrying. I heared a seagull cackle and had to shake the shiver outten my spine. Them seagulls be nasty birds what eats the garbage and the leavings, a bird no better'n a vulture, just whiter.

Harriet was sweating and trying not to scream. I was sweating and trying not to scream. It were gray daybreak when finally, with a whoosh, out come the baby and we both laughed and cried, with the baby's cry louder'n us, like we was all singing the same song. Master Doc was flashing them white teeth and clapping me on the shoulder, and I was full up with tears and wonderment that left no room for my fears. I joined Harriet on the bunk, wrapping my arms about her and the baby. There was that smell in the room of birthing what usually pinched my nostrils, but this time the smell was somehow familiar and right. It were the smell of my own baby gal, and I drunk it down like wine. The three of us was a family. For the first time in my life, I was part of a whole, complete family.

Master Doc was pleased with hisself. "Mother and child are fine," he laughed. He was standing, his shadow falling across the three of us, and he said, "This is wonderful! Everything's looking bright. I'll leave you all now and go tell Irene we have a little girl."

He was gone, but his words shadowed over us like he was still there. Me and Harriet both felt the sweat on our skins go chill, and we shivered till the baby begun to cry again. Neither of us said nothing. Harriet tried nursing the baby. I watched this beautiful tiny gal with a face just like Harriet's fumble at the breast, and Harriet patient-like guiding that little mouth. I done expected my fear would dry up when the baby come out, but my stomach flipped over thinking how my wife and child needed my protection. Master done said "We have a little girl," and the fear were sitting on my chest like a anvil.

The baby fell quiet and suckled. Harriet cradled her, humming soft:

Mary, what you call your pretty little baby
...mmm-mmmm...mmm-mmmm
Some call him one thing, I'll call him Jesus
...mmm-mmmm...mmm-mmmm

I knowed that song, but I didn't want to sing it 'cause Master Doc's words done made it plain: we didn't know what she'd be called, and we knowed we wasn't the ones to get to choose, neither. A trapped feeling begun building in me, and when Harriet gave the baby over to me—so small and warm and trembly—I near fell to my knees holding that child, thinking: how will I keep my baby gal safe?

Harriet must've seed the fear on me, and she gentled me the way you do a horse: handling the fears and jitters one by one; first just the smell of the leather headstall, then the sound of the bit when it clanks, then the touch of it, and on and on until you can throw on a saddle and finally sit atop that beast and begin to get somewhere. She gentled me, giving me the smell and sound and touch of my own fears yet leading me straight on.

She talked of how much we already loved this little baby, and how we was gonna raise her up with all the loving from both our lives. She talked of Gran and the strength of our kin. "This be our baby gal," she said. "No master nor missus neither gonna change that. I'd druther die and go to hell with my baby in my arms than ever let it be otherways."

From outside come the moan of the wind, and I heared Gran's voice telling the story of her mother, Njeri. For the first time I full understood Njeri's mothering. I full understood how the dark waters of the Endless Lake was the onliest and best protection she could offer her babies in a world where the white man claims your very name.

My tiny baby gal looked at me then, right in my eyes, and I recollected a morning when I was just a boy. I opened my eyes and told Gran I done seed them baby twins in a dream, and it were nice, like they come to play with me. "Twins," she told me, "be special. They can come and go in this life when they want, and Njeri knowed this. Njeri took comfort knowing them babies could come back if they wanted. I think in your dream, they wanted to come back to be with you."

I looked back at my baby gal, looked deep down through her eyes, wondering if them twins, one or both of them, done come back. "Let's us give her a African name," I said. "Her secret name, what we'll tell her when she's growed."

Harriet smiled at me bright and beautiful, just like them northern lights. "You recollects one?" she asked. "A special one?"

"Nzinga," I said. "From the water."

"Nzinga," Harriet crooned, kissing the sweet crown of our sweet baby's head. "Nzinga, born on the river."

"River running North," I said, hugging my baby close to my chest, and it were as close as I ever come to praying.

Chapter twenty-two

Battle Lines

On a small scale, you could liken me and Harriet's troubles with Missus Irene to the warfare betwixt the Dakota and the Chippewa. And Master Doc be like the fort—there to keep the peace yet blinkered to the mischief brewing. A whole mess of trouble were going on at Snelling when we returned in the autumn of '38. First was a bunch of new settlers what wasn't 'biding by the law against trafficking liquor amongst the Indians. Next some Dakota got liquored up and went pouncing on some Chippewa bands. Finally come Major Plimpton, inviting to the fort the Chippewa chief, Hole-in-the-Day, to talk him into not striking back. But the Major acted kind of dim-eyed and overlooked clearing it with Major T. or the Dakota, resulting in Hole-in-the-Day and his braves getting ambushed right outside the fort.

Well, Major Plimpton no sooner gets the guilty Dakota braves punished when a small band of Chippewa retaliates against the Dakota, this time using the fort as a sort of HQ for the counterattack—and Major Plimpton was blinkered to that, as well. He should've seed it coming, and Major T. about bust his spleen over it all. He was hot as stove iron and yelled at Major Plimpton that instead of cooling the hotheads, he was bellowing the fires.

That's how I's saying it were with Master Doc. Instead of helping things betwixt us and the Missus, he made them worser, mostly by acting blinkered to the truth. Now, I ain't leaking no sympathy for Missus Irene, I's just stating a fact: she was a unhappy woman, and we bore the brunt of that. She regretted leaving her papa's fine house for the rugged fort life. Regretted leaving her brother and sisters and missed having them to baby her. Regretted leaving her girlhood for a man what couldn't yet give her the life she wanted. Fact is, once all the hullabaloo and parties was done, her and Master Doc didn't suit each other. And I believe she resented how me and Master Doc got along easy. She whined that he spent too much time with me. I believe that's why she taken the notion we be stealing from her.

It's a certain truth that most everywheres you go, a white woman what's angry against her husband will take it out on the slaves. And the husband don't want to draw his wife's heat, so he lets her abuse go unchecked. So it were me and Harriet against Missus Irene, only me and Harriet counted things different on this score. Onliest times me and Harriet spatted was over that woman's treatment.

See, Harriet always looked for the Christian way, even with white folk. Harriet had goodwill, but Missus Irene done trampled all of mine. What I's gonna say maybe sounds mean and low, but a body can't take abuse and lies without bowing under them—you got to find ways to push back and straighten your spine. I pushed back. All the vinegar that woman squeezed out, I collected it up and poured it right back. I matched ambush for ambush.

There be slave ways of reckoning. As a instance, Harriet come upon the Missus pawing through our clothes one day, even l'il Eliza's, looking for hidden pockets. 'Course, she didn't find no hidden pockets 'cause we ain't thieves. But that didn't satisfy her. She begun spitting on all the leftover food, so's we wouldn't take none of it. Well, that be a two-lane road, sure 'nough! Harriet scolded me every time she catched me at it, but I wouldn't stop. Iffen the Missus spit after one meal, I spit 'fore the next one.

Still, Missus accused us outright of thieving. Any time she

266

mislaid something, she come yelling how we's filching from her. I got so tired of it I begun hiding things on her, just to see her fret. Let her rant half the day, then put the thing out in plain sight, so's she'd almost trip over it. Got so's she doubted her own eyes, and inside a month she stopped all that foolishness about stealing.

But there's no winning a war like that. Like the Chippewa and Dakota: you win this battle, you lose the next. Her new line of attack become pulling me offen working for a officer and ordering me to fill her cistern or some such thing, then lie to that same officer that she didn't know where I be, calling me a "lazy nigger." Well that put my boots on and laced them up tight, 'cause it cut into the wages I could earn, stretching out how long it would be 'fore I could buy my freedom. I can't prove nothing but there's no different thoughts to be had about it: Missus purposeful tried to cut into our wages and hold onto us longer than was right.

I complained to Master Doc. He heared me out, then shut the door for a private council with the Missus. When they called me on the rug before them, she laid her larceny on me, shameless, and laughed at my words when I spoken my side. And Master Doc believed her. So 'course, there weren't nothing I could do. It brought Master Doc down a peg or two in my sights, 'cause he be trying to weasel outten the truth. He knowed I didn't scuffle round, that my backbone was bent toward getting my family free. He just wouldn't brook no argument with his wife.

It sparked me and Harriet to talk a second time of running. This time we both carried a burden of doubt. We had a baby now, it weren't just her and me. Also, I felt tied to that money we already had toted in our favor toward buying freedom—we had four year of labor put into it by that time. I asked Master Doc and he said he reckoned we done had about two hundred dollars by then. I figured by me working extra, maybe I could make our price in another four year. This time we didn't argue. Harriet and me both agreed to wait, and right soon things changed in our favor so as to look like maybe I could do that extra labor.

In 18'n40, Master Doc got hisself sent to Florida, to help put down the Seminoles. He didn't want me along on this trip, didn't think it'd be for long. I was mighty glad for it, 'cause I seed Master Doc's leaving as a solid opportunity to quicken my pace toward freedom. I'd have less work from him and could hire out more of my time to others at the fort. Sure, the Missus kept on ambushing us whilst he was gone, but it were two against one now. She had nobody else taking her side or backing her up, 'cause me and Harriet was on better terms with most the fort people than the Missus was. I was certain I could get them to give me that extra work and see that Master Doc got the record of it. According to my lights, with Master Doc gone there were one less rock to clear outten the way of where I be plowing.

I was sowing my dreams into my labor, sure 'nough. No matter I was a slave—my dreams was bigger and brighter than those of my Master and Missus, whose hopes and dreams was so stunted they didn't allow for the big changes like I be planning. I was looking to jiggle and shake my world. I was looking to reap freedom. I seed that as my opportunity and my responsibility. Everything about me had one aim: to get free. 'Cause now I had a wife, a partner, a whole person walking beside me every step of the journey. I had a new child in my life. I had the love and trust of my family. I had the responsibility for my baby's laughter and my wife's peaceful sleep. Everything I did mattered.

⁂

Nothing mattered. John Emerson slumped down upon the smooth-sheeted hospital bunk, making a deep depression in the taut, white linens. It was the last time he would lie there. Today his discharge had been made official and tomorrow he would return to St. Louis, to his wife, to civilian life. He worried about his prospects for re-establishing a creditable medical practice in the face of the rumors. Even if Irene remained discreet about the scene she believed she had witnessed during her visit with him, there seemed no way he could stifle the gossip about the hospital funds. He had managed to avoid a dishonorable discharge, but the investigation into his culpability with the missing funds was now a matter of record. One or the other scandal was bound to spread like a sickness. Lying on his back, he covered his eyes with his arm and tried not to think about his disgrace.

268

As a young man fresh out of medical school, he thought he would do such good in the world. Helping and healing, restoring vitality to the vulnerable, he felt superior to powerful men. He was the doctor, second only to God in his abilities to alter life. He had felt pride in healing the troops and the tribes; in being a part of peace negotiations; in contributing to the amazing expansion of a great country.

Reality had humbled him: he had inoculated several hundred Indians, but smallpox wiped out ten thousand in '37. His words had been written into peace treaties, but those treaties were always broken. And the great, expanding United States had shamefully proven its heartless treachery in this Seminole War, time and again. The Dakota will always war with the Chippewa, he thought, as the last dying Seminoles will sustain their desperate ambushes upon the whites, and we all will fall prey to greater powers like God, disease, and the implacable, unreasoning might of the U.S. armed forces.

John Emerson felt old. With his arm still shielding his face, it occurred to him that finally he would get to make St. Louis his home. Ironically, he no longer cared if he ever got back there. He had long since stopped writing letters to the Surgeon General. Nothing mattered. Not even being married or starting a family. He was pretty sure Irene was pregnant. Before she left Florida, she had been experiencing the nausea and abrupt changes in her eating habits. She hadn't let him examine her, though. After she walked in and saw him with the orderly, after she denounced him publicly, she stopped speaking to him altogether, not even saying goodbye when the coach arrived to carry her back to St. Louis. He fervently hoped she would resume speaking to him once he, too, returned to St. Louis; not because he cared about his marriage. Mostly he didn't want to face people and have to make excuses for the contempt she so blatantly exhibited.

With a groan he pushed from memory the scene that had triggered his downfall. He buried his face in the pillow, wishing he had never brought Irene to Florida. After his first year and a half in the desolate swamplands, with an end nowhere in sight, he had longed for companionship, someone to talk to at the end of the day. While home on furlough during Christmastime, he had insisted his wife return with him to the fort. Irene demurred until he spoke of taking Dred back with him instead. Then she consented to make the journey. So he left the slaves in St. Louis and proudly escorted his pretty young wife across half the United States, only to regret the decision before they ever arrived at Fort Pickens. Irene detested the inconveniences of travel. Like him, she found the company of the troops too coarse. In consequence, she clung to her husband, demanding all of his time and attention, only to squander it by complaining.

By the time he had her settled at the fort, he was grateful to accompany the regiment on a mission to roust the "guerrilla" bands of Chief Micanopy, even though it meant marching through the swamps. They spent grueling days slogging through the mire, jittery about being bushwhacked, led by a Seminole scout that no one trusted. After General Jesup's treachery—offering Chief Osceola peace talks, then jailing him—everyone felt nervous about using the Seminole scouts and informants. For three days the regiment trod miles and miles through slime and humidity and mosquitoes, and though they failed to find the enemy, the enemy had not found them, either.

Lying on the bed, Emerson sighed in resignation. The scene would not be denied. It wormed its way back into memory, and he stopped fighting it. He remembered the regiment's return to Ft. Pickens. For most of the troops, it meant they could relax and refresh themselves. For Emerson it meant more work, caring for injuries incurred on the trek and tending to the bedded patients in the hospital. It was after midnight when he finally retired to the "watch room," a small, private hospital room where he had his own bed. Whenever critical cases required constant monitoring, Emerson would sleep in this room rather than return to his own quarters. If he had had Dred with him, he could have left, trusting Dred to summon him in case of an emergency. But Dred was in St. Louis. Only his wife was here, and he actually welcomed the opportunity to sleep away from her. He couldn't bear any more complaints.

Involuntarily Emerson's mind replayed the fateful scene. He rolled onto his side, curling his knees into his chest. As he was now, he had been on his bed then, exhausted from the day's work. Private Mulligan had appeared, offering to bring him hot water and a washcloth. Mulligan was just a boy, with a boy's frightened confusion in the face of brutality. Throughout the whole, barbaric campaign, Emerson had noticed Mulligan's innocence and hesitation, and he had requested him as an orderly. At first, he meant only to save the boy from crueler duties. Yet when the commander corralled the Seminole prisoners into pens unfit for animals—exposed to the harsh Florida sun and left for days without medicine, food, or water—Emerson formed a more conspiratorial bond with the boy. Together they smuggled food and medicine to the captives. Together they managed to administer some small dose of compassion in that callous world.

That night when Mulligan brought the towel dampened in hot water, Emerson did not reach for it. He looked up from the bed, drowsily registering how slender and boyish the orderly was. An unexpected tenderness surged within him, and when Mulligan sat beside him on the bunk to swathe his forehead, Emerson closed his eyes and accepted the comfort. He let his arm fall across the boy's lap and, feeling the well-muscled flesh of the boy's thigh beneath his hand, he again experienced an exquisite vulnerability.

At that moment, Irene walked in. Whatever she intended to say died on her lips. She stared in mute outrage as he removed his hand from between Mulligan's thighs. Emerson might have succeeded in convincing his wife the contact had been harmless, but the boy grew apoplectic with guilty embarrassment. Emerson had had to dismiss him in order to cut short all that gulping and quaking. Then he faced the full brunt of his wife's indignation. She castigated him so loudly that every patient in the hospital heard her accusations.

Thinking back on it, Emerson felt confused and ashamed. He felt he had been treated unfairly—by his wife, and subsequently by his commander. He had done no real harm. He was doing his best to live up to his duties in the midst of a ruthless, rigid, military campaign, yet his one brief, innocent and misunderstood gesture had become the target of redress.

Nothing honorable can survive this war, he thought. My good intentions, my past efforts, my clear record, all count for nothing in

the commander's eyes; and in my own they count for less than nothing. Not because of Mulligan, no; but because I have become a tool
in this cold-blooded operation called "resettlement."

Agitated, Emerson sat up and looked around the room. He
was quite alone. He had never before been so alone. His wife would
not be walking in on him this time. She had returned to St. Louis
three days following the scene with Mulligan. The day after Irene's
departure, Mulligan was transferred out as well. Now he himself was
discharged—honorably, but summarily—thanks to the rumors Irene
had set in motion. However, because no one would come out and say
it plainly, let alone accuse him officially, they had gone snooping for
other grounds to boot him. They found a discrepancy in his records,
and gave him the choice: a court martial or summary discharge. He
accepted the discharge. He knew he didn't stand a chance with a court
martial—even if he successfully argued that the misappropriated hospital funds and supplies were used to help the Indian prisoners, that
would hardly exonerate him in their eyes.

He was packed and ready to leave by first light, but he had no
illusion that he might find sleep before dawn. He stood and looked
down at the impression his body had left on the sheets. The bedding
remained sunken where he had lain. The sheets were wrinkled and
uneven. He stooped and placed his palm on the top sheet; there was
no warmth. With both hands he smoothed the sheets and erased the
impression of his being there.

⁂

Whilst Missus was down in Florida, me and Harriet lived and worked
in the household of Missus Irene's papa, old Alexander Sanford.
When Missus come back we heared all about the flap in Florida
'cause she cried to her papa and she cried to her sisters and she cried
to her brother. When Master Doc come back, he seed we knowed
his shame and he wouldn't look me in the eye much no more. He
was hang-dog. Put me in mind of Gran, like Gran was after we got
to Alabama: shrunken down. I felt sorry for him, 'cause I didn't hold
with what the Missus be saying. Didn't I work aside him all them
years? You get to know somebody, working that close. I didn't hold

with him having misdealings with young men. And as to the stealing, well, I understood his pity on them Indians. He done a good turn but got a bad twist.

By'n by when he taken up writing the Surgeon General again, I was glad for him—thought he was getting back some of his old grit. He felt he had to clear his name and he wanted back into the Army, so he writ to explain how he only used them hospital funds to the benefit of the Indian prisoners, what needed medicine and food. He writ all through '42 and into '43, but by that summer they turned him down flat as a griddlecake. He been skunked, and the stink was sticking.

Him and Missus had they little girl, Henrietta, by then, and he decided to move us all over to his land in Iowa—St. Looey weren't being no more forgiving to him than the Army. That were in the fall, and it were right 'fore Christmas when Master Doc died. Started out with the flux and a slight fever, ended with what he hisself said were blood poisoning. It's the onliest case I ever come across, so I didn't know much about it—just done everything as Master Doc told me. Tried leeching, tried powders, but that big man just wasted down. Inside a month he was gone.

I wasn't over-sad about his leaving this world—on account he proved hisself just a fair-weather friend in the face of Missus Irene's storms. But I sure 'nough come to feel nervous for all them dollars he been setting aside toward my freedom price. 'Fore he died I asked him could I see the dollars. He laughed at me. Flashed them big teeth and said it ain't done that way. Then he showed me a book where it was writ down—all the money me and Harriet earned, next to the bit he set aside toward the price of my freedom. I asked how much was writ down there. He said, "Nearly $400—you're almost there." I asked him how long 'fore I would get all the way there. "A couple of years or so," he answered. Finally I asked, delicate as I could, iffen Missus knowed how to tote these sums—in case. I didn't say in case of what. He flashed them big teeth again and said, "Dred, I surely hope to be there the day you reach $500, but if I'm not, Missus Irene knows what to do." Still that didn't calm my jitters none, and he seed that. Right solemn he put his hand on my shoulder and said, "You've been my little fella, Dred. Don't you worry about a thing. I'll even write it down in my will, so it's plain for everybody to read."

'Course, I never seed his will, and I'll never know whether he writ it down or he didn't. I wouldn't be willing to wager much money one way or t'other. All I know is Master Doc passed and left me and Harriet eyeball to eyeball with the Missus in our war with her, and her next attack were to divide and conquer.

Chapter twenty-three

Casualties

T he horse, moving only its eyes, watched with military dignity while Dred sang and jigged around it. He was cleaning out the stall, stomping a rhythm with his feet, choosing his own words to replace the shout's usual phrasing. His feet scattered the straw as his exuberance mounted, and he sang for his family:

> *How do you do, my dear Harriet*
> *How do you do, how do you do*
> *How do you do, l'il Eliza*
> *How do you do, how do you do*
> *I don't come to worry your patience*
> *I just come to bring jubilation*
> *How do you do, baby Joe, how do you do.*

Dred was happier than he had been for weeks. Harriet was coming. In the three long months since Master Doc's death, the Scotts had been separated because Irene Emerson had hired out Dred to her brother-in-law, Henry Bainbridge, at Jefferson Barracks; but she retained Harriet and Eliza with her in St. Louis. It was the longest separation Dred and Harriet had endured. Each felt the other's absence acutely, especially since Harriet was pregnant again. As her time to deliver drew near, Dred's anxiety peaked. He explained to Captain Bainbridge that his presence beside his wife was crucial, because Harriet's pregnancy three years back had ended tragically when the baby, a son, died at birth with the umbilical cord about its neck. That loss had haunted them both, and Dred begged to be with his wife.

Bainbridge was not a man swayed by tender sympathies. He would not relieve Dred of his duties. "There's no way to know when she'll deliver, and I can't let you go indefinitely. Surely you can understand that. I'm in the midst of very important combat exercises, and I need you. I won't be able to leave and visit my own family until next month, at which time I will try to arrange for you to see your family." Unlike Master Doc, Captain Bainbridge was an officer, first and last. He followed regulations as well as orders. He was young; he had seen no battle, and his martial discipline shielded his inexperience like a warm cloak.

So Dred did not learn he had a son until a week after the birth. He managed to sneak off during the night and travel the ten miles to St. Louis on foot. He barely had time to hug his wife and daughter, then hold his wriggling little son, before departing to be back at the barracks by reveille.

Dred was back at his duties just two hours when Captain Bainbridge told him that Irene Emerson had decided she no longer required Harriet and Eliza in St. Louis—they would arrive in camp the following day. Dred was too excited about the reunion to read anything more into the Captain's stiff and halting delivery of the information. He would once again have his whole family with him. Permanently. Or at least until Irene Emerson changed her mind again. He knew he shouldn't let his hopes mount too high, but he couldn't stop himself from making preparations as though the reunion would be inviolable. He had negotiated with other slaves for a whole room that his family could enjoy as their own, private abode. He rushed about, frantically trying to beg, borrow, and steal enough mattresses, blankets, cooking utensils, and other household necessities to make their "homecoming" cheerful. Despite his best efforts, he had to admit their new home was bleak. As a finishing touch, before he began his dawn chores, he collected a nosegay of crocuses that, like his son, had emerged just about two weeks ago. Dred felt wonderful: it was spring; it was warming; his family would soon be whole again.

Because the Army made allowances for the orientation of newly-arrived personnel, even slaves, Bainbridge relieved Dred of his mid-morning duties in order to greet and settle his family. Dred waited excitedly at the compound gates, the song and dance from his dawn chores sporadically breaking forth again. Finally he saw the buggy approaching. His little Eliza was up on the seat beside the driver. He couldn't see clearly, but assumed the bonneted shape behind the driver was Harriet, holding their infant son. He gave a jubilant whoop, waved his arms energetically, and stepped to one side as the carriage neared and rolled by him, slowing to a halt.

Before the buggy wheels made their final rotations, Eliza hopped down and ran to her father. Laughing, Dred scooped up the six-year-old in his arms, hugging her tightly, his smile radiating out over Eliza's shoulder, his eyes seeking his wife and son. There was Harriet, turning slowly to face him. Yet her arms and the space beside her were empty. As she met his gaze he saw in her eyes his own smile fading from his face. Harriet's head fell back as though searching the heavens, but her eyes were closed. Her mouth fell slack. The light caught the wetness pooled in the hollow beneath her eyes, and tears of fear clouded Dred's vision. As anguish quaked through her father, Eliza also burst into tears and buried her head in his shoulder.

Later, in their little, one-room home, Dred learned the details of his second son's death. As with the first, there was no reason, no clarifying explanation for why a child comes to term, struggles out of its mother's body into loving embraces, only to leave so abruptly. Baby Joe, barely ten days old, died in his basket without a sigh. Harriet had put him down before stoking all the fires, and she checked on him immediately after. She found him sweetly, peacefully resting, but there was no breath in his body. He was gone.

Throughout that night, Harriet released to Dred the desolation that consumed her. She relived the shock of that terrible moment.

"He was still warm," she protested. "My baby was still warm!" Sobbing and blaming herself, she agonized over why it happened. Dred wrapped his arms tightly about his Harriet, and when her spasms of misery subsided, he tried to assure her it wasn't her fault. Dred had no answers, although when he worked beside Master Doc he had seen other such sudden deaths among newborns. It was little comfort.

Exhausted by her grief but unable to sleep, Harriet talked through the night. "Remember, Dred? Our joy the night of our wedding day—seeing them beautiful lights? I knowed then that we couldn't always be that happy, but I never knowed how deep a heart can crack and still go on beating. There been times since baby Joe passed that I wished my own heart would just stop."

Dred cradled Harriet in his arms, stroking her hair and softly pressing his lips to the top of her head. "I recollects that night as iffen it were last night," he said. "I recollects you saying how them lights shined for our wedded joy, but it be the stars, ever and forever in the velvet night sky, what shined for our love. And I know that to be true."

Harriet's eyes were closed. She rested and drew strength from the sound of Dred's voice. He continued, "And you know what, Honeybee? When I think on them northern lights now, I liken them to our sons, what also come into our life with so much beauty. That beauty left too soon, but we seed it. Not everybody gets to see such beauty, but we sure 'nough did. We done had a rare chance to see something too beautiful for this world—even held it in our arms for a spell, letting it fill us up with joy. And that means we will always see it in rememory. Always."

Harriet cried silently on his chest, hugging him and nodding. "That's how I think it's gonna be for us," he concluded. "We's gonna miss them beautiful lights and ache for them sometimes, but we's also gonna have the rememory of holding them. And we's gonna have all the love betwixt us of each other, of Eliza, and maybe other children, too. And all together, as a family, we'll conjure up the beauty of them northern lights what couldn't stay."

Throughout the long night they rocked each other and cried. The other slaves in the quarters, learning of their grief, brought breakfast in the morning. Even Captain Bainbridge's rigid code of duty yielded before the couple's grief. He excused Dred for the rest of the day, cautioning him, however, that he would expect Dred back at his chores the next morning.

Healing came to the distraught family when Lizzie Scott was born the following year, and the newborn seemed determined to reassure her anxious parents that she was robust. She ate heartily, slept noisily, smiled early, and clapped often. She giggled and gurgled. She kicked and bounced. She bubbled with life.

The only cloud, a slight one that particularly irked Harriet, was that the Missus had named yet a second child after herself—Eliza was Missus Irene's first name, and Lizzie a nickname. Harriet begged Dred to come up with an African name for their second daughter. He remembered Afrya, from a tale Gran once told of a child born to a king and queen, and because Afrya was blessed by the gods, the kingdom enjoyed peace and prosperity.

Eliza, now seven, was a tender older sister. She was grateful to the infant for relieving the distress that had hung over the whole family like a shroud. She called her baby sister "Missy Lizzie," sometimes pronouncing it Mizzy-Lizzie, sometimes Missy-Lissie. She made up songs and rhymes, to which Harriet hummed in harmony and Dred rattled his bones. The baby especially loved the bones and clacked them riotously whenever she grasped them in her pudgy hands.

Dred and Harriet now enjoyed days unencumbered by the twisted manipulations of Irene Emerson or the rigid expectations of the Captain because after the death of baby Joe, Irene Emerson wanted Harriet out of her sight. She couldn't bear Harriet's grieving and turned the Scotts over to her brother-in-law. Henry Bainbridge was away from the barracks for half the year on a reconnaissance mission, but he arranged to hire out the slaves and collect their earnings. The Scotts returned to St. Louis and began working regularly for Adeline Russell, a young wife whose husband, a lieutenant, was stationed at the barracks. The Scotts treasured this arrangement; not only were the Russells congenial, they allowed the Scotts to work extra hours to earn extra money—money Dred believed would hasten the day he could purchase his family's freedom.

Unfortunately, this stability and harmony ended in July 1845. Bainbridge returned from Texas, announcing he was soon going back to the Rio Grande to battle the Mexicans, and he planned to take Dred with him.

⁊⊱

I protested and pleaded, for all the good it done me—Captain Bainbridge turned a deaf ear. I found my loneself on that Rio Grande River, missing my Harriet and my little gals something fierce. I become "lone star," sure 'nough. It tore me up thinking how my baby gal would be growing and walking and talking, without me there to be part of it. It tested me and sat begrudgeful in my heart that Missus Irene and the Captain could decide on how and where my family should live. I headed south with the Captain, and Harriet and the girls went back to St. Looey to be with Missus Irene, who now wanted Eliza and Lizzie as playmates for her little Henrietta. Missus expected us to feel sorry for Henrietta 'cause she had no papa. Eliza, she was tender-hearted, and she did feel sorry for her. I'll say this much: that little white gal took after her dead papa more'n her living mother, and that were a blessing for my gals. They growed right friendly. Henrietta was about five, Eliza was almost eight, but they played nice, one t'other, and they taken care of baby Lizzie, too. Was my poor Harriet what had the worst time of it, 'cause Missus Irene went right back to her old ways of rumpus and ruction.

I was worried sore, seeing how this mess down in Texas were heating up. It looked to turn to war. The Mexicans, already angry over Texas, was ready to fight over California, too. But them Texans was a bull-headed bunch, sure 'nough, and the U.S. kept plowing west—they wasn't giving up territory without a fight. I got afeared that me and the Captain would be down there a long whiles, years maybe. The thought of being years apart from my family squirmed in my gut like a tapeworm. I do believe it would've ate me hollow iffen the Captain hadn't gone and got serious injured.

No matter how long I live, I probably won't never get used to how quick things can change. One second I's pining for my family, tied to a man what made the Army his career, a young man eager to

280

do his duty on the field of battle. Next second I's still tied to that man, yet he's headed home—against his own wishes but in satisfaction of mine. Sure 'nough, we was down in Texas only three months when Captain Bainbridge got throwed from his horse and busted his leg, a bad break. Had his shinbone poking right through the skin.

I helped carry him in to the hospital, and the doctor ordered him direct onto the operating table. This doctor's apron were soaked in blood, and I seed the Captain's eyes go wild, like a horse what smells coyote. The doctor took one quick look and said to his assistant to prepare to amputate.

The Captain be nearly knocked out by the pain, but he pushed up on his elbow saying, "No, wait." Then he turned to me.

I seed right away where things was headed 'fore he even opened his mouth. So did the Army doc, and his jaw got rigid. Captain fell back flat, the pain drawing all the blood from his face, choking off his voice. He whispered, "Dred, what would Doc Emerson have done?"

I'll say this for old Master Doc—he didn't always do things the same as other docs, but then he had him a keen sense for the body and what it could bear. In the ten year I worked for him, I seed him twice save a man's leg just like Captain Bainbridge's by using splints and plasters. So I told the Captain how Master Doc done, intending only that maybe this Army doc might consider doing the same. I didn't even have the last word outten my mouth 'fore that Army doc said no, it were too risky.

"Right now," he said, "I can chop from the knee down. If you pursue another treatment, rot could set in and we'll soon be talking about amputating clear up to the thigh."

Now the Captain did pass out. He was a brave young man and was bearing up under considerable pain— I think it were when he looked away from the doc and, bad luck for him, spied a nurse carrying off a foot from the last amputation this doctor done. The Captain's eyes just rolled to the whites. I could see he was out but the doc took his silence as agreement and set to work. He begun moving the bone, but the pain snapped the patient awake. The doc probably regretted he done so, 'cause the Captain turned to me again.

I know, I know it sounds peculiar: a white man putting hisself in the hands of a slave over the hands of the white doctor. But iffen you ain't never seed a man facing amputation, you can't know how desperate it make him. I know men what would druther die than face a Army surgeon in his bloody apron, wielding that hacksaw, with feet and arms still littering the hospital floor.

Captain Bainbridge turned to me, gritting his teeth. "Dred, I know you assisted Doctor Emerson—did you assist with the bone fractures, too?" I told him I done so.

The doctor looked ready to spit he was so angry, and he flew hot as the devil to the commander and tried to stop where the Captain was headed, but the commander liked the Captain and said it was his flesh, his choice. Far as the commander cared, Captain was already no more use to him as a soldier, so what did it matter?

Captain wasn't paying that doctor no mind, neither. "Do you think you could do it yourself?" he asked me. I told him I recollected what to do, clear as iffen Master Doc done the treatment yesterday, yet I allowed how I didn't have the know-how of Master Doc. I didn't know how he decided in one case to amputate and in another to splint.

He waved his hand, as if to say that weren't a consideration. "Seems to me," he said, "the odds are in favor of splinting—even if I agree to an amputation, I could just as easily succumb to hospital gangrene. I might as well gamble on the splints and hope for the best. I am inclined to do so if you tell me that you can really do it."

I seed he was giving me the choice—Captain was asking me as to whether I felt I could succeed, and I easy could've told him no. But I was torn in two directions. I was tempted to test my skills, 'cause I deeply felt I could do it. I wanted to know the full stretch of my ability. Yet I had no desire to help the Captain. Didn't seem right that I should benefit a man what tore me from my family without regard for my feelings or concerns. Still, I done walked this earth long enough to see when I had a advantage. So I choosed to speak right on and ask him plain: "Captain, you know I didn't want to come here. Iffen I saves your leg, is we likely to stay on through this war what's coming up?"

My ginger taken him by surprise and he almost laughed; then

he thought better of it. "I take your meaning," he said. He was in so much pain he could barely keep his eyes open, but he went on. "This is how it stands, Dred: currently I am of no use to the Army. With my leg amputated, we'll most certainly be sent back to Jefferson Barracks. You'd like nothing better, I suppose?"

I nodded. He shifted and groaned as a pain shot through him, and a part of me felt sorry for him—but the most of me was thinking of my family.

The pain kept its grip on him for a long minute, and he couldn't continue. Finally he said, "If you succeed in restoring to me the use of my leg, the Army might keep me here. I really don't know. I concede that I wish to remain in the Army as a soldier. But more than anything I want to save my leg. So I will strike this bargain with you, Dred: do your utmost to allow me to keep my leg, and I will dispatch you back to St. Louis, to Irene. While I cannot guarantee what she will do, I will recommend that you and Harriet be hired out together and not separated. And in the event I am posted back here, I shall refuse to have you accompany me."

That's what I wanted to hear, sure 'nough, and I begun rattling off the supplies I'd be needing. 'Cept that Army doc wasn't about to let me work in his hospital. We had to get men to carry the Captain to his quarters and I worked on him there. Worked quick, too, 'cause we done wasted a lot of time getting to this point. The doc's assistant was with us, and he helped me get the bone pushed back under the skin, and I think that boy was impressed by how well I managed. I was working quick and sure, feeling confident in my doings, only feeling doubt about whether I could trust the Captain's word. For the first time I seed clear why the white man loves his paper and pencil, 'cause he knows some men's word ain't enough. But I was a black. I couldn't get nothing in writing anyways, so I set to work on his leg.

I cleaned the wound as Master Doc would've done and dressed it with a patch of linen dipped in a iodine solution. Then I splinted it and told the Captain how to hold his leg and not to move. He was a good patient and stayed in that one position four whole days, till he couldn't take it no more. I undressed the wound and was glad to see no pus. The skin were red, though, so I dressed it again, using less iodine now, and done that over and over for another week. Each time the redness was less'n less till it were gone. Then I made a weaker ointment and used that for another week, and the scarring started, looking normal. By'n by the Army doc come in. He was still angry but when he looked at how good the leg were, he couldn't say nothing bad. He went and looked over my supplies, I seed him take note, but he never asked me no questions.

Anyways, about eight weeks after he fell from his horse, the Captain and me was on the dock, waiting on the steamboat what was gonna bring me home to my wife and gals. I was going home! Seemed to me ever since I left Alabama I been traveling up and down rivers—in particular that Muddy Mississipp', what I never done trusted nohow. I ached to be on solid ground with my family about me, and never more to roam.

True to his word, Captain Bainbridge left me no doubts he would help me settle down with my family. He gone so far as to arrange with Missus Irene to have Harriet and my gals already waiting at Jefferson Barracks. When we arrived in St. Looey, it were January '46. I recollects there was snow and ice on the ground, and the carriage were swaying like a bobsled, and my heartbeats was slipping around in my chest, too. I felt just like a wandering prince in a story, returning to his home and his kin.

We rode through them gates and there was my Harriet, my Eliza, and my l'il-gal Lizzie—waiting on me just as I done waited on Harriet and Eliza that sorrowful day after baby Joe died. This time I knowed the joyful reunion I was expecting that earlier time. We was all laughs and hugs, and whatever tears there be was tears of thankfulness. I slept that night with all three of my gals surrounding me, and it were the best sleep ever.

Captain got me and Harriet hired out to officers, just like before. I didn't even see Missus Irene for about a month, and I surely didn't miss her. Enduring that month, Harriet couldn't believe the change in the Captain. Mostly it were 'cause I saved his leg, but also he changed in the way a patient will soften toward the man what tends to him day and night for a long time. He truly be my ally then, and I asked him direct for support.

See, it were 18'n46, and I been keeping track since 18'n36, when me and Harriet married. It were close on to ten year and I reckoned my price should be near about made, so I wanted to talk to the Missus about getting my family free. I knowed she wouldn't give in easy, but right were right, and I didn't reckon she'd go against her dead husband's wishes. Anyways, I put my case to the Captain, asking would he bring it 'fore the Missus.

He was surprised. "Aren't things now as you desired them to be? Isn't this what you said you wanted?"

I done my best to let him know I was grateful for him keeping his word, but I had to make him see that I had business with Missus Irene what went beyond that.

"Freedom may not be so easy," he warned me. "You're not a young man, Dred. You're forty-six? With two young daughters? It could be tough out there on your own."

He meant well, so I didn't take his words hard, but I had to speak plain. "Captain," I said, "I done heared white folk what hold us blacks can't make it by the twist of our own wrist. There be white folk what sees this whole slavery thing like a cozy little nest for black folk. What they don't know is that many a chick learns to fly 'cause it gets crowded outten the nest by so much mess piled up in there. Think on it: them birds be trapped in one litsy-bitsy nest, just eating and crapping all day. Nests ain't all that cozy for a grown bird, Captain."

He was on my side then, agreeing to speak on my behalf. Only he allowed how he never heared Missus Irene nor old Master Doc say nothing about freeing me. So I laid out the history, all the way back to Major Taliaferro. Told Captain how our marriage was official-writ in Major T.'s book, and likely the Major would write a paper regarding our freedom, too. I said I was certain we could send a letter to Major T. and get him to witness for us.

Captain got me to agree to wait on Major T.'s letter 'fore going to the Missus, saying that would give me a stronger argument. He knowed Missus Irene weren't gonna be welcoming this turn, neither. Well, it taken nearly two months 'fore word come back—Major T. done left Fort Snelling—but Major T. finally writ, agreeing with all

I said. Only he allowed how there weren't no official paper regarding our freedom. Said only that Master Doc ten year ago done stated that as his intention.

So then we went to Missus Irene, him and me, and Captain spoken up for me. Soon's she heared this talk were about my freedom, she called in her brother, John Sanford, what handled the settling of Master Doc's will. He said Master Doc never writ nothing in his will about my freedom. John Sanford did most the arguing for his sister till she couldn't keep her mouth shut no longer. She said, "It's insufferable that slaves should know more happiness than I do."

I harkened back in my mind to that gal in Alabama what said to me, "Don't you just love it when white folk envy us?" But these words of the Missus, full of envy and spite, sent a cold chill up my spine and I could hardly believe a white person could admit to feeling like that. I thought I'd done seed it all till then. Missus made it plain she wasn't going to honor her dead husband's wishes. Made it plain she was gonna keep me and my family as slaves.

I was sunk down in my heart. I didn't know what to do or think when I heared her say, "That so-called marriage document? That wouldn't stand up in court. Neither would Taliaferro's letter."

The Captain done his best. He argued back, saying how Major T. and Master Doc had a agreement, and even though it weren't writ down, a judge might still consider it binding.

Then John Sanford stepped up. "That agreement," he said, "terminated with John Emerson's death. The slaves now belong to Irene, and she made no agreement with anyone about freeing them. A judge would unquestionably find that binding."

Missus near-about crowed. "I'm within my rights to hold them. I'm within my rights to sell them. I'm within my rights to sell one and keep the others. Whatever I want, that's what I'll do—and I'll thank you, Henry, not to interfere in this matter further."

Till that moment, I never reckoned I could kill a man or a woman. Even when I fought Peter Blow, I wasn't aiming to kill him, only stop him. But I felt the hot blood of them warrior women boil in my veins. My heart sounded like a great drum, and when my fists clenched, no thumbs was tucked under. 'Course, I knowed I couldn't kill her and I knowed even iffen I did, it wouldn't help my family. But I also knowed, for a dead certainty, I was gonna find a way to win this war.

Chapter twenty-four

Deciding to Sue

Missus Irene seed we had a ally in the Captain, so she pulled us right away from him. We landed back in St. Looey in her papa's house, under his thumb and hers. They didn't really need us and kept us busy doing chores what didn't need to be done. I hated it. Soon they begun hiring me out around town—mostly at the docks, like I done before. It messed me up; I become jittery as a cat with new kittens. Every day I feared coming back to find my family gone. I couldn't eat without feeling like my belly was gonna flop over. I couldn't close my eyes without feeling like I was being drownded in that mighty Mississipp'. Onliest way I could sleep was to have my little gals and Harriet tucked beside me in the bed.

No question in my mind that my gals be in harm's way so long as we be slaves, and soon my mind were full up on thoughts of running. At night me and Harriet whispered over it, looking on things different now than back 'fore Master Doc died, when thoughts of running looked to be too risky, 'cause of little Eliza. Now there looked to be more risk in not running.

One night we talked of getting over to Illinois, and I told Harriet how them Blow boys done tried helping me back in '32. I begun thinking how maybe I should try to find Henry and Taylor. The old pharmacy were gone, but I was hopeful one or t'other of them boys might yet be living in the city somewheres. This much were clear: me and Harriet was gonna have to do something quick. I had to protect my family. I had to fight the Missus.

But I didn't have no firepower, and I knowed it. I was at a loss till Harriet come skipping home from church meeting one day and put a cannon in my hands.

She come calling out to me 'fore she even got inside the gate. I hurried out to meet her but stopped dead still for the pure delight of seeing my Harriet run. She come lightly up the walk, with her Sunday skirts gathered in one hand and the other clapping her bonnet to her head. Oh, she was a picture. A pretty woman running toward you is a sight to fill your heart—that's the sweetest kind of running!

She dropped her skirts, peeled her bonnet from her head, tossed it in the air, and grabbed my hands. "Honeydew, we done got us a way to get free, and get the girls free, too. Reverend Anderson's been telling me all about what they call a 'doctorin.' The white folk got lots of doctorins but the one that helps us is called 'once free, always free,' and it means any slave what lived for any time in any free territory shouldn't never have to go back and be a slave no more. Can you believe that?"

I was confused 'cause I thought she be talking about doctoring, like Master Doc done, and I didn't see the sense in that. Only later did we learn it was a different word. Confusion didn't stop me from laughing with her, though. She was as excited as a child at Christmas, and more beautiful than the angels I done seed placed atop the yuletide tree. That gal glowed.

Being Sunday, we had a little time to ourselves. We walked out away from the house, and Harriet explained how the courts stand by this doctrine. A slave what lived some time in free territory and gets took back into slave territory, like we done, that slave can go to the courts and ask for freedom. Reverend Anderson done told Harriet more'n a hundred slaves done got free this way! So Master Doc, when he brung us to live in Illinois and the territories of Iowa and Wisconsin—all that were free soil. Atop of that, the Reverend told

Harriet how our Eliza done had a double protection over her, 'cause she got born onboard the Gypsey, north of Missouri, in free waters. Our Nzinga, child of the river!

This was wondrous news. Yet powerful strange, too—the things the white man done writ since he pulled the pencil and paper from outten the satchel! Sets me to wondering what other "doctrines" they got out there what might be to our good. No wonder the white folk don't like us to read nor write nor congregate. If it weren't for Reverend Anderson's church meeting, we probably never would've heared of this "once free, always free."

We talked it over all that week, hushed-like, careful not to tip our hand to the Missus. 'Course, with me working outten the house all day, we had precious little time for whispering over new plans. Then the more we huddled and hushed, the more risky it begun to feel to me. After I got past the first excitement, doubts begun nipping at me like bedbugs. By the end of that week, them bedbugs growed to be wolves, with fangs tearing great chunks outten my confidence.

My first worriment were the issue of money. We was gonna have to spank down a bond to cover the court costs. We had such little money to set our hands on, and Harriet said these cases could drag on a couple of years. Where was I gonna get enough money?

Next were the troublement of what Missus Irene might do once she learned what we was up to. That woman was a poison to us, no doubts about it. We just didn't know what she might be able to get away with. Maybe it would spur her on to sell us apart quick, for spite.

Finally were the question of how was we gonna live iffen we did get free? I seed enough of these St. Looey free blacks, struggling to make a living against the poor whites and new immigrants. Times be harder now for the free black then they was when I first come to St. Looey. Any work not done by slaves went first to the relatives of the grandees, then to poor whites—and only last to free blacks.

My thoughts turned again to finding the Blow boys. I knowed they would help me iffen they could, at least help me to see what stretched out beyond slavery. I pure didn't know what freedom really might be like. Could I live as a free man? Could I make it in the world that way? Could I be for my wife and children what they would need of me?

My heart stopped beating like a war drum. Fear muffled it. I lost the feeling I be rooted to my warrior kin. The more I dug at the root and branch of this court thing, the more it seemed I was planted in sandy soil. I felt ready to topple, like a tree on the banks of that muddy Mississipp', and the current done ate away at the soil I stood on. Iffen I fell one way, on the rocky ground of slavery, Missus could chop us up and sell us apart. Iffen I fell the other way, into the churning waters of freedom, we could still get dashed to pieces.

I haven't said this out loud to many people, but I'll confess it now: I hold a powerful fear of that Mississip'. "The Great Sewer," they calls it, though it hardly never stinks 'cause the water just flows too fast for a nose to catch an odor. It flows deadly fast, with a power like a great scythe, chopping away at whatever's in its way. It's a fact: there be people go to bed on the east side of the river what wakes up on the west side of the river, 'cause the Mississip' decided to take a short cut on its way and slice through they bit of shore. And that's how I felt about this doctrine: following its flow could be like getting sucked into the Mississipp': maybe we'd be lucky and go to bed on one side of the law a slave, then wake up on the other side of it, free. But you never knowed what that river might do. I couldn't be certain where it might carry us. It could sink us. It could smash us on the rocks. Or maybe it would carry us to that bright land so many songs promise. I had no way of knowing. I was a small thing swept up by a mighty force, and it trembled me.

Harriet, though, she be her own kind of force. She be like salt in water what makes you float easier. Harriet showed me the strength, got me moving in the right direction. And all along the way, right up to this very day, any time my fears sucks me down, Harriet lifts me back up. Oh, I knowed from the first I laid eyes on her, Harriet would change my life. She made me believe that the broken bundle of twigs that was my heart really be a fine-wove basket, just the right size and strength to hold her loving. Harriet changed my world, she did, and by the time she come running and talking about Reverend Anderson and the doctrine, about the courts and the free black folk walking around St. Looey today what was slaves just a few years ago, well, she swept me up.

I recollects we was sitting on our little, narrow bed, with our gals sleeping peaceful across the room. We done talked through all the ifs and mights, leaving me feeling like that tree about to topple. I had my arms crossed over my chest and my head hanged down. Harriet rubbed my back and set my spine straight, saying how we both knowed we was standing on the edge of the cliff, but we was standing together. She kneaded my shoulders and pulled them square, saying how together, we was the strength and protection for our gals. She smoothed my brow and set my sights looking deep into her spar-kling brown eyes, till I believed. My hands was closed tight there on my lap, and she picked up one and then t'other. Caressed and kissed each fist, caressed the tucked thumbs, teased them out of their hiding places, eased my tension. Then she laced her fingers through mine, and our two hands together made a fist. "This be the fist we's gonna fight back with," she said. "We's gonna give it the full might of both of us, never stopping till our gals be free." Now I had two little gals, and the world was just as mean as ever. I was no bigger than I used to be, and I was no less scared. But holding my Harriet, looking over her shoulder at my two sleeping daughters, I knowed I was stronger. And right then I knowed I was just gonna have to change the world in which we was living, or die trying.

⁂

Standing in the middle of the towering library, Dred slowly turned, looking up. The domed ceiling rose twenty feet, and the walls were lined top to bottom with books. A railed promenade cut these in half, while a ladder on rollers could swivel from one access gate to another. Small footstools dotted the lower shelf area. Plush leather chairs and reading lamps were stationed by both bay windows and around the central hearth. The rest of the room was appointed with two writing desks, a globe, a bookstand with an enormous dictionary, and, incongruously, a child's wooden rocking horse.

"That the one I made you?" Dred asked, pointing to the horse.

Henry Blow patted the horse's wooden head. "Yes, my son rides it now. He likes to spend time with me in here, and I want him to grow to love books as much as I do."

Craning his neck to take in the columns of books, Dred whistled softly through the gap in his front teeth. The room amplified the sound. "You done well for yourself, Henry."

Henry Blow looked pleased. He was quite proud of his station in life, and his library was the symbol of all he had accomplished. He was only twenty-nine, and he was out in front of all his peers and many of his seniors. With Dred, though, he modestly replied, "I cannot take credit—I merely backed the right speculators in Colorado. Other than this room, however, the house isn't so very lavish. Yet I wanted this property because of this room and the books it contained."

"You done read all these books?"

"Not all—but I will some day. Look at them, Dred, the great books of our civilization, written by men with hearts and minds that were enormous. Philosophers who blazed the long trail to Enlightenment; scientists who brought us into the modern era. That whole column there? All those books are dedicated to the writings of Thomas Jefferson, as well as editions that are listed among Jefferson's library holdings at Monticello."

"Guess I done heard enough about Jefferson—your own grandpapa was a admirer. That's why your papa named his St. Looey boarding house the Jefferson. Did you know that?"

"Yes, I'd heard that story."

"Me, I don't know much. But I know Jefferson wrote 'all men be created equal.'"

"That's right."

"And I know he was a man to keep slaves hisssself."

"Yes. Regrettably. Sometimes the men who write the words can't live up to them. It's as if we still have to grow into our hearts and minds. We are dwarfed by what we can aspire to, just as we are dwarfed by the books in this room."

Dred clapped Henry on the shoulder and said wryly, "Take it from me, son, size ain't but half the story."

They settled comfortably into two chairs in front of the fire. Though it was spring outside, the air indoors remained chilly. Dred looked appraisingly at Henry, and Henry worried he had sounded pompous until Dred said warmly, "Henry, when last I seed you, nearly fifteen year gone now, I taken a notion as to the kind of man you was to become. It does my heart glad to see I wasn't wrong."

"As it does my heart glad, just seeing you again. When you appeared in the doorway of the store yesterday, I could scarcely believe my eyes. Last report I had of you, you were up on the frontier somewhere with Doctor Emerson. Then I learn that you're here, you're married, you have a family—I want to hear all the stories."

"The world is a pregnant woman, as Gran would've said." Suddenly Dred looked tense. Lines creased his brow and his chin dropped. He took a deep breath and asked, "Henry, can you tell me news of Gran?"

Henry met Dred's gaze with sympathy. "I wasn't there, of course, but I did hear from my cousin that she died at Uncle John's, in '34 I believe."

"Was it easy on her?"

"In her sleep, easy as anybody could wish." Dred became too emotional to speak, and Henry added kindly, "She was a grand woman."

Dred cleared his throat and agreed, "Sure 'nough, my Gran were a big woman."

With a lighter note in his voice, Henry said, "Just the other evening, dining with Taylor, he refused to eat the asparagus because there was dirt in it, and he said, 'Remember how Gran never served a stem of asparagus that had grit in it. Never.' And I could clearly recall the way she washed each stalk: she'd cup the tips and squeeze the water through to flush out the grit."

"Gran never served up nothing bad," replied Dred. "She always offered over what she done made better through her knowing and her doing. She possessed power, much as the sun itself; backbone, like a ox; and she knowed just about everything worth knowing," he paused, smiled wryly, and waved a hand at the towers of books, "without ever opening a book."

Henry looked slightly embarrassed, which wasn't what Dred wanted. He said, "Henry, I appreciates deep in my heart you giving me peace of mind over Gran. Many a night I worried on how her last days was spent. I thank you, and I mean it sincere when I say this reunion touches me deep. Seeing you and Taylor yesterday, still side by side, helping each other along. And I appreciates how you arranged to hire me out today—Missus Irene sure 'nough gonna flap her jaws when she finds out who you be and why you hired me out." He grinned briefly and his fingers danced noiselessly on his thigh. Again his face became serious, and he said, "But I's under that woman's thumb, and she got no tenderness in her heart for me and mine. I got to act fast, Henry. I sorely needs to know how you and Taylor decided upon my request."

Henry walked over to the window, grabbed a hunk of drapery and held it up before him as he answered. "I've remembered much of what you taught me, Dred, but I know I will never forget your last lesson. I knew even yesterday I would do all I could to help you secure your freedom. But I did desire to talk it over with Taylor, and also my brother-in-law, Charles Drake, who is an attorney."

Dred remained seated by the fire. He remembered clearly that day when a pudgy fifteen-year-old allowed himself to be wrapped up in the drapes. The tall, square, well-muscled man before him now would never allow it, Dred was sure. Henry had become a man of influence and consequence. The transformation amazed him, but it also lifted his hopes that he had come to the right place for help.

With his next words, Henry confirmed Dred's hopes. "Charles says that your information is accurate—the courts here in St. Louis have been disposed to granting slaves freedom on the basis of 'once free, always free.' Better than that, he thinks your case falls well with the precedent—" Henry saw the questioning look on Dred's face and explained, "Your reasons for suing for freedom match those reasons set down by the court for granting freedom. Charles thinks this will be a rather simple and straightforward case."

"I's relieved to hear it from a lawyer. So far we just been taking the word of Reverend Anderson—a good man, but his stomping ground be the church, not the courthouse." Looking steadily at

Henry, Dred stood to face him. He tilted his head back, as though trying to identify a faint odor. "So now I know what you think and what a lawyer thinks. What about Taylor?"

Henry frowned. "Taylor wanted to be here to speak for himself, but his wife has been ill. Anyway, you should know that Taylor and I hold quite different political beliefs. Taylor, well, he still holds slaves." Henry paused to gauge the effect of this news on Dred.

Dred responded, "Folks averagely conduct theyselves according to they learning, so the surprise to me ain't that Taylor got slaves—it's that you ain't."

Henry felt relieved. His own ideals concerning slavery were so rigid he had imagined Dred might eschew support from a slave owner. Henry continued explaining for his brother. "Whereas my mind was made up right away, Taylor needed to think it over. He's concerned about the way others might view his involvement—if he owned you, it would be different. This, he feels, is meddling with someone else's..." Henry didn't know how to complete his sentence.

Dred completed it for him. "Property."

Henry flushed. "Yes. Taylor can't help but see that aspect."

Dred sat down heavily. His gaze fell upon the rocking horse, and he thought he could hear the childish laughter of two young boys. "I don't aim to come betwixt you and your brother," he said. "Not after all these years."

Henry paced quickly over to Dred and sat beside him. "Oh, no. I think you misunderstand me. Taylor needed to think it over, but he has decided to help as well."

With those words, Dred realized he had been taking shallow breaths. He inhaled deeply and took Henry's hand in both of his. "You's both with me?" he asked cautiously.

Henry laughed and placed a hand on his shoulder. "Yes. Both of us are with you—and we'll muster others, if need be."

Dred laughed too, with relief. "It sure feels mighty good to be back with you two boys."

Simultaneously both men rose. Dred held out his hand, and Henry accepted it in a firm, brisk shake. Finding that unsatisfactory, Dred pulled Henry to his chest and they embraced, awkwardly at first, and then it was warmly familiar. "I feel like that time after your papa died and you two boys helped me to run," said Dred.

"You helped us more times than we helped you," grinned Henry. "Like the time you helped us sneak off and shoot our first rabbit—"

"Even though your papa done forbid you to use a gun," Dred interrupted.

"How about that time you caught me and Taylor at a peep hole in one of the upstairs rooms, rented to those people with the pretty red-haired daughter?"

"Sure 'nough, you two was into mischief every time I turned around," Dred chided.

"Yet you never tattled on us. Even when we were wrong, you kept it among us. And that's what Taylor wanted me to tell you, Dred: that loyalty outweighs all other considerations."

Seeing the love in Henry's eyes, Dred was seized by a powerful realization that, in some strange way, he had become to these boys the father they needed and the father he himself had always wanted.

Henry continued, "Taylor particularly wanted me to remind you of that time you rescued us from those bullies behind the court-house."

"Oh, I recollects that clear as yesterday," said Dred. "That were our first year in St. Looey, a blusty day in late October if I recollects rightly—that time of year when the trees look about ready to lift up they roots and strut round in they royal colors, and the sun still be sending down its heat but the winds are chilly."

Henry, recognizing the familiar story-telling tone, returned to his seat by the fire to listen while Dred conjured the past. Dred readily obliged. "That particular day, the wind were coming in fits. It played with the trees, making them dance. It played with the clouds, too, and the sun were hop-scotching over them clouds, sending down light and shadow like a lunatic opening and closing the shutters. One second I was standing in the sun, feeling its warmth, next second the sun were hid behind a cloud, and that cold wind be shaking leaves down in my hair. A day like that be full of spirits—mostly good spirits what makes you feel like you might oughta discover something—but a little impish, too. And it be a impish kind of spirit that moved you boys to go where you knowed you got the least reason to be."

Grinning boyishly, Henry said, "Little squirrels, isn't that what you called us?"

"Sure 'nough, you two was scamps. 'Cept I got to take responsibility on this day, 'cause I recollects I was exercising my jaw and lost track of you little squirrels for a spell. When I finally go looking for you in the usual places: no luck. Then I spy some white boys running and yelling to each other, puts me in mind of a pack of hounds urging each other on to tree the possum, and a cold burst of wind tells me something ain't right and I should follow those young'ns.

"I followed them round behind the courthouse and what did I see: you standing with a stick as thick as my arm and twice as long raised above your head, shouting something at this pack. Taylor's standing behind you, his little face all crowded with scared, worried, and mad all at the same time. You was looking snappish as a fice dog, yet there must've been nigh on a dozen boys, some bigger'n you, all kinda quiet and menacing and edging in.

"That's when I felt my hackles rise. Now, I knowed they was white boys. I knowed I be asking for trouble to run in amongst them, but I felt that sudden, protective kind of heat. You was my boys, and you was in trouble. I moved so fast I burned a path through the grass. But still I arrived late. Them bullies already done closed they circle clear round you two. Was nothing for me to do but shoulder my way in. Even though I was smaller'n some of them, I was twice as old as most of them—and I do believe those crackers was so surprised at being shoved by a black man that they up and froze for a minute. Which happened to be just long enough for me to spur you two on. I pulled you along behind me, moving through that circle of white boys like a harrow through old stalks of corn. They even begun to rustle like corn as we got clear of them, and I set you boys to running, me bringing up the rear."

Henry slapped his thigh and finished the story. "I remember we ran through some trees for a while, then stopped and climbed a nice old maple, with branches low enough to get up on. If I remember correctly, my flush of victory turned into a flush of shame when you chided me for not taking better care of Taylor."

"Brothers got to look out for each other," said Dred.

"Yes," Henry replied soberly. "And you've looked out for us, all through our childhood, like a brother. More: like a father. And that's why Taylor brought this up. Taylor said now that the bullies are surrounding you, Dred, it's our turn to shoulder our way in and pull you out."

That evening after dinner, Dred told his family about the meeting with Henry. Harriet asked, "And Henry's reason for helping us is for loyalty, too?"

The family was gathered about their little hearth, and Dred was packing a pipe—rather, Eliza was packing it for him, according to a nightly ritual that often accompanied shared stories about the day or reminiscences of the past. Dred pulled a stick from the kindling pile, set its tip aflame, and passed it to Eliza as she passed him the pipe. As he sucked on the stem, she heated the tobacco. Baby Lizzie was crawling at their feet.

To Harriet's question, Dred replied, "Henry said it were to right a wrong."

Harriet raised her eyebrows and nodded. Eliza, nearly eight, asked, "What wrong?"

Easing back into his rocker, pulling on the pipe steadily now, Dred hoisted Lizzie up onto his knee with a fake groan. "Wouldn't you know I got just the right story to answer that question?" Eliza scooted over closer by her father's chair. Sitting on a cushion, she leaned against her father's leg. Harriet settled down in her rocker, too.

"It seems a long time ago," began Dred, "in faraway Africa, lived two sisters named Lamusi and Mawusi. They father had bad luck with his crops for three year running, and he falled so bad into debt that he had to give over his two daughters as slaves."

"In Africa," said Eliza, drawing her baby sister's attention away from the buttons on Dred's vest and pretending to educate her, "slaves ain't always slaves for life. Sometimes they just pays off a debt and then goes back to being free."

"That's so," said Dred. "'Cept 'fore these gals got outten slavery, they father died, and so they be stuck with a master what was a awful, mean man. This master sold the sisters and split them up. Oh, how they cried and screamed at the parting." Instinctively, Eliza reached up and clasped her sister's leg, which was dangling over Dred's knee.

Dred continued, "It taken two full-growed men to separate them, and each gal had to be tied down and carried away blindfolded, so they wouldn't know where they was going or what direction the other one went in. They screamed to each other for miles—long after they couldn't even hear each other no more—promising to find one another some day. 'Course, the new masters, to stop them from finding one another, both decided to give the girls new names, which they did.

"Well, the years rocked by. Turns out that Lamusi wound up in a good house. She worked hard, but she was treated with a easy hand and they even gived her some learning. She growed into a good-looking woman, captured the heart of the young master, and by'n by they got married. Now she's the mistress of the house, and she figures she needs slaves herself. So her husband, out on his travels one day, buys her a maidservant from a distant village. And though nobody knowed it—guess who he brung home?"

"Mawusi!" gasped Eliza.

"That's right! Mawusi. Now, Mawusi all these years been living a hard experience. She been made to sleep in the dirt and eat bugs and leaves, and she worked like a mule and got beat for things she never knowed what for. By the time she come to Lamusi's household, all the hard work and beatings she taken made her look like a old woman, even though she was the younger sister by two year.

"Well, things got much better for her in Lamusi's household, 'cause she got a pallet to sleep on, enough food, and she didn't have to work so hard. She just have to mind the baby and cook the meals. She thinks she got it pretty good, now. Only troublement is Lamusi treats her with spite and can't seem to be satisfied with nothing she does. Mawusi don't get beatings, though: just tongue lashings, every day: complain, complain, complain."

"Is Lamusi like Missus Emerson?" Eliza asked.

Dred and Harriet exchanged grins over the girl's head. "Yes, she's a bit like the Missus," said Dred. "And Mawusi, she early on thinks herself better off 'cause her body ain't being tormented, but what she come to feel is that her spirit just can't take this daily abuse from Lamusi. 'Cause Mawusi tries real hard to please. She wants to please. But nothing is ever good enough. Mawusi is all toughened like leather on the outside, but inside she a soft-natured gal. And in a few years, she feels just as miserable as she did before, and she gets to remembering how happy she was as a little gal with her parents and her sister, how they played and sang together in the sunshine. She about wears her soul out, longing for them happy days.

"Then don't you know: one day Mawusi is cooking a soup. As she stirs the pot she gets lost in recollecting them long-gone good days of her childhood. She stands over the fire, just humming one of the little tunes she and Lamusi done made up theyselves when they was young and happy.

"Now into the kitchen comes Lamusi, and she hears that little song and exclaims: 'Why, nobody knows that song but me and my sister! Where did you learn it?'

"Well, Mawusi can hardly believe it. She drops the ladle and stammers: 'Me and my sister, Lamusi, made up that song when we was just babies together.'

"Lamusi understands and she cries: 'Mawusi! My sister!' And they run to each other's hugs and hold tight for dear life. They hug till the soup boils over. They hug till the fire dies down. They hug till the sun starts to set. They can't let each other go. They be laughing and crying and singing the old songs. Finally Lamusi apologizes for all the meanness she done heaped on her sister, and after that they live together just as happy as when they was babies, and each one agrees to share the work of the household and not buy no more slaves."

Eliza, like an apt pupil, said, "So Lamusi got to make right the wrong she done to her sister."

"Yes," said Harriet. "And it ain't often in life a body gets the chance to right a wrong."

Eliza looked puzzled, though. She looked up at her father and put a small hand on his. "Did Mr. Blow wrong you, papa?"

"Mr. Blow owned me," he answered.

"Like Missus Emerson own us?" Eliza asked.

"Yes."

Eliza mulled this over. "That's the wrong he done you," she finally said. It wasn't a question.

"Yes," said Dred.

"So how's he gonna make it right?"

Dred rubbed the bridge of his nose and looked at Harriet. She reached over and laced her fingers through his, making a fist. "Mr. Blow ain't gonna make it right," he answered. He reached down his other hand and laced his fingers through Eliza's, making another fist. He continued, "Your mama and me is gonna see to that, sweetpea." Eliza now reached out her free hand to Lizzie, making a third fist, and Harriet closed the circle by taking Lizzie's other hand. As they raised their clasped hands, Dred said, "Your mama and me is gonna get us all free. Mr. Blow just gonna help, is all."

Tucked in her bed, Eliza Scott was too excited to sleep. Free! She didn't really know what it meant, but it made her mama and papa as happy as the sisters in the story. Eliza knitted her fingers together and wiggled them, reliving the feeling of their hands all connected in a circle.

Twice her mother had told her to close her eyes and sleep, and she really was trying. But sleep would not come. She scrunched her lids tightly, but still could hear her parents talking about Gran, who had gone back to Africa, back to their kin. Her papa murmured softly, a sad smile in his voice, "Wish I could've been there, to see her safely across."

Gran was papa's grandmother. That was kind of difficult to understand, too. Anyway, she was an old lady but she was one of the warrior women, so she never really got old.

All fell quiet, except for the snapping of the fire and the creaking of a rocker. Drowsily, Eliza heard her mama begin to hum. The tune seemed familiar, and she realized it was a song she heard the day they buried baby Joe. To Eliza's ears it was a lullaby, not a dirge: a sweet, soft, simple tune, with words so soothing. With her papa singing those words, Eliza slipped off into sleep.

I am a poor, wayfaring stranger
Wand'ring through this land of woe
But there's no sickness, toil or danger
In that bright land to which I go
I's going home, to see Njeri
She said she'll meet me when I come
I's only going to my kinfolk
I's only going to my home.

Chapter twenty-five

Technicalities

April 6, 18'n46—the day I taken my family down to the courthouse to ask the judge for freedom. That morning Harriet ate nothing, and I ate too much, so the whole way to the courthouse my belly were talking so loud that I had Eliza convinced I be carrying a little animal under my coat. We played a game of peeky-boo, and that were good 'cause it taken my mind offen what we was about to do. Oh, Harriet and me was so nervous and excited it seemed neither one of us could hold l'il Lizzie without making her fretful, too. By the time we was at the courthouse, we gived the baby over to Eliza 'cause she the onliest one not wriggling like a Christmas custard.

That day the sky were lowering. You couldn't tell the thunderheads from the clouds of steamboat smoke rolling in offen the river. The thick air were greasy, and the daylight were like twilight. Yet when I looked up at the courthouse, it kinda bust through all that, big and solid and so white it looked to me to be soaking up all the light around it. The courthouse weren't complete built yet. Still, it were a mighty impressive building. Eliza looked up and her mouth dropped open.

"Is that where they keep the freedom, papa?" she asked. Oh,

that gal! She were smart as a whip, from the time she were a baby. I scooped her up, her and l'il Lizzie both, spinned them around.

"That's it, baby gal, and we's walking up them stone steps, and we's gonna stand 'fore the judge, and we's gonna ask him to give us some."

"For me too?" she asked.

"For you, Lizzie, Mama, and Papa. They got to give it to all of us or none of us."

This were an election day, so groups of immigrants was being herded in to swear the oath of allegiance, then hustled off to cast they votes as new citizens. Folks was swarming in and out like bees in a hive. In the rotunda, people moved in a rush, footsteps fell loud, and sounds bounced round the walls. We met Henry and Taylor along with the lawyer, Mr. Murdoch. He was the one with us just at the beginning, 'fore having to go off and settle a claim he had in California. I liked him: a tall, beanpole of a fella what liked to hear the sound of his own voice. But I liked the sound of his voice, too—very deep for a skinny man, deep as well water. I was hoping the judge might drink it down.

Any time Mr. Murdoch wasn't 'fore the judge, he spoken with a straw jiggling from his mouth. He used words strange to me in them days, but what I soon got the hang of. He said we got to claim Missus Irene "bruised and beat us"—seems just slapping us, shaming us, and making my pregnant wife stand for hours on swole-up ankles weren't serious enough for the court to mind.

Mr. Murdoch taught me a lot in them early days, and I appreciates that. The legal way is a whole different way of looking at things. See, I thought we should complain how Missus Irene robbed us. 'Cause me and Harriet done worked seven year for Master Doc, with him putting aside one dollar every week to pay against my selling price. And we continued working hard after he died till we come near gaining the full price, and she wiped all that out. She robbed us of all them wages and robbed us of the freedom Master Doc promised. Mr. Murdoch said he couldn't argue that way, though. He said there be a recipe, like baking a cake. "Once free, always free" be the main ingredient, and so long as we stuck to the recipe we'd be enjoying our slice of the cake.

That's how he explained it. He hitched up his waistband and tilted his head to one side so as his top hat—one of the tallest of them chimney-stack hats I ever seed—looked ready to tumble down. "It's the language of the court," he said, "and in our judicial system the language of the court must necessarily be broad. It is designed to include and embrace the largest number of people." That made me laugh: bruised, beat, and embraced—what a recipe!

Still, I writ my Xs on the papers and so did Harriet. That's when we got introduced to "technicality." I come to know a good many technicalities since that day, but this were the first: see, Mr. Murdoch done writ our names on the papers, and we was supposed to sign our Xs by our names, but the clerk in the court scratched out Harriet's name—said she couldn't be called Harriet Scott, 'cause that would be recognizing our marriage. Said she just had to be put down as "Harriet, a woman of color." I didn't like it none and Harriet liked it less. Still, we made our marks and that were the beginning of the case.

There were no great fanfare, just Harriet slipping her hands in mine. We circled our arms round our gals—Eliza was standing betwixt us, holding l'il Lizzie.

Eliza tugged my vest. "Papa, Papa," she said.

"Yes, l'il gal?"

"Is that it? We got freedom now?"

I picked her up again. How I loved the small, solid weight of my baby gals in my arms, how they balanced me and set my backbone straight. "Not yet, l'il gal. This be the start, but it could take a whiles more yet."

"How long?" she asked.

"Likely it's gonna take more'n the time it takes to come to your next birthday."

Mr. Murdoch bent low to look in Eliza's face, and she pulled close to my chest, shy of him. "Eliza," he said, "we got to give Missus Irene a chance to answer our papers—and then maybe we'll have a few more papers to bring to the judge—but I'm hoping by Christmastime we'll have freedom for you and your family wrapped up with a bow."

Then Henry and Taylor, what plunked down the bond for all this, they hugged me and shaked hands with Harriet. They wished us luck, agreeing with Mr. Murdoch on how it were gonna be a piece of cake. They all talked about freedom just like that. Even Harriet talked about freedom as iffen it were a solid thing what you could point to and say: that's a rock, or that's a tree, with everybody knowing the difference and everybody agreeing.

'Cept me—I been a black man in the white man's world too long to believe it were gonna be that simple. That's why my belly were talking. The little animal playing peeky-boo was doubt, and I didn't know it then but it were gonna grow much bigger as the years stretched out and rip up my insides with worry.

We all left the building, and I paused there at the top of the steps betwixt them tall, white pillars to see if the world looked different. It done showered whilst we was inside. The buildings was slick and the streets all muddied. A dark thunderhead blocked the sun. It were high noon but it seemed like night as I looked over to the levee and seed the steamboats belching them great, rolling clouds of black smoke our way. The courthouse wasn't soaking up light no more; it looked gray and begrimed. I looked down that hill of steps and watched all the people hurrying up and down: lawmen, politicians, immigrants—folk from all stations looking to find justice from the court, just like me.

Then I heared the cold, hard clanking of chains, and I seed a coffle of slaves, hobbled at the ankle, shuffling up the side of the stairs. Harriet pulled Eliza behind her skirts and I stepped up in front of my family. Auctions of slaves be regular conducted right there on the courthouse steps—I done passed by it many a time. Lynch's slave pens be right down the next block, so they chain them and lead them to the courthouse to be sliced up and sold away from they kin. In this group of about ten, I seed a spindly little gal stumble. An old man in front of her called to halt the lead slave. The whole coffle stopped; a deputy with a wooden cattle prod swore; the old man stooped and reached his arm under the gal and put on her feet. She were crying without no sound. The line moved on.

Oh, them Lynch slaves be the sorriest-looking slaves in all of

St. Looey. The misery in they faces just burns the eyes. And there I stood at the top of the steps, my mouth watering for my piece of freedom to be served up, and them other slaves was clanking along, knowing nothing of doctrines but hungering for freedom just as keen as me, of that I was certain. The doubt in my belly growled, and Mr. Murdoch noticed.

"What's wrong?" he asked me.

I couldn't answer right away. The air seemed too thick and clogged. I couldn't get enough of it into my chest. I throwed my head back to take a deeper breath, and I seed at the top of the courthouse that somebody done forgot to lower the flag once the rain come. It draggled from the pole all gray and dripping. Finally I said, "I feel like somebody just smote a nail in my coffin."

He laughed and clapped me on my back and boomed, "Don't you worry, Dred. I've never handled such a simple case. You mark my words."

Well, I marked his words, but it were well past Eliza's birthday 'fore Missus Emerson gave the judge her response— "not guilty." I guess it took her a long time just to cool down after learning what we was up to.

See, after that first day in court, she still didn't know we was seeking freedom. Everything rocked along as usual: me and Harriet was hired out, and Missus collected our wages. Every day I looked for signs of the Missus knowing about our court papers, but every day was just like the ones before. Finally, the first week of May, the sheriff delivered the papers—the Missus turned red as a Louisiana crayfish in hot water and lit out after me so fast that I was deeply thankful the sheriff was there to hold her back. He took away me and Harriet and our little gals right there, right then, explaining not to us but to Missus Irene that's how the judge ordered it. The fight begun in earnest then, and time and turmoil ate away at my little slice of cake 'fore I got nary a taste.

Oh, there's been a good many folk what has stepped up to lend us a hand along the way. It fills my heart that we done seed the benefit of so many folks what don't even know us personal-like. Yet they knows the Blow boys, and for that they's willing. My little squirrels sure 'nough stuck by me. Them boys was making it possible for us to live through this fight. They paid the court fees and found the lawyers we needed. They gived us this little house where we all could wait out the storm together. And they gived us food and money what didn't have to go to the sheriff. See, all through the fight, me and Harriet continued hiring out our time but we couldn't collect our wages. Till the court decided iffen we was free or not, all our wages was held by the sheriff. Iffen the court said we was slaves, Missus would get our wages and we would continue working as her slaves. Iffen the court said we was free, we would get all our wages, and then I hoped maybe to pay back the generosity of Taylor and Henry.

More'n everything else, though, them boys helped keep alive in me a cautious hope, a hope as frail as the little puff of smoke you conjures up with a flint and a wad of cotton—you get that tiny whiff of smoke and guard it, protecting it till it become a flame.

Looking back over everything, that flame might've caught. We might've been all right iffen we done got that first case decided for us quick. But we didn't get that early win. Should've but didn't. See, Mr. Murdoch left St. Looey 'fore we ever heared from Missus Irene. Henry and Taylor next got Mr. Charles Drake to lawyer for us. He was married to Patsy Blow, and he done all the work for us without pay, so I's grateful to him. But turns out he tripped over another "technicality," and that set us back.

Once Missus told the judge "not guilty," we all had to go into court and argue. That didn't happen till the summer of '47. Mr. Drake brung to court the testimony of Mr. Anderson, what hired me and Harriet at Fort Snelling—that were to prove that we done lived in free territory. Then he brung the testimony of Mr. Russell, what hired me and Harriet after Master Doc died—and that were to prove that Missus Irene done held us as slaves. It were that simple. But Missus Irene's lawyer put questions to Mr. Russell and it turns out he didn't hire us—his wife done it. So Judge Hamilton couldn't free us right then 'cause he had to hear from her that we was hired. Everything got held over till Mrs. Russell could be brung to the court, and that turned out to be a long time, what with the normal pace of the court being slower'n a prairie winter passing into spring, then the waterfront fires of '49, followed by a bad cholera outbreak. Everything shut down. The judges, the politicians, the lawyers, and half the business folk left town. Even Missus Irene left town, and that's when her brother, John Sanford, begun handling things for her—which only tangled things thicker.

We lost Mr. Drake, too, and that were another delay till the Blow boys could find us new lawyers. The new ones got us back on track, and also told us it were gonna be simple, and not to worry. But you can bet I worried. They tried to make up for that last technicality by "deposing" most everybody in my life. Everybody white, that is. Ghosts from my past was flying round thicker'n flies in summer. They writ down the testimony of the Russells, the Blow boys, officers and they wives from Fort Armstrong and Fort Snelling—even the captain of that steamboat we took from Loosiana, when l'il Eliza was birthed.

Still things didn't fly no straighter'n a boomerang, 'cause Missus Irene and her brother begun arguing back, filing papers in the higher court and confusing matters. They higgled and haggled nigh on four year from the time we first entered the court, and all that time Missus Irene got to continue holding onto us as slaves simply 'cause nobody yet done proved to the court that she held us as slaves—when it were plain to anybody with eyes. The lawyers explained how a black man can't stand in court and witness against a white, and how courts always holds first that a black man must be a slave and if he say otherwise, he's got to prove it—which kept most free blacks outten the courts, 'cause they could be hauled off as runaways. Oh, that statue of lady justice, she be blindfolded, sure 'nough, and it could surely only be a white man to make her be that way!

Seemed to me if anybody was having any cake—and getting to eat it, too—it were the Missus. From where I was standing, there weren't nothing simple nor sweet about this court business. What begun as a small hill to climb soon loomed large as a unending mountain range of technicalities, complications, setbacks, and outright lies. I know nothing iffen I don't know by now that a court case be little more than a game of hidey-seek, with the devil keeping score.

It put gray hairs on my head. And the grumble in my belly

got tired of waiting on cake, crawled on up and started nibbling at my lungs. Yes, the consumption ris up and got a grip on me enduring this time. Not bad at first, just some spells of cold and cough. They passed, yet never left completely. Kept coming back, each time wearing me down more'n the time before. Yet as my body weakened, my will toughened. Like heating iron and plunging it in cold water, all that tangling with the court hardened my will. The more I understood the language of the court and the reasoning of the law, the more I seed the right of my family being free. It were writ in the white man's law books, plain for all to see, and I was bound and determined to reach into the white man's satchel and take what he hisself said I was due.

It were January 18'n50, by the time that happened. We was all there—Harriet, the gals, the Blows, the lawyers—sitting there 'fore the Judge. Judge Hamilton was a wrinkly old man, looked like a sleepy lizard sunning itself. Even with his eyes open he looked sleepy, 'cause he had so many folds drooping under his eyes. But when he finally said "you's free," all them folds looked like Fourth of July bunting, and fireworks shot off from his eyes. He said I was free since the time Master Doc first taken me to Fort Armstrong. And Harriet was free since Fort Snelling. And our children was the free offspring of free parents. We was free Negroes, free blacks, free citizens of color. Harriet could be Harriet Scott again, and my children and their children and all forever after would be free. And I thought of my kin, free back in Africa before the Oyo catched them. Gran and Njeri and Nyota, and the little twins what drownded—they was out there somewheres, freed now, too, by the declaration of Judge Hamilton of the St. Looey Circuit Court.

That ruling come right following my fiftieth birthday—the best birthday present a man could hope for. Harriet squeezed the breath right outten my body, she was so happy. Me, I was proud and overjoyful. I felt taller'n a tree, and I knowed now my roots stretched down far and deep enough to stay standing no matter how fierce that river of slavery flowed by me. I held my family safe up high away from them churning waters, and I felt proud. We was a family together, safe and free. We had won the fight, and the prize were freedom.

The Blow boys gave us a feast that night, and we drunk some spirits till we got silly. I stood up and said, "Tomorrow, I ain't gonna do a lick of work." I turned to my Harriet and I said, "Tomorrow, you ain't gonna do a lick of work." We was all giggling like children, and I turned to my little gals and said, "Tomorrow, you's gonna do all the work what needs to be done." Everybody bust up laughing, enjoying the joking and enjoying the idea of living free.

Living free.

But that's all it were: a idea.

We did play all the next day, sure 'nough. Even had us a picnic. Though it were winter, we picnicked right in our front room, on the hearth. But freedom didn't come to us then. It were still playing hidey-seek. 'Cause Missus Irene done tied another knot in the blindfold on Lady Justice. She quick filed papers, calling for a new case in the higher court, and nothing could be done till that court heared the arguments and reached they own decision.

We went back to living as we done been living—hoping, doubting, waiting. There were no sweet taste of nothing, only bile hanging in my throat. Consumption sat heavy on my chest the rest of that winter, and I couldn't do much work. Harriet did all she could and more'n she should've. The gals looked after me whilst I was bedridden. And the Blow boys stuck by us. But we was all grim 'cause whatever the state court said was the final say—iffen it come down against us, we knowed we couldn't push no more appeals.

⁂

Though it was only November, the winter of 1851 was shaping up to be a brute. A nor'easter off the Massachusetts coastline swept curtains of rain inland. The town was awash in mud, but Irene Emerson would not postpone her wedding. She was marrying Calvin Chaffee, a Springfield physician and Republican Congressman, one of the best catches in all of Massachusetts. A swooping wind snatched her veil as she skipped from the church, but Calvin gallantly caught one end and wrestled it back. Laughing and running, they tumbled into a white carriage and hurried to her sister's house for the party.

Irene adored parties, particularly those held in her honor, but she dallied upstairs, determined to make her entrance well after everyone from the church had gathered. She insisted that the last speck of mud be cleaned from her damp wedding gown, then pestered her sister to re-do her wind-tossed coiffure twice before being satisfied. Reviewing her appearance in the mirror, she mused out loud that every girl should have the opportunity to marry more than once, and finally declared herself ready to join the party.

Still snickering at her sister's embarrassed response to her last comment, Irene paused at the top of the stairs to sponge up the cheers and congratulations. Her gaze swept the room full of happy faces and rested unhappily on her brother, John. Hunched in a corner, almost hidden by the upright piano, John stood in that childish posture of drooping his shoulders while at the same time pulling them forward—a habit developed over the years in a futile attempt to make his small head appear more in proportion to his body. As a boy he had been teased mercilessly, and there were still some back in Virginia who referred to him as "pin-head" and "pea-brain." His anomaly had been bad enough in his youth, but it had become more pronounced as he aged and acquired bulk. Now in his mid-forties, and with a rotund figure, John Sanford looked like an old, fat house cat.

Irene huffed. His isolation in the midst of her party annoyed her. This was her wedding, she should have no worries. Yet there he was. Before dismissing him from her thoughts, she made a mental note to find a quiet moment to confer with him about the court case before she and Calvin embarked on their honeymoon. Calvin, she had almost forgotten Calvin. There he was, pushing through the crowd to escort her into the parlor.

Hours later, Irene again noticed her brother. He was yawning; worse, he didn't cover his mouth and a silver string of saliva sparkled between his gaping lips. Mortified, she dragged John over to a small group of businessmen with whom she thought he might have shared interests. But when the conversation turned to the new Fugitive Slave Law, she grew alarmed. Like her husband, these men were abolitionists.

"I happen to be involved in a case in St. Louis," John began, then noticed his sister's eyes widen in silent caution, and he abruptly changed course. "But this is no time for dry political discussions. Today my sister has wed, and I would like to toast her happiness." They all raised their glasses, and Irene accepted their good wishes with a curtsy.

"John," she said, "Calvin is anxious to depart. May I have a word before we go?"

John Sanford jerked his head to the men in lieu of a bow—bowing, he felt, drew attention to his small head. He said formally, "Gentlemen, will you excuse us?"

Behind the closed door of the study, Irene said, "I'm eager to hear news about the case, but we cannot discuss it among the people here. We are surrounded by abolitionists, you know." Going to the sideboard, she poured two glasses of brandy and gave one to her brother.

"Good thing Father is already at his rest," John said lightly. "He'd have raised quite a ruckus with this bunch."

Irene flipped her hand airily. "Oh, to think of Father and Calvin going at it! Calvin lectures on and on about abolition just as Father droned on about slavery and states' rights."

"So your new husband still hasn't learned you own slaves?"

"Technically, he owns them now," she giggled mischievously, "but no, he hasn't learned—and he won't learn, so long as you continue to handle that end of my affairs."

"You know I am eager to help you in every way, Irene, but I confess it makes me nervous to keep such a large secret. What if Calvin happened to meet another Southerner who knew you?"

Irene stuck out her chin and declared, "Highly improbable. Like most abolitionists, he cloisters himself amidst his own kind. Calvin has no true sense of what "South" means—he's never traveled further south than Connecticut. Besides, what if he should find out? Well, we're married now, aren't we? There'd be some unpleasantness, but divorce would be a bigger scandal. He couldn't afford that and still hold office."

"Well, he can't very well hold onto his seat in Congress as a slave owner, either."

"True, but if the worst should happen, I'm confident he would allow me to quietly transfer ownership of the slaves to you. If he tried to stand on principle and make me give them up, I'd just remind him that he couldn't withstand any publicity on this matter." With a kick of her skirts, she sat on the divan. "Don't you worry, John, I know how to play this game and I will not lose. You and I have fought too long to give up the fight over these slaves." She raised her glass to salute him.

John remained standing. "Technically," John countered, "the slaves are no longer slaves."

Irene groaned. "Tell me, John, that it won't last long." She clenched a fist and looked up at him. "Tell me our appeal stands strong."

"It won't last long, I promise. I have very good news about the appeal." He took a seat beside her, and she rested her head on his shoulder.

"Oh, I tell you, John, I've lost sleep over that St. Louis judge's ruling." Her voice became indignant. "That the Scotts should just walk away free! That we should lose all those back wages, which rightfully belong to Henrietta's trust fund. That our family should be embarrassed by losing such a suit. Perhaps I should have remained in St. Louis."

John put his arm around his sister. "It was right and expedient that you left. Staying for a bunch of slaves could have meant your life. Besides, the Scotts have been freed in name only. In actuality, they are as fettered as ever. Little has changed. Their wages all go into escrow. The only benefit they enjoy, if it can be said to be enjoyable, is that they still live in that little shack that those Blow brothers have put them in."

Irene uttered a snort of disgust. "The Blows—what a foul and malicious task they have undertaken. I met Mary Anne Blow once, and she seemed normal. But those brothers! They're losing a pretty penny over this, and for what?"

"You needn't worry about them, either. As soon as Garland filed the appeal on your behalf, that put a halt to any real change for the Scotts, and the Blows are powerless to countermand that. Moreover, now that the Missouri Supreme Court has heard Garland's arguments, well, let's say I will soon have a very welcome wedding present to give you: the decision is certain to be decided in our favor."

Irene jumped up excitedly. "Then Garland argued persuasively?"

John laughed. "He did—he raised the issue of military jurisdiction and even managed to question the authority of the Missouri Compromise—he was in top form. But it wouldn't have mattered if a trained monkey delivered those arguments."

"What do you mean?"

"I mean," John said, proudly taking her hand and pulling her back to the divan, "that the judges in Jefferson City are poised to overturn the St. Louis circuit court ruling. They are hungry for a reversal, as hungry as they are to unseat Benton in these Senate elections. I tell you, Irene, we have the whole state court on our side—and that is my wedding gift to you: Judge Ryland has now reversed himself. The three judges have reached a unanimous decision in your favor. Their written decision is being drafted this very moment!"

Irene pulled John up off the divan, embracing him. "John, that's wonderful, wonderful. But how can you be sure? How do you know all this?"

With subdued pride John said, "Father's old connections. I haven't let them wither."

Irene clapped. "Oh, John, Father would be so proud! I know he didn't show it, but he was so pleased to see you following his footsteps. I'm proud of you, too."

John ducked his head, shy of the compliment.

"I can't thank you enough," she gushed, "for handling all that while I've been here in Massachusetts. You made it possible for me get on with my life. You shielded me from all that ugliness. You stood guard over my future. Henrietta and I owe you so much."

"Your happiness is thanks enough, Irene, truly."

He had finally lifted his head and she saw his sincerity, yet she sensed he was holding something back and urged him to speak up. Haltingly, he said, "Irene, this victory is not yet declared, but it is secured. Unless two of the judges die before they write their decision and announce it, your victory in the Missouri Supreme Court is certain. That is why I would now like to pursue my own plans. Ever since father died, the only reason I've stayed in St. Louis is for this case. I've been thinking of taking up residence in New York."

"John, that would be marvelous. You'd be so much closer!"

He looked relieved that she didn't require him to stay in Missouri

"Yes, I'd be closer to you, and as it turns out, more and more of my business is being conducted here in the east. In fact, before I return to Missouri, I plan to look at property in New York."

"Of course you must move, then. Don't you give another thought to those idiotic slaves and this case." Irene drank the last swig of brandy in her glass. She paced, full of a sense of victory. The Scotts thought they were so clever. They thought they could wrest the upper hand from a Sanford! Well, it had been a struggle, but it was resolving splendidly. She had her new marriage, an esteemed place in society, and a future with hardly a blemish; the stain of this irritating case would soon be dissolved. Soon, but not quite yet. As an afterthought, she added, "Of course, John, I may need you to wrap up a few details, once the judges do announce their decision. You won't leave me in the lurch, will you? Besides, I firmly believe you should have the pleasure of delivering the final blow."

"Of course, of course I'll see this through. I will be glad to conclude this business for you. I presume you will want me to sell them?"

"Positively. Their back wages and whatever price they fetch at auction will all be for Henrietta." She closed her eyes and inhaled deeply. Coyly, she said, "You know, Calvin is so dear with Henrietta, but we may wish to have children of our own—if the state of my health has not been compromised by the severe stress of this case. So it is eminently important to me to secure Henrietta's trust, to make certain that she gains every bit of her inheritance."

Irene's glass was empty, but John's was still full. He raised it in salute and said, "To Henrietta."

Irene raised her empty glass, clinked his, and echoed, "To her inheritance."

Chapter twenty-six

Nyasanu

Freedom were snatched from us before it hatched, like a egg spirited away in the night by a clever fox. We waited and waited, wondering what was ahead for us while that Missouri Supreme Court had some judges go and some new ones come. We heared the new ones was of the same stripe as the old ones, though, and I felt the chill of a strong, cold wind what snuffed out my whiff of hope.

In March 18'n52, word come down that the higher court done ruled against us. The three judges declared that if a slave was freed by another state or territory and stayed there, fine and dandy—but once that slave returned to Missouri, why he returned to slavery, 'cause Missouri felt no obligation to cotton to the laws of others states.

I thought it hard that white men should draw a line of they own on the face of the earth—on one side of which a black man was to become no man at all—and never say a word to the black man about it till they got him on that side of the line. I asked what about all them other slaves what got free under "once free, always free," and the lawyers told me the judges simply said that "times now are not as they were."

From March till June, I had a nightmare. Same one come

almost every night: I was walking outten the court building as I done that very first day when I first asked for freedom. Behind me come Harriet and Eliza and Lizzie, looking pretty as a picture. I was dressed in a clean white shirt and my shoes was buffed to a shine. I stepped out in front of them pillars, and a black cloud of steamboat smoke rolled over me, bringing me to my knees, coughing and hacking so I thought I might die. One old man helped me up, and I recognized the man what helped the spindly little gal in the coffle. Then I seed I was shackled at the ankle, chained myself to the long, straggly coffle of slaves from the Lynch slave pens. Harriet and the gals was way down the steps, reaching out and crying to me, but I was put for auction on them steps. I lifted my head to cry up to the sky but I had no voice, and I was dragged away like dirty laundry, with the sounds of my gals' crying still in my ears.

⁊⅌

In June 1852, Dred was summoned to the sheriff's office, where he met Sheriff Louis LaBeaume and Charles LaBeaume, brothers-in-law to the Blows. Charles, a prosperous lawyer who published abolitionist tracts, had been an especially helpful ally in the six years of legal proceedings, providing both financial and legal assistance. For the past year, he had hired out Dred and kept him busy as janitor in his own and other legal offices. Yet there did not exist between him and Dred the closeness Dred felt with the Blow brothers, and as Dred entered the sheriff's office, he was disappointed to discover Taylor was absent. Henry, he knew, was in Washington, pursuing his political career. Charles LaBeaume explained Taylor had been detained by important business, but would join them later. There was another man present, a stranger to Dred, but introductions were not made immediately. The three white men were silent and grim, and Dred felt his world was about to change horribly.

"It's bad news, ain't it?" said Dred.

The sheriff, who had come to like the old slave over the years of struggle, would not meet Dred's eyes. He looked out the window while passing a sheet of stationery to his brother. Charles was more direct. "Yes," he said, accepting the paper. "I hold here a letter from

Irene Emerson Chaffee, addressed to the sheriff, requesting your back wages be released to her."

It was clear to Dred that this was not the bad news. "And?" he prompted.

Now Charles did look down. He sighed deeply and spewed the words out quickly, "She indicates in this letter her intention to deliver you and your family to Lynch's slave pens for auction."

The impact of the news hit Dred in his gut; it knocked him back into a chair. A second later he ran to a wastebasket and vomited. Kneeling by the basket he moaned and squeezed his eyes shut. He trembled as Charles helped him to his feet and back to the chair. The sheriff brought a cup of water.

Dred clenched his jaw, and his mouth contorted as he fought back tears. Run, he thought. We's got to run and hope for luck. 'Cept we had such luck these six year gone, so much help and kindness, can I hope for more? Can there be that much goodness out there in that white world? He looked out the window, and two tears slipped down to his quivering lip. It was a splendid June day, and the beauty of the summer afternoon contrasted bizarrely with this hideous news. He pictured himself and his family: running hot, running soaking wet, running cold, running hungry. But his consumption had been worse lately. He felt old and sick. Painful memories of his aborted attempt to run with Sam arose, and he knew he would hold back his family if they ran. They would stand a better chance without him. Panicked, he thought, No matter what I do, I's gonna lose my Harriet, lose my gals.

A sob erupted from his chest. He covered his face with his hands and struggled for control. Everyone in the room was hushed. Dred's thoughts chased his feelings in a downward spiral, into a dark and narrow snake pit. *What have I done to deserve this? I know I ain't perfect. I's ashamed of things, but is that enough to warrant this? Is there any way this is just?*

Gran's voice echoed down into the pit, commanding, "I am Sanjo, my name means 'heed the past.'"

With a jolt he realized he had not thought of his kin, or of Africa, for long, long months. *I's a old man what can't sing African no more—hardly even tell the old stories.* He moaned again, thinking: I's a old man what let slip rememory—is that my wrong? And the kin be showing me my wrongs? Maybe the justice is that I let slip the ties to the past, so that the ties to my now and my tomorrow is being cut.

He felt terribly scared and alone, but Gran's voice came again, calmly this time: "You a slave cause of happenstance, and happenstance don't change who you be—only you can change who you be."

He found no comfort in that. He realized he had been thinking, planning, and living his days in the white man's world, the world of the paper and pencil. I don't belong there, he thought. Hollowly he wondered, Maybe it's all happenstance. Maybe there just is what is: just black and just white, and no changing none of it. No why and because. No "if" and then "so." Just doing and responding. The white man got the power, sure 'nough, and he'll fly high above the troubles, and the black man will be dragged through them. Maybe that's the only kind of justice there be—the unequal justice of the two satchels.

Gran's voice came to him one last time, a promise and a reminder: "Slavery can break a man, but iffen it don't—and I believe now it ain't never gonna break you, Dred—then a man become free inside hisself. He build inside hisself something strong that nothing on this earth can break nor silence—his own story. I's peaceful and proud in the knowing that my grandson is Nyasanu, man among men."

Her last words gave him something to hold on to. Nyasanu, man among men. Not man among black men; not man among white men. He was man among men, and he knew himself to be so. He felt himself to be so. It's what his whole life was about: becoming a man in spite of being a slave; facing himself and the world honestly; giving of himself, freely, to his friends and his family. In that instant he rejected the tyranny of the two satchels, tossed them aside, and in their place he discovered a boulder of hatred for Irene Emerson. Now he stood on that boulder and climbed out of the pit. He lifted his head, prepared to continue the fight.

Only seconds had passed, and he realized a hand was on his shoulder. It was Charles LaBeaume. Dred nodded, though no one had spoken.

Taylor rushed in. He already knew about the letter, and he impulsively embraced Dred. Standing now, composed, Dred said to Taylor, "I's glad you's here."

"Have they told you their new idea?" Taylor asked, and saw from Dred's confusion that they hadn't. He turned to the stranger in the room and addressed him, "Roswell?"

Roswell Field stepped forward to shake Dred's hand, introducing himself as an attorney interested in Dred's case. Charles interrupted to explain that Roswell had a legal strategy that might still win them their goal—freedom for the Scott family. "At the very least," Roswell said, "it will protect your family a while longer."

Dred thought he had disgorged the last of his hope in this tedious process of the paper and the pencil, yet the anticipation he now felt in his belly was surely hope. He perked up. "How?"

"We can file a new suit in the federal circuit court."

"I thought we done used up all our appeals," said Dred.

"That is correct, technically speaking. However, it is my contention that we might initiate an entirely new suit—and if we are so happy as to succeed in being heard, then your family could not be split apart while that new case is pending. I propose that the way to proceed is to sue John Sanford—the brother, not Irene Emerson herself—and we would be entitled to sue him in federal court on the basis of what's called a 'diversity suit.' That is, a resident of one state—you—sues a resident of another state—Sanford—and it takes place in federal court because it's a dispute involving the laws of two states."

Taylor voiced the question that was on Dred's tongue. "Why sue Sanford then? Why not sue Mrs. Emerson—I mean, Mrs. Chaffee—since she now resides in Massachusetts?"

Roswell paced while he laid out the strategy. "Chiefly because she does not wish to be associated with the case—"

"I see no reason to favor her wishes," Taylor interrupted.

"Of course not. Nevertheless, the reason we might decide to

323

help her remain hidden behind her brother is twofold: her involvement means Chaffee's involvement, and we gain little by nationally embarrassing a fellow abolitionist plus risk losing support amongst those who currently aid our cause. Second, if we back her into a corner, she may rashly proceed with selling the Scotts anyway. Given her victory in the Missouri Supreme Court and her connections, she just might be able to succeed, however unjust or illegal her actions may be. No, I feel strongly that we should approach Sanford—it will be bait he cannot resist."

Dred shook his head, not understanding. "Why should it bait him?"

Roswell smiled now for the first time and arched an eyebrow. "Again," he said, "the reason is twofold. First, John Sanford will endeavor to continue to protect his sister and her interests. Besides, once he stepped forward as executor of John Emerson's will, we legally obtained standing to accuse him of holding the Scotts in slavery—it needn't be the legal owner that we sue. Second, and most importantly, I believe John Sanford will want to face us in court because he is, according to the old saw, an acorn that has not fallen far from the tree."

Charles smiled knowingly. "Let's not forget who Sanford is," he said, "and who his father was. The Committee of One Hundred was the product of Alexander Sanford's hateful mind."

"The Committee of who?" Taylor asked.

"Of One Hundred," chimed in the sheriff. "You don't know them because they met in secret and quietly lobbied the judges and the legislature for all sorts of laws against the Negroes, to rid St. Louis of all free blacks. They instigated the riots back in '37."

"So that's where Missus get all her vitriol," said Dred.

"Yes," resumed Roswell, "and I believe her brother John maintains ties to the same rotten bunch—at the very least he is a tool of the New York Democrats. I am certain that faction would not pass up an opportunity to test these issues in court."

"What issues?" Dred asked, a bit sharply.

Charles replied excitedly, "Your case, Dred, has become representative of the issues that tear our country apart: the extension of slavery into the territories; the powers of Congress to legislate in the territories; the rights of Negroes to sue in courts, to be citizens, in fact. Your case has brought to light all of these issues, and now we have occasion to challenge the courts to rule on them."

Dred shook his head and murmured, "White men and they satchels."

The others were taken aback; only Taylor understood. "This case," he reminded the lawyers, "is first and foremost about a man trying to protect his family and keep them whole. It's not about a political agenda. It's about Dred and his family." His words dampened the enthusiasm that had been building. No one responded immediately.

Roswell, who also champed at the bit to test this case in the courts, took a deep breath and broke the silence. "Your case, Dred, is not clear and simple. It cannot and should not be regarded independent of the political climate. Even back in '46, the times were changing and cases such as yours were facing stiffer opposition from the bench. Your early lawyers, I'm afraid, failed to see that. Even these last two failed to respond to the clear political bent of the judges on the Missouri Supreme Court."

Dred liked Roswell. He seemed smart and truthful. Someone was finally confirming what he had felt all along, that this was not a simple matter. It was not a furry little kitten that could be taken in and petted. It was a fierce bobcat with fangs and claws.

Roswell saw he had Dred's attention. He continued, "The new case would still champion freedom for you and your family. But it will also argue the larger political issues. These two considerations can no longer remain separate. Tensions over slavery run so high in this country that I believe it is inevitable that the highest courts of the land will have to speak up. If you permit it, Dred, we will challenge them on the basis of your claim to freedom to do just that in the federal circuit court."

"So what kind of chance do you reckon we stand in the federal court?" Dred asked. "When it speaks, is it gonna speak up for my family?"

"Our chances are slim, Dred, I won't mislead you." Roswell held up a finger and wagged it. "But it isn't the federal circuit court that I have my sights set on. That's just the first step, a necessary step, and we'll more than likely lose there. However, a defeat there will allow us to appeal to the United States Supreme Court, the highest court in the land—and I fervently hope those justices will remain untainted by the seething politics that have polluted the lower courts."

Dred smiled sadly. "You think there be judges like that?"

"I know it," Roswell said definitively. "Right here in St. Louis we have Judge Hamilton—he's the one that ruled you were free. He's already received a copy of Irene Chaffee's request for your back wages, and he's denied it. In fact, it was in discussing this case with him that the strategy emerged to steer it toward the Supreme Court."

"And if we lose there?" Dred asked quietly.

Roswell looked grim, but he held Dred's gaze. "If we lose there, there are no other options through the courts. Your situation at that point will be this: you will have enjoyed several years of protection for your family that you would not otherwise have had. You will also be quite famous, and you may be able to use that to advantage. The Chaffees would be facing the same embarrassment then as they do now, only it will be so much more public. Any harm they cause your family will also cause harm to Chaffee's career and reputation."

Dred turned and stared out the window. In doing so, a small part of him smiled inwardly, recognizing with irony that he felt free enough to turn his back on a room full of white men. Outside, the sun was high, the shadows stunted. "How long will all this take?"

Roswell answered. "Two to four years—years that your family can't be sold apart."

Dred nodded again. "Let's do it then," he said, turning. "Let's do it and let's pray I live long enough to see it through." He sat down slowly, his mind revolving around all that had just transpired.

Taylor sat quietly beside Dred, while the two lawyers and the sheriff erupted into excited chatter about what to do first. Roswell Field wanted to know how to get in touch with John Sanford. The sheriff relished framing a retort to Irene Emerson Chaffee, and joked with the others about sending it to her husband. Charles LaBeaume proposed publishing an appeal on behalf of the Scotts to raise funds and public sympathy.

"We require something eloquent," LaBeaume said, "words that will vindicate our claim of freedom, justice, and equality."

Dred watched them tiredly. He felt older and wiser and black. The prospect of a new court case depressed him. Unlike the others, he held little hope that the outcome would be favorable. He didn't believe there would be justice or freedom at the end of the case, and he was quite sure there would not be equality. For him, a new court case was merely a way to play for more time.

In a voice so soft that Taylor almost couldn't hear, Dred said, "You all talk about ideals and principles. That's fine for white folk. But the only principle I stand by be the principle of my gals' future."

Chapter twenty-seven

Decisions

Roswell was right: the federal circuit court decided against us. He was right that the case next went to the U.S. Supreme Court. And he was right that it gived my family about four more year of protection. Till it come to be March 18'n57, and we was about to hear the decision of the highest court in the land.

All that time, the whole thing done gathered speed and pull—most the time I felt like when I was a boy playing on the slope what led up to the grape arbor: sometimes I runned down that hill too fast, till my top half be going faster'n my bottom half, with my little legs pumping just as fast as they could to keep me from tumbling head over heels.

You could say I already done tumbled. A whole slew of people jumped on our wagon enduring those four year, and I become no more significant to that passel of politicians and lawyers than the Xs I marked on all them papers the courts needed. In the end, I ain't been no more'n a mark, something what stands for something else, something small and easy to overlook. It weren't about my family and my little gals no more, it were all about slavery and abolition;

about the Missouri Compromise and the powers of the state; about citizenship for Negroes and iffen they got any rights—it were about white against black.

Then the world jiggled and shaked some more, and didn't I get more significance than I cared for? That's one more thing Roswell was right about: he was right that "the Dred Scott case" would get famous. Fact, the case got so famous that I do believe it will be remembered long after this poor old body gets laid in the ground. My tombstone likely will cast a longer shadow than I ever did.

After we got Mr. Blair to argue for us down there in Washington, why then all across the nation the newspapers was chock full of "the Dred Scott case." But all that did was draw the cranks and crackpots. You see, we become knowed. For ten year we was going up to that court house with nobody to say Boo. Once the Supreme Court got mixed up in it, though, even the dogs snarled at me. We become knowed to them what we just as soon would druther not. I see clear now why we was the first to go so high, 'cause the higher the case go in the courts the bigger target we become. The winter the brick flied in our window, we knowed we had to send the gals out of the city. They went to live and work in the next county north of here, with a family what's friendly with the Blow boys.

I was mighty grateful for the help, but it pained me considerable to have my family split like that. And it scared me when I heared folk say the court case be about abolitionism and federalism and every other kind of "ism"—the Blow boys and Roswell be the onliest ones to still see me as a man standing up for my family, to still listen to me as a father protecting my daughters. Them and Harriet, 'course.

Her and me had more talks, figuring on what we's gonna have to do iffen all them "isms" come down against us. Finally we come to be in agreement on running. With help from Henry and Taylor—what I knowed I could count on—running seemed the only last chance we might have to get free. No, I didn't want to run—I was hoping the Supreme Court was gonna free us—but a part of me begun to feel like running were just gonna be our fate. Only I didn't share with Harriet my deepest doubt, and I tried to hide how sick I truly be feeling. I didn't tell her when she looked into tomorrow and seed four of us running, I looked and only seed three.

⁂

On Friday, March 6, 1857, the Supreme Court read its decision in the much-debated case of *Scott v. Sanford*. Maddeningly, the Scotts waited all morning to hear word of what that decision determined for their future. Harriet and Dred busied themselves with their normal routines while they tried not to worry about the new-fangled telegraph wires blown down by winds or other delays in the news traveling across the country.

Harriet carried laundry to the backyard for washing. Dred was too sick to hire out, but well enough to continue weaving a basket that later could be sold. As he worked, Dred noticed the unpleasant smell of the fish they had been too tense to eat for dinner the night before. Most of it remained in the garbage pail. He rose wearily and lit a sprig of dried sage. Once the flame died out, the sprig smoldered, releasing a smoky ribbon of incense. Then he scooped up the garbage pail and headed out the back door. In the middle of the yard Harriet was vigorously thrashing a white shirt against the washing board. She saw him, wagged her head, and spoke the first real words between them all morning.

"Dred! You know with your cough you can't be chawing t'bacca. You trying to put yourself in the ground faster'n the devil's ready to take you? Are you just giving up? You get one good day where you feel good enough to go into town, and you go and chaw t'bacca!"

He had all but forgotten the incident with the tobacco when he had gone to town a week ago. Now her anger caught him off-guard. He lowered the pail to the ground and held up both hands before him, palms outward. "Now, 'fore you build any more steam in your pipes, know that I done kept my promise. I ain't chawed no t'bacca for over a year now."

"Then what's this stain here that I's rubbing my fingers raw over?"

He frowned, realizing he would have been better off lying. A

331

sudden spasm of coughing drooped him in a patch of sunlight like a wind-battered flower. He felt small inside his clothes, as small as a child dressing up in adult clothing. Harriet continued flagellating the shirt, furious with him. His eyes dithered, following her hands pumping up and down, and came to focus on that face, sweet even in anger, and still so young. It didn't seem fair that he should feel so old.

He recalled the incident outside the courthouse last week, and he didn't know how to tell that sweet face, nor how to keep it from her now. Dred had been heading home, but a sudden rain shower made him pause and debate whether or not to duck into the courthouse. Choosing this over getting wet, he hurried along the street muddied from earlier rains. Before he reached the courthouse, however, a thunderhead released its full weight of rain, and passing carriage wheels spewed a thin, dirty mist as they passed. That's when it happened.

After the incident, he remembered that there had been fighting words falling in the mist, too, such words as he had learned to ignore since the newspapers had begun printing his name nearly every week. The words sprinkled down as carriage wheels sprayed him with mud and stopped sharply right beside him. Then there was the unmistakable sound of a throat mustering phlegm, and he saw the slimy brown slobber hurtling in a downward arc from the drayman, as though the driver had tossed him a coin, and finally the driver's tobacco-fouled spit splattered on his white shirtfront. "Plead that before the judge, you piece of trash nigger."

How to tell this to a woman he loved, who already had more than she could bear?

Yet she read him like a book. She abruptly understood the stain as if he had spoken his memory out loud. She withdrew her hands from the icy water and shook them with disgust. "I see. So I's tiring out my arms over some hateful white man's spit." Her eyes were flat and her jaw bones jutted out. Bunching up the soaking cloth in a clawed fist, she hurled it into the smoldering trash pit, where it sizzled satisfactorily.

My only white shirt, Dred thought, but didn't say.

Again she responded to his unspoken words. "We ain't so poor as to need something that hateful," she retorted. Harriet strode past him and he followed her into the house, where the smoking sage emitted a single strand of perfume. He lifted the sprig and waved it through the air, awakening its red glow.

"The Sioux Mide men called this 'smudging.' Claimed it cleared bad spirits from the room." Setting the sage back down he faced his wife, and it felt now that his clothes fit him again. He felt ready to face whatever was coming.

Humorlessly, she smiled and said, "Wish we could wave some of this stuff in that Supreme Court—did you hear Roswell saying how that room was built to be a crypt? Think on it: a bunch of white men is sitting in a dark underground tomb to decide our fate—Hush!"

Dred sunk to his chair by the hearth in a fit of coughing that broke the sweat out on his forehead. Harriet moved quickly to bring him a blanket. He wrapped up in it and eventually the coughs subsided. He wiped his mouth with a slightly stained handkerchief. All of them at this stage were bloodstained; nothing got them bright white again.

They both jumped when Taylor's knock rattled the thin wooden door. As soon as he stepped into the room, his face delivered the bad news. Harriet kept her back turned to the room as she closed the door. Her forehead touched the door and her shoulders sagged. Dred stood and faced the grief lining Taylor's forehead, thinking how young and fair he had always seemed, a man who perpetually looked boyish, who today looked wizened and gray.

Without a word, Taylor placed an arm about Harriet and led her to Dred's side. Tears were on her cheeks and her hand trembled as she reached for Dred. He opened his arms and the blanket, wrapping her inside with him, and when he again began to cough, he sunk to his chair and Harriet wrapped him back up.

Dred's coughs jounced him a long time, and he couldn't speak. It was Harriet, motioning for Taylor to sit, who said, "Tell us."

Taylor sat on the edge of the chair, his hat still in his hand. Rubbing a spot on the brim and not raising his eyes, he recited in a controlled and solemn voice, "Justice Taney read a lengthy decision, for over two hours. Seven of the nine justices agree that Dred

333

Scott has no right to sue—in fact, that Negroes are not entitled to the rights of citizenship. Broadly speaking, he said that Negroes have no rights at all."

"All Negroes?" asked Dred, his voice wispy. "Or just slaves?"

Taylor pressed his lips together. "I'm not sure," he said. "There was something about the ancestors of blacks being imported as slaves. I think it means any black whose ancestors were slaves, whether free or enslaved now, still has no rights of citizenship. That's got to cover almost all the blacks in the country."

With deep sorrow, Dred said, "We's made it worser for all the blacks, not just ourselves."

Taylor opened his mouth to respond, wanting to tell him it wasn't his fault, but his words strangled in his throat.

Faintly, Harriet asked, "What about 'once free, always free?'"

"They struck that down, too," Taylor replied apologetically. "They allowed that though you may have been free in Iowa or Illinois, once you returned to Missouri, you returned to slavery."

Dred snorted. "We knowed that without the Supreme Court's say-so. 'Cept it didn't seem right or fair—by they own law books, it ain't fair."

"And it still isn't," Taylor said. Lamely he added, "What can I do for you, Dred? Harriet?"

They shook their heads in unison. Dred replied, "You can tell us them lawyers got another trick they ain't yet tried."

Taylor hung his head. He said, "This decision is final; there are no further options through the courts for preventing Irene Chaffee from," his voice cracked, but he continued, "well, doing what she will."

No one said "Lynch's slave pens," but everyone thought it.

Dred started to ask another question, but the consumption drowned it out. There was blood on his kerchief when he finally managed, "When will they come for us?"

Taylor's throat seized again, and he could barely breathe. He raised his eyes to meet Dred's gaze and said in a whisper, "Well, Irene Chaffee will have to go through the sheriff's office, so we'll know as soon as she starts anything. The LaBeaumes have already stated that they'll drag things out as long as possible. I imagine she'll try to get the back wages released to her first, then decide what to do, uh, about, well...." He trailed off pitifully and dropped his eyes again. He fingered the brim of his hat. He cleared his throat and in a voice a bit more steady he offered, "Of course, she still doesn't want her husband to know about any of this—and the papers haven't connected the Congressman to you. We may have a ray of hope there." He looked up, and now it was Dred's gaze that was scraping the floor. Taylor reached out a hand, attracting Dred's attention. With Dred looking at him, his arm still extended, he said with wrenching earnestness, "Henry and I are not giving up, Dred. Henry's in Washington right now, trying to arrange a meeting with Congressman Chaffee. If anything remains to be salvaged at this point, Henry will find it."

Tears brimmed in Dred's eyes as he responded, "You boys—" then he coughed briefly, struggled for control, and continued, "I hope you know my gratitude, 'cause right now I ain't able to tell it good."

A sob bubbled up from Harriet's chest. Tears flowed down her cheeks and chin, and she swabbed roughly at her face with Dred's blanket. Dred quickly clasped her hand, and she was shocked by how hot his hand felt. From force of habit, Harriet rose to make tea for him, but she moved sluggishly, with confusion. With an empty cup in her hand, she crumpled to the floor, keening like a distraught child. Still blanketed, Dred crouched beside her, wrapping her inside with him, then guiding her back to the hearth.

"I should come back later," Taylor stammered.

Dred nodded, but his gaze was still on Harriet. He caressed her face as she sat down. He shrugged off the blanket, leaving it wrapped around her. Turning to Taylor, he said, "We'd be obliged if you could loan us a buggy to go get our gals," he said.

"Oh, my goodness," Taylor said, startled. "I'd forgotten they're still away with the Morgans. Of course, of course. You'll want to go right away, to tell them yourselves. Of course. Well, I'll go get the buggy right away, if that's what you'd like."

Dred thanked him and walked him to the door. They paused and looked mutely at each other. There was nothing more either one could say.

When Dred returned to Harriet's side, she had quieted. She hugged herself numbly and rubbed her arms. Softly, Dred said, "Harriet, we ain't got much time 'fore Taylor returns with that buggy. We's got to talk."

Grudgingly she blinked her assent, but she remained tight-lipped.

"We got a decision to make, Harriet, and I aims to make it together, you and me, wife and husband. This cough tells me we'll be parted soon enough without us going in separate directions now."

The despair in her eyes flipped to pain. She winced, shook her head, and fought for control of her voice.

"You and me, Harriet, we be thinking the same thing about this here decision—ain't I right?"

Still shaking her head, she covered her face with her hands. He pulled her up from the chair and held her steady in front of him, waiting for her to lift her head again. When she did, he said, "Honeybee, you set this thing in motion, and I'll go to my grave grateful for the day you come skipping home from Reverend Anderson's meeting. You brung us the best chance we was to get to protect our family. You brung the abolitionists and the courts. We fought long and hard, for eleven long year, and it were a good fight. But now we's lost, we got to find another way to keep our gals safe. That means only one thing—running."

Weakly she said, "I feel so broke and empty, Dred."

"We's living in a house what's rottening down, sure 'nough, with one choice left us: tear it down and build fresh." He sucked his lower lip, reflecting, then spoke in a voice strong and sure. "You remember, Harriet, on the prairie, that time old man Jenkins had his house burnt to the ground, and all his crops and outbuildings?"

Harriet didn't look up. He continued, "You remember how he cried? Said everything he ever had in the world was put into that farm, and now it were all gone. But remember how after, he hoed all that good, black char into the soil, and in two year his crops was the best on the whole prairie? That's how we's gonna do. We's gonna build again from the good, black char what's left us."

Harriet still cried. "I can't face bringing such news to our gals.

I don't know what to tell them, how to do it without showing them this fear I carry."

"You saying you don't want to run?"

Harriet shivered, and he wrapped his arms around her. She tucked her head into his shoulder and in a muffled voice replied, "I's saying I's scared."

"Me too, Honeyberry, me too. Sure 'nough. The more I know, that's more I know to be afeared of. But something else been happening, too, along this eleven year. I been getting stronger. I been getting clearer on the onliest things what matter in this life. There ain't nobody more important than you, Harriet, and our gals. And there ain't nothing more important than seeing you and our gals safe. And that means running to freedom."

The couple sat again, now at their small wooden table. Each struggled with their emotions. Each stared hard at the grainy tabletop as though answers could be divined there. Dred reached out and cupped Harriet's hands between his warm palms.

Tears welled up as she accused, "I know how you be thinking, Dred, and I won't run without you." A hiccup of tension bubbled up from her throat. Her hands trembled in his.

Dred remained steady. He felt very certain and he let some of the desperation he felt come into voice, saying harshly, "We done talked this all through. You know the Missus is gonna sell us—sell us apart. Put our gals in chains."

She recoiled as though slapped. He pushed on, "So you got to run, Harriet, you and the gals. And you got to do it without me."

"I won't. They won't." She slipped her hands out of his, and reversed the position by taking his hands between hers. Her tears now pooled on the tabletop beneath her chin.

"We may have to lie to them."

"No. That's no good. A family can't hold together on lies. They'll only blame me and hate me later when they finds out the truth, and what do we gain by that? If that comes to pass, then that hateful woman wins anyway, 'cause our family still gets split apart."

Dred was resolute. "I's their father. I'll make them go."

"And how will you make me go? Dred, it's what we fought for

337

all these years, to stay together. What you's saying, it's what I's most afeared of—being without you."

"That's gonna happen soon anyways. Death ain't gonna wait on me much longer."

"I ain't ready," she cried. "I ain't ready."

He let her cry a while. He wore such a sad smile when he said, "You's so beautiful. You's the most beautiful thing this world ever made. And so good. So smart. I know you know that I ain't gonna make it. I can't run, that's all there is too it. I's too sick and too weak."

Harriet sobbed and dropped her head on her outstretched arm, but her hands remained clasped over his until he pulled away and moved around the table to hold her head, lifting it to look gently into her eyes. "Honeybear, I's too sick to run. I's even too sick to keep quiet in hiding. So it's plain: I can't get our gals to freedom, you can. You's the onliest one to do it, so you must. For our gals. For they future."

Harriet gave one last protest, "But what's the future worth without you in it? How can we be free if you ain't? Can't you see that? Without you we ain't gonna be free nor happy!"

Dred lifted Harriet into his embrace. As she sobbed against his chest he whispered, "But you can be safe. You can be safe, and you can be together, and from that will come happiness. By'n by. And that's why you got to run."

Harriet moaned. She sagged in his embrace.

"I feel right about this, Harriet," he persisted. "I feel right enough about this for the both of us—but I still want you to agree with me."

Harriet pulled away and sat down, exhausted. "I've lost sight of right and wrong," she said in a monotone. Dred stood behind her chair and stroked her hair while she continued. "Seems all I can see is win and lose. Together and apart. And a whole ocean of fear."

Soothingly, Dred crooned, "Gran used to talk of together and apart. Of kin and rootedness. Most my time with her, I didn't really know what she be saying. Took a heap of living 'fore I come to the full knowing of it. Took losing her to really know how you can still be with somebody, even if it's only in the heart. Iffen the bodies get pulled apart, the hearts can still stay connected, and that's the most important thing in life, 'cause life without that kind of connection, well, it ain't worth the breath in a ant's body.

"So I'll be with you and the gals in your hearts. You all ain't gonna forget me, is you? You ain't gonna stop loving me? No, you'll go on seeing me in your hearts, and loving me, and when all three of you's together, then I'll be there the strongest. And I will always, always keep you in my heart. Even when I pass over—then I'ma go up to that rich night sky, and I'ma join our sons and twinkle up there till you come to join us. I'll be shooting my rays down into your hearts. I'll be with you that way. And I know you know that in your own heart."

Harriet was quiet now. Her head rested against Dred's chest. She whispered, "I do know. I do know. But I's so afeared of when it's real. I don't know iffen I can really leave you—it's what I fear most in the whole world."

Still stroking her hair, he asked, "And what is it you most hope for in the world?"

"That we can stay a family."

He nodded, and now the tears sprung to his eyes and he answered, "That's how it be sometimes. To get what you most want, you got to face what you most fear."

The lull in tensions was fragile. Preparing to run, Harriet filled an old croker sack with blankets and extra socks. Then she wedged jars of preserves between the blankets. Next she squeezed in a pair of red russets that Eliza once wore, intending Lizzie to have the use of them. When she began to cram in a pipkin, Dred could contain himself no longer. He barked like a scared dog trying to sound fierce. "You ain't gonna be cooking up sauces so you don't need no pipkin! And Lizzie's already wearing a pair of shoes, so you don't need them russets. You got to take all that stuff out, Harriet, and cut it by half. How you think you gonna tote that big old sack for hundreds of miles?"

She squared her shoulders. "Don't you be telling me what we's gonna need and what we can do without, what I can carry and what I can't. I done carried enough baskets of laundry to know what

I's capable of carrying. When I's too tired to tote it any more, that's when I'll toss something aside."

"And who's gonna carry this carpetbag over here, then? The one you already filled to overflowing? Un-nnh. No. It's got to be one sack. Only the necessities. Use your head."

He knew better than to say something like "use your head," but it floated out of his mouth like steam from a tea kettle. He regretted it immediately, but only apologized after they had argued a while longer. Neither took the sparring to heart; each knew the strain the other felt. Harriet eventually acquiesced and began re-sorting both sacks. In the middle of the carpetbag her hand brushed something that rattled. Pulling out Dred's clacking bones, which he had hidden there, she said with a knowing smile, "Only the necessities, huh?"

Before he could defend himself, she laughed and turned to the croker sack. Reaching far down inside she pulled up the necklace Dred had carved for her when they first courted. "I's bringing this along for the same reason," she said. "'Cept I didn't know how to split it betwixt the gals. How's about I give the necklace to Eliza and the bones to Lizzie?"

The memory of their courtship melted whatever hard edges remained between them. Dred wrapped Harriet in a hug. "Wait for the right time," he said, "maybe the end of a long day when everybody's tired. Maybe a time when the gals is feeling real low. Give them the gifts we once gived each other. Tell them to remember they needs to always stay together and work together and give to each other."

The tension and argument had left them both, but now their thoughts slipped into sorrow. Feeling the firm warmth of Harriet's flesh in his arms, Dred knew it would be one of the last times. He gripped her so tight she grunted, but she was gripping him just as tight.

꙰

We surprised ourselves on how easy it were to get ready for running. The blessing in being poor is you don't have so much to pick and choose from. We had everything whittled down to one bag by the time I heared a commotion outside, coming from a distance.

"It's Taylor," I said. Then a chill worked up my spine when I realized he was coming on his horse, not in the buggy.

Harriet had the same thought. "We's too late," she moaned. "They's coming to get us now and it's too late to run. Oh my good Lord, will we ever see our gals again?"

I runned to the porch. Taylor was pounding up the alleyway on his horse, throwing off waves of mud and still yelling from a block away. My heart twisted up in my chest painfully as he come nearer.

Taylor was dripping mud when he hopped down and came running. Then I seed his face and my heart begun thumping again. His face was shining like the sun.

"It's good news," he cried out. "It's great news!"

He runned up to us and lifted me clear offen my feet and spinned me around. He grabbed Harriet next and did the same with her. We was all giggling like fools, it were so confusing yet also we felt a burst of joy and hope, just offen Taylor's shining face.

Laughing, nearly singing, Taylor shouted, "You're going to be free, Dred, you're going to be free. You and Harriet and the girls are all going to be free!"

Harriet was crying, the water streaming down her cheeks clear and beautiful and not pained for a change. We held each other while Taylor danced around us like a child in a ring game. Then I begun to cough so rough I had to sit. I couldn't talk, but I motioned for Taylor to spill his news.

"You're going be free," he repeated. "Henry struck a deal with Congressman Chaffee. I told you, Dred, if anyone could salvage this, it would be Henry—and he did it! He did it!" He hugged me again, and tears was streaming down my cheeks now. It were confusing and too sudden to be real, but there was no mistaking the powerful joy that washed over us.

Taylor went on to say how a Massachusetts newspaper found out John Sanford didn't really own us—and they found out who really did. When they printed in they paper that a abolitionist Congressman owned the most famous slaves in the nation, well he got pickled like a Alabama cucumber! And just as he was choking on the brine, Henry knocked on his door and suggested the best thing he could do was to set us free. Henry suggested what a feather in the cap that would be for abolitionists everywheres, and iffen he'd do that, iffen he'd free us all, then Henry swore he'd get all the abolitionist papers to write flattering stories about how Chaffee never knowed he had any connection to us.

"The Congressman jumped at that offer," crowed Taylor. "And here's the best part—in order to free you, Dred, Chaffee first has to sell you to somebody who's already a citizen of Missouri—one more 'technicality' of the courts. So Chaffee has agreed to sell you, Harriet, Eliza, and Lizzie to me, and I will have the privilege of accompanying you to the courthouse to sign the papers granting you and your family freedom!"

And 'course, that's just how it went. Took a couple of months, but on May 26, 18'n57, Lizzie, Eliza, Harriet, and Dred Scott was all freed in the St. Louis circuit court, in the very room where it all started back in 18'n46, by the very same judge, Judge Hamilton, what told us we was free back in 18'n50! Then all the crashing waves of our worry and struggle washed up to the shore and melted like seafoam on warm sand.

Now, ain't that a fine way to end a story?

Chapter twenty-eight

Downriver

That was not the end, though. Another story waited patiently for its turn.

After being declared a free man in a St. Louis Court, Papa lived another year and a half working as a porter at the Barnum Hotel. And as Roswell Field had predicted, he was famous. Guests of the hotel and people just passing through town for an afternoon stopped to congregate in the hotel lobby to hear the griot conjure his tales. He carried his history, not merely the bags of guests. His strength was opening new possibilities, not hotel doors. He crafted stories where honesty could breathe, get up from its confinement, discover its legs were still sturdy, and walk about freely.

In true griot tradition, Papa shared his stories and his history both. He began with a creation story that foretold the ending: the white man with paper and pencil would prevail in a universe where an injudicious god set up such divisions. Yet Gran's dream had also proved prescient: her grandson's music indeed would jiggle and shake the world, rupturing North from South. The tremors emanating from his history reverberate yet through our history.

Papa's great talent was to redraw his world. His portraits were colored with upriver tales of fables and folklore and the fabulous history of kin. Then he highlighted those in downriver versions resplendent with ghost stories and love epics; memoirs and dreamscapes; a medical guide, a travel journal and ultimately, a legal record that, for centuries to come, no history book covering this period will be able to omit.

There are many heroes in his stories, though Papa never saw himself as one. He wasn't a leader of men. He wasn't an abolitionist bent on ending slavery. He was merely a man whose nature and gift was to inspire others. He was a man who insisted on telling his own story, on speaking freely.

Dred Scott was merely a man—a man among men. He journeyed to define his own truth. He cried out to share it with all who would listen. That was his freedom, and he didn't require a court to help him find it. It was his birthright.

He himself may or may not be called a leader, but who can dispute that his story will lead generations of people closer to truth and freedom?

ﷺ

Goodbye, Papa.

September 17, 1858, you lay dying. Your body, always small and light, was now reduced to a skeleton jutting grotesquely under a sky-blue quilt as your chest heaved in spasms that jerked your body about. And that dear face, typically alight with humor and compassion, was emaciated and embossed with pain.

An embrace was out of the question; you would have suffocated. Instead, I held your hand. It was feverishly warm, and those tapping fingers were heartbreakingly still. So many times throughout your long illness I had sat at the bedside uselessly while you coughed up blood, desperate to help but unable. My vigils should have prepared me for goodbye, but they didn't. The end was so much worse. I was only thirteen, but I knew you were drowning, your lungs so swampy they no longer accepted the air you struggled to suck down.

Long into that night, Mama took my place and told me to rest

344

myself. I laid down beside Eliza, who slept fitfully. I held my own breath as I listened to the fearsome noise of your terrible struggle with that remorseless beast. Eliza awakened. Sensing death's engagement, we rushed back to your bedside.

You abruptly became quiet and Eliza reached out to you, but I was frozen with the fear that you were dead. "It's all right," Mama reassured me. "Papa's just resting."

After a while you smiled and said something I couldn't hear. I looked to Mama, who put her arms around Eliza and me. She pulled us together tightly. A shiver ran through her to me as she said, "Papa's going over soon, girls." You motioned weakly to Mama, who brought a slender pouch and offered it to Eliza and me.

My throat constricted with emotion, and I didn't want this gift. I wanted no farewells, no more tears, no more heartache. Eliza opened it and pulled out a long, slender piece of wood, like a ruler. It was covered all over in carvings, and at the bottom of one side I recognized a coiled snake design. I had seen it only once in my life, but I knew its story well. My tear-clutched throat relaxed and I said, "This is old Joe's age-stick."

Your lips moved, and I leaned down close to hear you scratch out, "Sure 'nough. I want you gals to have it. To tell all the tales yet to tell."

I had been trying not to cry, but a few devious tears wriggled to my chin. I covered my face with my hands, but I heard you urge, with as much insistence as you could muster, "Tell me a tale." You grappled for more air. "Let it go, let it come."

I looked to Eliza who handed me the age-stick. It quivered in my hands like a divining rod, seeking out subterranean streams of stories, but only tears flowed there. Mama held me while Eliza gave you a tale.

In a shaken voice she gave back the tale of Adebanke, the poor little Fon slave girl who was captured with Gran and made to work in the Oyo village. She worked very hard for a rich farmer. Her job was to carry the water to the fields to keep the soil moist for the growing of the yams. Her master owned many acres, so she carried water from sunup to sundown to get all the fields watered. Adebanke was all alone in this hostile place; her kin were all back in Dahomey, and the only thing she had of home was her head scarf.

In the carrying of water, Adebanke used a head cloth to balance the jugs on her head. But the cloth she wore on her head was the cloth made by the farmer's wife, who would not allow the slaves to wear the cloth of Dahomey. Only at night, when she slept, could she wrap the cloth of home around her head. And each time she wrapped the cloth of home around her head, she traveled in her dreams back to Dahomey, back to her kin.

This wasn't just a dream, she really went there. She could talk with her kin and give them news. She could play with her sisters and snuggle down next to her mother. As soon as the sun rose, though, each morning she awoke back in Oyo. She wrapped her head in the Oyo cloth and returned to the work of watering the fields.

When the time came of the long march to the slave fort, Gran and Adebanke managed to walk side by side. Nyota and Njeri protected Adebanke as they did their own children. But Adebanke never made it to the prison by the shore, and she was not on the slave ship. Nor did she die, nor was she taken somewhere else.

Adebanke escaped.

After the first day of marching, as the slaves collapsed into sleep, Adebanke wrapped her head in the Dahomey cloth, and in the morning both the girl and her magical head cloth were gone. She had found a way to return home and never leave.

Eliza finished the story with a gentle pit-a-pat on her skirt. I saw your delight, Papa, and I lifted my hands to my own head scarf. You watched me unwrap it. I gave it to you with steady hands. You crushed it to your chest, then wrestled mightily to hold it up. You succeeded, saying clearly, "This will carry me home."

Papa, you left too soon. I was only thirteen, Papa. You should have been here to see me grow to be a woman. You should have been here to protect me through the War. You should have helped me choose a husband. You should have had the chance to hold your grandson, at least once.

My son will never sit with his beautiful face lifted to yours,

Papa, entranced by the griot's tales. All we have now are the stories Eliza wrote down—and even though some of the pages are as lost as your dear embrace, memory has helped me restore them. I hope you would be pleased. I have tried to speak as plainly and truly as you, tried to speak right on despite what others think, regardless of convention and modesty. I have tried to tell the whole story. This is your legacy.

A story! A story! Let it go, let it come.

In 1957, thanks to the research of the Rev. Edward J. Dowling, S.J. and the contributions of Mrs. Charles C. Harrison Jr. of Villa Nova, PA. (granddaughter to Taylor Blow), a headstone was finally erected over Dred Scott's grave. An unveiling ceremony was held on September 17, 1957, ninety-nine years after he died.

The headstone inscription reads:

DRED SCOTT

BORN ABOUT 1799

DIED SEPT. 17, 1858

Freed from slavery by

his friend Taylor Blow

On the reverse side:

DRED SCOTT

SUBJECT OF THE DECISION OF THE

SUPREME COURT OF THE

UNITED STATES IN 1857 WHICH DENIED

CITIZENSHIP TO THE NEGRO, VOIDED

THE MISSOURI COMPROMISE ACT,

BECAME ONE OF THE EVENTS THAT

RESULTED IN THE CIVIL WAR

Acknowledgments

I t seems it took a village to raise this novel, and I am deeply grateful to many. To those talented fellow writers and hunters of words—Darwyn Carson, Trudy Harris, John House, Shannon Johnson, D.J. Kami, Wayne Lehrer, Rachel Levin, Monique Martin, Trista Tyson—for giving me a place to explore, trip, and move on; for tolerating tortuous (sometimes torturous) rewrites. Your talents, shared so generously, underpin every scene in this novel.

To my teachers, elders in skill level if not age, at UCLA Writers' Program, for demonstrating the craft and sharing your brilliance: Eve LaSalle Caram, Tod Goldberg, and Rachel Resnick. Special thanks to Les Plesko who encouraged me to look at my own life and challenged me to be professional.

To friends and family, kin and kindred spirits, who cheered me on, buoyed my doubts, and never grew bored: Claudia, Donna, Bob, Janet, Martin, Laurie, Dee, Susan, Mary, Jocelyn, Hannah, and Andrew. You each uniquely opened up possibilities that now are realities. Special thanks to Susie Arden for letting me adopt one of her delightful childhood memories; to Thomas Jones for his inspirational storytelling; and to Ellen Ruderman for helping me enjoy it all.

To the conjurers whose powers transmuted the base manuscript into this book: Matthew Miller for his prompt, hearty endorsement and lasting patience; Aloma Halter for her keen attention, compassionate reading, and deft editing; and to all the wizards at Toby Press.

These are the people whose touch and influence helped me write this book. Yet there are spirits whose powers were just as crucial: the descendants of Africans who told their stories of enslavement, and the writers of the Federal Writers Project who helped record their words; Walter Ehrlich for his valuable research and heuristic book, *They Have No Rights*; numerous contemporary historians, folklorists, and artists who keep alive a fabulous heritage, especially: Roger D. Abrahams, *African Folktales*; Harry Belafonte, *The Long Road to Freedom—An Anthology of Black Music*; B.A. Botkin, *Lay My Burden Down* and related works; Daryl C. Dance, *From My People* and related works; Clyde W. Ford, *The Hero with an African Face*; John Hope Franklin, *From Slavery to Freedom*; James Neal Primm, *Lion of the Valley, St. Louis, Missouri*; George P. Rawick, *The American Slave* and related works; Henry D. Spalding, *Encyclopedia of Black Folklore and Humor*. Finally, to the Missouri Historical Society, Washington University in St. Louis, and the National Park Service, all of which keep alive the meager, personal information pertaining to a great man and his family.

About the Author

Mary E. Neighbour

Mary E. Neighbour was born and raised in New Jersey, and spent her young adulthood in NYC. After attaining a BA in literature and creative writing from the City University of New York, she studied and trained as a psychotherapist before later returning to a career in writing. With her keen ear for first person narrative, she has specialized in helping individuals develop their own narratives, writing their memoirs and family histories. Her short fiction has won awards and has been recognized by the Sacramento Public Library, and *ByLine Magazine, Mid-American Review,* the *Alligator Juniper,* and the Whidbey Island Writers' Association. *Speak Right On* was one of the top prize-winners in the Pacific Northwest Writers' Association contest for unpublished first novels.

Ms. Neighbour and her husband live in Santa Fe, New Mexico. *Speak Right On* is her first novel.

The fonts used in this book are from the Garamond family

ELITES IN LATIN AMERICA

Elites
in Latin America

EDITED BY

SEYMOUR MARTIN LIPSET

AND

ALDO SOLARI

New York OXFORD UNIVERSITY PRESS 1967

To Jorge Ahumada (1917–65)
who worked for Latin American development

Preface

The term "elite" was first used by seventeenth-century shopkeepers to describe their best quality merchandise. By the latter part of the century the term had gained a broader application, as the "elite of the nobles."[1] In the nineteenth century the concept was gradually extended by various political and sociological analysts to refer to the governing or dominant strata. The use of the term by Pareto, Mosca, Michels, Lasswell, and Mills suggests various definitions, but a fairly clear consensus for its applicability seems to emerge. The most general usage refers to those positions in society which are at the summits of key social structures, i.e. the higher positions in the economy, government, military, politics, religion, mass organizations, education, and the professions. And within this more inclusive notion of the social elite, analysts such as Mosca and Pareto have distinguished between the political and governing elite—those who participate more or less directly in political decisions—and the nongoverning elite—those at the top of nonpolitical structures.

Elite analysis has to a considerable degree formed an alternative perspective to class analysis. The former generally assumes that in all societies, of the past, present, and future, institutional and societal power will be held by a relatively small minority, since the structure of complex society and organization prevents the mass from directly exercising power. Hence from elite analysis it is concluded that what-

[1] See T. B. Bottomore, *Elites and Society* (London: C. A. Watts, 1964), pp. 1, 15; Renzo Sereno, "The Anti-Aristotelianism of Gaetano Mosca and Its Fate," *Ethics,* 48 (1958), p. 15; Harold Lasswell, Daniel Lerner, and C. Easton Rothwell, *The Comparative Study of Elites: An Introduction and Bibliography* (Stanford: Stanford University Press, 1952); Suzanne Keller, *Beyond the Ruling Class. Strategic Elites in Modern Society* (New York: Random House, 1963); Carl Beck, James M. Malloy, and William R. Campbell, *A Survey of Elite Studies* (Washington: Special Operations Research Office, American University, 1965).

ever the predominant economic structure of a society—feudal, capitalist, state collectivist, some other type, or a combination of types—the distinction between elites and nonelites will persist; this does not mean, of course, that it does not matter, from a political viewpoint, what the social base or origins of a given elite are.

Marxists and other class analysts have logically and consistently rejected elite and "ruling-class" concepts because these are antithetical to their assumption that economic power relationships form the essential character of a society. The criticism of C. Wright Mills's book *The Power Elite* by a number of Marxists arose from their rejection of elite theory. For though they welcomed Mills's criticism of the existing dominant power groups in the United States, some of them saw in his focus on the relationships among the heads of various American institutions a rejection of Marxism, a way of looking at power structures which could be used to derive equally negative conclusions about Communist countries.

In this volume, we are not concerned with the conceptual or ideological differences subsumed in these different approaches. Rather, we are interested in elites because of our larger concern with social, economic, and political development. And while there are many factors which affect the propensity of a nation to develop, it is clear that regardless of differences in social systems, one of the requisites for development is a competent elite, motivated to modernize their society. The essays here deal with diverse aspects of elites in Latin America. This focus on elites, however, is not intended to imply that the character of economic or political systems is less important, or that a policy-maker should be less concerned to develop the competence of the mass of the population than that of the elite. A basic assumption of this book is that factors affecting the calibre of the elites play a major role in determining the propensity of different countries for economic growth and political stability, and are worth analyzing in depth regardless of the importance of other variables.

This volume is the outcome of a Seminar on Elites and Development in Latin America held at the University of Montevideo, Uruguay, in June 1965. The conference was called jointly by the two editors to bring together scholars from all parts of the Americas, plus a few from Europe, who were concerned with problems of Latin American development. In planning the seminar, we decided to invite various people to lead discussions dealing with the value systems and economies of Latin America, the patterns characteristic of specific elite groups, and analyses of different aspects of the educational system on both the university and secondary-school level. As a follow-up to the seminar, a number of those involved were asked by the editors either to rework the papers they had prepared for the conference, or to write totally new ones for publication in book form. This work is a result of their activities. Hopefully, it will make a contribution to the beginning of research on topics which have been inadequately treated in the past.

Many of the chapters published here constitute rewrites of papers delivered at the Montevideo seminar. Others, however, those by Horowitz, Landsberger, Lipset, Quijano, and Scott, were written specifically for this volume. We are indebted to all of the authors for the rapidity and skill with which they responded to the editors' requests to modify their original presentations, or to write new papers.

The Montevideo conference was sponsored by the University of Montevideo, the Institute of International Studies of the University of California at Berkeley, and the Congress for Cultural Freedom. Much of the funds to pay for the seminar, as well as expenditures for translation and editorial services, were borne by the Congress from a grant for international publications provided by the Ford Foundation. During the past year, while this book was being prepared for publication, the English-speaking editor has drawn upon services supplied by the Center for International Affairs of Harvard University with which he is now associated. The Center should, therefore, be considered as a fourth sponsor of the volume. This volume on Latin American elites is part of a program of studies on Comparative National Development which began under Lipset's supervision at the Berkeley Institute and is now conducted at the Harvard Center. This program has been supported by the Carnegie Corporation and the Inter-University Study of Labor Problems and Economic Development, as well as state (California) and federal grants. Other books which are a result of the Comparative National Development project include Neil Smelser and S. M. Lipset (eds.), *Social Structure and Social Mobility in Economic Growth* (Chicago: Aldine, 1966); Glaucio Soares, *Economic Development and Political Radicalism* (to be published by Basic Books); and S. M. Lipset (ed.),

"Students and Politics," special issue of *Comparative Education Review*, 10 (June 1966), pp. 129–376 (also to be published by Basic Books in 1967).

We would like to express our sincere appreciation to Luis Mercier Vega of the Congress for Cultural Freedom who did so much to make the seminar and this volume possible. He was co-operative beyond the call of duty with respect to the practical tasks, and almost invisible with regard to affecting intellectual decisions. The editors accept complete responsibility for determining the format of the conference and the authors of the chapters. We would like to also acknowledge with gratitude the assistance of Sandra Winston in the final editing, proofreading, and indexing stages.

Cambridge, Massachusetts   SEYMOUR MARTIN LIPSET
Montevideo, Uruguay   ALDO SOLARI
June 1966

Contents

I

Economic Development and
the Business Classes

I

Values, Education, and Entrepreneurship

SEYMOUR MARTIN LIPSET

Discussions of the requisites of economic development have been concerned with the relative importance of the appropriate economic conditions, rather than the presumed effects on varying rates of economic growth of diverse value systems. Much of the analysis which stems from economic thought has tended to see value orientations as derivative from economic factors. Most sociological analysts, on the other hand, following in the tradition of Max Weber, have placed a major independent role on the effect of values in fostering economic development.[1]

Although the evaluation of the causal significance of economic factors and value orientations has often taken the form of a debate pitting one against the other, increasingly more people have come to accept the premise that both sets of variables are relevant. Many economists now discuss the role of "non-economic" factors in economic growth, and some have attempted to include concepts developed in sociology and psychology into their overall frame of analysis. Sociologists, from Weber on, have rarely argued that value analysis could account for economic growth. Rather the thesis suggested by Weber is that, given the economic conditions for the emergence of a system of rational capital accumulation, whether or not such growth occurred in a systematic fashion would be determined by the values present. Structural conditions make development possible; cultural factors determine whether the possibility becomes an actuality. And Weber sought to prove that

I am extremely indebted to Ivan Vallier and Neil Smelser for detailed critiques of the earlier draft of this chapter. I would also like to express my appreciation to Elsa Turner for research assistance.

capitalism and industrialization emerged in Western Europe and
North America because value elements inherent in or derivative from
the "Protestant Ethic" fostered the necessary kinds of behavior by those
who had access to capital; while conversely during other periods in
other cultures, the social and religious "ethics" inhibited a systematic
rational emphasis on growth.[2]

The general Weberian approach has been applied to many of the
contemporary underdeveloped countries. It has been argued that these
countries not only lack the economic prerequisites for growth, but that
many of them preserve values which foster behavior antithetical to the
systematic accumulation of capital. The relative failure of Latin American countries to develop on a scale comparable to those of North
America or Australasia has been seen as, in some part, a consequence
of variations in value systems dominating these two areas. The overseas offspring of Great Britain seemingly had the advantage of values
derivative in part from the Protestant Ethic and from the formation of
"New Societies" in which feudal ascriptive elements were missing.[3]
Since Latin America, on the other hand, is Catholic, it has been dominated for long centuries by ruling elites who created a social structure
congruent with feudal social values.

Perhaps the most impressive comparative evidence bearing on the
significance of value orientations for economic development may be
found in the work of David McClelland and his colleagues, who have
undertaken detailed content analyses of folk tales in primitive cultures
and of children's story books in literate ones, seeking to correlate degrees of emphasis on achievement values in these books with rates of
economic development.[4]

Among the primitive tribes, those which were classified as high in
achievement orientation on the basis of the content of their folk tales
were much more likely to contain full-time "business entrepreneurs"
(persons engaged in a market economy) than those which were low.
To measure the relationships in literate societies, McClelland and his
co-workers analyzed the content of children's stories read by early primary school children during two time periods, 1925 and 1950, in many
nations. Statistically significant correlations were found between this
measure of achievement level for 1925 and the extent to which the increase in use of electrical energy (a measure of development) was
higher or lower than the expected rate of growth for the period from
1925 and 1950, for a group of twenty-three countries. Similar findings

are reported for forty countries for the period 1952 to 1958. As Mc-Clelland comments, the latter "finding is more striking than the earlier one, because many Communist and underdeveloped countries are included in the sample. Apparently N Achievement [his term for the achievement orientation] is a precursor of economic growth—and not only in the Western style type of capitalism . . . but also in economies controlled and fostered largely by the state." [5] These findings are reinforced by two historical studies of thematic content of various types of literature in England between 1400 and 1800, and in Spain between 1200 and 1700. In both countries, the "quantitative evidence is clear cut and a rise and fall of the *n* Ach level *preceded in time* the rise and fall of economic development." [6]

Striking differences have been found by McClelland and his collaborators in the value orientations of comparable samples of populations in less developed as compared with more developed countries. Thus, research in Brazil and the United States analyzing the achievement motivations of students aged 9 to 12, with the Brazilian sample drawn from São Paulo and Rio Claro, and the North American one from four northeastern states, reports that "Brazilian boys on the average have lower achievement motivation than their American peers . . . [that] upper, middle, and lower class Brazilians tend to have lower achievement motivation scores than Americans of a comparable class. *What is more startling is the finding that the mean score of Brazilian boys in any social class is lower than the motivation score of the Americans . . . whatever their class may be."* [7]

On a theoretical level, the systematic analysis of the relations of value systems to the conditions for economic development requires concepts which permit one to contrast the relative strength of different values. Thus far, the most useful concepts for this purpose are Talcott Parsons's "pattern-variables." These refer to basic orientations toward human action, and are sufficiently comprehensive to encompass the norms affecting behavior within all social systems, both total societies and their subsystems, such as the family or the university.[8]

Distinctions which seem particularly useful for analyzing the relation between values and the conditions for development are achievement-ascription, universalism-particularism, specificity-diffuseness, and equalitarianism-elitism. (The latter is not one of Parsons's distinctions, but rather one which I have added.) A society's value system may emphasize that a person in his orientation to others treats them in

terms of their abilities and performances (achievement) or in terms
of inherited qualities (ascription); applies a general standard (universalism) or responds to some personal attribute or relationship (particularism); deals with them in terms of the specific positions which
they happen to occupy (specificity) or in general terms as individual
members of the collectivity (diffuseness).

Concepts such as these are most appropriately used in a comparative
context. Thus the claim that the United States is achievement-oriented,
or that it is equalitarian, obviously does not refer to these characteristics
in any absolute sense. The statement that a national value system is
equalitarian clearly does not imply the absence of great differences in
power, income, wealth, or status. It means rather that from a comparative perspective nations defined as equalitarian tend to place more
emphasis than elitist nations on universalistic criteria in interpersonal
judgments, and that they tend to de-emphasize behavior patterns
which stress hierarchical differences. No society is equalitarian, ascriptive, or universalistic in any total sense; all systems about which we
have knowledge are characterized by values and behavior which reflect
both ends of any given polarity, e.g. all systems have some mobility
and some inheritance of position.

In his original presentation of the pattern-variables, Parsons linked
combinations of two of them: achievement-ascription and universalism-
particularism to different forms of existing societies. Thus the combination of universalism-achievement may be exemplified by the United
States. It is the combination most favorable to the emergence of an industrial society since it encourages respect or deference toward others
on the basis of merit and places an emphasis on achievement. It is typically linked with a stress on specificity, the judging of individuals and
institutions in terms of their individual roles, rather than generally.[9]
The Soviet system expresses many of the same values as the United
States in its ideals. One important difference, of course, is in the position of the Communist party. Membership in the party conveys
particularistic rights and obligations. Otherwise both systems resemble
each other in "value" terms with reference to the original pattern-
variables. Both denigrate extended kinship ties, view ethnic subdivi-
sions as a strain, emphasize individual success, but at the same time
insist that inequality should be reduced, and that the norms inherent in
equalitarianism should govern social relationships. The two systems,
North American and Communist, diverge, however, with respect to

another key pattern-variable polarity, self-orientation vs. collectivity-orientation—the emphasis that a collectivity has a claim on its individual units to conform to the defined interests of the larger group, as opposed to the legitimacy of actions reflecting the perceived needs of the individual unit.

Conceptualization at such an abstract level is not very useful unless it serves to specify hypotheses about the differences in norms and behavior inherent in different value emphases.[10] Such work would clearly have utility for the effort to understand the varying relationships between levels of economic development and social values.[11]

The Latin-American system has been identified by Parsons as an example of the particularistic-ascriptive pattern. Such a system tends to be focused around kinship and local community, and to de-emphasize the need for powerful and legitimate larger centers of authority such as the state. Given a weak achievement orientation, such systems see work as a necessary evil. Morality converges around the traditionalistic acceptance of received standards and arrangements. There is an emphasis on expressive rather than instrumental behavior. There is little concern with the behavior of external authority so long as it does not interfere with expressive freedom. Such systems also tend to emphasize diffuseness and elitism. The status conferred by one position tends to be accorded in all situations. Thus if one plays one elite role, he is respected generally.[12]

Although the various Latin American countries obviously differ considerably—a point which will be elaborated later—it is interesting to note that a recent analysis of the social structure of the most developed nation, Uruguay, describes the contemporary situation there in much the same terms as Parsons does for the area as a whole. Aldo Solari has summed up some of his findings about his own country:

> It is clear that particularism is a very important phenomenon in Uruguayan society and it prevails over universalism. A great number of facts support this. It is well known that the prevailing system of selection for government employees is based on kinship, on membership in a certain club or political faction, on friendship, etc. These are all particularistic criteria. A similar phenomenon is present in private enterprise where selection of personnel on the basis of particularistic relations is very common. The use of universalistic criteria, such as the use of standardized examinations is exceptional. Quite frequently when such universalistic criteria seem operative, they are applied to candidates who have been previously selected on the basis of personal relationships.[13]

8

Ascriptive ties are also quite strong in Uruguay, linked in large part to the importance of the family in the system. Concern with fulfilling family obligations and maintaining family prestige leads propertied Uruguayans to avoid risking the economic base of the family position. The concerns of the middle class which tend to affect the expectations and norms of the whole society are for "security, moderation, lack of risk, and prestige." [14]

The sources of Latin American values have been generally credited to the institutions and norms of the Iberian nations, as practiced by an Iberian-born elite during the three centuries of colonial rule. Those sent over from Spain or Portugal held the predominant positions, and in the colonies "ostentatiously proclaimed their lack of association with manual, productive labor or any kind of vile employment." [15] And Spain and Portugal, prior to colonizing the Americas, had been engaged for eight centuries in conflict with the Moors, resulting in the glorification of the roles of soldier and priest, and in the denigration of commercial and banking activities, often in the hands of Jews and Moslems. Iberian values and institutions were transferred to the American continent. To establish them securely, there were constant efforts by the "Church militant" to Christianize heathen population, the need to justify morally Spanish and Portuguese rule over "inferior" peoples, Indians, and imported Africans, and the fostering of a "get rich quick mentality" introduced by the *conquistadores,* but reinforced by efforts to locate valuable minerals or mine the land, and most significantly by the establishment of the *latifundia* (large-scale plantations) as the predominant form of economic, social, and political organization.[16] Almost everywhere in Latin America, the original upper class was composed of the owners of *latifundia,* and these set the model for elite behavior to which lesser classes, including the businessmen of the towns, sought to adapt.

And as Ronald Dore points out, in *arielismo,* the Latin American scorn for pragmatism and materialism, now usually identified with the United States, "there is an element that can only be explained by the existence of a traditional, landed upper class." [17] The period of the predominance of *latifundia* social structure is far from over. In most Latin American nations (Mexico, Bolivia, and Cuba are perhaps the major exceptions), agriculture is still dominated by *latifundia.* Thus farms of 1000 hectares or more, which constitute 1.5 per cent of all farms in Latin America, possess 65 per cent of the total farm acreage.

Minifundias (small farms of under 20 hectares) constitute 73 per cent of all farms, but less than 4 per cent of the acreage.[18] The high-status social clubs of most major cities are still controlled or highly influenced by men whose families derived their original wealth and status from *latifundia*. In spite of repeated demands for land reform, little has been done to reduce the economic source of the influence of *latifundia* families.[19] Hence the continuation of pre-industrial values in much of Latin America can be linked in large part to the persistence of the rural social structure which originally fostered these values.[20] Even in Uruguay, which has long been dominated by the metropolis of Montevideo, one finds that much of the upper social class of the city is composed of members of powerful old land-owning families. Many of those involved in commercial and banking activities have close kinship ties with the large cattle-raisers and *estancieros*. And the upper rural class maintains considerable influence on the society as a whole through its control over the main agricultural organizations, and the continued strength of a widespread ideology which states that the wealth of the country depends on land, and on the activities of those who farm it.[21]

In many countries the prestige attaching to land ownership still leads many businessmen to invest the monies they have made in industry in farms.[22] A study of the Argentinian elite indicates that similar emphases are important there also, in spite of the influence of its cosmopolitan, six million strong capital city Buenos Aires:

> Insofar as the entrepreneurial bourgeoisie moved up in the social scale, they were absorbed by the old upper classes. They lost their dynamic power and without the ability to create a new ideology of their own, they accepted the existing scale of social prestige, the values and system of stratification of the traditional rural sectors. When they could they bought *estancias* [ranches] not only for economic reasons, but for prestige, and became cattle raisers, themselves.[23]

In Chile, too, many analysts have suggested that much of the behavior and values of the urban bourgeoisie reflect their effort to imitate and gain acceptance from an extremely conservative land-based upper class. Less than 10 per cent of the landowners own close to 90 per cent of the arable land; this group shows little interest in efficient productivity and sustain semi-feudal relations with their workers.[24] One possible "superficial advantage" of the close identification of the urban middle class with that of the old aristocracy has been suggested by a North American commentator. "Because this group has in its political, social, and economic thinking so closely reflected the attitudes of the aristocracy, there has been almost no disruption as middle sectors have won increasing power in Chilean politics." But he notes that, while producing political stability, this role "may also have contributed to economic and social stagnation." [25]

Similar patterns have been described by many students of Brazilian society to account for the strong emphasis on family particularism within industrial life there. Brazil, of course, as the last major country to retain slavery, as a former empire which ennobled its leading citizens, and as the most rural of South America's major countries, can be expected to retain many of the value emphases of an elitist traditional culture, even among the successful "new classes" of its relatively highly developed southern regions.

> Rather than considering themselves a new "middle class," these newly successful groups have come to share, with the descendants of the old landed gentry, an aristocratic set of ideals and patterns of behavior which they have inherited from the nobility of the Brazilian empire . . .
>
> One of these aristocratic values relevant to economic change is what Gilberto Freyre has called a "Gentleman complex"—a dispraisal of manual labor in every form . . . Just as in the past when manual labor was the lot of slaves in Brazil, it is considered today to be the work of the lower classes . . .
>
> [S]emi feudal relationships continue to dominate the social and economic relations of the simple rural worker . . . The traditional relationships between this small upper [landed] class and the rural peasant and the growing class of urban workers are important factors in economic growth. The institutions and the value system of this upper class affect the ideology of change, the entry of foreign capital into the country, the encouragement and development of appropriate skills, and other acts facilitating economic growth. To a large extent it is their "aristocratic" values and ideal which provide many of the life expectations and incentives . . .[26]

The stress on values as a key source of differences in the rate of development of economic and political institutions has been countered by some students of Latin America; they will point to the southern states of the American union as an example of a sub-culture which has been relatively underdeveloped economically, which has lacked a stable democratic political system, and which has placed a greater emphasis on violence and law-violation to attain political ends than the rest of the country. And as these scholars point out, the white South is the most purely Anglo-Saxon and Protestant part of the United States.

The American South resembles much of Latin America, including Brazil, in having an institutional structure and value system erected around a plantation (or *latifundia*) economy, which employed large numbers of slaves, and which after the abolition of slavery developed a stratification hierarchy correlated with variations in racial background. From this point of view, the clue to understanding the economic backwardness and political instability of Brazil and much of Spanish America lies in their structural similarities with the American South, rather than in those values which stem from Iberian or Catholic origins.[27] This argument is strengthened by analyses of the differences between southern and northern Brazil. The southern part of the country, which was much less involved in large-scale slave labor agriculture, can be compared with the north, in much the same way as the United States North varies from its South. Southern Brazil and northern United States are much more developed economically, and they place more emphasis on the "modern" value system—achievement, universalism, and the like—than the warmer regions of their countries.

There are certain similarities in another American country, Canada, and its internal cultural and economic differentiation. French Canada, historically, has been less developed than English Canada. Much of its economic development has been dominated by entrepreneurs from English-speaking backgrounds.[28] A recent analysis of French-Canadian businessmen, based on interviews, reports their economic value orientations in terms very reminiscent of the studies of Latin American entrepreneurs.[29] Though not as unstable politically as the southern United States or most of Latin America, Quebec has long exhibited symptoms of political instability (an opposition party system is perhaps less institutionalized there than in any other populous province); charges of political corruption, illegal tactics in campaigns, violations of civil liberties, and the like seem much more common in Quebec than in the English-speaking provinces.[30] Quebec is certainly Latin and Catholic (if these terms have any general analytic or descriptive meaning), but it obviously has had no plantation culture, nor a significant racial minority, though it could be argued that the English-French relationships resemble those of white-Negro, or white-Indian, in other countries of the Americas.

Various analyses of the weakness of democracy in Quebec do argue that religious-linked factors are relevant. As Pierre Trudeau has put it: "French Canadians are Catholics; and Catholic nations have not always been ardent supporters of democracy. They are authoritarian in spiritual matters; and since the dividing line between the spiritual and the temporal may be very fine or even confused, they are often disinclined to seek solutions in temporal affairs through the mere counting of heads." [31] And many have pointed to the differences in the economic development of the two Canadas as evidence that Catholic values and social organization are much less favorable to economic development than Protestant ones have been. As S. D. Clark has reasoned, "in nineteenth century Quebec religion was organized in terms of a hierarchy of social classes which had little relation to the much more fluid class system of capitalism, and sharp separation from the outside capitalist world was maintained through an emphasis upon ethnic and religious differences and through geographic isolation." [32]

These comparisons between the United States North and South, and English and French Canada, show that structure and values are clearly interrelated. Structure such as a plantation system combined with a racially based hierarchy is functionally tied to a given set of "aristocratic" values, and antipathetic to an emphasis on achievement, universalism, and hard work. But any value system derived from given sets of historical experience institutionalized in religious systems, family structures, class relations, and education will affect the pace and even direction and content of social and economic change.

If we turn now to studies focusing directly on the relationship between values and entrepreneurial behavior, the available materials from many Latin American countries seem to agree that the predominant values which continue to inform the behavior of the elite stem from the continued and combined strength of ascription, particularism, and diffuseness. Thomas Cochran has examined the literature from various American cultures, as well as from his own empirical research, and has conjectured that Latin American businessmen differ from North American ones in being:

> 1) more interested in inner worth and justification by standards of personal feeling than they are in the opinion of peer groups; 2) disinclined to sacrifice personal authority to group decisions; 3) disliking impersonal as opposed to personal arrangements, and generally preferring family relations to those with outsiders; 4) in-

clined to prefer social prestige to money; and 5) somewhat aloof from and disinterested in science and technology.[33]

Somewhat similar conclusions are reported in various surveys of managerial attitudes in various Latin American countries. These indicate that role specificity, i.e. separation of managerial from other activities, is relatively less common there than in more developed areas. A Latin American manager "is quite likely to devote part of his office hours to politics or family affairs." [34] Bureaucratic and competitive norms are comparatively weak. Personal characteristics are valued more than technical or organizational ability.[35]

Family particularism is much more common among Latin American business executives than among their counterparts in more developed nations. "Managers are frequently selected on the basis of family links, rather than specialized training." The entire managerial group often came from one family, and the "great majority of managers interviewed either considered this to be an appropriate arrangement under the conditions of their country, or had not thought of alternatives." [36] In Brazil, even the growth of large industries and corporate forms of ownership has not drastically changed the pattern. In many companies the modal pattern seems to involve an adjustment between family control and the rationale demands of running a big business. Either the children or the in-laws of the old patriarch are technically trained, or the company involves a mixed system of family members working closely with technically educated nonfamily executives. However, the type of managers employed by family groups are known as *hombres de confianza* (men who can be trusted), and have been selected more for this quality than for their expertise.[37]

Most analysts of Latin American business behavior agree that a principal concern of the typical entrepreneur is to maintain family prestige; thus he is reluctant to give up the family-owned and -managed type of corporation. Outsiders are distrusted, for the entrepreneur "is acutely aware that any advantage that may be given to somebody outside his family is necessarily at the expense of himself and his own family." [38] From this evolves an unwillingness to co-operate with others outside of one's firm, and a defensiveness toward subordinates, as well as toward creditors, distributors, and others. Such assumptions about the behavior of others are, of course, self-maintaining, since people tend to behave as significant others define them, thus reinforcing a mutual state of distrust. In the family-dominated firms which constitute such a large proportion of Latin American business, nonfamily, middle-management personnel will often be untrustworthy and inefficient, since they will lack identification with firms in which "the 'road upward' is blocked by family barriers," and they are given limited responsibility.[39] This fear of dealing with outsiders even extends to reluctance to permit investment in the firm. For many Brazilian "industrialists, the sale of stocks to the public seems to involve . . . a loss of property . . ." A Brazilian market research survey reported that 93 per cent of entrepreneurs interviewed stated "that they had never thought of selling stock in their enterprise." [40] As Emilio Willems points out, "such a typically modern institution as the stock-market in large metropolitan centers failed to develop because the most important joint-stock companies are owned by kin-groups which handle transfer of stock as a purely domestic matter." [41]

Although not statistically typical of Brazilian entrepreneurial behavior, some of the practices of the largest Brazilian firm, the United Industries, which in 1952 employed 30,000 workers in 367 plants, indicate the way in which family particularism and other traditional practices can continue within a massive industrial complex. In spite of its size, it is owned largely by the son of the founder, Francisco Matarazzo, Jr. and various family members. "The bleak and impeccably dressed Francisco, Jr., controls his empire from a pigskin-paneled office that is fitted with a buzzer system to summon top executives, who, on leaving, *must bow their way backward from his presence.*" [42]

The managers of foreign-owned companies, whether Brazilian or foreign, are different in their behavior. They tend to emphasize a high degree of rationalization and bureaucratic practice in running their firms. Although they are interested in securing personal loyalty from subordinates, it is not the basic requirement for employment. The executive personnel are ambitious and competent employees, concerned with their personal success, and valuing ambition in themselves and others.[43]

The lack of a concern with national interests or institutional development among Latin American entrepreneurs has been related by Albert Hirschman to what he calls an "ego-focussed image of change," characteristic of badly integrated under-developed societies. Individuals in nations dominated by such an image, "not identifying with society," will view new developments or experiences simply as opportunities for self-aggrandizement. Although seemingly reflecting a desire to get

ahead, this orientation, which inhibits efforts to advance by co-operation with others "is inimical to economic development, [since] . . .
success is conceived not as a result of systematic application of effort
and creative energy, combined perhaps with a 'little bit of luck,' but as
due either to sheer luck or to the outwitting of others through careful
scheming." And Hirschman, like other analysts of Latin America,
sees the inability to trust and work with others as antithetical to effective entrepreneurship.[44]

A 1960–61 analysis of the "technological decisions" of Mexican and
Puerto Rican entrepreneurs, compared with foreign-born managers of
subsidiaries of international companies, supports these interpretations.
"Differences among foreign and national enterprises in ways of attracting capital, handling labor relations, arranging technical flexibility,
channeling information internally and externally (and even willingness to respond to impertinent interview questions) are all consistent
with an interpretation that the native entrepreneurs view society as
probably malevolent and that the foreigners would have stayed home
if they agreed [with this view of society]." [45]

Attitudes to money similar to those frequently reported as characteristic of a nonindustrial, traditional population have been reported in
studies of Latin American business leaders. A short-range rather than a
long-range orientation is common: make money now "and then to live
happily—that is, idly—ever after." [46] This means that entrepreneurs
frequently prefer to make a high profit quickly, often by charging a
high price to a small market, rather than to maximize long-range
profits by seeking to cut costs and prices, which would take more
effort.[47] Although the concept of immediate profit "in industrial enterprises usually meant within one year or else after paying back initial
loans," this does not reflect a Schumpeterian assumption about the reward or encouragement necessary to entrepreneurial risk-taking.
Rather, the overwhelming majority of the Latin American businessmen interviewed argued that risk is to be avoided, and that "when
there is risk there will not be new investment," that investment risk is a
luxury which only those in wealthy countries can afford.[48] Reluctance
to take risks may be related to the strong concern with family integrity,
with viewing business property much like a family estate. "Where
bankruptcy might disgrace one's family, managers will be more cautious than where it is regarded impersonally as expedient corporate
strategy." [49]

It is important to note that these generalizations about the attitudes and behavior of Latin American entrepreneurs are all made in a comparative context. Those who stress their commitment to particularistic and diffuse values are generally comparing them to North Americans, or to a model of rational, bureaucratic, competitive enterprise. However, as contrasted with other groups within their societies, Latin American entrepreneurs, particularly those involved in large-scale enterprise, tend to be the carriers of "modern" values. Thus one analysis of Colombian businessmen points out: "They are urban people in a rural country. In a relatively traditionally oriented society, their values are rational and modern." [50]

The impact of Latin American orientations to entrepreneurial behavior has been summed up in the following terms:

> Comparatively the Latin American complex: 1) sacrifices rigorous economically directed effort, or profit maximization, to family interests; 2) places social and personal emotional interests ahead of business obligations; 3) impedes mergers and other changes in ownership desirable for higher levels of technological efficiency and better adjustments to markets; 4) fosters nepotism to a degree harmful to continuously able top-management; 5) hinders the building up of a supply of competent and cooperative middle managers; 6) makes managers and workers less amenable to constructive criticism; 7) creates barriers of disinterest in the flow of technological communication; and 8) lessens the urge for expansion and risk-taking. [51]

The emphases on the value orientations of entrepreneurs as a major factor in limiting economic development in Latin America may be criticized for de-emphasizing the extent to which the values themselves are a product of, or sustained by, so-called structural or economic factors. Thus, it has been suggested that the unwillingness to delegate responsibility to nonfamily members reflects the objective dangers of operating in unstable political and economic environments. Such conditions dictate extreme caution and the need to be certain that one can quickly change company policy so as to avoid major losses or bankruptcy as a result of government policy changes, change in foreign exchange rates, and the like. An "outsider" presumably will not have as much interest in the finances of the firm, or the authority to react quickly. Rapid inflation, high interest rates, and other instability factors would all seem to inhibit long-range planning and encourage a quick and high profit. There can be little doubt that such structural factors help to preserve many of the traditionalistic practices. And such a conclusion would imply the need for deliberate government policies to create a stable environment, such as planned investment policies, regulation of inflation, and restrictions on the export of capital.

But if the existence of interacting supportive mechanisms, which will inhibit economic support is admitted, the fact remains that similar generalizations have been made about the effect of values on attitudes and behavior of other groups and institutions. For example, an analysis of Argentine politics points to the effect of these values in preventing stable political life. "Argentina's class-bound politics assume that no public measure can be good for almost everybody, that the benefit of one group is the automatic loss of all others." [52] Although Argentina is, after Uruguay, socially the most developed nation in Latin America, highly literate and urbanized, its citizens still do not accept the notion of, nor do they show loyalty to, a national state which acts universalistically. Argentina is instead characterized by the "survival or localistic, sub-national views and loyalties archetypical of the traditional society . . ." [53] Similarly in the largest country in Latin America, it "is a well known fact that local government, party politics, and bureaucracy in Brazil still largely reflect family interests which are of course at variance with the principles of objective management as dictated by democratic rule." [54]

Efforts to "modernize" values and behavior are not solely, or even primarily, located in the economic or political spheres. Rather, those professionally concerned with ideas and values, the intellectuals, may play a decisive role in resisting or facilitating social change. As John Friedmann has pointed out, the intellectual in developing countries has three essential tasks to fulfill, "each of which is essential to the process of cultural transformation: he mediates new values, he formulates an effective ideology, and he creates an adequate, collective (national) self-image." [55] In Latin America, however, the large body of literature concerning the values of the extremely prestigeous *pensadores* or intellectuals, whether creative artists or academics, agrees that they continue to reject the values of industrial society, which they often identify with the United States. A survey of the writings of Latin American intellectuals points up this conclusion: "There is no school of literature in Latin America, which argues that technology and technological change represent values which should be adopted, cherished, and used as a means to a more meaningful life." [56] Even when modern technology is accepted as a necessary precondition for social betterment, it is often described as a threat to the traditional values of the society.[57]

Some of the factors which sustain these attitudes, even in the face of the recognized need of the nations of Latin America to change to get out of the "humiliating" status of being considered "underdeveloped" or even backward, have been suggested in an interesting comparison of the different ways in which Japan and Latin America reacted to similar concerns.

> When seeking to define a national self-image in a nationalistic frame of mind, one is most likely to seize on those features which supposedly differentiate one from one's major international antagonist. For Japan this point of counter-reference, the thou than which one has to feel more holy, has been the West generally and in the twentieth century America more particularly. For Latin America, since the beginning of this century at least, it has been almost exclusively America. But in differentiating themselves from Americans, the Japanese could point to the beauties of their tight family system; their patriotic loyalty to the Emperor contrasting with American selfish individualism; the pacific subtleties of Buddhism contrasting with the turbulent stridency of Christianity; and so on. But it was not as easy for a Latin American to establish the Latin American differentiae in terms of family, political, or legal institutions. He had to fall back on "spirit" and attitudes; and since the most visible American was the businessman, he tended—*vide arielismo* as Ellison describes it—to make his dimension of difference the materialist-spiritual one. Thus by scorning American devotion to technology and profit, he made something of a virtue out of the stark fact of economic backwardness. For their part the Japanese had enough superior arguments with which to fortify their uncertain sense of their superior Japaneseness without resorting to this one, with its inhibiting effect on indigenous economic growth.[58]

While much of the anti-United States sentiment is presented in the context of left-wing critiques, *pensadores* of the right—those who uphold the virtues of tradition, Catholicism, and social hierarchy—also are aggressively opposed to North American culture, which they see as "lacking culture, grace, beauty, as well as widespread appreciation of aesthetic and spiritual values." [59] And a report on the writings of Chilean conservative intellectuals states that over one hundred works have been published which "are as hostile to basic United States social, economic and political patterns as to Russian communism." [60]

The values fostered by the *pensadores* continue to be found as well in much of Latin American education. Most analysts of Latin American education agree that, at both university and secondary school level, the content of education still reflects the values of a landed upper class. Even in the second most developed Latin American country, Argentina, a study of national values points out that the traditional landed aristocratic disdain for manual work, industry, and trading, continues to affect the educational orientations of many students. When an Argentine seeks to move up, "he will usually try to do so, not by developing his manual skills or by accomplishing business or industrial feats, but by developing his *intellectual* skills. He will follow an academic career typically in a field which is not 'directly productive' from an economic point of view—medicine, law, social sciences, etc." [61]

As Jacques Lambert has put it, "A ruling class deriving its resources from landed property looks to education for a means not of increasing its income but rather of cultivating the mind. The whole public education system has been organized as a preparation for higher education, and more particularly for the type of education provided in the faculties of law, which gave instruction not only in law but also in political and social science, for a class of political leaders." [62] There is considerable resistance at both secondary and university levels to changing the curriculum to adapt to the needs of mass education in an urban industrial society. President Lleras of Colombia, for example, has complained that students in the secondary schools "are studying the same courses as in the 19th century." [63] The Brazilian sociologist Florestán Fernandes suggests that the "democratization" of education in his country has meant "spreading throughout Brazilian society the aristocratic school of the past." [64] The school here reinforces the disdain for "practical work," and diffuses these values among the upwardly mobile. As he puts it:

> Education has remained impermeable to economic, social and political revivalist influences. Misunderstanding and contempt of popular education has subsisted, and the excessive prestige enjoyed by the humanistic culture of the old upper class, as patrons of a corresponding type of anti-experimental book-learning has been perpetuated. The school continues to be an isolated institution divorced from man's conditions of existence and specializing in the transmission of bookish techniques, potted knowledge and routine intellectual concepts. Formal education, in a word, is guarded from any impact that would adjust it to the constructive social functions which it should properly carry out in a society aiming at homogeneity and expansion. [65]

In Chile, one prominent educator, Julio Vega, wrote in 1950 "that education must begin to emancipate itself from the social prejudices which lead 99 per cent of those entering the *liceo*—somewhat the equivalent of the United States high school, but organized around an entirely different curriculum and dedicated to a different social purpose —to want to be professionals, so as to gain access to the world of the aristocracy." And many have argued that the educational system has taught middle-class Chileans "to think like an aristocrat of the past century and to hold in disdain manual labor and those who perform it." [66]

These generalizations about the strength of the traditional humanist bias in Latin America may be bolstered by reference to comparative educational statistics. Latin America as an area lags behind every other part of the world in the proportion of its students taking courses in engineering or the sciences. As of 1958-59, 34 per cent of all West European undergraduates were studying science or engineering, in contrast to 23 per cent in Asia (excluding Communist China and India), 19 per cent in Africa, and 16 per cent in Latin America.[67] The comparable figure for the major Communist countries including the Soviet Union and China is 46 per cent.[68] China now trains more engineers per year than any country except the Soviet Union and the United States. And 90 per cent of all China's scientists and engineers have been trained since 1949.[69] In Uruguay, on the other hand, slightly over half the students in higher education have been enrolled in faculties of humanities, fine arts, and law, about ten times as many as in the scientific and technical faculties. In Chile, in 1957, less than one-sixth of the students were studying science or engineering, and the increase in the numbers in these faculties between 1940 and 1959 was less than the growth in total university enrollment. "In Communist countries, of course, the proportions are almost exactly reversed; Czechoslovakia had 46 per cent in scientific and technical faculties and only 6.4 per cent in humanities, arts, and law." [70] Among Third World nations, only Israel with 42 per cent of its students in science and engineering, and Nigeria with 40 per cent, approached the Communist nations in degree of dedication of higher education to development training objectives.[71]

The situation is now changing in some Latin American countries; but it is significant that a recent comparative analysis of trends in higher education completed for UNESCO notes particularly that, as compared to other regions, in Latin America there "has been no concerted efforts . . . to strengthen interest and achievement in science and the related fields." [72] In the largest Latin American country, Brazil, enrollment in universities has increased ten times, from 10,000 to 101,600, between 1912 and 1961. However, the percentage of the total studying engineering was 12.8 in 1912 and 12 in 1961.[73] A study of students in seventeen middle schools (*ginásios*) in São Paulo indicates that the large majority hoped to enter one of the traditional prestige occupations. And Brandão Lopes comments that his findings indicate "the permanence of traditional Brazilian values relating to work in an environment in which economic development demands new specialties." [74] The absence of French-Canadians in leading roles in industry has been explained as a consequence of Canada's educational system, which resembles that of Latin America. Until the 1960's secondary education in Quebec was largely "based on private fee-paying schools," whose curriculum reflected "the refined traditions of the classical college. In the main, French Canadian education was never geared to the provision of industrial skills at the managerial or technical level. The educational system was inappropriate for the kind of society that by 1950 Quebec was becoming. It was an outstanding example of institutional failure." [75]

Another reflection of the strength of "aristocratic" values in the Latin American educational system is the phenomenon of the part-time professor. It has been estimated that less than 10 per cent of the professors at Latin American universities receive salaries intended to pay for full-time work. As one Uruguayan professor once said to me, "To be a professor in this country is a hobby, a hobby one engages in for prestige." Obviously when men spend most of their time earning their living away from the university, often in an occupation such as the law which is unrelated to their academic work, they cannot be expected to make major contributions to scholarship, or to devote much time to guiding students.[76]

To describe this system as "aristocratic" may seem ironic, but comparative research on other subjects indicates that the "conception that social service is performed best when [one] . . . is not paid, or is paid an honorarium, is basically an aristocratic value linked to the concept of *noblesse oblige.*" Conversely, inherent in equalitarian ideology "has been the principle that a man should be paid for his work." [77] In a comparative analysis of the position of leaders of voluntary organizations in the United States and various European nations, I presented data which indicated that there are many more full-time paid leaders of such groups in the United States than in much of Europe. And I concluded:

> The inhibitions against employing a large number of officials permeate most voluntary associations in the European nations and reflect the historic assumption that such activities should be the "charities" of the privileged classes. The absence of a model of *noblesse-oblige* in an equalitarian society fostered the American belief that such voluntary associations, whether they be the "March of Dimes," social work agencies, or trade unions, should be staffed by men who are paid to do the job. In a sense, therefore, it may be argued that the very emphasis on equalitarianism in America has given rise to the large salaried bureaucracies which permeate voluntary organizations.[78]

In the early days of the Latin American and European universities, they were staffed either by members of well-to-do families or the clergy. Such academics required no financial support from the university.[79] The high prestige of the university in Latin America is to some extent linked to its identification with the elite, with the assumption that professors and graduates, "doctors," are gentlemen.[80] However, such an identity is not dependent on the universities' contribution to society, and is clearly dysfunctional in any society which seeks to develop economically, or to make contributions to the world of science and scholarship. And it may be suggested that the resistance to "modernizing" the curriculum and to "professionalizing" the professoriate stems from the desire to maintain the diffuse elitist character of the role of the intellectual.[81] In contemporary times, when relatively few professors in fact can support themselves from family income, the diffuse elite status of the professor encourages him to use the status to secure wealth or power outside the university. Thus the professoriate as a status, as the equivalent of an aristocratic title, may be converted into high position in other dimensions of stratification. As one recent study of the Latin American university concludes about the behavior of the *catedrático,* the chairholder:

> With his name, title, connections, civil service status and life-long position ensured, he is often tempted to use his chair as a mere rung on the long social climb to power. Once made "catedrático," he no longer has to worry much about teaching and even less about research. Aided and sustained by his university post, he is at last free to launch up on a successful professional or even political career.

It is expected that a full professor will amass a modest personal fortune in the exercise of his profession as a lawyer, doctor or engineer . . . [Sometimes] these professional activities are also used as further stepping stones on the road to administrative, political or diplomatic positions . . .[82]

Economic Growth and the Role of the "Deviant" in Anti-Entrepreneurial Cultures

The argument that Latin American values are antithetical to economic development can, of course, be pitted against the fact that a considerable amount of economic growth has occurred in many of these countries. Clearly, in the presence of opportunity, an entrepreneurial elite has emerged. The logic of value analysis would imply that the creation or expansion of roles which are not socially approved in terms of the traditional values, should be introduced by social "deviants." This hypothesis is basic to much of the literature dealing with the rise of the businessman in different traditional societies.

In his classic analysis of economic development, Joseph Schumpeter pointed out that the key aspect of entrepreneurship, as distinct from being a manager, is the capacity for leadership in innovation, for breaking through the routine and the traditional.[83] From this perspective the analysis of the factors which resulted in the rise of an entrepreneurial group leading to economic growth under capitalism is comparable to the study of the conditions which brought about anti-capitalist revolutionary modernizing elites of various countries in recent decades. The approach which emphasizes the theory of deviance assumes that those who introduce change must be deviants, since they reject the traditional elite's ways of doing things.[84] As Hoselitz puts it, "a deviant always engages in behavior which constitutes in a certain sense a breach of the existing order and is contrary to, or at least not positively weighted in the hierarchy of existing social values." [85] In societies in which the values of the dominant culture are "not supportive of entrepreneurial activity, someone who is relatively outside of the social system may have a particular advantage in entering an entrepreneurial activity. The restraints upon entrepreneurial activity imposed by the network [of social relations] would be less effective against such a person. Thus, an immigrant may be outside of many of the networks of the nation and freer to engage in entrepreneurial activity," in other words, freer socially to deviate.[86]

If we assume, in following up such generalizations, that within the Americas the value system of Latin America has discouraged entrepreneurial activity, while that of the English-speaking Protestant world of the United States and Canada has fostered it, then a comparative study of the backgrounds of entrepreneurs in these countries should reveal that those of Latin America are recruited disproportionately from sociological "deviants," while those of North America should come largely from groups which possess traits placing them inside the central structures of the society. An examination of the research data bearing on this hypothesis indicates that it is valid.

In many countries of Latin America, members of minority groups, often recent immigrants, have formed a considerable section of the emerging business elite. "In general it appears that immigrants took the lead in establishing modern manufacturing before World War I [in Latin America]." [87] Recent studies in various countries reveal comparable patterns. Frequently, these new entrepreneurs come from groups not known for their entrepreneurial prowess at home, such as the Arabs and the Italians, although Germans and Jews are also among those who are to be found in disproportionate numbers in business leadership. A study of Mexican business leaders found that of 109 major executives, 26 had foreign paternal grandfathers; among the "32 outstanding business leaders in Mexico, 14 reported a foreign paternal grandfather." [88] Analysis of the backgrounds of 286 "prestigeous" entrepreneurs, taken from the Argentine *Who's Who,* indicates that 45.5 per cent were foreign born.[89] However, many of those born in Argentina are "among the first generation born in the country." [90] Classifying the sample by origins, Imaz reports that only 10 per cent came from the traditional upper class, and they, as in many other Latin American countries, are concentrated in industries which processed agricultural products, so that their role in industry is an extension of their position as a landed class. Among the rest, almost all are of relatively recent foreign origin.[91] Data from a survey of the heads of 46 out of the 113 industrial establishments in Santiago, Chile, which employ more than 100 workers indicate that 76 per cent of them are immigrants or the children of immigrants.[92] An earlier study of the Chilean middle class reports that as of 1940 the overwhelming majority of the 107,273 foreign born in the country were in middle-class, largely self-employed occupations.[93] In Brazil also "the majority of industrial entrepreneurs are immigrants or descendants of relatively recent immigrants." [94] Thus in São Paulo, 521 enterprises out of 714 were owned by men in these categories.[95] In the other economically developed states, Rio Grande do Sul and Santa Catarina, "almost 80 per cent of the industrial activities . . . were developed by people of European immigrant extraction." [96]

Similar patterns may be found in the less developed and more traditional countries. Thus, in a recent study of Peru, François Bourricaud traces in detail the continued control of members of the ancient oligarchy over much of the economic life of the country, their maintenance in much of agriculture and traditional business and banking of the *patron* system, and family and clan control. However, in the new and risky enterprises, those which have produced the new rich of the country, one finds many recent immigrants.[97] In Colombia, a country like Peru with relatively little immigration, a study of the members of the National Association of Industrialists reports "that in 1962, 41 per cent of a sample of business leaders in Bogotá were immigrants from other countries." [98] In Panama, in 1940 before the decree "nationalizing" commerce, "nearly 45% of the men actively engaged in commerce or manufacturing were foreigners." [99]

The various studies of the backgrounds of the Latin American entrepreneurial elite indicate that on the whole they are a well-educated group, the majority of them in most countries are university graduates. And a study of the origins of students at the University of São Paulo suggests that much of the separation in career orientations between those of native background and others takes place while in school. Thus, the proportion of students of non-Brazilian background is higher among the students than in the population of the city; only 22 per cent are of purely Brazilian descent. Even more significant is the fact that students with a higher proportion of foreign-born ancestors tend to enroll in the "modern" faculties, such as economics, engineering, pharmacy, and the like. Those with preponderantly Brazilian family backgrounds are more likely to be found in the more traditional high prestige schools such as law and medicine. And the author of this study comments:

> The children of foreign-born parents . . . are more inclined to take advantage of the new opportunities in occupations which have emerged from the economic development of the city of São Paulo. One should consider the fact that in Brazil, the schools of Law and Medicine convey special social prestige to their students.

It is easier for a not completely assimilated adolescent of foreign
descent to ignore that prestige than for a "pure" Brazilian.[100]

Similarly, at the University of Chile, the School of Physics suffers
from low prestige, "which diminishes the attractiveness of the field
. . ." A recent study of Chilean university students reports:

> Who, then, are the students in this school? Why have they re-
> jected the natural and well-formed paths of career choice? The
> most obvious are those who are immigrants or sons of immigrants
> —primarily German refugees and Italian emigrés . . . A second
> and frequently overlapping group is composed of students who are
> critical of the traditional alternatives.[101]

Immigrant and minority groups have shown comparable abilities to
take advantage of, or to create, opportunities in other parts of the
underdeveloped world. Thus in sub-Saharan Africa, Arabs, Indians,
and to a lesser extent Chinese, form a large part of the commercial
world. In southeast Asian countries, Chinese constitute almost the entire business community; Indians were important in Burmese economic life before they were expelled. It should be noted that it is not
only "immigrants" who have been disproportionately successful. Minority religious groups such as Christians have entered the universities
in relatively large numbers in various Asian states, even where they are
a tiny minority in the entire population. In Indonesia, for example,
over 15 per cent of the new students entering Gadjah Mada University
in 1959–60 were Christians, although few people adhere to Christianity. In general in southeast Asia, there is "a relatively high proportion of youth from minorities enrolled in universities and [they have
a] . . . reputation as better academic achievers than youth from majority elites. Such minorities . . . include the Karens and the Indians
in Burma, the Chinese in Thailand, the 'burghers' in Ceylon, the
Bataks and Chinese in Indonesia, and other Christians in all these
countries." [102]

The creative role of the deviant, or the outsider, has in part been
conceptualized by the term "marginal man," those who for various
reasons are partially outside the culture in which they are living, are
less socially integrated in the structures which maintain conformity,
and are therefore not as committed to the established values of the
larger order. Hence they are more likely to be receptive to possibilities
for change.[103] An analysis of those who successfully took advantage of
the opportunity to shift the use of land in the vicinity of São Paulo

from subsistence agriculture to lucrative commercial crops (mainly the growth of eucalyptus for firewood) points up this process. Over 90 per cent of those who became small-scale, relatively well-to-do entrepreneurs were recent settlers in the area, "immigrants or children of immigrants . . . or members of a small but flourishing Protestant sect (the *Evangelistas*) . . ."

> Almost all of the recent settlers were as poor as the *caboclos* [the native, lowest status rural dwellers] when they arrived. They managed to see new alternatives when they arose, to buy up small plots of land and gradually increase their holdings, mostly at the expense of the *caboclos* . . . It is worth testing . . . the proposition that *participation in newly valued activities among members of low economic and prestige classes varies inversely with length of residence in a locality*. Old settlers at depressed levels have inherited habits of belief, a morality and expectation of role rights and obligations associated with their statuses . . . that they are only slowly adaptable in the presences of altered opportunities. One of the most striking occurrences in the changing situation within the *municipio* under consideration is the fact that several *caboclos* sold or were seeking to sell their properties of prospective entrepreneurs, and then turned around and hired their labor out for wages.[104]

The traits which are often associated with economic innovation lead their bearers to be frowned upon or even hated by those who adhere to the conventional traditions of the society, or who resent the success of others. Thus in Brazil, Gilberto Freyre reports that many of non-Portuguese descent have

> shown a lack of finer moral scruples which has given many of them the reputation of being morally or ethically inferior . . . [Their actions which lead to success in politics and business] are given as an example of the fact that the sons of "immigrants" are morally inferior to the sons of old Brazilian families as political leaders, businessmen, and industrial pioneers. Of course, sons of immigrants who follow such careers are freer than the members of old and well-known families from certain moral controls that act upon men deeply rooted in their towns or countries or regions.[105]

It is indicative of the extent to which Latin Americans identify entrepreneurial or commercial abilities as "alien" to their tradition and values that ethnic myths are invented to explain the success of those of native background who do succeed. Thus both in Colombia, where the citizens of Antioquia have evidenced entrepreneurial abilities far exceeding those of other sections of the country, and in Mexico, where residents of Monterrey have shown comparable skills, the story is widely believed that both groups are descended from *maranos,* secretly practicing Jews who publically changed their religion after 1492.[106] These stories have been disproven by historical research, but the fact that many accept them as gospel tells much about attitudes toward entrepreneurship. The same factors may be involved in Gilberto Freyre's report, citing various writers, that the major center of business enterprise in Brazil, São Paulo, is "probably the nucleus of the Brazilian population with the largest strain of Semitic blood." [107]

The logic of the analysis suggested here, however, does not agree with the thesis that innovating entrepreneurs in developing societies must be recruited disproportionately from the ranks of social "deviants," as some have interpreted data such as these. Rather it points with Weber to the fact that many minority groups have not shown such propensities. Clearly the Catholic minorities in England, or other Protestant countries, were much less likely than the general population to engage in entrepreneurial activity. In his analysis of the divergent consequences for economic behavior of Protestantism and Catholicism, Max Weber pointed to the greater business accomplishments of the Protestant *majority* as compared to the Catholic minority in Germany.[108] The key issue, as Weber has indicated, is the value system of the various groups involved. Latin America and some other less developed traditional societies are so vulnerable to economic cultural "deviants" because the predominant values of the host culture are in large measure antithetical to rational entrepreneurial orientations. Where national values support economic development, the Weberian emphasis on value would suggest that the innovating business elite would be drawn not from deviants but rather from the "in-group," from persons with socially privileged backgrounds.

An examination of the social characteristics of North American business leaders in both Canada and the United States bears out these assumptions. Compared to most other nations in the world, the United States and English-speaking Canada have been among the most hospitable cultures to economic development. The Protestant ethic as fostered by denominations spawned of Calvinist and Arminian origins strongly influenced all classes in these societies, the United States somewhat more than Canada. And a study of the business leaders of the

United States in 1870, the period of its take-off into industrial development, indicates that 86 per cent of them came from "colonial families"
settled in the country before 1777. Only 10 per cent were foreign born
or the children of foreign born.[109] Over 98 per cent of the post-Civil
War business elite were Protestants. Although the proportions of those
of non-Anglo-Saxon, non-Protestant, and foreign-born parentage have
increased over the years, they have always remained considerably lower
than their proportion in the population as a whole.[110] Canadian data
are available only for the post-World War II period, but it should be
noted that Canada's emergence as a major industrial society largely
dates from the war. Previously its economy somewhat resembled that
of Argentina, being largely dependent on agricultural exports. The
Canadian case is extremely interesting since the country is composed of
two separate cultures—English Protestant and Latin Catholic. And a
comprehensive report on the Canadian elite shows a clear-cut picture:
where cultural values congruent with entrepreneurship are ascendant,
the business elite will be recruited largely from the dominant culture
group, not from minorities. Thus those of Anglo-Saxon Protestant
background are over-represented, while those of Latin, Catholic, and
minority origins are under-represented.

> An examination of the social origins of the economic elite shows
> that economic power belongs almost exclusively to those of British
> origin, even though this ethnic group made up less than half of
> the population in 1951. The fact that economic development in
> Canada has been in the hands of British Canadians has long been
> recognized by historians. Of the 760 people in the economic elite,
> only 51 (6.7 per cent) could be classified as French Canadians al-
> though the French made up about one-third of the population in
> 1951 . . . There were no more than a handful who . . . could be
> classified as top-ranking industrialists in their own province.
> Ethnic groups of neither British nor French origin, which made
> up about one-fifth of the general population, were hardly repre-
> sented at all. There were six Jews (.78 per cent of the sample as
> opposed to 1.4 per cent of the general population) . . . [O]nly
> 78 (about 10 per cent) were Catholic . . . 43 per cent of the
> population in 1951 was Catholic.[111]

In seeking to account for the low representation of French Canadians in the economic elite, even within Quebec, John Porter points out
that the evidence does not fit the assumption that it is largely a result
of the greater power of the British Canadians. For French Canadians
do quite well in other power structures, e.g. politics, the intellectual

world, and religion. French weakness in industry seems related to elements in their culture comparable to those in much of Latin America.

The varying origins of the business elites of the American nations clearly indicate that "out" groups, such as ethnic-religious minorities, are given the opportunity to innovate economically when the values of the dominant culture are antithetical to such activities. Thus, the comparative evidence from the various nations of the Americas sustains the generalization that cultural values are among the major factors which affect the potentiality for economic development.

Although I have focused on the direct effects of value orientations on the entrepreneurial behavior of certain groups, it should be clear that any given individual or group supports the values of their effective social environment. Although national values may discourage entrepreneurial activities, ethnic or religious sub-groups, or links to foreign cultures may encourage them for those involved. One explanation of the comparative success of members of some minority groups in Latin America, such as the Anglo-Argentines, is that they continue to respect their ancestral national culture more than that of their host society. The fact that many ethnic minorities in some Latin American nations continue to send their children to schools conducted in their ancestral language and to speak it at home attests to their lack of acceptance of national culture and values.

The key question basically is whether one is involved in a network of social relations which sustain or negate a particular activity. Viscount Mauá, Brazil's great nineteenth-century economic innovator, though a native Brazilian, was adopted while in his early teens by an English merchant in Rio de Janeiro; his biography clearly indicates that he became an "alien" within his native culture, that English became his "native" language, the one in which he thought and wrote his private thoughts.[112] Conversely, as we have seen, many successful entrepreneurs are drawn away from total commitment to their business life by an involvement in social networks and reference groups which supply more prestige than their vocation. One of Argentina's most successful entrepreneurs, who was an immigrant, built up a complex network of industrial companies, took the time to study at the university, accepted an appointment as an associate professor of Economics and Industrial Organization at the University of Buenos Aires, when he was fifty years of age, sought to secure a regular chair three years later, and bought a 6,600-acre *estancia,* on which he spent much time.[113] To facilitate the emergence of a given new role in a society, it is necessary to help create social recognition for it within meaningful sub-groups. The leaders of Meiji Japan have provided an example of the way in which one nation did this. To raise the prestige of the business class,

> . . . social distinctions [were] granted to the presidents and main shareholders of the new companies. The presidents were given the privilege of the sword and family name. They were appointed by the government, as officials were. A president could walk directly into the room of a government official while common people had to wait and squat outside the building. Many other minor privileges were granted.[114]

It is important to recognize that the introduction of new activities by those linked to "foreign" cultures or minority religions is not simply one of the various ways to modernize a society. Innovations which are associated with socially marginal groups are extremely vulnerable to political attack from those who would maintain traditional values. Consequently efforts at economic modernization, changes in the educational system, or social customs which are introduced by "outsiders," may have much less effect in modifying the central value system than when they are fostered by individuals who are members of the core group, as occurred in Meiji Japan.

Although much of the discussion thus far has involved the presentation of evidence concerning *the* Latin American value system, it is obvious that there is considerable variation *among* Latin American nations, as there is among the English-speaking countries. Thus, many of the distinctions which have been drawn between Argentina and Uruguay on the one hand and Brazil on the other refer to the greater equalitarianism and universalism in the former two. Or the earlier and greater degree of working-class consciousness in Chile (indicated by the strength of Marxist parties) as contrasted with Uruguay and Argentina may be a consequence of the greater elitism, ascription, and particularism of Chile, which was a major center of population concentration under colonial rule, while the values of the latter two were modified by their later formation as immigrant cultures.

Uruguay (and to a somewhat lesser extent Argentina) differs from the rest of Latin America in being relatively committed to a historically rooted equalitarian ideology. This value orientation stems from the effects of widespread immigration, which helped provide a mass

urban base for reformist political movements. As Gino Germani indicates, immigration "played a great part in the destruction of the traditional pattern of social stratification." [115]

The emphasis on equalitarianism in both Argentina and Uruguay is
perhaps best reflected in the extension of their educational systems,
which have long led all other Latin American nations in the proportions attending school, from primary to university. This commitment
to education may have played a major role in facilitating economic
growth during the late nineteenth century and the first three decades
of the twentieth. However, when equalitarianism is associated with particularistic and ascriptive orientations, it seemingly serves to strengthen
the concern with security mentioned earlier, and early successful pressures (more in Uruguay than Argentina) for welfare state measures.
Both countries, today, face a major economic crisis, brought about in
large measure because governments responsive to popular pressures
have dedicated a large share of national revenues to welfare.

Efforts to do more than present loose illustrations of this type must
await systematic comparative work on all the Latin-American republics, as sociologists at the Di Tella Institute in Buenos Aires are now
doing.[116] They are attempting to codify systematically a large variety
of qualitative and quantitative materials, covering over a century, to
test out various hypotheses concerning the sources of differentiation
within Latin America.

Changes in Value Orientations

The evidence presented thus far would seem to indicate that, regardless
of the causal pattern one prefers to credit for Latin American values,
they are, as described, antithetic to the basic logic of a large-scale industrial system.[117] However, as noted earlier, it should be recognized that
these descriptions are all made in a relative or comparative context,
that Latin American economic behavior is evaluated either in comparison with that in the United States, or other developed nations, or
against some ideal model of entrepreneurship. The value system of
much of Latin America, like Quebec, has, in fact, been changing in the
direction of a more achievement-oriented, universalistic, and equalitarian value system, and its industrial development both reflects and
determines such changes. Many Latin American entrepreneurs are hiring nonfamily members as executives, and in various ways have acted

contrary to the supposed norms. To some extent this may reflect the fact that a large segment of the creative and successful entrepreneurs are members of minority ethnic groups. More important perhaps is the fact that bureaucratic corporate enterprise has an inherent logic of its own; those who build such organizations, or rise within them in once-traditional societies, are either "deviants" who have the necessary new orientations, or men who develop them. Paternalistic feudal attitudes toward workers are characteristically more common in the less developed Latin American countries than in the more industrialized ones, a finding which parallels the situation within Spain.[118] There, the more developed an area, the more "modern" the attitudes of its entrepreneurs.

Such developments have been analyzed by Fernando Cardoso in his study of the industrial entrepreneur in Brazil. The shift from the values of the *patron* to those of the modern professional entrepreneur occurred with the emergence of large-scale industries, such as automobile manufacturing or ship-building. He points out that the rapidity of the adjustment to modern orientations depends on the attitudes of the entrepreneurs involved. And the same individuals and companies often react in what appear to be contradictory ways. These dual orientations, modern and traditional, reflect in part the mixed character of the Brazilian economy, which may still be characterized as incipient industrial capitalism.[119] The heterogeneity of entrepreneurial environments and orientations has, as yet, prevented the emergence of a consistent ideology to which most adhere.[120] Hence, Cardoso points to changes in values with growing industrialization, although he does not challenge the general description of Latin American economic behavior, as still applying to much of the Brazilian present.

Values clearly change as societies become economically more developed.[121] Many of the generalizations made about Latin American or other relatively underdeveloped societies, in contrast to the United States or northern Europe, were made, and are still being made, about such countries as Spain, France, or Italy, when they are compared with more economically developed countries.

Only a short time ago, economic "stagnation" in these European Latin countries was interpreted as the consequence of values incongruent with enterprising behavior. That breakthroughs in development occur for a variety of reasons in different countries is obvious. Values dysfunctional to economic growth may inhibit but not prevent growth, if other factors are favorable. As the history of various nations has suggested, processes or conflicts about values may foster the emergence of groups motivated to achieve economically. But conclusions such as these do not offer any prospect for change, other than to suggest the need for detailed careful study of the relevant factors suggested by social science theory in each country, or to simply add to the amount of investment capital available in a given country. I would like, therefore, to turn to a discussion of the various ways which seem open to those who deliberately seek to change values so as to foster the emergence of entrepreneurial elites.

The experience of Japan, the one non-Western nation which has successfully industrialized, suggests that the key question may not be the creation of new values so much as the way in which cultural ideals supporting tradition can give rise to those supporting modernity, that the shift from tradition to modernity need not involve a total rejection of a nation's basic values.[122]

In discussing this problem, Reinhard Bendix notes that in Weber's *The Protestant Ethic and the Spirit of Capitalism,* a study of the resolution of the contradiction between the coexisting traditional and modern within a developing society, western Europe, the author observes that Reformers continued to be concerned with their salvation and accepted the traditional, Christian devaluation of worldly pursuits. The emergence of the "spirit of Capitalism" represented a direct outgrowth of this early antimaterialistic tradition of Christianity, a growth which occurred without replacing this tradition. Linking Weber's approach to the various analysis of the preconditions for Japanese development, Bendix points out that the Samurai under the Tokugawa regime became a demilitarized aristocracy loyal to the traditional Samurai ethic of militancy, even though the Tokugawa regime pursued a public policy of disciplined pacification, of the avoidance of conflict or competitive struggles to change a status or power relationship among the feudal lords. After the Meiji Restoration of 1868, the virtues of achievement were socially accepted. The traditional Samurai ethic applied to a competitive world now meant that any self-respecting Samurai was obliged to show his ability and desire to win. Thus in nineteenth-century Japan, as in Reformation Europe, "modern" economic orientations emerged through the application of traditional values and sources of individual motivation to new structural conditions, rather than the supplanting of one set of values by another. Since Japan and western Europe are the only two non-Communist cultural areas which have developed successfully on their own, the finding that achievement values seemingly emerged out of a redefinition of traditional values, rather than the adoption of new ones, has obvious implications for those contemporary underdeveloped cultures which seek to industrialize.[123]

In seeking for culturally accepted orientations which will lead a section of the elite to "split off" and endorse "modern" values, Talcott Parsons suggests that nationalism, concern for the international status of one's society, can motivate those who are most oriented to foreign opinion to press for new attitudes toward industrialization. And within the existing elites such people are most likely to be found among intellectuals, especially "those who have had direct contacts with the West, particularly through education abroad or under Western auspices at home." [124] In the name of fostering the national welfare, major changes may be introduced, which would be more strongly resisted if they were perceived as serving the interests of a sub-group within the society, such as the businessmen. In Uruguay, governmental actions which are justified by a nonrevolutionary national development ideology are seen by the workers as another rationalization of the ruling class to consolidate its power.[125]

If the source of new development concerns is to be nationalism rather than self-interest, then the means are more likely to be perceived in the political rather than in an autonomous economic arena.[126] And within the political arena, it is necessary to disassociate the policies advocated from any identification with possible foreign control. In Latin America today, support of "socialism" as opposed to "capitalism" becomes a way in which intellectuals may advocate industrialization without being accused of seeking to foster foreign "materialistic" values which are destructive of the spiritual values of the society.[127]

A "socialist" ideology of economic development may be conceived of as a functional alternative to the Meiji elite's use of loyalty to the Emperor, Shinto, and the nation, when seeking to industrialize Japan. "To an important degree, socialism and communism are strong because they are symbolically associated with the ideology of independence, rapid economic development, social modernization, and ultimate equality. Capitalism is perceived as being linked to foreign influences, traditionalism, and slow growth." [128]

The problem which can best be met by a revolutionary nationalist ideology justifying the rejection of the past has been well put by Gerschenkron:

> In a backward country the great and sudden industrialization effort calls for a New Deal in emotions. Those carrying out the great transformation as well as those on whom it imposes burdens must feel, in the words of Matthew Arnold, that
>
> > . . . Clearing a stage
> > Scattering the past about
> > Comes the new age.
>
> Capitalist industrialization under the auspices of socialist ideologies may be, after all, less surprising a phenomenon than would appear at first sight.[129]

In formulating such ideologies, Latin America is at a disadvantage compared with the "new nations" of Asia and Africa. Most of the latter have recently attained independence under the leadership of mass parties whose revolutionary ideology subsumes the values of equalitarianism, achievement, universalism, and collectivity-orientation. Traditional practices may be attacked as antithetical to the national interest and self-image. In much of Latin America, however, many traditional values and practices are regarded as proper parts of the national identity. Supporters of these traditional practices cannot be challenged as being anti-nationalist. Conversely the initial steps toward attaining a national economic system in the United States were facilitated by its being "in many senses an underdeveloped country when it was transformed into a new nation-state by a revolution led by a new elite." The new United States faced the need to break down the particularistic loyalties and values of the "indigenous aristocracy" of each little colony. And under the aegis of the ideology proclaimed in the Declaration of Independence, the revolutionary elite modified "the social institutions inherited from the British to the needs of a continental political economy."[130] Latin America, however, did not use its revolutionary struggle for independence to legitimate major social and economic changes; rather, independence often confirmed the control of the traditional landed class in power. Hence, as segments of the elite have awoken in recent decades to the need for such changes, they find it difficult to create the political institutions and national consensus needed to foster new values.

Perhaps Mexico is the best example of a systematic effort at value change in Latin America. The Mexican Revolution transformed the image and legitimate political emphases of the nation. It sought to destroy the sense of superiority felt by those of pure Spanish descent by stressing the concept of *Mexicanidad,* and by a glorification of its Indian past.[131] There are almost no monuments to Spaniards from Cortés to independence in 1814. Emphases on white racial descent is socially illegitimate. The values of the Mexican Revolution are similar to those of the other Western revolutions—the American, French, and Russian. Though Mexico clearly retains major elements of the traditional Latin American system, it is the one country which has identified its national ethos with that of equality and an open society. And with the sense of a collective revolutionary commitment to growth and egalitarianism, one finds that business activities, which are sanctioned by government approval, are presented as ways of fulfilling national objectives. A detailed account of the way in which the Revolution affected value change concludes:

> [T]he Revolution fostered a shift from ascription to achievement as the basis for distributing income, and from particularistic to universalistic standards as the basis for distributing political and economically-relevant tasks among performers . . .
> Finally, it is evident that the nationalistic character of the Revolutionary movement together with the broad area of congruence between politically significant new class interests and social goals has assisted the shift from self-orientation to collectivity orientation in the performance by the new elite of its social role.[132]

Many of the conclusions about the impact of the Revolution on Mexican society which have been drawn from institutional and anthropological research have recently been reiterated in an opinion survey focusing on the effect of the Revolution on political attitudes and behavior. The authors compared Mexican responses on a number of items to those of Italians, choosing the latter nation as another Latin, Catholic, semi-developed state which does not have a commitment to revolutionary ideals. Among their findings are:

> In Mexico, 30 per cent of the respondents express pride in some political aspect of their nation—ten times the proportion of respondents in Italy, where only 3 per cent expressed such pride. A large proportion in Mexico also express pride in its economic system—in particular, they talk of economic potential and growth. In contrast, few Italians express pride either in the political aspects of their nation or in the economic system . . .

> There is some evidence . . . that the continuing impact of the
> Revolution explains part of the attachment to their political system
> that Mexican respondents manifest. Respondents in Mexico were
> asked if they could name some of the ideals and goals of the Mexi-
> can Revolution. Thirty-five per cent could name none, while the
> remaining 65 per cent listed democracy, political liberty and equal-
> ity, economic welfare, agrarian reform, social equality and national
> freedom . . . Those respondents who mentioned goals of the
> Revolution were then asked if they thought those goals had been
> realized, had been forgotten, or were still actively being sought.
> Twenty-five per cent of the 614 respondents in this category think
> the goals have been realized, 61 per cent think that they are still
> being sought, and only 14 per cent think they have been forgot-
> ten.[133]

The Mexican Revolution, of course, did not involve simply a symbolic transfer of power, as has occurred in a number of other Latin
American countries. Rather it is the one major Latin American revolution in which genuine land reform has occurred. The old dominant
class of large landowners has been eliminated. "The large landholders
disappeared at the pinnacle of the social order, together with their luxury consumption, no-work value system and the belief in the innate
inequality of social segments." [134] The rapid economic growth rate of
Mexico in recent decades has been credited by many to the consequences of this revolution in changing the value system, in making
possible the rise of a middle class that is self-assured about its own role.
It "is fairly abstemious and frugal; it is devoted to modernization and
education and recognizes economic achievement as a worthwhile end."
Conversely, its neighbor, Guatemala, provides a case for "good comparative control" with a nation of similar social structure and history,
but which has not changed its basic agricultural system and consequent class structure and value system, and shows little economic
progress; the term retrogression would be more apt.[135]

The positive example of Mexico and the negative one of Guatemala,
and many other countries as well, suggest that those concerned with
Latin American economic development and social modernization
might best devote themselves to an analysis of the conditions for revolutionary transformation of class relationships, particularly at the current stage of development in the rural areas. Presumably the quickest
way to initiate major changes in values is through social revolutions which remove those dominant strata which seek to maintain their
position and traditional values. A recent study of sociological changes

in Mexico concludes that in the new middle class, "there is evidence that the Revolution, by reducing the level of affluence and power of *cacique* families and by redistributing hacienda lands, has had a considerable psychological impact on the population in the direction of strengthening attitudes of independence and initiative and, conversely, reducing those of submissiveness." [136]

Analyses of the ways in which revolutions have fostered value change have pointed to how new regimes have sought to encourage economic development by changing the content of their education systems, not only in terms of more vocational education, but also through introducing achievement themes. In Mexico, through "the ideological values in Mexican socialism, achievement motivation was accorded a key position . . ."

> The process of inculcating achievement values in 1939 through textbooks took at least two forms. First, the texts gave universalistic and achievement values to the worker movement. All workers were equal; their individual progress and status within the movement depended on their own aggressiveness and accomplishment on the job. This value orientation served to break down the traditional emphasis placed on social immobility and status achievement by birth and blood, both ascriptive-based values. Secondly, a high value was placed on the very activity of hard effective work, where men got their trousers dirty and their hands calloused. Work was a noble and honorable endeavor in life. These achievement values were to be absorbed by the children who read how the son idolized his hard-working father. Later, in 1959 . . . in the field of education, the central idea presented to the child was the need to study, to excel, and to improve one's intellectual self. Related to the progress of education and to achievement was the stress placed upon developing personal discipline and a sense of responsibility.[137]

The educational system of Communist China has similarly exerted strong pressure on very young children for individual competitive achievement.[138] The teaching materials used in Chinese kindergartens in stories, songs, and games, "reveal a highly sophisticated program of training conducive to individual achievement motivation." [139] These are apparently designed consciously to break down the "non-competitive, group-oriented environment based on compatible relationships" fostered by the traditional pre-Communist family.

David McClelland has analyzed the emphases on achievement in Chinese education as reflected in the content of children's readers for "three Chinas," the Republican era of 1920–29, Taiwan during 1950–59, and Communist China for the same period. The stories of the 1920's showed a very low concern for achievement. The achievement emphases are markedly higher in Taiwan and Communist China, with the latter showing China "for the first time . . . above the world average."

> The predominantly U.S. influence on Taiwan has increased the amount of achievement concern in stories used there, but not as decisively as among the Communists on the Mainland. The quantitative data are supported even more strongly by qualitative analysis of the stories themselves. For instance the achievement concern in the Taiwanese stories is largely concentrated in tales of Western heroes—e.g., Magellan, Alexander Graham Bell, George Washington—whereas on the Mainland it saturates stories dealing with local and indigenous Chinese heroes.[140]

Data from various other nations undergoing ideological revolutions suggest similar conclusions. Thus the analysis of the content of children's readers in 1950 as compared with 1925 indicates that a "wave of high n Achievement . . . is common in newly independent countries." [141] This finding points up the earlier generalization that the "old" underdeveloped states of Latin America are at a disadvantage compared to the "new" ones of Asia and Africa in seeking political consensus for anti-traditional values. Analysis of Russian children's stories in 1925 and 1950 also reveals a considerable increase in achievement themes between the two periods. And case studies of post-World War II Russian defectors "strongly suggest that n Achievement may be higher in individuals brought up wholly under the Soviet system since the Revolution than in an earlier generation." [142] A comparison of the actual n Achievement test scores of a sample of factory managers and of professionals in the United States, Italy, Turkey, and Communist Poland also suggests the positive impact of Communist ideology on such orientations. The achievement orientation scores of the Poles were close to those of the Americans, and both were much higher than the Italians or Turks.[143]

Education and the Motivation for Innovating Entrepreneurial Elites

Although revolution may be the most dramatic and certainly the most drastic method to change values and institutions which appear to be inhibiting modernization, the available evidence would suggest that reforms in the educational system which can be initiated with a minimum of political resistance may have some positive consequences. Changes in the educational system may affect values directly through the incorporation of modern values to which students are exposed; indirectly they may help to modify the occupational structure by both increasing the numbers trained for various "modern" professions and helping to increase the status of positions needed in a developing economy. Clearly the way in which nations conceive of elite status may affect the supply of talent available for leadership in economic development. Thus, a high evaluation of occupations associated with traditional sources of status—the land, the military, humanistic intellectual occupations, and the free professions—tends to direct talent into occupations which do not contribute much to industrial development. And in cultures with such occupational values, the children of the successful entrepreneurs of lowly, often foreign, origin, frequently go to university to find means of entering the learned professions, politics, the arts, or similar occupations. Such behavior is likely to reduce both the talent and capital available for entrepreneurial expansion.

To analyze the value system inherent in university structures in detail would take us considerably beyond the limits of this paper. A detailed effort to do just this by Michio Nagai, Japan's leading educational sociologist, argues that the values of higher education are in fact achievement orientation, universalism, and functional specificity, among others. Nagai derives the need for these value orientations in the university from a consideration of the requirements for genuine scholarly creativity. Universities which do not stress these values can not be oriented toward the attainment of scholarly goals, and cannot protect themselves from outside interference with academic freedom.[144] There have been, of course, many universities, particularly in Latin America, which have not adhered to these values. Links with politics or religion have involved diffuse role obligations in which faculty have not been free to teach or publish findings in violation of the ideologies of groups of which they are a part. Ascriptive appointive, admission, or grading policies have sometimes reduced the adequacy of educational institutions as trainers of innovative elites motivated to achieve within a competitive system. But one may suggest that the more the universities of Latin America or other parts of the underdeveloped world are absorbed into the international world of scholarship, the more likely they are to reflect the values of this reference group in their internal systems, and to teach these to their students.

There is, of course, no simple relationship between the values of modern science and the way universities or even industrial concerns and government agencies operate in different countries. The Japanese system illustrates a formula whereby a "modern" nation may maintain particularistic and ascriptive traits while also developing rigidly universalistic and competitive patterns which guarantee the recruitment of talent into elite positions.

Members of various Japanese organizations, business, academic, or governmental, are given particularistic protection once they are admitted to membership. There is little competition for promotion or salary increases; men move up largely by seniority. Similarly, within the school and university system, little competitive grading occurs; almost everyone is promoted and graduated. And the graduates of various elite institutions are accorded almost "ascriptive" rights by others, e.g. leading business firms and government bureaus tend to hire most of their executive trainees from a few select universities, much as they have done for decades.

Universalism enters into the Japanese educational and business systems at two stages, first at admission to university, and second at entrance into the lower rungs of business or government executive ladders. The entrance examinations for Japanese universities are completely competitive; admission is solely a function of how well the students do on them, and many children of university professors, politicians, and the wealthy do not qualify for admission to the prestigeous universities. Before admission, no one has any special claim to be accepted. Once admitted, however, grades do not serve as an important basis for future selection. While a prospective employer may not learn much about a student from his grades, he can be fairly certain that almost any graduate of Tokyo, Kyoto, Waseda, and other high quality universities will be among the very top group in the country in general intelligence, and in ability to benefit from higher education. And as a further guarantee of quality there is another impersonal level of competition; job applicants must often take examinations as a pre-condition for civil service or business employment.

The Japanese system, therefore, permits particularism to operate in every personal relationship, while recruiting in a manner designed to ensure that the elite will be both highly motivated in achievement terms and well qualified. A teacher will not fail a student—i.e. some one with whom he has a personal relationship—nor will an employer or supervisor subject a subordinate to a humiliating lack of confidence. But the competitive entrance examinations, in which the examiners judge people with whom they have no personal relationship or obligation, meet the requirements of both particularistic and universalistic values.

It is significant that other industrialized societies which have emphasized ascription and particularism have also worked out means to handle the dilemma. In Britain, entrance to university has not been difficult until recently, but final grading has been handled on a completely universalistic basis. Examiners from other universities are always involved in awarding final examination grades to assure that local faculty do not give special preference to their own students. And the grade which a graduate receives—first- or second-class honors, or lower—remains with him as one of the major attributes which defines his place in government, business, and other institutions for the rest of his life. In France there is universalistic competition in receiving grades and in being admitted to elite schools at various levels.

Conversely, it may be pointed out that a society which strongly emphasizes universalism and achievement in its values may permit a great deal of particularism and ascription. Political patronage has continued in America to a greater degree than in many more particularistic European nations; nepotism may be found in industry; influence and family background may affect admission policies to universities, e.g. the children of alumni and faculty are often given preference over those with better records even in some of the best universities. It may be suggested that where a society has strong norms which fulfill certain basic requirements of the system, it does not need explicit rules. North Americans will yield to particularistic obligations, but within self-imposed limits, to avoid harming the institution by helping incompetents. Hence the very emphasis on achievement and universalism in the North American value system would seem to reduce the need for the kind of rigidly universalistic examination system which exists in Japan, where all the normative pressure is in the direction of particularism. And North American institutions are much less inhibited about dismissing students or employees for lack of ability.

Thus it would appear that modernizing societies require either strong values or rules sustaining achievement and universalism. *They need not reject their traditional value system if they can work out mechanisms to guarantee that a large section of the elite will be composed of men who are highly motivated and able to achieve.* However, much of Latin America and some other nations in the less developed parts of the world have not succeeded in doing either. Men from privileged backgrounds may be admitted to university, take courses in which it is easy to pass and get a degree, and then secure a high position on the basis of whom they know, or through family ties. These countries have not yet found mechanisms to associate talent with elite status. And those reformist student movements which resist making admission and examination standards more rigorous are, in effect, helping to maintain the traditional order.

There is, of course, considerable pressure on many Latin American state universities to change because of the increasing numbers of applicants. Today, in some countries, large numbers fail to qualify for university entrance.[145] However, the entrance examinations have been subject to severe criticism in many countries for being biased in favor of those educated traditionally in private schools.[146]

An admissions system which is biased against the children of the less well-to-do also discourages enrollment in courses leading to "modern" vocations as distinct from the traditional elite ones. Studies of occupational choices of university students indicate that the career aspirations of the less well-to-do resemble those of youth from minority ethnic backgrounds. They are both more likely to seek to achieve through studying subjects like business, engineering, or practical sciences. The source of the class bias in recruitment to Latin American universities is not solely, or even primarily, in the preference given to those whose pre-university training is in traditional subjects. Rather it lies in the fact that the road to university graduation requires a relatively high family income. And in poor countries, where most families have no possible economic reserve, they will not be able to sustain their children through the higher levels of schooling. In Latin America, about two-thirds of all secondary school students attend private schools which charge fees, a factor which undoubtedly operates to increase class discrimination. As compared even to other underdeveloped regions, Latin America has done little to "identify and encourage able students . . . to provide programmes for part-time students, although it is known that a sizeable proportion of the students in higher education support themselves through employment, and there is no programme for external or correspondence students. Perhaps most important of all, the number of students who receive financial assistance must be discounted as negligible." [147] This situation, of course, means that the overwhelming majority of students at Latin American universities are from quite privileged backgrounds. [148] The distribution of class backgrounds may become more rather than less discriminatory in the future, if higher education does not expand rapidly. For greater selectivity brought about by a more rapid increase in demand than in places available will increase the relative advantage of those from well-to-do, culturally privileged homes, who can prepare for admission examinations after having attended good private schools, or having private examination tutors. [149]

Evidence that a deliberate policy to encourage students to take modern rather than traditional subjects can work in Latin America has been presented by Risieri Frondizi, former rector of the University of Buenos Aires, who reports that the initiation of "a program of fellowships, offered only in fields like science and technology," cut the number studying law in half within three years, while the modern subjects gained greatly. [150]

The rulers of Meiji Japan have provided an excellent example of the way in which a development-oriented elite consciously used the educational system both to provide the needed cadre of trained and highly motivated people and to enhance the status of those occupations needed for modernization. Shortly after the restoration, technical "education was introduced at the university and middle-school levels, and it covered a broad range of theoretical science and practical instruction in agriculture, trade, banking, and, above all, industrial technology." [151] In addition to the various government schools in these fields, Japanese businessmen helped start private universities such as Keio and Hitotsubashi, designed to train for executive business positions students who could absorb the norms of modern business rationality as part of their education. [152]

Another major problem of Latin American universities is the curricula and status orientations of students which encourage vast numbers to work for degrees in subjects which are not needed in large quantity. Educational policy often encourages such maladjustments by making it much easier to secure a degree in subjects such as law or the humanities rather than the sciences or engineering. Clearly it is an implicit policy-decision to pass students in the former fields for less and easier work than in the latter, a decision which says, in effect, "We will over-train and over-encourage a section of our youth to aspire to occupational roles which are overcrowded and which do not contribute to social and economic modernization." Malcolm Kerr's comment about such policies in Egypt applies to many underdeveloped countries:

> The passively accepted assumption is that in these fields, where tuition fees are very low and nothing tangible is sacrificed by increasing the attendance at lectures, freedom of opportunity should be the rule. In reality, of course, a great deal is sacrificed, for not only does the quality of education drop, but a serious social problem is made worse, and thousands of students beginning their secondary schooling continue to be encouraged to aim for the universities rather than for the secondary technical education which would be more useful to themselves and to the economic progress of the country.[153]

These comments are clearly relevant to judging how education, particularly higher education, supports the elite in contributing to political stability and economic growth. First, as Arthur Lewis has suggested, there is some reason to suspect that the status concomitants linked to education *per se* should vary with the proportion and absolute size of the population that is educated. A relatively small higher educational establishment will encourage the retention, or even development, of diffuse elitist values among university graduates, while if a large proportion of the university-age population attends school, the pressures should be in the opposite direction.[154] In much of Latin America, university students almost automatically "become part of the elite. It matters little whether a student is the son of a minister or the son of a workman. His mere enrollment at the university makes him one of the two per thousand most privileged in the land." [155] Conversely in the United States, with its mass educational system, few university graduates may expect to attain high status; many of them will hold relatively low positions in nonmanual work; and a certain number will even be employed in manual occupations. Where comparatively few attend university, as in Britain, graduates who fail to achieve a status comparable to most of their fellow graduates will feel discontented; their reference group will be a higher successful group. The same analysis may be made with regard to the different implications of education for status concerns in the Philippines as contrasted with Senegal. A Filipino who attends the massive University of the Far East must know that few of his fellow students can expect an elite position; Senegalese students, like many in Latin America, however, know that among their classmates are the future economic and political leaders of the country.

A related consequence of increase in the numbers who attain higher levels of education should be an increase in the amount of high achievement orientation in a nation. Studies of the occupational goals of college students in nations with tiny systems of higher education suggest that the large majority of them expect positions in government work.[156] Since some form of white-collar employment must be the goal of college and secondary students, a sharp increase in their numbers should make talent available for a variety of technical and entrepreneurial roles. As Tumin and Feldman have indicated: "From the point of view of a theory of stratification, education is the main dissolver of barriers to social mobility. Education opens up the class structure and keeps it fluid, permitting considerably more circulation through class positions than would otherwise be possible. Education, further, yields attitudes and skills relevant to economic development and such development, in turn, allows further opportunity for persons at lower ranks." [157] The thesis that sees positive effects from the expansion of universities has been countered by these arguments: a transfer of educational techniques from developed to underdeveloped societies sometimes results in dysfunctional efforts at innovation; an "overexpansion" of educational resources may create a frustrated, and hence politically dangerous, stratum whose political activities undermine the conditions for growth; the "educated" often develop diffuse elitist status and cultural sustenance demands so they refuse to work in the rural or otherwise "backward" parts of their country; the educated often resist doing anything which resembles manual employment; and rapid educational expansion results in many being poorly educated, while reducing the opportunities available to the small minority of really bright students.[158]

There is no doubt, of course, that the rapid expansion of an educational system may result in an over-supply of persons with relatively high expectations of employment, salary, and status. The increase in the numbers of educated people in a developing economy necessarily means that as education becomes less scarce it should command less status and income. The process of adjusting expanded levels of higher education to reduced rewards is obviously a difficult one, and often results in political unrest. And as W. Arthur Lewis has pointed out, "upper classes based on land or capital have always favoured restricting the supply of education to absorptive capacity, because they know the political dangers of having a surplus of educated persons."[159] One must, however, separate the problem of the possible political consequences of educational expansion from the economic ones. As Lewis indicates, "as the premium for education falls, the market for the educated may widen enormously . . . The educated lower their sights, and employers raise their requirements . . . As a result of this process an economy can ultimately absorb any number of educated persons. . . . One ought to produce more educated people than can be absorbed at current prices, because the alteration in current prices which this forces is a necessary part of the process of economic development."[160] The argument against expansion is largely political rather than economic, and calls for a detailed examination of the sociological consequences. Mexico affords an example of the way in which economic growth and emphases on new values may reduce the tensions inherent in rapid educational expansion. William Glade contends that though the educated were often frustrated in pre-revolutionary Mexico, "the more or less steady expansion of the private sector activity since the mid-1920's" has meant a continuing demand for trained persons. "Secondly, . . . with the over-all expansion of the social, economic, and political structure there came a widening range of socially approved channels for the realization of achievement."[161]

To sum up the discussion of universities, the expansion of the educational system is of unquestioned benefit in providing the requisite skills, aspirations, and values essential to modern occupational roles. Not only expansion is required but also the content of education should be broadened. Specifically, education should be directed toward inculcating innovative orientations and teaching problem-solving techniques in all fields of knowledge. This would mean emphasizing and rewarding creative and independent effort on the part of students. The problem suggested earlier of the potentially disruptive political consequences of overproduction of university graduates would presumably be reduced if expansion is accompanied by a modernizing of the educational system. Underemployed graduates with modern, innovative orientations, are perhaps less likely to seek traditional political solutions to their plight, and more prone to look for other possible avenues toward achievement.

Proposals such as expansion and curricula change are easy to make but difficult to put into practice. Proposals to transform radically and to expand the educational system would meet, first of all, the opposition of present elites who are identified to some extent with the present system, and see such changes as a threat. Considerable innovative skill may have to be applied to overcome such opposition.

The conclusion to this section on education also brings us full circle to a recognition of the need to change class relationships in order to foster a change in values. Governments and parties which are deliberately concerned with the need to change values must also seek for ways to foster the rise of new occupational strata to status and power, and the reduction of the privileged position of old power groups, such as the land-linked traditional oligarchies who have little interest in economic growth, social modernization, expanded opportunities for talent, or democracy and equality.

Notes

1. For an excellent general discussion of the relationships between values and economic behavior written in a Latin American context see Thomas C. Cochran, "Cultural Factors in Economic Growth," *Journal of Economic History*, 20 (1960), pp. 515–530; see also John Gillin, "Ethos Components in Modern Latin American Culture," *American Anthropologist*, 57 (1955), pp. 488–500.
2. Max Weber, *The Protestant Ethic and the Spirit of Capitalism* (New York: Scribner's, 1935).
3. See Louis Hartz, *The Founding of New Societies. Studies in the History of the United States, Latin America, South Africa, Canada, and Australia* (New York: Harcourt, Brace and World, 1964).
4. David C. McClelland, *The Achieving Society* (Princeton: Van Nostrand, 1961), pp. 70–79; McClelland, "The Achievement Motive in Economic Growth," in Bert Hoselitz and Wilbert Moore (eds.), *Industrialization and Society* (Paris: UNESCO-Mouton, 1963), pp. 79–81.
5. McClelland, "The Achievement Motive in Economic Growth," p. 79.
6. Juan B. Cortés, "The Achievement Motive in the Spanish Economy between the 13th and 18th Centuries," *Economic Development and Cultural Change*, 9 (1961), pp. 159, 144–163; Norman N. Bradburn and David E. Berlew, "Need for Achievement and English Industrial Growth," *Economic Development and Cultural Change*, 10 (1961), pp. 8–20.
7. Bernard Rosen, "The Achievement Syndrome and Economic Growth in Brazil," *Social Forces*, 42 (1964), pp. 345–346 (emphasis in original).
8. See Talcott Parsons, *The Social System* (Glencoe: The Free Press,

1951), pp. 58–67 and *passim;* "Pattern Variables Revisited," *American Sociological Review,* 25 (1960), pp. 58–67; and "The Point of View of the Author," in Max Black (ed.), *The Social Theories of Talcott Parsons* (Englewood Cliffs, N.J.: Prentice-Hall, 1961), pp. 319–320, 329–336. I have discussed the pattern variables and attempted to use them in an analysis of differences among the four major English-speaking nations. See S. M. Lipset, *The First New Nation* (New York: Basic Books, 1963), pp. 207–273.

9. See Parsons, *The Social System,* pp. 182–191.
10. A comprehensive specification of the norms and behavior involved in concepts of political, social, economic, and intellectual modernization may be found in John Whitney Hall, "Changing Conceptions of the Modernization of Japan," in Marius B. Jansen (ed.), *Changing Japanese Attitudes Toward Modernization* (Princeton: Princeton University Press, 1965), pp. 20–23 and footnote 19.
11. The pattern variables have been applied in various discussions of social and economic development. For examples, see Fred W. Riggs, "Agraria and Industria—Toward a Typology of Comparative Administration," in William J. Siffin (ed.), *Toward the Comparative Study of Public Administration* (Bloomington: Indiana University Press, 1959), pp. 23–116; Joseph J. Spengler, "Social Structure, the State, and Economic Growth," in Simon Kuznets, Wilbert E. Moore and Joseph J. Spengler (eds.), *Economic Growth: Brazil, India, Japan* (Durham: Duke University Press, 1955), esp. pp. 379–384; Bert F. Hoselitz, *Sociological Aspects of Economic Growth* (New York: The Free Press, 1960), pp. 29–42, 59–60; David C. McClelland, *The Achieving Society,* pp. 172–188; G. A. Theodorson, "Acceptance of Industrialization and Its Attendant Consequences for the Social Patterns of Non-Western Societies," *American Sociological Review,* 18 (1958), pp. 437–484.
12. Parsons, *The Social System,* pp. 198–200. For a comparative social-psychological study of the orientations of comparable samples of adolescents in Buenos Aires and Chicago where the findings are congruent with Parsons's assumptions about differences between North American and Latin American values see R. J. Havighurst, Maria Eugenia Dubois, M. Csikszentmihalyi, and R. Doll, *A Cross-National Study of Buenos Aires and Chicago Adolescents* (Basel: S. Karger, 1965). The authors report that the Chicago group differs from the Buenos Aires one in being "more self-assertive and autonomous . . . more resistive to authority . . . more instrumental . . . the Buenos Aires group are more expressive in their orientation to the world" (p. 79).
13. Aldo E. Solari, *Estudios sobre la Sociedad Uruguaya* (Montevideo: Arca, 1964), p. 162.
14. Ibid., p. 171.
15. Frederick B. Pike, *Chile and the United States, 1880–1962* (Notre Dame: University of Notre Dame Press, 1962), p. 78. The strength of these values may be seen in the fact that for much of the colonial period, at the University of San Gregorio in Quito, "Applicants for

entrance had to establish by a detailed legal process 'the purity of their blood' and *prove that none of their ancestors had engaged in trade."* Harold Benjamin, *Higher Education in the American Republics* (New York: McGraw-Hill, 1965), p. 16 (my italics).

16. For a collection of papers dealing with the social structure of *latifundia* in different parts of the Americas, see Division of Science Development (Social Sciences), Pan American Union, *Plantation Systems of the New World* (Washington: Pan American Union, 1959), and Charles Wagley and Marvin Harris, "A Typology of Latin American Subcultures," *American Anthropologist,* 57 (1955), pp. 433-437.

17. R. P. Dore, "Latin America and Japan Compared," in John J. Johnson (ed.), *Continuity and Change in Latin America* (Stanford: Stanford University Press, 1964), p. 245. He indicates also that the absence of such attitudes in Japan is related to "the attenuation of the ties that had bound the feudal aristocracy and gentry began at the end of the sixteenth century and was completed in 1870." For a discussion of the concept of *arielismo,* see Kalman H. Silvert, *The Conflict Society: Reaction and Revolution in Latin America* (New Orleans: Hauser Press, 1961), pp. 144-161.

18. United Nations Economic and Social Council. Economic Commission for Latin America, *Provisional Report on the Conference on Education and Economic and Social Development in Latin America* (Mar del Plata, Argentina: 1963. E/CN.12/639), p. 250.

19. Thomas F. Carroll, "Land Reform as an Explosive Force in Latin America," in John J. Tepaske and Sidney N. Fisher (eds.), *Explosive Forces in Latin America* (Columbus: Ohio State University Press, 1964), pp. 81-125.

20. Wagley and Harris, "A Typology of Latin American Subcultures," pp. 439-441; Frank Tannenbaum, "Toward an Appreciation of Latin America," in Herbert L. Matthews (ed.), *The United States and Latin America* (Englewood Cliffs, N.J.: Prentice-Hall, 1963), pp. 32-41; José Medina Echavarría, "A Sociologist's View," in José Medina Echavarría and B. Higgins (eds.), *Social Aspects of Economic Development in Latin America,* Vol. II (Paris: UNESCO, 1963), pp. 33-39; Gino Germani, "The Strategy of Fostering Social Mobility," in Egbert De Vries and José Medina Echavarría (eds.), *Social Aspects of Economic Development in Latin America,* Vol. I (Paris: UNESCO, 1963), pp. 222-229; Charles Wagley, *Race and Class in Rural Brazil* (Paris: UNESCO, 1952), pp. 144-145; Bernard J. Siegel, "Social Structure and Economic Change in Brazil," in Kuznets, Moore, and Spengler (eds.), pp. 405-408.

21. Solari, pp. 127-129, 113-122.

22. J. Richard Powell, "Notes on Latin American Industrialization," *Inter-American Economic Affairs,* 6 (Winter 1952), p. 83.

23. José Luis de Imaz, *Los que mandan* (Buenos Aires: Editorial Universitaria de Buenos Aires, 1964), p. 160.

24. Pike, pp. 280-283.

25. Ibid., p. 287. This book was published in 1962, before the victory of the left-wing Christian Democrats.
26. Siegel, "Social Structure and Economic Change in Brazil," pp. 406–411. See also Charles Wagley, *An Introduction to Brazil* (New York: Columbia University Press, 1963), pp. 126–131. A summary of a detailed study of Brazilian industrialists reports that other than European immigrants and their offspring, "Most of the new industrialists were simply large landowners diversifying into manufacturing. Those who did not actually retain their plantations, retained strong links with the land. Their style of life hardly changed; their social attitudes changed not at all." See Emanuel de Kadt, "The Brazilian Impasse," *Encounter,* 25 (September 1965), p. 57. He is reporting on the findings in Fernando Henrique Cardoso, *Empresário Industrial e Desenvolvimento Econômico no Brasil* (São Paulo: Difusão Européia do Livro, 1964).
27. See Sanford Mosk, "Latin America versus the United States," American Economic Association, *Papers and Proceedings,* 40 (1950), pp. 367–383. See also Gilberto Freyre, *New World in the Tropics. The Culture of Modern Brazil* (New York: Vintage Books, 1963), pp. 71–72, 82–87, 193–195.
28. See Bernard Blishen, "The Construction and Use of an Occupational Class Scale," *Canadian Journal of Economics and Political Science,* 24 (1958), pp. 519–531; Yves de Jocas and Guy Rocher, "Inter-Generational Occupational Mobility in the Province of Quebec," *Canadian Journal of Economics and Political Science,* 23 (1957), pp. 377–394; John Porter, *The Vertical Mosaic: An Analysis of Social Class and Power in Canada* (Toronto: University of Toronto Press, 1965), pp. 91–98, *passim.*
29. Norman W. Taylor, "The French-Canadian Industrial Entrepreneur and His Social Environment," in Marcel Rioux and Yves Martin (eds.), *French-Canadian Society,* Vol. I (Toronto: McClelland and Stewart, 1964), pp. 271–295.
30. One French-Canadian analyst has argued recently that "historically French-Canadians have not really believed in democracy for themselves." He suggests "that they have never achieved any sense of obligation towards the general welfare, including the welfare of the French-Canadians on non-racial issues," Pierre Elliot Trudeau, "Some Obstacles to Democracy in Quebec," in Mason Wade (ed.), *Canadian Dualism* (Toronto: University of Toronto Press, 1960), pp. 241–259. On the general problems of, and weakness of, democracy in Quebec see Herbert Quinn, *The Union Nationale* (Toronto: University of Toronto Press, 1963), esp. pp. 3–19, 23, 65–67, 126–129, 131–151; Gerard Dion and Louis O'Neill, *Political Immorality in the Province of Quebec* (Montreal: Civic Action League, 1956); Arthur Maheux, "French Canadians and Democracy," in Douglas Grant (ed.), *Quebec Today* (Toronto: University of Toronto Press, 1960), pp. 341–351; Frank R. Scott, "Canada et Canada Français," *Esprit,* 20 (1952), pp.

178–189; and Michael Oliver, "Quebec and Canadian Democracy," *Canadian Journal of Economics and Political Science,* 23 (1957), pp. 504–515.

31. Trudeau, "Some Obstacles to Democracy in Quebec," p. 245; see also Quinn, pp. 17–18.

32. S. D. Clark, *The Canadian Community* (Toronto: University of Toronto Press, 1962), p. 161.

33. Thomas C. Cochran, *The Puerto Rican Businessman* (Philadelphia: University of Pennsylvania Press, 1959), p. 131; see also pp. 151–154 and Cochran, "Cultural Factors in Economic Growth."

34. Albert Lauterbach, "Managerial Attitudes and Economic Growth," *Kyklos,* 15 (1962), p. 384. This study is based on interviews with managers in eight countries.

35. Eduardo A. Zalduendo, *El empresario industrial en América Latina: Argentina* (Mar del Plata, Argentina: Naciones Unidas Comisión Económica para América Latina, 1963. E/CN/12/642/Add. 1), p. 46.

36. Albert Lauterbach, "Government and Development: Managerial Attitudes in Latin America," *Journal of Inter-American Studies,* 7 (1965), pp. 202–203; see also L. C. Bresser Pereira, "The Rise of Middle Class and Middle Management in Brazil," *Journal of Inter-American Studies,* 4 (1962), pp. 322–323.

37. Fernando H. Cardoso, *El empresario industrial en América Latina: Brasil* (Mar del Plata, Argentina: Naciones Unidas Comisión Económica para América Latina, 1963. E/CN/12/642/Add. 2), pp. 25–26; for a description of the way in which *hombres de confianza* were incorporated into a major Argentinian industrial complex see Thomas C. Cochran and Ruben E. Reina, *Entrepreneurship in Argentine Culture. Torcuato Di Tella and S.I.A.M.* (Philadelphia: University of Pennsylvania Press, 1962), pp. 266–268; see also de Kadt, "The Brazilian Impasse," p. 57, for a summary of Brazilian evidence on this point.

38. Tomás Roberto Fillol, *Social Factors in Economic Development. The Argentine Case* (Cambridge: M.I.T. Press, 1961), pp. 13–14.

39. Ibid., p. 61.

40. Cardoso, *El empresario industrial en América Latina: Brasil,* p. 31; Siegel, "Social Structure and Economic Change in Brazil," pp. 405–408. Robert J. Alexander, *Labor Relations in Argentina, Brazil, Chile* (New York: McGraw-Hill, 1962), pp. 48–49.

41. Emilio Willems, "The Structure of the Brazilian Family," *Social Forces,* 31 (1953), p. 343.

42. Richard M. Morse, *From Community to Metropolis. A Biography of São Paulo, Brazil* (Gainesville: University of Florida Press, 1958), p. 229 (my italics).

43. Cardoso, *El empresario industrial en América Latina: Brasil,* pp. 35–39.

44. Albert Hirschman, *The Strategy of Economic Development* (New Haven: Yale University Press, 1958), pp. 14–19.

45. W. Paul Strassman, "The Industrialist," in Johnson (ed.), *Continuity and Change in Latin America,* pp. 173–174.

46. Lauterbach, "Managerial Attitudes and Economic Growth," p. 379; Fillol, pp. 13–14.
47. One report on Panama comments that "their business philosophy . . . is that of the gambler or plunger . . . They prefer low volume and high markup; they want quick, large profits on small investment. They cannot think in pennies." John Biesanz, "The Economy of Panama," *Inter-American Economic Affairs,* 6 (Summer, 1952), p. 10.
48. Lauterbach, "Government and Development," pp. 209–210. J. Richard Powell, pp. 82–83.
49. Strassman, p. 173.
50. Aarón Lipman, *El empresario industrial en América Latina: Colombia* (Mar del Plata, Argentina: Naciones Unidas Comisión para América Latina, 1963. E/CN/12/642/Add. 4), p. 30; Guillermo Briones, *El empresario industrial en América Latina: Chile* (Mar del Plata, Argentina: Naciones Unidas Comisión para América Latina, 1963. E/CN/12/642/Add. 3), p. 35. It should be noted that most of the above generalizations about Latin American entrepreneurs are based on interview data. And as Fernando Cardoso points out, such data may tend to variance with actual behavior. Many of those interviewed are well educated and aware of the nature of a modern entrepreneurial outlook. Cardoso suggests that the actual behavior of those interviewed is much less modern and rational than would be suggested by the interviews. Cardoso, pp. 47–48, 59.
51. Cochran, "Cultural Factors in Economic Growth," pp. 529–530.
52. Kalman H. Silvert, "The Costs of Anti-Nationalism: Argentina," in Silvert (ed.), *Expectant Peoples: Nationalism and Development* (New York: Random House, 1963), p. 350.
53. Ibid., p. 353.
54. Willems, p. 343.
55. John Friedmann, "Intellectuals in Developing Countries," *Kyklos,* 13 (1964), p. 524.
56. William S. Stokes, "The Drag of the *Pensadores,"* in James W. Wiggins and Helmut Schoeck (eds.), *Foreign Aid Reexamined* (Washington: Public Affairs Press, 1958), p. 63; see also Fred P. Ellison, "The Writer," in Johnson (ed.), p. 97.
57. Stokes, "The Drag of the *Pensadores,"* see the footnotes to these articles for reference to the large literature by Latin Americans and others emphasizing these points.
58. Dore, "Latin America and Japan Compared," p. 245.
59. Pike, p. 251.
60. Ibid., p. 254.
61. Fillol, pp. 17–18.
62. Jacques Lambert, "Requirements for Rapid Economic and Social Development: The View of the Historian and Sociologist," in De Vries and Echavarría (eds.), p. 64.
63. Robert W. Burns, "Social Class and Education in Latin America," *Comparative Education Review,* 6 (1963), p. 232.

64. Florestán Fernandes, "Pattern and Rate of Development in Latin America," in De Vries and Echavarría (eds.), pp. 196–197; see also Oscar Vera, "The Educational Situation and Requirements in Latin America," in De Vries and Echavarría, pp. 294–295; and Wagley, *An Introduction to Brazil*, pp. 103–104.

65. Fernandes, "Pattern and Rate of Development," p. 196.

66. Pike, pp. 288–289. "There is a lengthy list of works suggesting that the educational structure in Chile foments class prejudice, leading the middle class to shun labor and the laboring classes, while striving to emulate the aristocracy," p. 442, footnote. This work contains a detailed bibliography.

67. J. Tinbergen and H. C. Bos, "The Global Demand for Higher and Secondary Education in the Underdeveloped Countries in the Next Decade," O.E.C.D., *Policy Conference on Economic Growth and Investment in Education, III, The Challenge of Aid to Newly Developing Countries* (Paris: O.E.C.D., 1962), p. 73.

68. Frederick Harbison and Charles A. Myers, *Education, Manpower and Economic Growth* (New York: McGraw-Hill, 1964), p. 179.

69. Ibid., p. 88.

70. Ibid., pp. 115–119.

71. James S. Coleman, "Introduction to Part IV," in J. S. Coleman (ed.), *Education and Political Development* (Princeton: Princeton University Press, 1965), p. 530.

72. Frank Bowles, *Access to Higher Education*, Vol. I (Paris: UNESCO, 1963), p. 148.

73. Robert J. Havighurst and J. Roberto Moreira, *Society and Education in Brazil* (Pittsburgh: University of Pittsburgh Press, 1965), p. 200. And engineering in Brazil and other parts of Latin America often means the traditionally socially prestigious field of civil engineering, not mechanical, chemical, or industrial.

74. Brandão Lopes, "Escôlha ocupacional e origem social de ginasianos em São Paulo," *Educação e Ciencias Sociais*, 1 (1956), pp. 61, 43–62. This study is reported in Wagley, *An Introduction to Brazil*, pp. 125–126.

75. Porter, pp. 92–93.

76. Benjamin, pp. 60–66; 94–97; 120–123.

77. S. M. Lipset, *The First New Nation*, p. 195.

78. Ibid.

79. Stokes, p. 70.

80. Lambert, p. 64.

81. Ironically, the powerful leftist student groups in the various Latin American countries constitute a major force resisting university modernization. See John P. Harrison, "The Role of the Intellectual in Fomenting Change: The University," in Tepaske and Fisher (eds.), pp. 27–42. In Venezuela, they have opposed tightening up examination standards. See Orlando Albornoz, "Academic Freedom and Higher Education in Latin America." *Comparative Education Review*, 10 (June

1966), pp. 250–256. For a collection of articles dealing with various aspects see David Spencer (ed.), *The Latin American Student Movement* (The National Student Association, 1965).

82. Rudolph P. Atcon, "The Latin American University," *Die Deutsche Universitätszeitung,* 17 (February, 1962), p. 27.

83. Joseph Schumpeter, *The Theory of Economic Development* (New York: Oxford University Press, 1961), pp. 74–94.

84. Bert Hoselitz, "Main Concepts in the Analysis of the Social Implications of Technical Change," in Hoselitz and Moore (eds.), *Industrialization and Society,* pp. 22–28.

85. Hoselitz, *Sociological Aspects,* p. 62; Peter T. Bauer and Basil S. Yamey, *The Economics of Underdeveloped Countries* (Chicago: University of Chicago Press, 1957), pp. 106–112.

86. Louis Kriesberg, "Entrepreneurs in Latin America and the Role of Cultural and Situational Processes," *International Social Science Journal,* 15 (1963), p. 591.

87. Strassmann, p. 164.

88. Raymond Vernon, *The Dilemma of Mexico's Development* (Cambridge: Harvard University Press, 1963), p. 156.

89. Imaz, p. 136.

90. Ibid.; see also Germani, pp. 223–226; and Zalduendo, p. 10. The census of 1895 reported that 84 per cent of the 18,000 business establishments were owned by foreign-born individuals. Cochran and Reina, p. 8.

91. Imaz, pp. 138–139.

92. Briones, p. 10.

93. Julio Vega, "La clase media en Chile," in *Materiales para el estudio de la clase media en la América Latina* (Washington, D.C.: Pan American Union, 1950), pp. 81–82, as cited in Pike, p. 279.

94. Benjamin Higgins, "Requirements for Rapid Economic Development in Latin America: The View of an Economist," in De Vries and Echavarría (eds.), p. 169.

95. Emilio Willems, "Immigrants and Their Assimilation in Brazil," in T. Lynn Smith and Alexander Marchant (eds.), *Brazil. Portrait of Half a Continent* (New York: Dryden Press, 1951), p. 217. These apparently are largely from Italian, German, Jewish, and Lebanese backgrounds. See also Pereira, p. 316; Richard Morse, "São Paulo in the Twentieth Century: Social and Economic Aspects," *Inter-American Economic Affairs,* 8 (Summer, 1954), pp. 21–23, 44; George White, "Brazil: Trends in Industrial Development," in Kuznets, Moore, and Spengler (eds.), pp. 57, 60–62.

96. Wagley, *An Introduction to Brazil,* p. 87.

97. François Bourricaud, *Peru: Une oligarchie face aux problemes de la mobilization* (unpublished manuscript, 1965), Ch. I, pp. 29–31.

98. Aaron Lipman, "Social Backgrounds of the Bogotá Entrepreneur," *Journal of Inter-American Studies,* 7 (1965), p. 231.

99. Biesanz, p. 9.

100. Bertram Hutchinson, "A origem sócio-econômica dos estudantes universitários," in Hutchinson (ed.), *Mobilidade e Trabalho* (Rio de Janeiro: Centro Brasileiro de Pesquisas Educacionais Ministério de Educação e Cultura, 1960), p. 145.

101. Myron Glazer, *The Professional and Political Attitudes of Chilean University Students* (Ph.D. thesis, Princeton University, 1965), pp. 78–79.

102. Joseph Fischer, "The Student Population of a Southeast Asian University: an Indonesian Example," *International Journal of Comparative Sociology,* 2 (1961), pp. 225, 230.

103. See Robert Park, *Race and Culture* (Glencoe: Free Press, 1950), pp. 345–392; Everett Stonequist, *The Marginal Man* (New York: Russell and Russell, 1961).

104. Siegel, pp. 399–400 (emphases in the original).

105. Freyre, *New World in the Tropics,* p. 161.

106. Strassmann, p. 166.

107. Gilberto Freyre, *The Masters and the Slaves. A Study in the Development of Brazilian Civilization* (New York: Alfred A. Knopf, 1963), p. 36. Freyre does not evaluate this thesis; rather as with many other tales concerning Jewish traits and abilities, he seems to be gullibly accepting. "The farmers with a deep love for the land and a thorough knowledge of agriculture were sometimes abused or exploited in Brazil by those of their fellow countrymen whose passion was for commercial adventure and urban life—most of them probably Jews." Freyre, *New World in the Tropics,* p. 50.

108. Max Weber, pp. 38–46.

109. Suzanne Keller, *The Social Origins and Career Lines of Three Generations of American Business Leaders* (Ph.D. Dissertation, Columbia University, 1953), pp. 37–41.

110. See S. M. Lipset and Reinhard Bendix, *Social Mobility in Industrial Society* (Berkeley: University of California Press, 1959), pp. 137–138.

111. Porter, pp. 286–289.

112. Anyda Marchant, *Viscount Mauá and the Empire of Brazil* (Berkeley: University of California Press, 1965), pp. 81, 83, 208–209, 241.

113. Cochran and Reina, pp. 147–151. It is worth noting that his two sons studied for their Ph.D.'s abroad, and that both are professors, one in economics and the other in sociology.

114. Johannes Hirschmeier, *The Origins of Entrepreneurship in Meiji Japan* (Cambridge: Harvard University Press, 1964), p. 35.

115. Germani, "The Strategy of Fostering Social Mobility," p. 226. Argentinian cultural traits are discussed in Fillol.

116. See Torcuato S. Di Tella, Oscar Cornblit, and M. Ezequiel Gallo, "Outline of the Project: A Model of Social Change in Latin America," *Documentos de Trabajo* (Buenos Aires: Instituto Torcuato Di Tella Centro de Sociología Comparada, n.d.).

117. Alexander Gerschenkron has shown how entrepreneurial activities in nineteenth-century Russia "were at variance with the dominant sys-

tem of values, which remained determined by the traditional agrarian pattern . . . The nobility and the gentry had nothing but contempt for any entrepreneurial activity except its own . . . Divorced from the peasantry, the entrepreneurs remained despised by the intelligentsia." He argues, however, that such cultural values may "indeed delay the beginning of rapid industrialization," but they cannot stop it. Their effect, rather, is to hold back the pressures for industrialization so that they finally burst out in periods of rapid growth. However, he also concludes that in Russia, "the delayed industrial revolution was responsible for a political revolution," i.e. the Bolshevik seizure of power. *Economic Backwardness in Historical Perspective* (Cambridge: Harvard University Press, 1962), pp. 28, 59–62.

118. Amando do Miguel and Juan J. Linz, "Movilidad Social del Empresario Español," *Revista de Fomento Social,* 75–76 (July–December, 1964).
119. Fernando H. Cardoso, *Empresário Industrial e Desenvolvimento Econômico no Brasil* p. 157 and passim.
120. A very similar point is made about the heterogeneity of outlook among the Argentinian entrepreneurs by Imaz.
121. For a statement of the ways in which economic development may change values, see Albert O. Hirschman, "Obstacles to Development: A Classification and a Quasi-Vanishing Act," *Economic Development and Cultural Change,* 13 (1965), pp. 385–393.
122. For example, see Robert Bellah, *Tokugawa Religion* (Glencoe: The Free Press, 1957); James C. Abegglen, *The Japanese Factory* (Glencoe: The Free Press, 1958); Marion J. Levy, Jr., "Contrasting Factors in the Modernization of China and Japan," in Kuznets, Moore, and Spengler (eds.), pp. 496–536; and Hirschmeier.
123. See Reinhard Bendix, "Cross-Cultural Mobility and Development," in Neil Smelser and S. M. Lipset (eds.), *Social Structure and Social Mobility in Economic Development* (Chicago: Aldine Publishing Company, 1966), pp. 262–279. See also Bert Hoselitz, *Sociological Aspects of Economic Development,* pp. 8–82; and Hirschmeier, pp. 44–68.
124. Talcott Parsons, *Structure and Process in Modern Society* (New York: The Free Press, 1960), pp. 116–129.
125. Solari, p. 172.
126. See also Gustavo Lagos, *International Stratification and Underdeveloped Countries* (Chapel Hill: University of North Carolina Press, 1963), pp. 3–30, 138–160.
127. Ellison, pp. 96–100.
128. S. M. Lipset, "Political Cleavages in 'Developed' and 'Emerging' Polities," in Erik Allardt and Yrjo Littunen (eds.), *Cleavages, Ideologies and Party Systems* (Helsinki: The Westermarck Society, 1964), p. 44.
129. Gerschenkron, p. 25.
130. Robert Lamb, "Political Elites and the Process of Economic Develop-

ment," in Bert Hoselitz (ed.), *The Progress of Underdeveloped Areas* (Chicago: University of Chicago Press, 1952), pp. 30, 38.

131. As one student of Mexican politics comments: "[T]he distinctive feature of a revolution is that it establishes new goals for the society; it reorganizes society, but it must first reorganize the values which that society accepts; a successful revolution means the acceptance as 'good' of things which were not regarded as good before, the rejection as 'bad' of things previously acceptable or commendable . . . Prior to the [Mexican] revolution, the Indian was semiofficially regarded as an inferior being, to be kept out of sight as much as possible, being prohibited by Porfirio Díaz's police from entering the Alameda, the public park in the center of Mexico City, for example. After the revolution, Mexico's Indian heritage became a matter of national pride, to be stressed in her art and her history, to be studied at length in her universities." From Martin Needler, "Putting Latin American Politics in Perspective," in John D. Martz (ed.), *The Dynamics of Change in Latin American Politics* (Englewood Cliffs, N.J.: Prentice-Hall, 1965), p. 25.

132. William P. Glade, Jr., "Revolution and Economic Development: A Mexican Reprise," in Glade and Charles W. Anderson, *The Political Economy of Mexico. Two Studies* (Madison: University of Wisconsin Press, 1963), pp. 50–52; for a detailed account of the way in which the Revolution affected changes in values see pp. 33–36, 39–43, 44–45, and *passim*.

133. Sidney Verba and Gabriel A. Almond, "National Revolutions and Political Commitment," in Harry Eckstein (ed.), *Internal War* (New York: The Free Press, 1964), pp. 221–222, 229.

134. Manning Nash, "Social Prerequisites to Economic Growth in Latin America and Southeast Asia," *Economic Development and Cultural Change*, 12 (1964), p. 230; Pablo González Casanova, *La Democracia en México* (México, D. F.: Ediciones ERA, 1965), p. 41; Clarence Senior, *Land Reform and Democracy* (Gainesville: University of Florida Press, 1958).

135. Nash, pp. 231, 232–233. See also Frank Brandenburg, "A Contribution to the Theory of Entrepreneurship and Economic Development: The Case of Mexico," *Inter-American Economic Affairs,* 16 (Winter, 1962), pp. 3–23.

136. Glade, "Revolution and Economic Development," p. 43.

137. Walter Raymond Duncan, *Education and Ideology: An Approach to Mexican Political Development with Special Emphasis on Urban Primary Education* (Unpublished Ph. D. thesis, Fletcher School of Law and Diplomacy, 1964), pp. 167, 204–205.

138. John Wilson Lewis, "Party Cadres in Communist China," in James S. Coleman (ed.), p. 425; see also Richard H. Solomon, "Educational Themes in China's Changing Culture," *The China Quarterly,* No. 22 (April–June, 1965), pp. 154–170.

139. Lewis, "Party Cadres in Communist China," p. 425.
140. David McClelland, "Motivational Patterns in Southeast Asia with Special Reference to the Chinese Case," *Journal of Social Issues*, 19 (1963), pp. 12–13.
141. Ibid., p. 10.
142. McClelland, *The Achieving Society*, pp. 412–413.
143. Ibid., pp. 262, 288.
144. Michio Nagai, *The Problem of Indoctrination: As Viewed from Sociological and Philosophical Bases* (Columbus: Ohio State University Press, Ph.D. thesis, 1952, multilith), pp. 36–39 and *passim*.
145. Benjamin, pp. 67–71, 97–99, 123–127, 148–153.
146. Bowles, pp. 147–152.
147. Ibid., p. 148.
148. Burns, pp. 230–238; Kalman H. Silvert, "The University Student," in Johnson (ed.), pp. 207–210.
149. Havighurst and Moreira, p. 104–105.
150. Risieri Frondizi, "Presentation," in Council on Higher Education in the Americas, *National Development and the University* (New York: Institute of International Education, 1965), p. 30.
151. Hirschmeier, pp. 127, 128–131.
152. Ibid., pp. 164–171.
153. Malcolm H. Kerr, "Egypt," in Coleman (ed.), pp. 190–191.
154. For a discussion of the consequences of moving from a small elite system to mass higher education in Japan, see Herbert Passin, "Modernization and the Japanese Intellectual: Some Comparative Observations," in Jansen (ed.), pp. 478–481.
155. Atcon, p. 16.
156. See K. A. Busia, "Education and Social Mobility in Economically Underdeveloped Countries," *Transactions of the Third World Congress of Sociology*, Vol. V (London: International Sociological Association, 1956), pp. 81–89.
157. Melvin Tumin with Arnold S. Feldman, *Social Class and Social Change in Puerto Rico* (Princeton: Princeton University Press, 1961), p. 7.
158. H. Myint, "Education and Economic Development," *Social and Economic Studies*, 14 (1965), pp. 8–20.
159. W. Arthur Lewis, "Priorities for Educational Expansion," O.E.C.D., p. 37.
160. Ibid., pp. 37–38.
161. Glade, pp. 44–46; for a general discussion of the conditions which affect student participation in various forms of politics see S. M. Lipset, "University Students and Politics in Underdeveloped Countries," *Minerva*, 3 (1964), pp. 15–56; and S. M. Lipset (ed.), "Students and Politics," special issue of *Comparative Education Review*, 10 (1966), pp. 129–376.

2

The New Urban Groups: The Middle Classes

LUIS RATINOFF

The rapid growth of cities has created a new type of social structure in Latin America which has aroused great attention among politicians and scholars, and which can only be interpreted by reference to the changes that have taken place since 1945.

Large cities require new organizational functions, which to some extent influence the distribution of power, prestige, and wealth. The principal cities are *par excellence* the centers of mass communication, the symbols of "modernity," and the locale of the institutions which are concerned with matters of merit, efficiency, and equality. This has led to the conviction that the cosmopolitan cities of Latin America are centers of progress and social change, and that the new urbanized groups will take a direct interest in social development and will adjust their behavior to the demands of progress.

The recent social history of these cities indicates that new men and groups, virtually unknown until very recently, have begun to play a part in the political drama. In all Latin American countries where urbanization has reached a significant stage of development, the middle classes have now become a decisive factor in the structure of power. Any study of the part played by the middle classes tends to emphasize their increasing participation in the government.

Recent publications dealing with Latin America assume that a kind of progressive spirit is inherent in the individual members of the middle class, and that spirit is usually defined in terms of development.[1] In an article comparing the growth-rates in four different Latin American countries, B. F. Hoselitz[2] pointed out that nations with a large middle class tend to grow *less* rapidly than those with a much smaller middle class; the decisive factor, therefore, would seem to be not the size of the middle class, but its internal structure and the practical part it plays in the general combination of social forces, interests, and groups.

This suggests a revision of the customary picture of the middle classes as a fundamental element in the process of social, political, and economic change covered by the general term of "development." The facts pointed out by Hoselitz could be supplemented by others. Indeed, the alleged "progressive spirit" of these sectors favor democratizing the national institutions from inside, maintaining the stability and continuity of those institutions, and promoting the transformation and improvement of the social structure. According to the most generally accepted view, the development and the rise of the middle classes constitute two aspects of a single phenomenon.[3] However, the experience of Nazi Germany, the conservative tendencies displayed by appreciable sections of these classes in certain industrial countries, and, most of all, the history of Argentina in the last few decades oblige us to take a new approach to the problem of the middle classes and their role in the process of economic development.

An analysis of these examples presents us with a picture of the new forms of organization of social inequality which have emerged from the rapid urbanization in Latin American countries. The comparative confusion that seems to prevail in the discussion of this subject, and the dogmatism displayed, are due not only to a certain failure to discriminate in analysis between the examples and the practical behavior under study, but also to the fact that the examples themselves, and the implications to which they give rise, have seldom received proper attention or been thoroughly described. It may be worthwhile to attempt a brief description of the most generally accepted hypotheses regarding the role and significance of the middle classes in economic and social development.

I. The Customary Hypotheses

The customary hypotheses see a connection between the tendency of urbanization to create social inequality and the changes in the structure of employment which result from the growth of cities; particular reference is made to the varieties and requirements of modern production. The pattern assumes the preservation of a certain homogeneity and of a minimum continuity in the institutions in a given community.

According to this concept, the truly traditional structures are based on two principal classes, whose respective duties and rights are not equal. Modernization resulting from the growth of cities in the twentieth century has created an ill-assortment of families and individuals placed half-way between the traditional classes; while these middle sectors are the product of social mobility, they constitute the social area where vertical mobility produces the greatest economic and social consequences.

Urbanization has brought about the recognition of the middle sectors as a social institution; the inequality it produces varies to some extent, inasmuch as it creates machinery and institutions which speed up mobility. Industry and other specifically urban economic activities require flexible forms of social inequality, so as to meet their needs in personnel and thus ensure their efficient functioning. Only a municipal authority which encourages the expansion of the middle class can satisfy the requirements of modern productive activities.

The middle class faces two kinds of demands so compelling that they influence individual action. There are social demands, which tend to accentuate the values and norms favorable to social mobility, and there are also demands made by modern industry. Objectively, the social destiny of the middle class depends both upon the opportunity for expanding and rationalizing urban productive activities, and upon the establishment of individual merit as the stratification principle. That is why this urban sector is always oriented toward creating an "open" type of social organization. In pursuit of this aim, the middle class comes into conflict, and sometimes into open hostilities, with the traditional power groups of the community, who are linked with the agricultural system and whose status is hereditary and based on the family. In their struggle against these oligarchies, middle-class leaders seek the support of the lower classes in the urban community, and thus come to advocate the admission of those classes to the body politic and their more equal participation in the social and economic advantages of city life. Far from being the fruits of an ephemeral alliance, these objectives reflect the values upheld by the middle class: their ideal of an open society with firmly enforced standards of equal participation. As a result of the conflict with the traditional sectors, the middle class becomes

aware of the relationship between economic and social development
and stratification on the basis of merit. This ultimately leads it to take
part in the transformation of traditional structures and in the establishment of the institutions typical of industrial society.

According to this interpretation, the internal structure of the middle
class makes it a willing instrument in the transformation of social and
economic institutions. The predominance of small independent firms is
regarded as the most important explanation of the developmental dynamics of the middle class.

II. Application of the Customary Hypotheses to the Interpretation of the Latin American Middle Classes

In a book published a few years ago, an attempt was made to apply
the foregoing hypothesis to the development of the middle classes in
Latin America and their role in the process of social change.[4] On the
basis of very full documentation the author described the effects of the
emerging middle classes in Brazil, Chile, Mexico, and Uruguay, and
suggested that the future progress of those countries was likely to be
bound up with their development. This interpretation leads to the following conclusions:

1) *The emergence of the middle sectors has been closely associated
with technological change and with the expansion of education and of
public utilities.*

According to the dominant hypotheses, this shows that the political
behavior of the urban middle classes in the above-mentioned countries
has been determined by technological changes and by the need of other
social groups to obtain their political support. Thus, the growth of the
middle classes is attributed to the requirements of modern techniques,
to the expansion of education, and to the new welfare and planning
functions assumed by the state in that order.

2) *The middle sectors are to some extent the product of social
mobility.*

Taking the end of the First World War as the starting point for the
development of the middle classes, the author presents a well-
documented picture which shows development to have been closely
related to the demand for new skills which those sectors could not
meet from their own resources, so that they were gradually obliged to
open their ranks to new social groups.

3) The absence of any prolonged common historical experience and the heterogeneous character of newly assimilated members of the middle sector have done much to impede the formation of a class in the strict sense of the term.

Heterogeneity is clearly an outstanding feature of the middle sector. The diversity of social and economic origins and of their interests prevents the formation of a compact social stratum constituting a bloc for purposes of political action.

4) It would, however, be possible to describe the general political and economic action of the middle sectors in terms of certain common historical experiences.

The middle sectors have nevertheless displayed a certain degree of political cohesion and convergence of interests. Thus, it may be pointed out that:

a) Well-established urban groups have shown themselves favorable to national policies designed to promote urban growth and economic development by granting substantial public funds to the urban centers;

b) The middle sectors regard education as a factor which determines status, and they encourage expansion of public education. With industrial development and the entry of commercial and industrial workers to the middle class, classical education has given way, in part, to a scientific type of instruction. Once a means of preparation for the liberal professions exclusively, the educational system is now a means of vocational training as well. This, according to the writer, clearly indicates the increasing involvement of the middle sectors with the demands and requirements of industry;

c) Industralization has been a prime objective for the middle sectors, especially in the post-war period. The political leaders of the middle classes began by taking an interest in the development of the mining industries, and the experience of two world wars has led them to support national manufacturing and heavy industries, thus promoting domestic markets capable of expansion;

d) Because the middle-class intellectuals formulate nationalistic political and economic interpretations, those classes, when they come to power, make nationalism an official philosophy of public action;

e) State intervention has been fundamental for the political leadership of the middle sectors, which have used state machinery to promote industrial development and social welfare;

f) The urban environment favors all kinds of associations independent of parental supervision; the social emancipation of women, the involvement of the middle class in modern, impersonal economic organizations, and also the ease of social mobility have all combined to reduce the importance of the head of the family in determining individual employment; the political party has replaced the family as the source of political action. The growth of social organizations which reward merit is closely associated, according to the author, with the transfer of individual political loyalties to common, impersonal party objectives.

5) *As the middle sectors increase in political stature, nonprofessional groups begin to compete within those sectors for political rewards.*

In the nineteenth century university professors constituted the most important section of the middle class, both because of their culture and prestige and because they had a virtual monopoly in framing political doctrines. As a result of their success in democratizing the national institutions, their own importance has diminished. There has been an increase in the prestige and political importance of primary and secondary school teachers (particularly where the public realizes the essential role of education) and a tendency to give them better training.

Another development has been the increase in the number and the status of civil servants; social tasks formerly left to private initiative have now been taken over by the political authorities. The composition of the middle sectors also seems to have been considerably affected by the emergence and increase of the commercial and industrial sections of the community. These sections have, in fact, operated both as a check and as a constructive influence, and perhaps they do indeed play the dominant part within the middle sectors. Scientists, technicians, and business managers, inasmuch as they enjoy the benefits of economic development, have tended to identify themselves politically with their employers.

6) *The growing importance of the middle sectors has gone hand in hand with a decline in the relative influence of the Catholic clergy in national politics, changes in the social structure having altered the position of the Church and narrowed its sphere of action.*

The tendency of the middle sectors has been to transfer to the state the monopoly of education and social welfare, while at the same time they have promoted an intensive use of the modern mass communications media and, in general, of all institutions which accentuate, directly or indirectly, the secular aspects of social activity.

7) *The middle sectors have built up a body of reliable political experience, and their social, economic, and political influence is likely to increase with time.*

Now that economic problems have become the chief political concern in the majority of Latin American countries, the middle sectors, placed as they are in a strategic social position, have been able to acquire considerable practical experience in matters relating to economic and social development, and have apparently become the group best fitted to provide the impetus for effective industrial change.

The middle sectors have also acquired experience in the art of political compromise. By bringing extremist tendencies within the bounds of workable politics, they are acting as a harmonizing and stabilizing factor.

8) *In the course of their rise to power, the middle sectors have concluded political compromises with the working classes which have led them to create new social institutions with norms and values more effectively concerned with merit, and with competence in their internal operation.*

The rise to power of the middle sectors has meant a far-reaching transformation of the social structure. The new institutions they have created not only have made it possible to introduce new social values, but appear to have endowed them at the same time with a firm social basis.

III. Other Interpretations

In addition to the usual interpretations of the role of the middle classes in the process of development, there exist alternative hypotheses not always mentioned in the books and documents on economic growth. It seems appropriate to mention these theories as well, in view of the disconcerting fact, pointed out by Hoselitz,[5] that there are some countries economically at a standstill although at the same time they possess a large middle class.

According to this alternative theory, the existence of a middle class in cities not yet industrialized is in no way incompatible with the fact that its conduct conforms to certain traditional types. The middle classes may thus, in some circumstances, represent a force committed to maintaining the traditional social system, despite the fact that they appear to favor the introduction of various symbols of modernity.

Supporters of this hypothesis maintain that traditional forms are not necessarily "rigid" or "static" and imply that the relative flexibility of such structures may be the result of a certain break in continuity between the social systems of which they are composed. Consequently, the creation of new institutions may be perfectly compatible with the maintenance of traditional institutions and values. The assumption is that in these circumstances, and in changing situations in general, it is precisely the traditional structures of a complex society which provide the necessary social cohesion and adjust with a certain flexibility to the new, changing, and contradictory requirements. Modern institutions set up within a traditional system are said to display greater rigidity in their response to the requirements of change.

The expansion of the middle classes reflects to some extent a greater social mobility and opening-up of the existing structures; in this sense, the individual members of the middle classes are guided in their conduct by norms which govern personal mobility. Not all forms of social mobility, however, imply the existence of openly competitive values; this is said to be true, in particular, of highly industrialized communities. Mobility, in so far as it results from the growth of cities in a traditional society, seems to operate more successfully when divorced from generalized competition. Indeed, primary relationships are apt to play a very important part in the advancement and rise of the individual; to gain success in a career, it is at least as important to have "patrons" as to do one's job efficiently, if not more so. Primary connections, and primary or personal relations in general, are an effective means of maintaining and improving status, and they often take precedence over the impersonal standards of recruitment and promotion which, at least ideally, form part of the structure of institutions based on the principles of efficiency and merit.

The system of "patronage" is propitious for those individuals who conform most directly to the requirements and values of certain small groups in the higher social ranks who can deal out favors. Such advancement signifies the socialization of values in the privileged classes of the community, together with an effort to support the established order of things, and this tends to preserve the status acquired as a result of mobility. The degree of dissatisfaction in the middle classes depends largely upon the opportunities open to them for improving, or preserving, the positions they have gained. If the system provides a reasonable degree of satisfaction for such aspirations, the middle classes tend to model their behavior and standards on those of the traditional social elite. Any conflict between the two factions is, on the other hand, the result of dissatisfaction. Inasmuch as the middle classes do not represent homogeneous social aggregates, their individual members always find themselves involved in the traditional order of things, and such conflicts tend to adjust themselves and traditional structures are adapted to the new demands.

In this sense, the diminished rigidity of social inequality can only have the effect of preserving traditional strategic institutions and of subjecting the functioning of new institutions to their limitations and possibilities. Thus, the political alliances of the middle classes will depend on whether or not the social system proves capable of satisfying their minimum aspirations. Where that satisfaction is provided, the middle sectors will be likely to seek alliance with the powerful and privileged groups in the community, and will thus contribute to the maintenance of the existing order.

IV. A Clear Picture of the Middle Classes in Latin America

There is no dearth of studies and reports for tracing the development of the middle classes in Latin America to compare the hypotheses summarized above. It is now necessary to present a theoretical picture setting forth the reasons for alternative hypotheses, as a parallel to the customary interpretations of their role. I have chosen certain themes which lend themselves to a different interpretation of the evolution of the middle classes in relation to the process of modernization in the major Latin American countries. These themes revolve around the problem of the participation of the middle sectors in the system of power, and the tendencies displayed by those sectors in political, economic, and social matters.

A) THE MIDDLE CLASS AS A PRESSURE GROUP

The political ascension of the middle sectors has followed a comparatively simple course. Descriptions, varying in their degree of detail, exist for several Latin American countries, and in all of them, notwithstanding notable differences of locality and period, we are struck by the presence of certain identical features recurring in every process of urbanization.

It is generally agreed that the middle-class political movements began their rise to power by enlisting the support of the working-class masses, and that as they went along they created various institutions whose "manifest" purpose was to improve the social and economic status of the workers. The "latent" effects of these institutions, however, appear to have promoted the expansion and prosperity of the middle classes themselves. Evidence shows that under their leadership there was a gradual expansion of the various social levels and sectors which make up the middle classes. This phenomenon is probably to be attributed not only to the growth of the population in urban areas, the creation of new institutions and productive units, and the general process of modernization, but also to the need to satisfy certain social and economic aspirations which made possible the political mobility of the middle sectors. Despite their initial working-class trend, the middle-class parties frequently gave priority to the demands of their members and of the social groups connected with them. This fact is a consequence of the composition of the movements, and of their commitments toward the relative satisfaction of their members' social and economic aspirations.

The vaguely "didactic" ideological tendency of these movements goes far to account for the "social" or "working-class" orientations in the early stage of their existence.[6] By gaining the support of wider social sectors, the middle-class parties and leaders brought pressure to bear on the groups traditionally in power, and paved their own way toward greater participation in decision-making and in the handling of public affairs.

The ascending process seems also to have been based on systematic recourse to certain traditional institutions, and on the creation of new institutions as a means of consolidating and improving the status achieved; in response to immediate and direct social pressure from the lower urban classes, the new middle classes committed themselves in politics to "interventionist" ideologies. In many cases the confidence they placed in state action was not so much an ideological reflex as a real means of action with a view to social organization. The "interventionism" of the middle classes carried with it an uninhibited expansion of the state machinery, greater educational facilities, a policy of economic stimulation, measures of social security, legislation for the protection of workers, and it had the result of introducing new social sectors into the body politic. The fundamental effect of these institutional transformations was the direct or indirect creation of new middle sectors, which ultimately made up a numerous middle class of considerable social importance.

In the course of this process the political tendencies varied. The "workers' movement" and the "people's movement" were watered down in time into compromises with the different demands of the existing order, and were converted into middle-class political movements. According to some writers, this provided an illustration of the middle sectors' skill in what has been called "the capacity for political compromise," a concept which might equally be applied to the economic and social spheres.[7] This tendency toward compromise is said to characterize the second phase of the middle-class movements, when they appeared to abandon their revolutionary tone and become the spokesmen of the middle classes as such, who at this stage were politically, socially, and economically committed to the maintenance of the existing order. Officially in favor of constitutional government, anti-militaristic, with a spontaneous faith in the natural perfectibility of institutions and in gradual economic progress symbolized by industrialization, middle-class movements began to seek allies in the traditional sectors and to give up the idea of a far-reaching and radical transformation of social institutions.

In this connection it is important to take into consideration the natural process of economic expansion, and its probable incidence upon the tendencies and values of the middle classes during the period 1945–60. The fact that the demand for posts halfway up the social ladder considerably exceeded the supply, does not appear to have led to the institutionalization of free competition, based on objective qualifications, as the method of recruitment and selection. On the contrary, the exchange of favors, family connections, "protective" relationships, the distribution of sinecures through the political party, and other forms of primary relations, formed a complex network through which "patronage" continued to operate in favor of the middle-class status. If we study the distribution of careers among individuals employed at these levels, we often form the impression that social mobility was playing its part, but people were always ready to avail themselves of the advantages of a partially closed system of relations—facilitating the offer of opportunities in the form of sinecures—and, in general, that the various middle groups in the community were probably not enjoying equal opportunities. Competition, merit, and efficiency do not always seem to have played the leading part in the selection of individuals for social advancement. To judge from the various sources of information, mobility and the maintenance of acquired or inherited status did in fact frequently operate in association with "patronage." This latter, as an institution, was so prevalent in the different sections of the social structure that from the standpoint of the individual, success often depended on the efficient manipulation of the comparative advantages made available to him by the social organization. Competition often took the form of rivalry in the skillful use of connections, or the prospect of improving one's personal relations and influence. The importance and social prestige of some groups were maintained in many cases by their ability to confer favors on their members and "protégés," regardless of their ostensible purposes.

It seems likely that the internal conflicts and the lack of cohesion which often characterized the middle classes in Latin America reflected not only the existence of certain relatively opposed interests, but also the fact that certain groups' advancement were impeded. Closed relationships were maintained with the purpose of appropriating at least the best opportunities, for certain small groups, thus barring the way for anyone who did not belong to the closed circle. Sporadic action undertaken by middle-class individuals and groups to transform the social order might be interpreted as certain pressure to compel these exclusive circles to open up and allow the little group of "rebels" to share their monopoly of opportunities. Many descriptions of the way in which the groups advocating change actually applied their ideals and programs once they reached power have stressed their interest in self-advancement; once that advancement was guaranteed, there was a tendency for the "revolutionary" impetus to diminish gradually in intensity and scale.

Since the institutions comprised in the state machinery in Latin America developed parallel to and in association with the middle classes, this did much to determine the conduct of those social sectors. The view of the state as the supreme dispenser of opportunities had its practical foundation in the "interventionist" activities of the governments in which the middle sectors played a part. The direct or indirect dependence of the most varied sectors and levels of economic activity upon state action has been no unusual feature of Latin American development; both the "dependent" and "independent" classes have been obliged, to a great extent, to base their social and economic possibilities upon the various policies of the state. This applies to the processes of modernization, to the creation of new institutions and productive units to the improvement of living conditions, and to the expansion of the market and of opportunities in general. Moreover, owing to the persistent demand for various social services for the white-collar sectors as well as for workers, there was a continual opportunity for widening the scope of the public institutions; it is not surprising that the groups composing the middle sectors—even those who openly advocated "free enterprise"—should have found themselves committed to and interested in "interventionism."

During the initial period, political power was probably the most effective social lever facilitating middle-class access to social opportunity. It was frequently by this means that business enterprises sought the protection of the state and succeeded in creating certain special positions for themselves. As a result, industrial firms appear to have often been so closely associated with the highest levels of political power that to speak of the state and industry, as though they were two mutually exclusive systems, is an exaggeration hardly consistent with the conditions in which economic activity really took place. Generally speaking, moreover, the defense and improvement of the status of the dependent middle classes rested, in the last analysis, with the groups which operated and took decisions at the top levels of the central power structures. These circumstances build up a picture of a social structure in which the various institutional circles were closely grouped around the political functions and institutions by means of a network of primary relationships. All this made it possible to have "semi-public, semi-private" autarchy, keeping its "clients" to some extent separated and ensuring the necessary autonomy for its different structural units, to function with considerable flexibility without the need for modern forms of social co-ordination.[8]

The two stages noted in the rise to power of the middle classes—viz. the period of access and that of compromise—contribute to the part played by the middle sectors in the transformation of Latin American society.

The "revolutionary" and "populist" impulse which characterized the middle-class movements at the initial stage does not appear to have aimed at the introduction of structural changes incompatible with the traditional order. The history of the individual movements and the analysis of their aims suggest that the intention, in each case, was to set up a certain number of new institutions and generally to improve those which already existed. The middle classes took the view that the form of democracy applied by the traditional power-groups should be improved by widening the bases of power.

The middle sectors tended to assume that the extent to which new political institutions developed into effective social structures depended upon their own more active participation in the political system and in economic organization. Consequently, they directed their principal efforts toward breaking into the circles in which power was vested. Through an interventionist policy they participated in the economic structure. The protection afforded them by the authorities enabled some of their members even to join the traditional upper class social circles. Although each successive step entailed a compromise with the established order, this should not be interpreted as increased conservatism: the middle classes came to be identified with the institutions they had themselves helped to create, and through these, with what remained of the traditional order. The changes made had by now been assimilated by the social system. In short, to support the new institutions no longer implied a position of hostility to and rejection of traditionalism in its contemporary form.

The incorporation of the middle sectors of society into the structures of power did not seem to entail the complete replacement of the traditional elite; it simply meant that they had to share the power with these newcomers—to come to terms, to compromise or to negotiate.[9]

B) THE ORIENTATIONS OF THE MIDDLE CLASSES

If we strive to go beyond the few stereotypes usually applied, to draw upon the variety of available information, to observe some general features common to the history of the different nations, we find that the tendencies of the middle classes have varied in emphasis and leadership in the course of urbanization, in proportion to their commitment to the established order and achievement of the necessary numerical and social importance. The contradictory features and the absence of a definite trend, which are typical of the middle classes in Latin America, suggest that the different tendencies which manifested themselves during the process, far from replacing one another, were superimposed upon one another and thus diluted, resulting in some degree of ambiguity.

One after another solutions were offered for specific social situations, but no theme was sustained for long, because of the heterogeneity of the middle classes, the emergence of new middle sectors in competition with those already existing, and the critical attitude of some of their strategic groups. Indeed, it has repeatedly been asserted that the middle classes, unlike those in the English-speaking countries, lacked a real sense of direction. Vascillating as they did between the working-class ideologies and the attitudes of the traditional social groups, the urban middle sectors apparently proved unable, when they achieved power, to set a clear and direct course for change in the majority of Latin American countries. To put things in this way is to oversimplify the problem of middle-class tendencies. It is an explanation which may, indeed, account in some instances for the ambiguity displayed in the definition of aims and values, and for the vascillation and changes of emphasis. But most of the evidence suggests that the picture is more complex; for while the middle classes undoubtedly showed a tendency to favor changes in the traditional structures, this did not mean that their purpose and action were directly calculated to bring about the radical transformation of those structures. On their way to power, the middle sectors successively adopted values and trends compatible with those of other groups and levels of society; but while it is possible to point to certain coincidences, which in some cases are tantamount to complete identification, there can be no doubt that they pursued their own objectives and trends on most occasions.

Reaffirmation of the rule of law   The defense of the rule of law as the ideal form of national organization has been described as the most important trend displayed by the middle classes in politics. The reaffirmation of "constitutionalism" as the method of distributing power and conferring it upon the different social sectors, has dominated the thinking of the majority of middle-class movements, especially since the Second World War. Put briefly, the political ideal upheld by typical groups in the middle sectors was an elected civil government in contrast to the military regime originating in a *coup d'état*.[10]

Any study of the "legalistic" ideological tendency observed among the middle classes makes clear their stress of individual rights and protection for the right of ownership and for freedom of contract as against authoritarian action by the state. Nevertheless, the individual guarantees which are central to the legal concepts are usually re-cast by the middle-class groups in the course of their ascent, their aim being to give a social character to those guarantees.

During their period of access to power, the middle sectors seem to be ideologically committed to establishing social limits to individual guarantees. Hence, there were the new and complicated state regulations concerning freedom of contract—particularly in the sphere of labor and social welfare—the introduction of legal provisions to control the free operation of markets—whether aimed at creating favorable conditions or at preventing undesirable effects—and the placing of new tighter restrictions upon the right of ownership. The new institutions usually reflect this initial "social" trend among the middle sectors; at a later stage, however, the growing tendency to compromise somewhat diminishes the urgency of great social rights.

This conception of "social justice" is said to be closely associated with the principle of state intervention. It is probable that in the view of the middle classes, political power should be kept within bounds by individual rights and private ownership, one of their most important functions being to ensure the protection of those rights—while at the same time creating a strong central government, capable of playing an active part in the guidance and control of the community and of the economy, and of ensuring a more equal distribution of benefits and opportunities among the population. These ideas usually make an ideological appeal to the political groups most representative of the middle classes, and particularly to the elements seeking a wider access to the power circles.

It would seem from the available sources that during this period the dual concept of a "modern national" and "nationalist" state is developed—namely, that of a political authority with the theoretical and practical function of representing the great mass of the population and defending the general interests of its own republic in an international system where an unequal distribution of power and wealth is the dominant characteristic. It is the duty of the national state to promote welfare and improve the general standard of living, to intervene in the economic machinery, and to ensure greater social justice by protecting the underprivileged groups in the community. The concept of the national state lays stress on intervention by the political authority, favors the restriction of individual rights in the spheres of social justice for which it assumes responsibility, and undertakes to promote the great collective aims. It might be called an "entrepreneur" state, not merely in its strictly political aspects but also in economic matters, in social changes, and even in cultural questions. Sufficient stress has not always been laid on this initial ideological approval of state control among the middle sectors, which equates the ideas of advancement and of social and economic progress with the predominance of state initiative in the various fields of human activity. Thus, for the middle classes, the concept of progress has been linked with their faith in collective action by the state.

It may be pointed out that, during their rise to power, the middle classes openly identified themselves with different forms of state control, but during the phase of consolidation of their newly won positions, they tended to lay stress on the rights of ownership and on individual guarantees. The change of attitude should not be interpreted as a substitution of more typically "liberal" or "individualist" concepts for that of state control. In fact, both attitudes existed side by side within ideological systems characterized by ambiguously formulated principles and doctrines. What has just been said only means that some attitudes were more strongly marked than others. The concepts of private enterprise and public action were intermingled—in association, in conflict, or simply co-existing among the standards regulating the most diverse levels and areas of behavior. It cannot be denied, however, that periodically certain middle sectors, finding their access to higher social positions systematically barred, have tended to identify themselves with a "state socialism" concept of progress.

Nor can it be asserted that all the component groups of the middle classes have uniformly advocated the rule of law, though this has been generally true. Some important groups have frequently taken part in revolutions and *coups d'état*, both during the period of rise to power and at the stage of compromise. Similarly, the concepts of the revolutionary state and the corporative state have received considerable attention from many middle-class intellectuals in certain Latin American countries. It would hardly be correct to say that these represent dominant attitudes among those social sectors, but they may perhaps indicate the dilemma confronting some of those social groups when the need and the demand for social change find no response in existing institutions, when cultural traditions are wholly pre-industrial, or when the absence of a consensus on fundamental problems tends to promote radical ideas and action.

The introduction of political changes along constitutional or legal lines has not always been favored by the middle sectors who shared political power. Policies of maintenance in office, arbitrary appoint-ment, the exclusion of certain political leaders and sectors, and even the single-candidate system, have all repeatedly been supported by small middle-class groups firmly established in the state institutions. Never-theless, whatever may have been the actual conduct of those sectors, the various sources of information point to the conclusion that in most cases they derived the ideological justification for their actions from the concept of the rule of law, vaguely based on traditional individual guarantees and from the concept of the state as the purveyor of social justice.

Toward a more developed economy The greater importance at-tributed to individual guarantees in middle-class legal and political theory does not seem to have been accompanied by a sharply individu-alistic concept of economic activity. It has been pointed out often that Catholic traditions, which place the general welfare higher than indi-vidual interests, have been a factor of no small importance in the middle-class acceptance of liberalism.[11] In point of fact, the liberals did not always fully grasp the social and economic implications of their creed, though many of them felt committed to its internal logic.[12] It has often been declared that the middle-class political movements favored state control in economic and social matters, but that their politics were liberal.[13]

The period during which the middle classes were gaining access to power usually seems to have been characterized by "the quarrel with capitalism." This so-called quarrel, sustained and fomented to a great extent by the new leaders, reflects the profound mistrust of economic liberalism felt by the rising middle classes. According to the terminol-ogy most frequently adopted, capitalism produced exploitation, parasit-ism, immorality, and poverty. The aims of human solidarity pursued by the Latin and Spanish culture were declared incompatible with the materialism and individualism of the capitalist system.

Thus, certain middle-class Catholic groups proposed the establish-ment of an economic system in which the "common welfare" would take precedence over "individual interests," because capitalism had a "dehumanizing, corrupting and poisonous" effect. In its extreme forms, this doctrine sometimes implies that individualism and economic and political liberalism are unacceptable in the Christian life and the spiritual essence of society can be preserved only by setting up a popular system of government on a non-liberal basis. It is agreed that in some cases property should be socialized and controlled by Christian planning, and in general, that the new social organization should be authoritative, "popular," and planned: a kind of halfway house between capitalism and socialism.[14]

The political goals of the emergent middle classes were directed toward the establishment of a new economic system organized to serve social and cultural ends. There was an unquestionable ideological tinge in their earliest somewhat utopian undertakings. Thus, the problem of the necessity of the "capitalist phase" in the advance toward the desired type of society was a quite important topic of political discussion among leading groups in the middle classes. Since to leave out "the capitalist phase" altogether was liable to lead to open revolution, the leaders and intellectuals often contemplated the transition stage in terms of a mixed economy which would ultimately lead to the establishment of a kind of socialism.

It is worthy of note, however, that as some of the principal groups in the middle sectors found their way into government institutions, their programs and behavior became progressively more vague with regard to the productive structure or the reallocation of resources expressing only general good wishes. Rather than considering the economic process in its complexity, requiring systematic programs for its modification or improvement, the middle classes looked upon the economic structure as an accomplished fact, and set about using the state machinery to create exceptional circumstances for the benefit of certain groups. Generally speaking, there was a phase of "social conquests" when various groups, particularly among the middle classes, exercised direct pressure to acquire special benefits.

The growing demand for new "social conquests"—both among the middle classes and at the "dependent" levels of the urban community —and the crises affecting the great international economic centers, made it obvious that a new structure of production must be set up. Three promises—improvement in the standard of living of the masses, economic nationalism, and industrialization—were the main features of the new middle-class political economy, once they had left behind the idea of mere participation in the benefits of the system. This new policy was frankly popular in the urban areas, where the factories came to be accepted as the only true symbols of progress.

At this stage the middle-class political parties were in favor of much more direct and far-reaching state intervention in the economic system. Political economy was often regarded as a species of state capitalism or socialism; it might be said that in many countries the "benefactor" state now became the "entrepreneur" state, which was expected to promote, encourage, invest, take risks, and carry out almost all managerial functions in the economic sphere. The new conceptions sometimes led to a markedly commercial view of economic activity. The need to "protect the national industry," the protection of the workers, capital, and resources, was implicit in the activities of the "entrepreneur" state. It has been pointed out that the dominant note was a kind of economic nationalism, based on an optimistic estimate of the positive and beneficial effects of all kinds which modern industry must bring.

Although there was a vague, generalized feeling that the intervention of the "entrepreneur" state was rendered necessary by the dearth of private contractors, the idea of planned activity kept its place in principle. One gets the impression that there was an almost blind faith in the "naturalness" of that process. The consequence of this was that without co-ordination the political authorities intervened in the most varied areas and sectors of the economy, but sporadically, inconsistently, and halfheartedly.

The middle sectors were apparently unwilling to commit themselves to a frontal attack to effectively transform the economic structure. Everything suggests that they preferred to introduce partial modification, hoping that the new productive institutions would lead to natural changes in the economic structure. In many countries the ideological and doctrinaire tone of interventionism gradually dwindled in importance, making way for a conception that the function of the state should be to create favorable conditions, and to stimulate and coordinate activity within a semi-liberal system thus promoting social welfare and economic progress.

Thanks to this policy of industralization and economic nationalism, specific middle-class groups gradually advanced to influential economic positions. The regulation of foreign trade, credit control, the use of financial machinery as a stimulus, direct investment in specific projects, and various other state activities helped them to accede to and participate in the management of commercial, financial, and industrial affairs. As these groups became actively involved in the different institutions of the economy, interventionism lost its initial "doctrinaire" tendencies.

In most cases, the policy of industrialization originated with the promise to improve the general standard of living. Those who preached industrialization as the sole effective source of prosperity were assuming that a better domestic distribution of revenue would automatically result from industry, that the national economy would thus expand considerably, and that the participation of the state in industry would create the public confidence needed to attract private investment to this sector. Industrialization as the general policy of the different governments, with the participation of the middle sectors, was held with high optimism and a great faith and confidence in the future. Initially it was identified with the political plans of the popular sectors in the large towns. For the middle and working classes, in fact, the pursuit of "social conquests" and that of industrialization formed a single strategy directed toward modernizing the traditional structures.

As a result of the application of the various programs of industrialization, with their sometimes contradictory results, the policy of "social conquests" recovered some of its force and independence in certain cases. It was taken up by many groups which set themselves up to represent the interests of the popular sectors and the underprivileged sections of the middle classes.

The policy of industrialization did not fully justify the hopes placed in it; only at the initial period did it raise the purchasing power of the masses and hold out promise of ending the urban unemployment. The differences between the poor and the rich increased. Dependence upon the fluctuations of the international market and the international policy of great economic centers was a basic factor in the evolution of those Latin American countries in which the middle class had achieved importance and had urged a policy of industrial development. Some authorities consider that state participation in industry, together with a protectionist policy, undoubtedly produced effects, but only partially succeeded in channeling private capital toward industry, while at the same time these policies had an unfavorable effect upon foreign investment. State intervention in the economy, and the attempts to promote social welfare, usually sent up government expenditure at a rate which outstripped the growth of the national income. The economic picture characteristic of the industrialization program often displays certain

typical features: an adverse balance of payments, chronic inflation, private capital displaying greater interest in speculative investment than in industry, organized pressure by various groups on behalf
of their own interests and ambitions. The working classes frequently
reacted in defense of the purchasing power of wages and of employment security. The middle classes felt the effect of the general economic instability, which affected both the purchasing power of their
salaries and their aspiration for improved status and its accompanying
symbols. The business sectors, for their part, demanded a series of
more definite measures to solve their currency and credit problems. In
most cases the demands of these different sectors were found to be incompatible, and it is likely that they often served to put the brake on
industrial growth. However, it must be recognized that these conflicting demands probably had a dynamic effect in accelerating the break
with the traditional system.

The sometimes disconcerting results of industrialization programs
very likely produced a sensation of living in a period of economic and
social chaos. The typical attitude of the middle-class governments in
economic matters was an adjustment to this state of affairs, achieved by
oscillating between a so-called policy of "social conquest." Beneath the
surface, a more comprehensive concept of the process of economic
transformation was taking shape, and there was a recognition of the
need to co-ordinate production, trade, and financial activities. The term
"economic development" ceased to be the password in industrialization
programs: it was replaced by the action of the public sector, and in certain cases even by economic action on the part of the private sector.
Development planning, in other words the planned co-ordination of
the various mechanisms contributing to economic growth, reverted to
some extent to the doctrines which had encouraged the middle class to
advocate "interventionism" in the early days, but the functions of the
entrepreneur state were kept within comparatively narrow limits, while
private enterprise and foreign investment began to play a more important part.

Probably the idea of development planning resulted from the comparative failure of the partial programs of industrialization, and the
manifestly critical situation engendered by the alarm of different
groups over economic instability. On many occasions the middle-class
groups in power moved gradually toward policies of economic "stabilization," which were considered the only alternative way to create the

conditions for industrial growth. The social and psychological sources of the stabilization policy were not deep, merely reflecting the desire of workers and employees to defend the purchasing power of their wages, and the weariness of general instability. The failure of the stabilization policy left no alternative but the return to general instability under a policy of "social conquests" and industrialization, the effects of which were more or less familiar. Development planning was intended to provide a new alternative which, while ensuring reasonable stability, would be conducive to industrial growth and help to improve the living standards of the population.

A study of economic trends among the middle sectors suggests that during the period of their rise to power, they usually identified themselves with a policy of social conquests and social claims favorable to interventionism and sometimes to a markedly doctrinaire form of state management and avowed economic nationalism; in contrast, during the phase of compromise there was a tendency to stress the importance of private initiative, the free play of markets, and the need for foreign investment to accelerate development, though without detracting from the leading role played in economic matters by the political authorities. The middle classes gathered around the state institutions; the new entrepreneurs came to the fore under the protection of the state; the various levels of white-collar workers kept up pressure on the political authorities, or used the public machinery to improve their economic situation. Until this time the "progressive" spirit among the middle classes had been associated with a vaguely interventionist dogmatism. The great majority in these sectors probably supposed that these terms were adequate for a transformation of the economy.

Toward greater social justice When the middle classes entered the political arena, they were committed to general principles of social justice. Until they came to power, the leading middle-class groups kept up a more or less permanent quarrel with the "privileges" of the established order. Starting with a basically equalitarian attitude, middle-class intellectuals became the most vigorous critics of the traditional institutions, while fighting for the establishment of a more perfect social organization. From various "populist" ideologies they built up the idea of social justice in the sense of freedom based on material equality of all human beings; at the same time, however, they hoped for a selfless community of citizens which might serve as a guide to action. It has been pointed out more than once [15] that the middle-class political movements in Latin America came into existence with a definitely anti-oligarchic orientation, prepared to launch a frontal attack against the traditional social order. But this impulse grew progressively weaker as these social sectors had to accept one political compromise after another.[16] Hence it has sometimes been suggested that although the middle classes, in their rise to power, introduced all kinds of innovations, they did not commit themselves to the establishment of a social order based on "middle-class values." [17] The more their leading groups rose to political, economic, and social power, the less contrast remained between their concepts and those of the old elite. Once in power, the middle-class political groups retained traces of their earlier tendencies for a considerable time; presumably the present social order developed from the measures taken by the middle-class political elite to improve social institutions. Thus, whatever controversial features the established order might display, it represented at this moment, for the middle sectors, "the best of all possible orders." To this it should be added that the strategy pursued by the middle classes in order to achieve their proposed improvement of social institutions appears to have been prompted simultaneously by civic values and by those of social justice.

The extension of civil rights to the dependent urban sectors generally compelled the traditional order to accept the admission of the middle-class political and social groups to some power and influence.[18] The leaders of the ascending middle classes must soon have learned that their opportunities, and those of the other groups rising with them, depended first and foremost upon the incorporation of new social sectors into the political community. To judge by the information relating to the periods of ascent by important middle sectors—and in some cases to the period when they were consolidating their recently acquired positions—there was a noteworthy extension of the suffrage to comparatively marginal social strata; this was generally accompanied by a series of social measures aimed not only at creating the minimum social and economic conditions required for the effective exercise of civic rights, but also at putting an end to the discriminatory effects of the system prevalent in the traditional community. The social policy of the middle sectors usually found expression in the creation and relative reinforcement of certain typical social institutions.

The leading middle-class groups identified themselves, first and foremost, with the establishment of a set of legal provisions and institutions to protect workers and improve the general hygiene and social security. All these were introduced as fundamental aspects of civil rights, and as means of limiting the effects of the privileges inherent in the social structure.

This strategy of equality had as its focal point the extension of the right of association to the trade union organizations. Governments in which the middle class participated used the state organization openly for the encouragement of the trade union movement among urban workers. The workers' protests were channeled and legally controlled by means of institutional frameworks closely linked to the political power structure; this probably helped also to consolidate the positions recently acquired by the new pressure groups. This becomes even clearer when it is remembered that the trade union movement was not confined to the workers. Employees' unions, and even certain associations of university professors, held an important place in the Latin American "fraternity" movement. In the early stages the workers' unions were indeed organized and financed by middle-class politicians occupying government posts. Although this does not seem to have been so in all cases, there are grounds for thinking that the political tendency displayed by the workers' movement in its initial phase sometimes coincided with the ascent and consolidation of the middle sectors.

The expansion of educational facilities was a favorite feature of the social policy framed by the leading middle-class groups. "Education for everyone" really meant a consolidation of the public education system, and more specifically the abolition of illiteracy, the gradual extension of school attendance among the population, the construction of schools, the introduction of scientific teaching, and, in general, the access of a greater proportion of the population to culture. Various changes were made in the curricula, and there was some expansion of public education and a far-reaching transformation of the system as a whole. The most important changes led to the systematic centralization of the institutions concerned. Generally speaking, the local authorities were losing, one by one, their powers in the educational sphere, all responsibility being left to the central government—that is, under the direct influence and control of the new groups in power. In most cases the middle classes defended and advocated state intervention in education, to the point of approving the establishment of a veritable state monopoly. Free, compulsory, and nondenominational education was undoubtedly one of the outstanding themes propounded by the middle-class ideologists and intellectuals, especially during the period when they themselves were rising to power.

The aim of the social security programs was to enable the mass of the population, through state action, to attain a minimum standard of living. It has been said that these programs served as a means of partially paying the debt to the workers which the middle classes had contracted during their rise to power—though in many cases most of the benefit went to the dependent sectors of the middle classes themselves. This aspect of the action of the middle-class groups in power gives the clearest illustration of their ideal of social justice, according to which the state took direct responsibility for changing the system of distribution of rewards deriving from the social structure, by creating exceptional situations in favor of certain groups, as a means of restoring equality. The social security programs were at first nothing more than sporadic and often inconsistent measures, adopted under pressure of the needs of the moment and forming a heterogeneous body of new institutions under state supervision. The control, management, and administration of these institutions were usually entrusted to the political representatives of the middle classes in power.

A general view of the social policy of the middle sectors during their rise gives the impression that whatever may have been their ostensible tendencies, their basic intention was to extend the bounds of citizenship as an essential condition of the satisfactory functioning of a centralized national state.

The new concepts relating to the patterns of community organization, which inspired the social policy of the middle sectors, tended to stress the value of a direct relationship between the subject and the political authority, and to reduce and restrict, in principal cities, the social foundations of the "intermediate authorities" who had become influential in the traditional system. The extension of suffrage and of public education, state control of trade unions, and social security administered by the state, to mention only the principal features of middle-class social trends, tended to bring the dependent or marginal sectors of the urban population into direct association with the institutions of the national state. The national state was to be the focus of loyalties, and each of its institutions was to be closely bound up with the world of labor, the family, the voluntary associations, and the various branches of leadership and decision-making. In short, the centralized state was to be symbolically and literally connected with every sector of national activity.

The results of this social policy do not seem to have come up to expectations, though they frequently illustrate the scope and the nature of the specific means by which the proposals have been translated into realities.

The introduction of universal suffrage did not lead to the mass incorporation of the marginal sectors into the body politic. Existing data indicate that while it undoubtedly produced successive extensions of the urban electorate, the participation of marginal social groups in the new sectors created was by no means proportionate to their numerical importance. The legal and social institution of universal suffrage served to regulate the civic participation of the population, and thus gave legitimacy to the political system. At the same time, to judge by available evidence, the fundamental effect of the increase in the electorate was to augment the active participation and influence of the middle sectors of the population politically. This had many consequences, the most important being the probability that the development of the institutions of the nation-state was aimed solely at the effective incorporation of the middle-class groups, inasmuch as the access of the lower levels was in practice regulated by a system of concessions.

The encouragement of the trade union movement by the governments in which representatives of the middle classes took part was only moderately successful. It certainly gave rise to very serious and well-organized unions, nearly always of a nationalist character; but the membership never included the great majority of the wage-earning sectors.

In many cases the various social security programs benefited the middle-class wage-earners first and foremost, and were of much less help to the lower classes. Owing to the enormous difficulties encountered in the enforcement of labor legislation and social security projects, the greater part of these got no further than an expression of good intentions on the part of the leading middle-class groups. For the great mass of urban workers this meant the introduction of the payment of wages in cash, the right to association in trade unions, the right to strike, and the right to a minimum of medical attention. In addition, this legislation helped considerably toward a realization that the urban masses were entitled to general respect and possessed certain rights which should be guaranteed by the state.

Despite the notable advances in education, the expansion of the system was fundamentally restricted to urban areas, and did not give the state a real monopoly of education—not even of primary schooling. This initial impetus, however, led to a considerable increase in literacy and analysis of school drop-out figures suggests that the expansion of public education chiefly affected the middle-class families, so that its benefits were not felt at all levels of society.

As for the policy of the redistribution of income introduced by the middle-class leaders, its chief result was probably to redistribute the national income for the benefit of the middle classes themselves. It is also probable that one effect of their social policy was to enlarge the groups and sectors of the community which had access to the advantages of civilization. Above the level of the lower classes, the conditions in which the community institutions functioned were more fluid; but where they existed, they seem to have made no considerable difference to the lower classes of the community.

During the periods of compromise, the social attitudes of the leading middle-class groups varied in emphasis and tendency. Far from insisting on the complete elimination of the "intermediate authorities" and of traditional society, they sometimes accepted the necessity of their survival. In other words, the equalitarian impulse seemed at this stage to find expression in more pragmatic terms. Thus, universal suffrage ceased to be a fundamental principle in the eyes of some middle-class groups, and became a kind of necessary evil: they were attentive to the abuses of trade unionism and the need to set bounds to the advances of the different associations; they advocated an educational policy of assistance to private and denominational education; the expansion of the security and social welfare services was sometimes used as a means of eliminating unrest among the underprivileged urban sectors; and the creation of privileged situations for new social sectors tended to be replaced, as a principle of political action, by the rationalization and co-ordination of the social welfare and security institutions. It may be that the actual effect of all this was to "freeze" the positions achieved during the immediately preceding period. Compared with the period of accession to political and economic power, during the stages of compromise with the established order the middle-class policies simply preserved the established positions and recognized poverty as a "fact" of the social system. The impulse toward a better distribution of power, prestige, and wealth steadily declined in importance, and the middle sectors showed more interest in securing for themselves the advantages of the desired status, in a social organization where the presence of poverty heightened the privileges of the groups in power.[19] Inasmuch as the social mechanism promoted the unequal distribution of duties and rewards, to the advantage of the new middle classes, the latter presumably identified readily with the established order.

V. Balancing the Alternative Hypotheses

In the present state of our knowledge we cannot be certain which of the foregoing accounts of the development of the Latin American middle classes is more correct. Keep in mind first that each of the hypotheses constitutes a sum of ideas, and that for analytical purposes various elements from one or another of them have to be considered.

No student of Latin American development can fail to observe that the growth of the middle sectors is apparently associated with the complex processes of urban modernization which have been taking place in the last few decades. New social institutions, the principles of political democracy, and the various industrialization programs have been associated with men and groups from those social sectors. It can readily be deduced from this that the Latin American middle classes found themselves extensively committed to the values of a fluid society, based on social norms which stipulate that merit is to be the reason for reward, above any other consideration.

Despite the dearth of information concerning social mobility in the countries of this region, it is most likely that the growth of the middle sectors usually resulted from the absorption of mobile individuals from other levels of society. These social sectors may thus have been the chief purveyors of the attitudes and trends favorable to, and closely bound up with, the phenomenon of mobility. Industrialization and urbanization also have had a fundamental effect on the middle sectors of the population, who were quicker than others to find their situation, individually and collectively, improving as a result of industrial progress and the modernization of urban organization.

On the other hand it cannot be overlooked that the middle sectors were frequently dominated by trends other than those conducive to competition and reward for individual merit. It is thus not surprising that the analysis of the results of a survey[20] of the relationship between social mobility and national identification concluded that the type of social mobility involved seemed to be more significant than mobility itself.[21] Moreover, the nature of urban modernization and the fact, more than once mentioned, that modern productive structures are not always competitive in their economic activity, make it necessary to re-examine the problem of the Latin American middle classes, their attitudes and expectations, and in general their role in the process of economic and social development. The suggested hypotheses provide criteria for assessing the conduct of individuals and groups in the middle sectors. It is probable that some of them approximate more closely than others the predominant social reality in certain Latin American countries, or that they are more characteristic of a particular economic and social pattern at one moment or stage of development. Both interpretations provide an analytical perspective for considering the relation between the behavior of the middle classes and the transformation of a society moving toward industrialism. It should not be taken for granted that this is a necessary relation; it is possible to conceive of a dynamic process of development resulting from causes other than the absence or presence of middle classes on any particular scale, though those social sectors would in any case expand as a consequence. Without going deeply into the examination of this question, the hypothesis can be made that the process of development, being a natural one, would be likely to influence the formation of certain attitudes in individuals belonging to the middle classes.

There are, however, certain limits to the above interpretations. First and foremost, they are essentially statistical, for they relate to isolated pictures of observable behavior in an isolated sector of society. This accounts for such inconsistencies as the assumption that a functional connection exists between economic and social progress and middle-class expansion, on the one hand, and the association of the stage of compromise with the predominance of a general state of stagnation, on the other. The second limitation is due to the fact that in both interpretations—though this may be unconscious—the behavior of the middle classes is analyzed as though they constituted hard-and-fast groups. In point of fact, generalizations of this kind are possible only insofar as they synthesize the forms of behavior characterizing the separate groups within these social levels—as when dealing with typical behavior patterns or general tendencies.

These limitations suggest the need for a dynamic picture to interpret the evolution of the middle sectors from beginning to end of the development process. This might well show that the absence of openly competitive social mobility is not incompatible with economic growth and social progress, and that fluid general conditions are an incidental feature, rather than a necessity, of development. A picture of this type would show which middle-class groups have been most active in the transformation of society. To put it another way, what class situations are most conducive to progressive or conservative action? Expressed in general terms, such a picture would show how the commitment of certain middle-class groups at a particular moment would lead other groups, in turn, toward the creation of an industrial system.

The formulation of the dynamic model thus proposed, which could be used to interpret the part played by the middle classes in the process of Latin American development and modernization, must depend to a large extent upon the results of empirical historical research. Only in the light of an examination of such findings—which in some respects has scarcely begun as yet—shall we be able to answer the questions relating to this aspect of the economic and social development of Latin America.

Notes

1. See, for example, J. J. Johnson, *Political Change in Latin America: The Emergence of the Middle Sectors* (Stanford: Stanford Univ. Press, 1958), and the Pan-American Union, *Materiales para el estudio de la clase media en América Latina* (6 vols., Washington: 1950–1951). The reader is also referred to Doc. E/CN. 12/CCE/176/Rev. 2, a study prepared by Marshall Wolfe, of the United Nations Bureau of Social Affairs, for the Committee for Economic Cooperation of the Central American Institute of ECLA. This last publication gives a useful inventory of the data available in 1960, establishes criteria for its evaluation, and draws a picture of the probable behavior of these social sectors.

2. "Economic Growth in Latin America," a paper presented at the first International Conference of Economic History (Stockholm, August 1960) and published by UNESCO in *Contributions* . . . (Paris: Mouton & Co., 1960).

3. E. Stanley, *The Future of Underdeveloped Countries: Political Implications of Economic Development* (New York: Harper & Brothers, 1961), pp. 223–225. The author considers that the middle classes play a really "providential" role.

4. Johnson.

5. Johnson.
6. Many middle-class intellectuals showed a tendency to embrace the concept of "working-class culture," expressed in theater, literature, periodical press, and in cultural centers and centers of action for the workers, all of which mirrored trends typical of the early stages of the trade union movement in several countries. The "people's universities," where students, professors, and intellectuals strove to act in conjunction with the urban masses, may be considered as reflecting ideologies centered on the need for a revolutionary transformation or change of the social order.
7. Johnson, p. 194.
8. See A. Leeds, "Brazilian Careers and Social Structure: A Case History and Model." (Revised version of the paper presented by this author to the Anthropological Society, Washington, on 16 October 1962.)
9. A. Pizzorno has recently advanced certain hypotheses concerning the relationship between urbanization and the process of development, pointing out that the accelerated growth of the big cities, at a time when the medium-sized and small towns and the country districts remained in a state of arrested development, is probably related to the fact that the urban middle classes were beginning to share political power with the traditional sectors. This, he suggests, had many consequences, one being that the traditional groups will occupy a place of their own in the new economy, thus lessening the reformist pressure from the middle class. See A. Pizzorno, "Suiluppo económico e urbanizzaziones," *Quaderni di Sociologia,* Vol. XI (1962), pp. 21–51.
10. See, for example, F. F. Palavicini, *Política constitucional* (Mexico City: Ed. Beatriz de Silva, 1950); G. Plaza, *Problems of Democracy in Latin America* (Chapel Hill: University of North Carolina Press, 1955); J. Posada, *La Revolución democrática* (Bogotá: Ed. Iqueima, 1955); G. Arciniegas, *Entre la libertad y el miedo* (10th edition, Buenos Aires: Ed. Sudamericana, 1958); and J. Johnson.
11. See, for example, W. S. Stokes, *Latin American Politics* (New York: Thomas Y. Crowell Co., 1959), pp. 156–157.
12. Ibid., p. 156. The reader is also referred to L. Correa Prieto, *Aspectos negativos de la intervención económica* (Santiago de Chile: Ed. Zig-Zag, 1955); F. Ayala, *El problema del liberalismo* (Mexico City, D.F.: Fondo de Cultura Económica, 1941); J. Silva Herzog, *El pensamiento económico en México* (Mexico D.F.: Fondo de Cultura Económica, 1947).
13. See, for example: A. Manero, "El fomento industrial en México," in *Memoria del Segundo Congreso Mexicano de Ciencias Sociales* (Mexico City, D.F.: Artes Gráficas del Estado, 1946), pp. 171–293; A. Pinto, *Hacia nuestra independencia económica* (Santiago de Chile: Editorial del Pacífico, 1953), p. 52; S. Oria, *El estado argentino y la nueva economía política* (Buenos Aires: Ed. Raigal, 1954); G. R. Velasco, *El mayor peligro, el Estado* (Mexico City, D.F.: Associación de Banqueros

de México, 1950); R. Laherre, *Reflexiones sobre la economía chilena* (Santiago de Chile: Ed. Zig-Zag, 1953).

14. See, for example, C. M. Londono, *Economía social colombiana* (Bogotá: Imprenta Nacional, 1953); A. Silva Basonnan, *Una experiencia social cristiana* (Santiago de Chile: Editorial del Pacífico, 1949); V. A. Belaunde, *La crisis presente, 1914–1939* (Lima: Ed. Mercurio Peruano); A. Amoroso Lima, *O problem do Trabalho, Ensaio de Filosofía Econômica* (Obras completas, tomo 20; Rio de Janeiro: AGIR, 1947); S. Dana Montano, *Justicia social y reforma constitucional* (Santa Fe, Argentina: Instituto de Investigaciones Jurídico-Políticas de la Universidad del Litoral, 1948); A. Ponte, *Como salvar a Venezuela* (New York: 1937), pp. 320–334. There is an extensive bibliography on Mexican synarchy.

15. See Johnson, pp. 181–183.
16. Ibid., pp. 183, 190 and 192–194.
17. Ibid., pp. ix, 3–4 and 195.
18. Ibid., p. 181.
19. On this view, see A. Leeds, pp. 22 and 38.
20. K. H. Silvert and F. Bonilla, *Education and the Social Meaning of Development* (New York: American Universities Field Staff, 1960).
21. K. H. Silvert (ed.), *Expectant Peoples: Nationalism and Development* (New York: Random House, 1963), p. 11.

3
The Industrial Elite

FERNANDO H. CARDOSO

I

The problem of the industrial elite in Latin America is presented in specialized literature as an aspect of development. In a few works that have been published on this topic, all the basic hypotheses stress that in order to have development the thinking of entrepreneurs must be brought up to date. There is also an attempt to describe the entrepreneur's role in the light of the forms of behavior manifested in industry as a whole, as a closed social system.

These studies have an implicit reference to what might be called a "general theory of the industrial elite." This is simply the theory derived from an analysis of how entrepreneur groups are formed in Europe and the United States, where "original development" occurred.

Industrialization in Latin America needs both a change of the individual entrepreneur's behavior in the individual industry as well as more dynamic action in the national economic system. But to put the problem in this way tends to produce a mere analogy of form, or else an expression in tautological terms. In the former case, the interpretations fail to account for the structural and historical differences that entrepreneurial activity has taken in Latin America; nor do they explain the limitations of that sector as a pressure group and a political force.

The first aim of the present study will be to set forth briefly the fundamental differences of historical structure which determine the possibilities of action and the mode of existence of the Latin American industrial elite, as compared with those of Europe and the United States. The distinction thus drawn will be illustrated by behavior of Latin American entrepreneurs. I shall then indicate what conditions appear to govern the different froms of action which have taken place in Latin American countries where sample surveys have been conducted among leading industrial figures.[1] In conclusion I shall discuss certain results of research conducted in Latin America and attempt a few hypotheses to explain the different patterns of behavior and social mobility in Latin America as opposed to Europe and the United States.

II

In the nineteenth century, industrial firms were managed and controlled by private individuals. It is true that the state played a comparatively important role during the initial period, when capital was being assembled and the world market organized; but the fact remains that the private firm was the characteristic unit of the economy. In this sense, the traditional middle class not only became the "conquering bourgeoisie" in the sphere of foreign affairs, but also provided the impetus for domestic development. Furthermore, the national states which came into being under capitalism were not confronted with the problem of the existence of states capable of opposing them, so that private industry was not hampered by strong pressure from outside.

The historical, social, and economic conditions which determine the possibilities of action of private industry in the present-day underdeveloped countries are very different. Economically, the basic features of production and marketing appear to be laid down *a priori* by the already developed economies (technology, trading methods, type of enterprise, etc.). Socially, the entrepreneurs find themselves confronted by other component groups of the industrial community who bring pressure to bear to restrict industry's freedom of action, whether directly or through the state. Politically, the expansion of the market and the adoption of a policy of industrial development have ceased being the nation's main goal. Instead the central government is concerned with ending the domination of the large landowners and in securing international agreements to advance the industrialization of the country—something which usually encounters the opposition of the big international combines and of the nations which dominate the world stage.

Within this framework, the problem of the entrepreneur as "demiurge" becomes meaningless if considered in isolation. For economic creativity no longer finds expression in terms of the "enterprise"—as in the economic system based on private enterprise—but moves to a larger scale, becoming a matter of formulating and implementing a "development policy."

The typical entrepreneur in underdeveloped countries is no longer merely an industrialist striving to introduce new manufacturing or marketing methods so as to increase profits (a process which has its limits, owing to the state of technological subordination in which the entrepreneurs in the underdeveloped countries are placed), but a man with the ability to steer his activity in such a way that he can benefit from the social and economic changes. Therefore, industrial activity is taking on political implications.

Hence any study of the entrepreneur system, while it must take into consideration the typical "characteristics" of the entrepreneurs themselves and the social conditions governing the emergence of the industrial middle class, must not ignore the practical circumstances of the entire community in each of the countries where an entrepreneur group exists.

The theory usually advanced to account for the emergence of entrepreneurs in the countries now industrializing, assumes the slow but steady development of the traditional system of craftsmen and artisans, which played a decisive part in countries whose foreign market conditions were propitious. The slow speed of the process of change is declared to be the fundamental variable which accounts for the *backward* responses of the entrepreneurs as a group when confronted with the exigencies of the situation: their assimilation of new patterns of behavior is not immediately apparent, and even if it were, it would not be vigorous enough to modify their attitude toward society as a whole.

This theory, however, does not pay sufficient attention to situations in which the entrepreneurs' behavior is more advanced than that of the workers or of the productive system, e.g. Colombia. It is also unable to take account of the possible coexistence of different types of entrepreneurs *from the beginning* of the process of industralization. In Argentina from the late nineteenth century, for instance, the type of employer who was a convinced supporter of rational, but not progressive, business values seems to have existed in the food-processing sectors, while industrial growth was fostered by dissatisfied and dynamic groups belonging to the agricultural and ranching sectors.

Our first task, therefore, will be to examine the basic features from which to derive a classification of the two fundamental types of business action. The essential thing is to arrive at an understanding of the problems of development as produced by the structural adjustments of relations among the workers, the entrepreneurs, and the state; thus, our main criterion for distinguishing between the different types of entrepreneur must be the contrast between the collective (or public) interest and private interests. The collective view will be the necessary condition for *development,* while the individual enterprise will be the unit yielding prosperity as such, given the conditions required for industrialization and moderization; these conditions include leadership among workers (with a maximum of vertical mobility and assimilation, which we shall symbolize as $M+$; $A+$), as well as initiative among the entrepreneurs for both prosperity and national planning. This is the ideal situation in which the state committed to development derives legal authority and maximum consensus from the social forces which support it.

We can formulate a typology of entrepreneurs based upon their differential orientation to the society as a whole and their individual enterprise (S = society; E = the enterprise). (1) $S-$, $E-$: This is the extreme case of the speculating entrepreneur, whose prosperity is based on bold strokes, the manipulation of stocks, opposition to the tendency for wages to rise (recourse to casual labor), etc.; (2) $S-$, $E+$: Here we have the "puritan" entrepreneur whose inclination may lead him to introduce more rational methods within the individual enterprise; this category includes the "captain of industry," who usually began as an old style master-craftsman; (3) $S+$, $E-$: This is the progressive but speculating entrepreneur; he manipulates the system of taxation and the machinery of trade at state level and accumulates capital by more or less fraudulent maneuvers, but has no interest in planning technical improvements in industry, or in manipulating wages in the factory; his chief efforts are directed toward winning a place for himself in a kind of independent system of economic development which will work to his own advantage; (4) $S+$, $E+$: This is the modern entrepreneur, interested in planning at the level of the community and in rationalization and the introduction of bureaucratic methods at the level of the enterprise.

By regrouping the above types, we see that the entrepreneurs may follow either of two tendencies in their form of action at the level of the community or of the enterprise. At the community level: (a) "economists": puritan entrepreneurs ($S-$, $E+$) and modern entrepreneurs (S +, E +); (b) "the politician": progressive but speculating entrepreneurs (S +, E —). At the level of the enterprise: (a) the "founders of enterprises": the puritan entrepreneurs (S —, E +) and speculators (S —, E —); (b) the "organizers of enterprises": the progressive speculators (S +, E —) and the modern entrepreneurs (S + E +).

This second grouping, at the level of the enterprise, suggests an observation which is important to the study of the industrialization process. It will be noted that both groups fit into the historic sequence in which the "founders of enterprises" precede the "organizers of enterprises." However, as I pointed out at the beginning, we must be on our guard against unilateral interpretations, based on the course of development in the "central" countries. The likelihood of this sequence is mitigated by at least two factors:

(a) the presence of foreign capital, which may be employed from the very outset among the general group of "organizers of enterprises,"

(b) the creation of industrial complexes based on initial technical requirement of extreme rationality and bureaucratic structure. The indivisibility of investment in the capital goods sectors is quite a distinct problem from that of industrial development in the "central" countries and it calls for special attention, because even where ample protection vis-à-vis foreign capital has been provided, the type of business activity thus introduced may create serious difficulties, which only the state can solve.

In accordance with our initial hypotheses, a particular *phase* in the practical development of a country cannot be inferred simply from the types of entrepreneurs then in action, but from the interaction of the different sectors in the industrial system. It seems advisable also to try to draw up a "panel" by which to detect which categories have been dominant at different times. To give a further illustration of this procedure, it may be maintained that in Argentina, before the time of Perón, business activity was carried on mostly by "creators of enterprises," with a relative preponderance of the "puritan entrepreneur"— chiefly because the absence of standards for industry at the level of the community tended to encourage an "economic" withdrawal into the enterprise rather than the expression of its interests in terms of "political action."

The war and state support rapidly changed this picture by facilitating the second stage, a notable increase in the "speculator-entrepreneur" (as evidenced in the spectacular development of the textile industry, for example), coinciding with the lack of commitment to economic development which has already been mentioned with reference to the state. The third stage, shaped by the crisis with which the 1950's opened, further demonstrated this maladjustment between the official efforts to promote development and the prevalent type of industrial action, which operated to the principal advantage of the "progressive speculator."

III

In the method I propose to follow, the analysis of these different types of entrepreneurs is not in itself significant. In other words, the predominance of one particular type of entrepreneur, such as the "speculator," in a particular country does not decisively affect that country's prospects of development and modernization, since the other social forces and the particular historical circumstances also have to be taken into account. These other factors have to be considered, firstly because the transfer from one type of entrepreneur to another may well result from economic and social changes which are often brought about by the actions of entrepreneurs of the "traditional" type who find themselves obliged to change their attitude or to break new economic ground,[2] and secondly because in Latin America the market situation and the process of development are not solely or directly governed by business conduct. We shall not deal with the first point in the present study, but it is obvious that it must produce certain effects upon the process of industrialization and modernization of the community; in other words, the action of what might be called traditional entrepreneurs, in the light of the general theory of industrial activity, may produce changes favorable to development.

The second point deserves fuller consideration, owing to its bearing upon the theory of industrial activity in the underdeveloped countries. The basic criterion for defining such activity is that of the entrepreneurs' attitude toward the market and toward the state. Any consideration of the circumstances in which markets and nations came into existence in Latin America makes it evident that the countries were brought into the world market in one of three basic ways:

(a) Through the introduction of foreign economic elements, as illustrated by the Central American plantation, the mines of Bolivia and Chile, or the oil wells of Venezuela.

(b) Through an economic system based on the exploitation of resources by local producers, as in the coffee plantations of Brazil and Colombia and the stock-breeding economies of the South.

(c) Through the enforced substitution of imported goods: this resulted in an expansion of the domestic market initially created by economic development following the second type of integration into the foreign market.

In the first two of these types of development there is a very clear connection between a dominant local class ("political" in the first case, "landowning" in the second) and the representatives of the central economies. These political classes, or oligarchies, seem to have been both a means and a condition of emergence as a nation. The connection between the market (which was *foreign,* and which had existed, as we have seen, from the very earliest days of Latin American history) and the local interests was mediated through the state, which was itself controlled either by the non-productive local oligarchy or by the landowning producers, to the exclusion of the other classes and social groups. Reference to the nation (the whole body of society) was in the nature of a recourse to outside pressure, for the purpose of bargaining with foreign groups in the case of situation (a), or to provide the agricultural classes, in the case of situation (b), with the political instruments they required, in an international trial of strength, to bargain over quotas and export prices.

Therefore, only the third case of the integration of the Latin American countries in the world market (situation c) appears to provide conditions in which the industrial entrepreneurs and merchants could emerge as the protagonists of national development. According to the previously mentioned theory, prevalent in Latin America, which draws an analogy between the course of development in Europe and the United States and that in the developing countries, the groups of entrepreneurs, as representatives of the urban and industrial economic classes, should have lent impetus to industrialization and national development and turned into the avant-garde groups in Latin America. This interpretation assumes a dual analogy with the original circumstances of development—it assumes the modernization originated among "puritan entrepreneurs" (in the style of Weber) and that the autonomy of the entrepreneur class conformed to the political behavior patterns of the European-bourgeoisie during their rise to power. The significance of the first assumption is diminished by the importance of the other types of entrepreneurs in Latin America, who were in no way characterized by economic asceticism. As for the second assumption, it has not been confirmed by research.[3]

On the contrary, the first two types of Latin American integration in the world market, though led by the traditional and landowning classes and by the state which had been created to serve those very classes, demonstrated the possibilities available to the urban industrial elite which was bound up with industrial development. The plan of development [4] observable in the most industralized countries of the region was decisively marked by the following successive circumstances and social pressures.

(a) Intensive urbanization, preceding industrialization, as a consequence of the favorable economic results produced during the period of development.

(b) Formation, as the result of (a), of lower-class groups who pressed for access to the market and a place in political life, through the actions of popular movements (led by Vargas, Perón, Gaetano, etc.).

(c) Formation of urban middle-class groups (civil servants, professional men, military men, civil engineers, etc.) who gained some control of the political machinery, because of the imbalance created in the traditional power structure by the *presence* of the masses, even where they were not active, during export crises. The middle classes obtained this partial control of the machinery of government whether through movements of their own (radicalism in Argentina and Chile, *Battlismo* in Uruguay, etc.) or through "anti-oligarchic" movements which, however, had the support of certain sectors of the oligarchy (*Tenentismo* in Brazil). The first type of movement appears to have been linked to a new middle class, of immigrant origin, while the second was allied to pressure groups in the traditional middle classes.

(d) Within this politico-social framework, where the export oligarchies were beginning to lose their absolute dominance, the groups created by industrialization (to meet the expansion of the domestic market which had resulted from the success of textile and foodstuff exports) *began to have marginal participation in the national political system*. In fact, when the entrepreneur groups came to the fore here was already an active state organization and an established market, and the other social forces—the urban masses and middle-class groups, the oligarchies and exporters—were competing for control of the state machinery, and thus for the possibility of influencing decisions relating to investment and consumption.

(e) The "technological" sectors of the middle classes (economists, army men, engineers, etc.) appear to have been concerned about the "unbalance of power" resulting from pressure by the masses and the danger implicit in it. Once they were to some extent participating politically in the state machinery, they began to favor an industrial policy based on public investment and aimed at achieving national independence and at creating a sufficient demand for labor to offset the disruptive effects latent in mass pressure.

(f) Not until somewhat later did the entrepreneur groups take over responsibility for industrial development. Even then, they did so under the protection of the state, and therefore, with the benefit of the expansion resulting from government investment (in energy, oil, iron, and steel), which opened up new sources of profit for private investment as a substitute for imports.

This picture, applicable to the principal industrialized countries in the region (Brazil, Chile, Mexico, and with less consistency, Argentina), indicates the content and values of entrepreneur action in Latin America. In this instance, the existence of markets did not involve such values as free competition, productivity, etc., because the market was "protected" by state measures which benefited the industrialists. Similarly, our reference to society does not imply, in the conditions prevailing in Latin America, that a deliberate scheme existed for controlling the politico-social situation; much less does it imply commitment to the construction of a democratic community for the masses, on the terms usually attributed to industrial societies. In point of fact the entrepreneur groups were emerging from a comparatively marginal politico-social situation at a time when other social forces, including the traditional exporting class, the middle groups, and the masses themselves, occupied key positions already in the political game. Moreover, these entrepreneur groups found their options restricted by the ambiguity of the situation: either they joined forces with the masses to bring pressure on the state in opposition to the exporting groups, or else their chances of political and social authority might be disturbed by mass action. In some circumstances they supported the state in its development efforts; in others, they competed with the state in the attempt to wrest certain fields of investment from it, or joined with foreign capitalists because of the technological dependence characteristic of underdeveloped countries. On occasion they sponsored measures for the extension of political rights; on other occasions they allied themselves to the oligarchy and its narrow interests because, as a propertied class, they were afraid the control of the community might pass to the masses. It is essential to analyze the responses of entrepreneurs in the dependent economic systems in terms of the problems which arose, limiting their options especially because of the existence of *underdeveloped* masses of population in the countries concerned. We shall examine later the problems in this. All that can be done for the moment is to point to their existence, in the absence of any consistent empirical analysis.[5]

Three basic problems appear to be involved: In what economic and social conditions, and under the thrust of what social movements, did the modernizing entrepreneur groups emerge and take action? What tendencies and characteristics of economic action put new dynamism into the Latin American businesses? What type of structure framed the basic choices these groups adopted with regard to social change, and to what extent did their desire to gain power dispose them to accept popular pressure on the one hand, or to placate the traditional governing classes on the other hand?

To answer these questions would require an elaborate historical and social analysis of industrialization in Latin America. On the basis of existing work, one can say that once launched, industrial growth followed a twofold pattern in almost all the countries of that region. First there was a slow growth of the handicrafts and manufacturing system, usually reinforced by the expansion of the domestic market (related, of course, to the increased exports of raw materials and the growth of towns, the latter accelerated by immigration resulting from the expansion of the export trade). Secondly, there was the rapid and increasingly dynamic process which set in whenever market conditions were favorable (war, devaluation for the protection of exports, etc.). Sustaining these stimuli depends to a great extent upon the ability of the leading groups to frame an adequate policy of investment in the basic sectors, to accept the views of the technical sectors which lay down investment policy. From the sociological standpoint the chief problem is to discover how well the social forces have taken advantage of the influences favorable to the automatic growth of the market (either in the slow, traditional manner, or with the speed produced by exceptional circumstances) to transform that process into a development policy, and the conditions in which this occurred. Did the industrial entrepreneurs create and exploit the opportunities offered by a development policy? Did it prove possible to harmonize the interests of the various dominant groups, and how great are the divergencies between the different classes participating in the development process? What form was taken by and what solution found for, the divergencies between the groups concerned in the export sector and those concerned with production for domestic market? What opposition was there between foreign economic interests and the national groups, and how was it overcome?

Here again, the answer must depend on a concrete analysis of typical social situations: the initial impulse was sometimes provided by general, widespread, and violent pressure exercised by the urban populace against the established forms of domination (Mexico). There was sometimes an alliance between the popular movements, the traditional interests, and the entrepreneur groups (Brazil under Vargas). Elsewhere, conditions approximated a phase of vigorous entrepreneur action at the economic level, including action by the exporter groups, together with comparative isolation and political antagonism of those groups in the face of mass pressure (as in Argentina under Perón). There were situations where the entrepreneurs' pressure in favor of development met with indifference from the other social groups (as in Colombia). What were the effects of these different circumstances upon opportunities for development? In what conditions did the entrepreneur classes manage to steer toward development the impulses for social transformation of other groups or classes whose objectives were different?

It is true that an analysis of these questions naturally involves summing up, referring to, the structural, economic, and social characteristics mentioned. However, we still need to restate, in terms of the Latin American situation, the classical problem of entrepreneur mentality and action. How did modernizing groups come into existence, always at the level of the enterprise? What types of entrepreneurs, recruited from what social groups, guided by what values, and stimulated by what social and economic pressures, had an important influence on development?

A study of this last group of problems should undoubtedly concentrate chiefly on patterns of investment and the mechanism of action by the entrepreneur sector. In the type of industrial growth which exists in Latin America, the composition and functioning of the economic classes are largely determined by use of the managerial capacities of immigrants who are active in smaller industries, or by manipulation of favorable market conditions by entrepreneurs whose original activity was linked to the agricultural-export sector—both groups representing small firms of the "family" type. Among these, the need to obtain quick financial results restricts the possibility of large investment in basic enterprises, and impedes the creation of modern economic organizations. The latter can dispense with quick profits owing to their rational methods; and their efficiency is measured by their ability to guarantee long-term advantages based on increasing differentiation of production, technical expertise, and the economies resulting from mass production. How is it possible to advance, at the level of the individual firm, from the old pattern of managerial activity to a new and more dynamic one? What role does the "foreign firm" play in this process? By what values are the former heads of enterprises impelled as they turn into captains of industry or modern industrial managers? To what extent has this process resulted from internal developments in the employer classes as they modernized themselves, and to what extent was it accelerated by pressure from outside the entrepreneur sector? What restrictions does the state of "dependency" place upon the process of industrial modernization?

Starting with the assumption that development is an inclusive process which derives its impetus from sources outside industrial economy and depends on the formulation of a policy for society as a whole, we will discuss the general problem of the tendencies displayed by the entrepreneur groups in their dealings with the state and with the community. Here we should concentrate our attention on the possibilities and obstacles confronting the entrepreneur class in Latin America for taking action outside the business sector in order to promote the necessary "conditions of development" and to transform itself into a dominant middle class (bourgeoisie), and the obstacle to such action. From this angle there are two problems which take precedence: the extent to which the entrepreneurs come to terms with policies deriving from the "traditional situation" (with the corollaries of abstention from political activity, restriction of state action, opposition to trade

union interference in public life, the search for foreign capital, etc.);
and the extent to which the entrepreneur groups show themselves able
to formulate a "social scheme," recognizing the right of other progressive groups to share in framing development policy. That is to say, to
what extent are the entrepreneur groups willing to let rivalry for the
future of investment be carried from the business to the national level?
And to what other groups are the entrepreneurs prepared, for structural reasons, to allow a share in defining national policy? In what
conditions can a "nationalist policy" have meaning? What are the
prospects that popular pressure for development will coincide with an
investment policy controlled by the entrepreneur groups, and within
what limits can this happen? The general theory underlying these
questions is that the traditional dominant classes can be permeated by
the effect of social change. It would be an oversimplification to suppose
that the entrepreneur groups represent "modernity" and that their
alliance with the lower-class pressure groups is therefore natural, and
sufficient in itself to alter the traditional balance. On the contrary, the
history of Latin America demonstrates the flexibility of "traditional
society." Consequently, the theme of the "traditional classes" has to be
considered in any analysis of development which does not start from
the preconception that the progressive industrial groups can alone, or
in alliance with popular pressure, break up the traditional framework
of society and redirect development in such a way as to secure a better
distribution of income, greater economic dynamism, and a fuller participation of the masses in the national political and economic decisions.

IV

These questions cannot yet be answered on an empirical basis. However, the results of certain comparative studies undertaken for research
in Latin America, the United States, and elsewhere, will serve to show
in what way it will later be possible, in my opinion, to make use of the
theory propounded above.

In any case, the information given in Table 1, concerning the percentage distribution of fathers' occupations, shows that the typical features displayed by the entrepreneurs, and the social conditions in
which the Latin American bourgeoisie came into existence, do not bear
out the general theory that, as in North America, this sector was recruited from among the urban draftsmen or industrial workers.[6] The

difference between the two regions may be explained by the fact that in
North America industrialization took place comparatively long ago.
But the difference persists even when we compare the Latin American
data with the results observed during the initial stages of industrialization in the United States.[7]

TABLE I

Percentage Distribution by Fathers' Occupation *

	CHILE [a]	COLOMBIA [b]	ARGENTINA [c]	NORTH AMERICA [d]
Industrials	38	45	24	69
Tradesmen	17	20	36	—
Employees	12	7	20	3
Professional men	28	15	12 [e]	11
Farmers	5	0	4	5
Peasants	—	—	0	4
Workers	0	10	4	9
	100	100	100	100
	n = 46	n = 61	n = 27	n = 106

Sources:

a) Guillermo Briones, *El Empresario Industrial en América Latina,* ECLA, 1963.
b) Aarón Lipman, *El Empresario Industrial en América Latina,* ECLA, 1963.
c) Eduardo A. Zalduendo, *El Empresario Industrial en América Latina,* ECLA, 1962.
d) S. M. Lipset, and R. Bendix, *Movilidad Social en la Sociedad Industrial,* 1963. Table 4.2, years 1891–1920.
e) In this case, military officers.

* This and the following tables are based on data obtained from various surveys. This table can give only a general impression, owing to divergencies between the categories selected, the characteristic of the samples, and the dates of the surveys.

The differences between these two situations, and the variations
which occur from one Latin American country to another in respect of
the social groups from which the entrepreneurs originate, can be explained only by reference to the historical framework and the different
ways in which the national economies were integrated into the world
market. For example, the concentration in Argentina (Table 1) of
entrepreneurs whose fathers came from the trading sector, points
clearly to an explanation on these lines. Similarly, the high proportion
of entrepreneurs in that country whose fathers were soldiers, is some-

thing that would seem unaccountable except in terms of the interplay of power as it has existed in Argentina.[8]

The hypothesis that relatively little real change was effected through industrialization, appears to be substantiated by the available data for educational levels. Thus, comparing the educational level of industrialists in Latin America with those in France, England, Spain, and the United States, we find, as shown in Table 2, that, above the

TABLE 2
Education Standard of Entrepreneurs

	ARGENTINA [d]	CHILE [e]	COLOMBIA [f]	U.S.A [a]	FRANCE [a]	SPAIN [a]	ENGLAND [a][c]	SPAIN [a][b]
Higher	11	0	2	15	1.5	20	4	1
Primary	25	40	48	28	15.1	42	16	19
Secondary	63	60	50	57	83.4	31	80	78
	100	100	100	100	100.0	100	100	100
	n = 27	n = 46	n = 61	n = 136			n = 248	

Sources:
a) A. Miguel and Juan Linz, Nivel de Estudios del Empresariado Español, *Revista Arbor*, No. 219, May 1964.
b) Entrepreneurs employing over 1000 workers.
c) Entrepreneurs under 50 years of age.
d) Eduardo A. Zalduendo, *El Empresario Industrial en América Latina*, ECLA, 1962.
e) Guillermo Briones, *El Empresario Industrial en América Latina*, ECLA, 1963.
f) Aarón Lipman, *El Empresario Industrial en América Latina*, ECLA, 1963.

primary level, Latin America entrepreneurs seem to have a high level of school attendance, comparable to the United States and Spain. However, when the variable scale of industry is taken into consideration, Spain, like the other European countries, also shows a different pattern from the United States. It would thus seem that Latin America tends to perpetuate standards equivalent to those which prevailed during the industrialization of the old European countries, where there was an aristocratic type of society. True, differences exist between the Latin American countries themselves; Argentina, for instance, comes close to the North American pattern.[9] *In all cases,* however, it remains clear that the type of educational pattern appears to shape the emergent industrial system; for in Latin America intermediate and higher education give greater prominence to classical teaching and to the liberal professions than to courses which are strictly technical or related to industry, and the same applies to the preferences of the entrepreneurs, as shown by the information obtained in the interviews conducted during this research.[10]

This seems to fit the hypothesis that on the one hand there is a "traditional class" which controls industry as a form of adaption to modern methods (most evident in Chile and Colombia), while on the other hand values of the traditional type are still observable in the trends displayed by the new industrial groups, who begin to adopt patterns from the pre-industrial community in their effort to assimilate themselves to the long-established dominant groups.

Even when we consider the directors of enterprises by themselves, we still find the tendency to maintain these same criteria during the process of individual integration in the industrial structure; the straightforward condition of "ownership" as a means of securing a director's position, occurs in 40 per cent of the cases considered during the surveys in Chile and Colombia (see Table 3). These results are

TABLE 3

Methods of Access to the Position of Manager

	CHILE [a]	COLOMBIA [b]
Promotion within the firm	23	20
Proprietor	37	40
Appointment by the shareholders' committee	18	30
Agent or representative of the family	8	2
Recruited by the firm for the post	15	10
Other methods	0	5
	100	100
	n = 46	n = 61

Sources:
a) Guillermo Briones, *El Empresario Industrial en América Latina*, ECLA, 1963.
b) Aarón Lipman, *El Empresario Industrial en América Latina*, ECLA, 1963.

confirmed by the interviews we have carried out in the Latin American countries under consideration: the effective control of the enterprises is still exercised on a family basis and through the selection of persons who enjoy the "confidence" of the shareholders in the light of non-professional criteria and relationships.

There are similarities in the entrepreneurs' responses to questions
about their motivation: in countries where industrialization has been
restricted within the limits of the "traditional society" they reply in
terms of dominant values asserting that industry offers possibilities, for
"helping people" and obtaining "social prestige," while in Argentina
priority goes to values such as "individualism" and "financial security,"
as shown in Table 4. This type of question also serves to illustrate the

TABLE 4

Incentives of Entrepreneurs *

	COLOMBIA [a]	ARGENTINA [b]	CHILE [c]
Opportunities for helping people	40	23	33
Financial security	27	46	33
Social prestige	2	0	15
Opportunity for risk-taking	0	6	2
Opportunity for being in authority	7	0	6
Personal independence	24	23	11
No reply	0	4	0
	100	100	100
	n = 61	n = 27	n = 46

* The first choice was taken for the following question:
Which of the following factors interest you primarily in your work as entrepreneur?

Sources:
a) Aarón Lipman, *El Empresario Industrial en América Latina*, ECLA, 1963.
b) Eduardo A. Zalduendo, *El Empresario Industrial en América Latina*, ECLA,
   1962.
c) Guillermo Briones, *El Empresario Industrial en América Latina*, ECLA, 1963.

danger that arises when questions are put without a theoretical frame
of reference; a tautological generalization finally appears—that the
universal values and patterns of industrialism are present in a higher
degree in the more industrialized countries.

However, bearing in mind the specific differences between the markets and communities from which the entrepreneurs derive their orientation and values, information on such individual points as personal
characteristics may acquire meaning. For instance, the Latin American
entrepreneurs attach slight importance to the "spirit of risk" (see
Table 5), and although at first glance this seems a flagrant exception

to the general theory of industrialists' behavior, or a sign of traditional-ism, it is in fact merely a realistic assessment of the practical conditions of industrialization in Latin America, which have already been de-scribed. The protection of the market in the first instance, and in the second instance the association with foreign monopolies, restrict the practical scope of economic risk-taking for Latin American entrepre-neurs.

TABLE 5

Personal Characteristics of the Entrepreneur *

	ARGENTINA [b]	COLOMBIA [a c]	CHILE [d]
Persistence	10	—	18
Working capacity	10	20	9
Capacity for taking risks	3	—	3
Initiative	27	42	37
Practical ability	18	—	11
Capacity for taking decisions	15	28	6
Capacity for making plans	15	—	11
No reply	—	—	—
	100	100	100
	n = 27	n = 61	n = 46

* The question was: What, in your opinion, are the principal attributes or personal characteristics an entrepreneur should possess? (The first choice was taken.)
a) Adapted from another source. The results were not tabulated.
b) Eduardo A. Zalduendo, *El Empresario Industrial en América Latina*, ECLA, 1962.
c) Aarón Lipman, *El Empresario Industrial en América Latina*, ECLA, 1963.
d) Guillermo Briones, *El Empresario Industrial en América Latina*, ECLA, 1963.

Finally, the surveys carried out to determine the actual characteristics of the entrepreneur seem to be restricted by a certain sterility of pur-pose, as mentioned earlier in this study.[11] Indeed, the analysis given in Table 6 indicates a wide divergence of views among the entrepreneurs themselves as to the definition of their role. This disagreement reaches its highest point in Argentina, and seems to diminish in the other countries considered, following the declining curve of industrializa-tion. The diversity of roles thus appears to be so great that analyses confined to modes are bound to be inconsistent; once again the avail-able data indicate the necessity of a historico-structural viewpoint in any interpretation of the Latin American entrepreneur's behavior.[12]

In the foregoing study I have offered a tentative description of the structural factors which constrain the action of the entrepreneurial section of Latin American society. In so doing I have been led to speak of the degree of control and participation attained by the entrepreneurs, in the markets and in the community, in economic systems which are striving to establish themselves on a national basis despite the existence of a world market which opposes the formation of national decision-making centers of investment and consumption. We must take these historical and structural peculiarities into consideration if we claim anything more than a merely descriptive significance for the differen-

TABLE 6

Self-definition of the Entrepreneur *

	ARGENTINA	COLOMBIA	CHILE	PARAGUAY
Innovator	20	7	14	9
Executive	33	33	40	18
Organizer	20	35	22	18
Imitator	0	2	4	55
Financial specialist	15	5	4	0
Co-ordinator	12	10	2	0
Traditionalist	0	2	8	0
No reply	0	4	0	0
Other definitions	0	2	3	0
	100	100	100	100
	n = 27	n = 61	n = 46	n = 16

* The question was: To which of the following types would you say you belong?
Source: E. Faletto, El Empresario Industrial en América Latina, Paraguay, 1964.

tiation made in this study between speculator-entrepreneurs, puritan entrepreneurs, progressive entrepreneurs, and the modern directors of enterprises.

I shall attempt to use the few and uncertain empirical results in order to illustrate the limitations of the methods followed by certain types of analysis, and at the same time, to demonstrate the need for further research, within a more complex frame of reference. Explanations which are valid in accounting for the behavior of social groups in the highly industrialized countries with central economic systems, cannot be merely transferred to provide an adequate interpretation of the formation of industrial communities in the peripheral countries. The permeability of the traditional dominant classes and the special circumstances in which the industrialization is taking place in Latin America, make it difficult, if not impossible, for industrialists and businessmen to play the same dynamic role that they have sometimes taken up elsewhere in the development of capitalism and the formation of an industrial society. At the same time, it would seem that the explanation of the mentality, values, ideology, and course of action of the Latin American entrepreneurs, both as directors of firms and when organized into a social class, requires analyses in terms of two sources of variation: the practical factors—ambiguous and sometimes contradictory—which determine the market conditions; and secondly the pressures and demands of society. Further research should proceed along both lines of inquiry.

Notes

1. This study was originally sponsored by the Centro de Sociologia Industrial y del Trabajo of the University of São Paulo, for the study of industrial managers in Brazil. Subsequently, thanks to financial assistance from the Latin American Social Science Research Center, at Rio, it was expanded to include interviews with industrial managers at Buenos Aires, Santiago, and Mexico City. The investigation of the subject is now being continued under the auspices of the Latin American Institute of Economic and Social Planning, not as a survey, but through the analysis of systematically chosen samples of entrepreneur groups.
2. See F. H. Cardoso, "Tradition et innovation: la mentalité des entrepreneurs de São Paulo," *Sociologie du Travail,* 5 (July–September, 1963), pp. 209–224.
3. See F. H. Cardoso, *Empresário Industrial e desenvolvimento económico no Brasil* (São Paulo: Difusão Européia do Livro, 1964).
4. This is not the place to refer to the economic explanations of Latin American development, which are well known, chiefly from the writings of Raul Prebisch and Celso Furtado. It is obvious that the initial factors in industrial development are related to the depression of the 1930's and to the world war. The disruption of the world trading system, later aggravated by the scarcity of hard currency, facilitated and stimulated the market (independently of any economic policy) and were favorable to industrialization.

5. The questions mentioned here are taken from a study program on the subject which the author submitted to the Latin American Institute of Economic and Social Planning.

6. I should like to take this opportunity to thank Carlos Filgueira for his help in preparing the tables and discussing the data.

7. See S. M. Lipset and R. Bendix, *Movilidad Social en la Sociedad Industrial* (Buenos Aires: Eudeba, 1963), Table 4,2, p. 141. It should be remembered that this table refers to entrepreneurs in general and not specifically to industrial entrepreneurs, which strengthens our argument.

8. On this point, see José Luis de Imaz, *Los que mandan* (Buenos Aires: Eudeba, 1964), esp. pp. 126–163. This is one of the few books on the formation of an elite in Latin America, and it provides valuable and original data and interpretations.

9. Similarly, the distribution in São Paulo is as follows: primary school 13 per cent, secondary school 43 per cent, higher education 44 per cent; see Cardoso, *Empresário Industrial,* p. 100.

10. Whereas in Argentina the surveys were not confined to large enterprises, in São Paulo they were, and these data add to the appropriateness of the explanation given here—though it must still be remembered that the unreliability of the available data makes caution necessary.

11. Nevertheless, the tendency in Argentina conforms more closely to the pattern of the highly industrialized communities, and changes in this direction are beginning to occur in Brazil as well. But the "modernization" of educational patterns is more apparent than real: classical studies are being replaced by a type of polytechnic and many-faceted science teaching which is not specialized and has no really analytical spirit, approximating in style to the traditional "polytechnics" or schools of economics.

12. See also Alexander Gerschenkron, "Social attitudes, entrepreneurship and economic development," in his *Economic Backwardness in Historical Perspective* (Cambridge: Belknap Press, Harvard, 1962).

II

Functional Elites

4
Political Elites and Political Modernization: The Crisis of Transition

ROBERT E. SCOTT

During the transition from traditional politics to a more modern political system elites play a crucial role. Elite activities determine the speed and effectiveness with which the polity can move toward national integration and political modernity. The characteristics of this modernity are rational and universalistic norms, a consensus of political values and expectations, and viable political structures that can operate to resolve internal differences and mobilize against external threats; a participant citizenry, holding government responsible and at the same time assuming its own obligations, helps to achieve this end. The attitudes and actions of the elites control when, if, or to what degree each characteristic will become part of the operational system.

In the more developed countries political modernization resulted from conditions arising from the Industrial Revolution. So is it in the emerging states today, with one important difference. The accumulated wonders of science and technology have so speeded up the rate of political change that for most practical purposes its very nature is altered.

In Europe and the United States well over a century ago the growing complexity of social and economic life produced a great number of groups with specialized functions, each led by the more able, alert, and politically minded members of the traditional ruling classes or by the same elements in the emerging sectors. At the beginning of the industrial era these new elites caused a certain amount of disequilibrium in the existing political structures, but they evolved sufficiently slowly and their pressures for political participation were pitched in a low enough key that they could be readily integrated into the existing political system.

Divisions between social strata gradually became blurred as widespread education, improved transportation, and mass communications brought farmer and city dweller together, led to contact between the upper and lower classes, and broke the long-established dominance of the landed gentry by placing power in the hands of a new breed of financiers, businessmen, and industrialists. Over the years new groupings further down the social scale appeared, and elites representing middle-class professions, shopkeepers, small farmers, industrial workers, ethnic groups, even obscure religious sects, to name a few, sought entry into the political decision-making process. Technological advances produced a more rapid expansion of wealth in the early developing nations, and so spokesmen for the masses were able to take a greater role in policy decisions deciding how goods and services were to be allocated, while at the same time the older elites retained their influence. If the traditional elements had not slowly and grudgingly accorded political legitimacy to the new elites and the latter had not shown political moderation and responsibility when they received this status, the political systems of modernizing countries might well have not been able to adjust to the shocks of change.

Actually political change was neither fast nor peaceful. The word "disequilibrium" comprises riots, murders, and civil wars. The term "allocating goods and services" evokes a long history of strikes, depressions, and the suppression of political movements. But even with this violence and struggle, most modernizing states have over the years been able to reform their political structures to meet new conditions. Within these structures both traditional and challenging elites have revised their values to fit new situations and establish new relationships. With a growing consensus the battles shifted to specialized political structures.

Politics increasingly became the responsibility of full-time, professional politicians, more or less neutral brokers who utilized political parties as aggregating mechanisms to resolve the competition among the many functional interests. Since the elites shared political values with the vast majority of their fellow citizens and since they found they could trust the integrity of the professional politicians, they no longer had to concern themselves quite so directly and so unceasingly with politics. As a consequence, they were not so highly politicized as they once were. They now could separate administrative and technical questions from basic policy matters, leaving the former to the technicians and concentrating their political energies on the latter. Thus they had to all intents become part-time political elites.

In no modern country have these elites withdrawn completely from the political arena. But they usually concentrate on improving the efficiency of their organizations so that they can exert as much pressure as possible on the decision-making process, albeit indirectly. These functional elites also operate largely within the rules of the political game, partially because the political culture conditions them to do so but mainly because internal control devices have evolved that force the elites to follow the rules of fair play established by the political system if they are to operate effectively.

The average citizen represents a strong control device in the modernized polity. General education and the knowledge engendered by the mass media of communication, together with lowered class and social barriers, make a high proportion of the population aware of politics and the part they can play in it. These citizens not only vote for candidates nominated for public office but take some part in selecting them, and many of them show concern for public affairs between elections. Because most citizens are motivated by a diversity of interests—regional, religious, social, economic, emotional—an elite representing a single functional grouping cannot achieve political influence by appealing to particular interests but must recognize the broader norms of the society.

The situation is very different in the rapidly modernizing countries of today's emerging world. The demonstration effect of political patterns in the developed states upon which the emerging states pattern themselves is intensified by rapid internal social and economic change engendered by technology and all of the consequences crowd in upon the political system. Diversification of functions produces new interests and their resulting elites so fast that unless some *modus vivendi* can be worked out with the traditional elites, the energies of the political system will be spent in resolving their rivalries for power rather than in serving the people. Unless some means of integrating the attitudes of the competing elites can be found, structural disequilibrium soon will turn into structural inadequacy, as political mechanisms are swamped with demands they are unable to process and satisfy.

The problem is intensified by the speed with which this process of

change is taking place, for the persons controlling the political structures in these countries often are quite unable to reorient their thinking
and action to make room for the new elites. Without some degree of
shared political norms and a willingness to compromise, it is most
difficult for the society to make a proper transition to universalistic and
rational norms. This breakdown of interaction between old and new
(and frequently among new) elites hampers government performance that is sufficiently effective in range and volume to assure political
stability. If this occurs, new, more particularistic non-governmental
auxiliary structures often evolve to rationalize the activities of the various interests and their elites. The difficulty here is that the non-
governmental structures tend to be specialized and limiting in their
operations rather than universalistic and generalizing, so that political
action then tends to move in traditional instead of modernizing channels.

In most of Latin America today, where political change takes place
under conditions of forced draft speed, the political elites play a quite
different role from that envisioned for them by European theorists such
as Mosca and Pareto, who wrote in more sedate circumstances. The
functional elites have remained political elites. Despite the beginnings
of an "expert society" in many parts of Latin America, none of the
countries has political "experts"—that is, full-time, professional politicians who can be permitted to undertake basic political decision-
making. The so-called *politicos* have less influence within the national political system than their public role indicates. In a transitional
situation where there is no general political consensus, political parties
or movements cannot function as neutral, brokerage intermediaries between the various elites. Instead, such parties represent the particularistic interests of the traditional elites or serve as vehicles for badly fragmented and competitive emerging interests and their elite leaders.

The basis upon which most Latin American political parties attempt
to expand their membership indicates that neither the general citizenry
nor the elites are yet ready to operate politically through generalizing
and instrumental aggregating mechanisms. Rather than seeking to attract large numbers of individual members through a broad national
program, the parties adopt a rigid ideology which appeals only to a
small group of dedicated supporters, or else set up labor, farm, youth,
or women's organizations designed to rival those of some other political movement.

Since the principal political initiative in Latin America is held by functional elites which act or hope to act directly upon the political process, this study will deal primarily with these groups and with the political structures through which they work. It will not, however, attempt to repeat substantive data on recruitment, membership, activities, or the like of particular elites, which are available in this volume and elsewhere.[1] Neither will it attempt to recast in political terms general statements about value systems either of traditional societies or of Latin America in particular.[2]

These comments on the limited influence of professional politicians, as compared with the political role of the functional elites, refer primarily to national political systems. Some very limited and scattered evidence exists to suggest that under local political conditions party leaders may wield considerable influence.[3] Sometimes this results from their ascriptive roles as landowners or from other traditional high-status positions rather than from the party position they hold. More commonly, such political power comes from an appointment as a government functionary, with all the legal authority such positions entail, particularly in countries where a high proportion of economic activity is controlled by the state. Since the *político's* influence reflects the government office he holds rather than his party role, his reputation for political power disappears rapidly when he leaves office.[4]

The role played by most Latin American elites, particularly the traditional elites, does not meet the needs of their countries' national political systems. Rapid change has produced a cultural lag. At one time the political triumvirate of large landowners, army, and Church was a real power elite, in C. Wright Mills's sense of the term. The hierarchical relationship between the masses and the ruling clique was based on a wide and almost insurmountable gap, with political power concentrated at the top. The officer corps and the religious leadership were recruited from the landholding class, and all three agreed about the proper functions of government and about those who should participate in the political process. In such a highly stratified system, these rulers more nearly resembled a ruling caste than a governing class.

Today, in Latin America's politically least modernized states—Honduras, Paraguay, Ecuador, the Dominican Republic, Nicaragua, and even Colombia—somewhat the same pattern persists. Similarly, in most of the other countries the traditional value system, with its emphasis on localism, inherited standards, and deeply etched patterns of political action, its mistrust of impersonal government and distant national authority which negate the tried and warm relationships of family and the mutual trust shared by *hombres de confianza,* continues to support the elite principle. But modern influences have become so pervasive that not even the strong bonds of traditional culture can hold together the old triumvirate as a monolithic, unchallenged power elite.

Social and economic development have put the three traditional elites more often than not in conflict with each other over the proper role of government in their society. Although the elites do often agree on certain questions involving perpetuation of their political influence, they agree less and less on other issues. At the same time the three traditional elites themselves have fragmented, as functional differentiation occurs and as their members have disagreed over the nature of their institution and its relation to society in the light of social and economic change.

The political views of the *hacendados* are dependent upon the use to which they put their land. Marginal producers, whose estates are worked by tenants or whose cattle and sheep raising are done inefficiently, have a very different attitude toward the government than landowners who employ large numbers of wage-earners and produce money crops for domestic consumption and export sale. And different money crops require different kinds of government support or create different kinds of attitudes on the part of the producers. Cotton-growing, which is seasonal, sugar production, which can be year round, banana cultivation, which is dependent upon foreign-controlled marketing arrangements—each requires a different kind of political support. Landowners' attitudes are also strongly affected by such considerations as labor relations, necessary social services, import duties on machinery and export taxes on agricultural products, dealings with foreign firms, credit resources, land distribution, and agricultural reform.

Similarly, patterns of recruitment for Church leaders and the military officer corps are rapidly shifting throughout Latin America. As older patterns of upper-class status change and new opportunities for middle-class mobility multiply, recruits move down the social scale; they tend to be drawn increasingly from the lower middle class and the upper lower class and come not from the center of the capital but its slums or from the smaller cities and the villages. Despite socialization into the ongoing traditional value systems of the two institutions by existing elite cadres, the forces of innovation are constantly at work. In every part of the world, modernization has meant secularization of society; in Latin America, even before the Ecumenical Council, it also meant a large voice in Church affairs for the laity, through Catholic Action and other groups. For the military, modernization has meant professionalization and increased technical competence; such new specialties as motorized cavalry and communications units have been developed, not to mention an entirely new and separate service, the air force. These new conditions, the distinct early life experience plus increased opportunities for outside contacts—through mass media, or with North American and other non-Iberian priests, or through advanced technical military training outside their traditional milieu or foreign military missions—reinforce each other in supporting generational differences in attitude toward generals and the hierarchy in the political system.

The social gospel and the military civic action program may not undermine religious obedience and military discipline, but they do challenge the inherited values of the Church and the military and question the assumptions on which the two forces feel they are free to intervene at any time in the political affairs of their respective countries. But the fact that the clergy, the top military, and the landed gentry engaged in different activities or changed their attitudes somewhat does not mean they automatically adopted modern political egalitarian and innovating values. Not only do the elites of the old triumvirate dislike the leaders who represent emerging interests because they pose a political threat, but they also continue to deny them equal status because of differences in culture which the elites put great store in. The elites react sharply to any alteration in the hierarchical relationship between the old *gente* at the top and the "others." For tactical reasons they may have to include elites representing the new wealth in their ruling coalition, but they continue to deplore the materialistic outlook of forces representing commerce, industry, or other forms of new economic achievement. Middle sector elites asking for a voice in government raise even stronger resentments in the old triumvirate. Even less attractive to them are the new elites representing mass interests, for reasons we shall consider presently.

Powerful commercial and industrial leaders may escape this resentment against the challenging elites, for many of them are spin-offs from the old ruling groups, and they were not identified with the lower classes. Not only do they dress and speak like the members of the older elites, but they tend to share many of their traditional political values. They may be economic innovators but they are not political ones. As a result of this muted approach to political modernization, these financial elites have often worked out a kind of armed truce with the traditional interests. We should note, however, that strong denunciations of the "oligarchy" come from comfortable members of the Church, military, and landowners as well as from the lower class.[5]

It is hard to assess the position of the intellectuals in relation to the traditional ruling elements. Perhaps this is because they really do not consist of any single identifiable sector of the population or represent the interests of any homogeneous constituency. As in other developing countries, in most Latin American states a village schoolteacher, newspaper reporter, political polemicist, university professor, or even one of his students, may be identified as an intellectual, and be accorded a certain degree of status. This does not necessarily mean high political status, for that depends upon the other roles the individual plays. Through most of this region being an intellectual is not a full-time occupation, or at least not one that can support a family. His other activities and the interests to which they bind him type a man politically and win him the support or the suspicion of the old-line power group. Indeed if an editorial writer and party cell organizer who works for a Communist publication can be considered an intellectual, so can a landowner who writes poetry, a priest who teaches in the university, or a colonel who publishes a military history of his country. In a society where many people's occupational and avocational patterns are multifaceted, who can determine which aspect of a person's activities enhance his political influence? All one can suggest is that those intellectuals whose other roles reflect high political standing seem generally to have more influence than other intellectuals.

Another potentially politically influential part of the citizenry hard to classify consists of members of the learned professions, including semi-professional teachers, middle range bureaucrats or managers, and small businessmen. The active *políticos* emerge primarily but not exclusively from the ranks of lawyers. Although a small sprinkling of physicians, engineers, and others from this stratum get caught up in politics, the striking fact is how large a proportion remains apolitical, at least until their privileges are threatened. Many then vote with their feet, moving out of the country rather than becoming politically active.

Such passive attitudes are explained partially by the vocational environment within which they operate. Where neutrality or support of the government can have a profound effect on one's professional career, and where politics is apt to be both highly partisan and cyclical, it is wiser not to become too strongly identified with any particular political posture. More important, per'laps, is the fact that most persons in professions take on traditional elitist norms, particularly as they are strongly upward mobile.

It appears that politically people in the professions are not a "group" sharing a single set of norms. Nor are they a set of groups divided on functional bases, for not even the structure of their professional associations seems to unite them on political matters, unless immediate and personal interests are involved in an issue, as was the situation during the 1965 doctors' strike in Mexico. Once again, as with the intellectuals, it is not so much the occupation as ascribed social status or the nature and effectiveness of the movement in which he participates that accounts for the professional man's political position.

No such ambiguity exists when we try to estimate the degree of acceptance accorded the elites representing emerging mass interests—organized labor, small farmers, urban and rural unskilled workers, or small shopkeepers. Whether these spokesmen are persons moving up from the lower class, with few of the social skills and little of the assurance demonstrated by the members of established ruling groups, or individuals who can pass social muster, either because they are of upper or middle class origin or because they hide humble origins in acquired graces, they are not likely to be granted an unqualified welcome into the political councils of the old establishment.

This is not simply a matter of denying political legitimacy for fear that participation by representatives of mass interests will in time swamp the smaller upper classes, though, of course, this does enter the picture. The fact is that the established elites are well aware that the emerging forces do not present as immediate a threat as their numbers might indicate. In the first place, the functional groups are badly balkanized into competing units whose personalistic leaders relate to different regional, ideological, or political reference groups. In addition, economic insecurity produces a kind of popular elitism. Skilled workers will not organize with unskilled laborers, *minifundistas* will not make common cause with farm day laborers, white-collar *empleados* have separate unions from blue-collar *obreros,* and they all hate the small shopkeeper and the moneylender. Again, the politically able and skilled citizens are found more frequently in the upper classes than in the popular sector. Often the mass-based organizations find it hard to man the positions of formal political leadership, much less to balance the leaders' political initiatives with rank and file competence which might assure responsibility to the general membership. This, incidently, is a major source of the oligarchic relations in these structures that contribute to elitist sentiments. The members of the upper-class functional interest associations, on the other hand, have so much political competence that they can operate formally through the legal governmental agencies and at the same time reinforce these operations through informal political channels.

The potential but not yet imminent possibility of the popular elites' capturing the political process is only one reason for denying them easy access. Another is that the traditional ruling elites simply do not want to see a change in their dominant power position, for elitist reasons. They cannot conceive that the masses, those "animals," those Indians "who have no souls," should have the same political rights as a cultured aristocracy. Nor should the elites who presume to speak for these common people. In a culture where elite status is bestowed across the board, political elite status may be delayed until popular elites can meet all the necessary conditions for social acceptance.

One might suspect *a priori* that refusal to accept these new elites results from differences in values, especially in attitude toward political modernization. It could be said that the masses and their spokesmen have had little opportunity to be socialized into traditional upper class values, that they are apt to be political innovators and therefore anathema to conservatives. I tested this hypothesis in Mexico and Peru a few years ago, in a still unpublished study. It proved incorrect there, and I believe would not test out in most other Latin American systems either. Too many members of the challenging elites have adopted the ruling groups' elitist norms and conservative tendencies and have sold out their followers in the popular organizations. A fair number of these turncoats have been accepted by the establishment as "tame reformers," but more important most of their followers accept this symbolic participation in the political process with little protest, despite the lack of any practical payoff for them. In time, of course, more dedicated and frequently more radical leaders appear in an attempt to displace the betrayers, but surprisingly few of these potential political innovators succeed. The truth is that the masses are too fearful and suspicious of change to welcome the destructive tactics of such leaders. This is by no means a rare attitude in poor countries where the marginal population has learned to survive under present conditions but has no reserve to fall back on in case an experiment in political theory fails.

In short, the one thing that most of the political elites seem to have in common is a sense of insecurity engendered by rapid change. The long dominant elites fear the threat to their power position from the surging new interests and reject the egalitarian pretentions of the challenging elites; the lower class leadership resents a situation in which they are denied effective access to the political process and feel a growing pressure from their constituents, who may not demand political change but are increasingly restive under social and economic deprivation. And all of the elites are in mortal competition with each other. In the face of particularly strong pressure from below, varied interests found in the establishment may close ranks for a time, and the challengers may react with a temporary coalition, but co-operation soon will come to an end. Each of the elites is seeking to maximize its political power and to protect the perquisites of power—material benefits, social and political status, and a sense of being able to control one's own destiny.

Clearly then, no power elite of the sort envisioned by C. Wright Mills exists in Latin America. Perhaps the continuation of a sharp hierarchical division between the leadership cadres at the top and the masses below, coupled with a weakness in the political structures that assure the counterbalancing of forces usually associated with pluralistic democracy, accounts for the widespread vogue Mills's approach enjoys among Latin American intellectuals. Certainly they can see from their own environment that in most functional groupings the lack of effective interaction between leader and follower does produce a series of independent and frequently irresponsible elites. Frustrated in their search to participate in the exercise of power, many intellectuals see those who wield authority as a monolithic force, identifying the historic pattern of the old triumvirate with the modern situation. They reason that the traditional elites have co-opted the leaders appearing in mechanized agriculture and in finance, commerce, and industry, citing the co-operation among these groups on certain kinds of political issues.

Actually, this situation is true only for certain types of issue. On most other matters of national policy the dominant elites are so competitive that they cannot act the way a ruling class might be expected to act—in agreement over a broad range of issues. The best they can do is to limit the speed and extent of advance in the political process by the challenging elites by setting up informal boundaries within which the government (usually personified by the president) may act quite independently but beyond which it steps only with great risk.

Given the multiplication of interests and the burgeoning of elites throughout Latin America, the pressing political problem is not so much to counteract a power elite by encouraging pluralism but to find ways to unite the many elites and their followers and to harness their political activities for constructive national integration. Neither the party systems nor the legislatures seem to be able to perform this aggregating function in a neutral and nation-building manner and, as we have just seen, even the chief executive, who generally is considered the strong man of Latin politics, is limited in performing this unifying role. This leaves the function open to more particularistic non-governmental structures, organized by their elites to protect the interests of specific functional groupings or coalitions of groupings. These private governments protect society from the consequences of open clashes, but they represent a very expensive form of protection for the great proportion of the population that is not politically competent enough to organize and operate such structures efficiently. What mechanisms are available to defend their interests?

Certainly not the majority of political parties which operate in the region. Parties, like any other political structures, are likely to perform the functions required by the citizens who man them. During the transitional political period through which Latin America is passing, the parties reflect the lack of cohesiveness within the masses and the intense competition among political elites. They are highly specialized political structures—small, particularistic, class- or function-oriented, often regional. They are elitist in the sense that political initiative resides in a restricted leadership group, frequently consisting of the elites who control the functional groupings which are brought into the political movement en masse with minimal consultation of the rank and file. The number of individually affiliated party members is limited, and political activists even more so. On the surface most parties are ideologically rather than programatically motivated, but in practice the ideology seldom remains operative after a party captures power because political movements tend to form around a personalistic leader and his coterie.[6]

Most such party leaders are not ideologically minded, or, if they are, their followers are not. In a rapidly changing political environment the psychological need for the sort of symbolic reassurance an ideology can provide, a frame of reference for the disoriented, is enormous. At one level an ideology is very attractive to the citizen seeking a sense of security because it supplies a kind of instant integration within a crumbling world. At another level the citizen tends to reject the universalism represented by ideology. Because of his sense of insecurity, he is much more attracted to the pragmatic and immediate. Pie in the sky is nowhere as attractive as bread in the hand. Ideology suits the more intellectualized who can reason by analogue and learn by the experience of others; those less educated in a formal sense are apt to be moved more by first-hand experience. The intellectual reasons over a longer period and on a broad range of policies; the harassed "doer" reacts to individual policy questions on a bread-and-butter basis. This rejection of ideology at the operational political level applies to the better educated and economically more comfortable members of the upper classes. For most of them, their ideology is subconscious and unintellectualized, reflecting deeply embedded elitist and particularistic values imposed by the socializing structures of the traditional political culture.

Under such circumstances the political elites who control a political party will speak ideologically but act pragmatically. They will not undermine their own authority with the rank and file and abandon the immediate interests of the functional groups they represent in order to turn the party into a more neutral and broadly based aggregating mechanism. In the long run, such a change might be advantageous to both the elites and the interests they serve, as well as to the country at large, but conditions do not encourage this kind of thinking. Not only does the highly particularistic set of values which individual members have carried over from the traditional culture preclude such co-operation, but the cut-throat competition for scarce economic resources among competing functional interests means that any group attempting to compromise the effectiveness of its protective bargaining device may be courting suicide. It is precisely because so many intellectuals in Latin America misjudge the importance of these mental and material considerations to potential political constituencies that as a group the intellectual elite has remained peripheral to the political power structure. They allow their support of ideological formalities or abstract future goals to stand in the way of the kind of direct and immediate representation in the decision-making process that a functional interest must have to survive.

These characteristics apply equally to the so-called mass-based parties or movements, such as *Aprismo, Peronismo,* the *fidelista* parties, some forms of Christian Democracy, or the more or less evolutionary reform movements of Mexico, Peru, and Bolivia. As Lipset points out in Chapter I, independence was attained in the new states of Africa and Asia "under the leadership of mass parties whose revolutionary ideology subsumes the values of equalitarianism, achievement, universalism, and collectivity-orientation. Traditional practices may be attacked as antithetical to the national interest and self-image. In much of Latin America, however, many traditional values and practices are regarded as proper parts of the national identity." Without the mystiques of a successful revolt against a colonial power to build support upon, the leaders of Latin America's popular movements utilize such abstract concepts as *indianismo* and nationalism as unifying catchwords. But the first smacks of a return to a more primitive era, which goes against the economic aspirations of the masses, and the second is a concept outside their ken and therefore suspect. The more demagogic leaders also use such terms as "the oligarchy" and "Yankee imperialism" as rallying cries, but words alone do not have much sustaining power in the struggle for political supporters.

In every country where a mass party has operated one can find large numbers of former members who grew tired of trying to identify their personal stake in the party's maneuvers for power or who grew disillusioned with the failure of promises once the government was captured. These people either become apolitical once again or if they remain activists move on to another party. Those who remain with the party do so because the political system offers them no adequate alternative of satisfying their political needs, as with the *peronistas* in Argentina.

The leaders and followers in such mass parties simply cannot find a common set of goals. At the top, the aims are either so general—the end of the *status quo,* national integration—or so personal—capture of office or enhancement of individual status—that they are not likely to motivate the man in the street. Below, the mass following is unable to articulate its own desires for economic improvement and a sense of individual dignity, much less to organize itself to obtain them. The politically ineffective citizens are manipulated by the party elite, often through slogans and promises that portend social justice, economic reform, and political democracy as ends, while at the same time the party itself operates through largely undemocratic means. As long as the masses remain uneducated and inarticulate and so unable to hold their leaders responsible, both the mass parties and the functional interest associations which include large numbers of the lower class will continue to be dominated by oligarchical elites. Under such conditions neither the smaller parties representing specialized functional interests nor the mass parties composed of many members with little in common as a basis for joint action can provide the unifying and integrating function political systems require.

If individually the parties cannot accomplish this function it is hardly possible that they will accomplish it collectively as a party system. In no Latin American country save Mexico, and there in limited degree through a dominant single party, does the party system act as an effective aggregating mechanism to force compromise and cooperation among the elites which represent divergent interests. As a consequence, in most countries the Congress is unable to fulfill its formal role in the decision-making process because of the uncompromising demands made upon it from the outside and the irreconcilable interests within the body. The legislators elected as representatives of specialized interest parties find it hard to approach their tasks in a broader context, and the very questions which are debated are formulated within a particularistic framework rather than in terms of a general welfare or long-range national goals. Little wonder then that much of the initiative for general policy-making is left to the chief executive, who must see to it that some sort of decision is made because he and his subordinates are faced with the services to be rendered and the problems to be solved.

Considering the Latin American presidency in this context produces an apparent paradox. Concentration of political power in the hands of the executive in order to provide some sort of integrating political structure tends to strengthen an already dominant president and to weaken the more popular party and legislative structures. That is to say, the status of an already powerful superordinate elitist figure, the president, is enhanced at the expense of what already are subordinate agencies, despite constitutional provisions and popular expectations to the contrary. It might be argued that because the parties are closer to the people and because the legislatures consist of a large number of elected officials, they are both more likely to provide opportunities for training the citizenry to become civic-minded and political participants and in time evolve a more representative form of organization that would result in more generally accepted political norms and ultimately could lead to an aggregating function. In fact, such has not been the case.

We already have seen that most political parties function in a particularistic manner because of social, economic, and political conditions outside their control. These same conditions, reinforced by the weakness of the party system as an integrating mechanism, reduce the possibility that the legislature will easily change the way it operates. Moreover, there is no guarantee that involving more individuals in the activities of party and Congress will make them more representative of a general interest. Remember that these parties are spokesmen for specialized interests and/or elite groups. The persons elected by them to the legislature can hardly be counted upon to adopt some new integrating norms merely because they have taken the oath of office. If the leaders and the rank and file follow traditional norms, it is because their environment socializes them into these value systems. It takes a continuing and compelling change in conditions to force them into new attitudes and patterns of action. The cultural lag that damps down the fires of political modernization affects even most of the more activist citizens.

It seems probable, however, that the president may stand a better chance of bringing about political modernization than the ostensibly more popular political mechanisms; this is due to his special role in the political process and particularly to the nature of the constituency to which the chief executive addresses himself. In constitutional theory he serves the interests of all the people and in political practice his administration has to meet the demands advanced by all the competing elites, whether or not they have been accorded political legitimacy. Until recently there was relatively little chance that a forward-looking president would ally himself with the integrating elements in the country to provide the kind of nation-building activity that would limit the divisive special-interest-serving actions of the functional elites. The man who reached the top, and especially one in a position to act as a strong man, was a product of his own political environment. He usually represented some alliance of the *status quo*-minded elites and thought in such terms himself. Today, in a few cases, evidence exists to suggest that innovating politicians who understand the need for a more neutral brokerage function not only can run for president but be elected.

But limiting devices upon the power of such a president often are built into a country's political process. The very act of seeking consensus in order to balance interest demands inhibits his freedom to act. At the same time the traditional elites still retain enough power to offset very nearly the chief executive's inherited authority as personification of the state and as constitutional head of the government. The old establishment and its new allies still control the preponderance of information, organizational skill, moral influence, and physical force in the country. Therefore the image of a strong president, unlimited in his power and able to keep the contending elites in balance, may be deceptive. The executive still has wide power within rather clearly defined boundaries, but he may risk his position crossing them. These boundaries differ in each state, depending on how much political influence the challenging elites have captured and on how closely the traditional elites have managed to co-operate in defending their established positions.

A number of innovating presidents—significantly, many of them influenced at some time during their lives by foreign experience,[7] though a few developed largely at home [8]—have been able to make a good start toward balancing the competing interests. At some point in his administration, however, each found himself pulled up short and his program disrupted by elements who objected to his moving into areas they deemed out of bounds. In some cases the innovator survived, in others he was ousted. In every case he crossed a forbidden boundary, most commonly offending the conservatives but sometimes the liberals. Perón and Quadros are examples of the former type, Rojas Pinilla of the second. A few managed to run into trouble from both right and left, sometimes because the consequences of rapid change piled up so fast no leader could balance contending demands and other times because of personality problems, or both. Gallegos, Bosch, and Paz Estenssoro fit this category.

The inability of Latin America's "political" structures to act as efficient integrating mechanisms as long as the functional elites which act as political elites remain fragmented and static suggests that the only real solution in the long run is to alter the value systems of people. If both elites and followers can be modernized, the existing integrating political structures—parties, party systems, legislature, and presidency —will adjust themselves to the changes, or new working structures will evolve to perform the function.

To be sure, a modernizing and more democratic political pattern depends mainly upon the ability of the political elites to change. This in turn rests squarely upon the ability of the rest of the population to make it possible for the elites to accept change, or even to require it, by amending their own attitudes toward the political process. If enough politically motivated citizens demanded, in a continuous enough way to institutionalize the shift, that their spokesmen support an aggregative policy in the legislature, the elites would have no choice but to comply. But in real life this simply is not going to happen, any more than the political activists among the populace are going to change their allegiance from special interest-oriented parties to nationalizing-integrating parties. At least it will not happen until either some kind of political revolution so upsets the present pattern of interest representation that a centralizing political structure can take over the aggregating policy of decision-making, as occurred in Mexico after 1930 with the PRI, or until evolutionary change continues to such an extent that the average citizen acquires such diverse interests that he can transfer his primary political ties from one or two specialized functional interest groups to a more neutral brokerage political party.

Meanwhile, during the phase of transition from traditional society, the sector of the population which conceivably might have some influence over the attitudes and actions of the functional political elites is hardly speeding up the process of modernization. In most Latin American countries the participant citizen is rare, simply because most citizens are unaware of politics. Lack of adequate communications, poor formal educational facilities, and particularly the rules of the game of politics, which call for a minimal role for the man in the street or on the *hacienda,* reduce activism. In some countries, Brazil and Peru, for example, the game is further rigged by literacy requirements for voting, which deprive a large portion of the adult population of even this formal influence.

A further complication. The relatively small part of the populace who are most likely to be political activists—not the operating politicians, but the informed, concerned, and politically skilled citizen who knows enough and has self-assurance enough to exert political pressures and to make the elites politically accountable—are not necessarily modern-minded. If any group should be so in terms of the standard indicators, it is these university-trained professionals, urban dwellers, consumers of mass media, relatively high-income earners, and purchasers of status-conferring items, those who in economic matters slightly incline toward entrepreneurial experimentation. The limited research available indicates that while such persons are somewhat more flexible than most of their fellow citizens, they are not in general political innovators, probably because they are insecure in the face of rapid change.[9] In fact, we already know that surprisingly few businessmen, physicians, engineers, or even lawyers participate directly in party politics or, as we shall see presently, in "private governments."

This pattern is exacerbated, but not necessarily caused, by the fact that the most venturesome of the university-trained professionals in Latin America are lured away from their original political setting by the so-called "brain drain." Many of the best prepared minds have been persuaded to leave their countries by the better economic opportunities, greater political stability, or other inducements available in the United States, Europe, in international agencies, or in other more developed Latin American states where they remain outside the political process. A recent United Nations study showed, for example, that during the past decade some 14,000 professionally trained Argentines had emigrated. Although in technical activities some of the physicians and engineers may be replaced by Paraguayans and Bolivians, who can supply the political participation that this large nucleus of educated citizens might have provided? Where are the activists who might have supported integrating party leaders or legislators who seek a general interest? Who can tell what pressures these absent citizens might have brought to bear to force more modern norms on the functional elites who double as political leaders?

This loss of potential modernizers among the participant citizenry and the tendency of many of the rest toward conservatism continue to leave the generalizing political structures weak. The same factors which make the party, the legislature, and the presidency ineffectual in their functions as national integrators make the functional elites politically independent. More important, they force these same elites to become politically stronger, not simply because the elites are power hungry but because some kind of organizing mechanism is required to perform the functions left undone by government. Under these circumstances, it is no accident that the functional elites have set up their own informal political structures to act as control devices over their own activities and as offense units in the battle for political power.

The notion of non-governmental, private structures of power is not restricted to developing areas or to Latin America in particular. In the United States, for instance, the so-called "interests," not only agriculture, business and labor, but also education, private social welfare, and a host of other functional groupings, operate such structures.[10] They have dual authority—internal, insofar as they mobilize, organize, and police their own members, and external, insofar as they act to influence the political policy making process. In a stable and modern political system with a high degree of consensus, such private structures can wield influence but they are always bounded by the limits established by the widely accepted concepts of general interest and welfare embodied in law and enforced by neutral government agencies. Thus their inherent particularistic tendencies are counteracted by the broader environment in which they must operate.

In rapidly changing environments, where consensus is shallow and the governmental agencies and political structures perform their integrating functions poorly, little reliance can be placed upon such mechanisms to limit the divisive role these special interest organizations play. Even if laws operating in the general interest are passed and executive agencies set up to enforce them, they offer little more than symbolic assurance to the populace that the nation exists. The real business of politics often takes place in a more specialized environment, with the private interest structures taking on the functions of private governments, practically unhampered by the constitutional government.

This situation obtains throughout most of Latin America. For the reasons already adduced, some method of structuring the operations of each separate functional interest and of rationalizing the activities of its leadership is essential, if only to maximize its defensive capacities in a battle not delineated by rules set up and enforced in a wider context of formal law.[11] That such structuring tends to enhance particularism and crystallize the *status quo* at the expense of national integration and constructive change may be regrettable, but it is one of the facts of political life in an unstable political environment. That it also tends to reorganize a kind of power elite following the demise of the triumvirate of traditional elites, denying real representation in the political decision-making process to all those who are not as well organized, also is regrettable but equally inevitable.

The elite in control of each set of interests establishes its own organization, attempting to pre-empt as much decision-making authority as possible from the government, which frequently allows its power to go by default. In fact, in many Latin American countries these organizations are granted semi-official status. By law certain tax receipts may be earmarked to support an organization's program, or groups engaging in the particular functional activity may be required to become members of the association. In some cases an organization may be permitted to nominate voting representatives on government control boards or agencies. Acting as a control device over its own clientele, the organization resolves internal struggles and internecine disputes which might weaken the interest represented in its external dealings with other private governments or with the agencies of formal government.

Many areas of policy decision, which in other types of political system might be considered the proper, primary, or exclusive concern of the constitutional agencies are determined here by the private government. The matter is taken to formal government only in the rare event that the organization's leadership cannot handle the internal stresses involved, or when the tensions between several such organizations grow to such extent that some outside agency must resolve the differences. Generally, however, government is presented with a policy decision already made; the constitutional legislature and executive are merely asked to ratify the decision.

The gradual formalization of these organizations from such earlier forms of reciprocal relationship as *compadrazco* or, in Brazil, of more complex social and economic mutual aid systems as *cabide, igrejinha,* and *panelinha* suggests that the private governments satisfy a functional need in the transitional political systems.[12] To some extent labor unions, rural co-operatives, Catholic Action and/or Opus Dei perform these functions for their memberships. So do professional associations of lawyers, physicians, engineers, and the like, but the most effective are the organizations of more complex and stronger economic interests which, as we have noted, are most likely to operate within a framework of particularistic and inelastic political norms.

The most traditionally oriented private governments probably are the Jockey Clubs of Argentina and Colombia and similar societies of large landowners wherever they may be located. Somewhat more innovative but hardly advancing rapidly toward political modernization in the sense of encouraging expanded formal government control over their actions are such functional organizations as associations of cotton growers, petroleum and mineral producers, or coffee harvesters, not to mention Industrial Chambers and Chambers of Commerce. One might even include the military, in the sense that most Latin American governments leave armed service affairs strictly to the respective staffs and a Minister of War or Defense, who frequently is an officer selected by the military itself. In a few countries law or custom assures the services some automatically fixed proportion of the budget, making them an almost completely independent government. There are two weaknesses in the inclusion of the officer corps here, however. In the first place, the military does not always remain a "private" government. In the second, the military is not inevitably a traditional force. Although the preponderance of bias lies toward the *status quo,* acting as a "moderating force" the armed services have at times forced some sort of reconciliation between the competing established elites and their challengers. On balance, however, Latin America has produced few modernizing Nassers or Ataturks.

Not all systems of private governments have gone as far as Peru's. There the established *Fuerzas Económicas Vivas* have become so structured that the presidents of some ten functional associations hold regular meetings where they discuss differences among member organizations, attempting to resolve disputes privately whenever possible.[13] At these meetings reactions of the several participating groupings toward proposed governmental action also are considered and collective action is decided. Publicly this action may take the form of statements by the heads of individual organizations or even full-page newspaper advertisements signed by the presidents of all of the member groups explaining their collective position and sometimes containing veiled hints at untoward consequences for the economy of the country and the jobs of their employees if their advice is not heeded. These private governments acting in concert can generate a tremendous amount of covert pressure, for their members pay a very large share of all taxes collected in Peru and have many other ways of making or breaking a particular regime.

In countries where the organized elites are less structured than in Peru, their influence is nonetheless impressive, probably because during the period of political transition they are essential as a co-ordinating device. In Mexico membership in the Chambers of Commerce and of Industry is compulsory and although their ties to government are un-official, through the presidency, they are very real.[14] In most other countries the tie is less obvious, perhaps, but no less effective. While speaking of the political boundaries within which the chief executive must operate in the transitional Latin states, we noted that an inno-vator's freedom of action is limited. To this we must now add the fact that for practical purposes whole areas of governmental activity have been pre-empted by the functional elites.

All this suggests that the rapid spread of complexity and the inelas-ticity of political culture norms are producing in many of Latin Amer-ica's political systems a potentially dangerous structural inadequacy. The mechanisms for making the emerging elites work together and for updating their viewpoints patently are not functioning well enough. In a very few countries some combination of time and re-sources (human and material) have permitted at least partial solu-tions. Of these Mexico probably has been most successful, for it got an early start in modernizaton, before the pressures born of mass com-munication and easy transportation could overwhelm its initial efforts toward integration. Moreover, abundant material resources are being exploited by a fairly large portion of the population that is educated and positively oriented toward modern norms. And most of this valu-able work force is remaining in Mexico because conditions are quite favorable. Finally, the Revolutionary Party and the government it sup-ports are strong enough to limit the most destructive aspects of elite competition and to force the specialized interests to accept the na-tionalizing-integrating values the political system has adopted. None-theless, it must be pointed out that the shift from traditional to modern political culture values has been very slow and still is not accomplished, after over fifty years of persistent effort by the revolutionary leaders.[15] Only now are the masses beginning to think and act like participant citizens who bring effective pressure upon the political elites to de-mand responsible representation for their interests.

To some extent Venezuela has been able to substitute money for time or adequate human resources in its search for constructive nation-building. Petroleum exploitation produced a new kind of elite based on wealth rather than land and tradition. This aristocracy may not share all of the egalitarian values of the *Acción Democrática* or COPEI parties, but it is able to understand the advantage of effective national government. Oil income also has given the government financial strength to experiment in social reform without disturbing the economic position of the traditional elements too extensively. As schools and roads appear, as new local industry in mining and in food processing develop, the masses may find themselves caught up in modernization and provide the popular foundation needed by a government seeking to broaden the role of its integrating political structures. Jorge Ahumada is rather optimistic about this possibility. He finds that Venezuela's social-political problems are those of any country "where traditional social structure is disintegrating without its having fully acquired and consolidated the key features of a modern society." [16] Meanwhile, despite the advantage of its oil wealth, Venezuela is undergoing the disruption of a minor civil war, as *fidelista* dissidents challenge the authority of the integrating central government.

Other Latin American states have handled the problem of deficiencies in the integrating political structures in different ways, some quite successfully and others less so. There is no easy way of generalizing their experience or of suggesting social and economic indicators to help forecast the pattern of success or failure. A country like Argentina, which early in this century seemed well on its way to developing a consensus and absorbing the mass of citizenry into political participation, has been unable to complete the process. Apparently such indicators as high literacy, an elevated per capita income, an integrated European culture population and ease of physical movement within the nation do not counteract the accidents of political history or the rigidity of the traditional triumvirate of power. The same is true to some extent of the pattern of change in Chile, El Salvador, and even Costa Rica. A few countries, such as Honduras or Paraguay, have not yet been exposed to the full force of structural inadequacy because the consequences of rapid change have not yet been felt widely. But in most parts of the region the political systems are struggling with the problem; their political leaders are only too aware of the problem but unable to do much to resolve it because the systems are overloaded with demands upon them and lack either time or resources to satisfy the competing interests.

The "crisis of elites," [17] as it is becoming known in Latin America, is one of the basic political problems of rapid change. We know that where the rigidity of traditional elites produces pressures too great for the political system to handle, extreme and revolutionary solutions occur. This happened in Mexico, in Bolivia, and in Cuba; it very nearly happened in Guatemala and the Dominican Republic, and symptoms are in evidence in Venezuela, Peru, and Brazil, among others. Unfortunately, extreme solutions do not necessarily resolve a country's political problems. Mexico took a long time to recover from its Revolution of 1910, and when the traditional elites were ousted from political dominance in Cuba and Bolivia the action proved counterproductive, in that not only social and economic development suffered badly, as the nucleus of trained manpower left the country, but the political structures were also emasculated. A similar pattern occurred in the Dominican Republic during 1965 and 1966, when large numbers of citizens abandoned the country to its fate.

This raises a fundamental question about the role of functional elites in the evolution of modern and democratic political systems for Latin America. In most states these elites tend to be particularistic, uncompromising, and strongly attached to the stratified class system. They appear to be unwilling or unable to make the adjustments necessary to permit constructive change. As evidenced by the cases of Bolivia and Cuba, and to a certain extent by the actions of the emigrating professionals throughout the region, many members of the elites are unlikely to stay in their own country to fight the hard fight to assure a workable political system. There exists ". . . the constant danger that if asked to give up their privileges, they will simply emigrate, leaving their country without the expertise to run it." [18] Rather than providing the impetus for political evolution, these elites hold on to their traditional political roles until the system cracks, and then move on to greener pastures.

It is easy for the outsider to suggest that individual members of the elites accept their responsibilities by helping to bring about changes in the political system before it is overwhelmed, or that they remain in their countries even though economic opportunities beckon elsewhere, or that in a revolutionary situation the educated and advantaged sectors stay to act as a moderating influence upon the political reformers. But if they do not, who is to do so? By the time the revolutions broke out in Cuba and Bolivia, it may have been too late; the frustrations of the long-thwarted emerging interests and the pent-up hatreds of decades may have made the position of the old ruling elites untenable. But many of the Mexican aristocrats remained in that country during and after the Revolution of 1910 and in so doing not only won an important place in the expanding economy by entering new types of economic endeavor, but continued to play a constructive if indirect role in the political evolution of their homeland. In the countries now undergoing the "crisis of elites," the political elites can try to head off revolution by accepting the inevitability of change and channeling it into evolutionary rather than revolutionary patterns.

The operations of private governments meet a functional need of the political system, and perhaps so does the freezing of an unstable situation by military takeover, but these are merely delaying measures or temporary stopgaps. The real solutions lie in the activities of innovating leaders who attempt to solve the problems of inadequacy of the generalizing political structures. Whether such leaders can accomplish their goals is anybody's guess. In a few states they have succeeded, in others they are trying, with some hope of success. Cárdenas in Mexico, Betancourt in Venezuela, Figueres in Costa Rica, Belaúnde Terry in Peru, and Frei in Chile offer evidence that the attempt can be made.

For all the terrible array of problems they have to face, the political modernizers have a few weapons on their side. Not the least important is the constructive example of Mexico and the frightening evidence from Bolivia and Cuba, together with the all too present alternative of the "crisis of elites" through which so many of the countries of Latin America now are passing. More specifically, and despite the less than positive examples offered here, a few political systems have provided instances of a reduction in the rigidity of some of the traditional elites, granting the innovators a little working room. As some landowners move into the mainstream of world commerce, as others in the oligarchy build relations with outside businessmen and suppliers, as modernizing sectors in the military develop, and as the Roman rather than the Iberian elements in the Church begin to gain prestige, the boundaries within which the nation-building political leader can operate begin to widen.

The most precious allies for the organizer are time and goods. The latter will ease popular pressures and the former permit dissemination of new ideas. Both would permit the restaffing of the national integrating mechanisms with a new breed of political elites. But in the final analysis the answer to the question of success or failure cannot be written here. It lies in the mixture of imponderables which each of the twenty republics faces alone. The correct type of leader, coming to power at a time when there is a proper balance among the traditional and challenging political elites, may be able to manipulate the situation. Only history can say whether such a combination of conditions will appear in a given country, or how long the process of transition will take if it does. But history also tells us that during the long story of mankind political systems have passed through many crises of change and somehow society has survived.

Notes

1. Latin America's elites have been discussed widely, both as such and as the leaders of functional interest groups. In addition to sources cited in the other studies in this volume which deal with specific functional elites, and the works listed later for specific countries, one can mention the following as illustrative: John J. Johnson (ed.), *Continuity and Change in Latin America* (Stanford, 1964); J. J. Tepaske and S. N. Fisher (eds.), *Explosive Forces in Latin America* (Columbus, 1964); J. D. Martz (ed.), *The Dynamics of Change in Latin American Politics* (Englewood Cliffs, N.J., 1965); Claudio Veliz (ed.), *Obstacles to Change in Latin America* (London, 1965); J. J. Johnson, *Political Change in Latin America; The Emergence of the Middle Sectors* (Stanford, 1958); W. V. D'Antonio and W. H. Form, *Political Influentials in Two Border Cities* (Notre Dame, 1964).

2. Of necessity any worthwhile study of a country's political process must contain some consideration of the elites. Among those utilized in this paper, the following were most helpful in relating the elites and the political process to each other. They are arranged in order of country: Argentina—José de Imaz, *Los que mandan* (Buenos Aires, 1964); Torcuato S. Di Tella, *et al., Argentina, Sociedad de Masas* (Buenos Aires, 1965); Alfredo Galletti, *La Realidad Argentina en el Siglo XX; La Política y Los Partidos* (Mexico-Buenos Aires, 1961); Rodolfo Puiggros, *Pueblo y Oligarquía* (Buenos Aires, 1965); Torcuato S. Di Tella, *El Sistema Político Argentino y la Clase Obrera* (Buenos Aires, 1964). Brazil—Raymundo Faoro, *Os Donos do Poder; Formação do Patronato Político Brasileiro* (Rio de Janeiro, 1958); João Camillo de Oliveira Tôrres, *Estratificação Social no Brasil* (São Paulo, 1965). Chile—F. B. Pike, *Chile and the United States, 1880–1962* (Notre Dame, 1963); Federico G. Gil, *The Political System of Chile* (Boston, 1966). Peru—François Bourricaud, *Peru; Une Oligarchie Face aux Problemes de la Mobilization* (unpublished manuscript, 1965). Guatemala—Mario Monteforte Toledo, *Guatemala: Monografía Sociológica* (Mexico, 1959). Mexico—R. E. Scott, *Mexican Government in Transition* (Urbana, 1959); R. E. Scott, "Mexico: the Established Revolution," in L. Pye and S. Verba (eds.), *Political Culture*

and Political Development (Princeton, 1965); Pablo González Casanova, *La Democracia en México* (Mexico, 1965).

3. In addition to many of the studies cited in footnote 2, see D'Antonio and Form; A. H. Whiteford, *Two Cities of Latin America; A Comparative Description of Social Classes* (New York, 1964); and Gary Hoskin, *Community Power and Political Modernization: A Study of a Venezuelan City* (Unpublished dissertation, University of Illinois, Urbana, 1966).

4. Hoskin, Chapter 8.

5. Despite numerous journalistic and polemical commentaries on the upper classes and a few studies of the power structure of the *oligarquía* (e.g. César Augusto Reinaga, *La Fisonomía Económica del Perú*, Cuzco, 1957), almost no serious studies of the general and political value systems which motivate them are available, with the exception of the incidental coverage Oscar Lewis gave in his study of the newly rich Castro family in Mexico in his *Five Families* (New York, 1959). In my opinion, one can get some sense of these attitudes through reading certain novels. For Mexico see Carlos Fuentes, *Where the Air Is Clear* (*La Región Más Transparente*) (New York, 1961); for Argentina, Beatriz Guido, *End of a Day* (*El Incendio y las Vísperas*) (New York, 1966).

6. For a discussion of party types, internal organization, and structure, as well as functions in the region's political systems, see Robert E. Scott, "Latin American Parties and Political Decision Making," in J. LaPalombara and M.Weiner (eds.), *Political Parties and Political Development* (Princeton, 1966).

7. To cite a few examples, Gallegos and Betancourt of Venezuela, Galo Plaza of Ecuador, Belaúnde Terry of Peru, Frei of Chile, Bosch of the Dominican Republic, and Paz Estenssoro of Bolivia.

8. Vargas and Quadros of Brazil, Perón in Argentina, Arbenz in Guatemala, Figueres of Costa Rica, and Rojas Pinilla of Colombia, again as examples.

9. See G. Almond and S. Verba, *The Civic Culture* (Princeton, 1963), *passim,* for comments on Mexico. My own research in many Latin American countries for a forthcoming study on Latin American universities and political change supports their findings.

10. See Grant McConnell, *Private Power and American Democracy* (New York, 1966); Corinne Lathrop Gilb, *Hidden Hierarchies; the Professions and Government* (New York, 1966); and W. A. Glaser and D. L. Sills (eds.), *The Government of Associations* (Totowa, New Jersey, 1966).

11. "Rationalizing" and "rational," as used here and throughout this paper, are highly elastic terms. They seem to have been adopted by social theorists from the economists' concept of the rational economic man, and applied to government in general and to political modernization in particular, as though some single standard of rationality in politics exists. It does not. As used on this page, for example, rational applies

to maximizing the peculiar advantage of a given interest or set of interests, but what is rational for, say, large landowners is not necessarily rational for the national interest. The sense of the term depends completely upon the context in which it is used.

12. See Anthony Leeds, "Brazilian Careers and Social Structure: A Case History and Model," *American Anthropologist,* 66 (1964), pp. 1321–1347.

13. Probably the most important of these is the National Agrarian Society, which has numerous sub-committees for various kinds of agricultural and animal industry activities. It receives tax moneys to help support a form of agricultural extension service (which seems largely concerned with the problems of the bigger commercialized producers) and, like some of the other organizations, names members to seats on governmental control bodies. Some of the other groupings include the National Mining and Petroleum Society, the National Industrial Society, the National Fishing Society, the Chamber of Commerce of Lima, and the Association of *Comerciantes* of Peru.

14. See Frank Brandenburg, "Organized Business in Mexico," *Inter-American Economic Affairs,* 11 (Winter, 1958), as well as R. E. Scott, *Mexican Government in Transition* (Urbana, 1959), p. 24 and *passim.* Compare C. C. Menges, "Public Policy and Organized Business in Chile," *Journal of International Affairs,* 20 (1966), pp. 343–365.

15. See Robert E. Scott, "Mexico: the Established Revolution," in Pye and Verba, for a discussion of the reasons for this slow development.

16. "Hypothesis for the Diagnosis of Social Change; the Case for Venezuela," *International Social Science Journal,* 16 (1964), p. 193. An updated version of this article, together with several extremely valuable studies of Venezuelan elites, may be found in Frank Bonilla and J. A. Silva Michelena (eds.), *Studying the Venezuelan Polity* (Cambridge, May, 1966).

17. See, for example, L. A. Costa Pinto and Waldemiro Bazzanella, "Economic Development, Social Change and Population Problems in Brazil," *The Annals,* 216 (March, 1958), pp. 121–126.

18. James Beckett and Keith Griffin, "Revolution in Chile?" *The New Republic,* 147 (December, 1962), p. 10.

5
The Military Elites

IRVING LOUIS HOROWITZ

Any social scientific examination of military systems in Latin America must recognize at the outset several distinguishing features which set them apart from military establishments in the highly developed portions of the world. These features can be conceptualized in terms of two coordinate sets. First, the Latin American military focuses almost exclusively on internal control rather than on international territorial struggle; thus however refined in weapons or organization it becomes, it functions as a political rather than a professional elite. Second, Latin American military systems act as the unique guarantor of sovereignty in their own nations; yet however firm this ideological nationalism may be, the military is functionally dependent upon foreign support and foreign supplies for its actual place in the national power structures.

Only by appreciating the contradictory roles and demands of the Latin American military, the strain between domestic legitimacy and international dependency, can the core problems of Latin American militarism be probed.

I. The Military Elite: A Source of Stability and Instability

Nothing seems more unpredictable than government stability in Latin America. Or rather, nothing seems more predictable than government

This chapter constitutes a synthesis of my work in the area of the military sociology of Latin America. Previous materials drawn from are: "Militarism in Argentina," *New Society*, II, No. 39 (1963); "Palace Revolutions: The Latin American Military," *Trans-Action*, I, No. 3 (1964); "Revolution in Brazil: The Counter-Revolutionary Phase," *New Politics*, 3, No. 2 (1964); "United States Policy and the Military Establishment," *The Correspondent*, No. 32 (1964); and above all, *Three Worlds of Development* (New York: Oxford University Press, 1966). No part of this material may be reproduced in any form whatsoever without written permission from both the editors and the author.

instability in Latin America. If we formulate the problem in the first way, we tend to throw up our hands in despair, for who is so bold as to predict the survival of a political system in an area of the world where *golpes de estado* are commonplace. On the other hand, the very predictability of instability opens up a genuine avenue of research in the natural history of military interaction with other sectors of state authority.[1]

Within a fifty-month span, from 1962 to 1966, eight constitutionally elected regimes have toppled: Miguel Ydígoras Fuentes in Guatemala, Carlos Julio Arosemena in Ecuador, Juan Bosch in the Dominican Republic, Ramón Villeda Morales in Honduras, Arturo Frondizi in Argentina, Manuel Prado in Peru, Víctor Paz Estenssoro in Bolivia, and the biggest "fish" of all, João Goulart of Brazil. Force of arms has knocked the props from under Pan-American rhetoric, and political schisms have crippled social alliances, for progress or otherwise.[2] In each case, a military counter-revolution effectively prevented a nation from taking its first vital steps toward development, the mobilization and integration of the masses. And in each case, the counter-revolution was made in the name of anti-Communism and national honor.

On the other hand, the dramatic—if often transient—role of the military in fashioning revolutionary movements in Mexico (1910–20), Guatemala (1950), Bolivia (1952), Cuba (1959), and Brazil (1962) is adequate testimony to the fact that in function and structure the Latin American military is by no means inextricably committed to the maintenance of the economic *status quo* or to preserving stagnant political factions. The military can function both as an agency for radical social change and as an institution preventing such change, therefore a precise inventory is needed for revolutionary indicators. The military establishments of Latin America perform different roles in different countries; at the same time, they can be contradictory in the performance of such roles even within a single country.

In Latin America, the military is often turned to as a court of ultimate national redemption, even while at the same time it is recognized that the military has often crushed democratic and constitutional processes. The military has been the traditional bulwark of anti-Communist crusades; without it, as several analyses make plain, nearly every Latin American republic would stand politically to the Left of where it now is. At the same time during the 'sixties, while Left-wing mass civilian politics declined everywhere except in Chile, Bolivia, and perhaps Venezuela, military Leftism has been growing in such diverse political climates as Mexico, Guatemala, Brazil, and Cuba.

"Socialism from above" is just as much a rallying cry among some military elites as the "anti-Communist crusade" was in the last decade. The military, in the *caudillo* tradition, remains an exemplar of lawlessness in its public behavior and of undemocratic processes in its political action. Yet it always makes its *golpes* in the name of law, legitimacy, order, and security. Finally we might mention that the Latin American military, as a self-seeking and self-promoting segment, has no peer throughout the continent; yet it is equally insistent (and sometimes properly so) that it alone is entitled to perform the role of guardian of the national morality and of the national treasury, since it alone has established international connections.

II. Comprehensive Types of Military Elites

Two broad types of military establishments are possible in any mature nation: a *professional* military under the direct supervision of civilian political leaders, and a *political* military which considers itself responsible for the definition and delegation of political authority. With the exception of the United States, Canada, Uruguay, Mexico, and Costa Rica, all American governments have political military forces.[3] In general, there is a high correlation between an advanced stage of economic development and professional specialization of military roles, which may be one reason why, *in the past,* the politically autonomous Latin American military establishments were loath to act as promoters of economic growth. In the absence of such stable developmental patterns, military men formulate policy—irrespective of constitutional "safeguards."

Within this framework of internal military establishments there are important and considerable variations. An astute commentator on Latin American affairs has singled out five types: The Caudillistic form, in which the national leader is invariably an officer in the armed forces; The Trustee form, in which power resides in the military but party politics is allowed to exist in civilian style; The Orienter form, in which deviant forms of politics are prevented from seizing power, while traditionalist or constitutionalist norms are not interfered with; The Consensual form, in which civilian government exists with the tacit consent of, but without interference from the military; The Veto form, in which the military acts as a faction in and for itself, but is otherwise without political power.[4] Thus, one can see that there is only a rough distinction between professional and political military elites—a fact which is just as true of the United States as any other state in the Western hemisphere.

It is characteristic of socio-economic classes of Latin America that each holds its own interests supreme in defining the national interest. National interest is thought to be nothing but a composite of the special interests. Labor unions believe their interests deserve absolute priority; the Church acts as a special interest with longstanding privileges; and the commercial classes consider themselves entitled to similar priorities. While every sector attempts to generalize its particular aims as being in the national interest, the Falangist shadow of special concerns is too long and too distinctive to deceive anyone.

The army has a well-defined ideology of national salvation and redemption. It views itself as the only force able to weld a national policy and enforce this policy on sectional interests through force of arms, if not by force of law. The armed forces believe themselves the stabilizer in a contest between social classes embittered by the gap between poverty and wealth. In Brazil and Mexico, this doctrine of the stabilizing factor leads the military to act as watchdogs over nationalized enterprises and entrepreneurial groups.[5] This stems from the directly nationalistic origins of the modern Brazilian *Tenentismo* movement and the peasant and proletarian pressures upon the Mexican army. In Argentina and Peru, the military functions to prevent the dominance of any radical mass political party, like the *Peronistas* and the *Apristas* respectively. This military balancing action in turn has its source in the uneasy coalition between the oligarchical origins and present-day middle-class base of the Argentine and Peruvian armed forces.[6]

There is little evidence to support a view of the military as a democratic force. Militarism rests upon the despotic use of force to repress extreme political movements, stemming from military claims of being the only truly national force. In fact, the claims of the military are usually no less partisan or parochial than any other. Too often, nationalism has been confused with radicalism. Nonetheless, Latin militarism is neither uniform in its goals nor in its sources of organizational inspiration.

The military has increasingly surrendered direct political control, ex-

cept for short interim periods. It has enough power to prevent governments unfavorable to itself from exercising authority, but not enough
to rule for any length of time. This then is a basic reason for
the instability of Latin American governments, which in turn may
help to democratize these governments by preventing the hardening of
any political complex and by minimizing the effects of already over-
developed bureaucracies.

Even where the forms of Latin American military organization tend
to imitate European military styles, the social structure and class
sources of power hinder the military's assimilation. Thus, Peronism,
which has obvious ideological affinities with the fascist style and
organizational affections for the German Nazi style, cannot really be
studied as a carbon copy of either. As has well been noted: "Perón
assumed power primarily as a consequence of his military position and
the previous actions of the armed forces. But of course both Hitler and
Mussolini assumed power in some measure despite the military, and
employed their armed might for war, a purpose alien to the ideas of
Perón, despite brave words about Argentine hegemony in the Southern
part of the Continent. It would not be unfair to state that the military
functioned in almost directly opposite manners in the Argentine and
European experiences." [7] It should also be added that not only did
Perón assume power as a result of his militiary position, but that he lost
power precisely because he lost his military pre-eminence. This too is
distinguishable from the European fascist phenomenon, where Hitler's
Nazi party apparatus all but wrecked the traditional military system as
well as the constitutional bases of power. [8]

III. Militarism and Violence

The more recent Latin pattern has been for the military to nullify an
election or intervene in the operation of an already established regime
rather than to engage in a prolonged *cuartelazo*. Then, after a relatively brief time, it returns the reins of government to civilian authority, usually to a more conservative faction than the regime ousted in
the *coup*. This was the pattern in Peru and Argentina in 1962 and in
the Dominican Republic and Ecuador in 1963. The *prima facie* reason
for the quantity of barracks uprisings is simply that after each one
government reverts to civilian authority. Since such civilian authority
often lacks countervailing sources of power, it must constantly come

up against the stubborn opposition of one or another military faction. Executive power cannot long mediate the claims of the entire society if it owes its existence to a solitary bureaucratic machine.

Today the military is strong enough to cancel democratic norms but cannot maintain political order for an extended period. With every other social sector in a like position—i.e. also powerful enough to disrupt governmental operations but without the strength to rule

TABLE I

Incidence of Internal Wars in Latin America—1946–60 *

	WARFARE	TURMOIL	RIOTING	TERRORISM— SMALL SCALE	TERRORISM— LARGE SCALE	MUTINY— MILITARY	COUPS— MILITARY	MILITARY ADMINISTRATIVE COUPS	QUASI-PRIVATE COUPS	MILITARY PLOTS	TOTALS
Argentina	1	1	10	16	1	5	1	8	1	13	57
Bolivia	1		23	2		5	3	3		16	53
Brazil			27	4	1	2	2	7	1	5	49
Br. Guiana			3								3
Br. Honduras			1								1
Chile			8	1				6		6	21
Colombia	1	1	30	8			2		5	5	52
Costa Rica	3		5	8						3	19
Cuba	1		26	48	2	2	1	7		13	100
Dominican R.			1		1			2		2	6
Ecuador			14	2		6	4	2		13	41
El Salvador			2				2			5	9
Fr. Guiana			1								1
Guatemala			12	10	7	2	1	5		8	45
Haiti			12	13	3		4	3		5	40
Honduras			5	2		1	2			1	11
Mexico			22	5						1	28
Nicaragua	1		2	7	1	1	1	1		2	16
Panama			17	2	1		3	2		4	29
Paraguay	2		6		1	3	7	1		9	29
Peru			11	2		5	2	2		1	23
Uruguay										1	1
Venezuela			15	2		5	4	2		8	36

* Materials drawn from *Internal War: The Problem of Anticipation* (Appendix 1), a report submitted to the Research Group in Psychology and the Social Sciences, by Harry Eckstein (Smithsonian Institution, January 15, 1962).
Original Source: *The New York Times Index.*

exclusively—the degree and magnitude of political disorder are a consequence of this unstable class framework. The best reflection of this instability is the extent of internal warfare, rioting, terrorism, and military and administrative *coups* (see Table I). Whether the originating source of such violence stems from the "force" of the state or the "violence" of those opposed to state authority is often difficult to ascertain. But the facts of such "internal warfare" are clear enough.[9] And every indication is that such forms of military confrontation are increasing in number and deepening in their violence.

The high incidence of military-induced civil strife, combined with an absence of international warfare, makes it clear that in Latin America the military has traditionally been used for internal repression rather than for overcoming external threats. The fiction that such military regimes, by virtue of their rightist characteristics, solidify hemispheric defense simply ignores the decisive fact that, as a potent deterrent against foreign aggression, the military establishment of Latin America is an extremely costly fable. Only if one is addicted to the ancient penal theory that an increase in the armed minions of "law and order" leads to a decrease in the quantity of departures from legal norms can one maintain that the military has been a tension-reducing factor in each nation of Latin America. It is more likely the case that to promote military solutions is inevitably to increase the ferocity, not to mention the extent, of civil conflict in Latin America.

A military establishment does not move without support. There is a consistent belief within the Latin American elite that the use of the military is justifiable for the preservation of patriotism, if not of politics. Many of the more well-defined social classes welcome the present military ascendancy as a visible display of national development.

As might be expected, the landed oligarchy and the conservative business elements view militarism as a means of national redemption—a way of recapturing, or perhaps capturing for the first time, a slice of international prestige, while at the same time protecting their own special interests. Nostalgia runs deep in Latin America; and the military elite is considered the preserver of national tradition and class privilege.

The middle classes, including a large and remarkably inept bureaucracy, support the military out of a fear that any civilian regime which would run its natural course, naturally and inevitably, yields its power to the numerically superior popular classes. An informal bargain is thus reached which exchanges political democratization for a fundamental integration of society along middle-class lines. Since military career patterns and bureaucratic advancement are also basic forms of middle-class mobility, the fusion between military and business elites becomes solidified.[10]

At the other end of the spectrum, urban working class and socialist elements see in the military elite at its worst an ambivalent force, and at its best possibly a positive force for national redemption. They seem to await a military messiah who can perform for the Latin American area what President Nasser achieved in Egypt or what Premier Sukarno sought to achieve in Indonesia—a socialist construction imposed from above.[11] This belief was reinforced in Brazil and Argentina by the populist (yet military) appeals of Vargas and Perón. As a result, the pivotal role of the military cannot be seriously challenged because it does have, contrary to sentimental belief, a broad base of popular support. Quite possibly this popular base of support may vanish once the failures of Ben Bella, Nkrumah, and Sukarno himself sink in.

Undergirding this broad base of support is a vast network of armed soldiers (drawn from the popular classes) and officer corps (drawn from the middle and upper classes) who deflect a considerable portion of the national budget and national manpower to solidify the military establishment, but who yet represent a prime form of social mobility.

IV. The Size and Budget of Military Establishments in Latin America

Table II indicates that the army continues to maintain at least a numerical dominance over the other service branches. What is not shown is the general rise in strength of the air force with respect to the other services. Cuba, for example, which hardly boasted an air force in 1960, had the largest air force in Latin America in 1963. In many nations of Latin America the size of the total military operations is frozen by constitutional edict. These maximum units are guarded over with particular zealousness by the army—which stands to lose to the other service units if these ceilings on military size and percentages are revoked or ignored. It should be mentioned, however, that the modernization of the armed forces has been only slightly hampered by inter-service rivalries, since the army has simply added air units to its already sizeable numbers.

Even the large figures in Table III showing recent budgets for

TABLE II

Distribution of Regular Armed Forces According to Branch of Service *

DATE	COUNTRY	ARMY	NAVY	AIR FORCE	TOTAL	% OF ARMY TO TOTALS [d]
1963	Argentina	75,000	21,500	12,000	108,500	70.0
1960	Bolivia	9,500	—	1,510	11,010	86.5
1960	Brazil	190,000	42,700	30,400	263,100	72.0
1965	Chile	21,500	17,000	7,210	45,710	45.0
1964	Colombia	15,000	6,800	1,100	22,900	65.0
1964	Costa Rica [a]	1,200	10	20	1,230	99.0
1963	Cuba	45,000	9,000	25,000	79,000	57.0
1963	Dominican Rep.	12,000	3,000	2,200	17,200	70.0
1963	Ecuador	6,000	3,780	3,500	13,280	45.0
1961	El Salvador	6,200	100	350	6,650	93.0
1965	Guatemala	8,000	—	500	8,500	94.0
1965	Honduras	2,500	500	1,200	4,200	59.5
1964	Mexico	41,800	7,500	3,550	52,850	79.0
1963	Nicaragua	3,300	200	600	4,100	80.5
1964	Panama [b]	3,374	—	65	3,439	99.0
1964	(Canal Zone) [c]	10,400	—	—	10,400	100.0
1962	Paraguay	8,400	300	400	9,100	92.5
1963	Peru	32,000	6,640	6,300	44,940	71.0
1963	Uruguay	9,000	1,470	2,640	13,110	69.5
1962	Venezuela	15,000	2,240	5,000	22,240	69.5

* *Sources:* Information drawn from figures supplied by military attaches of the various nations of Latin America; United States Defense Department estimates; *Statesman's Yearbook, 1965–1966;* and *World-Mark Encyclopedia of the Nations, 1963.*

(a) Figures refer to civil guard.
(b) Officially armed forces are under the control of police.
(c) Represents United States troops stationed in the Canal Zone.
(d) Percentage of army personnel is based on comparison with navy and air force units only. Figures do not calculate for special service units.

armed forces in Latin America are conservatively estimated. One expert has said that "in most of the Latin American countries the military receive 20% or more of all the funds expended by the respective governments in a given year." Argentina, Chile, Peru, and Venezuela are cited as nations having military budgets of between 25 per cent and

50 per cent.[12] In addition to such direct military allocations, there are the "private" armies under the direct aegis of local, regional, and state leaders which do not get calculated into the national budgetary allowances. We can only point out that in every Central and South American nation, there exist such security and para-military forces directed toward maintaining internal "order." [13] As will be noted in Table IIIB,

TABLE IIIA

The Total Budget of Latin America's Armed Forces *
(includes foreign assistance)

COUNTRY	POPULATION [a] OF COUNTRY	TOTAL [b] BUDGET	MILITARY [c] BUDGET AMOUNT	MILITARY BUDGET PERCENT
		(in national currency)		
Argentina	20,959,000	180,260	23,882	13.2
Bolivia	3,509,000	510,000	60,000	11.0
Brazil	70,528,625	477,249	54,793	11.4
Chile	7,339,546	98,100	17,800	18.0
Colombia	14,768,510	2,660,100	—	—
Costa Rica	1,237,217	345,751	471	1.0
Cuba	6,500,000	1,657,000	—	—
Dominican R.	3,013,525	125,990	33,300	26.0
Ecuador	4,396,300	1,922	—	—
El Salvador	2,612,139	184,900	22,994	12.0
Guatemala	3,759,000	121,029	—	—
Haiti	4,000,000	30,400	7,285	23.0
Honduras	1,953,138	100,400	7,700	7.0
Mexico	34,923,129	12,319,800	1,267	1.0
Nicaragua	1,593,007	253,214	—	—
Panama	1,067,766	66,802	—	—
Peru	10,857,000	104,830	1,916	18.0
Uruguay	2,800,000	842,500	733	1.0
Venezuela	6,607,475	629,260	5,221	8.0

* *Sources:* Information derived from *Statesman's Yearbook for 1963;* and from *The World-Mark Encyclopedia of the Nations, 1963.*
(a) Population figures based on the latest available census data.
(b) Budget figures are in national currencies, and given the fluctuation of the exchange rate, there is no feasible way of translating these figures into United States currency with any uniformity.
(c) The percentages of budget allocations for the armed forces do not include those monies spent for "para-military" or "security" purposes, which ostensibly are part of civic administration.

the figure for military allocation as part of the Gross National Product of each nation is considerably lower than that given in Table IIIA. The reason for this is that in defining the GNP foreign loans are not included, whereas in computing national annual budgets such foreign loans and grants are included. Where the figures cited include the amount of foreign assistance, the amounts shown for military purposes are considerably higher—in certain instances 300 per cent higher than when the GNP figures alone are used. Thus, Latin American militarism, if not a creation of foreign loans, is at any rate greatly aided by such carefully budgeted assistance.

TABLE IIIB

Expenditure on Defense as a Percentage of G.N.P *
(excludes foreign assistance)

RANK	COUNTRY	DEFENSE EXPENDITURES AS PERCENT OF G.N.P. PERCENT	DECILES	DATE
22	Paraguay	4.50	IX	1959
30.5	Dominican R.	3.20	IX	1961
33.5	Peru	3.00	IX	1959
37	Haiti	2.90	IX	1960
39.5	Chile	2.80	IX	1960
39.5	Nicaragua	2.80	IX	1960
44	Argentina	2.60	IX	1959
44	Venezuela	2.60	IX	1959
46	Brazil	2.50	X	1959
53.5	Ecuador	1.96	X	1959
57.5	Cuba	1.76	X	1957
61	El Salvador	1.58	X	1960
62	Guatemala	1.52	X	1959
66	Honduras	1.30	X	1957
68	Colombia	1.18	X	1959
69	Uruguay	1.02	X	1960
73	Mexico	.72	X	1959
77	Costa Rica	.53	X	1959
79	Panama	.27	X	1959

* *Sources:* Information derived from Bruce H. Russett, "Measures of Military Effort," *The American Behavioral Scientist,* VII, No. 6 (February 1964). Original materials drawn from *Economic Data Book,* Washington, D.C., 1962; and *United Nations Statistical Yearbook for 1961,* New York, 1962.

Foreign military assistance to Latin American nations is extremely high—in proportion to total budgetary allocations—totaling at least 25 per cent of all United States government aid. Thus, while the direct proportion of military expenditures as a part of the Gross National Product may not be considered exorbitant, the indirect proportion is exorbitant. Military loans, like other loans, are subject to repayment. And the purchase of hardware is, from an economic point of view, nonproductive; it falls into the category of consumer merchandise. Like consumer goods, military hardware also has a rapid rate of obsolescence, a high initial cost, and provides little opportunity to produce fresh capital.[14] Thus, the drainage effect on the national economies of Latin America is considerably higher than that indicated by the tables. Further, since repayments tend to lag badly behind military purchases, the interest, no less than the principal, is not repaid. Hence, the degree of indebtedness rises politically and socially, no less than economically. And this adds further strain to the functioning of Latin American social systems. Not only are they trapped between conservative and radical aspirations from within, but also by national commitments to development in contrast to international military aspirations.

V. The Integration of the Military in Latin American Societies

The Latin American military is not an alien force amidst democratic norms. As we have pointed out, it has a large base of support. Legendary mass heroes are often culled from military history or military mythology. More significantly, each social sector views the military as performing, potentially at least, a positive social function. Were this not the case, no amount of military aid could perform its intended "civic" mission. For beneath the contentment is also suspicion of the military. Under conditions of duress, the urban proletariat sees militarism as an extension of bureaucratic power at its expense. The bourgeoisie is displeased by the heavy costs of militarism which it must shoulder. The landed oligarchy is fearful lest military elites upset the feudal principalities. Despite an acceptance of the military as arbiter in the struggle of vested political and economic interests against one another, political ambivalence exists everywhere, which is in itself a basic reason for the instability of Latin American governments.

The military is largely recruited from the middle class whose values are currently oriented toward rapid economic development with a minimum of state intervention. Thus, while the military surveys and supervises political operations, it is constrained to do so in a framework of middle-class legality. In addition, excessive military intervention is effectively curbed, for civilian authorities have "weapons" of their own. They can act as a countervailing power to the military in many ways. Businessmen can either prevent or stimulate the flow of needed capital to foreign companies. Labor leaders can either repress or support general strikes. The bureaucracy can either restrict or encourage the import of machinery through variable tariff policies. Hence, in more developed Latin nations, the role of the military as mediator of political policies has very definite limits. Furthermore, if the people are made so apathetic that they retire from public affairs, or become so cynical about the future that they refuse to work diligently, the value of military intervention would be (and, as a matter of fact, is) seriously impaired.

This is a risk that few military elites can afford. The exceptions are Paraguay and Haiti, with their garrison states, hypocritical repression of the majority, complete abuse of civil liberties, rigid class structures, and complete collapse of political dialogue. These countries act to remind the more enlightened military of the high risk of armed intervention followed by thorough bureaucratic control. They are not usually models to be emulated, since this would only place the military in the position of advocating permanent backwardness and dependence on foreign capital. To do this would be a violation of their *raison d'être*—which is to act as a force for national unity and independence.

One of the prime features of instability in many Latin American regimes is the immature conception of constitutionalism as a juridical *limit* to personal sovereignty rather than as a device for guaranteeing maximum personal maneuverability. Democratic norms of political behavior come up against a feudal inheritance in which superordination and subordination are respected ingredients in politics. In the ideological sphere, the argument between Catholic "altruism" and Enlightenment "egoism," between medieval and industrial values, has never been resolved.[15] The highly personal world of the "big house" of feudal estates, where obligations as well as rights are individually assigned and understood, is a factor in political instability even in urban environments. The idea of constitutionalism, or a contractual society based on impersonal law, is held to be counter to the notion of the human being as a valuable individual entity. Perfect rationality moves toward a view of society which restricts charismatic values and the functions of informality so prevalent in Latin politics. Thus, basic to political instability is the persistence of traditionalistic patterns of culture inherited from the agrarian feudal society.

Another major cause of political instability is the use of constitutionalism for conservative ends—as a legal limit to personal sovereignty rather than as a guarantee for maximum personal liberty. In Brazil, for example, parliamentary members are directly linked to the landholding classes. As a result, constitutionalism effectively blocked major legislation concerning voter registration, literacy drives, and land-reform measures. It was only with a return to "presidentialism," with its maximization of executive power, that any substantial agriculture development programs were made possible.

In many parts of Latin America there is a powerful strain toward direct action, direct responsibility, and direct links to power sources, particularly under conditions of presidentialism, i.e. direct charismatic political control. The North American idea of constitutionalism based on impersonal law and commonly recognized authority moves against the impulse of class interests to preempt the mantle of national interest. This reflects a more fundamental fact of Latin American life: politics is a game played by classes comprising the money economy to the exclusion of those classes, such as the rural peasantry, which remain outside the money economy and firmly embedded in the master-servant, patron-worker system characteristic of neo-feudalism.[16] In a world of highly personalized work and social relations, it is little wonder that the rural masses see their solution as requiring an equally personalized world of political relations. The attraction of a personalized charismatic authority stems just as much from this feudal character of landed classes as it does from an inherent propensity of constitutionalism to perform as a conservative buffer to social change.

Where the shift from ruralism to urbanism, from agriculture to industry, shows an extremely uneven pattern, the military functions to balance legality and extra-legality (or constitutionalism and personalism). Men like Getulio Vargas and Juan Perón are, paradoxically, agents of both constitutionalism and personalism. They represent legality in their basic commitments to the idea of order and equilibrium. They also represent illegality, or charismatic authority and extra-legality, in their frequent intervention in the affairs of state and society.[17] Here the military elite feels compelled to maintain a delicate equilibrium between the legal superstructure and extra-legal revolutionary movements. Ideally, it must do so in such a way as to prevent the formation of a secular behemoth, while avoiding the possibility of total disintegration and breakdown of legal authority as such.

VI. Social Stratification and Military Elites: The Example of Argentina

The study of the military elite is drastically limited by an absence of concrete data. Because of this, the researches into the officer corps of the Argentine military made by José Luis de Imaz are particularly significant.[18] While it may be difficult to generalize from the Argentine case to the rest of Latin America, it is an excellent starting point precisely because of the presence of information unavailable for other national military elites.

First, it is interesting to note the extent to which the Argentine military has been "urbanized" along with the rest of the population. As can be seen from Table IVA, Argentine generals largely came from rural regions in pre-war years, but by 1961 only half of them did. It should also be kept in mind that the provinces of Entre Ríos and Corrientes are the most urbanized outside of the capital city.

TABLE IVA

Place of Origin of the Generals with Respect to
Regions and Age Groups

REGION	GENERALS ON ACTIVE DUTY				
	1936/41	1946/51	1956/61	TOTAL	% OF TOTAL
Greater Buenos Aires	16	42	48	106	42
Entre Ríos, Corrientes	7	17	8	32	13
Córdoba	—	6	10	16	6
Northeast, traditional provinces	5	7	12	24	10
Other provinces of the country	14	31	24	69	29
TOTAL	42	103	102	247	100

Table IVB makes it even plainer that the rural background of the Latin American military is, for Argentina at least, largely a matter of the past. This table, not being restricted to generals and not necessarily testing only for those higher echelon officers in active service, shows the urban impact on the military with unmistakable clarity.

TABLE IVB

Higher Officers of the Armed Forces with Respect to Branch and Place of Birth

	OFFICERS OF ARMED FORCES PERCENTAGES		
PLACE OF BIRTH	AIR FORCE BRIGADIERS	ADMIRALS	ARMY GENERALS
Greater Buenos Aires	64	67	42
Entre Ríos, Corrientes	7	4	13
Córdoba	1	4	6
Traditional Northeast	6	5	10
Other	22	20	29

Second, it is clear that the armed forces are becoming increasingly national and decreasingly drawn from ethnic origins outside of Argentina. There is a close correspondence between the urbanization process and the nationalization process. Table IVC shows the constant numerical rise of those with an Argentine background compared with all other national origins. Table IVD displays the same results in percentile terms.

TABLE IVC

Parental Nationality of the Higher Officers with Respect to Age Groups

	GENERALS ON ACTIVE DUTY			TOTAL OF
PARENTAL NATIONALITY	1936/41	1946/51	1956/61	CASES
Argentine	24	45	70	139
Italian	5	20	11	36
Spanish	1	10	8	19
Latin American	3	3	2	8
German	1	6	—	7
Various & lacking data	8	19	11	38
TOTAL	42	103	102	247

The great fear of the Argentinians in the 1920's that their country was being "Italianized" has of course proved quite groundless. The Italians, like other immigrant forces, became absorbed in the Argentine ethos by the second generation. Indeed, it is more likely that the similarities

TABLE IVD

Place of Birth of the Higher Officers with Respect to Branch

NATIONALITY	ARMY GENERALS (PERCENTAGE)	AIR FORCE BRIGADIERS (PERCENTAGE)
Argentine	62	68
Italo-Spanish	24	20
German	4	2
Various & lacking data	10	10

in Latin values and styles made the Italians more susceptible to "Argentinization" than ethnic groups from other Northern and Eastern European countries. Thus, as both the above charts reveal, the Italian factor tends to sharply diminish in the present period.

Third, real differences between the military elite and the rest of the population manifest themselves most sharply in occupational backgrounds. Only two members of the military elite examined came from working class origins; the rest came from middle-class backgrounds,

TABLE IVE

Parental Occupation of the Higher Officers

ASSUMED LEVEL	TYPE OF OCCUPATION	ARMY GENERALS	AIR FORCE BRIGADIERS	TOTAL
Higher middle class	Landholders	5	5	10
	Trader-Industrialist	18	10	28
	University Professional	12	2	14
	Military	16	4	20
	Administrative Head	1	2	3
	Self-employed	4	—	4
	Home Builder	—	1	1
	Rentier	2	2	4
Dependent middle class	Journalist	1	—	1
	Employee (white collar)	17	4	21
	Photographer	1	1	2
	Farmer	3	—	3
	Retired	1	—	1
Working class	Mechanic	1	1	2
		82	32	114

with an overwhelming majority having roots in relatively upper middle-class occupations as can be seen in Table IVE. This would tend to support the claim of a recent commentary that the Argentine military is not so much rooted to a defense of the landholding classes as it is concerned with the bourgeois system as such.[19]

Fourth, even the notion of military class composition, while offering more interesting contrasts than either the urban or ethnic variables, does not explain the current situation. What is forgotten is that an elite group strives for autonomy, and not just a role supportive of other elite sectors or other class forces. This striving for autonomy is well reflected in Table IVF. It shows that while studies at the military colleges remain relatively stable from 1936 through 1961, there is a quite noticeable jump in studies at Higher Technical Schools. Indeed, studies at such technical institutes are patently a post-World War Two phenomenon.

TABLE IVF

Generals and Higher Education

HIGHER STUDIES	GENERALS ON ACTIVE DUTY					
	1936	1941	1946	1951	1956	1961
Military War College	18	27	36	53	32	28
Military Technical College	—	1	1	12	6	18
Some special course	—	—	—	4	5	6
Without higher studies	1	4	4	13	14	8
TOTAL	19	32	41	82	57	60

Imaz indicates that a third of the generals are now military engineers. He says that this transformation from strictly miliary to technical concerns is "logical," for it represents a shift from a dependent to an independent institutional role.

Evidently, the manifest function of the Argentine military has not changed much over the years; it remains the armed force of the state. But its latent function is to provide cohesion and national integration to the successive stages through which the state passes. The difficulty is that the real functions of the military are not genuinely exercised by the Argentine (or by other Latin American) military: to preserve the national boundaries against foreign enemies. Thus, the military elite turns inward, and becomes concerned with its direct role in the state. It tends to seek functional roles—even if such a function demands a constant series of *golpes*.[20] Thus, the very autonomy of the military, far from leading to internal tranquility, accelerates the aggressive nature of the Argentine military. The hoped-for "professionalization" of the military has indeed taken place. But what has not occurred is its expected "Americanization." For in the absence of an internationally significant role, the military has fastened onto national issues. And this tends to work against the normalization of civilian politics. Instead, all outbreaks of political deviance are treated as national threats and as causes for direct and open military intervention. Thus it is that although the forms of militarism in Argentina have changed over the years, the functions of the military have not—thus heightening rather than healing the rift between civic and military elites.

Argentine social structure is undergoing a profound crisis of legitimacy. It is unable to establish legitimacy since its politics are guided by narrow class concerns. No single sector is able to develop a generalized rhetoric or a common ideology which would legitimize the social system as a whole. The role of the military is ostensibly to supply political normalization. However, the latent impact of constant military intervention has been to prevent *any* civilian authority from being generally accepted. The pattern of palace revolts is thus a response by one or another sector of the Argentine military elite to the possibility of social cohesion evolving into constitutional, nonmilitary terms. For this reason, the overthrow of constitutionally elected presidents in Argentina does not follow a Left to Right pattern, but is simply an assault on civilian rule as such—whatever its political orientation. Thus the liberalism of a Frondizi is as subject to military criticism as is the conservatism of an Illía. In this sense, military elitism contributes, in its very nature, to the destabilization of Argentine society.

VII. Revolution From Above and Revolution From Below

The military elite must guarantee the existence of legality. Because of this the extra-legality involved in military revolutions involves little violence. The balance between legal and extra-legal mechanisms of control is, nonetheless, breaking down. Charismatic authority contributes little to the long-run possibilities of social stability, so the precipitous actions of the military tend to be self-defeating. Because of the immaturity of constitutional and democratic norms, the possibilities of military intervention increase in proportion to the failure of most Latin American states to break decisively with the inherited political dualism of personalism and constitutionalism. Since Latin politics is a contest between classes from which the masses are excluded, and since the military elite is part of the larger class structure as well as being an autonomous bureaucracy, the possibility of revolutions from above, involving, but not necessarily affecting, relatively few people, is extremely high.[21] Where large masses participate in politics and government, on the other hand (and this means participation of representative forces within the state apparatus, and not simply regular voting), the possibility of palace revolutions is minimized. In Mexico, despite the historic sharpness of political and economic cleavages and despite its consistent one-party domination, mass participation has greatly reduced instability. In Argentina and Peru, where such barracks revolts are not held in check by a countervailing system of political power, their effects are considerably minimized. The wide gap between economic "haves" and "have-nots" is not as significant at this level as the gap between political "haves" and "have-nots." Military conspiracy is as frequent in highly modern Argentina as in tradition-dominated economies.

The phrases *revolution from above* and *revolution from below* define basic military extremes in Latin America. A revolution from above is a "class" change, while a revolution from below is a "mass" change. Where revolutions from below have taken place, or where political enfranchisement is both voluntary and high, as in Mexico, Chile, Uruguay, Cuba, there is a relative absence of a politicized military. In its place there has evolved a professional military or some kind of civilian militia which offsets the political military. However, too much emphasis on this distinction between professional and political military elites would be unwarranted, since the overlap between them is becoming increasingly pronounced. What is important is that revolution from below brings social stability and political integration after the revolutionary period, whatever the fundamental economic character of the revolution.[22]

A central feature of Latin American instability is its ecological-demographic unevenness. Historically, the coasts are well settled and heavily developed while the rural and interior regions are sparsely settled. There are many reasons for this, including geography, climate, and the prevailing attitudes of the people toward work. But whatever the reasons, the net effect on stability is disastrous. The center of political power is often the core of economic power, commerce, shipping, trade, and culture. Even more significant, the capital city, or the urban center, is most frequently the center of military operations. This high concentration of military power in one area sharply increases the potential for "spontaneous" revolutions from above. Revolution from below is less affected insofar as it depends for its success on the "historyless masses" who inhabit the countryside and who have traditionally operated outside the monied economy or the legal-political norms. It simplifies matters considerably to make a revolution from above, if the military encampment is only ten miles from the capital city rather than one hundred or one thousand miles away. Military concentration close to the vital centers thus encourages *coups*.

Brazil and Mexico are the only Latin nations to take serious account of the danger in such proximity. In Mexico, ecological diversification was achieved through the introduction of the state system as a counterweight to the capital city. In Brazil, too, the power of states is considerable. A special and noteworthy instance of planning for political diversification was the creation of Brasília (the inland capital city). Whatever its bureaucratic effects, it has introduced a new element into the nation. With Rio de Janeiro remaining the cultural center and São Paulo the financial center, the logistics of revolution from above become more difficult—although hardly impossible, as shown by the events following Jânio Quadros's renunciation in 1961 and also by the overthrow of João Goulart in 1964.[23]

The effect of the military depends not only on its ecological proximity but also on its symbolic threat to the execution of civil policies. There is a narcotizing effect on public action in the military presence. Such a presence compels revolutionary parties or reform movements to become more extreme than the situation may warrant. Thus, in intimidating the public as well as crystallizing radical opposition, the military, which fears revolution from below, only stimulates mass resentment by its own disregard of constitutional norms.

It must be remembered the military elite holds a favored occupational stratum under the present class-mass division. It represents the moving force in the bureaucratic apparatus; the direct link between political and clerical factions; and the product of traditionalist life styles. In these ways, it has an intimate line to the apparatus of political succession. But with industrial expansion, urbanization, and the increasing demand for educational reform, pressures are building for greater political democracy and the breakdown of the distinction between mass and class. This would harm the military elite more than any other group, since it is most removed from the values that come with industrialization. Even if the military establishments remained absolutely powerful, their relative influence would decline with such industrial expansion, as would the need for their political involvement.

While the military might fear social and economic development, its very survival in more developed Latin American states at least is contingent on its ability to ride the crest of development, and to see that its traditional advantages are not destroyed in the process.

The military elite has a long-standing fear of precisely the kinds of social changes that are necessary for Latin America and that are in the process of occurring. Most immediately it fears civilians bearing arms, for they would be least subject to its control. This brought on the *coups d'état* in Honduras and the Dominican Republic. The military elite also fears that the urban working class might organize and become a semi-military force, as it did under Vargas in Brazil and Perón in Argentina. The military elite would have great difficulty combating or controlling a large force trained in guerrilla tactics and strategies.

The military elite is neither totally opposed to socialism nor entirely in favor of capitalism. As a matter of fact, there are clear indications that the Mexican and Brazilian military are solid defenders of the nationalized sector of the economy—the petroleum industry, communications, steel, and electricity. Nevertheless, military nationalism does not necessarily entail a general radicalization of the political structure. Support for the Guatemalan regime of Jacobo Arbenz Guzmán (1950–54) depended upon the aid of the military and its willingness to support a policy of confiscation and land reform; but when such support threatened the political balance the military withdrew to its traditional conservatism.[24] Given the middle-class orientations of many military blocs within each nation of Latin America, military elites tend to stand in the way not of economic development as such, but in the way of those reforms which entail a threat to the higher bureaucracy. However, they can occasionally make a partial adaptation even to this. In Mexico, as noted, the political military of fifty years ago has become highly professionalized. In Cuba, a militia more or less absorbed the older officer corps—and destroyed what it could not absorb. Likewise, in Bolivia, mine-workers had a countervailing military system of such power that the economic system itself collapsed. In Costa Rica, the military has been abolished in favor of a civilian militia. In each of these countries, except Costa Rica, this transformation took place through violent social upheaval and reorganization.

In part, the high incidence of revolutions from above in the 'sixties reflects the growing desperation of military establishments—a fear that in post-feudal society they will no longer have special prerogatives and rights. Stability requires that these suspicions be lulled—even while the *political* military as such is eliminated. This is not easy. What can be anticipated is not the destruction but the transformation of the military elite and its redirection toward much greater mass support.[25]

The mass demands of Latin Americans have been transformed from class urgings for industrialization into demands for land confiscation and radical redistribution of business profits. The historic mission of the military to act as a watchdog over politics, to prevent exaggerated development of one economic sector over another, has been decreasingly viable. Militarism has weakened the chances of a peaceful resolution of the land distribution problem and has reinforced traditionalist patterns of behavior. We can anticipate a period of bitter strife between deracinated military and the "newer" sectors of Latin American society, particularly those that are no longer bound by the economics of nostalgia or by machine-gun politics. Until this battle is fought, Latin America must remain, for all of its riches, a portion of the social universe described by that dismal word "underdeveloped."

Policies concerning the military must take seriously the oligarchical tendencies of organizations—which include the drive to survive, however "dysfunctional" life may render such a body. The Mexican situation affords an interesting model for studying how the military can be pacified during the transitional period from ruralism to industrialism and urbanization. The first stage is to meaningfully involve the military in problems of executive decision-making as part of the larger political apparatus. The second stage is to evolve a pattern of countervailing powers, in which labor unions, commercial agencies, religious institutions, as well as directly elected political officials, share power. The third stage is to *advance* and upgrade requirements for membership in the military elite; in short to link professionalization with skill specialization. The fourth stage is to develop a juridical apparatus which would effectively carry out political decisions without recourse to armed intervention. These stages may be sequential or simultaneous, depending on local conditions and on the nature of the power "mix."

The specific military situation in each nation is important if we are to come to meaningful decisions concerning administrative reform. In Mexico, and to a lesser degree Brazil, where the military are attuned to national public sector interests and ecologically dispersed, civilian rulers might initiate the third and fourth stages. In Peru and Ecuador, the task may have to begin slowly and remain at the opening stage for a long time. In Argentina and Chile, where the military are already in the councils of government, perhaps too much so, the needs may be to concentrate on the second stage, on strengthening countervailing pressure groups such as labor, which will be able to compete on equal terms with their uniformed adversaries. But in conditions such as those in Haiti and Paraguay, perhaps nothing short of total revolution could start the implementation of these four stages.

But much of this elite manipulation from above requires reconsideration of United States treaty arrangements and fiscal policies with each Latin American nation. This in turn will be effected only by the initiation of further "revolutions from below." No general solution to the problem of military elites will be forthcoming unless and until militarism per se is seen to be a structural defect in modern democracy and not simply part of a special temperament or passion in Latin America,

The study of Latin American military establishments has lacked a significant body of empirical information concerning their organizational performances or ideological perceptions. Unlike studies of the United States military, such as those by Stouffer [26] and by Janowitz,[27] we have no comparable studies of the actual mechanisms of command and consensus, of bureaucracy and ideology, in the Latin American military. What we know tends to be restricted to general studies on the interaction of military rulers with government functions, and some crude data on the size of military budgets, the allocation of these budgets to various branches of the service, and the number of people engaged in military service. But even here, our knowledge is for the most part more official than real.[28]

We know very little of the rivalries between military factions or military services, at either the organizational or ideological levels. We know, for example, that as a general rule the army will be more liberal in its position than either the air force or the navy; however, we don't really know why. It might well be that this liberal-conservative dichotomy has nothing to do with Latin American characteristics, but is simply a function of the land-based nature of both army and civil functions, giving to its policies a realism perhaps less present in other branches of the armed force geared to operating in the "unnatural" environments of air or sea.[29]

While studies are now underway to determine the recruitment practices, class, religious and ethnic backgrounds, and types of educational systems relevant to the Latin American military, these have thus far not been linked to political behavior.[30] We can hardly be sure that such sociological information is even relevant to an understanding of schisms within the armed forces now evident in nearly every nation of the hemisphere, including our own.

VIII. Qualitative Indicators of Latin American Militarism

Statistics on the Latin American military are very important. Doubtless, the better our factual information is the more we will appreciate the objective circumstances of military power. But for a sufficiently accurate index of military determination of political events, we have to examine the qualitative problems as well. The social structure of military establishments has yet to be examined with the exactitude necessary to give us a better insight into the complex nature of the problem of Latin American militarism.

1) THE PROBLEM OF SPLENDID ISOLATION

In Latin America there is neither a particularly pronounced militarization of the civilian population as there was in Nazi Germany, nor is there any attempt at a "civilianization" of the military, as there was in India under Gandhi and the early years of the Nehru government. In Latin America the separateness of military from civilian functions is underscored by the proximity of the military encampments to the civilian population centers. Often the barracks are close to the main cities, but rarely are they actually part of the main cities. This symbiotic relationship tends to underscore the watchdog properties of the military, their constant surveillance over the political situation. While on the surface this would enable one to study the national military more readily, their furtiveness, their fear of negative publicity, and their bureaucratic discipline at the officer level all serve to make the study of national military establishments quite difficult, particularly in times of relative tranquillity. For the most part, barracks revolts and *golpes* are rare enough and short enough in duration not to upset this self-imposed Olympian isolation.[31] The ecological proximity serves to reinforce Bonapartist attitudes so that even radical military sectors tend to be highly elitist and undemocratic in character.

2) PROBLEM OF A ROSE BY ANY OTHER NAME

The definition of what actually constitutes a military system often shifts. The military has made use of military, gendarmes, and even traffic police for its duties in nations such as Costa Rica, where in 1965 the civic militia was sent into battle during the Dominican Civil War.

In Buenos Aires, for example, political activists fear the riot-prevention techniques of the city police far more than the activities of the ordinary, ill-kempt, unconcerned infantry conscripts. Indeed, the distinction between the police and army troops in Buenos Aires begins precisely with the physical appearance of both groups. It is plain to see that the smartly styled police are far more feared by the civilian population than are the ragged army troops; and for quite sound reasons. The existence of legally sanctioned but localized para-military units raises the problem of what actually constitutes an army. Since the civilian functions of the police are subordinate to its military functions in terms of such events as riot control, it is quite difficult to know the actual distribution of military power even within orthodox uniformed troops in charge of defending law and order.

3) THE PROBLEM OF THE PRIVATE ARMY

Some large latifundists, often in co-operation with the local heads of power or state governors, run their own armies—a remnant of feudalism. This was made particularly plain in the Brazilian *coup* of April 1964. Unlike the United States, these state militias are basically uncoordinated with each other or with any of the national armies. Their actual military activities may be much like a Reserve Corps, functioning in terms of weekly drill patterns, while the rest of the time they function for the plantation economy. But their presence is felt beyond the military mobilization period. They constitute a shadow military force. How forceful they can be is reflected in Adhemar de Barros's command of 40,000 privately controlled troops during the uprising

which deposed the Goulart regime.[32] Thus it is that the feudal sector
of the economy has itself generated a feudalistic pattern of armed establishments. To the best of my knowledge, these private armies have
never been studied or accounted for in the literature of social science.

4) THE PROBLEM OF A PEOPLE'S ARMY

There are of course insurrectionary forces. The rise of guerrilla insurgency in Cuba, Venezuela, Paraguay, Peru, Guatemala, and even in
countries such as Argentina and Brazil, may also be considered a remnant of feudalism, or at least a response to backwardness. These
guerrillas are not so much para-military as they are semi-military. Like
the private armies run by the big landholding estates, the men in these
forces often function in terms of peasant activities and peasant modes
of production. Like the private armies, they too tend to be unconcerned, unintimidated by the stable armies mobilized within the big
urban centers. People's armies differ structurally from private armies in
several important details. Private armies oftentimes have their leadership recruited from local sheriffs and police officers who control the
rural areas. The leadership of people's armies tends to be drawn from
city intellectuals who completely submerge their old personalities into
the needs of the People's Front and who oftentimes manage to work
out arrangements with local potential leaders among the peasant
masses. Without intending a parody, people's armies search for high
achievers, men who may be frustrated in their present style of life but
who prefer to fight rather than to migrate. The membership of these
people's armies has only the barest capacity to engage in sustained conventional wars. Their military training is ragged and at the worst simply an informal assignment of rank. Oftentimes training can initially
take place with brooms, mops, or local agricultural implements, indicating a lack of weaponry no less than of discipline. The strength and
élan of a people's army is oftentimes partly the result of stealing
weapons from the regular armed forces. The length of the actual build-
up period of a popular army is in some sense determined by the
amount of weapons which can be siphoned off from regular armed
forces. Weapons of North American manufacture are in particular
demand, since their parts are standardized and easily interchangeable.
An arms cache invariably yields a high proportion of United States
manufactured weapons.

To determine what constitutes a "people's army" is complicated, since there are times when people's armies may originate from or even become bandit outlaw armies. Such is the case in the backlands of Colombia.[33] Outlaw armies that may be adjuncts of either private or people's armies, arise in conjunction with kinship disputes. Their form is oftentimes quite obscure until the final phases of a conflict. The same was the case in the early stages of the Mexican Revolution, where similar outlaw armies flourished; as indeed they did in Texas during the period of statehood struggles. The ambiguous status of a "people's army" is a strong reason for avoiding a definition of the situation beyond what is analytically worthwhile.[34]

In sum, the four structural types of armed forces in Latin America are: (1) The regular national army under the control of the government. (2) Para-military units sometimes known as civic action groups, which are also officially sanctioned and are distinguished from the regular army by their regionalism and by their ostensible internal rather than international functions. But since it is clear that all military activities in Latin America serve an internal purpose, this distinction is merely formal. (3) The private army under the control of a local or regionally powerful latifundist supplied by the estate and responsible to his leader or at the most to a regional governor, but generally not responsible with respect to federal laws or troops. (4) The people's armies, the guerrilla insurgents, whose leaders may be drawn from urban sectors, but whose masses are recruited from the rural peasantry.

IX. United States Attitudes Toward the Militarization of the Hemisphere

Behind statistics stands policy. And behind the size and strength of the military in Latin America stand the policy decisions of the United States. It has been shown that in good measure, the entrenched military establishments of Latin American countries are underwritten by the United States; that such underwriting is made in the name of international or hemispheric security, irrespective of the actual uses of the military for internal repression; that the United States foreign-aid policies have increasingly shifted from a civilian to a military base; and finally that such policies are basically of recent derivation and do not represent a long-term orientation. Hence, they are subject to reorientation.

TABLE V

U. S. Military Assistance to Latin America *

U. S. OVERSEAS LOANS AND GRANTS–NET OBLIGATIONS AND LOAN AUTHORIZATIONS **

PROGRAM	Post-war relief period 1946–48	Marshall Plan period 1949–52	Mutual Security Act period					Foreign Assistance Act period			Total 1946–64	Repayments and interest 1946–64	Total less repayments and interest
			1953–57	1953	1959	1960	1961	1962	1963	1964			
Military assistance program	—	0.2	134.9	44.9	45.1	43.2	57.1	61.4	58.0	56.4	501.2	54.4	446.8
Other military assistance	—	—	10.1	—	8.5	10.3	51.4	70.6	5.7	12.5	169.1	--	169.1
Total military	—	0.2	145.0	44.9	53.6	53.5	108.5	132.0	63.7	68.9	670.3	54.4	615.9
Loans	—	—	13.6	2.3	14.0	11.1	12.2	6.8	6.2	4.7	70.9	54.4	16.5
Grants	—	0.2	131.4	42.6	39.6	42.4	96.3	125.2	57.5	64.2	599.4	—	599.4

* Data drawn from *U.S. Overseas Loans and Grants and Assistance from International Organizations* (July 1, 1945–June 30, 1964). Special Report for the House Foreign Affairs Committee (Washington, D.C., 1965).
** Computed for U.S. fiscal years and in millions of dollars.

The United States approach to foreign military appropriations is, in the main, linked to its political aims in dispensing general appropriations. Thus, for the years from 1945 until 1952 (the Marshall Plan years), aid to Latin America was kept to a minimum, while the form of such aid as was provided was usually nonmilitary. Between the years 1953 and 1963 (the Alliance for Progress years), foreign aid to Latin America increased tremendously, while a relative parity of military to nonmilitary appropriations was maintained. The present period is one in which the mix has gone over to the military direction, with a sizeable increase in the quantity of aid provided, and a noticeable increase in the military hardware under the newer programs. Indeed, it now appears that international trade has been absorbed by considerations of overall military strategy.

As an indication of the present mood of American aid and trade policy toward Latin America, we may note James R. Schlesinger's recent statement that "the threat to restrict trade has a clear limitation as a strategic weapon in that, like a missile, when it is employed it is gone." [35] The trend toward military assistance over civic assistance is further underscored by his remark that "in this era the 'supply effect' has shrunk in importance relative to the 'influence effect' in using trade strategically. In order to gain influence, one must put other nations in a position in which they have something to lose if they are uncooperative." [36] Thus, the concept of development as an instrument of national interest has given way to development as an instrument of American interest.

The military is not simply, or even primarily, intended to support a feudal structure. Quite the contrary, the notion of the armed forces as a modernizing institution, as an institution stimulating certain forms of capitalist development, when the domestic middle classes become impotent in the face of other challenges to implement such development, is the cornerstone of United States support for military elites. The contradiction is that any firm, clear-cut decision to maximize private investment would minimize military assistance, since the armed forces are part of the government sector. The task then becomes to convince the military to support those measures stimulating free enterprise and to oppose those measures, such as land reform and factory expropriation, which would lead to socialism. At this point, the other pole of the contradiction appears. The military are the dedicated upholders of the national tradition. And in nations such as Brazil, Argentina, and Chile, this means support of the public sector of the economy—particularly utilities and mineral wealth—in contrast to, even in opposition to, the private sector.

The existence of contradictory drives among Latin American military elites has been ignored by most United States policy-makers. For while evidence exists of these contrary push-pull factors on the military, the United States has increasingly come to regard support for the military as insurance for its general political lines, and for the execution of its economic wishes in the area. In nations such as Brazil and Argentina, when "showdowns" with civilian-oriented, public-sector dominated regimes did occur, the United States' faith in military conservatism did pay off. However, the examples of Mexico, Chile, and Uruguay would indicate that the military can just as easily perform the role of guardian of the public and civic sectors. United States policy has increasingly come to appreciate the difference between nationalism and radicalism. To the extent that the military operates within this bifurcation, and can link nationalism with conservative political aspirations, there is little doubt that the policy decisions of the United States will continue to be based on military grants and aid.

While United States foreign aid may not be directly used for repressive ends, it at least supports the military elites in the style to which they have become accustomed.[37] Of course, certain intangibles are extremely difficult to measure quantitatively, such as the ideological allegiances developed by mechanisms like the Mutual Defense Assistance Pact and the International Treaty of Reciprocal Assistance. The loyalty of old military elites to the established regimes are no doubt a function of their economic support, but the extent or efficacy of such loyalty is questionable. The strategy of "revolution from below" often entails a political strategy of "hyper-nationalism," since to eliminate the established military elite is to eradicate a prime recipient of American financing. This strategy places the Latin American military structures in a policy bind, since they are confronted with the choice of supporting the United States policy of using the military for counter-insurgency purposes and thus jeopardizing their self-created image of national redeemers, or supporting national redemption and jeopardizing their foreign aid supports. This dilemma defines the present state of most military establishments south of the border, and helps to explain why the military contributes to the continued political unrest in these nations.

Table V demonstrates that direct military assistance on a large scale is not a perennial feature of United States foreign policy but rather a very recent development. It represents the victory of "hard line" Defense Department views that the military is the most reliable and stable force in Latin American society. Prior to World War Two, New Deal policy was to eschew military aid. Despite some small departures during the war, the principle of nonmilitary aid held firm. In 1946 and again in 1947, the United States Congress refused to pass military aid bills. State Department attitudes at that time were elucidated by Spruille Baden and then Under-Secretary of State Dean Acheson, both of whom took the "soft line" view that military aid would prove detrimental to Latin America's economic development.[38] More recently, after the full cycle of Eisenhower Republicanism had run its course, pressure for a reconsideration of military aid policy built up once more. A special subcommittee study mission of the Foreign Relations Committee urged a de-emphasis of military assistance in its 1960 report, and John F. Kennedy promised a cut in military aid in his campaign speeches of that year. The issue remains in dispute.

The situation noted, what are the rationalizations and rejoinders of United States policy-makers concerning military aid programs? Essentially, they come down to four propositions.

Boomerang thesis: It is argued that if the United States does not supply arms to Latin America this will prompt Latin American rulers to turn elsewhere for weaponry and we will have made "enemies" out of "friends." This is the most frequently applied rhetoric and to the best of my knowledge has been openly challenged within government circles only by Senator Wayne Morse.[39] What advocates of this position fail to recognize it that the predominant position of United States nonmilitary assistance could easily curb any propensity to purchase arms elsewhere—with penalty of forfeiture of all economic assistance.[40] It should also be noted that Latin American elites are by no means thirsting for additional arms. Over the past several years, such erstwhile moderate leaders as Juscelino Kubitschek of Brazil, José Figueres of Costa Rica, Jorge Alessandri of Chile, and Lleras Camargo of Colombia have made strong appeals to the United States to direct more funds into economic development programs and less into military assistance programs. Thus, the boomerang argument is often lacking support even amongst those whom it is intended to preserve.

Bulwark thesis: It is argued that the Latin American military is the best defense the United States has against Communism. The argument has been put most recently and most forcefully by John J. Johnson, who maintains that without the military, every government in the Latin American orbit would be further to the left than it is now.[41] Ignoring the assumption that this resistance to any and all Left tendencies is a good thing, what real evidence is there for this statement? Very little. Military tyrants such as Fulgencio Batista, Pérez Godoy, Juan Perón, and Rafael Trujillo had little trouble with the Communist Left. Nor did the Communists have difficulties with the military regime.[42] It is the non-Communist Left, men like Juan Bosch of the Dominican Republic and Miguel Arrais of Brazil, who most often suffer at the hands of the entrenched military. On the other hand, as we have already pointed out, there are cases on record in Guatemala and in Chile where the military stimulated Left tendencies as part of a Nasserist or Bonapartist ideology. Thus, the bulwark argument lacks weight, either as science or as policy.

Hemisphere thesis: It is argued that the arms supply and training of military cadres are part of the overall United States strategy for defense of the Western hemisphere in the event of attack. This argument is heard with increasing frequency. However, since no Latin American military establishment could withstand a major conventional invasion, much less a thermo-nuclear attack, it is plain that the military are being trained for internecine counter-insurgency attack. This is obvious from the types of armaments shipped to Latin America by the United States—and from the rise in ideological "training."[43] This makes the notion, cherished by many hemispheric-minded government officials, that the military can be uniformly relied upon as a stabilizing agency simply preposterous. The hemispheric defense argument is the old Congress of Vienna "spheres of influence" doctrine spruced up to meet increasing guerrilla activities.

Developmental thesis: It is argued that the military can perform all sorts of civic action. The army, by virtue of its unique level of discipline and organization, can take part in essential projects for economic and social development—everything from public works to health and sanitation programs. The further aim of civic action is to counter claims that the army is by nature and function an illegitimate instrument. "As the interdependence of civil and military matters is increasingly recognized, the social and economic welfare of the people can no longer be considered a non-military concern."[44] Even a superficial look at Latin American military history will show that civic action often turns into anti-civic action, into conspiratorial acts against legitimately constituted governments. But there are other more weighty grounds for declaring this latest and most sophisticated approach pernicious as well as unrealistic. First, the costs of the military are exorbitant with respect to the minimal possible output they may make. Second, the character and structure of the conventional armed forces of Latin America are peculiarly ill-suited, in size and training of the officer corps, in temperament of the enlisted men, and in the outlook of the entire military organization, to perform legitimate economic roles. They are what they are by virtue of their political roles; it is difficult to understand why or how or under what compulsion they should become developmentally oriented. The myth of middle-class salvation has given way to the myth of military salvation. But as long as either sector remains structurally unaltered, the developmental hopes pinned on either force are pipe dreams. Finally, civic action, developmental programs, have the effect of making the military more political and less professional in their concerns. To the extent that they become policy-involved, they must become policy-oriented. And this means a deepening cleavage between the army and the people; between political and professional roles.[45]

Evidently these four rationalizations for maintaining and expanding hemispheric militarism are weighted differently. While each of the Latin American military elites might employ such theses to justify its own behavior as a way of joining a *raison d'état* to a *raison d'être,* basically they represent supposed United States needs in the area. This supposition is in itself the most decisive aspect of the present situation—namely, the breakdown of neo-colonialism and its replacement with imperial politics of a more classic vintage. The present turn to counter-insurgency as a style of politics marks a return to military solutions of economic problems, rather than economic solutions to military problems. While the form of colonialism may be classical, the content is quite new. The Marxian notions concerning the economic bases of imperialism seem quite outmoded and farfetched, given the economic costs and penalties of the present military actions undertaken or underwritten by the United States, with scant chance for an economic "pay-off" even in the distant future. Thus, while the form of imperialism has gone back to an earlier model, its substance is political rather than economic; it is more concerned with the balance of terror than with the balance of payments.

The age of Latin American *coups d'état* may very well be drawing to a close. They are no longer allowed to unfold naturally, because even the most conservative of them may have unanticipated international consequences unfavorable to the metropolitan center. What has taken place in increasing degrees is the external or foreign management of internal conflicts in Latin America. The study of this transition requires a supple methodological approach—one able to control for the degree to which the current "four-fold" military division within Latin American countries is either autonomous of or dependent upon external intervention.

To be sure, conflicts are still likely to be generated by the internal conditions within each of the Latin American states. But they can rarely, if ever, remain local in character any longer. The tendency is increasingly to transform such local conflicts into international struggles of power. Prior *golpes* were shaped by both internal and external forces. National and imperial forces performed a vital service of mutal reinforcement in overthrowing the regimes of Pérez Jiménez, Juan Perón, Fulgencio Batista, Manuel Odría, etc. But it was clearly understood that the external influence had self-imposed limits. The foreign power would provide economic supports, while the internal interests would be responsible for providing the ideology and the organization of the new system of government.

With the rise of overall strategies on a grand scale, with the assertion that the basic purpose of American national policy is to promote and secure a structure of world relationship compatible with the values of the United States and the Free World, local control, idiosyncratic regimes, and classical Latin strongmen can no longer be considered compatible with this master plan for a *Pax Americana*. This emphasis on overall design has led to higher degrees of planning and co-ordination in hemisphere military activities. For this reason chinks in the armor of design become intolerable. Factional military squabbles in the Dominican Republic obviously pose no threat to the United States or the Free World *per se*. They do threaten the *gestalt* of the grand design. And after all, the much feared domino effect can take place only in a context where cohesion and consensus are seen as total, and where any chink in the armor is seen to threaten the "system of mutual defense" as a whole.

United States policies of military globalism tend to make obsolete earlier efforts at a standard form of Latin American military styles based exclusively on internal political affairs. The decisive variable has become foreign rather than domestic, centralized power rather than autonomous authority.[46] Perhaps this is what Juan Bosch, former president of the Dominican Republic, was thinking about when he poignantly said of the United States military intervention: "This was a democratic revolution smashed by the leading democracy of the world, the United States. That is why I think my time is over. I belong to a world that has ended politically." [47]

The following nine-fold table will perhaps clarify the "external"

TABLE VI

TYPES OF PHYSICAL ENVIRONMENT (E)

O E 1:1 War against an enemy who has much the same technical sophistication as the United States in an environment with extensive industrial development and highly developed transportation facilities. Cross-country movement of mechanized forces flexible.	**O E 1:2** War against enemy who has technical sophistication, in an environment with high industrial development, but with only moderate to poorly developed transportation and communication. Cross-country vehicular movement is possible, but difficult.	**O E 1:3** War against enemy who has technical sophistication, in an environment with high industrial development, has little or no development of transport and communication facilities, and in which surface cross-country movement of mechanized forces is impossible or possible only in local areas.
O E 2:1 War against an enemy able to organize and operate armed forces using fairly modern weapons and equipment. Artillery; tactical air force; in an environment with extensive industrial development, highly developed transportation facilities. Cross-country movement flexible.	**O E 2:2** War in an environment with some industrial development, but with only moderately to poorly developed transport and communications. Cross-country vehicular movement is possible, but difficult. The enemy in this war is able to organize armed forces using fairly modern weaponry.	**O E 2:3** War in an environment which may have some industry, but little or no development of transport and communication facilities, and in which surface cross-country movement of mechanized forces is impossible or possible only in local areas.
O E 3:1 War against primitive forces most likely to engage in guerrilla warfare. Lack of technological sophistication; no aircraft; no radar; rudimentary communication system; in an environment with extensive industrial development, including highly developed transportation facilities.	**O E 3:2** War against guerrilla forces in an environment with some industrial development but with poorly developed transportation and communication. Cross-country vehicular movements possible, but difficult.	**O E 3:3** War against primitive guerrillas in an environment which while it may have some industry, has little or no development of transport and communication facilities. Surface cross-country movement of mechanized forces is impossible or possible only in local areas.

TYPES OF PROSPECTIVE OPPONENTS (O)

characteristics of North American involvement in Latin America. The key item in the internal chart is political *sponsorship*; the key item in the external chart is economic development.[48] In other words, the doctrine which asserts the legitimacy of "limited war" also, and parenthetically, asserts the need for unlimited intervention. It is on these grounds that the issue of colonialism and development in Latin America is joined in its full fury.

X. Militarism, Peace, and Revolution

It might be thought that since many of the weapons and weapon systems of Latin American armed forces are obsolete, combined with their "inner directed" perspective, they therefore pose but a small danger to international peace. While it is correct that such weapons may be five to fifteen years behind the latest forms of weapon technology, they are being used in nations which are fifty to five hundred years behind the latest forms of social relations. Thus, the modernity of a weapons system does not uniquely determine the extent of the dangers posed to national tranquillity. As long as little parity between weapons technology and social management exists, the threat to equilibrium remains high. The fact that the missile system installed by the Soviet Union in Cuba between 1961 and 1962 did not reflect the latest stage in weapon sophistication in no way minimized the United States perception of a threat to its own shores.[49]

Of even greater significance is the fact that the types of guerrilla and counter-insurgency operations now underway in countries such as the Dominican Republic, Guatemala, Colombia, Peru, and even more advanced countries like Brazil, Venezuela, and Argentina, do not require the most advanced form of military technology. They need relatively well known and easily accessible or purchaseable hardware—helicopters, flame-throwing equipment, and chemical goods for defoliation purposes.[50] Therefore, the issue of Latin American military armaments cannot be dismissed on technological grounds. Indeed, the weapons now available correspond precisely to the kinds needed for the conduct of rural-based jungle or mountain warfare.

To say that we live in an age of rapid development is more of a truism than a significant observation. What is of critical importance is the exact character of the transitional process—not only in the sense of where we were and where we are heading—but no less the human agencies to get there. To favor multiple over singular causation is not to take seriously the possibility that some factors are more important than others in the development process. The commitment to rapid change is not necessarily well correlated with strategies for effectively bringing about the desired changes.

Without wishing to indulge in philosophic debate over the nature of determinism or causality, it is evident that from the social science perspective there are some variables which can explain a greater degree of variance than others. The political apparatus of sixteenth-century Italy and the economic system of eighteenth-century England are obvious cases where one or another factor is "basic." It is my belief that the military apparatus of twentieth-century developing nations has the same kind of "deterministic" properties. To be sure, like any system of determinants, it has its limits and perhaps even its deficiencies as an explanatory system. However, with the collapse of international binding agencies, from the Socialist International to the United Nations, and the corresponding strengthening of national sovereignty as a condition and touchstone for measuring political development, the role of the military has become absolutely central.[51]

The Latin American complex offers an excellent laboratory for showing the extent to which the military determine the game of politics in the Third World. The rise of guerrilla activities has been spectacular. Yet, it might well be the irony of hemispheric affairs that counter-insurgency units precede in time the formation of insurgency units. This, at any rate, seems to have taken place in the Dominican Republic. When aspirations of the popular classes are frustrated by military action, and when newly formed, foreign-sponsored counter-insurgency units spearhead the ouster of legitimate regimes, then a rise in guerrilla action is likely to follow. The exact causal sequence is important. If it is the case that counter-insurgency precedes the formation of insurgency units, then the self-fulfilling prophetic aspects of United States foreign policy may well turn into self-destructive action.[52]

Nor is this the only irony. It may well be that the emergence of insurgency units actually cement the relationships of the military to conventional civilian types of regimes. For example, after the parties of the extreme Left in Venezuela began a guerrilla campaign, the military elite, far from performing its usual role of canceling electoral norms, actually formed military sub-organizations (such as the *Fuerzas Armadas de Cooperación*) which undergirded the Rómulo Betancourt regime. In other words, the loyalty of the military elite to the parliamentary system was achieved by insurgency threats from the Left, rather than any reform of the military from within.[53]

It might well be that for ecological, sociological, and political reasons, insurgency forms of revolutionary activity will either be unsuccessful or simply unfeasible. The patent failure of insurgency in the big nations of the hemisphere, particularly in Brazil, Venezuela, and Argentina, makes it clear that insurgency warfare as outlined by Mao Tse Tung or Ernesto Guevara is not necessarily operational in highly urbanized and industrialized sectors. On the other hand, it must also be borne in mind that the deployment of regular troops, either of a home-grown or colonial-imported variety, does little to resolve fundamental demands made by revolutionary movements. If it takes between twenty and thirty thousand troops to maintain a cease-fire agreement in one small Caribbean nation, or ten times that number to hold a small slice of Asia, it becomes evident that it would take at least one hundred times that number to maintain an equilibrium in the face of revolutionary tides. All of which should provide sober food for thought to those devotees of *Realpolitik* who still believe that those who rely on international, legally sanctioned organizations are dazed romantics, or that the art of compromise is equivalent to the diplomacy of capitulation.

The study of the military in Latin America remains in its earliest phase, not because statistical information has been scanty but because theoretical issues are only now being raised. Is the military itself a determining pivot, or is it part of a general system of interest groups? Is the military ideology determined by the training system of the armed forces, or by the traditional social backgrounds of the officer-recruitment system? Is the military still tied essentially to old landholding classes, or is it performing middle-class tasks which its ineptness throws into the hands of a caretaker system? Can the established military ever perform a radicalizing or developmental role; or is the evidence of Mexico, Cuba, and Bolivia conclusive proof that only a massive frontal assault on the established military will achieve nationalizing and radicalizing ends? These questions can only be answered concretely when a great deal more information has been amassed than is presently available, and when the Latin American military shows a sort of candor which has thus far been noticeably absent.

Perhaps sociologists are finally catching up with the novelists of Latin America, who have long known that the key to Latin American societies are the uniformed men—whether they appear as night-riders on horseback or as sky-riders on wings.

Notes

1. For an appreciation of the possibilities in the scientific study of the Latin American military, see Lyle N. McAllister, "Civil-Military Relations in Latin America," *Journal of Inter-American Studies,* Vol. 3, no. 4 (July 1961), pp. 341–350.
2. See Edwin Lieuwen, *Generals vs. Presidents: Neomilitarism in Latin America* (New York: Frederick A. Praeger, 1964).
3. It must be mentioned, however, that "buffer" nations such as Uruguay and Costa Rica, while not having a political military, do not have a professional military either. They might be described as limiting cases—nations without a noticeable military pivot.
4. K. H. Silvert, "Political Change in Latin America," in *The United States and Latin America* (second edition), edited by Herbert L. Matthews (Englewood Cliffs: Prentice-Hall, 1963), pp. 73–75. For a more general study along the same lines, see K. H. Silvert, "National Values, Development, and Leaders and Following," *International Social Science Journal,* XV, No. 4 (1963), pp. 560–570.
5. For several significant monographs on the function of social classes in select areas of Latin America, see Helio Jaguaribe, *Burgesía y proletariado en el nacionalismo brasileño* (Buenos Aires: Editorial Coyoacán, 1961); and Miguel Othón de Mendizábal, *Las clases sociales en México* (Mexico, D. F.: Sociedad Mexicana de Difusión Cultural, 1961); and Pablo González Casanova, *La democracia en México* (Mexico City: Ediciones Era, 1965).
6. Cf. Robert J. Alexander, "Brazilian *Tenentismo,*" *Hispanic American Historical Review,* 36, No. 1 (May, 1956), pp. 229–42; and Edwin Lieuwen, *Arms and Politics in Latin America,* rev. ed. (New York: Frederick Praeger, 1961).
7. K. H. Silvert, "The Costs of Anti-Nationalism: Argentina," in K. H. Silvert (ed.), *Expectant Peoples: Nationalism and Development* (New York: Random House, 1963), pp. 364.
8. For an account of the uneasy alliance of the National Socialists and the German General Staff, see John W. Wheeler-Bennett, *The Nemesis of Power: The German Army in Politics, 1918–1945* (New York: St. Martin's Press, 1954).
9. See on this Harry Eckstein (ed.), *Internal War* (New York: The Free Press of Glencoe, 1964).
10. The strongest case yet made for the essentially middle-class character of the Latin American military is that of José Nun, "A Latin American Phenomenon: The Middle Class Military Coup," in *Trends in Social Science Research in Latin American Studies* (Berkeley: Institute of International Studies, March 1965), pp. 55–91.

11. Cf. Irving L. Horowitz, "Militarism in Argentina," *New Society*, 1, No. 39 (June, 1963), pp. 9–12; also Gino Germani and Kalman H. Silvert, "Politics, Social Structure and Military Intervention in Latin America," *Archives Européenes de Sociologie*, 11, No. 1 (1961).

12. Robert J. Alexander, *Today's Latin America* (Garden City, New York: Doubleday-Anchor Books, 1962), pp. 183–184.

13. For more information on this see the collection of papers edited by John J. Johnson, *The Role of the Military in Underdeveloped Countries* (Princeton: RAND Corporation Research Study, Princeton University Press, 1962); see in particular Johnson's own study on "The Latin-American Military as a Politically Competing Group in Transitional Society," pp. 91–129.

14. For details on United States foreign military expenditures, see United States House Committee on Foreign Affairs, *Staff Memorandum on Background Material on the Mutual Security Program for Fiscal Year 1960* (Washington, D.C.: Government Printing Office, 1959), p. 132; and United States Senate Committee on Foreign Relations, *Control and Reduction of Armaments: Disarmament and Security in Latin America* (Washington, D.C.: Government Printing Office, 1957), p. 15. For an informative general discussion of the military aspects of the Latin American policy of the United States, see Lieuwen, *Arms and Politics*, pp. 175–225.

15. Cf. Frank Tannenbaum, "The Political Dilemma in Latin America," *Foreign Affairs*, 38, No. 3 (April, 1960), pp. 497–515.

16. See on this Anthony Leeds, "Brazilian Careers and Social Structure: A Case History and Model," in Dwight B. Heath and Richard N. Adams (eds.), *Contemporary Cultures and Societies of Latin America* (New York: Random House, 1965), pp. 379–404.

17. For a comparison of the Brazilian and Argentine situations, see Heráclito Sobral Pinto, *As Forças Armadas em Face do Momento Político* (Rio de Janeiro: Editorial Ercilla, 1945); and Alfredo Galletti, *La Política y Los Partidos* (Series: La Realidad Argentina en el Siglo XX. Mexico-Buenos Aires: Fondo de Cultura Económica, 1961).

18. The various tables which follow are derived from the data supplied by José Luis de Imaz, *Los que mandan* (Buenos Aires: Editorial Universitaria de Buenos Aires, 1964), pp. 55–65.

19. See José Nun, "A Latin American Phenomenon: The Middle Class Military Coup," pp. 55–91.

20. See Merle Kling, "Towards a Theory of Power and Political Instability in Latin America," *The Western Political Quarterly*, Vol. IX, No. 1 (March, 1956), pp. 21–35.

21. Anisio Teixeira, *Revolution and Education* (mimeographed and circulated by the Pan American Union, Washington, D.C., 1961). Also, a very important monograph explaining this mass-class split in terms of "internal colonialism," Pablo González Casanova, "Sociedad Plural, Colonialismo Interno y Desarrollo," *América Latina*, 6, No. 3 (July–Sept., 1963), pp. 15–32.

22. See Daniel Villegas Cosio, *Change in Latin America: The Mexican*

and Cuban Revolutions (Lincoln: University of Nebraska Press, 1961); and Robert J. Alexander, *The Bolivian National Revolution* (New Brunswick, N.J.: Rutgers University Press, 1958).

23. Cf. Irving L. Horowitz, "Revolution in Brazil: The Counter-Revolutionary Phase," *New Politics,* Vol. III, No. 2 (Spring, 1964), pp. 71–80. Also see his *Revolution in Brazil* (New York: E. P. Dutton, 1964), pp. 279–304. In part, the problem is the late and still only halting development of Brasilia. The military *coups* in Brazil still need only the two big coastal cities to capture effective political control of the entire nation.

24. P. B. Taylor, "The Guatemalan Affair: A Critique of United States Foreign Policy," *American Political Science Review,* 50, No. 4 (1956), pp. 787–806; and for an impressionistic "insider" account, see Juan José Arévalo, *The Shark and the Sardines* (New York: Lyle Stuart, 1961).

25. On the bureaucratic potential of the military, see Víctor Alba, *El Ascenso del militarismo tecnocrático* (Mexico, D. F.: Estudios y Documentos, 1963).

26. Samuel Stouffer, Edward A. Suchman, Leland C. DeVinney, Shirley A. Star, and Robin M. Williams, *The American Soldier: Adjustment During Army Life,* Vol. 1, and *Combat and Its Aftermath,* Vol. 11 (Princeton, N.J.: Princeton University Press, 1949).

27. Morris Janowitz, *The Professional Soldier: A Social and Political Portrait* (New York: The Free Press of Glencoe, 1960).

28. Several efforts at collecting basic information on a regional level have been recently undertaken. On the Middle East, see Morris Janowitz, *The Military in the Political Development of New Nations* (Chicago: The University of Chicago Press, 1964); and on Latin America, Irving L. Horowitz, "United States Policy and the Latin American Military Establishment," *The Correspondent,* No. 32 (Autumn, 1964), pp. 45–61.

29. See the studies by Mario Horacio Orsolini, *La Crisis Del Ejército* (Buenos Aires: Ediciones Arayú, 1964); and Imaz.

30. While a number of recent studies have called attention to the socioeconomic aspects of military recruitment, to my knowledge none has thus far linked the service rivalries with differential status or mobility rates. For some first attempts, see John J. Johnson, *The Military and Society in Latin America* (Stanford: Stanford University Press, 1964), pp. 102–133.

31. Indeed, when outside foreign interference occurs, these barracks revolts are capable of being transformed into civil wars, and escalated far beyond the original intentions of the competing factions.

32. Cf. Horowitz, "Revolution in Brazil: The Counter-Revolutionary Phase."

33. Germán Guzmán-Campos, Orlando Fals Borda, and Eduardo Umaña Luna, *La violencia en Colombia: estudio de un proceso social,* 2nd edition (Bogotá: Ediciones Tercer Mundo, 1962).

34. For a sensitive essay on the need to select variables so as to highlight

differences in military response to specific circumstances, see Davis B. Bobrow, "Soldiers and the Nation-State," *Annals,* 358 (March, 1965), pp. 65–76.

35. James R. Schlesinger, "Strategic Leverage from Aid and Trade," in David M. Abshire and Richard V. Allen (eds.), *National Security: Political, Military, and Economic Strategies in the Decade Ahead* (New York: Frederick A. Praeger, 1963), pp. 701–702.

36. Karl Brandt, "Developed and Underdeveloped Ideas," in Abshire and Allen, pp. 707–728.

37. This in not to deny that the United States, at the turn of the century, had a full-blown imperialist policy—see for instance the papers reprinted in Louis I. Snyder (ed.), *The Imperialist Reader: Documents and Readings on Modern Expansionism* (Princeton, N.J.: D. Van Nostrand Co., 1962), pp. 385–413. However, this policy was abandoned by Franklin D. Roosevelt in his Good Neighbor Policy.

38. John Gerassi, *The Great Fear: The Reconquest of Latin America by Latin Americans* (New York: Macmillan, 1963), pp. 287–298.

39. See Wayne Morse, *Report on a Study Mission to the Committee on Foreign Relations, United States Senate* (Washington, D.C.: U.S. Government Printing Office, 1960).

40. This is the argument by two former State Department officials in their recent book on Latin America. See Karl M. Schmitt and David C. Burks, *Evolution or Chaos: Dynamics of Latin American Government and Politics* (New York: Frederick A. Praeger, 1963), pp. 36–8.

41. Johnson, *The Military and Society in Latin America,* 1964, pp. 143–4. See on this my critique of this position, "The Military of Latin America," *Economic Development and Cultural Change,* XIII, No. 2 (January, 1965), pp. 238–42.

42. Cf. Robert J. Alexander, *Communism and Latin America* (New Brunswick, N.J.: Rutgers University Press), 1957.

43. Cf. Schmitt and Burks, *Evolution or Chaos,* p. 38.

44. See U.S. Department of Defense, "Civic Action: The Military Role in Nation-Building," *Armed Forces Information and Education: For Commanders,* Vol. III, No. 14 (January 15, 1964), pp. 1–3.

45. For a critical evaluation of the developmental thesis, see Orsolini.

46. Prior to the occupation of the Dominican Republic, the Department of Defense issued a statement to President Leoni of Venezuela requesting permission for the installation of naval bases at Paria and Goajira, both in Venezuela. The statement shows the sort of global military determinism which is becoming increasingly standardized as policy: "The grave fact that a considerable sector of the Armed Forces have been seduced by ideologies dangerous to the national interests of Venezuela compels us to look forward to that time in the future when our own forces will have to guarantee the defense of the country; in support of perhaps that weak and small sector of the military which has not succumbed to the seductive voices of oppositional sirens." See Department of Defense, Request to the Commander of the Vene-

zuelan Navy to Install Naval Base, P-2, 16-2-65, Series 009, printed in *Marcha,* 26 (March 26, 1965), p. 15. In this same issue see Gregorio Selser, "El Pentágono conmina a Leoni."

47. *The New York Times,* Saturday, May 8, 1965, p. 8.

48. For the final design of this nine-fold table, I am indebted to the work of Seymour J. Deitchman, whose model of a limited-war matrix is surprisingly parallel to my own attempts at linking modern non-nuclear war and the level of the developmental process. But given the priority of publication of Deitchman's book, no less than its formal precision, I have adopted his model, with some serious modifications. See *Limited War and American Defense Policy* (Cambridge, Mass.: M.I.T. Press, 1964), esp. pp. 103–7.

49. For some idea of the immense power at the disposal of the Cuban armed forces, one has merely to note the following: from 1961 to 1963 the size of the combined military forces more than doubled—from approximately 35,000 to 79,000. Its air combat craft went from 86 to 325, and its 24 missile sites are fully equipped with ground-to-air missiles (SAMS). In addition, Cuba has 420,000 members of the civilian militia on a combat-alert basis.

50. The rapid accumulation by Argentina, Brazil, Colombia, Peru, and Venezuela of Bell, Sikorsky, Dinfia, or Alouette types of helicopters is indicative of this counter-insurgency phase to present military operations. It is hardly accidental that these countries have witnessed considerable guerrilla activities over the past five years.

51. See Stanley Hoffmann, *The State of War: Essays in the Theory and Practice of International Politics* (New York: Frederick A. Praeger, 1965).

52. See on this the recent work by Lieuwen, *Generals vs. Presidents,* esp. pp. 7–9, 126–9, 136–41.

53. See Robert J. Alexander, *The Venezuelan Democratic Revolution: A Profile of the Regime of Romulo Betancourt* (New Brunswick, N.J.: Rutgers University Press, 1964), pp. 105–17.

6

Religious Elites: Differentiations and Developments in Roman Catholicism

IVAN VALLIER

I

Religious elites and professional holy men hold a more distinctive place in history than warriors or kings. As experts in things sacred, their influence is visible in every society and in all civilizations. Moreover, as guardians of spiritual values and moral authority, religious elites emerge as key points of ideological ferment in periods of crisis and social transformation.[1] The revolutionary situation in contemporary Latin America is no exception. Thus special attention to its religious elites is warranted.

For the purposes of this chapter, "religious elites" in Latin America refer to the Roman Catholic Church and its varying, but evolving, patterns of leadership.[2] Within these generous boundaries, two problems are defined: one has to do with the elites' role in the adaptation of the Church to a changing situation; the other involves the bearing of these Catholic adjustments on the wider processes of secular development. Paralleling my restriction of religious elites to Catholicism, I make certain requirements of the term "elite." I do not limit its use to the top positions in the religious system—cardinals, bishops, and pivotal positions in the orders or diocesan clergy. My defining criterion for religious elites, especially in the context of social change, is the capacity of either individuals or small nuclei to exert a decisive influence on the development of the Catholic system or the wider social order, whether this influence is resistive, innovative, or neutralizing.[3] Consequently both laymen and clergy, by virtue of certain behaviors, ideas, personal qualities or position, may be included. Put another way, the problem of defining elites in relation to modernization or change must be examined in terms of capacity for influence and/or power.[4] My second thesis is that elite phenomena must be viewed within a historical context, i.e., within the institutional framework which gives social meaning to their activities. In the case of Latin American Catholicism this framework is the Church in relation to its history and thus to its evolving connections with levels and spheres of the social structure. Unless one understands the priorities, pressures, and demands that have grown out of the Church's problems of survival and adaptation, its current elite developments are left hanging in mid-air.

My argument in broad terms gives Catholics a strategic place in Latin American social dynamics. In this I shall make it clear that this role is not merely one of reactionary conservatism. Moreover, instead of viewing the liberal or progressive sector of Catholicism as a homogeneous, undifferentiated movement, lines of unmistakable division are isolated and described.[5] In addition, the sources of these various elite movements are only meaningful and explainable in relation to the Catholic Church's present attempts to rescue itself from a threatening, crisis situation. Finally, I maintain that the pivotal role of Catholicism in Latin America cannot help but give the new Catholic elites a formative influence on secular change in the wider society.

II

To know what the Church is and what lines of change it is now taking, we need to know what it was and where it stood in the traditional social order. The changes that are reportedly occurring in Latin American Catholicism today cannot be separated from its earlier characteristics nor from the mechanisms it relied on to achieve its objectives. This task of identifying the traditional Church's essential features, however, presents risks, since it is necessary to deal in historical abstraction. In order to avoid complete disaster, I shall limit my attention to several patterns which, in my judgment, are both distinctive and also relevant to contemporary elite developments.[6] Special attention is given to the traditional Church's connections with society, its organizational style, and its characteristic modes of dealing with problems. The things I point to are not meant as a constructed ideal-type, though together they may serve some of the utility of that device. Four patterns bear examination.

Pattern 1: During the seventeenth century, a deep cleavage began to

develop between the Church and the "Catholic" religion. Due to shortages of clergy, to the hierarchy's fusion with the ruling classes, and to
the missionaries' conception of Christian conversion, the Church soon
lost its potential for capturing and holding the formal loyalties of the
people. This gap between ecclesia and religious needs became institutionalized.[7] Although the Church continued to anchor its activities in
the cathedrals and chapels, Catholicism became grounded in non-
ecclesiastical social units: in the family, in the brotherhoods, in the
community, and along informal lines that bound individuals into their
everyday world.[8] A major part of the people's religious needs came to
be focused on and satisfied through extra-sacramental practices, private
devotions, "contracts" with divine personages, and by participating in
festive, religious social activities. The priest and his sacramental authority have thus tended to be peripheral to man's quest for salvation.[9]

Pattern 2: The Church, as a policy-making and administrative
organization, has undergone minimal degrees of qualitative development. The traditional system may be described as decentralized, extremely unco-ordinated in its regional and diocesan activities, and
structurally awkward. The Church emerged as a series of isolated
ecclesiastical units, each one focused almost exclusively on its local,
immediate situation. Lines of authority, channels of communication,
and notions of priority were weak, clogged, and confused. The
Church's activities were not tied to a set of central and shared religious
objectives. Autonomous, long-range policies did not emerge. Routine
administration and ad hoc problem-solving superseded planning and
programming. In short, the Catholic Church in its traditional make-up
was hierarchically undeveloped, internally divided, and relatively incapable of using its canonically based legal framework as an effective
system of command and action.[10] Consequently, its elite groups have
not been able to muster a clear and unified stand as *religious* leaders.

Pattern 3: Traditional Catholic elites have been subjected, over most
of the last four hundred and fifty years, to secular control. The
Crown's privilege of the *patronato*, its exercise of the *placet*, its control
over the Church's budget, and its jurisdiction over the opening of new
missions placed the religious elite in a continuous, frustrating situation.[11] Thus the hierarchy had to work through the non-Church elite in
order to initiate Church activities or develop strategies of survival. In
this situation, the clergy's energies were largely consumed by short-run
maneuverings, by building up viable coalitions with other power

groups, and in bargaining.[12] Survival, as well as visibility and status, depended on the elite's capacities for "politics": a maximization of short-run gains when conditions were favorable, the exercise of restraint in periods of uncertainty, and readiness to be inconsistent if the situation demanded it.

Pattern 4: By virtue of their image of the Church's mission and by reason of their various ties, involvements, and subordinations with secular society, Catholic elites failed to create and institutionalize a religious-moral foundation for the growth of an agreed-upon system of values. The bishops' and clergy's potential capacities to symbolize, foster, and demand conformity to a higher moral order were constantly weakened by their maneuverings and inconsistencies bred, for the most part, by the institutional features of the society. Instead of functioning as creators of a religiously based value system and as impartial leaders in the moral realm, the Catholic elites actually fomented moral confusion.[13] Consequently, a decisive and enduring tie was established between secular political strength and moral legitimacy. Latin American politicians have not only modified standards of the "good" to fit their needs of the moment, but have also tended to assume that power can create moral leadership and an agreed-upon system of values. This unfortunate perspective has interrupted the whole process of differentiation found in other cultures between long-range value-orientations about the nature of the good society and the mechanisms of its attainment. Politics has not emerged as an arena in which competition can take place over "who is best qualified to lead" but as a "religious" battle over ends. There is little doubt, at least in my mind, that this early tie-in between secularly based power elites and moral authority has played a key role in creating the political turmoil that is constantly being expressed in contemporary Latin America.

The central idea which emerges from these generalizations about the historical Church is that its achievement of influence and social control did not depend on its capacities as a Christian religious system. This is meant at the broadest level, since in certain isolated instances ecclesiastical power did come from strictly religious activities and the charisma of the clergy. But in the main, the Church and its leaders drew their importance from the support they gave to the existing powers and from their multiple involvements in education, social welfare, and administration. The scope of the Church's functions was very wide, each one dependent on the maintenance of the *status quo*. During the colonial period, the Church was linked fully with society. It was supported, protected, and given special privileges. In turn, the Church served as an agency of colonial expansion, as an administrative and economic organization, and as a key institution of social control. Vigorous local congregations and a responsive spiritual life were not imperative for its status or survival.[14] In the next major period, covering roughly the first century of political independence, the Church was drawn completely into the liberal-conservative struggles that cut through Latin America. This period served to align the dominant elements in the Church with the conservative sector, thereby forcing it to rely on the status, wealth, and power of these groups to carry its influence and to assist its defense. This was the Church's principal survival strategy as it entered the twentieth century.

III

The traditional Church, especially during the past fifty years, has in one Latin American country after another encountered trends and events that are forcing its elites to recognize a state of bankruptcy. The credits of the Church, built up over the years through political coalitions, a permissive morality, property involvements, and other worldly promises, are largely depleted. This crisis is partly due to the anticlerical attacks of the nineteenth century that forced the Church out of key areas of public life, but more importantly to a series of subtle sociological trends that have more recently cut across the whole social order: the growth of an urban-based working class, population shifts, a strengthening of technical and scientific centers in secular universities, and the emergence of aggressive interest groups making clamorous and immediate demands on the resources of these societies. Old and familiar lines of power, influence, and status are weakened and confused, if not totally broken.

Out of these general changes, brought on by both the evolution of Western civilization and by indigenous strivings, three developments have appeared to render traditional Catholicism's position of influence especially problematic: new value movements; a changed basis of social control and group integration in society; and certain pressures of non-Latin American Catholic hierarchies on the leaders and laity of the national churches. Each of these threats deserves separate comment.

Local—New value movements Until the turn of this century, Catholicism held a dual monopoly. It stood, on the one hand, as the official national religion of these republics (and in some cases, still does). In addition, Catholicism held an undisputed dominance as a general religious culture. Most of the value-orientations, ways of thinking, and notions of rightness were part and parcel of the Catholic religious framework. Even anticlerical intellectuals of the nineteenth century willingly evidenced deep respect and feeling for this overarching religious phenomenon.

Two kinds of radical movements, both arising within the past half century, have helped to break this cultural monopoly of Catholicism: political movements of the left [15] and salvation-oriented Protestant sects.[16] Both movements preach a new reward system, assume a militant posture against the existing social order, and articulate a cohesive set of anti-Catholic values. The rapid growth of these movements between the First World War and 1950 severed the Latin American value system, at least in some countries, from the Catholic religious system. Chile, of course, stands out in this respect. Mexico, somewhat a special case, went through the same process, though with violence and abruptness. Brazil would appear to be almost as far along as Chile. But the important thing is that, for the first time, a line was cut between a value system fused with Catholicism and a non-Catholic value system. Where the earlier anticlerical movement had forced the Church, as an organization, out of certain public spheres, these new value movements forced the religion to take a competitive position at the level of major values. In one sense, Catholicism was pushed down one level of social control, taking on the color of an ideology for the conservative groups. One outcome of this shift was the Church's new position where its fortunes rested with a limited segment of society and one which, in terms of rapidly growing social trends, was on the decline.

But the competition at the level of values turned out to be only one of the threats posed by those new value movements. Besides offering a whole new framework of "salvation," new meanings, and new categories of evaluation, they also provided the adherents with a "program" and a "strategy of action" in society. Moreover, both the Communist-Socialist movement and the Protestant Pentecostal movement sponsored a lay-type organization that gave new members, as well as veterans, key statuses that linked enthusiasm with group responsibility.[17] Thus, the Catholic Church was up against morally oriented action systems that both penetrated society at the grass roots (and among groups that the Church could not even attempt to recognize) and also provided the membership with "opportunity structures" which, in most instances, served as effective bridging mechanisms between commitment and key organizational tasks. The layman, even the novice, found himself with a definite status, a set of meaningful activities, and with delegated responsibility, e.g. contacting potential members, "selling the gospel," and so on.

The traditional Catholic system, as I have already indicated, is ill-equipped to counter these militant, focused, sect-type value movements. For more than four centuries, the "ordinary member" was overlooked as a religious system resource. No attempts were made by the hierarchy either to integrate the layman into the religious organization or to provide him with a set of meaningful responsibilities. This is not surprising. Theological reasons aside (having to do with the *official* status of the layman), the traditional Catholic system in Latin America has not had to groom the layman as an instrument of religious influence or anchorage, since, in fact, the whole Catholic system was sponsored, protected, supported, and cradled by the total society, especially its political machinery. Why, then, should the grass roots, or the laity, be shaped, organized, and delegated to "win the neighbor"? All the neighbors were baptized Catholics, so were the people of the next village, so too were *patrones* and slaves, peasants and military officers. In short, the building up and channeling of a membership-based religious enthusiasm were not essential to the operation and viability of the traditional Catholic system.

One further characteristic of the new value movements deserves attention, for again it is something that the traditional Catholic system is unable to offer. I have in mind the emphasis placed in these new value movements on strong person-to-person bonds or "horizontal solidarity," implicit in such phrases as "from each according to his ability; to each according to his needs" and "we are all brothers in Christ: no priests, no servants, no rich, no poor." The Communists and Socialists, as well as the Pentecostal sects, stressed these dimensions both ideologically and structurally. Contrast this with the traditional conceptions of status in the Catholic organization: priest above people, bishop above priest, and pope above all. Even within the laity, the social lines of division (class, family, ethnic, etc.) were allowed to hold their distinct visibility. Those who worshiped regularly within the same church building did not constitute a solidarity-based congregation, but a random assortment of differential social statuses juxtaposed in proximity for the duration of the Mass. Traditional Catholicism cannot provide the membership with religious conceptions that link men to other men in a form of familiar solidarity. For this type of gratification, the Catholic had to turn to family, friends, co-villagers, and extended kin. It is not surprising then to find that in Latin America these socially meaningful relationships are resistant to change and modification.

National—The emergence of a new rhythm and a challenge The second major stimulus that is increasingly pushing the Church toward self-evaluation, new strategies, and differing alignments with the secular world is less easily defined and conceptualized. But it is no less significant. For want of a better term, I shall refer to this second stimulant as the aggregate effects of a modern society's rhythm—that is, there is a characteristic tendency for a modern, nationally focused society to move and adapt, as a total system. As the Latin American countries develop economically and politically, a qualitatively different type of institutional interdependence emerges, binding all specialized functional units into a more functionally integrated whole. Thus, the *primary* integrative level of an industrializing country is found at the level of the total society, not in terms of regional or local (community, family, ethnic) units. This broad and often loose form of national integration characteristically generates its own peculiar dynamic which is expressed variously through geographical and social mobility, through the interplay of organized group interests, and in the continual adjustment of old norms to new emphases that emerge in the wake of innovation, structural change, and population shifts. National events dominate the rhythm of social life and are quickly transmitted, with varying repercussions, to all levels of human activity. This means that special interests, such as influence-oriented religious groups, require clear-cut national strategies and forceful national organizations if they are to make an impact. Furthermore, behaviors in key institutional spheres are highly segregated, thereby decreasing the possibility of controlling and influencing people through a single type of public activity. Thus, in order for a Church to "get at the people," more is required than programs of limited, local dimensions; more is required than ad hoc, short-run coalitions and maneuverings. Similarly, a program that is developed to gain influence at one point in time or in one geographical area may have to be quickly modified and/or shifted in location and emphasis, simply because residential and social involvements constantly undergo change, often quite abruptly. The web of life is difficult to hold in focus, except at the national level, and even more difficult to control. Transiency, flux, and movement—even though patterned within a broad institutional setting—give the modern, industrial society the mark of a ceaselessly flowing current.

Threats emerge from all sides: increased competition with secular, public agencies in areas of human need, the loss of control lines or connections with strategic centers of social control, and a reduced visibility in the sphere of religious leadership. In all of this, there is a marked uncertainty about "religious needs," an ambivalence over the proper functions of the Church, a confusion over priorities, a search for new resources, and a deep frustration bred by a vision of possibility and a simultaneous realization of inadequacy.

These developments hold a number of basic implications for an ambitious religious system. Several organizational tasks become imperative.[18] First, the religious impact has to be planned, developed, and aimed along lines that catch hold of the total society's trends, rhythms, and problems. Second, gains or attempted gains require action—a conscious reaching out to society and co-ordinated maneuvering. Loyalty must be generated, not simply gathered. Third, religious programs must meet at least two organizational criteria: a steady, long-term sense of direction and a short-range, local flexibility. Specialization and performance must be matched by centralized decision-making and effective co-ordination.

Traditional Catholicism, accustomed to maintaining its position through ad hoc problem-solving, local adaptations, and alignment with prominent status groups (now on the way out), possesses limited organizational capacity to deal with this new rhythm of social life, particularly with regard to achieving an effective competitive position in a web of social control that has been radically altered. The Church is still, in many cases, given to passivity and informal maneuvering, and is still susceptible to norms and pressures in many particular situations. It is thus extremely handicapped. From its long years of accumulated involvements with multiple, concrete aspects of traditional life, it now finds the task of gathering itself together for purposes of building an overdue offensive next to impossible.

International—Non-Latin American Catholic hierarchies Unbeknown to some observers of contemporary Latin American Catholicism, the Church is being put under heavy pressure by the various hierarchies of international Catholicism. Astute Roman Catholic leaders, representing the entire spectrum from the papacy to various national episcopal conferences (in France, Belgium, Germany, Canada, and the United States), are evidencing a first-order concern with the Church's problems in Latin America.[19] Pressures are thereby placed on Latin American prelates to put their house in order. There are several reasons for this outside interest. Latin America not only encompasses more than one-third of the Church's total baptized membership but, as well, appears to be particularly susceptible to political seductions of the Communist variety. Equally important, the Second Vatican Council, initiated in 1962 and now completed, is quite plainly focused around issues, policies, and innovations that bear directly on the problems found in traditional Latin American Catholicism. No one can overlook the connections between the current emphases on liturgical innovations, the principle of collegiality, theological reforms, or extra-Catholic ecumenicity and the present crisis of the Church in lands south of the border. Since Latin America undoubtedly stands as one of the key "test sites" for contemporary Catholicism, and since the Second Vatican Council is considered to be the major instrument for "bringing the Church up to date," it follows that the test of the Council is to be found in what happens to Catholicism in Latin America. Thus, the question is not, as one writer has put it, "Is not this council the last chance for Latin American Catholicism?"[20] but, rather, is not the Latin American situation the last chance for the Catholic religion? A recent Latin American spokesman put the problem quite well when he wrote that "Latin America is in fact the 'test' of the Council: will it give Christians the means by which to overcome the Church's difficulties?"[21]

IV

Under these pressures, Catholic leaders are desperately seeking formulas and plans of action that will both strengthen the Church's spiritual life and give it new bases of influence in the wider institutional order. By consequence, new ideas, diagnostic appraisals, and proposed "solutions" proliferate. Some of these plans are utopian and visionary; some are pragmatic and moderate; others tend to be regressive. Manpower problems are crucial, not only in terms of lowering the ratio between clergy and members but also in terms of the Church's special intellectual, administrative, and "political" needs. Talent and leadership, including theologians (*periti*), sociologists, planners, educators, and "efficiency" experts, are being drawn from many places throughout the world, notably Western Europe. Some of these specialists arrive, of course, with their own notions of priority and more than a little personal charisma. They increase already present internal divisions as well as the general atmosphere of uncertainty.

The patterns that are emerging from this new phase of the Church are shadowy and largely unformed. Information is hard to come by, not only due to communication barriers that often exist between outsiders and Church elites, but also because many of the members of these elite groups do not themselves know what direction to take or where to place priorities. They have "hunches" and can group some of the surface activities into recognizable patterns, but the nature of the new Church is far from decided at this point. As Troeltsch put it more than fifty years ago, with reference to the future of Christianity in Europe: "What the new house will look like, and what possibilities it will provide . . . no one at present can tell." [22]

In this indeterminate period, elite developments may appear random unless approached with definite analytical frames of reference. Here I make use of two such frames: elite patterns connected with changes in ecclesiastical organization, Catholic ideology, and membership responsibilities which, in combination, flow from the Church's formal efforts to bring about an effective type of adaptation; and elite patterns that crosscut these manifest themes, emerging more along diffuse, informal lines and stemming essentially from a search for viable solutions to the problem of the relation between Catholicism and the social order. [23]

TRANSFORMING THE CHURCH AS SYSTEM

Considerable amounts of energy and leadership talent in the Latin American Church are being channeled into tasks that are aimed toward shifting the traditional Church into a new phase of relevance and effectiveness. [24] The first theme may be called "centralization," since the activities involve the establishment of tighter linkages within the hierarchies and the enlargement of the *de facto* powers of national and intra-Latin American episcopal conferences and councils. The whole pattern of vertical integration within the Church is being overhauled. The former autonomy and local isolation of the bishops have been reduced through the co-ordinating activities of high-ranking episcopal commissions, national and regional secretariats, and new departments with specialized functional responsibilities. The local clergy are rapidly being drawn into a series of new policies which orient them and their pastoral work to the needs, goals, and activities of the total Church. Communication networks are growing around such long-standing problems as vocations, pastoral methods, liturgical customs, and the lay apostolate. In Chile and Brazil, definite gains are evident in setting explicit goals and defining long-range policies that provide a direction of action above and beyond the demands of everyday, routine administration.[25]

Other themes of elite activity are emerging. The creation of a socially relevant Catholic ideology is generating one important cluster. In this matter, priests and intellectuals draw heavily from the social encyclicals and the new theologies that have been produced in the Church over the last seventy-five years.[26] Leo XIII's *Rerum Novarum* (1891), Pius XI's *Quadragesimo Anno* (1931), and John XXIII's *Mater et Magistra* (1961) are frequently quoted documents. In the latter, set forth on the seventieth anniversary of *Rerum Novarum,* specific attention is given to "social matters," the "applications of social teachings," the task of the layman, the place of Christian "action and responsibility" in the world, and the need to maintain respect for "the hierarchy of values." Along with these papal teachings, a number of modern Catholic theological works figure prominently in building up the Church's new social ideology. The names of Maritain, Congar, Rahner, Teilhard de Chardin, Kung, Suenens, and Henri de Lubac—all Europeans—are household words among the socially progressive sector of the Church. Current leaders of Christian Democratic parties, such as Eduardo Frei Montalva of Chile, received some of their most important "political" orientations from the writings of Maritain. Congar, writing in the 'fifties, gives special attention to the theological problems of the laity and their place in the apostolic mission of the Church.[27] In a series of brilliant essays, Rahner develops the concept of the Church as "diaspora" and spells out the implications of this advancing minority status for the institutional development of Catholicism.[28]

But perhaps the greatest source of ideological strengthening for the agents of change within the Church has come from the ideas and proposals produced by the Second Vatican Council. This Council has given the liberal side of "the Catholic problem" so much publicity and popular reinforcement that those who earlier hesitated to act are gaining remarkable confidence.[29] The decisions and debates of the assembled prelates have given a new legitimacy to ecumenical conversations, liturgical reforms, and may now give the idea of episcopal collegiality canonical status.[30] Out of these broad developments, a small group of Latin American Catholic liberals (cardinals, bishops, clergy, and laymen) have fashioned an increasingly powerful and appealing ideology. The core concepts are "social justice for the deprived," "fundamental institutional reforms" (often shortened to "revolutionary reforms"), social action in the world as the key means of Christian influence, and a concern for man and the human community.

One other theme of elite activity bears brief mention—the Church's attempts to mobilize a new missionary labor force. The key to this new endeavor is the layman. Growing threats to Catholic influence not only call for the building of a strong organization and a meaningful Christian ideology but, equally important, for the mobilization of religious proselytors who can serve as apostles for the Church in everyday contexts. The broad term that identifies this movement is the lay apostolate. For generating this new level of religious activism in secular society, the layman's association, directed by a priest, is the key social mechanism. Each of these apostolic groups is given responsibility for meeting the problems of people in a particular sphere: trade union work, family life, and so on. In the early phases of formation, one lay group may concentrate on a number of interests. The action programs begin around a small nucleus of concerned laymen, similar to a "cell." In this nucleus, the layman is educated and persuaded to infuse his daily relationships with Christian principles and to relate to those outside the Church in ways that will foster their interest in an active, sacramental life. This is not an easy assignment, for it requires the usual passive layman to promote Catholicism in his daily round of activities as worker, friend, club member, or family member. In short, the lay apostolate is a missionary movement of the changing Church aimed toward re-Christianizing the dormant masses—an attempt to regain for the Church a prominent place in a changing society.

Around these three themes of Catholic activity development—administrative, ideological, and apostolic—new leaders and elite nuclei are in evidence. Some of these developments are products of new specialties that have become necessary as part of the Church's operation, e.g. experts in social research, chaplains to Catholic Action groups, and mass-media technicians. Out of these additions, strains often develop between line and staff—between occupants in the canonically defined hierarchial offices and the new men who serve as consultants, who are in contact with new group activities, and who come with special kinds of knowledge and skills. Some of the traditional tensions between diocesan clergy and the religious orders, as well as those stemming from the priest-bishop relationship, are being eclipsed by these incipient divisions.

FORMING NEW LINKAGES WITH SOCIETY

In my judgment, these functionally generated differentiations do not adequately portray the entire scope of the Church's internal dynamic nor the direction it will likely take in the future. There are several crosscutting elite developments that have more to do with the Church's strategy of survival and its role in social change than with internal jurisdictions and criteria of authority. These elite developments are based on analytical considerations other than functionally defined spheres. They are viewed as lines of differentiation that stem primarily from political and cultural priorities and from the various definitions of Catholic imperatives within these. Four types are identified: three are "new" elite developments; the fourth represents the traditional core out of which the others have emerged. Since each of the new elite groups is in varying kinds of tension with the traditional elite, I shall begin with this latter type.

Traditional Catholic elites in Latin America are oriented to the power structure of secular society. They look to outside groups for support, protection, and legitimation. Their chief strategies for achieving influence are: skillful maneuvering, short-run coalitions, and making the most out of ad hoc situations as they arise. Hierarchy within the Church is important in the same way that it was in the fifteenth century: a set of formal, recognized positions from which the clergy or bishops can establish themselves as influential in the wider community. The laity are ignored. Rituals are carried out *pro forma,* the sacraments are available to those who can pay the fee, and social evils are defined as implicit in the human situation. The new pressures that have come from the Second Vatican Council, having to do with changes in the liturgy, relations with other faiths, and lay involvement, are strongly resisted, even satirized. The reference group of the traditional elite is the upper class, from which many of them come. In return for the loyalty of this stratum, the Church gives its members the responsibility for dispensing charity. Because of the Church's interlocking connections with the polity and because its fortunes rest on strategies of manipulating public opinion and power groups, I shall refer to this traditional elite as the "politicians."

Among the three new elites, there are first the "papists." Not meant with any opprobrium, the term stands for a militant, modern Catholicism aimed toward "re-Christianizing the world." Since the Church's main objective from this perspective is to regain former religious influence, the bases of elite differentiation are at least two: first, roles that have to do with the "penetration" of the social milieu; second, roles that give the Church internal strength, organizational power, and a new tie with rising status groups, especially the urban proletariat. The major orientations of the "papists," as an elite, are three: hierarchy, action, and sacramentally based religiosity. Rejecting traditional sources of political involvement, the "papists" focus on building a Church that relies on its own authority and its own resources to achieve influence and visibility. Direct political involvements between the Church and political parties are eschewed, even forbidden. Thus the hierarchy, the clergy, and the laity constitute a missionary elite concerned with expanding the frontiers of Christian-Catholic values. The principle that underlies the laity's participation is "collaboration with the Hierarchy," that is, full obedience to and full supervision by Church authorities. Religious action is accordingly defined and given meaning within traditional Catholic premises on such matters as the nature of the Church, the validity of its dogmas, and its monopoly of religious charisma. Hierarchy extends beyond the local or national level to Rome. The validating point of ecclesiastical authority is "ultramontane" rather than "Gallican."

This militant, apostolic conception of modern Catholicism's relation to society has grown out of the Western European situation over the past two generations. The most decisive expression of this new mission emerged during the pontificate of Pius XI, though it was well under way by the end of World War I. By the mid-'thirties, this frame of reference had been adopted, with some modifications, in the Latin American Church. Youth programs, apostolic units, and episcopally directed strategies emerged. These developments produced a segment of hard-core Catholic apostles who, in communication with their European counterparts, turned to the tasks of converting the Latin American masses. Actual successes have been minimal, not only be cause of the lack of lay response to their new missionary status, but also due to the fact that the "militant Church" provoked latent forms of clericalism that were incongruent with the social and political ideas of the time. Less-than-expected gains have not, however, weakened the spirit of the "papists." The "action ideology" of this elite group is very strong in countries such as Colombia, Argentina, and Mexico.

Beyond these two elite groups there are at least two further divisions. These are the "pastors" and the "pluralists." The "pastors" are a small but growing group of bishops and clergy who see their main task as that of building up strong, worship-centered congregations. They are searching for a formula that will effectively weld priest, people, and the sacraments into a spiritual body. The priest's role is elaborated beyond his place as isolated ritual leader to include the tasks of preaching, counseling, and mingling. In many ways, the liturgical movement is a symbol of this new elite. Worship is focused on the Eucharistic Mass. Side altars and images, as well as personal piety, are intentionally played down. Laymen are encouraged to take active roles in the liturgy, both by assisting the priest in reading the Word of God and by singing psalms. Solidarity within a religious congregation is one of the major objectives. In order to promote this religiously based social bond, parish boundaries are being reduced in size, an affinity of status among the members is considered important, and new church buildings are designed to reduce the physical distance between priest and worshippers. The ideological themes in this elite's vocabulary are caught up in such words as "co-operation," "community," "communication," "pastoral care," and "the meaning of the sacraments." I take this development to be one of the most significant changes in the religious life of the Latin American Church.

The fourth elite group, the "pluralists," seem to be at present a very mixed and changing group. The central premise of the "pluralists" is that Catholicism in Latin America is a minority faith—one religion among many others. Their major objective is to develop policies and programs that will allow the Church to assist the institutionalization of social justice on every front that provides the opportunity. Thus, the center of attention is moved away from traditional concerns with political power, from hierarchy and clericalism, and from worship and the sacraments to grass-roots ethical action in the world. Coalitions with the "good" are to be made wherever and whenever possible. Community enterprises, aimed to further economic development and social integration, are viewed as essential religious tasks. Special attention is given to the needs and the deprivations of the poor and the exploited. Ecumenical ties and co-operative undertakings are established with other faiths. Planning is long-range and the scope of social interest wide, and is not limited to immediate, local situations. With respect to the social revolution, the Church "must find her place" and "play an important role therein"; not as a "political party," nor as an anxious guardian of established privilege, but as a differentiated, grass-roots agency of moral and social influence. Small groups of this persuasion are found in all of the major centers of Latin American Catholicism. They refer to the conforming, clerical Catholic Action elite as "sacristans" or "goon squads." They talk with bitterness about the traditional "políticos" and their maneuverings. Those whom I have called the "pastors" are not discounted, but the latter's exclusive concern with the Church's inner life calls out criticisms of "escapism," "retreatism," and "withdrawal."

These groups do not exhaust the kinds of elite differentiation to be found in contemporary Latin American Catholicism. Nor are these types meant to be full empirical summaries. But the differences mentioned involve two major dimensions of analytical importance. The first has to do with the choice of the sphere from which the Church is to gain its major source of influence—whether from its "internal" resources (its organization and its rituals) or from its involvement with secular groups and events ("external"). The other dimension identifies the organizing principle of religious-social relationships, whether these occur within the Church or outside. One of these principles is termed the "hierarchical"; the other "co-operative." A fourfold typology is built from these distinctions:

FIGURE I

Typology of Catholic Elites

Structural principle of
Catholic activity

		HIERARCHICAL	CO-OPERATIVE
Sphere from which Church influence is to be drawn	EXTERNAL	Politicians	Pluralists
	INTERNAL	Papists	Pastors

A number of questions, both theoretical and practical, arise from these identifiable types: What are the conditions for the emergence and growth of each type? How influential is each type and how do these strengths vary from country to country? Which elites hold the greatest adaptive potential for the Church in the contemporary Latin American situation? Or the greatest dangers for its long-range capacity to survive and grow? What kinds of tensions emerge within and between each type? What is the layman's role in each type? Answers to many of these questions require considerably more information than we have at the present time. Others involve difficult problems of measurement. But despite these restrictions, certain broad patterns and relationships can be identified.

With respect to the conditions of the "new" elites' emergence ("papists," "pastors," "pluralists"), two patterns are clear. First, the strength of the politicians in the national hierarchy limits the growth of the papists and the pastors—both emphasizing a development of the Church's internal capacities—but accelerates the growth of the plural-ists. The strength of the politicians, in turn, appears to be strongly cor-related with Church-state ties or connections. Where constitutional clauses buttress regalism or where concordats guarantee Catholic monopolies, the politicians hold the power. This is not surprising. As noted earlier, the traditional modes of binding the Church into the political system provoke Church leaders to rely on short-run, top-level power strategies. Basic changes in the leadership style of the Church thereby depend on changes in the broader institutional fabric of the so-ciety. Unless the hierarchy is assured of autonomy, neither the upgrad-ing of the Church as an apostolic organization, nor the re-structuring of worship and parish life is possible, or even necessary. It works both ways. At the same time, however, the prominence of the politicians in any area or country is certain to prompt the pluralist movement. Progressivism becomes a reaction against the political posture. Counter-elites develop and tend to take a radical grass-roots, social justice direction—a result of deep-felt hostilities on the part of clergy and laity against the hidebound, stereotyped, and ambivalent stands of key Church leaders.

From another perspective, the papists appear to be a key transition elite for the effective development of the other two new elites: pastors and pluralists. With their emphasis on political detachment, improving Church organization, involving laymen, and on defining an articulated set of theologically based conceptions of "mission in society," the papists form a bridge between the traditional politicians and the new pastors and pluralists. In short, the development of the Church as a militant, missionary system functions to prepare the conditions for the pastors and the pluralists. Thus one can hypothesize a sequential pattern of Catholic elite developments, moving counter-clockwise from the top left cell.

Therefore, although pluralists may emerge directly as a reaction to the traditional strategies and established powers of the politicians, they cannot be effective, either as contributors to the long-range adaptation of the Church or to the development of society, until a series of other changes takes place in Church organization, conceptions of religious action, laity motivations, and ideas about mission. Institutional change in Roman Catholicism requires the *imprimatur* of the hierarchy. Structural modifications may be pressed by lower strata, but they usually fail, serving only to breed frustration and chronic dissent, unless they gain official sponsorship. Consequently, the pluralists who strike out on their own to bring about a social and religious revolution must either anticipate disciplinary measures or leave the Church. On the other hand, if the Church system has undergone a series of structural and ideological changes—including a "liberalization" of the hierarchy—the pluralist strategy becomes a fully integrated part of a total mission and thus may add both to the strength of the Church and to the positive development of the society.

So far as the potential contributions of these various elites for the effective adaptation of the Church, I see the possibilities for a working combination between the "pastors" and the "pluralists," if they can bring the organizational capacity of the "papists" into their camp without having to accept their emphases of authoritarianism, monopolism, and ultramontanism. Unless the two more radical groups recognize the importance of centralized co-ordination and certain types of international linkages, they run the risk of dispersion and thus defeat. The "pastors" and the "pluralists" actually have the long-range advantage, since the trends in Latin America toward sociological pluralism and increased religious competition are well developed in certain areas. In short, the Church will have to forego some of its rigidity and emphasis on ritual and organizational uniformity if it is to capture important segments of the population. Even with the development of Catholic Action, it cannot respond easily to special groups, new classes, and minorities. The institutional dilemma, of course, is how to achieve the advantages of "denominationalism"—that is, internal religious, ritual, and ideological differentiation—without falling into a pattern of Protestant fragmentation. With the forthcoming changes in liturgy and the growing strength of the national episcopal councils, and with the impetus that the Second Vatican Council has given to the collegiality principle, some of these needed sources of flexibility may be gained. Interestingly, just as the Latin American Catholic Church faces squarely the problem of building up viable lines of internal religious variation, the Protestant churches in the United States are moving toward fusion and comprehensive mergers.

The strength of these elites varies from country to country. Colombia, Argentina, and Peru are strongholds of the politicians. As expected, radical pluralist breaks have emerged in each. The papists are also strong in Argentina and Colombia, as well as in Mexico. Brazil, Venezuela, and Chile, on the other hand, are the main centers of solid pastor-pluralist developments. Strong pastoral emphases are also found in certain sections of Bolivia and Guatemala. These are, of course, subjective estimates. With more information, qualifications would undoubtedly need to be made.

Within these limits, the broad comparative picture suggests two generalizations: first, elite developments in Chilean and Brazilian Catholicism appear to be on the threshold of a new phase, having partially broken the "political" mode and, in turn, moved through a modified papist period. Thus, an institutional basis for effective pastoral and pluralist developments exists to some degree. This may also be true in certain Venezuelan and Argentinian dioceses. Second, the pastoral and the pluralist elites gain in importance as Christian Democratic parties are formed and assume a place in the national political system. Christian Democracy, as a Catholic-inspired political movement, serves to absorb political-type strategies within the Church and also allows the pluralists and pastors to concentrate on religious values and religious action. Moreover, in Christian Democracy, the papists find a fully institutionalized role for linking political action to Catholic values without formally involving the Church in politics.

A fourth issue is illuminated by the typology. We hear a great deal in the Church today about *aggiornamento* or "bringing the Church up to date." From these phrases and the ideas that accompany them, the observer tends to see the whole dynamic of the Church's development

in terms of the struggle between the "conservatives" and the "liberals."
Journalists are particularly prone to see things this way. But within the
present typological distinctions, it is possible to clarify the crucial distinction between "bringing the Church up to date" (or "renewal")
and "reform" of the Catholic system. Many Catholic leaders and laymen champion Pope John XXIII as the most advanced point of the
"liberal" camp. But this is a mistake. His major emphasis was on
"renewal"—on raising the internal effectiveness of the Church's structure and adjusting traditional ideas to the modern times. He was not
bent on making deep structural changes in the Church—such as those
taken seriously by the pastors and the pluralists. To "renew" is not to
"reform." Consequently, one of the most critical tasks of the new
Catholic elites is how to secure basic structural changes that bear decisively on the special religious problems and social issues in Latin
America. The "happy days" of John XXIII created a phase of risky
optimism that has already suffered some deep shocks.

V

Turning now to the role of the new Catholic elites within the total
context of Latin America progress, the process of development may be
seen as a three-stage sequence. In the first stage, the problem of development is to find, or to create, frameworks of meaning that legitimate
the notion of change, especially to status groups that hold a vested interest in the *status quo*. Many groups, including the industrial workers,
the technicians, and segments of the middle class, do not need to be
convinced that change is necessary—they are already committed to the
principle. But their readiness for change, however much this is pub-
licized and rewarded, is not always sufficient to swing the society into a
new direction. Some broader legitimating ideology is needed—one that
can tie traditional symbols of authority and meaning to the idea of
change—one that fuses the past with the future in the context of
familiar elements in the culture. Thus the burden falls on ideologists,
who have the capacity to link the sacred to change, to fuse religion
with the idea of social revolution.[31]

The second stage of Latin American development centers upon the
problem of translating the ideological commitments to change into behaviors and social arrangements that bring together heretofore unco-
ordinated scarce resources, that promote lines of co-operation and

compromise, and that mobilize the population to actually engage in common developmental tasks. This is precisely the point where many Latin American sequences run aground. Key sectors of the society hold a vigorous commitment to change, to modernization, and to revolution, but they find it impossible—even if they gain formal leadership positions in national politics—to get the "system moving" and to work these energies and capacities into a steady, disciplined pattern of growth. The mechanisms of mobilization,[32] revolving around the pooling of resources, the delegation of authority, and the capacity to "trust the system," are terribly weak, in some instances relatively absent.

The third phase of Latin American development appears as full-fledged modernization—a phase in which the mobilization problem has reached some degree of institutional support and where change, both on the level of ideology and at the level of behavior, is accepted by all the major groups in society. In this third stage (i.e. modernization), old forms of solidarity, meaning, and anchorage are shattered. Local and informal identities are broken. People are "on the move," both in physical and social space. Extended kinship boundaries no longer exist as a protective, and encapsulating system. The individual stands pretty much alone in relation to society. Thus, the problem is to establish a new level of social integration, both vertically and horizontally, that is congruent with the demands of modernization.

Thus a sequence of societal development poses three major imperatives: (1) shifting the focus of meaning away from tradition to the idea of change (change is good, it is right, it is necessary); (2) shifting the population's acceptance of the "idea of change" into behavioral modes that actually mobilize resources and latent capacities ("doing" instead of "talking"); and (3) developing new modes of integration and solidarity that support and sustain full modernization (initiating social forms and lines of activity that can replace traditional bonds that were provided by family, tribe, and community). I think these imperatives, although they stand somewhat to the side of the familiar notions of "developmental requisites" (capital, industry, voting franchise, etc.), call attention to the deeper types of transformations that development entails. Whether we refer to these problems as the need for an "integrative revolution," the absence of a "binding factor," or the need for certain types of community, the sociological point is clear: Latin American development is precisely a problem of re-structuring meaning systems, action systems, and the bases of hierarchy and solidarity. Unless this three-level modification takes place, it is unlikely that the chronic problems that emerge around production and politics will be solved.

Taking this three-stage model of Latin American development as a point of departure, we can make several broad suggestions that link the new Catholic elites to the process of social change. In my judgment, each of the new elite groups—the papists, the pluralists, and the pastors—has a special contribution to make to Latin America's development. The papists, stressing the noninvolvement of the Church in politics and, at the same time, adhering to the social encyclicals of the recent popes, perform at least two critical functions in the context of social change. First, they forge a linkage between traditional Catholic values and the concept of social change, thereby providing the loyal Catholic with a solution to a key dilemma. Papal authority can be called upon to bring Catholics into a mood for change. Second, they promote the idea that the Church, as hierarchy, will not impose its conceptions of the good society on others by taking a traditional, political position. The Catholic social ideology is not to be promulgated through a new wave of clericalism but by the laity who, in working back and forth between the Church and society, act as carriers and agents of the new values.

In Latin America, where Church and secular interests have been historically fused in a very extreme way, these two functions of the papists reduce the notion that the Church is committed to a total preservation of the *status quo*. In addition, the papists draw a decisive line between religion and politics. They have the indirect consequence of lending the Catholic system's prestige and influence to the process of social change without throwing the Church into direct political alignments. Of course, these broad norms have not been fully institutionalized; but it would be a mistake to underestimate the "symbolic importance" of the papists' position. Their principles have entered into the modern Catholic's ideology and thus into the central orbit of Latin America's dynamics.

The particular relevance of the papists' contributions comes at the early stage of social development: the point when the Church is under heavy attack because of its tendency to "interfere" and to resist change. In this sense, the role of the papists is essentially that of giving a Catholic legitimation to social change, thus helping to dislodge sources of conservatism. Moreover, the papists' stress on building up the internal spiritual resources of the Church within a traditional hierarchical framework, readies the Catholic system for the competitions that a modern, pluralistic society entails. In short, the papists help pull the Church out of politics, link it to society through the laity, build up its internal spiritual resources, and provide the basis of a Catholic ideology of social change. These contributions are especially relevant at the point when the society begins its first major phase of development.

The second type of new Catholic elite—the pluralists—emphasize the principle of building-up programs and liaisons with non-Catholic groups in the interest of furthering social justice. Grass-roots enterprises of an economic nature, technical training schools, literacy classes, and health clinics represent this activity. At the professional level, especially among businessmen and in the universities, Catholic priests and laymen join with non-Catholics to foster social change and modern practices. Again, however, the direct participation of the Church, as hierarchy and as religious authority, is played down. Priority is given to mobilizing Catholics, at various points in the society, to undertake a co-operative role in furthering social development. This pattern of co-operation, even though decidedly modest, holds an enormous "mobilizing" potential, since committed Catholics join with non-Catholics in common tasks.[33] At certain levels, this involves relationships with leaders from the Protestant and the Jewish communities. In other instances, it takes Catholics directly into activities that are normally associated with the secular left. Thus it is no surprise to hear the more conservative Catholics refer to the pluralists as "more Communist than the Communists." But if this pluralist strategy emerges after the papist developments, the risks of losing contact with the Catholic anchorage are reduced. The pluralist approach to be effective appears to depend on incorporating some prior emphases of the papists, i.e. the norm of lay responsibility in the world, the support of an ideology that links Catholicism to change, and an acceptance of the principle that the Church refrains from direct political activities. In their efforts to bring about social justice and to aid other reforming groups, the pluralists assist the second stage of development—mobilization. Their work adds the stamp of religious (Catholic) legitimacy to co-operative action and to disciplined performance, both of direct relevance to solving practical problems on society.

Again, as with the papists, this is an ideal picture. The pluralists are not a single, cohesive group within the Latin American church. They have not joined hands to form a social movement. But they are an identifiable line of differentiation, and they do undertake activities within a general and shared system of meanings and priorities. Moreover, their willingness to form coalitions, to initiate social justice programs, and their interest in promoting social development suggest that the pluralists play a decisive mobilization role at certain points in the larger society. This hypothesis takes on particular importance in light of Latin America's "problem of development." Recent theorists who focus on this area of the world draw attention to certain problematic features of Latin American institutions, namely, the lack of strong support for interpersonal co-operation, the vulnerability of social consensus, even when attained, and the absence of functional lines of integration between levels of social structure—between the person and formal organizations, between the community or village and national institutions, and between the family and the wider society. The fragility or "underdeveloped" state of Latin American institutions at these basic junctures of the social order obviously paralyzes the possibilities of many social activities that bear directly on the process of development. In short, many of Latin America's problems of development have their source in these patterns that weaken the growth of co-ordinative and co-operative links on which a modern society depends. Silvert points to the weakness of solidarity bonds beyond those of the family.[34] Hirschman sees the problem of Latin America's economic underdevelopment in terms of a "lack of the cooperative element in entrepreneurship" [35] and the absence of a "binding factor" in social behavior.[36] Other observers speak of the "absence of community" [37] and the Latin American's tendency to assume that the "system" cannot be trusted.[38]

These diagnoses strike at the roots of the developmental problem. More importantly, they direct attention specifically to the need for innovations and programs that can establish new types of crosscutting co-operative relationships. In this context, the pluralists' attempts to bridge traditional cleavages in the service of social goals, lending Catholic support to common endeavors, may be taken as one important aspect of mobilization. Their contribution is especially important in the second stage of secular development, when the forces of change have been initiated and when aspirations have been turned toward new possibilities, but when at the same time mobilization efforts fail because of strife, factions, and established differences. This is not to say that the new Catholic elites which have been identified as pluralists hold the salvation of Latin America in their hands. But it would be ungenerous to discount the symbolic role this Catholic participation plays in social development.

Put another way, a Latin American society that undergoes the first phase of development, in which the idea of change becomes legitimate and focal, often finds that this commitment to change is frustrated by chronic problems of competition and disharmony. It is in this second phase that the problem of mobilization becomes critical. The mobilization of existing motivations and resources is only possible if compromises and coalitions are formed and held. Groups that hold a prominent symbolic position in society, such as Catholic elites, can assist by showing their readiness to join with others.

The third line of differentiation among the new Catholic elites involves the pastors. These leaders concentrate on strengthening the internal spiritual life of the Church. They also initiate activities and legitimate roles in the liturgy and worship that strengthen the parish church's capacity to weld members together as a religio-social unit.[39] The broader problems of society's development and the threat of pluralism are subordinated to the task of building up the Church as a grass-roots stronghold. The pastors are aware that Catholic strength in the modern world depends on membership commitment and participation, not on political alignments with the state and not on using the Church's resources to compete with other agencies in the solution of social ills. In these respects, the pastors turn inward toward strengthening the religious capacities of their members. They aim to reshape the parish church so that it becomes a source of identity and a basis of social integration for the member.

The contributions of the pastors to the broader process of long-range social development are more indirect than in the previous two cases, but nevertheless important. The new parish church, centered upon spiritual and social activities, provides individual members with an extra-familial integrative system and thus a group identity that stands between immediate social relationships and the wider society. This type of opportunity structure, linking Latin America's religious tradition with new forms of social integration, is particularly functional for people and groups that have become parts of the mobile, urban mass. The Church's operations in most places cannot serve the socio-religious needs of these people. In its traditional form, the parish church and its ritual tend to be aloof, impersonal, and formal. By contrast, the pastors focus on the spiritual problems of the members and initiate activities that allow their expression. If this "pastoral" trend takes root in Latin America, the parish church will gradually come to have many of the same functions that local churches have in the United States: combining roles and meanings that provide social identity, religious expression, and cultural anchorage.

This kind of religious unit becomes especially important when societies have moved into the third phase: full modernization. In this phase, old patterns of identity and association have been broken. Economic opportunities and the attraction of the cities spur migration and mobility. Family relations, especially in terms of the extended kinship system, are de-emphasized and weakened. The local church, providing it answers to the needs these modern conditions raise, takes on special importance as a unit of solidarity, as a framework of religious identity, and as a mediating mechanism between the person and society. But this role should be seen as a further development beyond the first two stages of social change. Whereas the papists function to tie Catholic values to social change and to dislodge the hierarchy from its traditional political involvements, and whereas the pluralists serve as leaders in forming new lines of inter-group co-operation, the pastors function as creators of small religio-social systems on the local level which answer some of the problems stemming from mobility and social isolation.

Matching the three-stage model of Latin American development with the levels of the socio-cultural system and the new Catholic elites, we gain a total picture. Figure 2 presents the hypothesized relationships:

FIGURE 2
Role of New Elites

		Stages of development		
		t_1 LEGITIMATING CHANGE	t_2 MOBILIZING RESOURCES	t_3 RE-INTEGRATING SOCIETY
	CULTURE	Papists		
Levels of the socio-cultural system	INTER-GROUP		Pluralists	
	PERSON-SOCIETY			Pastors

Colombia, Argentina, and Chile represent examples of these groups at work in concrete cases. Colombia, despite its recent programs for land reform, its coalition government, and its coffee export trade, is held to be the prototype of a traditional Latin American country. Roman Catholicism is the official religion, guaranteed by the Concordat of 1887. The Church has a major grip on the country's educational system. Bogotá is the home of the conservative Jesuit university, Javierana. The clergy walk the streets and enter public places with a casualness that can only come from a secure position in society. In a very deep sense, Colombia is a clerical country. It is also a country that is not yet committed fully to the necessity for social change. Many sectors of the power structure not only resist the idea of change but also dampen and obstruct minor types of social reform.

Regarding the new Catholic elites, two patterns are undeniably present in Colombia. There is, on the one side, a solid core of pluralists, engaged in programs that bear directly on the solution of common problems in the society. On the other side, there is a growing, volatile group of pluralists who want to make a direct, frontal attack on changing the social order, through revolution if necessary. During this past year, this second type of pluralist has come to occupy the forefront of the nation's attention. One priest, recently killed, "renounced his priesthood," openly criticized the Cardinal, and published a manifesto for social revolution. His position was one that gained rapid support since he claimed that true Christianity is not possible under Colombia's present social and political conditions.[40]

This radical development is, in my judgment, a concrete reflection of a "missed stage" in the evolution of the Church. The crucial contribution of the papists has not been realized. Instead, the new Catholic elites are turning directly to secular forms of participation without the support of a Catholic-based social ideology that condones development and modernization. This is a tragic situation for both the Church and for society. For the Church and its traditional hierarchy, the legitimation of the more radical kind of pluralist strategy, at this time, is too destructive of their own authority. They cannot give way and maintain their own dignity. At the same time, key sectors of the society are not prepared to confront the problems that the new priests and a new laity are defining to the public. If, on the other hand, the traditional sectors of the society, both the hierarchy and the secular groups, had been prepared by a phase of contact with the modern Catholic ideology, the pluralists would now be able to tie their efforts into a meaningful movement of social action. Over time, of course, the "new Church" will win out. There is too much now under way to keep it down. But the possibilities for stabilization and a re-integration of the Church are extremely weak at this moment. Part of the solution, according to the present theory, is to be found in a "pulling back" by the pluralists—at least in those cases where action has become a true rebellion—and a refocusing of their energies to effect changes at the level of the whole cultural system, which means in terms of an ideology that will help link traditional Catholic loyalties to the imperatives of social change. If this can be accomplished, then the pluralists will be able to move out again into their programs of direct social action.

Argentina presents a different set of developmental problems. Many of the dominant groups are oriented to change and growth. The economy has a history of vigorous production bursts. Much of the infrastructure for a modern society exists. Urbanization and technology are basic features of the society. With respect to the Church, Argentina maintains a form of regalism. Thus key changes in the hierarchy must meet the approval of the politicians. In broad terms, the leadership of the Church is traditional without being reactionary. Many of the top positions are filled by the sons and grandsons of the Italian immigrants. One discovers thereby a curious combination of an Italian-type Catholic orientation and a nationally-focused Church: ultramontanism mixed with particularism. At the lower reaches of the Church, the papal encyclicals that spell out a social doctrine of change are fully diffused. Catholic Action groups are relatively strong, especially among students and some of the middle-class professional groups. Problems of social change have been a main focus of these group interests since the 1930's.

Argentina, however, has not sustained a steady pattern of development. There is commitment to change, but a weak basis for long-range mobilization. Things get started and then slip backward. Energies and resources are depleted because of factionalism, non-productive competition, and distrust. The Peronist era, raising the skilled workers to a new level of prominence and economic gratification, set norms that were unrealistic for Argentina's long pull. These groups are now unwilling to let go of the gains they have won. From another side, the major urban region of Buenos Aires and its environs is an intense arena for certain kinds of religious tensions. Both the Protestants and the Jews constitute sizeable minority groups. Their presence is a social fact that cannot be ignored. These and other indications suggest that Argentina's central problem of development is one of "mobilization" —drawing the already present commitments to change into a working framework of co-operative effort. The resources are there, but they remain uncombined and unaligned at strategic junctures in society. This is not merely evident in the economy, but is generally true throughout all major institutional spheres.

In this period of transition, the Church actually stands hesitantly between the position of the papists and that of the pluralists.[41] Catholicism and the idea of change have been fused at numerous points throughout the system. But very little action has taken place that symbolizes the willingness of the Church or its new elites to "join hands" or to lead the way in co-operative undertakings. Part of it stems from divisions within the hierarchy. Part of it stems from factions among lay groups. Thus the Argentine Church, like the society, is fragmented and unsure of its direction. The new Catholic elites of the pluralist variety thus appear to be one of the key agencies for building up the society's mobilization capacities. Their efforts are needed both within the Church and in the secular sphere. Small developments in Buenos Aires, focused on inter-faith programs, co-operative enterprises, and lines of dialogue, therefore stand as pioneering steps. There is no doubt but that a greater participation of the Church's elites in these joint ventures would have a major symbolic effect on breaking other forms of deadlock. In short, the Argentine society appears to require the institutionalization of a set of crossties that will form the normative basis for successful, long-range mobilization.

Other patterns call for attention in Chile. If present indications are in any way signs of the future, Chile is entering a full stage of modernization. This country has suffered chronic economic ills, experienced exasperating political battles, and has, as well, generated a rush of internal migration that bring it problems of "urbanization without full industrialization." Yet the political development, over the past fifty years, has been quite steady. Major coups and internal disruptions have been minor relative to other countries in the hemisphere. Social programs, including a health system and social security provisions, are regular features of the national institutional framework. A major land-reform program is now in its first stage of application. More recently, new arrangements between the Chilean government and the foreign owned mineral corporations have been worked out to the general satisfaction of most interested parties. Although it would be rash to make any long-range predictions, there is some basis for defining Chile as "on her way."

What about the Church? The Chilean Church is often referred to as "the most progressive Catholic system in Latin America." This is an appropriate description and one that has been earned. The hierarchy, at some of its most important points, is in the hands of the liberals. Traditional, conservative nuclei are certainly present, but they are not in control. From another side, the Chilean Church has developed and legitimated a powerful social ideology, formulated around such key concepts as "the Christian revolution." This ideological development got under way in the 'thirties but reached its most decisive phase of growth after 1950. In Chilean Catholicism, as in the society at large, the idea of social change is fully institutionalized. But this Catholic social ideology, working as it has to fuse tradition and modernity, does not exist in separation from action. Under the auspices of the progressive groups in the Church, several types of concrete programs of reform have been initiated: technical training for the *campesinos,* the distribution of Church lands to underprivileged groups, and the forming of credit and production co-operatives in some of the *callampas.* These pluralist-type thrusts have brought the Church into contact with other reformers who represent both private and governmental units. The recent victory of the Christian Democrats, both in presidential and the congressional elections, is largely a product of the Church's new phase.[42] But this leadership should not be construed as a result of the hierarchy's direct political participation, but rather in terms of the Catholic elites' rare capacities to give meaning to social change in terms of symbols that bridge past and present and, also their ability to give co-operation and various forms of social effort the benefit of religious legitimacy. In effect, the Church's new elites have shown that the Catholic system can build a floor for the processes of modernization.

Chile has gained one of the most important successes in mobilization. In this, the new Catholic elites—both papists and pluralists—have made a singular and important contribution. But it would be a mistake to conclude that smooth sailing is assured. The present moment is one of the most delicate situations in Chile's history. Much of the country's capacity to move through this period depends on what takes place in the Church. There is, on the one hand, the possibility that the new elites will become so enamored with their new influence that they will

want to tell the country how to grow. If this happens, the old temptation to move directly into politics will emerge. Having helped to bring
a new political movement into power, the new Catholic elites may
want to steer the ship, or even move into the captain's quarters. In my
judgment, this direction would spell disaster for both the new Church
and for Chile as a developing nation. The most positive line of development for the Church in Chile is to move the pastors' strategy into
the front line, which means to turn now to building up the local
churches as a new basis of religious and social solidarity. This move is
already under way, but not yet fully developed. This line of work takes
on even more significance when one takes time to look closely at the
strengths of the Chilean Church. Put briefly, the Chilean Church has a
strong, liberalized hierarchy but it does not have deep religious
anchorages among the people. The local church, for the most part, is
not a vigorous line of spiritual or social activity. Thus it comes as no
surprise to find that the Protestant Pentecostal groups have made solid
inroads in Catholic territory.

The three cases suggest that something more than a rough correlation can be discovered between the development of the Catholic system
and the development of Latin American societies. Where other sociologists have pointed to a relationship between economic growth and
democracy,[43] the emphasis here is on religious development and
societal development. But I think the foregoing analysis allows a further inference: Catholic developments are not merely correlative with
societal developments, but are requisites; they play a causal role. Both
Colombia and Argentina are being "held back" by the hesitancy and
"underdevelopment" of the Catholic system. Chile, on the other hand,
possesses a Catholic "floor" on which a modern society can be built.

In making these inferences, we give a major role to the Catholic religious factor and its sociological implications. I do not think this is unwarranted; but the importance of Catholicism is not adequately
indexed by measures of church attendance or the people's conformity
to the Church's official moral rules. Instead Catholicism's critical role is
to be judged in the context of men's loyalties to the "Mother Church"
(distinct from the hierarchy and clergy), the people's estimates of
their own capacities in problematic situations as against a belief in
supernatural interventions, their manifestations of dependence on
"higher authorities," and their conception of Latin America's destiny.

In these terms, Latin America is a Catholic-based social order. As

Ramos writes of his own Mexico: "The real motivation for our culture, given the nature of our psychic activity since the time of the Conquest, is religiosity. . . . Materially or ideally, the church always occupies a high vantage point." [44] MacKay, thirty years ago, traced out this Catholic religious theme of Latin American culture as expressed in categories of thought, artistic styles, customs and habits, and even in the writings of vocal, anticlerical liberals such as Bilbao, Montalvo, Prada, and Rodo.[45] Paz makes the point in another way when he states, "We are a ritual people." [46] Freyre's socio-historical analysis of Brazil underlines the importance of the Catholic theme: "Brazilian development views as a whole may be considered predominantly Christian. . . . It is also Catholic, or a branch of the Latin form of Christianity or civilization." [47] These deep and broad religious dimensions are being increasingly recognized by more recent Latin American scholars. Morse, in a short comment on social science research on Latin America, brings this whole point into clear focus with these questions: "Should not an inquiry into 'voting behavior' presuppose understanding of the relation of conscience to natural law in the Hispano-Catholic tradition? Must not an analysis of 'the decision-making process' involve knowledge of the moral function of casuistry in a Catholic society? . . . . how seriously have any of us dared require a steeping in St. Thomas Aquinas, Dante, and Suárez for those who would understand Latin America?" [48] In short, politics, production, and personal meanings are all indirectly imbued with Catholic dimensions and a redemptive *Weltanschauung*. In the midst of misery, confusion, strife, and disillusionment, these people look for a convincing eschatology and for membership in some beautiful crusade.

This Catholic culture and its corresponding Catholic psychology must also be linked to the impressive sociological features of the Catholic Church as an organization. First of all, the Church is the only formal organization that spans the four and a half centuries of Spanish-American history. The implications of this unbroken continuity in the central religious institution must not be underestimated when questions arise regarding the nature of the social order.

In addition, the Church is the only formal organization and value-transmitting agency that supersedes national boundaries. This is not a trivial observation. While one may easily distinguish the Church in Chile from the Church in Mexico, it remains true that the Latin American Church is an entity in and of itself; it possesses a distinct type of identity in relation to other sections of the Catholic Church, it maintains a visible dimension of solidarity, and it reaches a working basis of formal integration. At least two kinds of empirical relationships connect the various national Churches at the continental level: a formal set of structures, such as CELAM,[49] CLAR,[50] and FERES,[51] and a series of durable, functional informal relationships that have developed around friendly alliances, confidence structures, and common interests. From this perspective the on-going debate as to whether one can validly speak of a common Latin American culture can draw, on its positive side, considerable support from this overarching and operating unity of the Church. Since social scientists are aware that value orientations, cognitive standards, conceptions of authority, and relational modes are always heavily influenced by dominant religious systems, a more than fragile basis exists for the inference that a core religio-cultural unity is present throughout the continent.

One should also be alerted to the fact that within any given country or region the Church is the only organization that maintains close contact with both the "people" and the "rulers." Its vertical span goes from one end of the social scale to the other. The Church's hierarchical breadth is juxtaposed, as well, with a functional scope which encompasses ritual, educational, and social associations. In short, the Church is not only historically comprehensive and internationally continuous; but it is also vertically and functionally formed to meet social life in numerous places and junctures. Drawing on familiar contrasts, we can say that the Church in Latin America is both old and new, national and international, local and cosmopolitan, bureaucratic and communal, differentiated yet corporate.

If one chooses, other kinds of supports can be mustered to show that the Catholic Church is not a mere decoration on the cultural map. More than 90 per cent of the population has received the sacrament of baptism. More than one-third of the whole educational system, in varying amounts from country to country, is part of the Church. Clergy, sisters, and brothers constitute a group of more than 150,000 individuals. A large proportion of this group is highly educated and from the better classes of society. No less important, the leadership of the Church is filled with men who are oriented to international issues, cosmopolitan values, and literary-artistic-scientific pursuits. Thus the Church's labor force makes up a rather impressive status system in a continent that generally lacks education, is steeped in parochialisms, and tied to the ways of the past. In the present era the Church is developing special programs that bring it into a new type of contact with rural peasants, professionals, university youth, and urban poor. A vast network of radio schools, television studios, research institutes, and social service agencies (such as co-operatives, health clinics, and literacy programs) are now being promoted by the Church. Another relevant consideration is that the Latin American Church is now being viewed by outside Church hierarchies, in Europe and North America, as in need of urgent help. Thus the influence and resources of other Catholic systems are being diverted to this religious institution. From these few statements one can easily see that the Church is far from dead; in fact, it has never been more active and alive.

There is no intention here to build the Church up into some kind of a complete and absolutely unique system. My only consideration is that any approach to Latin America must include Catholicism, and any attempt to catch hold of this "Catholic factor" in Latin America must begin with the Church as a social system, historical and contemporary. In terms of the dimensions mentioned above, the Catholic Church is an extraordinary feature of that continent. Its potential lies along many routes and avenues. Within it, there are possibilities for both universalism and particularism, for both the long reach and the soft touch, for flexibility as well as stability.

VI

These optimistic appraisals of the developmental potential certain new Catholic elites have for Latin America imply three things. First, attention is called to the role religious elites may play in the process of total societal change, particularly at the strategic levels of symbolizing inter-group solidarity, legitimating institutional reforms, and drawing marginal peoples into values and relationships that form the basis of a modern society.[52] Ever since the enunciation of the Weber thesis, centering on the indirect consequences of religiously based motives for economic development, sociologists have been energetically searching other religions to see if parallels to the Protestant Ethic are present. Hinduism, Buddhism, and Islam have all been brought under scrutiny. If evidence for something like the Protestant Ethic is not found, the whole topic of religions' relevance to institutional change is dropped. Roman Catholicism, with its sacramentalism, its hierarchical system of authority, and its corporatist conceptions of society is, of course, auto-matically taken to be the complete antithesis to social change. Thus it is no surprise to find that we have had few sociological contributions to the study of Catholicism since the days of Comte and Troeltsch. But the Weber thesis has perhaps blinded us to the important theoretical point that religions may have various positive consequences in spheres of life other than the economic and through other mechanisms than the unconscious strivings of believers to transform the world in order to build the Kingdom of God. Catholicism in Latin America is the only religious theme that cuts across all the countries. Moreover, the very fact that it is an "elite" religion with great emphasis on authority, may mean its leadership can be of singular importance, if properly de-veloped.

This brings me to the second point. The capacity of the new Catho-lic elites to lever reform and assist other modernizing elites depends on their skillfulness to achieve "spiritual" authority in the secular realm without falling into a political strategy. The temptation is undoubtedly great. But I think any move in that direction would be regressive. Catholic elites in Latin America are faced with the task of developing themselves as *religious* elites—a task that involves freeing themselves from the coiled serpent of political power, and thus requires transform-ing their own values, modes of control, and conceptions of society.

Third, a wedge is being driven between Catholicism and the tradi-tional order. Sociological benefits are assured if this breach can be sus-tained. Consequently, Latin American development increasingly cen-ters around the secular reformers' willingness to tie their forms of production, their political objectives, and their concepts about social revolution to Catholicism's "new face." Unless this connection is made, Latin America will continue to show regressive swings, egregious political setbacks, and familiar patterns of disturbance and resistance. One cannot expect new conceptions of authority, attitudes toward per-formance, and notions of trust and co-operation to gain anchorage in the social order unless they are tied in with the new Catholic subsoil that is now being formed. In effect this new Catholicism is the point of Archimedean leverage between Latin America's past and its future. Put in more direct terms, those who want to help get Latin America moving may be placing their bets on the wrong horse—at least if things are taken in long-term perspective. Instead of simply more capi-tal or shiny tools, support is needed to help the new Catholic elites transform their system in order that the "Catholic" factor and its cultural power can be applied to the whole task of social development. In short, religious reform is a requisite of social reform. If this is valid, two levels of reference are always important for examining the process of Latin American change: reform in the Catholic system (including the Church as a formal organization) and reform of society. If these are held in tension, without creating conflict and stimulating recourse to traditional strategies, development is not only possible, but predictable. Thus the new Catholic elites may prove to be one of the most important "transition" elites for twentieth-century Latin America.

Notes

1. Of the many books dealing with religious elites and social revolutions, special attention is given in John S. Curtiss, *The Russian Church and the Soviet State, 1917–1950* (Boston: Little, Brown & Co., 1953); Mary A. Baldwin, *The New England Clergy and the American Revolution* (Durham, N.C.: Duke University Press, 1928); Guenter Lewy, *The Catholic Church and Nazi Germany* (New York: McGraw-Hill, 1964); Joseph N. Moody (ed.), *Church and Society: Catholic Social and Political Thought and Movements, 1789–1950* (New York: Arts, Inc., 1953); Leslie Dewart, *Christianity and Revolution. The Lesson of Cuba* (New York: Herder and Herder, 1963); Ernest Q. Campbell and Thomas F. Pettigrew, *Christians in Racial Crisis, A Study of Little Rock's Ministry* (Washington, D.C.: Public Affairs Press, 1959); Leonard Binder, *Religion and Politics in Pakistan* (Berkeley and Los Angeles: University of California Press, 1961); Peter Worsley, *The Trumpet Shall Sound: A Study of 'Cargo' Cults in Melanesia* (London: Mac-Gibbon & Kee, 1957); Clifford Geertz, *The Religion of Java* (Glencoe, Ill.: The Free Press, 1960), Chapters 11, 12, and 13; J. N. Farquhar, *Modern Religious Movements in India* (New York: Macmillan, 1915); Alexis de Tocqueville, *The Old Regime and the Revolution,* trans. by John Bonner (New York: Harper & Bros., 1856).

2. Most of the work on religious leadership, charismatic religious groups, and Church officials related to Latin America has taken one of four lines: (1) The role of specific Catholic clergy or groups in the shaping of the area's culture and institutions, e.g. Guillermo Furlong Cardiff, *Historia del Colegio del Salvador y de sus irradiaciones culturales y espirituales en la ciudad de Buenos Aires, 1617–1943,* 2 vols. (Buenos Aires, 1944); Richard E. Greenleaf, *Zumarraga and the Mexican Inquisition, 1536–1543* (Washington, D.C.: Academy of American Franciscan History, 1961); José T. Medina, *El tribunal del Santo Oficio de la Inquisición en las provincias del Plata* (Santiago de Chile, 1899); Peter Masten Dunne, *Early Jesuit Missions in Tarahumara* (Berkeley

and Los Angeles: University of California Press, 1948); Guillermo Fur-
long Cardiff, *Los jesuitas y la cultura rioplatense* (Montevideo, 1933);
Charles S. Braden, *Religious Aspects of the Conquest of Mexico*
(Durham, North Carolina: Duke University Press, 1930); Manoel S.
Cardozo, "The Lay Brotherhoods of Colonial Bahia," *The Catholic
Historical Review*, XXXIII (April, 1947), pp. 12–30; Lewis Hanke,
The Spanish Struggle for Justice in the Conquest of America (Philadelphia: University of Pennsylvania Press, 1949); (2) Studies of pio-
neer Protestant missionaries and the development of various types of
social service programs, e.g. James G. Maddox, *Technical Assistance
by Religious Agencies in Latin America* (Chicago: University of Chi-
cago Press, 1956); Kenneth Scott Latourette, *The Twentieth Century
Outside Europe*, vol. V of *Christianity in a Revolutionary Age* (New
York and Evanston: Harper and Row, 1962), in which Protestant work
is traced for each country in the chapter on Latin America; Kenneth
Strachan, *The Missionary Movement of the Non-Historical Groups in
Latin America* (New York: Division of Foreign Missions of the Na-
tional Council of Churches of Christ in the U.S.A., 1957); Rudolf
Obermuller, *Evangelism in Latin America* (London: Lutterworth
Press, 1957); *El Christianismo Evangélico en América Latina, Informe
de la Conferencia de Iglesias Evangélicas Latinoamericanas* (Buenos
Aires: La Aurora, 1947); Webster E. Browning, *The River Plate
Republics* (London: World Dominion Press, 1928); Webster E. Brown-
ing, John Ritchie, and Kenneth E. Grubb, *The West Coast Republics
of South America* (London: World Dominion Press, 1930); (3) The
types and functions of folk religious elites, e.g. Allen Spitzer, "Aspects
of Religious Life in Teopztlan," *Anthropological Quarterly*, XXX, 1
(January, 1957), pp. 1–17; Allan Kardec, *El libro de los mediums* (Mexico City: Editorial Orión, 1951); Joseph Bram, "Spirits, Mediums, and
Believers in Contemporary Puerto Rico," *Transactions of the New
York Academy of Sciences* (1957), pp. 340–357; Lloyd H. Rogler and
August B. Hollingshead, "The Puerto Rican Spiritualist as a Psychia-
trist," *American Journal of Sociology*, LXVII, 1 (July, 1961), pp. 17–21;
(4) Over the past few years, a *fourth line* of work has been developed
by Catholic sociologists on the evolution, structure, and composition
of the national hierarchies and bodies of clergy. These monographs
are valuable empirical additions to the subject of religious elites in
Latin America. See, e.g. Isidoro Alonso, *et al., La Iglesia en Chile*
(Madrid: Oficina Internacional de Investigaciones Sociales de FERES,
1962); Rutilio Ramos, *et al., La Iglesia en México* (Madrid: FERES,
1963); Gustavo Pérez & Isaac Wust, *La Iglesia en Colombia* (Madrid:
FERES, 1961). These reports on the ecclesiastical structure of the
national Churches are now available for nearly all of the Latin American countries.
3. This emphasis on the impact of elites for various systems of reference
differs from the tendency to limit power to the making of decisions.
Recent references to the relationship between decision-making and

power are found in Frank J. Munger, "Power Structure and Its Study," in Roscoe E. Martin, *et al., Decisions in Syracuse* (Bloomington, Ind.: University of Indiana Press, 1961), pp. 3–20, and in M. Herbert Danzger, "Community Power Structure: Problems and Continuities," *American Sociological Review,* 29 (October, 1964), pp. 707–717.

4. On this problem see David Apter, "Political Religion in the New Nations," in Clifford Geertz (ed.), *Old Societies and New States* (New York: The Free Press of Glencoe, 1963), pp. 57–104.

5. This essay hopefully shifts attention to characteristics of religious elites that avoid stereotyped emphases on priest vs. prophet, functionary vs. charismatic, and administrator vs. pastor. For a fuller treatment of religious differentiation, see Ivan Vallier, "Religious Specialists: Modern," *International Encyclopedia of the Social Sciences,* forthcoming.

6. In this section, I have relied chiefly on the following historical works and interpretative writings: Leandro Tormo, *Historia de la Iglesia en América Latina,* vols. 1 and 2 (Fribourg: Oficina Internacional de Investigaciones de FERES, 1962); Sergio Bagu, *Estructura social de la Colonia. Ensayo de Historia comparada de América Latina* (Buenos Aires: Librería "El Ateneo," 1962); J. Lloyd Mecham, *Church and State in Latin America. A History of Politico-Ecclesiastical Relations* (Chapel Hill, N. C.: University of North Carolina Press, 1934); W. H. Prescott, *The History of the Conquest of Mexico,* 3 vols. (Philadelphia: Lippincott, 1874); Richard Pattee (ed.), *El Catolicismo Contemporáneo en Hispanoamérica* (Buenos Aires: Editorial Fides, 1951); John J. Kennedy, *Catholicism, Nationalism, and Democracy in Argentina* (South Bend, Indiana: University of Notre Dame Press, 1958); two papers recently published in a section of the *Hispanic American Historical Review* entitled "Colonial Institutions and Contemporary Latin America," by Woodrow Borah, "Political and Economic Life," and Charles Gibson, "Social and Cultural Life," XLIII, 3 (August, 1963), pp. 371–389; L. N. McAlister, "Social Structure and Social Change in New Spain," *Hispanic American Historical Review,* XLIII, 3 (August, 1963), pp. 349–370; Leslie Byrd Simpson, *The Encomienda in New Spain* (Berkeley and Los Angeles: University of California Press, 1950); William J. Coleman, *Latin-American Catholicism* (Maryknoll, New York: Maryknoll Publications, 1958); Mary C. Thornton, *The Church and Freemasonry in Brazil, 1872–1875, A Study in Regalism* (Washington, D. C.: The Catholic University of America Press, 1948); Manoel S. Cardozo, "The Lay Brotherhoods of Colonia Bahia," *The Catholic Historical Review,* XXXIII (April, 1947), pp. 12–30; D. P. Kidder and J. C. Fletcher, *Brazil and the Brazilians* (Philadelphia: Childs & Peterson, 1857); Richard M. Morse, *From Community to Metropolis* (Gainesville: University of Florida Press, 1958); Luis Galdames, *A History of Chile,* trans. & ed. Isaac Hoslin Cox (New York: Russell and Russell, Inc., 1964), first published in 1941; and Frederick B. Pike (ed.), *The Conflict Between Church and State in Latin America* (New York: Alfred A. Knopf, 1964).

7. For a fuller discussion of this cleavage, see Ivan Vallier, "Roman Catholicism in Transition," in Ivan Vallier, *et al., Anglican Opportunities in South America* (New York: Columbia University, Bureau of Applied Social Research, 1963), Chap. III.

8. As Fransisco Vives writes of his own country: "Chile, a Catholic country according to statistics, is not so at Mass. . . . For those same souls, the sacramental presence of Christ in the Eucharist is not exactly and frequently validated. Instead of praying to Christ for our Holy Mother Church, they frequently asked for personal favors from some saint." See his "Chile," in Pattee (ed.), p. 195; and two sections by W. J. Coleman, "Diverse Catholicisms," pp. 1–3, and "Indices of Latin American Catholicism," pp. 23–33.

9. A number of descriptive articles and essays are available on these patterns, e.g. Thales de Azevedo, *Social Change in Brazil* (Gainesville: University of Florida Press, 1963), "Religion," pp. 57–81; Charles Wagley, *An Introduction to Brazil* (New York: Columbia University Press, 1963), pp. 232–251; John A. MacKay, *The Other Spanish Christ* (New York: Macmillan, 1933); Emile Pin, *Sociología del Catolicismo en América Latina* (Madrid: Oficina International de Investigaciones Sociales de FERES, 1962); François Houtart and Emile Pin, *The Church and the Latin American Revolution,* trans. by G. Barth (New York: Sheed and Ward, 1965).

10. A Catholic scholar summarizes these features by stating that one of the "great defects" of Latin American Catholicism stems from its failure to develop a "hierarchy capable of carrying on all the institutions of the Church." Coleman, p. 11.

11. In speaking of the *real patronato de las Indias,* Mecham states: "Never before or since did a sovereign with the consent of the pope so completely control the Catholic Church within his dominions . . . [This control] was not confined to ecclesiastical persons and temporalities, but even encroached upon the sphere of purely spiritual matters . . . The king . . . exercised quasi-pontifical authority." Mecham, p. 43. On problems of jurisdiction between bishops, governors, and tribunals, see Dunne, pp. 84–85. And Freyre, describing the plantation system in Brazil, notes that the priest or "chaplain" who served the household was, in fact, "a member of the patriarchal family, with the rank of bachelor uncle or an old and widowed grandfather, rather than that of a priest under the control of his bishop." Gilberto Freyre, *New World in the Tropics* (New York: Alfred A. Knopf, 1959), p. 87.

12. When a religious organization is placed in this kind of situation, its goal striving is heavily influenced by an unpredictable, short-run framework of the social process. In Parsons's terms, "political power-holders and power-aspirants are oriented to relatively short-run goals of the social system." Talcott Parsons, *Structure and Process in Modern Societies* (Glencoe, Ill.: The Free Press, 1960), p. 106.

13. A Latin American churchman asks: "Is it strange that the continent

which numbers a third of the whole Roman Communion has not produced a single outstanding theologian, or an important order, and very
few saints . . . ?" José M. Bonino, "Latin America," in M. S. Bates
and W. Pauck (eds.), *The Prospects of Christianity Throughout the
World* (New York: Charles Scribner's, 1964), p. 168.

14. This idea is developed further in Ivan Vallier, "Roman Catholicism
and Social Change in Latin America: From Church to 'Sect,'" *CIF
Reports,* III, 3 (May, 1964).

15. Robert J. Alexander, *Communism in Latin America* (New Brunswick, N.J.: Rutgers University Press, 1957); William Pierson and
Frederico G. Gil, *Governments of Latin America* (New York: Mc-
Graw-Hill, 1957); and K. H. Silvert, *The Conflict Society* (New Orleans: Hauser Press, 1961).

16. Strachan, *The Missionary Movement of the Non-Historical Groups
in Latin America;* Prudencio Damboriena, "The Pentecostals in Chile,"
Catholic Mind, 60 (1962), pp. 27–32.

17. Lipset underlines the decided parallels between religious sects and
Communist movements, particularly in terms of the status groups who
respond. This is shown on the basis of comparative data for America
and Western Europe. Seymour M. Lipset, "Extremism, Political and
Religious," from his *Political Man* (Garden City, N.Y.: Doubleday,
1960), pp. 107–108.

18. The relationships between religion, industrial society, and the organizational factor are developed comparatively for Roman Catholicism
and Protestantism in the United States, France, and Chile in Ivan
Vallier, "Religion, Organization, Industrial Society: Case Histories
and Theories," paper presented at the 59th Annual Meeting of the
American Sociological Association, Montreal, 1964, Mimeo.

19. For an introduction to this international aspect of Latin American
Catholicism, see Houtart and Pin, pp. 245–254.

20. *Informations Catholiques Internationales,* No. 176 (September 15,
1962), p. 1.

21. *CIF Reports,* I, 7 (December, 1962), p. 334.

22. Ernst Troeltsch, *The Social Teaching of the Christian Churches,* vol.
2, trans. by O. Wyon (New York: Harper Torchbooks, 1960 ed.), p.
992.

23. This section is based primarily on my field research carried out during
1962 and 1965 in Argentina, Uruguay, Chile, Peru, Bolivia, and
Mexico.

24. Most of these changes have followed the establishment of the *Consejo
Episcopal Latino-Americain* (CELAM) in 1955, with headquarters
in Bogotá.

25. For the details of the Chilean Bishops' Plan and Brazil's "Emergency"
Plan, see *Recent Church Documents from Latin America,* CIF Monograph #2 (Cuernavaca, Mexico: The Center of Intercultural Formation, 1962–63).

26. See Anne Fremantle (ed.), *The Social Teachings of the Church* (New York: Mentor-Omega Books, 1963).

27. Yves M. Congar, *Lay People in the Church,* trans. by D. Attwater (Westminster, Md.: Newman Press, 1957).

28. Karl Rahner, *The Christian Commitment,* trans. by Cecily Hastings (New York: Sheed & Ward, 1963).

29. For an empirical study of the second session of Vatican Council II, 1963, based on interviews with cardinals and bishops from all over the world, see Rock Caporale, *Vatican II: Last of the Councils* (Baltimore, Md.: Helicon Press, 1964).

30. This issue has now reached a historic point in Pope Paul VI's announcement of his decision to establish a synod of bishops "for consultation and collaboration." For a full text of this plan, see *The New York Times,* September 15, 1965, p. 14.

31. This relationship is given central attention in Robert N. Bellah, "Religious Aspects of Modernization in Turkey and Japan," *American Journal of Sociology,* LXIV (July, 1958), pp. 1–5.

32. The concept "mobilization" receives special attention in David E. Apter, "System, Process and the Politics of Economic Development," in Bert F. Hoselitz and Wilbert E. Moore (eds.), *Industrialization and Society* (Paris: UNESCO, 1963), pp. 135–158; and in Karl W. Deutsch, "Social Mobilization and Political Development," *The American Political Science Review,* LV, 3 (September, 1961), pp. 493–514.

33. Mark G. McGrath, Bishop of Panama, underlines this theme when he urges all Catholics to unite in every possible sphere with others who hold to the values of social justice and individual freedom. "The Teaching Authority of the Church: The Situation in Latin America," in William V. D'Antonio and Frederick B. Pike (eds.), *Religion, Revolution, and Reform* (New York: Frederick A. Praeger, 1964), p. 49.

34. K. H. Silvert, *Expectant Peoples. Nationalism and Development* (New York: Random House, 1963), pp. 347–372.

35. Albert O. Hirschman, *The Strategy of Economic Development* (New Haven: Yale University Press, 1958), p. 17 ff.

36. Ibid., p. 6.

37. H. A. Murena, "Notas sobre la crisis argentina," *Sur,* No. 248 (Buenos Aires: 1957), reprinted in Lewis Hanke, *South America* (Princeton, N. J.: Van Nostrand Co., 1959), pp. 159–161.

38. Roberto Fillol, *Social Factors in Economic Development. The Argentine Case* (Cambridge, Mass.: MIT Press, 1961).

39. See "The Pastoral Renewal" in François Houtart and Emile Pin, pp. 227–244.

40. For a defense of this case, see *El 'Caso' del Padre Camilo Torres* (Bogotá: Ediciones Tercer Mundo, July 30, 1965).

41. On the internal tensions within the Argentine Church, see John J. Kennedy, "Dichotomies in the Church," *Annals,* Vol. 334 (March, 1961), and *Criterio* (May 28, 1964).

42. Hugh O'Shaughnessy, "The Chilean Experiment," *Encounter,* XXV (September, 1965), pp. 87–89.
43. Seymour Martin Lipset, "Economic Development and Democracy," in *Political Man,* pp. 27–63.
44. Samuel Ramos, *Profile of Man and Culture in Mexico,* trans. by Peter G. Earle (New York: McGraw-Hill, 1962), pp. 77–78.
45. MacKay, *The Other Spanish Christ.*
46. Octavio Paz, *The Labyrinth of Solitude* (New York: Grove Press, Inc., 1961), p. 47.
47. Freyre, pp. 4 and 39.
48. Richard Morse, "The Two Americas," *Encounter,* XXV, 3 (September, 1965), p. 93.
49. *Conseil Episcopal Latino-Americain,* created by the Conference of Bishops at Rio in 1955. This council meets annually, with a permanent Secretariat in Bogotá.
50. *Confederación Latino-Americana Religiosa.*
51. International Federation of Institutions for Socio-Religious and Social Research. This organization has centers in Buenos Aires, Rio de Janeiro, Santiago, Mexico City, and Bogotá.
52. For another view on the incompatibility between Latin American religious-ethical orientations and economic development, see Roger E. Vekemans, "Economic Development, Social Change, and Cultural Mutation," in D'Antonio and Pike (eds.), pp. 131–142.

7
Cultural Elites

FRANK BONILLA

From the moment when the handful of scholar-soldiers who led Latin America into formal political independence passed from the scene, the fortunes of intellectuals have fallen and risen with the alternation of military and civilian power in government. The history of the region supports only too well the proposition that there exists some root incompatibility between men of ideas and men of action that makes clashes of temperament between the intellectual and the soldier inevitable.[1] It is not surprising then that at a time when the number of military regimes in the region seems to be approaching a new peak, intellectuals should find themselves under strong attack and in a state of disarray and dependency.[2] The point of this observation is not to suggest that all military regimes are implacably anti-intellectual or even that most of the difficulties faced by Latin American intellectuals are to be laid at the door of the military services. However, the ascendancy of the military has, by and large, meant the eclipse of all but a few favored intellectuals as well as diffuse constraints on intellectual activity. As the principal focus of cleavage in the nation and the most visible and articulate voices of divisive contention among and within parties, intellectuals are to the military political evil incarnate. The situation of the intellectual, not only as a political actor, but within his own defined spheres of special competence, is thus inextricably linked to the area's record of militarism—to the prevalence of the threat of force and the use of armed power as essential instruments of social control.[3] The number of military regimes in the region at any given time remains a good indicator of adverse change affecting cultural elites.

Anna Maria Sant'Anna of the Harvard-MIT Joint Center for Urban Studies gave valuable research assistance in the preparation of this chapter.

233

Because intellectuals for the moment symbolize disunity (and not only to the military), they are in the most controversial position of any elite group. Without pausing to define these groups or determine the degree to which they may overlap, we can clearly see that industrial, administrative, technical, and labor elites are in a more favorable or hopeful situation than cultural elites. While probably all these special-ized elite groups can be said to have some cultural functions and most would figure among intellectuals in any country, insofar as their des-ignations do set them off from these more generic categories, the labels themselves point to positive features of change in elite structures. That is, as newly invigorated groups, practically all can be said to be expanding in numbers, competence, and political influence. All are fre-quently said to be evidencing a fresh capacity and disposition to con-tribute to the solution of national problems. But the aura of optimism that embraces these technical, professional, managerial, and investment-oriented elites does not extend to the residual group, heavily freighted with those intellectuals whose concerns are primarily cultural. The intellectual is assailed from every quarter. Even the abuse heaped on intellectuals from their own ranks is rarely perceived as a sign of healthy self-criticism. It is taken rather as added evidence of fragmen-tation, dogmatism, and petty vindictiveness in the intellectual world. To the long-standing charges against cultural elites of barren sy-cophancy, imitativeness, and disconnection from local realities have been added the more contemporary accusations of disloyalty and delib-erate subversion. The intellectual at the moment commands more attention as a potential terrorist than as an active agent of desired cul-tural change or an established influence in politics.

Culture and Development

The question of the precarious status and possibly pre-insurrection-ary posture of Latin American cultural elites is of considerable impor-tance. Large-scale disaffection among intellectuals has, of course, been widely interpreted as a major symptom of imminent social upheaval.[4] But, more important here is to bring out the basic contradiction in Latin American society.

In the face of the area's chronic economic and political insolvency, Latin American self-esteem has leaned heavily on a sense of moral and cultural superiority to the United States. The high purpose and seriousness of Latin American society, according to this particular myth, are manifested in the lordly status and deference given learning and intellectual work. Inefficiencies in the economy and the machinery of government no doubt produce material disadvantages and inconveniences, but these are lightly borne by a people well disposed to pay a reasonable price so that the things of the spirit may flourish. Poverty, backwardness, corruption, and gross inequality are present but are substantially palliated by the wide scope given to individuality, the rich affect of family and friendship, the high priority over any practical consideration given to truth, morality, and beauty. However, since there is little at home to sustain the positive side of this idealized image, the evidence remains largely negative. Latin America, say the proponents of this view, is less materialistic than her northern neighbor because Latin America is poor; social relations in the region are more humane because white North Americans hate and exploit Negroes.

The issue at stake here has only a marginal relationship to the level of cultural achievement or decency of social relations in the two areas. Nor would the matter be of great consequence if it merely reflected a widespread, self-comforting delusion. The more arresting question lies in assessing the meaning for Latin American society of the jarring discrepancies between this culturally valued self-image and the obvious facts of social organization, power, and value dominance. The alleged primacy of cultural values has been readily accepted, despite the slender evidence that it actually exists in any department of social life. In Latin America, as elsewhere, apart from the extensive effort to diagnose educational problems, little serious attention has in fact been given to the role of culture or cultural elites in the process of social change and national development. Few writers have gone beyond noting the existence of a diffuse and obstructive traditionalism presumably deeply rooted in the value system.[5]

Current efforts to define and test for the presence of the attitude patterns through which this diffuse traditionalism manifests itself are refocusing attention on cultural aspects of change. Development, we are now told, since it requires a major restructuring of values and attitudes, is to be seen fundamentally as a cultural process. But is it the same to say that the development process is cultural as to say that cultural elites must take the lead in producing desired transformations? Is the modern intellectual really as crucial a figure in national development as Schumpeter's entrepreneur is taken to be for economic growth?[6] If the intellectual is to serve as an anchor of stability and a source of creative change during the transition to a higher order of national integration, what are the minimum conditions required for the organization of intellectual work on a fruitful basis? What role can the intellectual actually have in a society where conflicts of ideas are viewed with greater suspicion and intolerance than conflicts of interests?

The emphasis on cultural factors raises even broader questions for theory and policy. The new search for the cultural foundations of the successful industrial and democratic society implies that there is diminishing hope of achieving major and lasting change through economic innovation or reshufflings of the political order. The revival of the idea that a society cannot be more efficient or moral than the individuals who make it up may prove a useful counterbalance to theories that see the economy or political system as the main engines of change. However, education and socialization can prove a blind alley for policy if they become merely a way of skirting seemingly intractable problems of economic and political reform. There is, in point of fact, no true refuge for policy-makers here, whatever may be said about the attraction for conservatives of educational as against other forms of planned change. For it is specifically in the area of attitude formation and change—socialization, education, mass media effects, the creation and dissemination of ideologies, the search for noncoercive methods of mass mobilization—that theory is weakest, results least predictable, and success most dependent on the support and effectiveness of a divided, refractory sector of the elite.

It is precisely the elaboration of more extensive and effective means of such noncoercive cultural control—of cybernetics (i.e. internalized and self-adjusting mechanisms)—that Talcott Parsons sees as denoting the primacy of the cultural factor in development.[7] This higher order of social governor resting on the capacity to control information, communication, and standards of judgment is seen as superordinate to wealth and power. The main lines of modernization are to be observed in the gradual process of differentiation in the cultural system, first a shearing-off of religion from the social system followed by the successive secularization of aesthetics, politics, science, and law. Modern society in this sense is taken to have emerged only once, in Western Europe, all other cases being modern by diffusion.

All Latin America (along with all other post-Renaissance societies with Western European roots) is, by this definition, culturally modern. Parsons's formulation does not discriminate sharply among varieties of the modern, though, of course, he has extensively analyzed the U.S. case.[8] Nevertheless, his ideas provide suggestive points of reference for assessing the relative weight of the cultural sphere in Latin American society and for arriving at some sense of the nature and importance of cultural elites in regional life.

Assessing the Role of Culture and Cultural Elites

Whatever the importance assigned to the cultural factor in any development theory, it remains extremely difficult to answer the question of how cultural concerns and the relative power and prestige of cultural leaders actually predominate over other specialized elites in any specific society. At the heart of the vocation for culture, the humanist tells us, lies man's passion for truth and delight.[9] In more directly sociological terms, culture constitutes systems of belief and expressive symbols. Culture defines what is true and what is pleasurable; it provides canons for the discovery, creation, and evaluation of new truths and new forms of beauty and self-transcendence. Culture is manifest as objects (symbolic meanings) toward which action is oriented, as integral features of individual personality, and as institutionalized normative patterns.[10] Cultural elites are the elites *par excellence* in that the qualities required for high achievement seem to be rare, requiring long and concentrated cultivation to perfect. Moreover, the standards for creativity or virtuoso performance tend to be demanding.

A variety of *ad hoc* schemes for classifying types of knowledge and other cultural products have been offered; Scheler's typology ranging items along a scale of artificiality is probably the most elaborate.[11] The typology presented below, though clearly not exhaustive has the virtue of being systematically derived and almost fully satisfies the limited needs of this essay.[12] Each field of knowledge or culture is defined by three elements. Thus, science is seen to be concerned with existential propositions about the empirical world which are to be merely accepted or rejected (i.e. these are "truths" which have relatively low gratificatory significance and do not ordinarily require a response of strong commitment). Religion, on the other hand, deals with evaluative propositions about nonempirical matters in which a high priority is given to commitment as a response.

As has been noted, one would expect to find elite elements in each of these fields among those doing the principal creative work or performing with the greatest skill. To the degree that each activity engenders a specialized organizational apparatus, one would also expect to find a segment of administrators who might themselves possess little creative or performing talent but would nevertheless figure in elite circles. In a

FIGURE I

	EXISTENTIAL	EVALUATIVE	EXPRESSIVE
EMPIRICAL	Science	Ideology	Aesthetics
NONEMPIRICAL	Philosophy	Religion	Mysticism
	ACCEPTANCE	COMMITMENT	APPRECIATION

similar situation there would be a small number of critics, presumably equipped by their special knowledge and sensibility to orient public taste and monitor cultural production. Not formally covered by the typology are communicators as a class, particularly owners and administrators of mass media and other generalized communications facilities. This sector stands in a crucial relation to cultural elites but has a borderline position with respect to the basic values of the cultural sector as a whole.[13]

From this point of departure a variety of questions can be raised that help focus on cultural activities and institutions and assess their true place in Latin American society. One may ask what evidence of high achievement in the cultural sphere can be mustered, how many individuals are primarily occupied in such activities, what part of the society's resources go into such work, what degree of specialization and differentiation is manifest within the cultural sphere, how general are concerns with cultural values at all levels of the society, to what extent do uniquely cultural values spill over into and shape behavior in other spheres, how autonomous are cultural institutions, and how much of a role does cultural achievement or the control of cultural resources have in fixing individual prestige. Plainly only very approximate answers can be given to most of these questions. It should be plain as well that not all of them are equally relevant as indicators of the importance of cultural activities as such or for all types of cultural activity. Finally, of course, the questions themselves reflect culturally determined notions about how the importance of social facts may be established. Nevertheless, if Latin Americans as a people can in any meaningful sense be said to be centrally committed to values of truth, beauty, harmony and a richly textured individuality, one should reasonably expect to find important manifestations of that primacy in at least some cultural aspects.

The matter of achievement is among the most difficult to judge, both in terms of the absolute standards of individual or collective accomplishment and with respect to the significance for the society as a whole of exceptional performance by individuals. With respect to any given field of knowledge the second issue of recognition versus achievement arises. In a period when phrases such as cultural imperialism and cultural terrorism form a standard part of the lexicon of social analysis in the region, there is widespread sensibility regarding the international stratification of intellectual work and the distribution of honors for scholarly or artistic achievement. Plainly, the cultural product of the dominant countries has an unequal chance of prevailing by monopolizing attention and rewards.

What does it mean, then, that there has been only one Latin American Nobel Prize in science since the awards were first given in 1901? [14] Answers come more readily in this sphere since Latin American claims in the scientific field are certainly modest. Scientific research, outside of the field of medicine and in all but a handful of model institutions maintained as national showcases, is largely formalistic and ornamental. As recently as 1962 universities from the entire region reported a total of 939 graduates in natural science for that academic year. The equivalent figure from the same tabulation for the United States was 56,712.[15] The power of science is recognized and inspires awe, but this reverential attitude is balanced by a frank skepticism bordering on contempt.

But what is to be made of the fact that only three of the 158 saints canonized since the fifteenth century are Latin Americans? If science has flagged because its relativism, pragmatism, and subservience to industry and war have repelled a people sentimentally tied to a loftier universalism and other-worldliness, is it reasonable to expect stronger evidence of religious and mystical virtuosity? [16] Yet it is not only saints, but also theologians and outstanding Church administrators, that have been in notably short supply in the region. The more dramatic expressions of religious fervor are by and large throwbacks to more primitive forms of fundamentalism, marginal to or outside of the Catholic framework. Even when within the Church, they tend to be viewed with trepidation and reserve by modern Church leaders.[17] The low estate of the clergy—in numbers, quality of training, and cultural status—is one of the major problems of reorganization facing the Church. Contemporary Catholicism manifests greater vitality as a fountainhead of social ideology than as a spiritual force.

Thus, within these two most universalistic cultural fields—science and religion—where international communication is high, agreement on standards of performance well established, and the desire to distinguish outstanding Latin Americans no doubt present, regional achievement must by any criterion be seen as disappointing. Moreover, and particularly with respect to science, prospects for the future are not bright. As scientific endeavor moves increasingly into fields requiring the massive mobilization of resources and complex institutional arrangements, it is increasingly unlikely that regional scientists will somehow come into their own and take their place on an equal footing in the world community. Scientific manpower is meager in numbers and becoming more rather than less dependent on international opportunities for training and meaningful research. The possible impact of scientists as carriers of a new national or regional ethos seems slight indeed.

Science and religion, as universalistic systems, have been highly elaborated within the mainstream of Western culture, perhaps lending themselves less readily than other fields of cultural effort to distinctive innovation or readaptation. That is to say, the fact that both Catholicism and science represent in essence well-established bodies of dogma and method with an institutional evaluative apparatus makes them less likely than other fields of knowledge or cultural activity to be transformed in accord with individual and regional taste. Philosophy, ideology, and aesthetics have by contrast been more often defined as areas in which a people might legitimately search for those truths that could be regarded as uniquely their own. Though there have been efforts to make both science and religion more responsive to regional and national realities, the main pressure has been placed on social thought and artistic creation.

The history of social thought in Latin America can be seen as an unfulfilled search for a distinctive and compelling synthesis of ideas that might give sense, coherence, and dramatic expression to regional life for more than a select minority.[18] But the exaltation of indigenous cultures in order to affirm unique regional values and achievement has never placed a high value on the social or human worth of contemporary Indian populations. The continuing frustration of such efforts has been reflected in the persistent charges that writers and artists have lacked authenticity and have indulged in "cultural tranvestism" and other forms of subservience to foreign models and powers.[19] That Latin American intellectual life has been touched by every ideological and aesthetic current flowing from Europe and the United States in the last two centuries cannot be questioned. In a few countries, such as Chile and Argentina, the impact of formal ideologies on party organization and the process of government is plainly visible; more commonly the history of ideas in Latin America concerns itself with the intellectual byplay within small coteries of writers, artists, politicians, and social analysts. Chile is not alone in having been called a burial ground for ideologies, in the sense that all ideologies come to uneasy rest there. The prolonged skirmishing over defunct ideas, not directed to national problems in any concrete way, is often the best evidence that can be mustered to demonstrate the zeal of Latin Americans for ideas.

Ideological failure has stemmed not only from the disconnection with reality but from a failure of faith. Even the handful of luminary *pensadores* who have thought most deeply about the identity and fate of Latin America have alternated between black pessimism and ingenuous self-congratulation; intellectuals have never had more than a faltering conviction that Latin America was truly a promised land. But ideology has remained central because society has always been trying to transform itself—to locate the source of its chronic malaise and generate courage to take some prescribed cure. Because ideology, to return for a moment to the paradigm in Figure 1, is both empirical and evaluative, it not only defines the meaning of past and present; it is subject to partial verification and must therefore submit itself to some canons of proof.[20] To succeed, an ideology must not only be viable—i.e. propose imperatives for action that are realistic and produce results—but must have capacity to charm, that is, must create a future vision that captures the imagination. In this sense ideology is as much to be discovered as fashioned to please.

This polarity between the grim reality and the future vision has never been successfully resolved in Latin American thought. Only recently has the social scientist begun to supercede the man of letters in judging the state of society and providing the base for evaluating social conditions that underlie the ideologies. The results to date have not been sufficient to establish beyond dispute the superiority of the approach of the technician over that of the artist or the working politician.[21]

The ideological demands on the artist have also been great, though set against them has been the artist's own desire to transcend the limits of his own milieu and to discover a vision at once more private and more encompassing than national ideologies. Even before the emancipation of art and music from the salon, academy, the traditional conservatory, outside currents had their impact, and art was turned to social and political purpose. Today, major exponents of every contemporary literary genre and artistic style exist in Latin America. But the expectation that the post-war explosion of artistic production, the rising tide of international recognition of literary and artistic work, the appearance of a broader and more discerning public, the establishment of museums as vigorous centers of creative activity would become a prelude to development on other fronts has not been realized.

In short, it seems difficult to build a convincing case for the primacy of cultural values—concern with creativity or free expression—as a distinctive mark of Latin American society. Neither art, science, ideology, nor religion can be said to be decisive sources of motivation for change nor do they command much power as embodiments of cherished values. This of course does not mean that ideas have no role in Latin America today, or, especially, that the social and political significance of religious sentiment or of the Church as an institution can be denied. The point is rather that in all cultural action achievement has been spotty, investment in human and material resources slender, institutions weak and dependent (including those features of Church organization most directly tied to strictly religious functions). The prime values of culture are neither pervasive nor compelling, and the social status of all but the most distinguished actors in the cultural sphere quite insecure.

Some Fragmentary Data on Cultural Elites

All those with university training in Latin America have generally been regarded as within a superior class culturally, and higher education is equated with intellectual status. If the guidelines for identifying cultural elites set down in the foregoing pages are followed, the numbers within this elite in Latin America would be substantially narrowed. In fact, one of the virtues of the scheme is that it demonstrates how few of those commonly viewed as in the culture elite are more than marginally dedicated to cultural functions as defined in the paradigm. Friedmann, for example, using Brazilian data from the 1950 census, counts some 130,000 persons with advanced professional degrees

TABLE I

Holders of Professional Degrees and Persons Professionally Active, Brazil, 1950

	A. HOLDERS OF PROFESSIONAL DEGREES	B. REPORTED AS PRINCIPAL OCCUPATION	PER CENT A/B
Doctors and dentists	43,000	40,447	92%
Engineers	20,400	12,785	52%
Lawyers	31,300	15,556	48%

as among the intellectuals. Even by his generous definition, the group represented 0.5 per cent of the population over 20 years of age, a ratio of one intellectual for every 200 adults. By this standard there would be one intellectual for every 20 adults in the United States.[22]

A more recent analysis from the same Brazilian census shows some 362,000 persons ten years and older in technical, scientific, artistic, or similar activities. This number included 185,000 women, of whom 75 per cent were school teachers and 15 per cent nurses. The principal professions among males, after that of teacher (16 per cent), were physician, lawyer, dentist, pharmacist, and engineer (all in the neighborhood of 8 to 11 per cent).[23] A partial confrontation of the two sets of data suggests a further problem in using educational data as a means to estimate the approximate size and composition of the intellectual population. Some substantial differences emerge depending on whether one uses the ascriptive mantle of education or the active exercise of a profession as a criterion in establishing intellectual status. Where are the 15,000 lawyers who are not practicing law, the 7000 engineers with other occupations? How many of them are to be considered intellectuals?

Nevertheless, if one accepts a university education as an indispensable credential for cultural elite status, it is apparent that the recruitment base for elites remains heavily weighted with individuals trained in traditional professions (medicine, law, engineering) and those who prepare for teaching by studying the humanities and social science. In the figures given below for Latin American university grad-

TABLE II

University Graduates, 1962

	LATIN AMERICA		U.S.A.	
		Per cent		Per cent
Medicine, law, and engineering	25,915	42.2	81,149	16.5
Natural science	939	1.5	56,712	11.6
Fine arts and architecture	1,546	2.5	18,223	3.7
Humanities, education, etc.	33,029	53.8	334,544	68.2
	61,429	100.0	490,628	100.0

uates in 1962, there is substantial variation from country to country in the latter two categories but hardly any at all with respect to the proportions graduating in science or the fine arts (including architecture).[24]

A small study in Mexico focusing on a more narrowly selected group of intellectuals provides some details that corroborate the foregoing remarks on cultural elites and their situation. The 179 subjects were selected through what has been called the "snowball" technique. Interviews were undertaken with a list of 75 individuals who seemed to be unequivocally among the more prominent intellectuals in the nation, and each of these was asked to name three other persons whom they considered to be intellectuals. A deliberate effort was made to secure a broad spectrum of political opinion in the basic list.[25]

The group turned out to be entirely university trained; nearly four in five had university degrees, another 10 per cent had some university training. The median age of the group was about 43, about five years younger than a careful sample of Mexican legislators taken simultaneously. About one in five were women, this being nearly four times the proportion of women who had penetrated the legislative ranks. The proportion of bachelors (26 per cent) was also substantially higher than among legislators (6 per cent). The median income of the intellectuals ($400 per month) was about $150 less per month than that of legislators, who, of course, do not represent the top of the political elite in Mexico.[26]

TABLE III

Fathers' Occupational Field for
Several Latin American Elite Samples

	Mexican legislators	Mexican intellectuals	University of Chile professors	Catholic University (Chile) professors	Brazilian managers
	Per cent	Per cent	Per cent	Per cent	Per cent
Professionals	15	31	20	26	9
Business	22	30	49	36	54
Agriculture	42	11	6	13	9
Political-military *	8	10	5	8	2
Arts, communication, entertainment	—	7	2	—	1
Service and manual	13	11	18	17	24
(N) =	(96)	(179)	(85)	(82)	(174)

* About half came from each in every sample.

In terms of social origin, the Mexican intellectuals interviewed came largely from business and professional families (in contrast to the legislators, many of whom have rural beginnings), and parallel data on Chilean university professors suggest a similar pattern there. New business elites, if a Brazilian sample of managers can be taken to reflect broader trends in the region, are emerging heavily from business and secondarily from working-class backgrounds.

In terms of subjective class identification, Mexican intellectuals, as well as Chilean academics, almost unanimously count themselves as professional and middle class, as seen in Table IV.[27] More noteworthy, in view of the common lament that the material rewards of intellectual work are unfairly low, is the fact that one in four of the Mexican group and majorities in both samples of Chilean professors count themselves among the wealthy. There are no peculiarities in the distribution of income within the Mexican intellectual group that explain why somewhat more of them feel they belong among the rich than do legislators, who in fact command substantially higher incomes.

Of these elite groups, only the legislators choose to place themselves among the proletariat, and they do so far in excess of what might realistically be expected in terms of their class origins and self-designa-

TABLE IV

Subjective Views of Class
of Several Latin American Elite Samples

	Mexican legislators	Mexican intellectuals	University of Chile professors	Catholic University (Chile) professors	Brazilian managers
CLASS IDENTIFICATION:					
	Per cent	Per cent	Per cent	Per cent	Per cent
Rich	15	25	51	58	9
Modest	80	69	28	33	82
Poor	5	—	—	—	3
None	—	6	21	9	6
Professional or proprietor	75	86	88	91	53
White collar (*empleado*)	11	11	11	7	45
Worker	8	—	—	—	—
None	6	3	1	2	2
Upper class	2	9	4	23	10
Middle class	96	86	89	69	86
Lower class	2	2	3	—	1
None	—	3	4	8	3
Aristocracy	1	3	3	12	4
Bourgeoisie	30	59	66	63	68
Proletariat	43	11	9	4	14
None	27	28	22	21	14
(N) =	(96)	(179)	(86)	(82)	(174)

tion on the non-political scale. The three samples of intellectuals opt strongly for ranking as bourgeois or reject the political class scale entirely.

The predominantly middle-class identifications and pre-occupations of these intellectuals seem to be confirmed by other responses, as shown in Table V. In discussing the problems faced by people like themselves

TABLE V

Some Attitudinal Characteristics
of Several Latin American Elite Samples

	Mexican legislators	Mexican intellectuals	University of Chile professors	Catholic University (Chile) professors	Brazilian managers
PER CENT SAYING THEY:					
Are satisfied within own group	29	43	36	37	43
Are very happy or happy	86	78	79	88	91
Like competition	64	62	51	63	79
Practice a religious faith	81	66	56	94	62
(N) =	(96)	(179)	(85)	(82)	(174)

these intellectuals principally emphasized the financial difficulties of raising a family with due propriety, the problems of obtaining better training, more regular promotions, and broader recognition for achievement. Some of their other responses seem to counter familiar stereotypes of the intellectual as a socially marginal man. These Mexican intellectuals display few signs of being at odds with their middle-class world; in substantial majorities they report that they are happy, that they enjoy competition, and that they practice a religious faith. They do not seem to be any more preoccupied than the politicians or businessmen sampled about division with their own ranks.

The most dramatic signs of disaffection come in the sphere of politics—both in direct criticism of the political system, but more unexpectedly in the low sense of political efficacy and the very substantial withdrawal from politics indicated by their explanations why their own political opinions are of no significance.[28] Four times as many intellectuals as legislators affirm that the majority of Mexicans do not have an effective voice in government. Most of those who feel themselves out of the picture politically exhibited a bitterness and animus in their responses that was absent in all other parts of the interviews. The

TABLE VI

Political Attitudes and Behavior
of Several Latin American Elite Samples

	Mexican legislators	Mexican intellectuals	University of Chile professors	Catholic University (Chile) professors	Brazilian managers
PER CENT WHO SAY:					
Majority in nation do not have effective voice in government	15	64	—	—	37
Personal political views important	*	38	13	23	40
Worked actively in politics in last 6 months	*	30	10	12	7
Participated in a demonstration in last 6 months	*	18	22	16	15

* Legislators were not questioned about political activities or efficacy.

following are typical remarks: "In virtue of the fact that I am totally anti-political." "Because Mexico is a politically castrated nation." "Because politics are not governed by the opinions or activities of the people."

Preliminary data from a study of Venezuelan elites tend to confirm the over-all impressions of the Mexican data. The cultural sector within this national elite is trained principally in law and secondarily in medicine and engineering (43, 13, and 13 per cent respectively). Only 17 per cent received their primary training in the humanities. Besides a small sprinkling of prelates, all are important figures in the arts, sciences, education, and mass media. They spring almost entirely from the middle class—all of their family ties, original and those acquired in marriage, are to middle-class individuals of modest educational achievement. They began their occupational careers on the lower rungs of government, communications, and education, and slowly worked their way up to the positions of relative eminence they now occupy. Their high social mobility comes at a high cost; they emerge into the first ranks of their fields at a later age than politicians or businessmen. Even after achieving success, they remain dependent on salaries fixed primarily through decisions and allocations of resources made by political and economic elites. Their organization and communications are feeble and show a similar dependence on the more powerful political and economic sectors. Except for a special communications elite that commands the mass media—and, in effect, straddles the world of politics, business, and cultural production—the Venezuelan cultural elite by and large maintains a precarious hold on prestige and privilege and exists in an atmosphere of relative isolation, dependence, and profound frustration.[29]

Constraints on Elite Action

How is this statistical image of a fractious Babbitt to be squared with the multiple and more generous images of intellectuals prevailing in the regional folklore? Where is the man of letters, ornament of the republic, abandoning his private labors to lead the nation through a moment of crisis? Where is the committed militant turning his back on the bourgeois securities of career and family to make his life among the down-trodden? Where is the eloquent polemicist, burning conscience of the nation? All exist, and no one who has spent any amount of time in Latin America can fail to name intellectuals of high accomplishment, self-abnegation, and profound social conscience. The point is, however, that the Latin American intellectual has by and large never abandoned his middle-class roots. His political rebelliousness and protest, even his acts of insurgency and terror, are forays from a private world of submissiveness to the heavily sentimentalized bourgeois concerns with family life and social decorum as well as material comfort. It is a dizzy plunge in Latin America from the upper middle class to the bottom, and there is nowhere for the "declassed" to go.[30]

This bourgeois anchorage has made the social control of intellectuals, whether by military or civilian regimes, far easier than the region's record of instability would suggest. Though the roster of intellectuals who have given their lives in behalf of political principle is not inconsiderable, few have lived or worked for long periods under genuinely totalitarian controls. The black chronicle, past and present, of torture, arbitrary imprisonment, and other abuses of civil rights notwithstanding, these have not been the most characteristic means of cutting off elite dissent in Latin America. The intellectual confronts not highly organized repression but a diffuse and suffocating authoritarianism. This authoritarianism approaches the intellectual gently. It is permissive, pluralistic, shies away from total mobilization or ideological orthodoxy, allows considerable freedom of expression, practices co-optation with great refinement, prefers to grant a gilded exile to well-connected dissidents rather than to publicize internal rifts, remains forever open to quick and generous reconciliation. It rewards expertise and respectability.[31]

The intellectual effervescence of the early 'fifties raised the hope that the cultural elite in Latin America was finally coming of age, that it was about to take command of its own process of development and place it behind the larger project of national emancipation. The moment of self-discovery and regained self-confidence was said to be at hand. Cultural elites were to legitimize the social revolutionary ideal by formulating a convincing national ideology that would bind all in the nation together during the anticipated crises of national transformation.[32] These predictions now seem overly sanguine. The clear ascendancy of the soldier and the technocrat, with the partial admission into the power ring of the social scientist turned social engineer, are perhaps the most direct testimony of this failure. The social technician committed to profound change, who seeks escape by joining an international organization, only encounters a new form of frustration; he neither escapes politics nor gains added prestige by working *on* his country rather than in it. The path of revolution or terror, whatever its inspiration, is in essence an abdication of the intellectual role and an even graver symptom of the intellectual's dislocation in a society that pretends to prize his function.

If the task of national development truly hinges on massive cultural reconstruction—educational, ideological, moral, and scientific—and the present assessment of the status of cultural leadership is approximately correct, the prospect is disheartening indeed. The cultural elite is perhaps more obsolete than any other and is displaced from leadership even in its most sacred redoubts.[33] Yet it is only within some fragment of the present cultural elite or that of the future that one can expect to find the combination of skills, capacity to approach social standards critically, and motivation to create the ideological and moral instruments necessary to achieve the desired goals. Whatever immediate historical constraints there are on autonomous economic growth and political affirmation, the process of cultural transformation must begin within the intellectual himself. As long as he remains politically radical and socially conservative, he gains no true leverage on the shape of his own life, that of his class, or of his society.

Notes

1. In Venezuela, where the independence struggle ended with intellectuals largely relegated to the sidelines, the creation of an effective and stable civil counterbalance to military power is still short of consolidation. The antipathy between military men and men of letters in the last century is aptly pictured by Simón Rodríguez: "Rare indeed is the military man who can distinguish among men of letters, but rarer still is the literary man who will do justice to a soldier. For the military man without talent, all literary men are philosophers, and that is because subsumed within the idea of philosopher is the idea of cowardice. The vulgar man of letters views all military men as ignorant and pitiless." Introduction to "Defensa del libertador" in *Escritos de Simón Rodríguez,* compiled by Pedro Grases, 3 volumes (Caracas, 1954–58).

   The historical development of relations between the military and intellectuals in Brazil is a special case within the region though it has moved very sharply toward the common pattern within the last decade.

2. Edwin Lieuwen, *Generals vs. Presidents* (New York: Praeger, 1964) describes seven major coups over the period from 1962 to mid-1964. Countries in which the military are now overtly in control include Argentina, Bolivia, Guatemala, Ecuador, the Dominican Republic, Brazil, Haiti, Nicaragua, and Paraguay. Periodic and apparently well-founded rumors of incipient coups or potential military takeovers have repeatedly been reported during this period from Venezuela, Colombia, Salvador, and more recently, even from Uruguay and Chile.

3. On the "antipolitics" of the military see Morris Janowitz, *The Military in the Political Development of New Nations* (Chicago: University of Chicago Press, 1964).

4. Crane Brinton, *Anatomy of Revolution* (New York: Norton, 1938).

5. José Medina Echavarría, *Aspectos Sociales del Desarrollo Económico en América Latina,* Vol. II (UNESCO, 1963), p. 46 ff., reviews the main issues as presented in recent writings on the role of intellectuals

in development as these relate specifically to the Latin American situation. Several broad-scale efforts to analyze the process of cultural transformation required for effective national integration have come from the work of the now disbanded Instituto Superior de Estudos Brasileiros (ISEB). See Alvaro Vieira Pinto, *Ideologia e desenvolvimento nacional* (Rio de Janeiro: ISEB, 1960); Hélio Jaguaribe, *O nacionalismo na atualidade brasileira* (Rio de Janeiro: ISEB, 1958); Candido Mendes de Almeida, *Perspectiva atual da América Latina* (Rio de Janeiro: ISEB, 1960) and his *Nacionalismo e desenvolvimento* (Rio de Janeiro: Instituto Brasileiro de Estudos Asio-Africanos, 1963). Preliminary work toward a normatively anchored and empirically tested model of political development has begun at the Center for Development Studies of the Central University of Venezuela. See Jorge Ahumada, "Hypotheses for the Diagnosis of a Situation of Social Change: The Case of Venezuela," *International Social Science Journal*, XVI, No. 2 (1964), pp. 192–202.

6. See John Friedmann, "Intellectuals in Developing Societies," *Kyklos*, XIII (1960), Fasc. 4. Friedmann argues persuasively that intellectuals must be seen as key figures in mediating change and describes a four-step process of intellectual revolution that has interesting implication for the Latin American case. The intellectual, says Friedmann, departs from a position of moral superiority and moves toward a stage in which he undertakes experimentation with formerly rejected barbarian means, having come to believe that these innovations can be incorporated into the superstructure of his own thought and culture without too disruptive an impact. The largely frustrated concern with rationing, subduing, or exorcising technology is a related and persistent preoccupation among some Latin American intellectuals; see William S. Stokes, "The Drag of the *Pensadores*," in James W. Wriggins and Helmut Schoeck (eds.), *Foreign Aid Reexamined* (Washington, D.C.: Public Affairs Press, 1958).

7. Talcott Parsons, *Societies: Evolutionary and Comparative Perspectives* (New York: Prentice-Hall, 1966).

8. See especially *Structure and Process in Modern Society* (Glencoe, Ill.: The Free Press, 1960).

9. John U. Nef, *Cultural Foundations of Industrial Civilization* (Cambridge: Cambridge University Press, 1958) like Parsons traces the main impulse to modernization in Europe to the Renaissance. According to Nef, the drive to productivity, scientific endeavor, and improved technology was primarily aesthetic (rather than commercial) and was only subsequently turned to industrial purposes. Even then, the continued primacy of aesthetic concerns on the continent led to an initial emphasis on high quality production as contrasted with Britain's quick entry into the production of cheap goods for mass consumption.

10. See Talcott Parsons, *The Social System* (Glencoe, Ill.: The Free Press, 1951), especially chapters 8 and 9.

11. Max Scheler, *Die Formen des Wissens und der Bildung* (Bonn: F. Cohen, 1925). Arrayed from the least to the most artificial Scheler's

classes include: technology, philosophy and metaphysics, mysticism, religion, folk knowledge, myth and legend.

12. Though it does not appear in precisely this form in that volume, the typology presented in Figure 1 is taken directly from chapters 8 and 9 of Parsons's *The Social System*.

13. Educational elites will only be tangentially considered here and passing mention made of university problems.

14. An Argentine, Bernardo Houssay, in 1947 received a Nobel Prize in medicine and physiology. Professor Houssay subsequently resigned from the university under Peronist charges of incompetence. The Chilean poet, Gabriela Mistral, and the Spanish-born Puerto Rican, Juan Ramón Jiménez, received awards in literature in 1945 and 1956 respectively. Another Argentinian, Carlos Saavedra Lamas, won the Peace Prize in 1936.

15. *América en cifras,* Vol. V (Organization of American States, 1964). A more comprehensive picture of contemporary capability in Latin America for research in the physical and life sciences is given in David Bushnell, "The United States Air Force and Latin American Research," *Journal of Inter-American Studies,* 7 (April, 1965), pp. 161–178.

16. The factor of international stratification is probably not to be lost sight of even with respect to sainthood. Italy, France, and Spain alone account for 130 of the 158 saints canonized in the last six centuries. See John Coulson (ed.), *The Saints* (New York: Hawthorn Books, 1958).

17. Brazil probably presents the richest variety of syncretist and aboriginal cults. Protestant fundamentalist sects are also making inroads throughout the region.

18. See, for example, Harold Eugene Davis, *Latin American Social Thought* (Washington, D.C.: The University Press, 1961). Also William Rex Crawford, *A Century of Latin American Thought* (Cambridge, Mass.: Harvard University Press, 1961, revised edition); note especially his extensive bibliography. The literary histories by Pedro Henríquez Ureña and Arturo Torres Rioseco are helpful. Principal sources for Brazil are the works of Nelson Werneck Sodré and João Cruz Costa. John J. Johnson (ed.), *Continuity and Change in Latin America* (Stanford, Calif.: Stanford University Press, 1964) has informative articles on artists and writers.

19. Nelson Werneck Sodré, *História da literatura brasileira* (Rio de Janeiro: Livraría José Olympio Editôra, 1940). Also by the same author *Raizes históricas do nacionalismo brasileiro* (Rio de Janeiro: ISEB, 1960).

20. On the impact of the ideology of science on the building of national ideologies, see Apter's interesting essay in his *Ideology and Discontent* (New York: The Free Press of Glencoe, 1964). Clifford Geertz's "Ideology as a Cultural System" in the same volume emphasizes the opposing pull of cultural symbolism, figurative expression, and style in the formulation of ideological communications. The intricate balance between the "truth claims" and the more subjective elements of

ideology is explored in most of the ISEB publications cited earlier. Refer especially to Michel Debrun, *Ideologia e Realidade* (Rio de Janeiro: ISEB, 1959).

21. The most systematic effort to apply an interdisciplinary approach to the derivation of a national ideology of development is found in the work of ISEB. See Frank Bonilla, "Brazil: A National Ideology of Development," in Kalman H. Silvert (ed.), *Expectant Peoples* (New York: Random House, 1963). Though the *Isebistas* departed from a thorough diagnosis of the Brazilian situation, practically all of their predictions about how the complex array of interests they perceived to be at work would operate have, at least in the short run, proven inexact. The work of CEPAL, BID, and other similar agencies is another locus of pragmatic efforts to define realistic paths to national development and regional affirmation based on hard-headed assessments of economic and political realities.

22. Friedmann, "Intellectuals in Developing Societies," p. 520. The author argues both that the status of intellectuals is an ascribed characteristic of all those with professional training in developing societies and that professionals in such societies are by and large concerned with ideas to a far greater extent than is usual in the more developed West.

23. "Estudos Demográficos, No. 265," Instituto Brasileiro de Geografia e Estatística—Conselho Nacional de Estatística (mimeo, no date).

24. *América en cifras.*

25. The study was part of a large one covering four countries. The preliminary report (K. H. Silvert and Frank Bonilla, *Education and the Social Meaning of Development: A Preliminary Statement,* New York: American Universities Field Staff, 1960) did not include data on the intellectuals. The actual instructions to the core sample read as follows: "We have begun our survey with a small group of intellectuals whose deep concern for national problems is well known. Taking into account the very special nature of the intellectual community, we have chosen to leave to our first respondents the definition of who really forms an effective part of the intellectual group in Mexico. For this reason we ask you now to indicate the names of three persons that you know and feel merit the designation of intellectuals, keeping in mind that we are interested in consulting principally those persons who best express or have greatest influence on the formation of Mexican thought in all its varied forms with respect to contemporary social, economic, and political problems."

26. The comparisons with legislators are given to provide some point of reference with a specific group in Mexico itself. That has not been the main line of analysis in the original research. Details regarding the sample design for all groups shown in this paper can be found in K. H. Silvert and Frank Bonilla.

27. The Catholic University professors include more individuals claiming upper class status than any other of the samples shown here.

28. The sense of political efficacy of the intellectuals and the four samples

of educators in Chile were the lowest reported and even lower than that of people living in *favelas* in Brazil.

29. This very impressionistic summary draws heavily on preliminary analyses of the Venezuelan data by Prof. Julio Cotler of the Centro de Estudios del Desarrollo of the Central University of Venezuela. Much qualifying and specifying detail is required to place these impressions more concretely within the Venezuelan context. A description of the total research effort and some first findings will appear in a forthcoming issue of *América Latina* (Frank Bonilla, Julio Cotler, and José Agustín Silva Michelena, "La investigación sociológica y la formulación de políticas").

30. A poignant account of one young man's unsuccessful effort to navigate the distance is given in Eugenio González, *Hombres* (Santiago, Chile: Ed. Ercilla, 1935).

31. Juan Linz, "An Authoritarian Regime: Spain," in *Cleavages, Ideologies, and Party Systems. Contributions to Comparative Political Sociology,* ed. by E. Allardt and Y. Littunen (Helsinki: Transactions of the Westermarck Society, 1964), paints a full-scale portrait of this type of regime, which he sees as a distinctive form, neither an imperfect democracy nor a weakly organized dictatorship.

32. See the works cited in footnote 5.

33. "The pivotal force in the development of culture is now in the hands of doers rather than the thinkers and the centers are now the great corporations rather than the universities. It is in these new centers that new directions are charted. The danger that the entire culture may become technological is obvious. Even in the recent past the intellectuals, the professional intellectuals, knew they were the leaders of thought. But the doers are assuming this role and doing a better job than the intellectuals." Eli Ginzberg, *Technology and Social Change* (New York: Columbia University Press, 1964). Though the quotation refers principally to the U.S., it is appropriate in the present context, especially with regard to the isolation of the university from the councils of policy. The charge of obsolescence has been stated by Sergio Bagu, *Acusación y defensa del intelectual* (Buenos Aires: Colección Nuevo Mundo, Editorial Perrot, 1959). Bagu further charges intellectuals with lack of political skill, weak organization, feeble commitment to social reform, uncritical acceptance of slogans, and not meeting their obligation to heterodoxy.

8

The Labor Elite: Is It Revolutionary?

HENRY A. LANDSBERGER

I. Labor and the Concept of Elite

We shall assume that the ultimate purpose underlying this study of Latin American elites is not that of describing their internal structure and composition, necessary though this may be. Our purpose is, rather, to clarify a number of key problems concerning the influence of such elites. We shall study the influence of labor and its leadership particularly on national events of special importance to labor itself, for we assume that labor, like any elite, will above all try to affect this kind of decision. Its success or failure in influencing decisions crucial to its own fate may be taken as an index of the elite's maximum strength and power, for if an elite cannot affect even decisions of importance to itself, it is unlikely to have more influence on other decisions. In any case, the emphasis on the *status* of elites in the definition with which this volume began ("positions in society which are at the summit of key social structures") [1] needs to be complemented by an equal emphasis on certain aspects of the *role* of elites: their activities and attitudes with respect to, and their effect on, key social processes and decisions.

One step in such an analysis is to clarify the aims and goals which different Latin American elites have set for themselves: their content, breadth and level, and the intensity with which these goals are pursued. Aims may be high, for example, but rather narrow and specific. This, according to de Imaz, is the case of some Argentinian industrial elites who want a peculiar combination of freedom from restriction on

I am indebted to Professors James O. Morris, Robert Potash, and J. P. Windmuller for helpful comments. They are, of course, in no way responsible for any opinions expressed in this chapter.

the one hand and of government aid on the other, but only with respect to matters immediately affecting them. They apparently have little intrinsic interest in foreign policy and none even in major aspects of home politics which have no immediate impact on their interests.[2] This contrasts with many intellectual elites, who desire profound changes in a broad range of social institutions.

Second, an analysis needs to be made of the nature and the extent of the sources of power which a certain elite can utilize in the quest to achieve its objectives. What is the nature of its leverage and how strong is that leverage? Does its power rest on the control of economic resources, as in the case of industrial elites? of physical coercion, as in the case of the military? of mass support, as in the case of labor leaders? or of scarce human skills, as in the case of intellectuals? Does it rest on its identification with certain values which legitimate its intervention and its position on certain issues, as in the case of the Latin American Church and the "social problem"? What difference does it make to have one kind of power base rather than another?

A comparison of the goals subjectively sustained by an elite on the one hand and on the other, its objective bases of power, is of course crucial to the understanding of why some elites are "underachievers" (exercise less power than they could if they chose to do so) while others are frustrated—or are "overachievers" only because other groups have aided them. Indeed, clarification of the relationship between elites is essential for an understanding of their role. In this essay, for example, we shall have frequent occasion to refer to the relation between labor, middle-class groups, intellectuals, and the military. Also when assessing the power of an elite an examination of its internal structure and composition becomes relevant. Variations here—for example, too much ethnic heterogeneity, as in the case of Argentinian entrepreneurs [3]—may affect the extent to which potential power is converted into actual power.

Finally, and after the nature and level of goals as well as the objective sources of power of an elite have been clarified, it will be easier to understand the methods used by elites to achieve their goals, and the degree of success those methods have brought.

Before embarking on this more detailed analysis of goals, sources of power, and methods, and anticipating somewhat the section on sources of power, we must justify the fact that for purposes of this chapter, the concept of "elite" will frequently be broadened beyond positions "at the summit of key social structures." Much material on the "structures" themselves, i.e. on labor as a whole, will be presented.

The reason for such an extension is not alone, nor even most importantly, because of the absence of systematic and reliable information about labor leaders. Rather, it is due to the nature of the power of which labor leaders usually dispose. In all societies, but especially in Latin America, labor as a whole, and labor organizations in particular, are not tightly organized. With rare but, of course, important exceptions, labor is not automatically responsive to orders from its top leadership, and this is precisely one of the features which distinguishes it from several other important social groups.

Much of the power of the military elite, for example, comes from the fact that subordinates, accepting any order as legitimate, will obey their officers relatively blindly. As a result, the order-giver and only he—his values and attitudes, his abilities and objectives—become extraordinarily important, and hence worthy of study. Even in the case of the military, the obedience of subordinates becomes problematic after a certain point. But within astonishingly wide margins, the opinions of the "rank and file" may not be worth taking into account in any study of the military elite.

Much of the business elite, too, does not derive its power from its representation of the rank and file of business men. Its power and influence stem, by and large, from the wealth directly controlled by the top inner group and from the influence which that wealth and the personal connections based on it and on other considerations can buy.[4]

Intellectual elites, even more than the military and the business elites, are perhaps the extreme example of a group worth studying as individuals. The position ceded them by other groups in the process of policy formulation and implementation is due, by definition, to respect—warranted or not—for their personal knowledge and their skill in the realm of ideas, though sometimes also because of their influence on other key elites or directly on various publics.

By way of contrast with the above elites, the basis of the labor leader's influence on national decisions, in Latin America as elsewhere, is much more dependent than in the case of other elites on a highly problematic relationship with his "constituents."

In some instances—and we shall examine the characteristics of these situations below—the leader does in fact have considerable latitude, somewhat like a military leader. This allows him to operate with his own ideology or with his very personal interests in mind, as in the case of many labor leaders of the Perón era, and of Mexican labor leaders in their heyday during the 1920's. But even in these cases, this latitude needs explanation—and it is often stunningly limited.

The cases of Juan Lechín vs. President Hernán Siles of Bolivia and of John L. Lewis vs. President Franklin D. Roosevelt of the USA might serve as examples of the limitation imposed by members even on strong, charismatic leaders. It also serves to illustrate the greater severity of this limitation in Latin America as compared with the United States (although, of course, no conclusion can be based on one case). John L. Lewis, undisputed leader of North America's coal miners for many decades, was able to maintain the support of the miners and defy, through crippling strikes, a very popular president even in wartime—but only on economic issues. For even Lewis had lost that support when he had ventured to stake it on a personal feud fought out in the arena of politics in the 1940 election, at which time the miners voted for Roosevelt despite Lewis's orders. Lechín, on the other hand, while doubtlessly also idolized by Bolivia's tin miners, lost their support *even on an economic issue in which he was defending their interests.* In 1957, Lechín and the leaders of other major federations attempted to oppose Siles's economic stabilization program, which involved withdrawing subsidies from consumer goods, a wage freeze after an initial once-and-for-all adjustment, more freedom for private employers, etc. President Siles's plea to labor leaders in the *Central Obrera Boliviana* to accept these emergency measures was spurned and a general strike agreed upon. But the individual unions disavowed the strike call, and even the miners, after a personal appearance in the Oruro area by President Siles, ignored all their leaders, from local officials up to and including Juan Lechín in an extraordinary display of higher loyalty.[5]

But even instances such as those just cited, and others which we shall discuss in which labor leaders have considerable latitude, are not typical of Latin America, nor of other areas. The influence of labor is, for the most part, faceless, and insofar as spokesmen actually intervene in the process, their influence springs from the fact that they supposedly interpret the goals of their constituents. It is their—the constituents'—goals and values and their sources of strength that need to be studied, at least as much as the source of the leader's power within his constituency. As we shall see, this type of labor leader—the most frequent by far—cannot in fact ignore his constituents' goals for long and remain influential. He is much more dependent than is the military elite on the willingness of the led. Indeed, labor as a whole exerts tremendous influence on certain decisions without any of its leaders being close to the decision-making process, because those involved anticipate how "labor" —and not necessarily its leaders alone—would react if one rather than another decision were made. It is in this sense that we have called labor's influence impersonal and "faceless."

That even a government relatively friendly to labor may propose legislation affecting labor without ever consulting even the leaders sympathetic to it is illustrated by the fact that in Chile the Christian Democratic government proposed an Agricultural Reform plan in late 1965 which clearly had the rural worker in mind—but without previously consulting the *Unión de Campesinos Cristianos,* nor making substantial provisions for the participation of their leaders in the projected administrative system, as was vigorously noted at the time by UCC leaders.

Indeed, a pattern as typical as any other in Latin America—perhaps *the* single most frequent pattern—is for labor as a whole, or some neglected sector of it, to make its crucial first gains well before it is really established as a powerful pressure group. Rather, these early gains are often handed to it on a silver platter, in order to build it up as a source of support, or to forestall the growth of discontent.

In *Brazil,* mass trade unionism—as distinct from more limited, labor aristocracy unionism—was introduced from "above," in the *Estado Novo* of Getulio Vargas after 1937.[6]

In very much the same way, Perón deliberately fostered organization of the unorganized in *Argentina* in the first years of his regime: "during the 1943–1945 period, Perón threw his efforts into helping the labor movement expand. There had been perhaps 300,000 to 350,000 organized workers in Argentina when he took office. Within a couple of years this number was increased several fold. Perón forced employers . . . He personally led campaigns among packing house workers . . ."[7]

Bolivia's first labor code and its Ministry of Labor were established under the Provisional Presidency of (Col.) David Toro and made permanent under the subsequent government of (Lt. Col.) Germán Bush in the years following the coup of May 1936. While both presidents gave high positions to labor leaders, the real power base of the government was, of course, a group of young officers in the Bolivian

Army. The legislative benefits given to labor were more in anticipation of, and for stimulating, the future power of labor than the result of already existing labor power.[8]

In *Venezuela,* a declaration of labor's fundamental rights was for the first time included in the 1936 constitution, after the death of dictator Gómez in 1935. Labor at that time was more a potential than an actual force, so that its inclusion in the declaration can be attributed neither to the power of labor in general nor to that of its leaders. The labor movement did not become firmly established until the *trienio* interlude of 1945–48, sparked once again by a coup of young military officers (the *Unión Patriótica Militar*) together with the group of middle-class intellectuals represented by *Acción Democrática.* While labor did constitute an existing power by this time, it was still far enough removed from the central decision-making process, and still weak enough, for Martz to state that "the government of *Acción Democrática* turned to the workers as a major source of support, and labor was given sympathetic encouragement." [9] In other words, labor was outside, not inside, *Acción Democrática;* which in turn was the weaker of the two partners in the alliance with the military.

In *Chile,* increasing labor unrest (symbolized by the massacre of nitrate miners in the northern port of Iquique in 1907) and increasing labor organization (the *Gran Federación Obrera de Chile,* founded in 1909, was captured by the left and converted in 1917 into the *Federación Obrera de Chile*) were, of course, critical in convincing Chile's first non-oligarchic president, Arturo Alessandri Palma, to attempt to get parliament to approve a labor code in the early 'twenties. But this attempt was not the result of the lobbying activities and pressures of labor's leaders in favor of such legislation. Labor leaders were still far removed from the seats of power, or at best negligibly represented therein. The legislation was, once again, the result of estimates about the future of labor, and the result of compromises between various elite groups which did not include labor representatives nor have much direct contact with labor.[10] Labor leaders were, in fact, opposed to the new code.

In *Mexico* alone perhaps it might be said that labor's first charter—Articles 27 and 123 of the Constitution of 1917—was won in small part through the direct pressure of labor and its leaders, negotiating mainly with Alvaro Obregón, who was sympathetic and sensitive to, and influential with, the labor leaders of the *Casa del Obrero Mundial* although not himself a labor leader. However, the deciding factor even in the case of Mexico was the initiative of Obregón and other progressives, acting on the basis of their beliefs and not pressure from the leaders of the still relatively powerless working class.[11]

Thus, where labor codes have been adopted in the most highly industrialized Latin American countries (which are, of course, the ones with the strongest labor movements), we find that a wide range of situations existed with regard to labor's intervention, from the case of Mexico at one extreme, where labor's leaders played a definite role, to Brazil, where they played practically none. Yet there remains a very strong impression that most cases are more like the Brazilian than the Mexican. In most cases, direct pressure from labor as a whole, quite apart from intervention by its leaders, was quite limited or was non-existent. Among the many different reasons which have prompted existing elites, not including labor, to sponsor labor legislation seems to have been to forestall social upheavals *in the future,* to capture labor's *awakening* political power, to enhance national prestige by adhering, like other nations, to the conventions of the new international organizations of the post-Versailles period,[12] or because the elite's own ideology and value system stressed improving the position of labor.

Such being the nature of the influence of labor and of its leadership, the labor elite cannot be meaningfully analyzed without understanding its "clientele" or "constituency." This essay will, in fact, consider three groups of clients, in addition to labor leaders as such: each more encompassing than the preceding one, each less strictly an elite, and yet possessing some claim to be considered as such.

The first are those labor groups, generally unionized, whose position is exceptionally privileged and powerful. The second, wider and more diluted, is the organized sector of labor as a whole. And the third, most diluted, is urban labor, white and blue collar as a whole, organized or not; for it, too, is a favored group of relatively high influence from some points of view, as we shall demonstrate below.

It would be wrong, of course, to deny that the difference between labor leaders and other elites in their need to represent a constituency is only a matter of degree, however substantial. Military leaders, too, weaken their influence if they do not at least maintain the support of their fellow officers, and their failure to do so has sealed the fate of many a general, to mention but Juan Perón of Argentina and Rojas Pinilla of Colombia. And even a united officer corps, led by one of its elite representatives, cannot, in the long run, rule a country without popular support [13] or even maintain itself as an important sector of a larger elite unless it represents the aspirations of some group outside of itself. The instability of civilian intellectual elites on this score of unrepresentativeness is self-evident from events in Africa (Algeria, Nigeria, Dahomey, the Congo, Chad, etc.) and Asia (the weakening, of Sukarno *vis à vis* the army in 1965–66).

Nevertheless, a much more immediate dependency on his constituency is one of the prime characteristics of the labor leader as "elite" in Latin America, though, of course, that dependency is in turn not complete. To some, though to a lesser extent, the labor leader *is* like a military leader, and *does* have freedom to pursue goals not shared, or less intensely felt, by his followers. But his limits are much narrower, so that an analysis of the goals of his constituency and of the basis of *its* strength is essential to an understanding of the behavior and influence of the labor elite properly so called. To these more complex considerations we now turn.

2. The Goals and Ideology of Labor

What is most important is to clarify the exact sense and the precise extent to which the goals of labor in Latin America can be termed "revolutionary." Such an analysis links up easily with another: the correctness and the precise extent to which labor in Latin America can be regarded as "ideologized" and "politicized." Groups which explicitly have as their goal substantial changes in major social institutions, such as the property system or the system of access to political power, and which are in that sense revolutionary, generally seek their ends on the basis of explicitly formulated *ideas* about how society as a whole functions, how it should function, and what, if anything, needs to be done to reach this desirable state of affairs. In short, revolutionary goals are generally accompanied, and legitimized in the minds of their advocates, by an explicit, revolutionary ideology.

The idea that Latin American labor is revolutionary and that it is highly ideologized is widespread. In a recent article on labor leaders, Robert J. Alexander stated that:

> . . . labor itself is an integral part of the Latin American revolution . . . [and] has a wider scope of activities and different attitudes than the labor movements prevalent in the U.S. Latin

> American labor movements are not only interested in bread and
> butter questions but also in the whole process of achieving for
> its members full participation in the economic, social and po-
> litical life of the countries.[14]

and

> Organized labor in Latin America has had an essentially revo-
> lutionary role . . . [It is] part of the movement for basic eco-
> nomic, social, and political change, and has represented a group
> which was seeking a larger role in the general life of the com-
> munity.[15]

It is suggested here, first, that labor is revolutionary only in some,
albeit important, meanings of that term but definitely not in others. On
the contrary, Latin American labor—like U.S. and British labor before
it—gives some indications of being potentially quite conservative.[16] We
maintain that labor's basic aims are mundane ones: short-range, limited, economic, and not primarily the total reconstruction of society. In
this latter sense, labor is neither "ideologized" nor "revolutionary."

Second, it is our thesis that in the absence of ideologization, the ad-
mittedly intimate link between labor on the one hand and the state and
the political system, including political parties, on the other hand,
makes it essential to distinguish very clearly between "politization" and
"ideologization." Separate sets of causal factors for each of these quite
different phenomena need to be searched for. We shall seek to establish
these general theses by means of a series of factual assertions, supported
by historical data and the results of questionnaire surveys.

One final introductory point, dealing with the methodology of this
article and the use of evidence, before passing on to the arguments
themselves. We are very much aware that the use of historical examples may be sharply questioned when, as in our case, they are not selected by any scientific process of randomization. This danger can be
avoided only by including all instances of a certain phenomenon (e.g.
all "important" strikes) and sampling systematically from this "universe." This is, unfortunately, an impossibility, both practically and because of unsolved, conceptual or definitional, problems (what is an
"important" strike?). We have done our best not to bias the choice of
examples deliberately in favor of our hypotheses. But it is our profound
belief that the use of history, while rife with dangers, has the inestimable advantage of at least attempting to deal with what actually hap-

pened. For though historians may not have all relevant information and may dispute about much of it, there usually is agreement at least on the fact that something did happen! Questionnaire data, on the other hand, while superficially more attractive and systematic, are on many key issues ultimately less reliable.

3. Of Time and Revolutionary Fervor

The revolutionary fervor and ideological sensitivity [17] have declined over the years. In this first assertion, we do not maintain directly that labor today is not revolutionary or that it is not ideologized. We maintain only that it is *less* so than in the past. Our evidence or "index" for this is the relative infrequency with which one encounters today, as compared with the past, the existence of separate trade-union federations, each explicitly established in accord with some socio-political doctrine, generally of a revolutionary nature. This is particularly true for the more developed and industrialized Latin American countries, which have, of course, the more important and developed trade-union structures.[18]

In *Argentina,* for example, FORA, the *Federación Obrera Regional Argentina* was established in 1901, but split only two years later because the originally dominant socialists lost control to anarchists and therefore formed their own *Unión General de Trabajadores* (UGT). In addition, and earlier—in 1886—railroad engineers and firemen had organized themselves into a brotherhood, *La Fraternidad,* along U.S. (and, one might add, British) lines, explicitly oriented toward mutual benefit activities and collective bargaining. The anarchist unions in particular rejected bargaining and, for ideological reasons, advocated the use of direct action. In May 1910 the anarchist unions called for a general strike, again for ideological reasons far removed from immediate labor interests: to protest the celebration of the patriotic holidays—giving rise to a great deal of violence. From then until the early '40's, the history of the Argentinian labor movement consisted of a series of attempts to bring together anarchists, socialists, syndicalists, Communists, and "trade unionists," all of them ending in failure. CORA, FORA V, FORA IX, USA, COA, CGT, CGT1, CGT2: a bewildering variety of rival federations were formed, merged, split and re-established, substantially on an ideological basis, and strikes were called which had definite ideological overtones, or took on such overtones as a consequence of government suppression, as in the case of the *semana trágica* of 1919.[19]

This history of extreme factionalism on an ideological basis, so characteristic up to 1940, and the pervading influence of ideology on union tactics in the broader sense of that term—i.e. the attempt to produce a total change in institutional structure through strikes, direct action, and the refusal to bargain—must be remembered in order to see in correct perspective the degree to which Argentinian labor is ideologized today and the labor elite divided on that basis. No one can deny that some unions are today under *peronista* influence, others Communist, still others socialist, independent, Christian, etc. Nor would anyone deny that these ideological differences are sufficiently pronounced so that the adherence and non-adherence by individual unions to calls for a general strike, street demonstrations, etc., can be related to the political orientation of their leaders.

Nevertheless, the fact is that today, apart from independent unions, there is only one substantial federation—the CGT—instead of two, three, or four and that within the CGT there continue to work side by side, albeit with friction, union leaders with supposedly conflicting ideologies. In respect to union tactics and strategy, there appears to be a decrease in the importance of revolutionary ideology in the full sense of that term. Let us accept, for the sake of argument, that the *plan de lucha*[20] of the *peronista* unions in the 1964-65 period was *primarily* designed to bring down the government in order to help restore Perón and that its declared economic aims were merely a ruse (an extremely political interpretation of the *plan de lucha* which this author, and most other observers of Argentinian labor, would not be inclined to accept). Even so, the substitution of a Perón friendly to labor and necessarily relying on it, for the Illía regime, essentially laissez faire and backed by a right-wing military not friendly to labor—such a substitution is more in line with the tactic of rewarding ones' friends and punishing ones' enemies, than any indication of the desire to remodel society in accord with some grand utopian blueprint. No one in control of an important sector of labor strength is today advocating the abolition of the state and the socialization of all means of production. Both as regards union structure and tactics, therefore, the intensity and importance of ideologization and of revolutionary fervor have declined.

In *Chile,* the situation is very similar. There were, as in Argentina, early struggles between (1) anarcho-syndicalists, who in the 1890's established "Resistance Societies" eschewing bargaining (later merged into FORCH, the *Federación Obrera Regional de Chile*); (2) a group of unions with limited, "benefit society" aims accepting collective bargaining and based, as in Argentina, on the railroad workers, who established in 1909 the *Gran Federación Obrera de Chile;* (3) Marxist-oriented groups led by Recabarrén, who captured the *Gran Federación* and renamed it the *Federación Obrera de Chile* in 1917; (4) a second group of anarcho-syndicalists linked to the IWW and opposed to FORCH, despite their similar ideologies. In the late 'twenties, the surviving groups began to struggle against a new group of unions which had decided to accept and live under the labor code passed in 1924, and who established the *Confederación Nacional de Sindicatos Legales,* while the two anarcho-syndicalist groups merged to form the *Confederación General de Trabajadores*. But then the Communists divided, in addition to which a Socialist Party was established in 1932 which became involved in a murderous fight with the Communists over control of certain sectors of labor in the 1940's.[21]

Once again, no one would deny that a certain amount of friction continues within today's *Central Unica de Trabajadores* (CUT) between Socialist and Communist leaders, and even more between these two on the one hand and leaders with Christian Democratic affiliation on the other. The establishment of a separate Christian or non-Marxist confederation is within the realm of possibility. But CUT—which also includes Radicals—has held together since 1953. It has refrained from affiliating with any of the three (ideologically based) world federations of trade unions precisely in order to preserve internal unity. The break-up, should it occur, would not be over basic philosophic differences as to whether or not in principle to use collective bargaining, to accept the labor code, to plan for direct action, etc., but be rather over matters of organizational control and over co-operation with the Christian Democratic government. As with Argentina, we by no means deny the existence of ideological undertones, we maintain only that their virulence is far less than was once the case, as indicated by the absence of rival federations based on competing ideologies.

Finally, we refer briefly to the somewhat less clear-cut cases of Mexico and *Colombia*. In the latter, the two major federations were avowedly founded, originally, on competing ideologies. The UTC was established in 1946 by elements of the Conservative Party and the

Catholic Church as a counter to the CTC, founded by the Liberal
Party and, at the time, partly Communist-led. But by the 1960's, both
groups belonged to the same Latin American regional trade-union
organization, announced their intention to merge, and co-operated in a
number of educational ventures.[22] Insofar as independent and left-
wing unions have of late begun to grow up outside these federations,
this seems to be due to the success of their more aggressive bargaining
tactics, not to the attractiveness of their ideologies.

In *Mexico,* a period of "balkanization" of the trade-union movement
attended the decline of the *Confederación Regional Obrera Mexicana*
(CROM) in the late '20's and early '30's. Temporarily alleviated by
the founding of the *Confederación de Trabajadores de México*
(CTM) in 1938, splintering began in the late '40's and early '50's as
the CTM was weakened. This splintering was partly on an ideological
basis, but probably as much on the basis of dissatisfaction with the
conduct and management of the different federations and on the basis
of personal ambitions and incompatibilities. In any case, since the late
'fifties and early 'sixties, the tendency has unquestionably been toward
de facto consolidation. By 1963, the CTM was in any case numerically
dominant. But in addition, together with its erstwhile arch-rivals, the
remains of CROM, of CGT (a CROM rival founded in 1921), and of
CROC (*Confederación Revolucionaria de Obreros y Campesinos,* a
CTM rival founded in 1952), it formed the labor sector of Mexico's
ruling *Partido Revolucionario Institucional* (PRI). Labor groups
which differ sufficiently in political ideology from PRI not to support it
(CRT and the UGOCM) are estimated to have a membership of
well under 100,000.[23]

We conclude that the ideological sensitivity of labor and of its leaders and the intensity of ideological differences have weakened sufficiently over a period of time to permit the progressive consolidation of
the labor movements of different Latin American countries. Thus no
assertion is being made that, in any absolute sense, ideological differences have ceased to exist or that the different national trade-union
movements are unified.

4. Moderate vs. Extremist Ideologies and Labor Leaders

When a large sector of society for the first time exerts organized pressure through economic and/or political channels to improve its living
and working conditions, or when these conditions are improved by

other groups merely in anticipation of such pressure, then this in itself constitutes a revolution. For the nature of the decision-making process and the nature of decisions themselves have been altered. In this important sense, Latin American labor and its elite are revolutionary. The desire to pressure for improved conditions, and any success in doing so, is in itself revolutionary. But in the more extreme, more usual sense of this term—that of supporting ideologies which demand changes in power and property relations, explicitly as a necessary first step and not merely as an implicit concomitant of the recognition of labor's demands—Latin American labor has usually not been revolutionary. It is our thesis that in competition between two ideologies, one less and the other more revolutionary and extreme, the more moderate has tended to triumph, unless stifled by right-wing dictatorships. As Marx and Lenin recognized correctly long ago, labor and its leaders, if left to themselves, will not advance beyond the rather limited goals of "trade unionism."

When describing the evolution of *Argentinian* labor, we already noted that today's CGT is not only less divided ideologically and more unified, but that it is clearly less extreme than earlier anarchist, syndicalist, and socialist groups. In other words, Argentinian labor today is not revolutionary in any absolute sense of that word, which does not, however, mean that it might not support efforts to overthrow a right-wing regime which leaves it to its economic fate. In *Mexico,* we also noted that extreme left-wing groups have made little headway among labor against the distinctly moderate PRI.

The case of *Bolivia* is, however, especially instructive. Prior to the Revolution of 1952, Trotzkyist elements affiliated with the *Partido Obrero Revolucionario* (POR) had a strong foothold both in the tin mines and in various Bolivian industrial unions. The new government, composed of members of the MNR (*Movimiento Nacional Revolucionario*), proposed a moderate policy of compensating the expropriated tin mine owners. After a brief struggle in the *Central Obrera Boliviana* (COB), the previously very strong POR elements advocating outright confiscations were completely vanquished. At the same time, more independent extremist federations—the Communist (*Partido de la Izquierda Revolucionaria*) controlled *Confederación Sindical de Trabajadores de Bolivia* and the archo-syndicalist *Federación Obrera Local*—"virtually ceased to exist." [24] The MNR remained in almost total control of the Bolivian labor movement.

We would like to advance the thesis that sub-groups with really extreme ideologies among the labor elite have only attracted substantial allegiance—in these last decades of lessening ideological sensitivity and less extremism—when more moderately left leaders have turned to the right, or when such leaders have been suppressed by dictatorships.

In *Venezuela* the Communists' attempt in 1961 to found a labor federation apart from the *Confederación de Trabajadores de Venezuela* (CTV), when the dominant *Acción Democrática* (AD) was still vigorously reformist, was quite unsuccessful. They had also lost ground heavily in the *trienio* of 1945–48, when AD unions won many gains.[25] Yet in the last few years, as the AD has become more entrenched in power and less concerned with basic reforms, there are signs that its hold on the industrialized urban sectors is becoming less secure, and that it is turning increasingly to the peasantry for support. This process could also be seen in the case of the MNR in Bolivia, as it lost some of its earlier reformist zeal and with it some of its labor support.

In *Peru,* the relatively moderate APRA had little difficulty in holding its ground during the Bustamante period of 1945–48, its equivalent of the Venezuelan *trienio,* and it fared equally well during the more democratic second Prado administration of 1956–62. It was only under the earlier and less democratic Prado regime of 1940–45, that a Communist, Juan P. Luna, was elected secretary general of the CTP (1944), and he regained stature during the Odría dictatorship of 1948–56.[26] Of late, there are indications that extremism is once again increasing its hold, but this time both governmental disfavor toward APRA and the loss of aggressiveness on the part of APRA leaders themselves may well be the cause.

In *Cuba*, likewise, before 1959, extremist ideologies made rapid gains during their years of alliance with Batista in the late 'thirties and, in particular, during Batista's presidency of 1940–44. They lost control almost completely during the Grau San Martín and Prio Socarrás *Auténtico* regimes of 1944–52, to regain some of it under the second Batista dictatorship of 1952–58.

We must be careful, however, not to overstate our case. Just as Communist gains in Cuba and Peru were often due to strange alliances with right-wing dictatorships keen to restrain moderately left mass parties, so the gains of these less extreme groups were often due to favoritism from their respective governments, and to the repression of more extreme groups. The loss of Communist strength—under Prio

Socarrás in Cuba—was as much due to official hostility and to governmental encouragement of anti-Communists—i.e. *Auténticos*—as it was a "spontaneous" phenomenon.

However, if ever there was a test case of what labor's allegiance would be under genuinely free conditions, it was probably in Cuba in the eleven months following the fall of Batista on December 31, 1958. Despite the superior experience of the Communist leadership, the *Frente Obrero Humanista,* the labor sector of Castro's 26th of July movement, which was radical but anti-Communist, gained the vast majority of the union elections held in 1959. The anti-Communist Castro groups were in solid control of the CTC by the time its Tenth Congress was called in November 1959. A "unity" slate containing the names of three Communists was rejected by the Congress: a second one, with no Communists, approved. The later purge of anti-Communist leaders was a government inspired activity, not a spontaneous move on the part of labor.[27]

We conclude that in the competition for leadership, ideologically less extreme elements triumph over more extreme ones, provided they are vigorously progressive. The mass of labor follows extreme ideologies only where no genuinely progressive alternative exists, as in Guatemala, or where previously progressive leaders move toward the center or right or are replaced by individuals of this orientation.

5. Radicalism: Evidence from Attitude Surveys

There are available only two attitude surveys of Latin American labor elites sufficiently systematic to be taken as reliable sources of information. One is the study of conflict and consensus in Venezuela, conducted by the *Centro de Estudios del Desarrollo* (CENDES) of the Universidad Central de Venezuela in collaboration with Frank Bonilla of the Center for International Studies of the Massachusetts Institute of Technology.[28] The Venezuelan study is of regional and national leaders, and includes personnel from both the CTV ($N = 185$) and the more extremist CUTV ($N = 30$, which represents severe relative undersampling of the CUTV leadership universe, but may not be undersampling from the point of view of membership represented). The second study is the author's own survey of Chilean labor leaders. It is confined to blue-collar unions and covers presidents of local, plant-level unions.[29] There are no problems of political underrepresentation—

failure to respond was less than 10 per cent. In addition, we were kindly permitted to draw on Alex Inkeles's Chilean study which, apart from 37 union leaders, has the inestimable advantage of including also rank and file members both active and passive, a small group of non-unionized workers, and substantial groups of workers who had recently entered industry for the first time, as well as non-industrial and agricultural workers.[30]

TABLE I

Inkeles: "In your opinion, which of the following should be the most important task of a union?" (%)

GROUP	Improve economic position of workers (wages, pensions, etc.)	Broad program social activities	Awaken strong political attitudes and conscience	Improve physical conditions of work	TOTAL N
Union leaders	54	8	3	35	100 (37)
Union "activist" members	60	6	1	32	100 (112)
Union "passive" members	71	2	0	26	100 (260)
Non-unionized	71	0	0	29	100 (14)

My own study, designed especially for labor leaders, probed in considerable detail their goals. Designed to clarify their general conception of the function of the union (i.e. not limiting him to what it might obtain from the employer), my study asked what he thought the union should try to achieve in the next three to five years. The answer alternatives were carefully designed to permit the expression of a Marxist conception ("Arouse the workers' political consciousness") and of a traditional Catholic conception ("Improve the educational and moral level of the workers") as well as "economic betterment," "strengthen the union movement internally," "social activities," "improve physical working conditions," etc. In the Inkeles study, basically the same question but with fewer answer alternatives was asked.

The results thoroughly confirm each other: union leaders chose economic objectives as their most important in 54 per cent and 62 per cent of the cases (in the Inkeles and Landsberger studies respectively),

TABLE 2

Landsberger: "Thinking of the next three to five years, which of the following goals do you think should the union try to reach? From the following list, select three, putting a '1' against the most important, etc."

	1ST CHOICE	2ND CHOICE	3RD CHOICE	TOTAL
1. Obtain economic benefits such as salaries, severance pay, pensions, etc.	62	9	5	76
2. More weight and respect for the union in the industry; more influence in the administration of the company	5	12	9	26
3. The unification and strengthening of the union movement in Chile	10	19	14	43
4. Improve the education and spiritual development of workers	8	23	15	46
5. Make workers fully politically conscious	1	4	5	10
6. Develop more union spirit, participation, and more solidarity among the workers	6	15	15	36
7. Establish a full program of social activities	0	1	7	8
8. See that the influence of the union as a workers' organization, is felt in, and benefits the community, by taking an interest in schools and education, protect and create green zones, etc.	6	11	19	36
9. Obtain better physical conditions at work (lighting, temperature, space, etc.)	1	6	11	18
	100 (230)	100 (230)	100 (230)	

Source: Henry A. Landsberger, Manuel Barrera, and Abel Toro, "The Chilean Labor Union Leader: A Preliminary Report on His Background and Attitudes," *Industrial and Labor Relations Review,* Vol. 17, No. 3 (April, 1964), pp. 399–420 (Reprint Series No. 150). Reproduced from Table 6 on page 410 of the above article.

while arousing political awareness is seen as a first goal by 3 per cent (Inkeles) and 0.8 per cent (in Landsberger, seventh in importance!) Tables 1 and 2 represent the Inkeles and my data.

The remarkable fact is that 43 per cent of the union leaders professed to be sympathetic to the two Chilean Marxist parties, the Communist and the Socialist; yet they did not see the union in Marxist terms. And

23 per cent of the leaders professed sympathy toward the Christian Democrats; yet few emphasized education. Moreover, 73 per cent of the leaders described relations with management as very good or more good than bad and only 26 per cent as bad (3 per cent) or more bad than good (23 per cent). Once again, professing sympathy for Marxists made only a modest difference. Twelve per cent of Christian Democrats and apolitical leaders thought the company was trying to eliminate the union; and that figure rises to only 24 per cent for Socialists and Communists, and is overshadowed by the fact that 39 per cent of the latter felt the company was helping the union. Only 9 per cent of all labor leaders were sure that they would not be able to obtain their most important demand in the next round of negotiations with management, 45 per cent were sure that they would be able to obtain them, and most ascribed this to management's good will.

These answers, typical of many others which we might cite, make it quite clear that labor leaders, even when a substantial group of Marxists are included, see the function of the union as predominantly economic, and that their relationship to management is nowhere near as hostile as one might have expected it to be. Other data indicate that labor is also critical of management; that management could give more; that it does not concern itself as much with the interests of the work force as it should.[31] It is clear that there are some strong negative attitudes, but remarkable as it may seem, these are not as extreme as one might have supposed. Our aim has been to show that those most directly involved in labor management relations see the union chiefly as a tool to obtain economic benefits through collective bargaining; their Marxist or Catholic ideologies are not strong enough to guide them in their perception of the function of the union.

6. Radicalism on National Political Issues

The CENDES study makes it quite clear that, in Venezuela, a solid majority of labor leaders are not alienated from the existing political system and that they do not advocate drastic and immediate change. Fifty-nine per cent are opposed to the state's ownership of all industries, and only 37 per cent were in favor (p. 30).[32] Even the immediate nationalization of the (U.S. owned) petroleum industry was accepted by only 41 per cent of the leaders and rejected by 56 per cent (p. 30).

More than half of them want political parties to be above class and professional interests, and only 26 per cent want to see them represent specific classes (p. 67). Whereas capitalists were seen as a prime negative factor in Venezuela by only 18 per cent of the union leaders, 48 per cent saw Communists as such (by far the largest single percentage, p. 85). Thirty-two per cent (the largest single percentage) saw capitalists as a prime beneficent influence, and from 80 per cent of the respondents upward thought that anyone could reach various top jobs in the occupational hierarchy (p. 79). As for violence against the government, the largest percentage by far—48 per cent—saw it as justified only if the government itself stepped outside the law: only 16 per cent saw it as justified if the government "did not represent the interests of the people" (p. 75). One's impression is that there may be among the labor elite a hard-core extremist element of around 20 per cent, but that a substantial majority—perhaps two and a half to three or four times as much as 20 per cent, depending on the issue—is anything but extremist.

The two Chilean studies are not easily comparable to the Venezuelan one, since different questions were used. We noted above, however, that one issue where nationalism and economic radicalism fuse alluringly, so that one might have expected large "votes" in the radical direction—the issue of the immediate nationalization of the oil industry—was actually supported by fewer than 50 per cent of Venezuelan leaders.

In Chile, in the Inkeles study, respondents were asked whether, from their point of view, foreign capitalists had done good, harm, etc. (What oil is to Venezuela, copper is, of course, to Chile.) There are two astonishing results, both in line with our thesis that labor—and particularly its leaders—is more moderate than might be thought. Of the labor leaders, only 8 per cent said that foreign capitalists had done them "much harm," and 24 per cent that they had done "some harm," as compared with 41 per cent who said they had done good and 27 per cent who said they had done neither good nor harm. Secondly, and perhaps even more astonishingly, Inkeles's labor leaders (plant-level officials, as in our own study) are generally more moderate than any of his other eight groups! Percentages of those who feel foreign capitalists have done "much harm" are above 8 per cent, generally in the low or mid-'teens, and for newly industrialized, non-industrial and agricultural workers are in the upper 'teens and reach 20 per cent. Those who think that foreigners have done much good drop from 41 per cent for union leaders into the twenties for several other groups (although some groups exceed the 41 per cent figure).

But perhaps more central to the issue of extremism, unadulterated by nationalism, are questions about the extent and the rapidity of the structural changes which Chilean labor leaders believe need to be made for positive progress, and here we do find a good deal of radicalism. There is no question that the Inkeles and Landsberger studies confirm each other: in both, less than 1 per cent of the labor leaders want no structural change when asked what degree of change Chile needs in order to advance, and 33 per cent in the Inkeles study, and 34 per cent in that by Landsberger, want "total and immediate change." Groups of approximately similar size want lesser or less rapid changes, but still want substantial change in the not too distant future. Comparison with other groups (from the Inkeles study) shows that on this issue labor leaders are similar to other groups and neither more nor less radical.

We have no desire to overstate our case. We would not for a moment wish to deny that probably in most parts of Latin America labor is ready for "changes" in the general and rather vague sense. It should be noted, too, that between 1962 and early 1964 Chile had a center-right government under which inflation, briefly suppressed between 1958 and 1961, was once more underway. Labor felt quite alienated from this government (only just over 10 per cent of the leaders in the Landsberger study identified with one of the three government parties). By way of contrast, Venezuela's *Acción Democrática* is a "populist" party based in part on the working class.[33] This, together with Venezuela's objectively faster economic progress (despite, not because of, its foreign exchange situation),[34] might well have been responsible for the fact that 98 per cent of Venezuelan labor leaders thought that their country's situation would improve, while in Chile only 61 per cent thought so, and 20 per cent thought it would get worse. Also, rather ominously, 90 per cent of the Chilean leaders thought employers had a great deal of power in national decision-making, while only 10 per cent thought that labor did.

The sensitive relation within the labor sector between extremist ideology and economic or socio-political deprivation is also brought out in a recent article by Zeitlin, which demonstrates that those Cuban workers who had suffered most unemployment in the period before 1959, and those who were Negro, were most likely to support the Castro regime.[35] Does this show that there may be, after all, a substantial potential for support of change and of revolutionary regimes? After all, pre-1959 Cuban unemployment is quite typical of much of Latin America. It was perhaps less intense than in certain other areas, since Cuba experienced considerable economic growth in the 'fifties. And Chile's Alessandri government was definitely among the more progressive center-right regimes. If even these two situations can produce radicalism, a good deal of radicalism should develop.

There are two reasons, though, for not exaggerating the intensity and consistency of this desire for change. First, the Zeitlin results, plus the fact that a regime only as moderately left as *Acción Democrática* can produce, among the labor elite, a great diminution of revolutionary temperature, corroborates our main point. The underlying problem is economic, and a relatively mild improvement in economic conditions will remove the desire for a total qualitative institutional change. This is also corroborated by Kahl's study of Brazil and Mexico, in which socio-economic radicalism were found to be quite directly related to income—"Apparently our respondents are rather materialistic." [36] We express neither approval nor disapproval, nor joy or sorrow at this conclusion; we simply feel that the facts point toward it.

Second, caution is necessary because these revolutionary ideas are expressed with considerable, and puzzling, inconsistency. We have already noted that supposed Marxists do not visualize trade unions in Marxist terms, but have relations with management which are preponderantly favorable. This same inconsistency recurs in the realm of national politics. Forty-two per cent of the labor leaders with Socialist-Communist sympathies opted for the extreme alternative, "Total and immediate change," on the key question of what Chile needed in order to progress. This percentage was, of course, lower for leaders with other political orientations (22 per cent for those professing no political sympathies, 28 per cent for Christian Democrats).[37] But the main point for the present analysis—how intense are revolutionary ideologies? to what extent do they serve as orienting principles?—is surely that fewer than half of those who profess sympathy for Marxist parties subscribe to total and immediate structural change even when violence was deliberately not mentioned in order to make the statement acceptable both to "soft" Moscow-line Communists, hard-line Chinese supporters, and Trotzkyists, etc.[38]

These results are confirmed by a study of leaders of a Brazilian metal workers' federation. Lowy and Chucid obtained both the political party affiliation of their leaders and their opinions about a number of issues concerning social and economic policy. The latter permitted the leaders to be classified into "conservative and moderate," "radical," and "ultra-radical." Unfortunately, the authors do not present the absolute cut-off points for these divisions, but it seems unlikely that they would have employed the label "conservative and moderate" if that of "mildly radical" had been more appropriate, particularly since the authors' intent was clearly to prove that a process of "radicalization" of labor leaders was taking place. In view of this, it is particularly noteworthy that 25 per cent of labor leaders with Communist and Socialist affiliation were classified as "conservative and moderate" and less than half—45 per cent—as ultra-radical. Among the *Trabhalistas,* 60 per cent were conservative and moderate, and 7 per cent ultra-radical.[39]

We conclude—as did Converse [40] before us, in a study of the U. S. electorate—that the expression of all kinds of views, political allegiances, and attitudes, particularly on very general issues, cannot be taken at face value in Latin America. Such evidence as we have at the level of expressed opinions argues against the massive existence of a crystallized extremist ideology either among the labor elite or among labor as a whole. Where it does exist, it is a direct reaction to economic and status deprivation, responsive to relatively mild measures and subject to the influence of relatively mild reformist ideologies.

When labor's behavior and action are studied, rather than expressed opinions, the same conclusion is reached, as will be seen in the following section

7. Radicalism: Evidence from Behavior

THE CAUSES OF SEVERE STRIKES

To deduce motives and attitudes from behavior does, of course, create its own set of difficulties. To the extent that expressions of purpose are used, we are back with the problem of whether or not to accept these attitudes as genuine; but to deduce motives from actions directly is hazardous because we know that motives are generally mixed. The real question is: how much of each motive is present? This is precisely the kind of sophisticated question which is essential but very difficult to answer. For our purposes it is central, because our assertion is that labor is prepared to undergo the real sacrifice of a long strike or the possible danger of a street demonstration for economic rather than ideological reasons. Ideally, one should begin with a total inventory for all of Latin America of all strikes, or all "major," "long," or "important" strikes, and then classify them according to motive. But neither the inventory nor the classification is practicable. Instead we shall look at the outstanding changes in government known to have been of importance to labor, and briefly examine labor's role. Then we shall examine some of the best known strikes and elucidate what the issues were.

We will be weighting the scales against our own point of view as far as the first kind of evidence is concerned. For we do not accept that protecting a government with pro-labor policies against a *coup* by elements known to be hostile to labor can properly be called "ideological." Yet we shall find that labor has been relatively sluggish even in such crises and consistently energetic only on matters directly and immediately related to employment issues or matters directly affecting the standard of living.

In *Argentina,* where *coups* over the last 23 years have invariably had much significance for labor, labor has in fact not played a very active role—at least as much from lack of desire as from lack of power. The original June 4, 1943, coup which was the initial move toward the first, pro-labor Perón era was, of course, in no way pro-labor, and labor had no part in it. Labor had more of a role in protecting Perón from ouster on October 17, 1945, although Argentina's main labor body, the CGT, badly divided, did not officially declare a nationwide strike until late that day, after Perón had already won.[41] Alexander makes it quite clear, however, that ideology in any broad sense was not at all involved. "If the new government had made it clear that it did not intend to go back on any gains made by the workers under Perón, it could have asked for—and would very likely have received—the cooperation of the CGT and other trade union bodies. If, for instance, a labor leader of some distinction had immediately been made secretary of labor . . ."

In 1955, "the workers remained more or less passive bystanders during the drama of the overthrow of the dictatorship,"[42] and labor was once again "a passive bystander" when President Frondizi was overthrown in March 1962 despite his "last minute efforts to rally their support for his regime."[43] By 1955, Perón had antagonized much of labor by letting inflation outstrip wage gains, and Frondizi had likewise not proved as friendly as labor had hoped. Only when General Aramburu, known to be sternly right-wing and anti-labor, ousted General Lonardi, more friendly to labor, in November 1955 did labor even attempt to call a general strike. But it was a failure.[44]

This hesitancy may well be contrasted with the tenacity with which some sectors of Argentinian labor have attempted to better their condition, or to defend the conditions they had gained in the past. (The most protracted battles have, in fact, been defensive, both in Argentina and elsewhere, as we shall see.) During the last ten years, for example, by far the most widely reported strike which has taken place in Argentina has not been connected with any political event.[45] The 42-day strike of railroad workers in 1961 has all the elements common to the strikes which were taking place, or threatening to take place, on the railroads of Britain and the U.S. The issue was quite simply the job security of vast numbers of redundant employees, in other words: "featherbedding." With an increase of 30 per cent in the number of employees since 1948, and a wage bill which alone was 14 per cent more than the system's total annual income, the railways were in a sorry state, since neither freight tonnage, passengers, nor mileage had increased. The government had been footing the cost of the ever-increasing deficit but had at last appointed a commission to investigate and recommend proposals, which it did in May 1961. It proposed—as did a similar commission in Britain—the closing of uneconomic branch lines and also the elimination of auxiliary services—e.g. some of the hotel and restaurant system—which gave much employment and brought no net income. The elimination of 75,000 employees—one third of the work force—was recommended, and the government accepted these recommendations, promulgating them in a decree. After the maneuvering and bluffing which is usual in major crises of this sort, a strike finally broke out in late October, and was settled only with the mediation efforts of the Archbishop of Buenos Aires, Antonio Cardinal Caggiano, and after several (non-fatal) acts of sabotage, such as firing on trains. Lest it be argued that this is a union known for its economic orientation, let us counter that we simply do not know of any ideologically-politically oriented unions which have struck for 42 days for political reasons, let alone for ideological-revolutionary ones.

Labor's role in *Bolivia's* 1952 revolution and in the 1964 counter-revolution partly disproves our thesis, and we admit it. Labor support given to civilian MNR elements in 1952, both within La Paz and in

Oruro, was crucial in the days *after* the original police coup against the army was on the point of failing. This support was a genuinely revolutionary act: it was explicitly designed to overthrow a system of government and of class dominance.

Antecedents of the 1964 counter-revolution are less clear-cut. In the first section of this article we used the failure of the miners to support their leader, Juan Lechín, in 1957 as an indication of the limited influence held by a popular labor leader. It also shows, however, contrary to our thesis, the importance of ideological loyalties and/or political allegiances. For the miners' failure to support Lechín was in part due to their loyalty to the MNR as the embodiment of a new post-revolutionary society. Their failure was also due in part to the MNR's deliberate efforts, as a political entity, to undermine Lechín's growing, independent mass-base among the miners. And in this, there was an ideological, not merely a political element, since Lechín was the known leader of the left within the MNR, against the rightist tendencies of President Hernán Siles.

The 1963–64 tensions in the tin mines were in part the continuation of this fight for political control and ideological allegiance. By this time a third element—Communist leadership—had been added to the fight between Lechín and more right-wing MNR groups, now represented by Paz Estenssoro. Yet this struggle—which ultimately provided the rationale for the military take-over of November 2, 1964—would never have reached the intensity and bitterness it did but for an underlying economic issue.

The issue was precisely the same as in the case of Argentina's railways: job security in the face of obvious redundancy and featherbedding. The "Plan Triangular," under which technical and financial aid would be given to the Bolivian Mining Corporation (COMIBOL) to close old mines and to open and modernize others, was contingent on the Corporation's transferring and reducing its labor force. To this the miners refused to accede. The bitter strike of August 1963 was the consequence.[46] While Juan Lechín's political ambitions may have played a part, this was probably not a major factor for, first, he was out of the country at the time; second, the miners had disobeyed Lechín before (actually, on the same issue, in 1957); and third, in other Latin American countries, the elimination of redundancy has given rise to severe strikes in the absence of politically ambitious leaders.

In *Mexico,* we likewise find that the only episode of labor unrest in recent years which seems to have merited an entire article to itself was the feud between the *Sindicato de Trabajadores Petroleros de la República de México* and the Mexican government,[47] once more on exactly this same issue of job security and redundancy. After the nationalization of the oil industry in 1938, the union quickly took over a number of key positions. Attempts by the government from August 1938 onwards to reorganize the industry, release large numbers of socalled "temporary" employees, control fringe benefits, give top management greater freedom in the selection of employees at the managerial level, and restrict the operation of seniority in general, were bitterly opposed by the petroleum workers. A very protracted struggle followed extending over many years, several times involving the dismissal of union leaders and the intervention of troops.

Since it was in Mexico that labor had played a considerable role in the earlier, revolutionary years, it should be pointed out that many of the pre-revolutionary strikes which did so much to create a climate for the 1910 Revolution in fact involved quite strictly economic issues—for instance, the textile strikes gave rise to the Rio Blanco massacre of January 7, 1907. The upsurge of labor organizations in the early years of the revolution itself and their alliances with various revolutionary leaders in later years were likewise heavily based on short-run, limited economic issues, even though the influence of ideologically motivated outsiders, such as the Flores Magón brothers, was also present,[48] and political demands were made in the 1906 strike of miners in Cananea.

CORRUPTION IN LABOR ELITES AS AN INDEX OF MATERIALISM

Lipset,[49] in our opinion correctly, has used differences between trade-union movements in such matters as degree of bureaucratization, salaries of officials, and extent of corruption as indices of the value system sustained by these movements, and by the societies in which they are found. In particular, the existence of corruption is seen as an indication of the relative absence of idealism and collectivity orientation, and as an indicator of personal material aspirations.

Let it be recognized that one first needs to be able to measure corruption with some reliability. As this is clearly impossible, one is forced to rely on "impressions." Alexander states that the morals of the Latin American labor leaders "can be favorably compared to that of any other important group"—a somewhat ambiguous judgment, presumably deliberately so—and that it varies considerably from country to country, corruption being more common in some countries than in others. In our view, a somewhat more strongly worded conclusion might well be justifiable. Three of Latin America's most substantial labor movements—in Mexico, Brazil, and Argentina—have, after all, had major problems of corruption over critical periods of their histories.

The *Mexican* Federation of Labor (CROM) and its head, Luis Morones, clearly had an incomparable opportunity in the 'twenties—uniquely early for Latin America or any other area, for that matter—to obtain a body of favorable and practical labor law, to establish a broadly based and well-administered labor movement, and to improve the conditions of all labor in Mexico. The record is one of much personal enrichment and relatively little collective achievement—for example, a detailed labor code was not passed until the early '30's, by which time labor was no longer close to the seat of power.

Clark describes an astonishing variety of abuses, ranging from the misuse of strike, building, and welfare funds, to the blackmailing of employers; the signing of contracts with terms lower than might have been obtained in return for personal favors; the acceptance of bribes while holding official positions; and the use of governmental machinery to repress rival labor organizations. Luis Morones's personal wealth and the lavishness of his style of living became notorious.[50]

In *Brazil,* where the labor movement was weak before the Vargas period, the unions established by his *Estado Novo* were made so dependent on the Ministry of Labor and its labor tribunals, and they found the administration of the "union-tax" and of the social welfare and security funds so attractive, that there grew up a special, and very numerous, group of union officials contemptuously called *pelegos.* The Brazilian labor movement has still not recovered from the aura of corruption which surrounded it then.[51]

Finally, it is clear that in *Argentina,* when Perón moved in to gain control of the labor movement in the years following the 1943 coup, the blandishments he held out to some leaders were as successful, or more so, than the terror and murder he had to employ against many others. Once again, a notable sector of labor leadership used the opening provided by Perón for personal enrichment, and Alexander says that "petty graft undoubtedly ran riot in the lower echelons . . . Equally serious was the corruption in its upper strata," with Angel Borlenghi, Minister of the Interior and leader of the white-collar workers' federation, as the prime example.[52]

The tone of Alexander's assessment of labor leaders, cited at the beginning of this section, may also be contrasted with that of Víctor Alba, the distinguished Latin American analyst. Alba supports our impression of a steep decline over the years in ideology generally and in radical ideologies specifically.[53] He states that "until the 1914–1918 war, one can say that unionism was suffused by ideology . . . lack of confidence in the parliamentary system and hostility toward the state . . . and the desire to organize a society without classes on the basis of work-communities" (p. 15). Then industrialization and the rise of an educated white-collar group, as well as the rise of a working class which gets no pleasure from work, cause the union to "lose, above all its messianic tone" (p. 19). He complains that neither in members nor in leaders can there be found any appreciable influence of the nineteenth-century ideologies, nor is there any awareness of the problem of unemployment (p. 151). Concerning labor leaders, in particular those of working class origin, he cites Michels with approval, regarding the labor elite as separated from the members, devoid of idealism (pp. 137–138), and attached to a group only for personal advantages (p. 173 ff.).

We regard Alba's characterization in turn as much too sweeping and extreme. In particular it makes little allowance for those many leaders who are indeed selflessly devoted to the welfare of their members. Yet, in general, we have found considerable evidence that Latin American labor elites, both in their collective action—i.e. strikes—and in their personal behavior, are motivated strongly toward economic gains and much less strongly toward social reconstruction. Lieuwen has described how military reformist elements who have come to power with labor frequently help lose their enthusiasm both for real reform and for labor participation, and then adds, "Labor was then caught in a dilemma and, generally speaking, chose to accept the harsh alternative of more economic democracy at the expense of less political democracy."[54]

Why, then, despite this basic interest in economic rather than ideological issues, should there be such an intimate link between labor on one hand and political parties—often ideologically oriented but usually not led by labor—on the other hand?

8. The Weak Economic Base of Labor as a Mass

Up to this point we have sought to establish that the goals of labor, including those of its leadership, tend to be economic and quite limited. They are not ideological and revolutionary unless the absence of a reformist alternative drives labor to more extreme positions. Now we attempt to establish that the economic base of labor's strength is often, but not always weak, and that its political strength is generally greater. For this reason, labor very frequently uses political rather than economic means to achieve its economic goals, and certain uncontrollable factors in its relation to governmental policies reinforce this tendency.

Paradoxically Argentina's railroad workers, Mexico's petroleum workers, and Bolivia's tin miners have been here portrayed as employing economic methods with vigor. The contradiction to our present thesis—that labor generally uses political means—is resolved by returning to a crucial point made at the very beginning of this essay. Labor and labor elites should not be thought of as an undifferentiated whole, but as divisible into different sub-groups who vary, precisely, in economic and political strength and hence also in the methods they employ.

PRIVILEGED ISLANDS OF ECONOMIC AND POLITICAL STRENGTH

The relationship between economic and political strength is probably rather complicated. By definition, groups with great economic strength can hold their country up for ransom by interrupting the flow of taxes and foreign exchange (Chile's copper workers, Mexico's petroleum workers, Bolivia's tin miners) or by paralyzing internal commerce and manufacturing (railway workers and bank employers). By virtue of this very fact, they can exert political power, for they can force the government to pay attention to them. Since the government is responsible for the health of the economy, it usually has great interest in having work resume quickly, however brave the words at the beginning of bargaining sessions about "the time for a showdown has come." To all intents and purposes, the government acts like a weak employer. And in the case of state-owned industries, it is the employer, even formally. In other cases, its stake in continuing production may be at least as

great as that of the formal private employer, for the government's
"income"—in money or in terms of confidence and votes from a satisfied public—may be even more dependent on the industry than is the
prosperity of the owners.

These islands of economic strength are usually effectively unionized,
and they or their equivalents (i.e. in Chile, nitrate before copper replaced it) were probably the first to be unionized. Some of these
groups may be politically radical—the nitrate and coal miners and, to a
much lesser extent, the copper workers in Chile—and they may elect
radical leaders. But many are not ideologically radical—railway workers often are not—and in the critical test of action, they usually follow
their own interests and are in turn left alone by the rest of the working
class. General strikes called to support these islands-of-strength groups
generally do not materialize. This was so in the case of Argentina's
railway workers in 1961, and in Mexico in the case of the petroleum
workers. Conversely, these groups often do not support strikes called
by the trade-union movement at large. During the early 'sixties in
Chile, several general strikes called by tough-line Socialists of the *Central Unica de Trabajadores* were not supported either by their own Socialist colleagues among the copper workers or by the (moderate)
Radicals in the railway unions.

But this base of economic and political strength, and the organization to which it has given rise, has created a highly privileged economic status for these groups. Direct negotiations with employers, as
well as *ad hoc* state intervention and favorable permanent state laws,
have made these groups elites. Precise calculations of the extent of this
privilege are difficult to make because some at least of the income may
be in the form of such benefits as housing, subsidized food, medical services, or even (occasionally) job-security and low work loads, all of them
difficult to cost. Calculations made by the author in the case of one of
Chile's largest copper-mining operations indicated that labor costs to
the company might be as much as four or five times, perhaps even
eight to ten times, above those for the average industrial employer.

This highly privileged sector could also include certain white-collar
groups, particularly civil servants and those who are skilled and therefore difficult to replace, such as bank employees and the employees of
health services and hospitals. These white-collar groups may be much
more highly organized and militant here than those in the more indus-
trially advanced countries.

All groups in these islands-of-strength have in common not only that the executive finds it difficult to oppose them, but also that elected legislators will tend to vie for their favor. For while they may not be overly large in number, they do represent a bloc and a source of politically skilled activists (e.g. teachers) in an electorate where blocs are not easy to find, and for that reason worth wooing. In short, these groups use both economic pressure and political channels to strive—often successfully—to reach their economic goals.

THE BASIS OF MASS STRENGTH

For labor to exert much influence on the most important decisions affecting it, it must be numerous and strongly organized. Great labor movements generally have their mass basis in a big manufacturing sector—steel, chemicals, metal manufacturing, rubber, electrical goods. Small islands-of-strength are not enough. Yet the economic basis for such mass strength is, to a greater or lesser degree, absent from most Latin American countries. No understanding of labor in Latin America —sociological, political, or psychological—is possible without taking this fact into account. Hence the following factors weakening labor's strength must be cited.

First, the manufacturing sector is small when measured in terms of the percentage of the total labor force employed in it [55] (which is the relevant measure for our purposes, rather than other measures of the size of the manufacturing sector, such as its percentage contribution to gross national product). In industrialized countries, such as France or the U.S.A., manufacturing employs from 25 per cent upwards of the labor force, while in the United Kingdom it is 40 per cent. In Latin America only Argentina has reached the 25 per cent figure, and Argentina does indeed have the continent's largest, strongest, and most mature labor movement, with an estimated 2½ million union members in a labor force of 8 million. But in Chile, only 17 per cent of the labor force is in manufacturing, in Ecuador perhaps 14 per cent, in Colombia and Venezuela perhaps 11 or 12 per cent, in Honduras 8 per cent. It might be pointed out that 90 per cent of Latin America's total industrial production in terms of value comes from Brazil (36%), Argentina (28%), Mexico (15%), Chile (6%), and Venezuela (5%).[56] It is dubious that one can appropriately speak of "industrial labor" in most countries apart from these and Bolivia and Cuba.

There is, of course, nothing magical in the fact that the manufacturing sector has generally been the firmest basis for mass-labor strength. It is due to its relatively high skill requirements (thus making it difficult to replace "recalcitrant" labor), and it is due to its tendency to bring closely together large numbers of persons with common interests. In other words, manufacturing establishments tend to be large, and therefore the most easily organized apart from islands-of-strength and skilled workers. But this is not necessarily the case in Latin America, and therein lies the second factor weakening labor as a mass. Using as an index of size, within the manufacturing sector, the number of "employers plus self-employed" as compared with the number of "wage plus salary earners," we find that in the U.S.A. the ratio is 1:50, in the United Kingdom 1:35, France 1:10, and in Italy 1:4. In Latin America, Argentina, Brazil, nor Chile have published census figures on this point later than 1950. But Mexico—one of the more highly industrialized countries—shows a ratio of only 1:4½, while Venezuela has one of 1:2 and Ecuador of 1:⅔, i.e. there are more self-employed, and family workers and employers working in manufacturing than there are wage earners or salaried employees.[57]

Third, the manufacturing sector of many countries has been stagnant or at least growing only sluggishly over the past decade, particularly in the manpower terms which are of interest to us. In the face of a rising population and labor force, this means more competition for fewer jobs, and is therefore bound to undermine labor's economic strength. Between 1945 and 1950, so-called "secondary employment"—basically, manufacturing—grew at a reasonably satisfactory pace: by 21 per cent for Latin America as a whole; "tertiary employment"—commerce, services—grew by approximately the same percentage, 22 per cent. But between 1950 and 1955 the secondary sector grew by 14 per cent only, while the tertiary sector grew by 27 per cent, which would seem to indicate that some of this growth was hidden unemployment of persons who were looking for manufacturing jobs but could not find them.[58] In Chile, it has been estimated that the total in the manufacturing sector rose by only 1,000 or 0.25 per cent between 1952 and 1960 in the face of a labor force which rose by 10 per cent.[59]

Fourth and finally among the factors weakening labor's economic strength is unemployment, permanently high in Latin America. We shall not go through the ritual of citing figures and footnoting. The measurement of unemployment is notoriously difficult in Latin America for a multiplicity of reasons: conceptual (are reluctant shoeshine boys unemployed?), definitional (is two days a week "unemployed"?), administrative, political. Few who know the area put any confidence in published estimates, and, in fact, few countries even bother to publish estimates. Persons familiar with the area would probably think of 15 to 20 per cent of the urban labor force as being unemployed or underemployed, and the swollen tertiary, commerce and service sector would usually be cited as evidence of underemployment. For in few, if any, countries has the increase in the percentage of the population urbanized been matched by a similar increase in the percentage of the work force in manufacturing. In the industrialized countries—which can best afford a large tertiary, service sector of employment—the ratio of secondary to tertiary employment is $1:1$ or even $1:\frac{1}{2}$, but in Latin America—which cannot afford it—it is often $1:1\frac{1}{3}$ (Chile) or even $1:2$ (Honduras).

It is the frequently underemployed labor in this tertiary sector (except for groups such as well-organized government and bank employees), plus labor in the smaller, unorganized sub-sector of the manufacturing sector, that we regarded as a third, still weaker, but far larger "elite" than the second group: the organized manufacturing worker. How is it that either group—the organized manufacturing worker and this even weaker third group—can still be regarded as a privileged elite? The organized manufacturing worker does of course have some economic strength, although it is less than that of the "islands-of-strength" of the first group (miners, transport workers, etc.). That strength seems to be sufficient at least in a country like Chile to make union officers feel that they can get more out of direct bargaining with their employer (77%) than by involving Ministry of Labor officials or politicians in their disputes (11%).[60]

But the tertiary sector does not even have this modicum of strength, yet it is probably privileged in comparison with the rural population of the Latin American countries. Income from employment may or may not be more in the city than in the country. There is some doubt about this, though most observers would feel that it was higher even if the farmers' subsistence from home-produced food is taken into account. But the urban dweller is definitely privileged if not only income from employment but total income is included, particularly government aid such as access to education, sometimes health services and, increasingly, housing. The fact that this "income" is provided by the government and not by the employer is a clue to the fact that the strength of the urban mass is political not economic—as is the Negro's in the U.S.A. In sum: much of labor is economically weak, and for this reason alone tends to turn away from economic and toward political means to reach its economic goals.

9. The Political Orientation and Strength of Labor

There are two further reasons why labor seeks to achieve its economic aim via politics: that is, through complicated pressures on and exchanges with political parties and with the governmental machinery. First, these parties and governments have so designed the national system of decision-making that the economic status of labor is more affected by what government and political parties do than by what employers do. They therefore become the logical institutions with whom to negotiate: the locus of important decisions is in the political sphere, not in the economic. Second, labor's power in politics, both at the ballot box and elsewhere, is quite substantial and is certainly greater, relatively speaking, than its power in the economic arena. This is particularly true for the unorganized or weakly organized. Purely political groups with programs going far beyond labor's more immediate objectives have sought to harness labor's political strength.

The locus of decisions affecting labor   The three areas of decision-making which are most crucial to labor's welfare are almost entirely located in the realm of the state and the political, not subject to the employer's control. First, the structure of the union movement and of the collective-bargaining process in countries such as Brazil, Chile, Colombia, Ecuador, and Peru is regulated in great detail by the government and its agencies. Moreover, these regulations are of a very particular kind: they usually make the state an important participant in the collective-bargaining process and in internal union affairs. Second, the state regulates directly, by removing from the field of labor-employer determination, many of the most important working conditions: minimum wages (and, for government employees, wages in their entirety), overtime, length of vacations and holidays, severance pay, health and pension plans. Finally, major economic policies—inflationary and counter inflationary programs, taxes, expansion of industrial employment, import and foreign exchange controls—are in the hands of the government to the extent that they are in anyone's hands at all. Since they have a direct, critical effect on labor's standard of living, labor naturally attempts to exert influence on governmental decisions in these areas. To safeguard and raise its standard of living, labor turns to politics because that is where the decisions affecting it are made. Once labor turns to politics, the process starts anew and becomes self-perpetuating.

The vigorous role of many Latin American governments in determining union structure, the collective-bargaining process, and working conditions themselves has been well described by the International Labor Office.[61] The establishment of a union requires governmental action even in an industrialized country such as the U.S.A. But in many Latin American states—notably Brazil—the Ministry of Labor is given very broad discretionary powers, and this is not usual in the more developed countries. In the U.S.A., for example, government recognition of unions is also necessary before they can avail themselves of the protection of the law. But ground rules for doing so are promulgated and administered by a quasi-judicial body, the National Labor Relations Board, relatively independent of ministerial or political pressure. The broad discretionary powers given directly to ministries in Latin America naturally focus labor's attention on them, and in Brazil and Argentina, for example, was deliberately designed to do so.

The labor code of Chile makes it very difficult for unions to employ a professional staff and also makes negotiations above the level of the plant union difficult for any institution. In short, it practically rules out the effective use of national unions and federations. Labor naturally feels drawn into the political arena to change this and other restrictive laws in the same way the U.S. labor movement does to change Article 14 B of the 1947 Labor-Management Relations Act, and as did the British labor movement in 1945 to change that clause of the 1927 Trades Disputes Act which made it difficult for unions in collecting individual contributions for the Labour Party.

Concerning the regulation of the collective-bargaining process, many Latin American labor codes contain complicated but stringent provisions for compulsory mediation, strike votes, "cooling-off" periods, etc., and they often require that labor obtain governmental recognition of strikes. Such regulations tend, of course, to rob strikes of their effectiveness, to make labor dependent on the government, and to make many strikes illegal. The consequent threat of prosecution—frequently not exercised but always available—weakens at the very least labor's bargaining position, and certainly makes labor even more dependent on governmental goodwill and political protection, thus once again orienting it to politics.

Not only are "fringe benefits," such as vacations and holidays, sick and severance pay, in many instances fixed nationally, by legislation, but so often are two aspects of working conditions most critical to labor: wages and job security. In most Latin American countries, minimum wages are fixed if not by law then by tripartite boards whose pronouncements are binding, and who may take regional and indus-trial variations into account (indeed, they are frequently established by regions and industry).[62] Since in fact many wage rates are close to the minimum in Latin America, the impact of fixing minima is even greater there than it is, for example, in the U.S., where many rates are so far above the minimum that a change in the latter does not affect them. In Chile, these boards have in fact been guided in the annual process of wage fixing by the percentage rise in the cost of living dur-ing the preceding year; this percentage is frequently used by employ-ers to adjust other wages also.

In the area of job security, Peru is well known for having laws which make dismissal of workers, especially those with long service, very difficult and costly. But Mexico and Brazil have similar laws, and Chile has recently also passed such legislation. In short, labor finds most of its working conditions determined by the government and the parties and groups in control of it, and it is to these that it must turn.

Finally, labor inevitably looks to politics because it is deeply affected by all major governmental economic policies, even those not explicitly intended to affect labor. The failure to control consumer prices—e.g. an annual rate of inflation of 36 per cent, which is not too unusual for Chile, Brazil, or Argentina—can lose labor more in three months than any labor movement could ever hope to gain in real terms in one year through bargaining with an employer. Labor therefore pays as much or more attention to the government's price, tax, and foreign exchange policies as to the individual employer. The imposition of sales taxes in the absence of a progressive income tax or capital gains tax is properly the concern even of a labor movement which is fundamentally non-political and non-ideologically oriented. The permission by the govern-ment to have foreign exchange used to import luxury consumer items instead of machinery for industrial and employment expansion is, ob-viously, also a matter of legitimate concern even for a basically non-politically oriented labor movement.

We may cite three main reasons why Latin American governments and governing groups have seen fit to centralize these decisions in their own lands. The least important is that of legal and political tradition, both Spanish and French. Thus, the centralization of decisions concerning working conditions and detailed legal regulation of trade unions is seen as no more than a specific instance of a more general tendency to centralism, legislation, and codification.

More important is the government's desire to control labor by keeping it weak and unable to exert pressure. Both highly traditional elites —such as those which worked on the formulation of Chile's labor code in the 1910's [63]—and nationalist and intellectual elites interested in very rapid modernization have supported this policy. That is why in socialist countries unions are "transmission belts" for carrying out orders stemming from a central authority, or at best are "safety valves." Unions are not given free rein to exert the maximum pressure of which they are capable. All governments which attempt to adhere to some kind of economic plan—even more moderate governments such as the MNR of Bolivia or the Christian Democrats of Chile—sooner or later find themselves, like Britain's Labour Party, at odds with the trade-union movement and urban labor in general over labor's attempt to secure more benefits for itself.

Finally, decisions affecting labor have been given political connotations in order to convert deliberately labor's gratitude into politically effective "coin" and thus provide a source of political support for those who grant some of its demands.[64] This clearly was the motivation behind Perón's policy of locating the outcome of most labor negotiations, or union elections, ultimately in the hands of the Minister of Labor, or in those of his wife Evita. It has been an important motive in Brazil's labor policy, and to some extent in Chile's. On the surface it appears paradoxical that governments who have most desired to weaken labor and control its demands *beyond* a certain point (and are thus likely to incur its hostility) have been most desirous of gaining labor's gratitude for anything *up* to the point where control was deemed to be necessary. Only thus could sufficient goodwill be built up to make labor accept control without being alienated politically. While such a balance between concession and control is necessary both from an economic and a political point of view, it is, of course, very difficult to reach, as Perón among others found out.

The political strength of labor We have sought to establish why labor would wish and would need to be oriented toward political activities—alliances with parties, pressures and exchanges with the governmental machinery. But how does labor have the power to make its desires effective? We believe this power rests on two pillars: numerical strength at the ballot box when elections matter, and the threat of violence as the ultimate weapon when elections do not—and as a threatened additional weapon even where it does (as in Chile).

The political integration, at least in the formal sense, of the lower socio-economic classes is apparent in the rapidly rising percentages of the total population participating in elections. The most dramatic, but by no means the only case, has been that of Chile. The percentage of the population which voted went up from 18 per cent in 1958 to 32 per cent in 1964: it almost doubled not only in percentage terms in six years, but also in absolute terms (from 1,250,350 votes cast in 1958 to 2,530,697 in 1964).[65]

Literacy requirements—as well as the traditional apathy of lower classes—do keep down the political strength of the working classes in many countries such as Brazil, particularly in rural areas. Attempts to achieve a radical change in literacy requirements consequently stir up deep resistance from existing elites. Nevertheless, the tendency has been for an increase in the political participation of labor in the electoral process, and this has enabled it to make its views prevail more than heretofore in all areas of political life and government operations. The forms which this increasing strength will take is not clear. In Argentina, where extensive urban working-class participation is long established, di Tella describes one wing of Peronism as almost equivalent to a worker-led workers' party, thus breaking the tradition of labor serving merely as mass support for essentially middle-class elements.[66] But whether in other Latin American countries increased labor participation and power will similarly lead to the establishment of worker-controlled parties seems more doubtful.

Labor can also make its demands count by violence, either actual or, even more effectively, threatened. On this, many observers are agreed. Alexander has stated that "through the power of the general strike, the union can, if well organized and united, overthrow governments dominated by the military";[67] di Tella likewise draws attention to this group of weapons in labor's armory;[68] and more recently, the entire Peruvian labor relations system has been most suggestively interpreted as a model of "political bargaining" in a general setting of "democracy through violence."[69] Payne sees the rank-and-file worker as fundamentally non-ideological and oriented toward economic gain, and as exercising a restraining influence (by simple disobedience) on the more genuinely ideologically oriented labor leader. Violence is seen as normal and to be expected where voting does not function; the orientation to politics is seen by Payne as equally normal and expected for some of the same reasons adduced above.

A complete theory of the use and threat of violence by labor remains to be developed. Is it more effective against friends dependent on labor and fearful of a right-wing take-over, or is it more effective against the right wing itself? Under what conditions does labor use or threaten violence? Who does so—the weakest sectors, who have no other weapon—but may be too disorganized for this one also? or the strongest sectors, who may have no need for it—but have it available? or the sectors of intermediate strength—e.g. textile workers, as in Peru? These and other questions cannot be dealt with here. Within our context, it is only necessary to emphasize once again that violence is usually, but not exclusively or invariably, used in support of those who are ideologically to the left and against those ideologically to the right. But it seems that the rank and file cannot be convinced to threaten violence on a purely ideological issue, even if labor leaders wished to do so, unless there are genuine economic grievances.

10. Summary

We have sought to show in this essay that the role of labor in the making of those decisions which most closely affect it—let alone those which do not—cannot be usefully studied by focusing exclusively on labor leaders. The goals, means, and power of labor as a whole need to be analysed, given the fact that in Latin America as elsewhere labor organizations are political in the special sense that authority flows up, not downwards; given also the fact that labor is so weakly organized in Latin America that a military-type of obedience to leaders is not characteristic; and given further our knowledge that decisions affecting labor are not necessarily made with the participation of labor leaders but rather with the mass of labor in mind. It was then demonstrated in various ways that labor as a whole (including its leadership) is less ideological than in the past, and less extreme ideologically insofar as it still is ideological. Labor has not been consistently captured by extreme ideologies, as distinct from moderately reformist ones: only an extremely rigid *status quo* seems to produce such a tendency. Labor's goals are economic not ideological, but it seeks to use political means to reach these goals, because the decision-making process has been designed to lure labor into politics—often deliberately so. Moreover, many sectors of labor seem to have more political than economic power, partly because of Latin America's stagnant economic development and partly because of labor's rapid political involvement, through the ballot box or by violence, between 1920 and 1960. The military regimes of the middle 'sixies are, in part, intended as a curb on labor's growing, though still weak, economic and political power.

We have perhaps exaggerated somewhat the case for conceiving of labor as being basically non-ideological. But we have done so because this side of the case was urgently in need of statement.

Notes

1. See p. vii above.
2. José Luis de Imaz, *Los que mandan* (Buenos Aires: Editorial Universitaria de Buenos Aires, 1964), p. 145–7. The reference is particularly to foreign-born top managers and directors of foreign companies.
3. de Imaz, pp. 156–7.
4. The concentration of wealth even in countries as relatively pluralistic as Chile is well brought out in Ricardo Lagos's *La concentración del poder económico* (Santiago: Editorial del Pacífico, 1961), p. 181. In Argentina, according to de Imaz, the situation is apparently more complex, indeed almost paradoxical. Outstanding individuals of great personal wealth do not choose to exercise political power (p. 142); nor do the giant foreign enterprises except on restricted issues directly affecting them (pp. 146–7); while the industrial associations are, from our point of view, somewhat similiar to labor organizations: their leaders do not wield personal power but are representative and hence not overly important as individuals (p. 135).
5. For details, see Robert J. Alexander, *The Bolivian National Revolution* (New Brunswick, N.J.: Rutgers University Press, 1958), pp. 213 ff.
6. Robert J. Alexander, *Labor Relations in Argentina, Brazil and Chile* (New York: McGraw-Hill, 1962), pp. 59 ff.
7. Alexander, ibid., p. 174.
8. Alexander, *The Bolivian National Revolution*, pp. 25–27.
9. John D. Martz, "The growth and democratization of the Venezuelan labor movement," *Interamerican Economic Affairs*, Vol. 15, No. 2 (Autumn, 1963), pp. 4 ff.
10. James O. Morris, *Elites, Intellectuals and Consensus: A study of the origins of the industrial relations system in Chile, 1900–1938* (to be

published by the N.Y. State School of Industrial and Labor Relations, Cornell University, Ithaca, N.Y., 1966).

11. Marjorie Ruth Clark, *Organized Labor in Mexico* (Chapel Hill, N.C.: University of North Carolina Press, 1934), pp. 26 ff.

12. The influence on Latin America, particularly in the field of legislation, exerted by foreign "models" of labor relations, including the "model" (in a dual sense!) provided by the International Labor Organization, has been noted by many observers. See also Efrén Córdova, "Sobre la implementación del Derecho Laboral en la América Latina," *Journal of Inter-American Studies,* VIII, No. 3 (July, 1966), pp. 453–470.

13. This point is emphasized in all major analyses of the role of the military, e.g. Morris Janowitz, *The Military in the Political Development of New Nations* (Chicago: University of Chicago, 1964), p. 134.

14. Robert J. Alexander, "The Latin American Labor Leader," in William H. Form and Albert A. Blum (eds.), *Industrial Relations and Social Change in Latin America* (Gainesville, Fla.: University of Florida Press, 1965), p. 72.

15. Robert J. Alexander, *Organized Labor in Latin America* (New York: The Free Press of Glencoe, 1965), p. 12. The reader will note that throughout this chapter, we draw heavily on the work of Professor Alexander. Without his immense work there simply would not exist any account of the development of the various Latin American labor movements. Since we are taking quotations from two of his writings as the starting point of our discussion of the "revolutionary" nature of Latin American labor, we would like to make it absolutely clear that our intention is no more than that which we have stated: to clarify and make more precise the use of that word. We do not see ourselves as differing at all categorically or fundamentally from Alexander, though there is clearly some difference in emphasis.

16. The general thesis that labor is conservative was, of course, made famous for U.S. labor by Frank Tannenbaum in his *A Philosophy of Labor* (New York: Knopf, 1951), although we do not argue that Latin American labor is conservative in the precise sense in which Tannenbaum portrays U.S. labor to be. Our argument is more akin to that of the Commons-Perlman school (that labor fights for jobs) or to those who maintain that it fights for adequate wages and employment opportunities in general. See, for example, Solomon Barkin, "Labor Unions and Workers' Rights in Jobs," chapter 9 in Arthur Kornhauser *et al.* (eds.), *Industrial Conflict* (New York: McGraw-Hill, 1954), pp. 121–131.

17. We mean by this "ideological sensitivity" in the same sense as Lipset, Trow, and Coleman: to denote the tendency of individuals to perceive and define issues, persons, situations, etc., in the light of certain ideologies instead of in terms of their more immediate and practical implications. The ideologically sensitive person judges a candidate for office more according to whether or not the candidate adheres to a

certain ideology, and less according to whether he is suited to the position. See Seymour M. Lipset, Martin A. Trow, and James S. Coleman, *Union Democracy* (Glencoe, Illinois: The Free Press, 1955), pp. 306 ff.

18. The decline of ideology and revolutionary spirit in the course of industrialization is a central hypothesis in Clark Kerr, John T. Dunlop, Frederick H. Harbison, and Charles A. Myers, *Industrialism and Industrial Man* (Cambridge: Harvard University Press, 1958), see esp. pp. 208–210 and 293–294. We believe it is thoroughly applicable to Latin America, despite the region's precarious state of development.

19. Alexander, *Labor Relations in Argentina, Brazil and Chile,* p. 162 ff. See also de Imaz, p. 208 ff. De Imaz emphasizes the declining force of ideology in Argentinian labor.

20. A co-ordinated series of staggered strikes in which workers also took over factories.

21. Alexander, *Labor Relations in Argentina, Brazil, and Chile,* p. 254 ff.

22. *Labor in Colombia,* U.S. Department of Labor, Bureau of Labor Statistics Report No. 222 (March, 1962), pp. 43–44.

23. *Labor in Mexico,* U.S. Department of Labor, Bureau of Labor Statistics Report No. 251 (August, 1963), p. 91. See also Alexander, *Organized Labor in Latin America,* pp. 192 ff.

24. Alexander, *Organized Labor in Latin America,* p. 107.

25. John D. Martz, "The growth and democratization of the Venezuelan labor movement," pp. 9 ff.

26. Alexander, *Organized Labor in Latin America,* pp. 116 ff.

27. Ralph Lee Woodward, Jr., "Urban Labor and Communism," *Caribbean Studies,* Vol. 3, No. 3 (October, 1963).

28. *Estudio de conflictos y consenso, serie de resultados parciales I: muestra de líderes sindicales* (Caracas: CENDES, Universidad Central de Venezuela, 1965), p. 107. Also supporting our view of the weak radicalization of the working class is Daniel Goldrich, "Toward an estimate of the probability of social revolution in Latin America," *Centennial Review of Arts and Sciences,* Vol. V, 1962.

29. Henry A. Landsberger, Manuel Barrera, and Abel Toro, "The Chilean labor union leader: a preliminary report on his background and attitudes," *Industrial and Labor Relations Review,* Vol. 17, No. 3 (April, 1964), pp. 399–420. We shall cite unpublished results as well as results presented in the above article.

30. Apart from his own wide-ranging stock of questions, Inkeles kindly included some questions from the author's union leader study to permit comparison. Early results from Inkeles's Chilean study were calculated for us by Dr. Juan César García who had been in charge of the field work. We should like to express our warmest thanks to him. Monographs on the entire Chilean study, and on other countries included in Inkeles's study of values in modernization, are being prepared.

31. Landsberger *et al.,* "The Chilean Labor Union Leader," pp. 405–412.

32. Page numbers are from the CENDES report cited in footnote 28.

33. It is so classified by Torcuato di Tella in his "Populism and Reform in Latin America," in Claudio Veliz (ed.), *Obstacles to Change in Latin America* (New York: Oxford University Press, 1965), p. 60 ff.
34. See *Economic Survey of Latin America 1963*. 3. Growth rate by countries, Economic Commission for Latin America, Department of Economic and Social Affairs (New York: United Nations, 1965), pp. 13 ff.
35. Maurice Zeitlin, "Economic insecurity and the political attitudes of Cuban workers," *American Sociological Review,* 31, No. 1 (February, 1966), pp. 35–51.
36. Joseph A. Kahl, "A study in career values in Brazil and Mexico," p. 16 (mimeo, 1965).
37. Henry A. Landsberger, "The ideologies of labor leaders: do they really matter?" (mimeo, 1964).
38. The Chilean Communist Party pursued, and still pursues, a soft Moscow line, the Socialist Party supports a tougher ideology.
39. Michael Lowy and Sarah Chucid, "Opinioes e atitudes de lideres sindicais metalurgicos," *Revista Brasileira de Estudos Politicos,* No. 13 (January, 1962), pp. 132–169.
40. Philip J. Converse, "The Nature of Belief Systems in Mass Publics," Ch. VI, in David E. Apter (ed.), *Ideology and Discontent* (New York: The Free Press, 1964), pp. 206–261.
41. Robert J. Alexander, *The Perón Era* (New York: Columbia University Press, 1951), pp. 33 ff.
42. Alexander, *Organized Labor in America,* p. 47.
43. Ibid., p. 52.
44. Ibid., pp. 47–48. The failure of labor to take decisive action in political crises of importance to it could also be illustrated from the histories of Peru (the Odría coup of 1948, the Prado ouster of 1962), of Brazil (1964), Guatemala (1954), and Cuba (1952).
45. Morris A. Horowitz, "The trade unions of Argentina: a current picture," *Labor Law Journal,* Vol. 14, No. 9 (September, 1963), pp. 795–805.
46. Alexander, *Organized Labor in Latin America,* pp. 109–110.
47. J. Richard Powell, "Labor problems in the Mexican petroleum industry 1938–1950," *Interamerican Economic Affairs,* Vol. VI, No. 2 (Autumn, 1952), pp. 3–50.
48. Clark, *Organized Labor in Mexico,* pp. 11 ff.
49. S. M. Lipset, "Trade Unions and Social Structure: II," *Industrial Relations,* 1, 2 (February, 1962), p. 90.
50. Clark, *Organized Labor in Mexico,* pp. 106 ff.
51. Alexander, *Labor Relations in Argentina, Brazil and Chile,* pp. 65 and 75.
52. Alexander, ibid., pp. 184–5.
53. Víctor Alba, *El líder: ensayo sobre el dirigente sindical* (Mexico, D.F.: Cuadernos de sociología, Universidad Nacional, no date, 1956 approx.). Numbers in parentheses in text refer to page numbers in Alba's book. The translation is ours.

54. Edwin Lieuwen, "Militarism and Politics in Latin America," p. 138, in J. J. Johnson (ed.), *The Role of the Military in Underdeveloped Countries* (Princeton, N.J.: Princeton University Press, 1962).

55. See International Labor Office, *Yearbook of Labor Statistics, 1964*, Table 4A, pp. 14–65. Figures for individual countries are generally based on censuses taken in 1960, but sometimes earlier.

56. *Economic Survey of Latin America 1963*, Table 48, p. 73.

57. International Labor Office, *Yearbook of Labor Statistics, 1964*, Table 4A.

58. "Estudio preliminar de la situación demográfica en América Latina," presented to the ninth period of sessions of the Economic Commission for Latin America, Economic and Social Council, United Nations, held in Caracas, May 1961. Document: E/CN. 12/604.

59. "La economía de Chile en el período 1950–1963," Vol. II (Santiago: Instituto de Chile, 1963), p. 14.

60. Henry A. Landsberger, *et al.,* "The Chilean Labor Union Leader," p. 412.

61. "Labor legislation and collective bargaining in the Americas," *International Labor Review*, Vol. 84 (July–December, 1961), pp. 269–291. See also previous articles by Roberto Vernengo, "Freedom of association and industrial relations in Latin America, I and II," *International Labor Review*, Vol. 73 (May, 1956), pp. 451–482, and Vol. 74 (June, 1956), pp. 592–618.

62. "Labor legislation and collective bargaining in the Americas," pp. 270–271. See also "Minimum Wages in Latin America," International Labor Office, Studies and Reports, New Series, No. 34 (Geneva, 1959).

63. See Morris.

64. A most insightful discussion and classification of non-labor groups seeking to use labor strength by forming "populist" parties, and of the reaction of elements hostile to such alliances, is to be found in the writings of Torcuato S. di Tella. See his "Populism and reform in Latin America," pp. 47–74 in Claudio Veliz (ed.), and the final chapters of his *El sistema político Argentino y la clase obrera* (Buenos Aires: Editorial Universitaria de Buenos Aires, 1964).

65. *The Chilean Presidential Election of September 4, 1964, Part II*, Table 1 (Washington, D.C.: Institute for the Comparative Study of Political Systems, 1965), p. 2.

66. di Tella, *El sistema político Argentino y la clase obrera*, p. 108.

67. Alexander, *The Latin American Labor Leader*, p. 75.

68. di Tella, *El sistema político Argentino y la clase obrera*, p. 109.

69. James L. Payne, *Labor and Politics in Peru* (New Haven: Yale University Press, 1965), see especially pp. 3–11 and 268–283.

9
Contemporary Peasant Movements

ANÍBAL QUIJANO OBREGÓN

One of the most important elements that characterized the present process of change in Latin American societies, is the tendency of the peasants in some countries to differentiate themselves and organize and form politico-social movements to further their own interests. Sometimes the peasants are a highly organized group which exercises considerable influence over their respective countries.

In the past the peasants had always been a dispersed and isolated mass, characterized by atomistic and localistic loyalties. Despite occasional rebellions, they were only mobilized for ends unrelated to their interests and often conflicting with them. Today, however, a large proportion of the peasants seem to be developing the capacity to identify their interests, to establish certain organizations to protect their concerns, to distinguish the fundamental needs inherent in their social position. Consequently they have gradually developed certain orientations which allow them to distinguish among social and political interests well enough to identify their friends and enemies. They work politically either through independent organizations or in alliance with broader political organizations which advocate some of the most significant and immediate objectives of the peasants in their programs. Their specific demands for reforms and for radical changes are thus articulated and moderated by political parties or movements which seek to form the largest possible base of support.

It is true, however, that this phenomenon does not take place in all

The peasant movement which had an initial impact upon the Mexican revolution has not been discussed in this chapter because it is well-known. Our main interest is with present movements. Within our outline the Mexican movement would be placed under the classification of "revolutionary agrarianism."

the Latin American countries with a large peasant population. In addition, the existing movements differ according to their objectives, organization patterns, methods of action, leadership, and views of society. It is also obvious that this process of differentiation, of organization of their social interests, does not occur in either a uniform or a coherent way through all the sectors of the peasantry. We cannot expect that the development of the peasants' social awareness will take place at the same rate with the same characteristics as it does with urban workers. Peasant movements are not a new phenomenon in Latin America. Most of the countries, especially those in which the peasant population is mostly Indian, have experienced peasant rebellions throughout their post-colonial history. Nevertheless, with the exception of Mexico, such rebellions were always sporadic, ephemeral, inorganic, locally isolated, and generally were conducted according to political models which interpretated the situation along conventional lines. In addition, they tended to incorporate traditional objectives which only indirectly articulated the interests of the peasants.

Only in the last two decades have there emerged groups fostering long-range general peasant interests which go beyond the traditional emphasis on local concerns. These new movements are either characterized by a reliance on modern methods of organization or they utilize traditional ways for new objectives, developing greater social awareness among their numbers. In this sense, these peasant movements should be studied as a new phenomenon in Latin American social history.

This chapter is an attempt to develop an approach to the comparative study of peasant movements in Latin America.

Two Historical Stages of the Peasant Movements in Latin America

We still do not have sufficiently thorough studies of the social struggles of the Latin American peasants which present a clear idea of the various activities which could form the basis for an historical typology.

The present phenomenon of radical mass movements only partly arises from contemporary circumstances. In the long run it is the culmination of a prolonged process during which the peasants gradually developed the capacity to organize as a specific sector with defined social interests. For the first time today, they have found the means to crystallize their actual social needs in a politically relevant fashion.[1]

The available material does not allow any definite generalization concerning the nature and scope of the objectives of the various peasant movements, of their ideological models, of their political strategies, of their patterns of organization and leadership selection, and of the general trend of their development.[2]

Nevertheless, it is possible to divide the social struggles in Latin America into two main periods: the pre-political period, and the period of politicalization.

The pre-political movements did not call for a drastic and thorough reformation of the power structure of the society through the elimination or modification of the economic, social, and political factors which determine the social structure of the rural areas. On the whole, they pursued barely discernible objectives or intangible ends which dealt with the real situation in a fragmented way, or indirectly by implication. The few cases which went beyond this level were only able to see limited aspects of the problem without understanding the most important factors which actually conditioned the peasant situation. They were never able to perceive their social interests, and consequently, they never demanded drastic changes in the national power structure.

The dominant characteristics of the pre-political peasant movements reflect the prevalence of ideologies which prevented any realistic appraisal of the circumstances which led to the rebellions. These ideological models[3] may be called "feudal-religious," since they are largely based on a conception of social reality involving the relationship between man and the divine, or between man and a natural order of things which cannot be substantially modified. The movements maintained the same pattern of leadership and of organization as had existed in traditional structures. They rarely resulted in a definite integrated organization.

Their political strategies were in line with their limited objectives, and relied on traditional methods of organization and leadership. These limitations in their behavior were not so much the result of the decisions of the mobilized peasants as an adaptation to the dominant groups of the society and of the state.

Concrete Forms of Pre-political Movements

The various peasant movements may be classified historically as follows:

1. Messianic movements
2. Social banditry
3. Racial movements
4. Agrarian movements either traditional or incipient.

This typology does not imply a given historical sequence, or a natural pattern of development. Diverse types have existed in the same country at the same time, while there have been some overlapping elements in the same movements.

Messianic movements are those which attempt to change the relationships between men and the divine following religious models of interpreting reality and seeking expression through religious symbols. These movements are characterized by an emphasis on mysticism and even though loosely structured are organized according to sects or churches. Their leadership is considered sacred or becomes legitimate by sanctification. Their ideology stresses "retirement from the world" which often results in actual physical or spatial retirement from a world which is condemned as evil.

Social banditry, on the other hand, has essentially primitive ends. Even though clearly a form of social protest against the injustices of the most powerful, it never develops "a broader ideology" than revolt against specific abuses and oppression. Only exceptional cases have resulted in rudimentary protest organizations. On the whole, social banditry is characterized by violence by small groups. The acceptance of a leader will depend on his capacity to successfully organize such acts better than others. It does not seek to change society drastically. It differs from the other types of banditry in that its actions are largely directed against the powerful groups of the community, depend on the support and adhesion of the peasant masses, and are associated with the defense of the peasants against acts of oppression.[4]

Racial movements are defined as rebellious movements against domination by groups of different ethnic origin. Thus their objective is not a change in the social structure but the elimination of a specific dominant group, not so much because it dominates, but because of its different ethnic background. Their pattern of organization and leadership follows the traditional lines of kinship and caste more than the other movements do. They generally do not have an ideology, and in a certain sense their actions pursue a primitive objective. This type of peasant movement in Latin America has emerged in societies where ethnic differences correspond to differences in social power and prestige such as those in which a large proportion of the population are Indians living in utter poverty and isolated from the power structure of society.

Finally, the traditional or incipient agrarian movements are characterized by demands for social reform, but fail to understand the basic problems of their society. They do not seek to change the social situation of the peasants, but rather advocate the improvement of certain superficial specific aspects which vary according to circumstances. Within these movements one often finds some rudimentary elements of social awareness which indicate something about the nature of the game. However, these elements are not dominant, and are contradicted by other aspects which correspond more to feudal models of thinking about the situation. In their most developed stages the agrarian movements include patterns of organization and leadership which differ slightly from the traditional social patterns and are dedicated to the achievement of a concrete goal. They never result in permanent organizations with a reliable mass following. Their methods are always indirect, when they engage in violence it is often the result of reacting to efforts to repress them. This type is the closest to real politicalization, and under the right conditions can be incorporated in modern ideological movements, either of the syndicate (union) or revolutionary variety.

Latin America has not experienced other types of pre-political movements such as the "mafia" and the "millennial" ones which have occurred in other regions.[5] The Latin American messiahship does not seem to reflect either the characteristics or the objectives of the medieval European millennial movements.[6] Since we do not have sufficient information, it is impossible to determine a historical sequence among pre-political peasant movements in Latin America. Nevertheless, it can be said that messiahship and racism were predominant in nineteenth century, while social banditry and incipient agrarian movements have been more frequent in the twentieth century.[7]

Messiahship and racism cannot be incorporated into rational organizations of social criticism, or in broader political movements with a modern, reformist or revolutionary ideology. They are the most "archaic" and "traditional" forms of pre-political movements.

Despite its isolation and lack of a formulated ideology and an organized structure, social banditry does involve a slight abandonment of feudal-religious values. In a primitive way it is often the beginning of the secularization of social action. Since social banditry in Latin America has always been directed against the domination and the abuse of landlords, it reflects an incipient process of identification of the most important social enemy of the peasants.

Traditional or incipient agrarianism has, however, done more than the preceding movements in developing realistic social attitudes. In a traditional society, of course, this type cannot develop further. Nevertheless, it is only after this type appears on the scene that modern agrarian movements have developed.

Thus, contemporary trends in peasant movements are largely the crystallization of a new configuration of elements which have been slowly developing through a long process of experience in peasant struggles. Two of the most important currents through which peasant aspirations are channeled—revolutionary agrarianism and social banditry—are the development and modification of their pre-political equivalents, agrarianism and common banditry. These pre-political forms of peasant mobilization seem to have been predominant in Latin America until the 1930's when the development of a new type of social conscience among the peasants resulted in a new type of mobilization.

The Politicalization of Peasant Movements

Since the 1930's peasant movements have notably differed from the preceding ones in each of the analytical categories described presently. The result of these changes may be described as politicalization.

The notion of politicalization is used here to describe the behavior of all the social movements whose objectives, ideological models, organization forms, leadership and strategies of action, are mainly directed toward fundamental economic, social, and political change in the society.

Every system of social dominance uses political power as a mechanism of integration and, if need be, self-preservation. In addition, every social movement directed against basic aspects of the social order will seek a confrontation with the political power apparatus serving the system of dominance. During its development it tends to become either an independent political movement or to ally with broader political movements according to circumstances. The greater the elements of the power structure at stake, the greater the objectives of the movement, the more its influence upon the political order and politicalization.

The most important characteristic of peasant movements in Latin America throughout this period has been the tendency to question the basic aspects of the dominant social order, gradually including within their scope the most fundamental problems and calling for thorough changes in the social structure. The nature and the scope of these objectives encompass ideological models which are radically different from those which guided the traditional movements. While the earlier movements basically recombined feudal-religious values, the ideological models of the contemporary peasant movements allow them to understand the social situation in terms of the role of specific economic, social, and political factors.

It is evident that the more recent peasant movements have developed a system of organization and leadership very different from those which appeared before, though they often have adopted traditional forms of organization to new purposes. On the one hand, they have taken trade union patterns used in urban areas, which they have adapted according to their needs, or they have developed organizations *sui generis* such as peasant leagues, molded out of traditional forms of communal organization.

We must emphasize, however, that when we propose politicalization to differentiate the peasant movements of both periods, we are not implying that all the traditional ideological elements, forms of organization, leadership, strategies of action, and objectives have been completely eliminated and replaced by those derived from politicalization. This has not occurred. In fact, one can find the superimposition of elements from both periods. What is important, however, is that the fundamental tendency of this period of politicalization is the progressive relinquishment of the traditional traits or their re-elaboration in a new context. This can clearly be seen when one attempts to distinguish the principal forms of peasant activity in this later period.

Predominant Forms of Politicalization of the Peasant Movements

Based on the available information one can divide the more recent peasant movements into three types:
1. Reformist-agrarianism
2. Political banditry
3. Revolutionary agrarianism.

Unfortunately, this classification is only partly based on systematic and comparative studies, and is consequently rather limited in empirical underpinning. It is impossible to specify a temporal sequence among these forms even though the third seems to be the most recent. In addition, these categories do not exhaust all the national variations. Nevertheless, they do correspond to the principal current tendencies in the most important peasant movements of the countries in which they have been very influential.

Reformist-agrarianism is probably the most common tendency among the peasantry participating in agrarian revolts. Under this heading are included all those peasant movements in Latin America which seek partially to reform the social order, and propose the elimination of a few of the most oppressive effects of the existing power structure which affect the peasant sub-culture. On the other hand, they neither threaten nor question the power structure as such. Thus, their ideology accepts the legitimacy of the social structure and only seeks to improve the system. Their patterns of organization and of leadership are adopted from urban movements. Their methods of action closely follow the precedents of legal activities set by other underprivileged social groups, i.e. workers' organizations.

This reformist tendency has developed in different countries with two principal variants. The first consists in mobilizing the peasants to modify some specific negative aspects of the work situation. Essentially, organizations following this line of action resemble urban trade unions, and their method of action is the strike. This was the most common form of reform agrarianism until the 1950's. Its most important expressions took place in Venezuela, Bolivia, and Peru. In a less developed variety it was also to be found in Chile, Colombia, Brazil, and the Central American countries, especially El Salvador and Guatemala.[8]

On the whole, such peasant movements developed as a result of the systematic agitation of reformist political parties. They have become very effective political supporters of these parties. The most famous cases are undoubtedly the Peruvian and Venezuelan where the reformist-political parties, APRA and Acción Democratica, respectively, agitated for and helped organize peasant syndicates, eventually obtaining political backing from those rural organizations which they had helped to develop.

In general, the peasant syndicates of this period recruited their participants from rural workers in the most modern agricultural enterprises. That is, they tended to win support mainly from the wage-earning peasants or rural proletariat. They did not concentrate their attention on the other peasants. Thus, these movements largely developed in rural areas closer to the urban zones, and in those places where agriculture had been modernized and the countryside urbanized. Even though the majority of the peasants were not involved it is safe to say that in the long run these movements were very influential in paving the way for subsequent peasant movements.

Since these movements were created by urban based organizers linked to the urban parties, who molded their ideological orientation, they must be described as *dependent* peasant movements. This relationship, therefore, only partly modified, and sometimes prolonged, the dependency of the countryside on the city, the dependency of the lower strata of the population on the higher.

The *second type* of reformist-agrarianism has become more characteristic in recent years. It reflects the fact that increasingly peasants are not satisfied only with an improvement in their working conditions, a salary raise, and the other social benefits such as those which increase the standard of living of workers, but now demand a change in the land-tenure system, even though the fundamental problems of the rural power structure are usually not challenged or even questioned. This is the most prevalent characteristic of contemporary reformist-agrarianism. The fundamental objective is broader than an improvement of living and working conditions, but it still involves only a partial and limited change of the social order.

The new ideological models, of course, involve a total rupture with the traditional feudal models. The peasants no longer accept the existing power structure, although they do not propose a fundamental transformation of society. Although the new movements are aware that the peasant situation is mainly based on one factor, land maldistribution, their ideologies nevertheless remain reformist. They do not question the property system as such, or the social order of the countryside. Their methods of organization and leadership partly resemble those of previous movements. There is a tendency, however, to develop new models of organization.

The most aggressive agrarian reformists, those who are determined to reach their objectives rapidly, seldom utilize the traditional type of trade-union organization. Their organizations are the result of efforts to combine the urban-syndicate form with traditional rural organization models such as the characteristic case of the "Indian Communities" in Peru,[9] of the *ligas camponesas* in Brazil,[10] or the rural syndicates which have emerged since the events of the "Valle de la Convención" in Cuzco.[11]

Their action strategies accept in part conventional union methods. But while the strike is the characteristic weapon of the syndicates, in recent reform agrarianism the more prevalent tactic seems to be the direct appropriation of the land in a type of strike in which the peasants temporarily occupy the land.

Even though this new variant of reformist-agrarianism partly depends on support from the traditional reformist parties or sometimes revolutionary urban based groups, it is largely a more independent movement with its own leadership. It is not part of national political ideological movements, but rather has fragmented and temporary associations with one or more of them.

It differs also from the preceding type whose members were largely, and almost exculsively, recruited from the rural proletariat, in that its membership is much more heterogeneous, coming from almost all the social sectors of Latin-American rural areas, including non-agricultural groups such as merchants, artisans, and students.

Consequently, this new type of agrarian reformist movement is not only located in the rural areas contiguous to the cities or in the most developed rural regions, it also involves people from all socio-cultural strata and from all the rural areas. The more advanced movements of this type are often confused with revolutionary peasant movements, not only because their activities, their strategies, their forms of organization and objectives may eventually lead them to such a position, but also because they have begun to formulate total ideological models in order to interpret the social situation of the peasants. This type of reform agrarianism verging on the revolutionary, has been and still is characteristic of a majority of the recent peasant movements in Brazil, Peru, and Chile, although in the latter case in a rather ambiguous and incipient way during the last two years.

Revolutionary Agrarianism

Revolutionary agrarianism is, according to all signs, the latest phase of peasant movements which, in most cases, does not differ much from the most radical agrarian reform groupings.

It is characterized by the following elements:

1. Its purpose and objectives are not limited to reform or improvement of the land-tenure system as advocated by reform agrarianism, but it also calls for a substantive reform of the entire power structure affecting the peasant subculture. This includes not only the need for basic reforms in the economic aspects of the traditional order, but also the overthrow of the social and political systems linked to the economic system. Thus it is not only concerned with the redistribution of the land property, but also seeks the redistribution of authority and social prestige.

2. These policies imply that any effort to deal with the conditions of the peasants must attack all the fundamental economic, social, and political factors of society as responsible for the poverty of the peasants. They obviously involve a complete and definite break with the feudal-religious images, and with the reform models which call for changes in only a few decisive aspects, but do not advocate the global changes that will revolutionize the social system as such.

3. The methods of organization and leadership are adapted to the necessities of action in a revolutionary social and political context, though often involving a re-interpretation of existing models of organization. Thus these groups may find a new use for the model of the urban or rural syndicates or elaborate the organization model derived from the traditional pattern of community organization of a peasant population. At the highest level of action these are often turned into either military or pre-military organizations such as the militia, the band, and the guerrilla, as a reaction or a response to the repression by the state political apparatus that defends the traditional system.

4. Their strategies are mostly direct and often illegal including the seizure of land, the physical and social elimination of landlords, the destruction of the local political apparatus which is replaced by another power, and finally, armed defense or reprisal against the reaction of the landlord or the state.

In a few countries this tendency appeared separate from, but at the same time as, the development of reform agrarianism. In Colombia, for example, the experiment of the *"Repúblicas Rojas,"* of which Viata's is the most important, may be included in this category in spite of their later routinization and decadence. Even though available information is scarce, similar events seem to have occurred in El Salvador.

Revolutionary movements have become more widespread in recent years. The most developed case is the militant peasant syndicate movement in Bolivia after the 1952 revolution, emerging in a political context favorable to its growth, although it became dependent upon the political party which seized power.[12]

Others which emerged under different circumstances include the famous peasant movements of the valley of La Convención and of Lares, in Cuzco, Peru, under the leadership of Hugo Blanco. The present "red republics" (*Repúblicas Rojas*) are an example of the development of revolutionary tendencies though modification of what started as political banditry. We could also include the actions of the Brazilian *ligas camponesas* in this grouping.[13]

Undoubtedly, such tendencies are the climax of a process of politicalization among peasant movements. As these movements question the nature of the power structure, seize the local political apparatus which defends the established landed system, and create a new political power, they necessarily become politicized. These peasant movements, however, despite their association with revolutionary organizations tend to develop a clearer sense of the need for responsibility and relative autonomy from other groups. Thus, these movements often develop as an autonomous and distinct political force. An independent peasant leadership then emerges which, though it associates with broader national movements, does so on its own conditions.

The best example of a high level of peasant politicalization occurred in Bolivia. A peasant syndicate and militia movement was organized under the direction of the urban revolutionary group, and was then legalized and co-ordinated by the MNR. For some time its leadership depended almost completely on the governing party. Eventually, however, it acquired sufficient autonomy so that the government party found it necessary to negotiate with the peasant leaders in order to retain their support. Even though at the present, a large part of the radical peasant leadership seem to support the military chiefs who overthrew the MNR, they are not a dependent ally. Rather they demand considerable representation in the next parliament. Thus the movement functions as a peasant party.[14]

In the similar way, the Peruvian peasant movement has generated its own independent leadership since the events of La Convención. It has associated with the urban leftist political groups but only partly relies upon them to gain its ends.

The Brazilian *ligas camponesas* and the Colombian guerrilla groups seem to have developed in the same way. The large majority of the Colombian peasant movements, despite all their associations with political parties, are largely independent of them organizationally.[15] It is very significant that one of the most prestigious guerrilla chiefs appears as a member of the PCC (Communist Party), but his actions and statements usually contradict the official position of the party.

Political Banditry

The only important recent example of political banditry emerged in Colombia in 1948. Armed struggles existed in Colombia before 1948, since guerrilla campaigns had been conducted previously by the Liberal Party, as well as by some sections of the Communist Party. In 1948, however, various political events resulted in more intense armed struggle in the countryside than ever before.

A study of these events is limited by official government propaganda which has successfully conveyed the image of political banditry as being without any social and political purpose, and whose only objective is violence for violence's sake. Even though some academic studies have sought to gather information concerning the types, degree, and the amount of violence, they also use the term employed by all the official propaganda to describe the peasant movements, i.e. *violencia* (violence), without any qualifying adjectives. This term, ambiguous and yet conveying a preconception, emphasizes one of the elements of the problem, but ignores the content and the social and political importance of the struggle. On the whole, the ideas which are implicit in this form of political banditry reflect the social conscience of the countryside.

The majority of the students of the post-1948 phase of violence have pointed out that it originated from the political conflict between the two traditional parties in Colombia. Consequently, the first period can be described as a civil war between conservatives and liberals in which the majority of the peasants on each side participated according to their own background. But since the political groups were led by two factions of the dominant class, the interests of the majority of the peasant population were largely disregarded. Very often the interests of the dominating groups conflicted with those of the peasants.[16]

Afterwards, the participation of the peasants in the struggle gradually went far beyond the objectives of the leaders of the civil war until it reached the stage when it affected the interests of the landlords. Thus, the degree of violence eventually affected the landlords on both sides in such a way that it undermined the power structure in the rural areas. It seems likely that for the majority of the peasants participating in the conflict, the circumstances of the struggle and the degree of violence led them to question the *status quo*. The threat raised by the participation of the peasants to the class interests of the landlords was, however, more the result of exposure to frustrating events than a well-defined objective on the part of the peasants. Nevertheless, even at this stage in the development of the self-consciousness of the peasants, the existing patterns of social domination were not questioned seriously. *We can not legitimately talk, therefore, of a genuine peasant movement in the strict sense of the word.* The peasants were not fighting for their own interests, but for the interests of landlords. They were involved in the rivalries of their enemies.

Eventually violence was directed against all the landlords regardless of political affiliation, the development and exacerbation of violence had to affect the established order in the long run. As the conflicts took on this extreme course the frightened landlords initiated what became a mass exodus away from the struggles. They abandoned their lands and their centers of power. By these actions the landlords admitted that the struggle had surpassed the objectives pursued in the first phase of the civil war between the two political factions.

Since then the Colombian army has been largely responsible for the problem. Henceforth it became clear that the civil war was a struggle between the armed peasants, united without regard to previous political associations, and the army representing the state. From this moment a new phase begins, slow and irregular. The militant peasants are gradually united against a common enemy: the army. This does not mean, however, that partisan rivalry among the peasants has disappeared, but that as the scope of the civil war increased involving considerable cruelty through army attacks, peasants whether liberal or conservative recognized that unless they united to protect themselves they would be in constant danger.

Since the landlords supported the punitive actions of the army in the countryside because they feared that peasant violence could shatter the social order and threaten established political power, the peasants began to realize that they also had a common social interest, the expulsion of the landlords from the countryside. Consequently, they have come to face the problem of uniting against the army and the landlords. The development of the liberal-conservative civil war had thus led to a social struggle.

At the present, this new level of conflict seems to be predominant. The armed groups of peasants are either slowly dissolving or becoming guerrillas with definite socio-political objectives. On the rural level, a radical transformation of the national social order has begun.

The participation of the peasants in the Colombian *violencia* seems to have undergone three principal phases:

1. Dependent participation, marginal to their own interests and at the service of the interests of the landlords.

2. Socio-political banditry, in defense against the reprisals of the army and the landlords, leading to a progressive abandonment of traditional political dependency.

3. Revolutionary guerrilla warfare, in defense of their own interests and linked to the revolutionary movements.[17]

In the first phase the conduct of the Colombian peasants cannot be properly considered as peasant movement activity. The peasantry were mobilized and recruited by external forces, for ends which were foreign to their interests. They remained totally dependent upon landlords and urban political leaders.

Only in the second phase, when the peasants' action becomes more autonomous as a result of the exodus of the landlords from the countryside, can we talk of the existence of a true peasants' movement. This process constitutes a unique development among the peasants' movements of Latin America.

The third phase can be included under the heading of "revolutionary agrarianism" because of its objectives and main characteristics: the reorganization of the entire rural power structure, independent of official power and against it.

This evolutionary sequence of the peasants' behavior during the time of *la violencia* is not meant to imply an exact rational process. The sequence does not mean that the dominant tendencies at each stage uniformly embraced all the peasants participating in the struggle, or that the tendencies at one stage disappeared completely by the next one. However, it is possible to see a definite sequence in the formation and development of the main tendencies guiding the peasants' struggle. Most significantly, the present stage seems to involve that form of revolutionary agrarianism which has led in many places to guerrilla action.

This discussion is not meant to deny that one of the most prevalent characteristics of peasant action in Colombia has been violence for violence's sake, or that pure banditry exists. Certain traits of common banditry affect part of the peasants' behavior even in the context of political and social banditry, and among the revolutionary guerrillas as well. However, these aspects of common banditry do not seem to have determined the more basic character of the mobilization of the Colombian peasantry in spite of the considerable brutal violence. Many Colombian landlords and members of the army must also face the accusation of banditry. Cruelty and perversity cannot be solely laid to the agrarian rebels. And it may be argued persuasively that peasant violence is largely a reaction to the repressive violence of the army and the landlords.

Political banditry, as an aspect of a sector of the activity of the Colombian peasantry, is an isolated phenomenon in the history of the peasants' struggle in Latin America. The use of violence as a method of action, to facilitate defense or repression, has of course occurred many times. What makes Colombian peasant activity unique is that the efforts at defense and vengeance, found among every type of banditry, became social when defense and reprisal were increasingly directed against the most powerful *because* they were the most powerful. The "violence" became political when it confronted political power.

What is so notable in the Colombian case is that initially the resistance against the army and the local authorities was conducted by the peasants without any social or political content. The social content of the movement gradually developed in a slow, irregular and incoherent manner, as a consequence of circumstances. It gained momentum only when the confrontation with the army was accompanied by a similar confrontation with the landlords. This experience generated in the peasants the beginning of a view of the landlords as a hostile interest group. Only then did they learn the need for a new organization, which identified their closest enemy—the army—with their landlords. Thus, political banditry slowly became transformed into socio-political banditry, and ultimately into an alliance with revolutionary groups, or more accurately becoming itself the revolutionary tendency of the country.

It is important to recognize that Colombian political banditry, although an important tendency of a sector of the peasants, is a product of very special circumstances and does not necessarily reflect either the social structure or the degree of social awareness of Latin American peasants.[18] This is a pattern of development unlikely to be repeated elsewhere.

Relationship Among the Tendencies

Even though the most recent agrarian tendencies in Latin America are those involving the greatest degree of politicalization with programs calling for thorough changes, there is no regular pattern to the different peasant movements. They have not developed in linear fashion.

In addition, since very different types of movements coexist in the same socio-historical context, they necessarily develop a complex inter-dependent pattern. Examples of such interdependence are the elements of pure banditry to be found among the most developed groups of Colombian guerrilla, or the existence of elements of feudal-religious ideologies within the modern models of interpretating the situation which guide a part of the Indian peasant population in Peru.

But the best proof of the non-linear and irregular character of these tendencies is the fluctuation of the peasant movement between one and another tendency depending on the circumstances of the moment. Such fluctuations may be described by two characteristic cases: the Peruvian and the Bolivian movements.

In Peru the most developed form of revolutionary agrarianism originated and developed in the valleys of La Convención and de Lares through the actions of Hugo Blanco and the political group associated with him. The peasant movement not only seized the *haciendas* and eliminated the landlords, but also erected a new power structure eliminating the traditional economic, political, and social power structures.

The army, which invaded the region immediately after the *coup d'état* of 1962, eliminated through violence the revolutionary leaders of the peasants and drastically reduced their influence over the rural population. As a result, the now relatively weak peasant organization fell under the control of moderate leaders. Currently, the movement in these valleys supports reformist rather than revolutionary tendencies.

Since the revolutionary elements profoundly influenced the peasant population of that area, the present strength of the moderates does not necessarily mean the elimination of the revolutionary tendencies. They cannot simply be uprooted by repression. But clearly the revolutionary tendency is no longer dominant in the region even though their existence has probably deepened the reformist perspective of radical agrarianism which is presently supported by the peasants.

In Bolivia similar phenomena occurred. Participation by important revolutionary groups on the extreme left, in the initial stages of the revolution of 1952, permitted them to spread the idea of seizure of the land and organization of armed militia to defend the new situation. The triumphant party, the MNR, did not originally include a call for a radical agrarian reform in its program. It was forced to yield to the powerful armed peasants. At that moment the militia movement of the peasants became a powerful factor in radicalizing the national revolution. It organized a national power structure in the countryside and through a national chain of peasant syndicates displaced the traditional power structure in several regions.

The MNR was forced to identify itself with this rural movement. However, in order to consolidate its power, it gradually and systematically developed a policy of strengthening local "caciquism" through economic and political corruption. The peasant leaders were encouraged to contend with other pressure groups seemingly as a means of broadening the scope of the revolution in other sectors. By so doing the MNR successfully separated the peasant movement from the revolutionary movement of the workers. Undoubtedly one of the reasons for this new role of the peasant movement was the rather limited aspirations of the peasants holding revolutionary power, but it is also true that circumstances allowed and encouraged such developments. What must be stressed, therefore, is the fact that a highly developed revolutionary agrarianism was converted into a radical reformist movement, that it gradually yielded to a new national system of social domination.

As will be demonstrated later on, these fluctuations of the peasant movements among different tendencies indicate that the destiny of these movements definitely depends upon what happens in the national society as a whole.

General Patterns of Development
in Existing Peasant Groups

Although the concrete form of each peasant movement in Latin America is determined by specific historic circumstances, certain general patterns can be abstracted. In general, three principal phases can be established in the development of these movements:

1. Agitation and urban dependence
2. Increased participation and relative independence from the city
3. Co-ordination and centralization.

URBAN AGITATION

Although most of the traditional peasant movements have been the result of peasant initiative and action, the movements in this century have been organized by men involved in urban activities. In general these efforts were undertaken by urban based political groups or parties, who sent radical reformers, or revolutionaries, to the country.

Their influence was directed and restricted largely to the rural proletariat employed on large farms and to the rural zones most influenced by urbanization. Consequently the resultant peasant groups were dependent on the urban political parties and were controlled by them. No independent peasant leadership emerged. During the same period, the revolutionary movements also sought to agitate and develop their influence in rural areas, but except for a few isolated cases, they were ineffective until the end of the Second World War.

In Peru the Communist Party had managed to extend considerable influence in the departments of the southern Andes where it had penetrated peasant groups.[19] In Bolivia revolutionary agitation began with the growth of the PIR immediately before the Second World War and produced a rising movement of peasant unions in some zones. Later the influence of Trotskyist groups in the tin mines extended to the countryside and paved the way for the subsequent peasant mass movement.[20]

Under Vargas's first administration in Brazil, the Communists devoted considerable effort to agitating plantation workers. In Colombia revolutionary groups were able to influence and control certain isolated rural localities and to organize the precarious "red republics" shortly before the Second World War.

Although the early agitation of the revolutionary movements seems to have failed in that it did not produce a single stable organization, it did spread revolutionary models among some peasants and captured groups of militant followers here and there. The failure may in some part be credited to the refusal of the revolutionary parties to accept the idea that the peasants could and should have their own autonomous revolutionary movements.

Starting with the 1950's, however, years which produced a certain organizational maturity and increased strength in the radical agrarian reform movements, and to a lesser extent in revolutionary agrarianism, the urban based revolutionary agitation took on a different character and obtained different results. The urban revolutionaries now proposed to organize the peasants through developing peasant leadership, not necessarily dependent on the parties, although their objectives were still to control the peasant militants and establish party control over peasant organizations.

These new policies of the urban revolutionaries toward the peasants resulted from the fact that in a number of countries it became clear that revolutionary organization was no longer the exclusive heritage of formal organized groups or political parties, but that it was being carried on more successfully by groups or individuals with radical reformist ideologies, who were not even necessarily members of any party, or even if they were, acted on their own accord. As in the cases of Blanco and his followers in Peru, these were individuals or groups not necessarily linked to formal political parties. In Colombia the unchaining and mobilization of the peasant were due to action of the two traditional political parties, although the most radical tendencies in the emerging peasant movement can be related to the agitation of revolutionary political parties and groups. In Bolivia the work of professional agitators in the PIR, the POR, and the MNR, was decisive in helping to break the traditional chains. In Brazil the Marxist groups, the Catholics of the left, and above all the actions of Francisco Juliao, started the real peasant movement.[21]

In the stage dominated by the initial urban agitation, the peasant movements were characterized by dependence on and consequent control by urban groups. Even though there was little formal organization, the urban groups controlled the movement, oriented it, gave it structure, and proposed the most advanced objectives. It seems probable that the highest ranks of peasant leadership at the time were composed predominantly of militant party members.

INCREASED PARTICIPATION AND RELATIVE INDEPENDENCE FROM THE CITY

The second phase in the development of peasant movements is characterized by a large increase in support both geographically and socially, by the development of autonomous peasant action and initiative, and consequently also by the emergence of leaders free from political affiliation with urban groups. This does not mean that the influence of the urban parties or of their militant followers has been eliminated or has decreased. On the contrary, the participation of urban agitators, with or without party affiliation, has become even greater.

Nevertheless the new situation reflects the fact that the geographic and social extension of peasant participation and the development of an organization structure of considerable strength outstripped the capacity of the urban political organizations to control or directly influence the peasant groups, thus permitting the latter to develop a political force not easily manageable.

Various factors have resulted in the growth and relative independence of the movements, which though distinct have had comparable and reinforcing effects.

In the Colombian case, as we have already seen, the increased peasant participation in the armed struggle was largely the work of the traditional parties. The rise in peasant autonomy resulted from the landowners' retreat from the countryside to escape peasant violence which increasingly turned into a class war when the army backed by the landowners launched reprisals.

In the Bolivian case, the decisive factor seems to have been the efficiency and organization of the power structure created by the militia and the peasant syndicates. It resulted in a leadership group with immense power that could deal from a favorable position of strength with the party and state leadership. Increasing participation was principally the work of the peasants themselves when they adopted the revolutionary method of taking the land and organizing armed militia to protect the seizure. The revolutionary groups lacked the numbers and organization to control or directly influence the peasant organizations. The armed peasant militia also fostered peasant autonomy, even though the militia, corruption, and dealings between the local *caudillos* and the MNR limited the effectiveness of this development.

Nevertheless, the Bolivian peasant militia is the most significant example of autonomy in the peasant movement. It took the place of a peasant political party. This is shown by the fact that after the coup a large part of the militia leadership switched allegiance from the MNR to the *Frente Nacional*. It could break its seeming political dependence on the MNR since what existed was a political alliance, not peasant subordination.

In the Brazilian case, the growth of the confederations of "peasant bands" is the best example of the generalization that the successful organization of such groups has to be, above all, the work of the peasants themselves. The confederations originated in the action of one man without an organized political apparatus, and against the hostility of the reformist parties and the traditional revolutionaries. The movement of the peasant confederations covered a vast region and gathered hundreds of thousands under its banners. Juliao did not have a method which permitted direct participation in the rapid diffusion of his movement, nor was he able to control it once it had become so extended. Juliao is now outside of Brazil and no longer has any important influence. The peasant movement has declined under the new political circumstances. However, it still exists in an organized way and publishes the newspaper, *El Campesino,* and it remains completely autonomous depending on no other control than its own leadership.

The development of peasant syndicates of Brazil, formed principally by the left-Catholic groups and by the Communist Party, followed a similar course. Particularly in the case of the syndicates influenced by the left-wing Catholics, the organizations though originated and backed nationally by them, could not be controlled by those who fostered them. The expansion of the syndicates was too great for the left-Catholics, they could not be present everywhere. Under the general indirect stimulation of the left-Catholics, the peasants themselves now have control of an enormous syndicate movement. Pernambuco alone can claim 200,000 members.[22]

Reliable data are not available on the number of peasant syndicates that have been organized in Peru in the last ten years, following the lead set by Blanco, or how many land invasions have occurred since 1960 through syndicate or community action. The information available indicates that in 1962–63 alone, not less than two hundred such invasions occurred; in the majority of cases these were the work of "Indian Communities." Newspaper reports indicate that in every case between 500 and 3000 peasants participated; the land appropriated that has been retained by the peasants exceeds 50,000 hectares.[23] More than 200,000 belong to the Peruvian peasant syndicates supporting the seizures.

At the time, the urban radical parties violently opposed these land seizures. These parties and other revolutionary groups neither had nor have now the organizational capacity or sufficient members to intervene directly in these peasant actions.

The national expansion of the Peruvian movement in the last few years has been the work of the peasants themselves. The result is independence from urban party control and the existence of competent peasant leadership.

CO-ORDINATION AND CENTRALIZATION OF THE ORGANIZATION

The desire to co-ordinate and centralize has been present since the beginnings of peasant organization. However, this did not become evident until the stage of mass participation. It is important to emphasize that the co-ordination and centralization phase emerges from a convergence of efforts by different peasant organizations and the other groups and political movements which influence the core of the movement.

In the process of confronting the landowners and the repressive action of the governments, as well as in searching for an effective way to influence the political establishment, the peasant organizations are forced to co-ordinate their actions. At the same time, however, they seek the support of urban political organizations to achieve wider political backing. Each urban group, of course, attempts to channel the action of the peasant groups toward its particular side.

The process of co-ordination and centralization is often inchoate and incomplete. Since centralization under a leadership group who are members of a definite political group implies a political orientation, many peasant groups resist centralization, especially if they originally developed on their own and have been free from the influence of urban groups. Inevitably, however, various elements of centralization develop depending on the political ideological nature of the urban organizations that influence the particular peasant movements. It is significant, however, that in spite of variations, this phase is characterized by the ending of isolation among the different peasant organizations, the overriding of old local divisions, characteristic of a pre-political stage of activity.

The tendency towards co-ordination and centralization in the peasant groups has resulted in varying forms of organization in countries such as Colombia, Bolivia, Brazil, and Peru, i.e. countries with a well-developed peasant movement. These include federated syndicates, federations of peasant communities, tribunes of peasant bands, militia commandoes, and guerrilla commandoes.

In Peru the National Confederations of Peasants and the Regional Federations of Indian Communities are basically national peasant centers. In Bolivia the peasant militia is centered around regional militia commandoes and the syndicates are grouped in a Peasant Federation that forms a part of the *Central Obrera Boliviana*. In Colombia the bands and the guerrillas are unified into the Regional Commandoes that control and co-ordinate the action of organizations over vast regions. In Brazil, the Peasant Bands (*Ligas Camponesas*) are centralized in a Council of Presidents of Peasant Bands (*Consejo de Presidentes de Ligas Camponesas*) and the syndicates are centralized in regional federations.

These networks of peasant groups that have arisen in different countries represent the institutionalization of the peasant movement, of the appearance of a new power structure in peasant society.

In this way the once atomized and dispersed peasant masses of our societies have clearly begun a period of organized cohesion. They are capable of maintaining an active network of local organizations and have made their entrance into the Latin American arena of social conflict. The highest national leadership in these organizations are highly politicized, seeking to participate in the struggle for national power. This phase of co-ordinated effort through which the different peasant groups join together in opposition to the existing political power structure to further their interest is the most important development in the peasant movement in recent years.

Contemporary peasant movements in Latin America are thus characterized by *the ability to sustain a modern functioning organization capable of political combat, operation on a national scale, a co-ordinated and centralized structure, a break with traditional feudal-religious ideologies, growing politicalization on the most developed ideological level, and institutionalization of a new power structure that can compete with the traditional structures in the countryside.*

Notes on Contemporary Peasant Leadership in Latin America

One of the greatest gaps in the empirical material concerning the peasant movements of today involves the background of the leadership of these organizations. It is not possible to generalize even in approximate terms about the social-economic and cultural traits of the leaders,

or even to report the demographic structure of the group. Weak inferences can be made around their motivations, aspirations, attitudes or
opinions, the extent of their political-ideological independence, their
relations with the leadership of urban political organizations, very
little about the mechanics of organization and the way in which they
react to the tasks of being a leader.

For these reasons, the following conclusions should be viewed as partial and tentative hypotheses formulated with the desire to stimulate
research in this field and based almost entirely on Peruvian and, to a
lesser extent, Brazilian experiences.

1. Two demographic characteristics predominate in the peasant
leadership, they are male and young. While the first trait continues the
pattern that has always guided social relations between the sexes in this
continent, the second may be considered as a break with traditional
norms. I know of only one case of a woman leader in Peru, in the Department of Ayacucho, southern Andes. She was an illiterate about
forty years old who had the complete co-operation of her community,
directed the taking of nearby *hacienda* land, and traveled to Lima to
attend a reunion of communal leaders with the President of the Republic, about which she commented with terrible irony showing two
farm utensils that were given to her as a symbol of government support.

2. In Peru the leaders are quite heterogeneous socially although there
is much less variation in the most densely populated Indian zones.
There are, of course, some generalizations regarding the leaders of the
most important tendencies of the Peruvian peasant movement.[24]

The traditional agrarian movement is strongest among the rural
proletariat in the more modern and urbanized areas along the Peruvian coast. Consequently the leadership recruited from this particular
peasant group is culturally much more akin to the creole population of
the country than to the *cholos*. The higher echelons of leadership in
these organizations are quite urbanized and literate. Culturally, they
tend to be among the most homogeneous leadership groups in the
peasant movement.

The radical agrarian group recruits its support from the traditional
haciendas of the highlands, from the Indian communities and from
the *minifundiarios* who are part Indian. The leadership seems to be recruited at the middle socio-economic levels, from *colonos* without *hacienda* land, from large or medium property owners, and especially

from among some small businessmen and craftsmen outside of agriculture. From the cultural point of view, the leadership in general reflects the influence of the *cholos,* and is semi-urbanized.

The leadership of the agrarian-revolutionary groups does not differ much from the heads of the agrarian-radical tendencies except in a cultural sense; the former includes more *cholos* and is more urbanized.

Similar patterns seem to characterize also the leadership of the peasant communities and syndicates in Brazil, although the latter includes more men from the agricultural proletariat class.[25] The Bolivian militia leadership may also be described in these terms. No inferences can be made about the bandit or guerrilla leadership in Colombia.

3. The power of peasant leaders over their followers is related to the social heterogeneity of the masses. In Peru the more homogeneous the Indian group, the more it is able to influence its leadership. On the other hand, the more socially heterogeneous the masses in a given movement, the less control they seem to have over their leaders.[26]

4. The mechanics of recruiting leadership seems to vary with the type of organization.

The syndicates use traditional election procedures. In the militia bands and guerrillas, elections rarely occur, usually only in the lowest level of organization. In communally based organizations the election results produce leaders who reflect the usual social status criteria. Nevertheless, in Peru, a gradual displacement of leaders who possess these traditional social criteria by a new leadership is occurring. The latter are chosen for leadership abilities, and resemble those selected for leadership in the syndicates, militia, and guerrillas.[27]

5. In some areas, a lack of co-ordination and centralization in the movement tends to encourage the emergence of a pattern of local "bossism" (*caciquismo*) in the leadership. Such leaders are likely to be self-oriented, although to retain peasant support they will protect the general interest.[28]

The Sociological Significance of the Contemporary Peasant Movement

This account of tendencies in the peasant movement points to two processes occurring within the single living complex: differentiation of interests and organization of interests.

The notion of interest differentiation refers fundamentally to the development of a new type of social awareness in the peasant population of certain countries that is spreading. The traditional outlook of the Latin American peasant was dominated by what we have called a feudal-religious model. In Marxist terms it may be characterized as a form of false consciousness, of social psychological alienation. For centuries the dominating classes in the peasant culture, who usually corresponded to the upper classes on a larger societal level, were able to reinforce this interpretation of the social reality.

Continued influence of this model on the peasant consciousness was supported by the dispersion and atomization of this group, by the enormous social and cultural gap between the city and the country, by the absence of rapid and adequate communications, and by the repeated failure of isolated and precarious attempts at rebellion.

Today, however, the various indicators of peasant awareness as reflected in action, in the resolutions worked out at conferences, in the political literature of groups supported by peasants, reveal a growing rupture with the old ideological models, the emergence of new ways of defining the general social situation, and the peasant situation in particular. Although this new social consciousness is not yet thoroughly formulated, a tentative description of the process may be made.

1. The peasant class has created new patterns of action and interaction. From their most limited to their most radical forms, these organizations proceed with the specific aim to modify the rural power structure, first by seeking to change a few important sectors, and later through attempting the total modification of the local social situation by capturing total community power.

2. The organization of syndicates for improving working conditions implies a certain acceptance of the general social order. The confiscation of land and the organization of peasant community power structures that withdraw from the traditional local and national power systems indicate that many no longer define the social situation in the old way, but rather come to accept a model that explains their situation as a product of a given system of land ownership which is interdependent with larger structures of local or regional power.

3. This developing perception is linked to an awareness that conflicting social interests exist and leads them to identify their own social interests. The fact that action is taken not only against isolated landowners who have been particularly bad, but against landowners in general,

points to the process of interest identification which is developing, that enemies are not considered as special cases but as a part of another class with different social interests.

4. Finally, the support for centralized national organizations indicates that the peasants perceive a community of interests against an opposing class, and thus as a group they repress regional, ethnic, and cultural differences to unite for the common goal.

All this may be described as the emergence of realistic group consciousness among the peasant populations of certain Latin American countries replacing the traditional feudal-religious consciousness.

It should be obvious that the emergence of a new social consciousness does not occur as a linear or coherent process, that the different social, economic, and cultural groups cannot participate in the same way or on the same level, and that the new level of social consciousness is rarely formulated or expressed in a rational integrated structure in its early stages.

We find the superimposition of elements of the new consciousness on the traditional old consciousness even among the highest levels of peasant leadership. What is important is not the confusion, but the fact that there is a clear tendency toward the formation of a new type of social consciousness. Empirical investigations are needed to discover the limits of this tendency, its effective elements, and the variations in acceptance among the different sectors of the peasant population in various countries.

A new social consciousness must of course be linked to group or class organization advancing the interests of a stratum against opposing forces if it is to affect society. The emergence of the peasant class as a specific sector of organized social interest among the many differentiated sectors raises a problem of great interest to the sociologist. What is the nature of the group that is evolving in the peasant population?

In contemporary social theory, the different forms of fundamental social interests are grouped under the titles of *estamento,* caste, class, and status (*Stand*). At present in Latin America it does not seem correct to think of the emergence of *estamentos* or castes, nor does it seem appropriate to consider the segment of the peasant population that participates in the movement with its heterogeneous socio-economic, cultural, and ethnic composition as a status group. A more useful approach to the problem is inherent in the theory of social classes and class struggle derived from Marx. Essentially it may be said that the peasants of some Latin American countries are involved in the phenomenon of class formation. The processes of differentiation and organization are resulting in a new social class. In Marxist terms this process consists of the change of peasant population from the situation of class in itself (*an sich*) to that of a class for itself (*für sich*). The characteristic elements of this change are differentiation and organization of interests, or in other terms, the development of a group social consciousness includes a realistic interpretation of the power structure as well as the generation of the organized expression of social interests. To verify this interpretation is beyond the scope of this study. It has considerable implications for the Marxist theories of social classes and social change.

Marx himself was very dubious about the possibility that peasants would become a class because the system of production resulted in their social and cultural isolation, their involvement in local loyalties, and the lack of a system of intra-group communications which might permit the spreading to all levels and local subgroups of the basic elements of group social consciousness. Hence, he doubted that they could develop an organized system of class expression, a base for the representation of peasant interests.[29]

It is, therefore, very important from a theoretical point of view to discover the factors and new circumstances that have permitted the peasant to surpass these limitations and undertake the building of a class. From a political standpoint the assumption that the peasants are becoming a class in the Marxist sense points to a radically new phenomenon in the process of social change in Latin America. The consequences and implications of this process for the peasants and for the rest of society should be carefully watched and explored.

In a recent study of the Brazilian peasant movement, Benno Galjart argues that the theory of social classes does not help in interpreting this movement because the syndicates and other peasant organizations were started by urban political groups and remain linked to them as well as to the privileged strata. For this reason Galjart claims that the traditional hierarchical patterns between dominating and subordinate strata reflected in paternalism and client status continue within the peasant movements, that the peasants are still inferior, are still clients.[30]

It is true that all peasant movements have originated in urban groups. In some sectors it is also true that their growth was facilitated by a favorable attitude on the part of the government, and even by effective assistance in the form of specific legislation.

Galjart's arguments, however, may be countered by various facts: 1.

Government support helped peasant movements to organize in only a few countries, before the appearance of the important contemporary movements. The most important case occurred in Guatemala.[31] 2. The support given to the peasants by the Goulart government in Brazil was not the cause of peasant organization, but reflected pressure from the peasant movement, especially from the associations led by Juliao. 3. In every other important case, especially in Bolivia, Peru, and Colombia, pro-peasant governmental measures were the result of actions taken by the peasants: the militant tactics of the peasant militia in Bolivia which convinced the MNR to accept the land seizures, the carrying out by peasant bands of agrarian reform in Colombia, and the appropriation of *hacienda* land in Peru, forced the governments to accept reform. 4. The best evidence for the above interpretation lies in the fact that most genuine agrarian reforms in Latin America apply largely to those areas which have had the most intense peasant agitation and organization. Far from reflecting a paternalistic attitude government action in these four countries has resulted from fear, from the recognition that agrarian reform is necessary in order to conserve other parts of the system. 5. In cases where the peasant movement has been helped directly by the government as in Bolivia, or has benefited from a favorable government attitude as in Goulart's Brazil, the movement did not lose its autonomy simply because the government tried to further the general goals of the peasant. 6. While in all previous ages, peasants could be mobilized for forces alien to themselves, now they can seek to strengthen parties or governments whose policies correspond to their interests, especially agrarian reform. Clearly in none of the important cases cited by Galjart have peasants been found fighting on the side of their enemies.

Galjart's idea that the peasant movement is simply social imitation, that it is characterized by continuity of old patterns of client relations, paternalism under another guise, is not compatible with the facts already described.

The argument that peasant agitation originated in urban movements does not clearly undermine the class theory. The history of the development of subordinated classes, of their struggles for power, indicates that in all cases they were initially activated by members of the privileged classes. Marx was the first to show that the emergence of class consciousness among the members of a depressed population has always originated from outside the class. This was the case of the bourgeoisie in feudal society and of the working class in capitalist society. The claims for spontaneity and absolute autonomy of social groups that evolve into classes simply do not stand up to the facts of history.

The characteristics of a class are not merely determined by its role in the production process and its share of the benefits of society. These only describe a social situation that contains a group of elements that characterize objective class interests. Only when a population confronted with a given situation has developed the capacity to conceive of itself as a group in a common situation, with a community of social interests, and has learned to generate systems of communication and organization, as well as to subordinate the individual will to the will of the group is there a process which can be described as class development.

Only when a population in a certain situation develops the realization that its social situation is distinct from other groups, that certain individual interests are common interests, and an organized expression of these interests occurs, does class exist. Such developments are intimately related to a confrontation with other groups in a struggle for specific objectives. In this struggle the group learns to distinguish between allies and enemies. The group learns to conceive of itself as a group, to differentiate its interests from those of others, to generate group organization, to develop systems of intra-group communication and integration, to create normative institutions and form common symbols and cultural institutions. The last stage of class development is participation in a struggle for total power in society.

The Latin American peasants who participate in the most advanced movements show all the necessary characteristics of incorporating a group ethic, have generated an organized structure of interaction, but above all have organized themselves for a co-ordinated fight against the landowners. Viewing these events as the beginning of class formation seems to be a correct interpretation of the situation.

Some Factors that Affect Contemporary Peasant Movements

A widespread belief inside and out of Latin America attributes the growing peasant pressures for radical changes in the social situation to a combination of the demographic explosion and the increasing deteriorization of standards of living, especially in rural zones. These factors do engender protest, but they cannot explain the scope of the peasant movements particularly when the same events occur in many Latin American countries without such movements. Other factors must be found to explain why the phenomenon occurs in certain countries, and not in others.

Basically, a comparative look at the various Latin American countries suggests that the phenomenon of peasant radicalization is characteristic of societies in an intermediate or partial state of modernization which possess some degree of a democratic polity, particularly free speech and organization. The peasant class of such changing unstable societies have had their traditional values disrupted by contact with modern urban influences, but they are still involved in highly traditional socio-economic relations. The countries which qualify for this group are Bolivia, Brazil, Colombia, Peru, and, to a certain extent, Venezuela.

The slow molecular processes of change, more accelerated and general now, in the various societies began with the modernization of the urban sectors, and the social-psychological transformation that occurred there reached into the rural areas also.[32] These changes which flow from the increased power of the urban business sectors and bourgeois influence on the traditional landed class, as a consequence of changes in the economic structure, have resulted in various new relationships: (1) a slow modification of the traditional criteria of social evaluation that maintain and legitimize social stratification; (2) an increase in the channels of upward social mobility especially for the middle class; (3) the progressive loss of the social and economic power of the traditional provincial class of landowners as the small commercial bourgeoisie extend their influence to all areas of the rural subculture; (4) the massive growth in urban population involving a great peasant migration which indicates the weakening of the traditional rural forces keeping them in the country.

These changes have been followed by adjustments within the peasant population. The most notable elements of this process are: (1) social differentiation among the peasant class reflecting the new opportunities that the economic structure has created; (2) the appearance of numerous and complex intermediate social groups; (3) the emergence in the Andean regions of an intermediate cultural group, half-way between the dominant creole culture and the principal peasant subcultures; (4) the rapid diffusion of urbanization, as a cultural phenomenon; the widespread rural-urban migratory movement, which characterizes the last twenty years in Latin America, and especially the last ten, facilitates the process of cultural urbanization in rural areas.

This is not intended to be complete but rather presents a schematic list of some of the major phenomena that can be related to the emergence of contemporary peasant movements in modernizing middle-level countries of Latin America.

Some Considerations on the Future
Prospects of the Peasant Movement

Any effort to predict the future of these movements is very risky in the uncertain political-social scene in Latin America. The more radical class conscious tendencies discussed here will not necessarily prevail. Nevertheless it may be worthwhile to suggest some probable developments without implying a rigid scheme.

Previous historical experiences in which the peasant class emerged as a decisive factor in the struggle for political power, of which the Mexican Revolution is the prime example, clearly show that peasants may be eliminated from important political influence, seemingly on the verge of taking power. Their solidarity may be broken up by the atomization which occurs from a breakdown in the traditional rural structure resulting from the rise of the bourgeoisie to national power. The long-range possibilities from the consolidation of peasant movements as a political class which can take power in their own right are not very great anywhere.

The appearance of tendencies favorable to class formation in the peasant population of some countries is, as we have seen, largely the result of the ending of peasant's isolation which had so impressed Marx. Intra-group communications increase sharply the possibility for the development of a new social consciousness through peasant movements. It is possible that peasant predominance in revolutionary class movements may only occur over a short historic period during the period of political struggle undertaken by revolutionary groups centered in the countryside. As class conflicts increase, the urban context of the struggle becomes more and more decisive. The peasant, therefore, is reduced to the status of a supporter without effective participation in the leadership of the struggle. In most recent revolutionary efforts, the abstract and rationalist ideologies, which inspire the actions of the urban movements, focus their attention on the growth of industry and cities as synonomous with progress. Such behavior means that the movements seek to take a radically different direction from that which would be taken if the revolution were undertaken by and for the peasant class. Thus, although, the general ideological content of these movements is identified with the peasantry, they are actually more concerned with fulfilling the aspirations of various urban socio-economic sectors.

In Bolivia the government that arose out of the revolution of 1952 had no alternative but to legalize the land seizures of the peasants which occurred during the revolution. But as a result, the new government had the opportunity to divide the workers' militia, sympathizers with the revolutionary extreme left, from the peasant militia majority and the peasant syndicates, from whom they obtained support against further revolutionary changes in the cities. This Bolivian experience suggests that under certain conditions a partial and momentary satisfaction of the most immediate peasant demands for land—without a doubt the most powerful motivating factor among the masses—can be very successful in turning the peasant organizations into a force against more profound transformations of society.

It is important, however, to recognize that these experiences do not have to be repeated in other countries where strong peasant opposition movements now exist. In Bolivia itself the recent changes in the general political situation may inaugurate a new radical phase in the peasant movement. In a number of Latin American countries, the constraints inherent in the world political and economic situations and the ideology of the movements that fight for a genuine revolution are radically different from those which affected the course of the Mexican and Bolivian revolutions.

The Cuban experience, like that of China and Vietnam, shows clearly that under revolutionary and very coherent ideological direction, or under international circumstances which encourage the expansion of the objectives of revolutions initiated for more limited purposes, that the peasant class can become a genuine ally and most rigorous supporter of a deep and total revolution.

What seems to be clear is that the future success of peasant movements depends entirely on the success of other forces with similar objectives, that by their own means they are not capable of modifying the national situation and even have difficulty in making short-range reforms work.

From this perspective it would seem that the process of forming socially conscious groups among the peasants does not have the historic possibility of attaining full development. Circumstances, however, may require a change in this conclusion.

The official projects for agrarian reform in all countries of Latin America result only in the liquidation of certain sectors of the *latifundia* property and the class deriving an income from it, the formation of a small sector of small and medium bourgeoisie, and the proletarianization of the rest of the countryside. A better solution is still viable in some countries, which would permit an alternative for a considerable period. In those countries, however, where organized and politicalized peasant movements exist involved in the major revolutionary struggles, such a solution does not seem possible, and, indeed to find an effective and stable solution, there is no other path than the most thorough socio-political revolution.

If this is true, the peasant movements of today may well increase greatly in the near future, resulting in more intense peasant participation in the struggle for the revolutionary transformation of Latin American societies.

Notes

1. The term peasant, as used here, refers to the population of rural areas which belong to the economically and socially inferior strata, regardless of their specific roles: wage-earners, small landowners, small merchants, artisans, students, settlers, etc.
2. The concept of social movement refers to the tendency of one sector of the population to put pressure on some aspects of the structure of society with the objective of changing them deliberately in some way. For a good discussion of "social movements" as mechanisms and sources of social change see Jerome Davis, *Contemporary Social Movements* (New York: The Century Co., 1930).
3. Ideology, as used here, has a broad meaning and refers not only to rational systems of ideas about social order, but also to the unstructured models of interpretation of the social situation, based on the values and attitudes which are not necessarily either explicit or conscious. In this last sense one can talk of peasant "ideologies."
4. This characterization of social banditry follows the one given by Eric J. Hobsbawm, *Primitive Rebels. Studies in Archaic Forms of Social*

Movements in the 19th and 20th Centuries (Manchester: Manchester University Press, 1959), p. 5.

5. Ibid.

6. See Norman Cohn, *The Pursuit of the Millennium* (London: Secker and Warburg, 1957).

7. For a study of the messianic movement which occurred in Brazil in the nineteenth century, see the description by Euclides Da Cunha, *Os Sertoes* (Rio de Janeiro: Libraria Francisco Alves, 1944). For a study about racist movement in Peru at the end of the nineteenth century, see Ernesto Reyna, *El Amauta Atusparia* (Lima: Ed. de "Frente," 1932).

  The only available source on peasant banditry is narrative literature. See Ciro Alegría, *El mundo es ancho y ajeno* (New York: Crofts, 1945); Rómulo Gallegos, *Cantaclaro* (Barcelona: Araluce, 1934); Enrique López Albújar, *Cuentos Andinos* (Lima: 1920); and *Nuevos Cuentos Andinos* (Santiago: 1937). In addition see in epic poems, José Hernández, *El Gaucho Martín Fierro* (Buenos Aires: D. Viau, 1937).

  The best source of information about pre-political agrarianism is also the social narratives. References about the Indian movements in southern Peru can be found in Raúl Galdo Pagaza, *El Indígena y el Mestizo en Vilquechico,* Ministerio de Trabajo, Serie Monográfica, no. 3 (Lima: 1962).

8. For a report on traditional agrarian reformism in Venezuela, see John Powell, *Preliminary Report on the Federación Campesina de Venezuela, Origins, Leadership and the Role in the Agrarian Reform Programme* (Madison: University of Wisconsin, Land Tenure Center, 1964); for Bolivia, see Richard Patch, "Bolivia: United States' Assistance in a Revolutionary Setting," in Gillin *et al.* (eds.), *Social Change in Latin America Today* (New York: Vintage Books, 1961); Leonard Olen, *Bolivia: Land, People, and Institutions* (Washington, D.C.: Scarecrow Press, 1952).

  On Chile, see Gerrit Huizer, *Peasant Union, Community Development and Land Reform in Chile* (Santiago: April, 1966, mimeo); Orlando Caputto, *Las organizaciones campesinas* (unpublished thesis, Universidad de Chile, Santiago, 1965); Henry Landsberger and Fernando Canitrot, *Iglesia, clase media y el movimiento sindical campesino* (Santiago: Universidad de Chile, Faculty of Economics, mimeo); H. Landsberger, *Obstáculos en el camino de un movimiento sindical agrícola, Memorias* of the VII Latin American Congress of Sociology, Vol. 1 (Bogotá: 1965), pp. 386 ff.

  On Colombia, see G. Huizer, *Peasant Organization, Community Development and Agrarian Reform* (Santiago: 1966, mimeo).

  Finally there is a prolific number of recent studies on Brazil. See especially Robert Price, *Rural Unionization in Brazil* (Madison: University of Wisconsin, Land Tenure Center, 1964); Balden Paulson, *Local Patterns in Northeast Brazil* (Madison: University of Wisconsin, Land Tenure Center, 1964); Diana Dommlin, *Rural Labor Move-*

ment in Brazil (Madison: University of Wisconsin, Land Tenure Center, 1964); Marie Willkie, *A Report on Rural Syndicates in Pernambuco* (Rio de Janeiro: CLAPUS, 1964, mimeo).

9. The "Indian Communities" of Peru have been studied for more than twenty years. A comprehensive bibliography may be found in Henry Dobyns, *The Social Matrix of Peruvian Indigenous Communities* (Ithaca: Cornell University, 1964, mimeo). Concerning their participation in the present Peruvian peasant movement, see Aníbal Quijano, "El movimiento campesino del Perú y sus líderes," *América Latina,* 8 (October–December, 1965).

10. For further information concerning "As ligas camponesas" see Francisco Juliao, *¡Campesinos a mí!* (Buenos Aires: Cia. Argentina de Editones, 1963), and *Que são as Ligas Camponesas* (Rio de Janeiro: Civilização Brasileira, 1962); also see B. Paulson, *Difficulties and Prospects for Community Development in Northeast Brazil* (Madison: University of Wisconsin, Land Tenure Center), p. 42.

11. Concerning the peasant syndicates organized by Hugo Blanco, see Adolfo Gilly, "Los sindicatos guerrilleros del Perú," *Marcha* (September, 1963); Luis de la Puente Uceda, "Revolución peruana," *Monthly Review* (October–November, 1965); Hugo Neyra, *Cuzco, tierra y muerte* (Lima: 1963); Quijano, "El movimiento campesino," particularly the distinction between the urban or traditional rural syndicate and the contemporary peasant syndicate; R. Patch, "The Indian Emerging in Cuzco," A.S.F.S. Letter (Nov. 14, 1958), CIDA: Informe sobre *Tenencia en el Perú,* 1965.

12. About El Salvador, see Daniel James, *Red Design for the Americas* (New York: Day, 1954).

About the revolutionary agrarianism and the Bolivian peasant militias, see Patch, "Bolivia: U.S. Assistance in a Revolutionary Setting." For further information about the peasant syndicates in Bolivia see, Johan Vellard, *Civilisations des Andes* (Paris: Gallimard, 1963), pp. 224 ff.; Dwight Heath, *Agrarian Reform and Social Revolution* (February, 1963, mimeo); Marie Willkie, *Report on Boliva: on the Social Structure of Rural Areas* (La Paz: 1964).

13. Concerning revolutionary agrarianism in Peru, see Neyra, *Cuzco, tierra y muerte;* Gilly, "Los sindicatos guerrilleros del Perú"; Quijano, "El movimiento campesino del Perú"; and Hugo Blanco, *Tierra o muerte, venceremos* (Lima: 1964).

Concerning the "red republics," see A. Gilly, "Guerrillas y repúblicas campesinas en Colombia," *Monthly Review,* 17 (December, 1965), pp. 30–36.

Concerning Viota, see José Gutiérrez, *La rebeldía colombiana* (Bogota: Tercer Mundo), p. 86.

Concerning the revolutionary agrarianism in the "ligas campesinas" and the different behavior of the rural syndicates, see Paulson, *Difficulties and Prospects for Community Development,* "It is difficult to understand the orientation of the Leagues, but basically they want change in the *land tenure and political structure,* so the mass on the land is more favored" (underlined by A. Quijano), pp. 42–43. In addition see Lêda Barreto, *Juliao, Nordeste, Revolução* (Rio de Janeiro: Civilização, 1963).

14. The demands of the peasants' militias in Bolivia for participation in the parliament as a condition for supporting the National Front is mainly a verbal report of a Bolivian economist working in the Agrarian Reform.

15. Havens and Lipman state that "it began as a deliberate political manipulation to intimidate and destroy the opposition, but it gained momentum so fast that it soon spread throughout the country," Havens and Lipman, *The Colombian Violence. An ex-post facto experiment* (Madison: University of Wisconsin, Land Tenure Center, 1964).

16. A good study of the origins of the "violence" is in Guzmán, Fals-Borda, and Umaña, *La violencia en Colombia* (Bogotá: Tercer Mundo, 1962).

17. Guzmán, Fals-Borda, and Umaña, *La violencia en Colombia,* especially pp. 287 ff.; also Jorge Gutiérrez Anzola, *Violencia y justicia* (Bogotá: Tercer Mundo, 1962).

18. About organization systems, leadership and ideology in the Colombian movement, Guzmán, Fals-Borda, and Umaña, *La violencia en Colombia,* Vol. 2, particularly Eduardo Umaña, "Normas propias y actitudes del conflicto," pp. 55–202. Also Gilly, "Los sindicatos guerrilleros del Perú," which has a revealing quotation from Camilo Torres about the organization of the guerrilla movement.

19. The author heard a personal story from the Peruvian novelist José María Arguedas about a peasant meeting held in a village near Cuzco in 1941 to receive Prado, then President of Peru. More than 20,000 Indians attended the meeting organized by the P.C.P. and one of them gave a beautiful speech in Quechua, which was not translated for Prado. The text of the speech was kept by the novelist. In 1963 the author heard an old Indian singing the following song while he was drunk:

> "Hurrah Juan Barrios,
> I would give my life for Juan Barrios."

Juan Barrios was a professional Communist agitator in the rural areas of Peru during the Second World War.

20. See *Resoluciones del Congreso de Pulacayo* (La Paz: 1948). For the revolutionary point of view of the Bolivian situation before the Revolution, see the interesting essay by Ernesto Ayala Mercado, *La "realidad" boliviana* (Cochabamba, Bolivia: 1950).

21. Biographical data about Juliao may be found in F. Juliao, *¡Campesinos a mí!* Although Juliao appears as the author on the cover, with the exception of two "Letters to the Peasants" by Juliao, it is a text written by an anonymous Argentine.

22. Concerning the Brazilian rural syndicates, see M. Willkie, p. 15; B. Paulson, p. 43; Benno Galjart, "Class and 'Following' in Rural Brazil," *América Latina,* 7 (July–September, 1964), pp. 3–24.

23. John Strassma, "El financiamiento de la Reforma Agraria en el Perú,"

Trimestre Económico, Vol. 32 (July–September, 1965), pp. 484–500.

24. Concerning the Peruvian peasant leadership, see Quijano, "El movimiento campesino del Perú," and *La emergencia del grupo cholo y sus implicaciones en la sociedad peruana* (Lima: 1964, mimeo).

25. Concerning the Brazilian peasant leadership, see Geraldo Semansate, *Itabuna, Bahia* (Bahia: Instituto de Ciências Sociais, Universidade de Bahia, mimeo), pp. 9 ff.; Mario Alfonso Carneiro, *Sape, Paraiba* (mimeo), SPLAN, pp. 9 ff.; Galjart, "Class and 'Following' in Rural Brazil."

26. In the peasant movement of the Central Peruvian mountains, especially among the "Indian Communities" of the Department of Junín, the leadership is composed of the non-agricultural sector. See Quijano, "El movimiento campesino del Perú."

27. During the invasion of the Hacienda Paramonga, owned by Grace and Co., the formal leadership of the invaders, Pararin, was almost completely displaced by a young group which directed the actions and later became the effective though not the formal leaders. This was told to the author by Professors Edmundo Murrugarra and C. Benavides, of the Faculty of Social Sciences of the Agricultural University of Peru.

28. The best examples of *caudillismo,* a local caciquismo of the peasant leadership, are Colombia and Bolivia.

29. Karl Marx, *The Class Struggle in France 1848–1850* (New York: International Publishers, 1964) and *The Eighteenth Brumaire of Louis Napoleon* (New York: International Publishers, 1963). See also Friederich Engels, *Revolution and Counter-Revolution* (Chicago: Kerr, 1907).

30. Galjart, "Class and 'Following' in Rural Brazil," pp. 3 ff. In addition see a reply to Galjart by Gerrit Huizer, "Some Notes on Community Development and Rural Social Research," and an answer by Galjart, "A Further Note on 'Followings': Reply to Huizer," *América Latina,* 8 (July–September, 1965), pp. 128 and 145, respectively.

31. Concerning the peasant movements in Guatemala since the revolution of 1944, there is an extensive bibliography, see especially R. Adams, *Political Changes in Guatemalan Indian Communities* (New Orleans: Tulane University, 1957) and "Fomented Agitation in Rural Guatemala," *Economic Development and Cultural Change,* 5 (July, 1957), pp. 338–361. Also Nathan Whetten, *Guatemala, the Land and the People* (New Haven: Yale University Press, 1961).

32. Concerning the socio-economic changes of the peasant movements see Charles Wagley, "The Brazilian Revolution," in Gillin *et al.* (eds.), *Social Change in Latin America,* pp. 177–227 and C. Wagley, "The Peasants," in John J. Johnson (ed.), *Continuity and Change in Latin America* (Stanford: Stanford University Press, 1964), pp. 21–48. Also on Brazil, see Manuel Diégues, Jr., "Mudanças Sociais no meio rural latino-americano," *América Latina,* 6 (1963).

Concerning Peru, see Dobyns, *The Social Matrix;* William Mangin,

The Development of Highland Communities in Latin America (mimeo), a report presented at the Annual Latin American Conference of Cornell University (March, 1965), and the commentaries of Dwight Heath on this text; and Aníbal Quijano, *La emergencia del grupo cholo en el Perú.*

Concerning Bolivia, see R. Patch, "Bolivia: United States Assistance"; Ayala Mercado Ernesto, *La "realidad" boliviana* (Cochabamba, Bolivia: Imprenta universitaria, 1944).

Concerning the urban-rural conflict see Marshall Wolfe, *Recent Changes in Urban and Rural Settlement Patterns in Latin America: Some Implications for Organizations and Development* (Santiago: CEPAL, Division of Social Affairs, 1966); see Everett Hagen, "The Transition in Colombia," *On the Theory of Social Change* (Homewood: Dorsey Press, 1962); Orlando Fals-Borda, *Peasant Society in the Colombian Andes* (Gainesville: University of Florida Press, 1955), and *Facts and Theory of Socio-cultural Change in a Rural Social System,* Sociological Monographs, 2 (Bogotá: National University of Colombia, 1962).

About the modifications in the socio-economic and cultural composition of the Latin American peasantry and the rising urban-rural population, see Andrew Pearse, *Agrarian Change Trends in Latin America* (Santiago: ICIRA, 1966, mimeo).

III

Education and Elite Formation:
The University

I O

Universities and Social Development

DARCY RIBEIRO

I would like to be provocative at the outset. As everyone knows, there is no such thing as a genuinely Latin American university, just as there is no Latin America, in the sense of a homogeneous social and cultural unit. There is, however, a common basis sufficient to justify our speaking, in general terms, of one and the other. Perhaps not so much for what they are today, as for the common challenges they have to face, and their common struggle to develop, which may bring them into uniformity. This is the view taken in many studies of Latin American university problems.[1]

I. The Three Americas

It seems that the American nations can be divided into three blocs of different historical, cultural and economic formation, each of which in its different way is confronted with its own separate development problems. In the first group we have the *witness peoples,* the product of the encounter between the European conquerors and the original, highly developed American civilizations. These are the peoples of Mexico and of some of the Central American countries, and the peoples of the high plateaux of the Andes (Bolivia, Peru, and Ecuador), the former being survivors of the Mayan and Aztec civilizations, the latter of the Inca civilization. They all bear within them, even today, traces of the conflict between those ancient cultures and the European civilization. A second bloc consists of the *new peoples,* produced by the meeting of widely varied ethnic strains—chiefly the encounter of indigenous races and Negroes with Europeans—which subsequently underwent a process of cultural assimilation that gave rise to the new ethnical strains, not identical with any of their sources. Chile, with its mixed

343

population of predominantly indigenous origin, falls into this category; so do Brazil, Venezuela, Colombia, and the West Indies, where the population consists of a mingling of Negroes, Indians, and Europeans, the proportions differing in each case. The third group—setting aside the United States and Canada—is represented by Argentina and Uruguay, inhabited by *transplanted peoples* whose present ethnic configuration is conditioned essentially by the mass immigration of Europeans who took over and subjugated the original Gaucho strain formed before independence.[2]

Each of these categories affects not only an aspect peculiar to itself, but a number of specific development problems. Thus, the witness peoples and the new peoples are chiefly distinguished by the rigidity of their social structure, which is divided into five completely separate strata. In addition to three traditional social classes, they have also a supra-upper class and an infra-lower class. The latter comprises the great mass of those who have no place as producers and consumers in the national life, and play no part in the social or political life of the nation, owing to their backwardness and illiteracy. In the case of the witness peoples, they are chiefly remarkable for occupying a "cultural wilderness" in which they conform to traditional indigenous patterns and values, resisting integration. Among the new peoples, the infralower class are social rather than cultural rejects. Having been torn from its indigenous and African roots by a violent process of deculturation under the pressure of the slave system, this class has remained beyond the social and economic pale of the modern national community, its members living in the most backward areas or sometimes flung into the big cities, where they likewise find exceptional difficulty in fitting into the system of urban and industrial life and work.

The existence of this huge class of social outcasts, which exercises pressure on the national structures in the attempt to gain admission to them, imprints certain middle-class characteristics upon the lower class—of workers and minor employees, who are literate and receive at least the local minimum wages—because despite poverty the latter is placed in a privileged position compared with the emergent masses, and lives under the constant threat of returning to the state of backwardness and penury which is that of the majority of the population.

To a certain extent the three blocs also differ in their educational and university history. The witness peoples, as the first to be conquered, the owners of great mineral wealth, and constituting stratified communities whose members could be set to immediate productive tasks by the Spaniards, began in the very first decades of colonization to be a patrician class of mixed blood which soon had the advantage of educational institutions, including universities. The new peoples, who came into existence principally as part of the single-crop system of vast plantations worked by slave labor, although they produced an equal amount of riches during the colonial period, had to wait far longer for equal educational opportunities. Brazil, for instance, had no secondary schools until after independence, and these were not developed into universities until after 1830. The transplanted peoples living in the southern triangle, of more recent origin, went through a positive ecological process, under the leadership of an elite which had passed through the colonial educational institutions. Since independence, this system has been extended and enriched as the result of a state policy, more vigorous in these areas than in others, which has produced a more complete and efficient system of education. For the political leaders in this area, "to civilize was to populate" with Europeans—which amounted to turning the educational ambitions of the immigrants themselves toward compulsory school attendance.

Any generalizations about Latin America must at least allow for these three separate stages in our continent, each sufficiently different from the others to justify individual treatment. Thus, the transplanted peoples, brought into contact with a population culturally and socially integrated with the nation, saw the development problem essentially in terms of industrialization, of winning a more advantageous position in world markets in cereals, hides, meat and wool, and of achieving a domestic social organization which would ensure a more equitable distribution of the products of the nation's labors. The other two groups were faced with equivalent economic problems, and had to meet the further challenge of promoting the integration of their huge and growing masses of cultural and social outcasts and compelling the small privileged class to accept new social trends with the chief purpose of taking account of the others' interests.

All these countries are striving for economic, social, and cultural progress through industrialization and the consequent improvement of the technological level of agricultural production, anticipating that this will have the same effect in Latin America as everywhere else in the world—a transformation of the social structure and of standards of living, simultaneously with an enrichment of the community. But industrialization, being applied in such a widely different context in each country, encounters correspondingly varied obstacles and leads to consequences which also differ. In the case of the transplanted peoples, whose population is already integrated into the nation's productive system and political and cultural life, one of the principal consequences of industrialization will probably be to throw on the labor market manpower which is becoming redundant. This happened in Europe during the corresponding period, generating social tensions which were reduced in most cases by exporting millions of Europeans to the American countries—thus creating the transplanted peoples we are considering at the moment. These latter, however, will not be able to deal with the situation in the same way, and their surplus manpower will tend more and more to press for a structural renovation calculated to provide greater opportunities for work and progress.

In the other two groups, the human surpluses constituted by rural unemployed and by the uprooted urban population are in increasing danger of sinking back into the pre-existent mass of "outcasts." The integrated sectors of the population obviously have better prospects of bringing pressure to bear on the national institutions through the trade unions, and of expressing their own interests in political terms, than have the underprivileged masses. The arrival among these latter contingents of the formerly integrated may be expected to give them a new dynamism and make them, probably, less resigned and more combative.

This pressure for reform, and its expression in politics, is withstood by the united front of the three blocs, the oligarchies jealous of their privileges but unable, so far, to frame an inclusive national scheme for conciliating their own interests with the popular demand for progress. As reformist demands increase, the oligarchies resort more and more to measures of repression and to the foreign alliances which combine with the national and continental armed forces to maintain the *status quo*. The struggle for social development is taking on an international complexion owing to the self-defense of foreign interests in Latin America, the alliance among the Latin American oligarchies, and the association of these two groups of interests.

During the early stages of Latin American industrialization the national entrepreneurs were struggling to establish and enlarge their factories, in competition with foreign industry and imported goods, so that their interests were compatible with those of the general population. They could therefore claim protective tariffs and government aid on the grounds that these were necessary for the nation's progress toward autonomy and would lead to increased employment.

But when the international corporation leapt over the customs barriers and began competing on the various domestic markets in the guise of local firms financed by foreign capital, the big national firms, in most cases, either went into partnership with them or were swallowed up. Contributory factors in this surrender of independence were the advantages of association with firms that were larger and more profitable—even if the profits had to be shared—than the old individual businesses had been, and the technological fragility of the latter, which were not equipped to compete with factories run by big corporations with great numbers of technical and scientific personnel at their service.

Thus the net effect of the measures adopted in Latin America to remedy a basic shortcoming in development by the domestic production of goods formerly imported has been to create two new forms of dependency. One of these is economic—the domination of the national markets by industrialization directed from abroad, which is not only burdensome but does little or nothing to promote the training of senior executives. This results in a stultifying distortion of the economic structure, since it weakens the entrepreneur sector which should be leading the struggle for independent national development. The other is a technical form of dependency—an increasing reliance on foreign "know-how," without which no enterprise can survive, and which also has structural consequences, since it slows down the process of making good the national backwardness in technical and scientific matters, and the emergence of skilled technical experts.

Hence the internal barriers impeding development are thus reinforced by foreign obstacles which not only retard the industrialization of Latin America but reduce its power to bring a new order into social life. There is the further danger that these foreign pressures and their alliance with industrial interests may have the effect of reinforcing the out-of-date structure instead of reforming it.

II. The New University

These challenges have to be met in order to lay the foundations of a scientific understanding of the conditions in which industrialization is taking place and of the alternative possibilities of action open to each individual country; and they must be answered by mobilizing the best experts in all fields for a rational orientation of progress.

The universities, since they possess the largest body of expert personnel, have a decisive role to play in this rational effort to replace the old do-as-you-please system by the planned organization of economic, social, and cultural activities. But they can carry out that role efficiently only if they reorganize themselves for the purpose of acting firstly as active centers for the analysis of national problems and the elaboration of solutions covering all the interests involved, and secondly, as a nucleus for training expert staff in the numbers, and with the range of specialization, required for development.

All this signifies, in fact, that some more of the walls sheltering "academic freedom" will have to be broken down. This is imperative if the university system is shortly to achieve the maturity required for survival and action in a world where even the most famous and conservative universities have been drawn into the same process. In the past, the Latin American universities have been guided in their growth by the spontaneous interplay of factors which reflected the poverty and backwardness of the different countries, and dazzled by the great foreign houses of learning; now they are called upon to fit themselves for the rational pursuit of planning, or their own development, by setting forth the values to which they wish to remain faithful and by enumerating clearly the academic, social, and national aims they are helping to attain.

The walls isolating the universities have long been broken down in all parts of the world. The great battles of war are being fought today in the laboratories of the principal universities. Their study centers are pursuing objectives of an extra-mural character, which may be military, or designed to promote economic and political domination; and they are financing vast research programs. Their technical staffs are being enlarged to take part in work which goes further and further beyond the mere search for new knowledge and the transmission of existing knowledge, and is intended to serve national and group interests. In this new academic world, directed toward new tasks in war and peace, any university which is not perspicacious enough to realize where the others wish to arrive, and to review and determine its own course accordingly, is doomed to betray its own future and to fail its nation. Only by exercising such perspicacity can our universities avoid the outstanding dangers which threaten them today—

first, the danger of isolation maintained for fear of undesirable outside influences; second, an ignorant and foolish clinging to old ways, which involves their teaching staff in irrelevant projects.

This is a serious challenge to the independence of Latin American cultural development, which is condemned on the one hand to make sure of the international coexistence without which no scientific progress is possible, and on the other hand to guard against its own alienation and commitment to outside projects. In a world where within two hostile camps everything and everybody is involved in the conflict, science first and foremost, we are in danger of seeing our restricted research teams diverted from the task of national development and placed at the service of international science.

These threats are not illusory or premature, they are the daily experience of all Latin American university laboratories which having attained a certain scientific level, are continually urged to allow themselves to be financed for the purposes of the cold war. In each particular case it is necessary to examine how far this financial generosity is due to a common concern for scientific progress, and how far it is prompted by less direct aims.

The sole way to deal with this challenge is probably to frame a system of ethics to guide Latin American research scientists, reinforced by an appropriate set of moral sanctions, and defining what fields of research are to be given priority and subject to what conditions work on foreign projects may be undertaken—in order to ensure that our chief personnel and the scanty equipment and resources at our disposal shall not be turned aside from themes connected with development.

In this new world, so remote from the traditional "ivory tower," protestations of disinterested love of knowledge or outmoded university traditions have an old-fashioned ring. Nothing is more anachronous than certain expressions habitually used by those who, in their unhealthy obsession with academic erudition, degrade knowledge into something less than it really is—an instrument for changing the world. Or our university hierarchy will also be afflicted by the servitudes that run through the whole of our society.

There are many positive elements in the university life of Latin America, which is why these expedients are necessary. It is essential to bring fresh thought to bear on university life as a whole, reconsidering the old values in order to establish standards and convincing new goals for the professors and the students. For this reason we need to define our attitude clearly toward social renovation; because if young people, in their places of study, hear no echo of the popular anxiety for progress in which they share, they will inevitably listen to other voices and end by rebelling against their universities.

Only if they throw the weight of their real cultural achievements into the national debates, can the universities become leaders of their own students. The rebellion of the student body in the underdeveloped countries, which is nourished by a new awareness of the national poverty and a refusal to accept underdevelopment, is a necessary aspect for social progress. Its impact on academic life, so often advanced as a reason for ineffectiveness, is perhaps the least of the factors contributing to the backwardness of the Latin American universities. And as it is something that cannot be eradicated by disciplinary measures, it can be dealt with, and diverted to fully acceptable aims, only as fast as the universities overhaul themselves and transform themselves completely into responsible institutions for the rejuvenation of society.

This is a theme which has been ardently debated in recent decades, as a reflection, in the university sphere, of the controversy about the causes of the backwardness and poverty of our peoples. In present-day Latin America, everything is on trial. All political, social, economic, and educational institutions are being scrutinized and called in question with the urgent purpose of determining what form they are to take, or what part they can play in social life and in the struggle for development. Amid the present dissatisfaction with backwardness and public desire for progress, the universities, too, must speak out and take a firm stand.

In these circumstances, which everyone understands, the general aim of the pursuit, assimilation, and transmission of learning takes on additional importance for the universities of the underdeveloped countries, as a new means of serving national and social purposes. The debate has inevitably spread to professorial circles, perturbing those whose only wish was to enjoy learning for its own sake, and obliging them to take a stand. It is probable that this controversial atmosphere acts as a stimulus to rebellion among the students and is prejudicial to the strict observance of the curriculum. But it also undoubtedly provides a rare and valuable opportunity for a redefinition of objectives, which would otherwise be impracticable.

Foreign professors, and we ourselves, in our respective attitudes, reflect the stage of development of the communities from which we come and to which we belong. We should be showing a lack of judgment and of realism if we assumed them to be as confident as ourselves that tomorrow must inevitably be better than today, merely through our own efforts—or if we relaxed and adopted their position of Olympian indifference to political and ethical questions and to the national aspiration toward progress.

So long as the enormous present-day distance continues to exist between the advanced societies and ours, which are backward and at odds with themselves, all that is required of the genuine representatives of the two worlds is to cultivate a certain reciprocal tolerance. They must respect our passion for investigation, which throws doubt on everything, demanding that all institutions, norms and values shall be redefined in terms of their ability to serve our social aims. We should respect their national loyalties and the fundamental conservatism which makes them perpetually ready to seek an adjustment. The dialogue will always be difficult, as is natural between Crusaders and Moslems.

III. Cultural Autonomy

The economic and social progress of the fully developed nations was brought about by constant interaction between a body of scientific and technological knowledge on the one hand, and the nation's productive activities on the other. Within this system of forces, each side has been stimulated by the other's development. Thus, the expansion of production created financial resources which made it possible to strengthen the educational system and the research institutions. And these last, in turn, by consolidating knowledge and training new technical executives, influenced production and contributed to its progress.

This process established a body of scientific knowledge, applied in the technical sphere, which came to constitute the culture of the industrial community, taking the place of the rule-of-thumb precepts of the primitive society. Despite academic and institutional barriers and the pragmatism of the men of action, this body of knowledge steadily established itself; it was based on the university methods of research and formal transmission of knowledge, and on the opportunities and challenges that confronted producing circles in the practical application of newly acquired knowledge. Thus, as well as building up new sources of energy, new machinery and new methods, industrialization also produced a new culture and a new scholastic and university mentality.

Nevertheless, the universities were slow to adapt their structure to the new requirements of the modern industrial society, which called for intensified scientific specialization together with the training of more numerous and varied categories of executives for social welfare work, the civil service, and technical activities. Not until the twentieth century, in fact, was there any deliberate attempt to reform the universities, by including the basic sciences in degree courses, giving fuller scientific instruction to executive personnel, and widening the range of specialization in order to satisfy the demands of production.

The universities of the United States, which were the pioneers in this task and took a particularly keen interest in production problems, were the targets of mordant criticism from European university circles, which clung jealously to their position of detachment from all practical matters lying outside the customary limited range of the traditional professions. The Latin American universities, though their own backwardness kept them aloof from this problem, allowed themselves the luxury of enthusiastically taking sides with the European purists.

The need for a form of university studies with a scientific basis and a technological slant, suitable for the modern industrial community, became increasingly obvious as the underdeveloped nations began demanding to be guided, in their turn, toward industrialization. They had no technical personnel qualified to carry out the primary tasks of introducing and controlling the new productive processes, but above all, they lacked the ability to operate the new machines. They therefore adopted the course of importing industrial plant lock, stock and barrel, together with the engineers required to set it up and run it. Almost always, however, such plant "aged" rapidly, periodically requiring either complete replacement or else protective legislation to make it effective again and enable it to compete with the constantly modernized factories in the advanced countries.

Not until after the Second World War was there a general awakening to the existence of these phenomena and of the related need for university reform.[3] Meanwhile, the discrepancy between the "career" of an industrial plant in the developed countries and that of the same plant in the backward countries, had been growing evident. A factory exported from the United States to Germany and to Japan, for example, or to Latin America, would have a completely different history in each instance. In the former case it would fit into the local economic system, adjusting itself to raw materials and market conditions, being constantly brought up to date, and ultimately beginning to compete with the country of its origin. In the latter case it would soon lapse into obsolescence and in less than ten years its value would have declined to a fraction of the original cost. Climatic and racial factors could obviously not be held accountable for such a difference in "performance"; it gradually became evident that this was principally due to the existence in the first two countries of a highly skilled labor force, with a good background of modern scientific knowledge and an extensive system of technical and vocational education which did not exist in Latin America.

The Latin American universities now have to win their cultural autonomy in order to master the same scientific knowledge, and the promotion of technological progress, both in the sphere of original research and in teaching and training. An intensified effort will result in their modernization in a manner consonant with the movement of national renovation, and they will thus take up their proper function of generating knowledge and technological skills and training the scientific and vocational personnel required for development purposes.

All this means that in their struggle for progress the underdeveloped nations have to meet two related challenges—the artificially induced promotion of industrialization, and the conquest of cultural autonomy, also by an act of will. As for the general planning of development, programs for the expansion of production should be as numerous as the corresponding measures of cultural renovation, the latter including educational projects and more especially those relating to higher education.

These last, however, are the specific concern of the universities, and represent a challenge inasmuch as those institutions can probably only preserve their autonomy if they take the initiative in transforming themselves into vehicles of development. That is why the universities have to tackle the revision of their values, both expressed and implicit, in order to adapt them to the demands of national development; to renovate their own structure in order to master modern science and technology and apply them creatively to their national circumstances and problems; and to enlarge their facilities for training qualified personnel.

The Latin American universities, at the most varied levels reflecting the degree of national development and their own degree of maturity, are now confronting these challenges. They can all rely on positive experience which helps overcome their worst shortcomings; but they are all handicapped to a varying extent by structural difficulties which impede the solution of their chief qualitative and quantitative problems.

IV. The Modernization of the University

The two basic external necessities of any fruitful university life—freedom and support—have seldom been granted in a satisfactory form, or for any length of time, to the universities of Latin America. Freedom to conduct research, to criticize, and to teach has been denied by the intervention of dictators, or rendered impossible by orthodoxy enforced upon the private universities. At other times the funds essential to full-scale university activity have been lacking. Both freedom and funds have often been far below necessary minimum, owing to the social backwardness and poverty in the countries.

Apart from these external conditions, determined by extraneous factors, our universities have hitherto lacked, and still lack, the necessary internal conditions for the exercise of their functions and the adaptability required to change those structures to meet the new scientific, technical, and social demands.

We will consider more particularly these last shortcomings, which, since they lie largely within the compass of university decision-making, place a greater responsibility upon the university staff, and are probably more amenable to rational organization than the external requirements. Practically speaking, the three groups of requirements are indivisible. They can be considered separately for the purpose of analysis, if only in order to indicate more precisely the specific responsibilities of the universities—those which we must not fail to meet, and those which give society a greater respect for academic life, together with more adequate and regular financial support.

The university, regarded as a social system, is hampered by vested interests, traditions, customs, and habits which militate against rational reorganization. The most serious factor in this situation is that the resistance is entrenched in bodies of differing and indefined values, which are invoked to justify any and every attitude. For instance, criticism of inadequate educational opportunity is answered by invoking the need to maintain minimum standards for university qualifications. Criticism of the unsatisfactory basic scientific training provided for vocational posts and of the inadequate training of high-grade experts is answered by pleading society's need for vast numbers of university graduates. Thus, anything can be justified. The worst is that this is nearly always taken as an excuse for harping on external difficulties and avoiding discussion of the universities themselves and their limited capacity for mastering up-to-date scientific and technical knowledge and producing the types of personnel required for purposes of national development.

We will now consider briefly the principal structural difficulties impeding the revitalization of the Latin American universities, in the light of the national aspirations toward economic and social progress. The following considerations do not, of course, apply to all universities without exception, for many of them, conscious of their role in the community, have been striving for years past to overcome these obstacles and have achieved encouraging results. The important point is that this progress has been made only in cases where the preliminary task of diagnosing the trouble was courageously faced.

PROBLEMS OF ADMISSION

Very explicit economic and social surveys conducted in both capitalist and socialist countries, including the United States, Japan, England, and the Soviet Union, have shown the decisive importance to any development program of an educated labor force. They have also shown that the quality of the available labor force and the effectiveness of production techniques depend chiefly on the long-term increase in income achieved in fully developed economic systems.[4]

This means that increased expenditure on education at all levels— initially in the greater proportion on higher education, for this can rapidly improve the situation—must be included in Latin American programs of national development over the next few years. It is true that many countries already devote a considerable proportion of their national budgets to their universities and would find it difficult to give more—a fact which makes it incumbent on those universities to redouble their own efforts to reduce their expenses by a critical examination of their resources in terms of social profitability. This duty is all the more imperative for the Latin American universities since the extreme youth of the national population requires enormous expenditure on general education.[5]

For countries with great numbers of cultural or social "outcasts," there is a particular need to promote the education of those sectors. In the case of Brazil and Mexico, an idea of the enormity of this task can be gained by realizing that despite their educational efforts, the increase in the population so far outstrips the school enrollment, that the number of illiterates has increased instead of diminishing in recent years.[6] From the moment when our universities are not merely a by-product of the increasing national expenditure on development, but become an instrument of social renovation, these facts must be taken into account in all plans for modernizing the universities, so that this may be done at the least possible cost, as a minimum condition of their practical value and social usefulness. We are therefore confronted by a complex problem of educational planning which demands comprehensive action, concentrating on improved technical education and giving special consideration to the social factors implicit in the framing of any program.

The quantitative problems of the Latin American universities are now beginning to be dealt with scientifically, through estimates of the probable needs of each sector of activity in the matter of qualified personnel. The studies now available will make it possible to introduce a university policy of incentives to certain types of training and discouragement of others, in accordance with the requirements of national development.[7] For the individual, some universities are setting up centralized services to deal with selection and vocational guidance, which will ultimately put an end to the helplessness which is now often manifested by young applicants for university admission.

At present it is only by indirect means that the candidates for a particular university course can discover the extent to which it is likely to be socially useful. Armed with this very unreliable information, and influenced by the social prestige attaching to the various professions, they choose one career rather than another. This vague approach is coupled with a rigid university system which compels the young applicant to choose his course of study once and for all, before entering a Faculty, and with no objective information about the possibilities and the professional scope of his choice. The less informed candidates, without definite social views, are attracted to the subjects they consider most interesting, usually those "in fashion" at the moment, and obtain with difficulty some insignificant certificate of aptitude.

For many Latin American countries, the restricted educational opportunities offered to their young people by the universities constitute a serious problem. A typical example of the restricted university policy is the limitation, by a "numerical clause," of the number of annual admissions to each faculty, matriculation being determined on the basis of a competitive examination, regardless of national needs. The numbers are often fixed as the result of pressure from the teaching staff, who do not want to have to work harder. One only has to compare the equipment and teaching staff available in certain faculties with those of colleges of similar level in other countries well known for the quality of their tuition, in order to realize that existing resources in the former are not being used to the full.

The great disadvantage of this restriction is that it reduces the number of senior executives available for development tasks and thus makes it impossible to spread a knowledge of basic scientific technology throughout the different fields of activity. A parallel drawback is the great number of "mushroom" schools which come into existence because those which possess highly qualified staff, good libraries, and adequate equipment are voluntarily limiting their teaching capacity with no thought for even the most obvious social requirements.

Another result of the "numerical clause" system is the specious character of the matriculation examinations, which are devised with the purpose of admitting no more than the predetermined number of new students, who reach a certain required standard out of all proportion to the level of the average candidate. In some countries, particularly Brazil, matriculation candidates are obliged to take special preparatory courses, which are usually private and expensive, and this aggravates the effect of social barriers affecting admission to higher education. To all these obstacles must be added the disheartening effect upon young people of repeated examinations in a system so ridiculous that success is sometimes purely fortuitous.

The other solution, of free entry to the university, based on the recognition of the right to matriculate for all secondary school leavers, is likewise unsatisfactory. This is so because the universities, not being entitled to interfere in secondary education, would be faced with the necessity of accepting a mass of candidates for a year, or at most for two years, during which time they would pick out from the crowd those actually capable of carrying their studies further.

In the last few years, some universities have opened pre-university courses where closer attention can be paid to candidates for matriculation, thus making it possible to sort out for admission to the faculties those who have the ability to profit from the higher education. A satisfactory alternative is to set up a centralized selection service, providing one single preliminary examination for all candidates for matriculation, devised to reveal their degree of intellectual maturity or level of knowledge in the subjects taught in the secondary school, together with their profile of interests, so that suitable candidates can be steered toward the faculties for which they are best fitted.

In addition to providing an overall, unbiased view of the results achieved by the secondary schools, which could serve as a useful guide to the educational authorities responsible for that sector, the single examination would oblige the faculties to adopt uniform criteria of admission, each in its own field of study. This method, associated with a system of personal interviews, enables closer attention to be paid to the individual candidate and gives secondary school pupils a reliable idea of the standard that will be expected of them when they enter the university. The system also facilitates the granting of scholarships to particularly promising students.

One of the social achievements most highly appreciated by students in Latin America is that of free tuition at the public universities. This, however, presents serious drawbacks. In the first place it fails in its intention of ensuring a democratic system—as can be seen from the negligible proportion of poorer students matriculating. Secondly, it deprives the universities of the additional funds they could receive in the form of fees from students who can afford to pay their own expenses. There has recently been a move in the universities—beginning in Brazil—to levy a fixed fee upon such students, who are estimated to represent more than 30 per cent of the total, and thus build up a students' fund to provide scholarships for the rest. This would help to solve the problem of the poorer candidates in faculties which demand or recommend full-time study; such as those of Engineering, Medicine, and Science.

STRUCTURAL OBSTACLES

The major structural obstacle to modernizing the Latin American university is probably its own system of organization, which frequently gives it the form of a mere federation of independent faculties. The weakness of the corporative organization underlying the vigor of its components is something that leaps to the eye. This is due to the artificial nature of these universities, which were built up by the formal amalgamation of pre-existent schools, each with its own strong traditions. In such cases university life consists of a few solemn acts carried out collectively, and of a common approach to dealings with the government, chiefly in budgetary matters. Whereas everything connected with the recruitment of professors, the curriculum, and the system of student admission, is left to the decision of the individual faculties, each of which jealously guards its independence. In other cases, isolation is attributable to the way in which European universities were created in the last century, as an amalgam of separate colleges, each of which selected its own students and dealt with them from beginning to end of their studies, making no provision for inter-collegiate life or for the integration of the whole mechanism.

This system of watertight compartments makes it necessary for each college to provide instruction in the same subjects, with a consequent duplication of teaching staff, equipment, and teaching and research laboratories. In addition to the high cost of all this to the university, it puts a brake on original research by reducing every field of knowledge to the propedeutic or professorial level. Thus fragmented, mathematics, physics, dentistry, and biology, for example, require an enormous number of professors, scattered through the different faculties and included in the university statistics, but not consolidated to form a complete, creative team. As well as causing an unnecessary duplication of staff and equipment in the individual schools, this division leads to an expansion of the schools themselves, since it requires separate premises, a separate library, and separate lecture-halls for every new course the university decides to introduce.

This federative structure worked well enough in the pre-scientific days when the purpose of a university was to turn out theologians, doctors, and bachelors of arts; but it is incompatible with modern scientific developments, for the professional training provided at universities in the nineteenth century still took the traditional forms of integration into academic life as the common preparation, and the general disciplines were compulsory in all branches of study. Nowadays the professional capacities of a specialist, the professional level he can expect to attain, the adaptability he will need in order to keep pace with advances in his specific field, all depend essentially on his basic scientific training. This means that the universities must devote more time to the basic sciences, and above all, to tuition in science itself, instead of turning out the prefabricated instruction usually provided in professional courses.

The sphere of scientific knowledge—which is another basis of the modern university—in its turn requires special facilities if it is to be cultivated independently of its possible professional applications, and in circumstances propitious to original research; for there can be no "science" where nothing is provided except lectures on scientific subjects, and no serious tuition where original research is not carried on as well.

The most frequent solution in Latin America is either to scatter the teaching of basic science throughout the university by means of subsidiary groups providing professional courses, or else to concentrate it in special institutes or faculties of "higher studies." A ridiculous combination of both systems is in fact often used. Both present insuperable drawbacks in addition to those already mentioned. In the former case the scientist is compelled to withdraw from university life if he chooses a research career, instead of beginning with professional studies and going on to specialize.

Most students do both, in the interests of security—taking, for example, a complete medical course instead of deciding from the start to specialize in biochemistry. In the second case, which is even more disastrous, eighteen-year-olds, fresh from secondary school, are compelled to opt for some scientific career demanding highly specialized qualifications as to the nature of which they are completely ignorant.

The alternative solution would appear to be the unification of general preparatory studies in independent centers which all students would be required to attend before making a definite choice of profession. In this way the first year of science teaching would be entrusted to practising scientists, which is essential, and future specialists would be selected from the whole body of university students, according to their aptitude for scientific research. Thus the choice of a scientific career would be made with open eyes, with the help of adequate guidance, and would result in the continuation of the studies already begun, without the need to attend schools dealing with neighboring professional branches.

Another reason why it is preferable to provide general scientific tuition in the same institution where advanced courses are given, is that teaching is thus associated with practical research activity. Moreover, it economizes effort, because postgraduate students can be used on the teaching side. This is the pattern of the central institutes now being set up at the University of Brasilia.

The general courses organized in this way also offer more favorable conditions for providing the thorough scientific training at the advanced level which is becoming more and more necessary for those who can neither fit into a specific professional field nor take up a career in science, but are attracted toward the new sectors of production and services which require this type of training. The rapidly changing conditions existing in certain occupations of high technological level, due to the adoption of complex material such as electronic computers, will call in the future for scientific training in depth, rather than for the extension of the range of professional studies.

It is sometimes considered that these are problems inseparable from the stage of development reached by the most advanced countries. It so happens that the one "advantage" of underdeveloped peoples is that they need not necessarily follow the same course of technological progress, in the same stages, amid the same confusion, and at the same social cost, as the nations which are now fully developed. And it is probable that our one possibility of ultimately catching up lies in our capacity to absorb the system of modern industrialization, not only by importing up-to-date industrial plant lock, stock and barrel, but also by incorporating, through the universities, the body of scientific and technological know-how which produced that plant and is constantly improving it. The speed of Latin American progress will thus depend on the capacity to achieve real autonomy in cultural development, and this can only be done if the universities are as good as the best in other parts of the world.

The standardization of scientific training centers, and their independence of professional teaching, is advantageous to the latter as well. Once released from outside duties, this sector can concentrate more effectively on its own task. It will also help to get rid of the ambiguity so frequently engaged in by professors of applied disciplines, who, in the pursuit of false professional prestige, complicate their subjects unnecessarily instead of teaching them by "practical" methods. It is likely, too, that the professors who train students for the liberal professions will feel encouraged to expand the methods of training which are a social requisite in their various branches of learning.

The establishment of central institutes of science, equipped to provide basic courses for all students, with graduate courses and a curriculum leading to the master's or doctor's degree, gives the university the means of integration which it lacks at present. It also facilitates the reorganization of teacher training on a new basis. And in the entire field of traditional education, this is perhaps the branch in which the Latin American universities are most backward. The existing teacher training faculties barely suffice to train secondary-school teachers, without even coping with the demand for teachers for technical courses at that level. In no instance do they enable the university to make its fitting contribution to the solution of the problems of primary education, or to the training of the wide range of experts required for educational administration, educational guidance, educational planning, and so many other matters. Nor do they cover the field of teaching methods at the university level itself, which is left to the inspiration of individual professors, no provision being made for evaluating the experience gained. This is a shortcoming which is making itself tragically felt in connection with the teaching of new branches of knowledge, particularly science.

A further advantage of the system of central institutes giving preparatory courses for all university students, is that it enables the student to postpone his final choice of a career. Only at the conclusion of these preparatory studies is he required to choose between the profession toward which he was originally attracted and some branch of scientific specialization, if he reveals an aptitude for the latter; or to turn to the educational sector if he proves to possess a gift for teaching. Educational activities thus become a form of free choice open to all students, and the whole university is transformed into a system for training educators.

Another structural drawback resulting from the division of the university into independent faculties is that the system of tuition is based on rigid programs. This compels the university to recruit a fresh group of professors and to obtain new equipment whenever it plans to introduce a new course of study, because it is not possible to assemble students taking different courses into one class, even when they require the same basic instruction. The narrow range of facilities offered by the universities, and the high annual per capita cost of students, are chiefly due to this structural instability. The disadvantages of the system are obvious, particularly in view of the need to expand technical and vocational training to facilitate social development.

The alternative seems to be the inclusion of all university studies in a comprehensive system aimed at placing them as far as possible on an equal footing, together with the introduction of a central service to frame and approve the curricula and promote the full use of all the teaching possibilities of each university unit in the different courses included in its program.

The system of interchangeable admissions, which exists in the United States universities, provides an admirable model of curricular integration. By moving closer to this system, many Latin American universities could add new training facilities to the few they now offer, at a minimum cost in terms of staff and equipment. This would be possible for graduate or postgraduate courses, for specialized vocational courses, and for scientific training courses. The best results would perhaps be felt in the short-term courses made up of the combination of a number of subjects drawn from different syllabuses, with the aim of providing university qualifications for those taking up one of the countless activities in the field of development, which are now sparsely available in the form of in-service training or correspondence courses.

THE PROFESSORS

Another obstacle to the modernization of the Latin American universities, and one which is in many ways more harmful than those already described, is the institution of the university chair. We may take as an example, for the purposes of analysis, the case of Brazil, where the system is particularly rigid and displays all the principal defects.[9]

The occupant of a Brazilian university chair is a feudal overlord with absolute powers in university life, whose security from dismissal and right to life occupancy of his post are guaranteed by the Constitution itself. He obtains his *latifundia* in the learned world through a public competitive examination which represents a "bloodless tournament" in which no scholar would deliberately choose to take part. The candidate has to satisfy a most learned jury, orally and in writing, that he has a full and detailed command of his field, including any and every historical or collateral aspect on which he may be required to hold forth. This test, which is probably unequalled for severity anywhere else in the world, should, in the nature of things, have produced the world's finest body of professors. As it has manifestly not done so, something unusual must have happened. And in point of fact, the vast majority of university professors never sit for the examination, but take up teaching through one or other of a vast number of lawful stratagems. It also happens that when the examination is held, the occupant of a chair exerts his decisive influence beforehand to make sure that his favorite assistant has a better prospect of succeeding him than a more capable rival.

Thus, an ultra-rigorous legal mechanism exists side by side with an enormous number of parallel mechanisms facilitated by political bureaucrats and professorial favoritism. Strong in his discretionary powers, the reigning professor selects or promotes his subordinates, preventing all hope of a well-ordered career system which would enable junior professors to climb the ladder by means of successive tests designed to assess their teaching capacity, efficiency, and productivity.

The prerogatives of the university professor in Brazil, derived from the medieval tradition of *lente proprietario*, are reinforced by a constitutional principle; this attempt to protect freedom of teaching guarantees life-long occupancy of his chair and rules out all possibility of removing him whether or not he is still competent, whether or not he continues to teach.

Recent events in Brazil have proved to satiety that life-occupancy offers little or no guarantee of freedom to teach, and therefore that the two questions should not be confused. The guarantee that the professor shall be independent and free in his work is one thing—it is a guarantee that should be given not only to the university professor, but to teachers at all levels, and it depends essentially on the democratic freedoms existing in the country concerned. Security of employment is another thing, and it should be guaranteed to professors, as to the members of all other professions, after a certain number of years of work. But when the two principles are intermingled, they produce an autocratic mechanism which neither generalizes freedom of teaching nor gives security, but impedes the advance of learning by setting up a life-long, immovable and irreplaceable obstacle in the person of the professor.

The occupant of a university chair partly benefits and partly suffers from this system, which, although securing him certain privileges, at the same time puts him in chains. Compelled to act as though he commanded a field of knowledge in which he is not competent, he can only save his face at the expense of his professional honor, by relying on the formal authority with which he is invested and thrusting aside the young professors whose ability would show up his own weakness.

Such is the case of the aging professor, who might perhaps have been a respected member of some other profession, but who has now become a laughing-stock to his assistants and students.

The Brazilian professor, raised by law to such enviable heights, automatically becomes an operative unit of university life, multiplied whenever a new discipline is introduced, to form a new, independent feudal fief. This makes it impossible for experts in one particular field or one individual school to associate and co-operate among themselves.

Another result of this concept of the university chair is to condemn its occupant to the stultifying task of repeating the same lectures every year till the end of his days, to students taking the same course, usually at the same hours and in the same lecture-theaters. Inevitably the lectures end by ossifying into notes read out in rolling periods by the professor and taken down somnolently by the students. Many professors, of course, succeed in keeping abreast of their subject thanks to personal ability. But these are cases of individual merit, persisting in defiance of the shortcomings of the institution.

If the teaching work were divided among departments jointly responsible for teaching and research in each separate field, it would be possible to change the courses by obliging the professors to keep up to date and to take turns at the head of each teaching unit. It would also facilitate the attendance of students from different schools, thus reducing expenses and promoting intercommunication within the university, which is desirable from every point of view.

In addition to its defects as an institution, the university chair presents even greater drawbacks from the social viewpoint, since it gives its occupant a certain status, not only in university circles, but in the community as a whole. Thus, a medical practitioner who also holds a university chair will usually have a richer and longer list of patients, and the same applies to the engineer, the architect, or any other professional man. Consequently, the professor finds his reputation outside the university much more profitable than his salary, and his teaching becomes a secondary occupation, important chiefly for the prestige it confers. In these circumstances most occupants of university chairs in the traditional subjects are hostile not only to the introduction of a system debarring them from any outside activity, but in many cases even to the organization of teaching on a professional basis.

This situation changed, of course, with the appearance on the university scene of increasing numbers of scientific research personnel and of professors dealing with the new branches of study deriving from the basic sciences. Since these new professors could not find an outside market for their degree in mathematics, physics, anthropology, etc., they found themselves obliged to live on university salaries which had been fixed with a view to remunerating assistants rather than full members of the profession. This resulted in a conflict which divided the professors into two camps, that of the "liberals" who favored the *status quo,* or at most an increase of existing salaries, and that of the scientists, who pushed for the establishment of university teaching as a full-time profession. As the former represent established authority, their interests carry greater weight, retarding the progress of the universities and weighing them down with the burden of a general rise in salaries which benefits those who give least and have the smallest claim, without satisfying the minimum conditions laid down by the new teaching and research personnel, who are compelled by the nature of their subjects to regard teaching as their profession, yet prevented from dedicating themselves solely to university activities.

In the last few years, thanks to the efforts of the professors of basic sciences, these questions have begun to be openly discussed in the universities; this has led to certain progressive innovations such as the introduction of full-time teaching in some subjects, with a corresponding differentiation between the professional teacher and the traditional type of professor.

The universities of Brazil and of some other Latin American countries have recently been reviewing the professorial system, trying to organize teaching as an open profession with fixed stages of access on the basis of examinations. The hope is that this will increase the dedication of professors and researchers to their work, and oblige teaching personnel to keep their knowledge up to date. The most advanced regulations stipulate that titular professors must pass an examination every five years, in order to have their contracts renewed. In a few cases, too, the essential problem of the authority of the teaching staff is being tackled, through systems which subordinate professors of all categories in each branch of study to the united authority of the department, for whose approval they have to submit their annual programs of work. But these new systems offset the obvious advantages of periodic tests of efficiency and up-to-dateness by denying the professors that security in their posts which is desirable from every standpoint. In some Latin

American universities this is now one of the problems most keenly debated.

Another obstacle to the improvement of higher education in Latin America, indirectly related to the system of university chairs, is the dearth of high-quality books in the national languages. During the Middle Ages, university teaching was given in Latin so as to impart a body of traditional learning to a small elite. Later it was given in French, because the leadership of liberal thought had passed to France; and still later it was France which took the lead in the replacement of philosophical speculation by empirical and inductive methods of scientific thought. As the modern disciplines were introduced, teaching came to be given in most cases in one or another foreign language— usually English—because of the lack of works of reference in the national language, and on the principle that as all students sat for the preliminary examination in foreign languages, they must be familiar with them.

Desirable as this may have been, the immense majority of Latin American students can scarcely read their mother-tongue. What is to be done? Should languages be taught at the university to make good the deficiencies of intermediate education? Yes, where this is practicable. But that is not enough. It seems likely that we, like all the countries which have now achieved development, must recognize that the ordinary university student, struggling to obtain a degree, cannot be expected to study in any other language than his own.

This situation is natural and comprehensible when we consider the change that has taken place in the last few decades in the social composition of the student body. While it is true that most students come from the middle classes, it is also clear that they do not come from the aristocracy, nor do they reflect the results of the explosive increase in the numbers enrolled in the secondary schools, which has produced a crisis in their educational patterns. Likewise, in comparison with earlier generations, the new university entrants tend to display, among other deficiencies in their earlier education, less ability for foreign languages.

Once the new situation is recognized, with the further fact that the students prepare themselves for their examinations chiefly in the light of their class marks and of the famous "personal notes," all that remains is to tackle the problem. And the only solution, a long-term and tremendously costly one, is to induce the universities—perhaps in the framework of regional programs—to produce fundamental literature in all fields of knowledge at the university level. It is obvious that private publishers cannot do this by themselves, and that the present publishing activities of our universities, which are chiefly concerned with *belles lettres* and essays, will never fill the gap. The introduction of a system of departments, which would recruit the university teams in each speciality for collective undertakings, would create exceptionally favorable conditions for the solution of this problem.

THE STUDENTS

Those who have looked into the problems of the Latin American universities appear to be genuinely puzzled by the political activity displayed by the student bodies, and try to hold these responsible for the deficiencies of higher education in this part of the world. They sometimes complain so vehemently and so ingenuously about student agitation that they remind one of the doctor, enchanted with his ultramodern hospital, who thought the only thing wrong with it was—the patients.

I would like to point out that student agitation in Latin America is not only an inevitable result of our archaic social structures, but one of their positive aspects. Though it may perhaps be prejudicial to teaching, it cannot be blamed for the shortcomings of the university system. A much more serious drawback is the encyclopedic teaching range of the Latin American university, where the curricula are crammed with theoretical subjects. In some cases there is compulsory attendance for 25 or even 30 hours of lectures per week, with annual series of 10 or 12 subjects, all compulsory, so that the teaching is reduced to innumerable lectures and to examinations which merely test the students' ability to reel off multigraphed texts.

The students of poor countries, conscious of their privileged position as members of the tiny fractions—between 1 and 3 per thousand of their generation—who succeed in entering the university, keenly aware of national poverty and indignant about its visible causes, inevitably give expression to their attitude by acts of insubordination. They are differentiated from the young workers by a more actively rebellious spirit, due to their higher level of education, the amount of time they have to spare, and their social position, which to some extent protects them from systematic political repression. Thus, in their student days they take part in all the working-class struggles which are noteworthy for the social generosity of their aims—and indeed, often initiate campaigns which subsequently attract other sections of the population. Once they have graduated, however, they become equally involved— with the additional responsibilities inherent in marriage—in a working discipline which prompts them to a more conformist and conservative attitude. But the vast majority of them retain from their period at the university, as well as the knowledge they acquired with the view to obtaining a degree, a pleasant recollection of this political liveliness, which finds expression in a better-informed and more open-minded attitude toward the contemporary world and the national problems.

Since the Latin American universities confine themselves almost exclusively to providing general courses, seldom offering specialized instruction, they have no place or role for their graduates to fill. Some representatives of the alumni find their way onto the governing bodies of the universities; but they are generally chosen from those who have kept in touch with the institution because they hope to join the staff. There is consequently no regular give-and-take in the university precincts between the rebellious student body and the conforming staff, such as might lend dynamism to both sides.

It is impossible to understand Latin American university life and the functions exercised by the student body without studying the part played by the movement for university reform which has now been going on uninterruptedly for some fifty years.

This student movement came into existence early in the century. In 1918 it exploded into the proclamation of the "university revolution" at the provincial university of Córdoba, Argentina—which decreed an indefinite strike, together with the occupation of the professors' quarters in order to prevent the installation of a new rector who had been elected by a clique of reactionary clergy, and issued a fiery manifesto. This document, couched in red-hot language, proclaimed the battle for reform; and from then onwards the student bodies of the most mature university groups in all parts of Latin America united to fight the administrative system of the universities, their methods of teaching, and the concept of authority which was entrenched in every one of them. The eloquent terms of the manifesto became slogans still voiced by all the students: "the grievances we still have are the liberties denied to us"; "university democracy and sovereignty, the right to self government, are vested chiefly in the students"; "we know that what is true of us is—painfully—true of the whole continent." All this was accompanied by the conviction that the anachronistic feature of the university system was "the divine right to which the university professors lay claim."

Even apart from its fighting spirit, the Córdoba document is remarkable for its shrewd diagnosis of the way in which senescence was creeping over the Latin American universities:

"The public functions are exercised for the benefit of certain factions. The curricula and regulations have not been reformed, for fear that some people might lose their jobs as a result of the changes. The watchword 'today to thee, tomorrow to me,' has been running from mouth to mouth until it has become a tacit precept of the university statutes. Teaching methods have been vitiated by a narrow dogmatism which helped to keep the universities out of touch with science and all other modern studies. Lectures, reduced to the endless repetition of old material, favored the spirit of routine and conformism. The university bodies, jealous guardians of dogma, tried to keep the young isolated, in the belief that learning could be stifled by a conspiracy of silence." [10]

Everything that is new and democratic in the structure of our universities is due in great measure to the students' battle for reform, or to the fact that the student body has shown greater energy here than anywhere else in the world in confronting the problems of university organization and the composition of its governing bodies. Since then, the majority of the Spanish-American university organizations have been obliged to agree to increasing student participation in their governing bodies and in the election of deans and rectors.[11]

Far from resulting in anarchy and the disruption of the teaching hierarchy, as had been feared, this co-government by the students has shown itself to be a means of setting limits to agitation through the joint participation of students and professors in the search for solutions to university problems. It has thus become an instrument for the integration of the principal components of university life, and is gradually making it possible to set up democratic bodies to which the students' representatives make a variety of positive contributions. They encourage interests which limit the professors' tendency to favoritism; they revive the prestige of the teaching profession, the status of which is too frequently lowered by professors who appear to consider that erudition is incompatible with didactic probity; they keep an open mind toward investigation and criticism, which are requisites as a preventive of dogmatism; and they keep a keen and vigilant eye on every part of the university, strengthening the central bodies and the university policy against abuse and insubordination on the part of the subordinate bodies.

Co-government has also had an influence on the student fraternity itself, which has developed more maturity, renouncing its attitude of systematic opposition, and is beginning to take its share of the common responsibility for defending the university from any infringement of its autonomy.

Once co-government had been introduced, the students' action took two forms. Joint participation in the governing bodies of the university, which brought them into contact with complicated educational and administrative problems, became extremely technical in its character. This new activity, by compelling the students' representatives to make an effort to overcome their natural deficiencies and show themselves equal to the tasks devolving upon them, has led them to insist that the other academic bodies shall put their proposals more clearly and face up to the social aspects of each problem touched upon.

The other field of student action has been the college fraternity. Now that co-government is relieving them of their internal tasks, they are better able to take action in matters of policy without the former drawback of unnecessarily involving the whole university in each of their campaigns. The political activism which characterized the student bodies in the days before co-government still continues, therefore, reflecting the ideological maturity and natural rebelliousness of the privileged section of the young generation in the underdeveloped countries. Thus, co-government has had the effect of making student influence into a university institution, preserving and reinforcing the dynamic character of the students' militant attitude in politics—which is probably the very mechanism which will transform the Latin American universities into factors of social change, in contrast to what is happening in other parts of the world.

AUTONOMY

The obstacles to modernization of the Latin American universities usually tend to weaken their already precarious autonomy, which is lavishly recognized by legislation, but undermined by lack of independent funds and by the constant danger of government interference. It may, in fact, be wondered whether the Latin American university has ever really enjoyed the autonomy to which it aspires and about which there has been so much discussion.

The medieval universities had their own funds, but they were always subject to stringent ecclesiastical discipline. The universities of the liberal, French type, became state bodies at the same time as they became secular in character, so that their professors were transformed into civil servants and, as such, had to conform to the regulations applying to all government officials. The private universities in the United States were subject to pressure from the reactionary expectations of the wealthy industrialists who supported them, and now, increasingly, from the demands of the state organizations, military or civil, which finance their most costly programs. In the Soviet universities, professors and students are strictly subordinated to the official Party doctrine, which forms the basis for all assessments of merit, and the whole university life is dominated autocratically by the state.

Once the Latin American universities had won their formal independence of the state as a result of the reform, they went on to cultivate an anti-government attitude. In most cases they are independent of their governments as regards the appointment and change of staff members. An obvious measure of their dependence is the need for official subsidies. However, as this restriction gives rise to obligations in respect of the public interest, its effect is to liberate rather than to restrain, since it gives the universities a more suitable foundation than any other would for the exercise of their social functions. Moreover, this not infrequently results in a state of "peaceful co-existence" attended by hostility on the part of the state, which, finding its attempts at interference checked, tries to restrict the universities' area of influence. The dispute usually settles down into a struggle by officialdom to retain the leadership, and to interfere in other fields of activity, such as primary or intermediate education, teacher training, certain categories of technical training, technological and scientific research, and the creative work of intellectuals and artists.

By ceasing to be a state institution, the Latin American university lost much of its former influence, and became less representative of the nation. One result of the divorce has been the emergence of many private universities, most of them ecclesiastical, which take "freedom of education" as their *raison d'être* but lay more and more claim to public funds. This brings them into competition with the public universities for the available funds, which are always scanty, and the result is not so much to guarantee educational freedom, as to cause an uneconomic dispersion of the sums devoted by the nation to education.

Nevertheless, this university independence provides a better safeguard than any other system could do. It permits free discussion and enables the universities to embark upon political activities with an increasing absence of constraint—so that despite police repression, they are often the sole nucleus of national thought and recruitment for progress. In this respect the Latin Americans probably have more to teach than to learn from any other university in the world. We have built up a model of university organization which offers better guarantees for freedom of research and teaching, and a democratic form of university structure which ensures responsible joint participation by professors and students in the government of the university. The fact that the operation of these democratic safeguards is obstructed by dictatorial interference, is no more than a repercussion, at university level, of the institutional instability that results from underdevelopment. But when this occurs, our universities, thanks to their special structure, are nevertheless able to act as a main factor in resistance to tyranny and in the battle for a return to democracy.

Probably the great achievement of Latin American universities is that they have discovered a way to reconcile the official character of the public university with the desirability of not reducing it to a mere government agency. It is this which puts them in a position to play a dynamic role as institutions with an overall view of the nation and with the moral force to guarantee democratic functioning.

The exercise of these duties fosters an attitude of tolerance toward the ideas of others, and sets up mechanisms for a united effort to attain common aims; as a result, our universities have achieved the maturity needed for existing on good terms with other national and foreign institutions. All this has enabled them to provide their students not only with instruction, but also democratic teaching of the highest value. Since the nation's leaders in every field pass, almost without exception, through the universities, this education for citizenship is of the utmost importance, since it contributes to the gradual spread of democratic practices through all sectors of national life.

Some circles periodically express disapproval of this atmosphere of tolerance and free discussion in our universities, and their objections are nearly always couched in terms of the struggle against Communism. The falsity of their attitude becomes self-evident, however, when we reflect that they are thus attacking freedom in the name of democracy. The fact is, however, that at one time or another in the fluctuating existence of the Latin American democracies, nearly every social and political group has had occasion to appreciate the importance of the university as a refuge and stronghold of freedom. That being so, only the most hard-bitten reactionaries, the most resolute enemies of democracy and progress, can venture to challenge the university's conquests. Such people are, of course, the natural—and almost desirable—enemies of the universities, and the sole effect of their action is to strengthen and consolidate the university *esprit de corps*.

V. The Social Role of the University

The characteristics of the Latin American university structure, and the problems confronting the universities, are attributable in part to the difficulties of transplanting a type of institution from one community to another of a very different nature. Thus it is that the positive and negative peculiarities of the universities of Latin America reflect an individual background and a social dynamic proper to an institution which originated in a different cultural context. Seen from this angle, the development of our universities becomes comprehensible as the outcome of efforts to transplant a European model of higher education for the purpose of training national leaders. This was done by stages, over a considerable period of time during which the original model was gradually modified to meet the new aims consonant with the profound changes which had occurred in the European communities. Hence, by the time the transplanted model had overcome the initial difficulties and been adapted to the task of carrying out the functions it exercised in Europe, it had already undergone transformation in that continent by taking on qualities now accepted as pertaining to the new university ideal. The discrepancy between the two types of community—one fully industrialized and the other archaic and moving at a slower pace—tends to perpetuate this state of things. The result of every attempt to catch up with an ideal is that the ideal changes its shape, detracting from the usefulness of the results achieved and demanding fresh efforts. This process differs from the independent development of the university structure, because its chief impetus is external and causes a constant urge to excel and match up to a particular model.

It can be shown that at a certain period, many Latin American universities carried out their essential functions as efficiently as any other university of past times. Thus, the higher schools which were established or reformed at the time of Independence were unquestionably effective in training their students for the liberal professionals needed in the society of those days. From them emerged the jurists who were to create the legal framework of the new nations and settle disputes between oligarchic groups—the physicians who tended the rich with modern methods opposed to those of the quack-doctors to whom the mass of poor people still resorted—and the engineers, at first military and later civil, who were entrusted with building rich men's houses, highroads, and the most prominent public works.

The break-up of the archaic community—due to an extensive process of change which is not yet completed—led to a confrontation, within the state, of the general population with their rustic culture, and the educated oligarchy, and brought about a redefinition of university aims. It now became necessary to train experts not merely to contribute to government activities and serve the ruling class, but to reform the community as a whole; it was their specific task to promote the replacement of traditional by modern methods in all fields of activity. This extension of their functions carried with it from the very first a threat to the accepted standards, which were mistrusted and actively opposed by the university leaders, especially in the spheres where the greatest technical and scientific progress had been made.

This gave rise to ideas regarding the minimum qualifications of university professors, it being implicitly agreed that to restrict the spread of the new scientific achievements would be preferable than to lower the standard already reached or aimed at. In the case of medical studies, for example, this position was categorically adopted. Another factor which helped to raise the standard was the pride taken in training doctors of an even higher quality than those of the most advanced centers elsewhere. This, however, sometimes means that these highly specialized doctors, who are only trained to work in large teams, using extremely costly apparatus, fail to extend the benefits of modern medicine to the population as a whole.

Naturally, the insistence of this high standard is justified not only on grounds of academic ideals, but also in terms of the university's duty to master present-day science and technology at their most advanced level. Nevertheless, it should be possible to uphold these ideals and at the same time train a certain type of health officer in sufficient numbers to reach the entire population within a short space of time. The majority of the Latin American countries have always refused to train doctors of this type, on the plea that it would lower the university standards; but this excuse is a thin disguise for certain class interests, concerned with maintaining existing professional privileges.

This example illustrates the need of refusing to choose between one type of professional training and another, or to compromise between them, and of satisfying, simultaneously and in full, the demands of university training and those of social requirements. Once the resistance of certain academic circles has been overcome, both results can be achieved by a variety of methods. One method is that of the "intensive training" introduced during the war by European and North American universities for doctors, engineers, and other professional men. Another method—more suitable for countries waging an uninterrupted bloodless war against poverty and backwardness—is to set up different patterns of vocational training, with varying levels of qualification.

For instance, students studying medicine or engineering can take joint courses of basic scientific training and preliminary professional instruction, at the end of which they divide up to study their respective specialties. Those who have obtained the best results in their basic science courses will have the option of continuing scientific or professional studies with a view to reaching the highest possible level. Those who are less gifted, or whose social circumstances make them prefer a more rapid and practical form of vocational training, can be given the choice of courses leading to a somewhat lower level of qualification. This would be one way of obviating the tremendous wastage of human energy in the free-entrance universities, where a mass of students matriculate and only a small minority graduates—the remainder being forced out, with no attempt to provide them with any form of training for an occupation. This method would also lead to a better use of the universities' technical and human resources, which are generally underemployed.

In order to assess the possibilities of action in this sphere, we need only consider, for example, the enormous equipment for technical instruction which is available in many schools of engineering, and which, in association with industry, could train a great number of the technicians urgently needed for production; at present the equipment is used only for a few hours per week, during brief periods of the year. The professors responsible for these sectors of instruction are always ready and proud to display their wealth of apparatus to visitors, but they only make it available to students for a few demonstration classes, without ever considering the possibility of using it in the public interest.

This kind of procedure, acceptable in any university, is particularly advisable for the Latin American universities, which have to meet the challenge of attaining, simultaneously, the highest technological and scientific standards and the greatest possible effectiveness in satisfying the social requirement of training the most numerous practitioners for the widest possible range of professions, at the highest level. To adopt the new procedures would, however, necessitate far-reaching structural changes, beginning with an overhaul of the system of autocratic professors.

The best way of speeding up economic and social progress is, undoubtedly, to master present-day science and technology by training university leaders of the highest capacity as well as a more numerous and highly qualified labor force. And this is the principal task of the Latin American university, which is called upon to contribute its own, irreplaceable weapons to the arsenal of social renovation. Faced with the danger of finding ourselves falling further and further behind the fully developed nations, owing to our slower rate of progress, the universities are challenged to revise all their values and re-think all their programs, in the light of the national problems.

This fundamental need can be met only if the Latin American academic bodies adopt a really mature attitude in regard to the two basic loyalties which every university must respect—responsibility toward the international patterns of learning, and duty toward the social problems of the nation. A failure to preserve one of these loyalties cannot be made good even by the utmost devotion to the other, because it leads to irremediable distortions. Consequently, one of the basic problems confronting the Latin American universities in their effort to modernize themselves is that of combining both problems for accelerating progress.

In the foregoing analysis I have tried to show that resistance to renovation in the universities is due not so much to a failure to perceive the problems involved, or to a lack of practical plans for reform, but rather to institutional obstacles and to stubborn opposition from vested interests. But the pressure of the social environment is increasing, and it finds expression in a widespread dissatisfaction with the old type of academic life. This is now coupled with two internal forces: the dynamic role played by the representatives of science and the students' consciousness of the problems of the university and their bearing upon development, which is bound to reflect upon academic structures as the younger generation becomes increasingly clearsighted and exigent in expressing its combativity.

Faced with this dual pressure, from within and without, the universities may continue for a time to be bogged down in barren disputes; but they must end by redefining their role and their function in society. A decisive part will devolve, in this respect, upon the new-style professors of basic sciences, whose social circumstances make them the natural and inevitable foes of the old-style professor, who, with his two to four hours of lectures per week, is more interested in his clinic, legal practice, or factory than in teaching. But the new men will have to be fully conscious of the social requirements of development, and to show active loyalty in dealing with the problems of their nation and age, if they are not to surrender to the pressures already alluded to, and to those still entrenched in the defense of a spuriously scientific spirit which would be as disastrous as the now outdated "academicism."

In addition to the general problems discussed here, the Latin American universities all have others, peculiar to their respective environments. Argentina, Uruguay, and to some extent Chile, appear to have reached saturation-point with regard to training for the professions. Nothing less than structural reorganization establishing the productive system on a sounder technical basis, together with an improvement in the general standard of living, can make it possible to absorb the great mass of graduates which the universities of these countries are already turning out. In Brazil, Venezuela, and Columbia, scientific technology of university standard is only just beginning to be disseminated through the productive system, and even in the large cities there are not enough doctors, dentists, and other university-trained specialists to meet the needs of the population. In Mexico and the high plateaux of the Andes such shortages appear to be even more acute, and the spread of modern technology is impeded among much of the population owing to resistance from the basic indigenous cultural traditions. Only in Mexico, so far as I know, is a well-directed effort being made to train experts of university standard to deal with the living-conditions of the underprivileged classes.

In the sphere of the basic sciences, even the most modern of the Latin

American universities are seriously hampered by their inability to draw up scientific development projects of their own, adapted to their own circumstances and financial resources. In recent years many leading Latin American scientists have begun to emigrate to the great foreign universities, thus aggravating the shortage of research workers and science teachers, and defrauding their own countries of any return on the considerable sums spent on training them. A contributory factor in this exodus is the natural attraction exercised by the great laboratories and by internationally famous teams of workers—for a scientist contemplating his future career will consider that more creative work is likely to be possible in centers which have first-class equipment at the service of a small number of highly skilled researchers.

Another factor is the excessive and premature specialization among scientists, who are usually trained to deal with a narrow range of problems, based on the themes under consideration at the great research centers, and to approach them by the methods and with the equipment available in those centers. Thus, in the outlying regions, we find teams of young researchers being trained solely in pre-determined subjects, which often have no connection with any scientific questions relating to the actual conditions of their national development; this is due not so much to the demands of science itself as to the influence of the great centers.

The decisive factor in this exodus seems to be constituted by the difficulties encountered by scientists in making a worthwhile career in their own countries, which are slow to recognize their merits and to provide them with the resources they need for their best work. Further difficulties in the path of scientific progress arise from the division of the universities into isolated faculties and of these latter into independent chairs, the lack of give-and-take among the national universities, each of which has its own corps of professors, and the absence of facilities for intercontinental contacts. All these drawbacks call for urgent remedy, since they prevent the cultural autonomy which is essential to full development. They can probably be overcome only by means of comprehensive, nation-wide programs for the larger countries and regional programs for the others, which would make it possible to assemble the funds and human resources required to set up great research centers, with their own ample and independent teams of workers, to serve the cause of Latin American progress.

Many of the questions discussed above involve ideological postulates, that is, they require an elucidation of the values the university proposes to exemplify in respect of the community; and as such, they have an inevitable polemical content. But is it possible to set aside the question of values in social situations where such conflicting interests confront one another? The fact that they cannot be eradicated is proved by the unavailing efforts of many university generations to do so. The university inevitably reflects the community it is called upon to serve, and constitutes a melting-pot for the forces which will shape the future and those committed to the maintenance of privileges.

Hence, any scrutiny of university life reveals the presence of old and obsolete elements which not only struggle to survive there, but, in their way, to maintain the *status quo* they exist to serve. And together with these, there are the new elements which rise up and try to lead the university toward perfection and to enlist it in the national struggle against backwardness and poverty. Therefore, the fundamental requirement of university modernization is an explanatory review, to be undertaken in the form of a restatement of professed or implicit values and of their implications and consequences for the people and the nation. It is to this that I have striven to contribute.

Notes

1. Various books and articles published by: Luis Alberto Sánchez (Guatemala, 1949); Aníbal Bascunan Valdés (Montevideo, 1958): Gonzalo Aguirre Beltrán (*La Educación*, 18, 1960 and Yalapa, 1961); Rodolfo Mondolfo (*Universidades*, 3, 1961); Florentino V. Sanguinetti (*Universidades*, 3, 1961); J. Roberto Moreira (Boletín Claps, 1961); Nestro Eduardo Tesón (*Universidades*, 5, 1961); Rudolf Atcon (*Ecco*, 37–39, 1963).
2. Darcy Ribeiro, "O desafio brasileiro," unpublished.
3. The authorities of Chile showed particular concern for education, taking the lead among the countries in the group.
4. T. W. Schults, "La educación como fuente del desarrollo económico," doc. MIM No. 15 of the Conference on Education and Development in Latin America (Santiago: CEPAL [Commisión Económica para América Latina], 1962). H. M. Phillips, *"La economía de la educación,"* (Paris: UNESCO, 1961, mimeograph). M. A. Colin Clark, *The Conditions of Economic Progress* (London, 1957).
5. The percentage of the population between the ages of 7 and 10, which is 12.6 per cent in North America, rises to 20 per cent in Brazil and Mexico, while in Brazil 50.2 per cent of the population is under 18 years old.

6. In Brazil, between 1900 and 1950, the proportion of illiterates over 15 years of age fell from 65.11 per cent to 50.49 per cent, but their number rose from 6.3 million to 15.3 million. In Mexico, between 1930 and 1960, the proportion of illiterates over 6 years of age fell from 66.6 per cent to 37.8 per cent, while their number increased from 9 million to 10.5 million.

7. Detailed forecast of skilled manpower requirements in the different sectors have in fact been made, at least for Brazil, Argentina, Mexico, Chile, and Venezuela. Cf. Banco de México, "El empleo de personal técnico," *La Industria de Transformación,* 4 vols. (Mexico, 1958). A. Barbosa de Oliveira and Z. Sá Carvalho, *A Formação de Pessoal de nivel superior e o desenvolvimento econômico* (Rio de Janeiro, 1960); Miguel A. Almeida *et al., Los recursos humanos de nivel universitario y técnico de la República Argentina* (Buenos Aires, 1964), 2 vols. It should be pointed out that none of these surveys was initiated by a university body.

8. Darcy Ribeiro, "A Universidade de Brasilia," in *Educação e ciências sociais,* VIII, 15, 1960 (Rio de Janeiro); and *O plano orientador da universidade de Brasilia* (Brasilia: Ed. Univer. Brasilia, 1962); and "Role and function of Brasilia University," *Modulo,* 1963 (Rio de Janeiro).

9. A fuller study of the subject will be found in Darcy Ribeiro, *A universidade e a nação* (Ceará, Brazil: Ceará University Press, 1962).

10. Federación Universitaria de Buenos Aires, "La Reforma Universitaria 1918–58" (Buenos Aires, 1959), p. 26.

11. I should mention that despite my position as a militant reformer in many fields, particularly in that of the University, my past attitude toward student participation in university government was one of skepticism. As Minister of Education I discouraged the campaign launched by the Brazilian universities for its immediate introduction, and as organizer of the University of Brasilia, though I championed its inclusion in the Statutes, I did so with great caution, for fear it should lead to anarchy. Since living with the professors and students of the Universidad de la República Oriental, Uruguay, and enjoying the opportunities for studying the system of joint government, I have gained experience which convinced me of the great value of the system, not only as a contribution to the students' education, but for what it brings to university life as such.

II

Relations Between Public
and Private Universities

LUIS SCHERZ-GARCÍA

Our chief concern in this chapter is with the problems involved in the creation of elites, of persons capable of helping to improve the living conditions in Latin America.

We start from the well-founded assumption that the universities can be—as in fact they have been, though imperfectly—the chief institutions forming creative elites in this part of the Americas. We should therefore consider the problems which affect the universities in the performance of this particular task. Within this context, the relationships between public and private universities will be our main focus.

We shall analyze the nature of such relationships to find out what bearing they have upon the education and training of elite groups. What function, or counter-function, do these relationships exert upon the possible replacement of existing university structures by others which would lead to a more efficient and appropriate production of the desired elites? Reciprocally, how, or to what extent, do these relationships reflect the degree of transformation achieved by the universities? These are two significant questions, two aspects of the same reality, which we must ask ourselves and attempt to answer. The answers may give us a theoretical basis for developing a rational university policy adequate for training elites.

We begin by describing the universities of Latin America as they really are and emphasize those aspects which are most significant for our purpose. Then, we discuss the different types of relationships between the public and private universities, and assess how effective they are in training the desired elites and how nearly they reflect the democratic aspirations involved. Finally, we hope to outline some university policy which will help to encourage processes favorable to the education and training of leaders capable of constituting a new community in Latin America.

In our analysis we give special consideration to Chile, but make some mention also of other countries. This selectivity is due chiefly to the fact that Chilean universities form a useful basis of reference for our other Latin American universities, as we have already pointed out on a previous occasion.[1]

Universities in Latin America

PHASES IN DEVELOPMENT

A vast majority of Latin American universities belong to the type known as "Napoleonic-professionalizing," in other words to a type created by the inspiration of a pragmatic, liberal, and secular mentality.[2] They can be divided into three categories corresponding to three forms or phases evidenced by this type of institution during the present century.

The first of these phases will be called the *static* phase, the second the *critical* phase, and the third, the *dynamic-dualistic* phase. The *static* phase may mean either a time of harmonious adjustment to a stationary social system or a comparative state of quiescence of the university in a social system which is beginning to undergo structural changes.[3]

The *critical* phase occurs when the "professionalizing" university feels the impact of the processes of transition that are taking place in the social system. The *dynamic-dualistic* phase refers not only to the time when the university changes so that it can become an active force in producing social change, but also to the time when conditions in the social system are favorable for the creation of a new type of university. Such a university would be communitarian and co-ordinative, conferring importance upon those engaged in university work or research and providing for a close co-ordination of such groups among themselves and with the rest of society. Some of the structural elements of this new type of university, with new objectives and new functions, might infiltrate the existing university to become a newly emerging system contiguous or parallel to the old system.

In studying the university in each of these phases, we consider its official functions, the institutional units responsible for carrying out these functions, and characteristics of its professorial staff, its plans and programs of study, and, finally, the problems and conflicts which it faces.[4]

In its *static* phase, the university centers its effort exclusively upon the professional preparation of its students for traditional careers (especially in law and medicine). For this purpose, it is made up of schools (colleges), or faculties acting independently and without any co-ordination between themselves, and possibly located at different points in a city or area. The professors are usually selected on a competitive basis, and they combine university teaching with the exercise of their professions (which take up the greater part of their time). They are encouraged to expound professional techniques obtained from their practical experience, which the students are supposed to memorize for their examinations.[5] The university's problems and conflicts which do not affect its structural integrity, are usually concerned with financial difficulties or struggles for superiority between its institutional units.

In its *critical* phase, the university not only educates students for the liberal professions, now expanded to include economics, engineering, and teaching, but also emphasizes the so-called *extension* activities, directed toward society as a whole and designed to disseminate culture and social activities. This expansion is accompanied by a rapid, haphazard increase in the number of colleges or units composing the university, which now may be grouped on the same campus or in buildings used for common purposes. Professors are now employed for fulltime as well as part-time teaching, especially in the new schools or departments, and they usually have heavy teaching programs and diversified activities within the university. The curricula include systematic technologies and methodologies of a certain degree of abstractness. The problems and conflicts of the university in this phase usually result from structural inadequacies intensified by the population explosion,[6] such as a sudden influx of new students, and usually occur in an atmosphere of controversy

In the *dynamic-dualistic* phase, scientific research becomes very important. In addition to the existing colleges, faculties, and affiliated auxiliary institutions, centralizing units of scientific learning and research (often called, for example, Central Institutes), come into existence and set themselves up as sub-systems separate from the rest of the university. They introduce an institutional dualism into it. The research professors are entirely dedicated to their respective tasks, and they exercise them in a more or less isolated sphere of the university.[7]

In the program of study, pure science plays a fundamental role in technological subjects. At length, large numbers of students and younger instructors and lecturers become convinced of the necessity for a complete and radical conversion of the old university system to the new system, which has begun to infiltrate through the establishment of the research sub-system.

In Latin America as a whole, all three phases exist simultaneously, since the area's universities have not developed with the same rapidity in every country or region. It can be emphasized, however, that most of the universities of Latin America are in an advanced stage of the *critical* phase, and in an organizational situation susceptible to change. Likewise, many of the universities most strongly resistant to change, such as those situated in the capital cities, show simultaneous evidence of all three phases. If we were to take one of these universities as an example and examine it in all its diversified aspects, we would find it stratified into layers more or less representative of the different phases which we have mentioned. It is therefore not surprising that some student groups should be greatly influenced by inflammatory orators or political demagogues—a condition characteristic of the static university phase—and that, at the same time, the situation of some of the institutes of the university should be almost characteristic of the dynamic-dualistic phase.

Through the influence of the emerging "extra-mural" system and the international organizations providing technical assistance, all Latin American universities will most likely soon enter the *dynamic-dualistic* phase. Here we can note the possibility of a new kind of a university emerging compatible with the aspirations of Latin Americans as a whole.

A NEW MAN FOR A NEW COMMUNITY

Many eminent academic leaders have made statements and delivered addresses about the new direction which higher education in Latin America should follow.[8] They contain a few key proposals which show the scope of their views and the scale of values they are ascribing to the new university.

The statements of these leaders show their realization that we shall have to live in a world subject to change, which, it is believed, may lead to the creation of a new social order in Latin America and perhaps in the entire world. The positive part which science is playing, or could play, in these social movements is brought out too. The statements also stress that it is an obligation of the university to aid in the formation of the new rules and patterns of future Latin American culture and life.

These statements usually contain a reassessment of certain religious and traditional values, which often is not very explicit, and reveal an eagerness to reconcile them with elements associated with "modernism." Beyond that, we find a multidimensional, broad, and dynamic image of the human individual. In fact, this creation of a "new type of man" (in the pedagogical sense) appears to be the goal toward which they believe all efforts in the field of higher education should be directed.

With such an educational ideal as their standard, the universities must organize themselves into institutions able to accomplish this purpose, and must carry out the basic, closely interrelated functions essential to achieve that goal. These functions include education for the professions, scientific research, and the dynamic creation and coordination of new cultural patterns effective in society as a whole.

The leaders also declare that the universities must not only prepare people to master professional and technological skills—their almost exclusive objective up to now—but must inculcate them with the qualities of social leadership and civic interest which will enable them to carry out the needed changes in society and culture. They also insist that the universities must take a share in increasing scientific knowledge and must use such knowledge to advance their educational and socio-cultural purposes.

The great majority of the educational leaders' statements are based upon a democratic outlook, and they agree that higher education should be accessible to the great majority of young people of university age.

These educational leaders conclude by stressing the desirability and necessity of finding a definite formula and a means of operation for the new university.

THE SPONTANEOUS ROLE OF THE STUDENT GROUPS

University students are potential members of the new elites; in addition, some of their organized representatives assume important roles in the intelligentsia.

During the *static* phase, student organizations show a deep awareness of the social injustice existing in the lower socio-economic strata of society. Student minorities in the universities have begun to carry out a function not fulfilled by other social groups, that of denouncing the injustice of the established order and agitating for total change. Thus the university is considered by the youthful intelligentsia primarily as an instrument of political agitation.

During the *critical* phase, society as a whole sets itself in motion and drags the university along with it. Both are subject to the tidal waves of social change which arise without definite direction. New social factors cause the gradual weakening of the student movement under the ideological forces on the extreme left.[9] There are also groups outside the university who denounce social injustice and clamor for its elimination, and the university groups then assume a secondary role. It is also to be noted that in this phase large numbers of students and former students (generally of good background) associate themselves with student political activities. The newly emerging leaders do not wait for a change within their own social sub-groups before beginning their attack on society as a whole. They declare that the university was not fulfilling certain needs, and they launch a rather confused campaign for reform. At the same time they foment and put into effect a policy of social action in the large towns and cities.

In the *dynamic-dualistic phase,* there is increasing awareness among students that a radical change of the social system may also find its point of departure in alterations of the society superstructure, bringing pressure to bear upon the rest of the social mass. Politically active student minority groups take the initiative in a spontaneous way—although now their attitude contains a considerable element of thinking influenced by the introduction of science into academic halls—by concerning themselves first and foremost with the university itself, which represents for them the major problem.

We should not leave this aspect without mentioning that each one of these phases is characterized by a different type of student leadership. The chief asset of the leader in the *static* phase is his oratorical ability, in the *critical* phase his organizational ability, and in the *dynamic-dualistic* phase his visionary aspect, for he is usually convinced that man's spiritual capacity will triumph and so provide proper orientation for human action and for the achievement of social progress.

A CHALLENGE TO THE UNIVERSITY

Some of the fundamental points on which the Latin American university is challenged by the most active professors and students are the following: it should be democratized and open its doors to all those who desire to obtain a higher education; it should provide its graduates with a complete and well-rounded education by means of a more flexible and better co-ordinated institutional structure; it must give greater importance to scientific research and to the training of teams prepared to carry out such research; it should take a firm stand to maintain its independence against the pressure of the external powers which help to finance it; and it should answer the need of society to exercise a guiding role in this period of great change, and so provide an element of leadership and stability in Latin American social and cultural progress.

All these goals are perfectly compatible with the need to train elites. Here we will emphasize the matter of the independence of the university. This is closely involved in the actual relationships between public and private universities.

Inter-University Relations

If we admit that universities within a relatively homogeneous sociocultural sphere (i.e. in the same country or region) have similar degrees of structural change, we can then devote our attention to relations between universities which are in more or less the same phase, especially in the *static* or *critical* phase.[10]

In the introduction we posed the question of how the relations between universities reflect the degree of change reached by their respective structures. It is obvious that in the matter of relationships, universities still in the *static* phase will present a different picture from that of universities in the *critical* phase. We also asked what part those relationships play in the alteration of university structures.

First of all, we must mention that the distinction between a public and a private university is not always clear. A public university, sometimes called a "national," "official," or "State" university, has the legal status of a public person and a financial subsidy from the government, which either founded it or has nationalized it. A private university, which may be either religious or secular, was founded by private individuals and usually acquires a juridical entity in the form of a private legal-person status.

In speaking of inter-university relationships, we must also consider the attitude of the government toward universities of different legal status—public or private. The vertical relationship of each university with the state has a reciprocal effect on the horizontal relationships between universities. This factor strongly affects the relationship between public and private universities within the national educational system. A vertical relationship also exists between the state and all the universities of the nation considered collectively

Universities which are in the *static* phase are generally state institutions without competition of any kind.[11] It can even be said that only one of these universities exists in an entire country or that, at the most, it has branches in different provinces or regions.[12]

The state does not intervene in the establishment of the ultimate objectives of a university in its first phase, but it does make its hand felt by keeping the right to ratify the university statutes, to authorize or appoint the rector and other authorities, and, in some cases or on some occasions, to approve plans and study programs and to recognize the academic titles or degrees granted by the university.

The few private universities existing in this first phase are generally Catholic institutions which have been created as a reaction against the purely secular spirit of the state university. They are, however, near replicas of the state universities, except for their structure of authority. They are subject to state laws and ordinances in respect to the granting of degrees and the validity of their examinations, plans, and programs; and their graduates must appear before boards or commissions of the corresponding official university. Nevertheless, the private university may determine its own objectives and designate its own authorities, professors, and administrative employees, without interference on the part of the state or the presence of state representatives on its councils.

A public university can be considered as a government service, but, through a jealously defended tradition of academic freedom and a privileged legal status, it usually enjoys at least the guarantee of free academic expression. It is, in other words, a semi-autonomous part of the government. A Catholic university is, on the other hand, a part of the Church. The state confers upon the official university a privileged economic status, while controlling the use of its funds through indirect channels. In the event of political independence on the part of the university, the government may exercise reprisals of a financial nature,[13] but in the face of tradition and of the university's legal guarantees, it rarely goes so far as to risk any other type of punishment.[14] The Church must, in its turn, find means of financing its institutions of learning, if and when they receive no subsidies from the state.

Because the state gives the public universities power to control to some extent the work and activities of private universities, relations between the two kinds of universities are definitely antagonistic. The face-to-face stand-off of the two types of university is one outlet for the expression of the religious-ideological struggle involving the anticlerical, or secular, and the clerical, or Catholic. It is a shadow cast by the latent struggle between the Church and the state. It may be added, however, that the possibility of creating a Catholic university despite such an atmosphere of tension is one of the foremost indications that the conflict between Church and state has been reduced to a mere formality.[15]

A public university in its *critical* phase has enlarged its sphere of autonomy with respect to the state without having given up its legal and financial privileges. On the contrary, the government continues to look upon it as an institution which is informally a part of the state itself. If the university gets out of line politically, the government can always make its authority felt in the matter of finance. With respect to the private universities, the government has abandoned an attitude of belligerency and its relations with them are the expression of a regularized situation. The private universities, both Catholic and non-Catholic, are even assisted financially from public funds, although on a lower scale, of course, than the official universities.[16] The growth of the population and the effect of industrialization have greatly increased the number of university students. Not being able to absorb this growing number in its more closely affiliated institutions, the government has been forced to allow the foundation of private universities. Many of these came into being as a result of industrialization in order to provide professional training in the fields of engineering and business. Others were created under the pressure of regional groups, since the large national universities are situated in the capital cities. And some of them were founded through the efforts of ideological groups in order to ensure, paradoxical though it may seem, a freer expression of the secular spirit in view of the increasing number of Catholic universities.

Bearing in mind that the principal threat to the independence of the universities is now financial, since most of the funds for their operation are supplied from state subsidies granted with severe restrictions, let us now turn our attention to university financing in the *critical* and *dynamic-dualistic* phases.

As is the case in almost all countries, the Latin American universities look to the government for most of their financial support, and, in fact, the state universities are almost entirely financed from sums provided by the government in the form of a budget appropriation, a subsidy or income from special taxation or from bond issues. Private universities now also obtain an increasing share in such funds, but they must nevertheless depend to a greater or lesser extent upon income from tuition fees, which are therefore usually rather high and are comparable in many cases to those exacted by universities in the United States.[17] In addition to these sources of income, some receive private grants (from the Church in the case of the Catholic universities).

We must not overlook the financial and technical aid from international sources which has had a catalytic effect on the establishment of systems and sub-systems of higher education in most Latin American countries. Major sources of this type of aid have been the government of the United States, the Organization of American States, the Inter-American Bank for Development, and certain foundations such as Ford and Rockefeller.

Universities in the critical phase are not isolated but are to some extent in contact and communication through institutionalized channels with other universities undergoing either the same phase or the *dynamic-dualistic* phase. This fact undoubtedly has an effect upon the relationships of the universities with the government and on the international relationships of each one of them. (This also applies to universities undergoing the *dynamic-dualistic* phase.)

THE EXAMPLE OF CHILE

So that we may observe more accurately the relationship between public and private universities, and their relationship to the state, particularly in the *critical* phase, let us examine a few aspects of the Chilean university system, a system which offers a satisfactory degree of integration.

At the end of the year 1964, there were eight universities in Chile— two of them public or state universities, three Catholic, two supported mostly by regional organizations, and one permanently financed by a foundation.[18] The two state universities also have a network of branch institutions which are administratively semi-autonomous.

Both state and private universities enjoy practically complete administrative and academic autonomy. In the field of scientific investigation, however, the autonomy is only partial since research is intimately connected with the financing received by each university from the state, and such funds are very often earmarked for some specific purpose.[19] The state universities receive 100 per cent of their normal income from the government. The other universities receive government subsidies[20] which comprise up to 80 per cent of their income. This financial aid is, however, not fixed or standardized, and it must be solicited anew each year by the rectors of the universities.

The internal dynamics of the universities, most of which are in the advanced *critical* phase (the University of Concepción being in the final phase), the impact of some of the external challenges we have mentioned, and the influence of international aid have combined to bring about the creation and institutionalization of co-operation among Chilean universities and co-ordination of their activities in order to achieve certain common objectives.

This co-operation has received legislative endorsement in the form of a law creating a Council of Rectors composed of the heads of all Chilean universities. Assisting the Council is an Advisory Board composed of representatives from each institute of higher learning, from employers' associations, and from government departments or agencies concerned with the industrial and agricultural development of the country. This Advisory Committee is concerned with facilitating and promoting the co-ordination of inter-university activities and of university-industrial relations, with obtaining internal and external aid for the development of the university, with encouraging the career opportunities needed in national development, and with pointing out problems in university preparatory instruction and in postgraduate training. The Committee also sponsors a clearing-house for scientific information and documentation.

The same law set up through special taxation a National University Building and Survey Fund.[21] However, the law limited the application of that fund to the financing of university activities found to be compatible with the development plans advocated by the Chilean government.

Such are the aims and such the composition and operation of the

Council of Rectors and the Advisory Committee. As to the way in which these bodies carry out their functions, it is useful to quote or summarize the opinions of the majority of the participating rectors,[22] as this will give us an inside view of the relations between the universities represented in the Council. We can thus obtain some idea of the form and content of the conflicts and opposing attitudes which place difficulties in the way of a smooth development of inter-university relationships.

All the rectors are of course agreed as to the advantages offered by their association. They see in the creation of the Council of Rectors a decisive step toward the improvement of relations between the universities and toward the accomplishment of the objectives of each of the institutions. One rector expressed it in this way: "I am convinced that a great step forward has been taken in our country by the creation and functioning of the Council of Rectors, as it is undoubtedly true that gathering around a table all those who direct the institutions of higher education has already brought about the great advantage of making our universities better acquainted with each other, additional advantages will undoubtedly accrue in the future from the co-ordination of efforts which this permanent contact will bring forth."

Most of the rectors are nevertheless conscious of the fact that the Council is not yet a cohesive unit and that only by overcoming considerable latent resistance can it be converted into an effective working body. One rector interpreted this fact in the following way: "It is evident that much still remains to be done, but it is not easy to set aside years of misunderstandings and recrimination between institutions which are apparently guided by different principles and which have in fact launched violent attacks upon one another in the past."

The latent sources of conflict that arise in the course of the Council's work are sometimes ideological, sometimes related to the co-ordination of work, and at other times the result of a struggle for leadership or authority or for obtaining and distributing funds.

The Catholic institutions are wary of possible ideological disagreements with the other universities, but the others, except perhaps the older state universities, do not consider the religious character of the Catholic institutions a great problem, and they feel that there should be a little religious tension in the Council, if, in a spirit of tolerance, it confines its work to matters directly concerned with higher education. The rector of a private, secular university remarked in this respect:

"Some degree of conflict probably does exist between the aims of the religious universities and the secular ones, or between the former and the state universities, but even if such a discrepancy does exist I feel that it can only limit our co-operation in a particular aspect and cannot affect it in the educational field itself—which is the most important."

The representatives of the private institutions consider it essential that university activities be co-ordinated in an atmosphere free of external pressure, and that the autonomy of each be limited only by considerations of common benefit; hence, they consider it appropriate to co-ordinate the activities of the Council of Rectors with those of the National Planning Authority. All the members admit, however, that they have not yet been able to reach an agreement as to the order of priority for the Council's activities. This is doubtless due to the preoccupation of each university with its own objectives.

The individual university authorities do not attach to the Council the importance which it was hoped such a body would have. As one rector pointed out, the effectiveness of its work is hampered by the self-interest of each university and the fear that co-ordination may mean a restriction of the university's plans for expansion. Another university head expressed the opinion that some time will pass before the university authorities attribute to the Council of Rectors its real significance, which requires personal dedication and absolute sincerity in facing such common problems of university policy, budget financing, and outside aid.

Tension in the Council also arises between the small universities and the larger and older ones (and also among the latter themselves). Basically, however, the older state university represents the point of convergence of the deeper tensions affecting the co-operation between the Chilean institutions of learning.[23] The head of a private, secular university has said: "The history of higher education in Chile is marked by the effort of the private universities to free themselves from the ordinances forcing them to follow governmental policy even when that policy is wrong. The University of Chile, for its part, has never voluntarily given anything, and it has ignored the existence of the private universities even when making decisions which of necessity affected them in some way."

Alluding to the financial aspect of the struggle (the distribution of funds granted by the government), another university leader remarked: "There is an antagonism always in the background: a suspicious, defensive and, at the same time, self-absorbed attitude on the part of the University of Chile and a cautious attitude on the part of the private institutions, [which are] watching for an opportunity to grab whatever still remains on the plate." [24] This same rector added that "this mistrust, dissimulated by good manners and by cordial personal relationships, takes away much of the effectiveness of the possible co-operation among Chilean universities through the Council of Rectors."

As has already been suggested, there has been no change in the cordial nature of the members' personal relations despite the conflicting interests on the Council. The informality of contact and the friendship gradually developed among the rectors (or already existing through bonds of kinship or of ideology, etc.) serve as moderating elements when dissension arises.

There are doubtless times when a rector, feeling himself torn between two loyalties not yet entirely compatible with each other (university vs. Council; state vs. Church), will adopt a position of compromise which eases tension but does not entirely solve the problems blocking the optimum integration of the university system. That is why the Council of Rectors may sometimes deserve to be called inefficient or indecisive in accomplishing its objectives and in overcoming the differences which stand in the way of good relationships between the universities represented.

INTER-UNIVERSITY RELATIONS AND THE SYSTEM OF HIGHER EDUCATION

It is not difficult to observe (or to deduce) the effect of structural characteristics of individual units upon the nature of the relationships between universities. For example, the ideological claims of each university in its *static* phase and the conflicts between its faculties and schools leave their traces on inter-university relationships. But let us leave this point and examine more closely relationships within the university structures.

We have already suggested the positive part which these relationships can play in the development of systems of higher education constituted by universities of given socio-cultural areas. Let us examine the processes involved in that interaction.

The process of inter-university action evolves from a stage of conflict, passes through a phase of institutionalization or settlement of conflicts, and culminates in a stage of free and co-ordinated co-operation. It is significant that the presence of Catholic universities among the state institutions of higher education in the *static* phase develops between and within the universities a confused and conflicting set of values characteristic of the *critical* phase. It is likewise true that contact and communication between universities at different stages of the *critical* phase create a situation of adjustment of relationships very close to that of the final phase—a situation which, moreover, helps to formalize the conflict between universities of different legal status. It might be expected, then, that the relations between universities undergoing the dynamic-dualistic phase should be those of units integrated in a system having standards and activities characteristic of the new type of university. It can therefore be asserted that the standards regulating inter-university relationships (and which can be interpreted as the index of the system formed by them) are generally at a more advanced stage than the respective set of standards of each individual university in the group.

There is a parallel process of development and integration of the university system in each country and in Latin America as a whole—an evolution which is moving from an informal and scarcely integrated system through a diffused system without very clear-cut or well-defined objectives and relationships, toward an integrated system with clearly specified objectives, structures, and functions.

The correlation between the two processes is obvious, but we must establish the sense of interdependence of the two. The development and integration of the overall system depends to a very large extent upon the dialectics of inter-university relationships, which in turn are conditioned by the inherent dynamics of each university and by exogenous factors, such as international aid and social challenges. We can tentatively affirm that once the atmosphere of conflict pervading university relationships has been done away with (with explicit identification of the conflict), a process of integration begins in the field of inter-university communications and, as a result, integration of standards and, subsequently, of functions of the system it facilitated.[25]

It is not within the possibilities of this analysis to go into further detail about the machinery by which inter-university relationships act upon the development of the overall system. But we can say that, together with the impact of exogenous factors and the internal dynamics of the universities, the flow of communications between them plays a paramount role in the overall integration of the system.

Present State of Relationships and University Autonomy

There are also groups very similar to—but not always as inclusive as—Chile's Council of Rectors in Argentina, Bolivia, Brazil, Colombia, Mexico, Peru, and Venezuela. In Central America there is a council of all the "national," or public, universities. Since all Latin American universities will in all probability emerge into the *dynamic-dualistic* phase within the next few years, we have reason to believe that Chile provides a significant model. Furthermore, the system in each country can be considered a sub-system of a general Latin American university system which is gradually beginning to acquire a homogeneous pattern. On the basis of these assumptions, we shall attempt an assessment of the degree of autonomy achieved by the various Latin American university sub-systems and, from there, an approximation of the autonomy achieved by their member universities. From the amount of autonomy, we can judge fairly closely the nature of the relationships between the universities of a given country.

UNIVERSITY AUTONOMY

Every university, as a social institution, has a certain degree of autonomy and self-determination in its operation and its structural changes. The degree varies: sometimes it is quite restricted because it is subordinate to an extra-university system; or it may have greater scope because it belongs to a system where it can co-ordinate its activities with the rest of the member units. (It should be kept in mind that the individual university is also a system, although of lesser magnitude.)

When we speak of autonomy, we mean the powers possessed by a system, sub-system, or institution to carry out its activities and make decisions without outside control. The limits of these powers are determined by the number of persons or groups composing the system or institution, the knowledge and experience accumulated by its members, the organization and distribution of rights and duties among its components, the quality and quantity of its instruments of social influence and its financial resources, and—lastly and fundamentally—by the degree of integration in the system concerned.[26]

To the extent that the university system of each country maintains its connections with similar institutions in other Latin American countries, its powers are increased. Isolation weakens it, in Paraguay and

Panama, for example. Systems which have built up a tradition and contain within their universities a concentration of outstanding intellectual and professional people are assured a certain degree of social authority, as in, among others, Argentina, Chile, Mexico, and Uruguay. An organizational or structural system which does not have a well-balanced distribution of rights and duties presents a weak flank to other non-university institutions in each individual country. Such lack of balance exists to a greater or lesser extent in each of the national systems of higher education, because the oldest state university generally dominates the other universities. The Councils of Rectors of the latter do not have executive powers or the authority to enforce agreements which they reach in their meetings. With respect to these systems' means of influencing society, we can say that in Latin America each university system relies upon the influence and the action of its graduates and, above all, upon the support of public opinion. Through these channels, and due very largely to their role as the principal vehicle of social change in Latin America, the scope and the intensity of the social power of these universities appear to be greater than those in Europe or the United States.

When we speak of financial resources, we touch upon another aspect which affects the powers and the autonomy of the university system or systems in Latin America. These funds are mostly granted by the state, but they are granted with the attitude of conferring a favor rather than of fulfilling a public service, and as we have observed, there is no lack of discrimination or favoritism in the distribution of these resources. This undemocratic attitude can always occur in favor of the strong and against the weak. In addition, the majority of these systems do not have a high degree of integration. The actions of individual universities do not necessarily contribute to the integration of the overall system. A state university succeeds in ensuring for itself a privileged budgetary position regardless of the efforts of other universities, and it attempts to do the same with regard to obtaining money from educational foundations, agencies for technical assistance, or from foreign governments. The private universities, each one for itself, pursue a similar goal. And so we find ourselves facing a vicious circle: the absence of an integrated system impels the agencies of international aid, the state government, and the Church to act independently of the university system as a whole—and the system therefore cannot be consolidated.

THE UNIVERSITY SYSTEM IN CONTRAST WITH OTHER SYSTEMS

We see, then, that a university system of unconsolidated powers is faced by other social institutions whose actions affect it. These include the national government, international aid, and the Church. All three of these institutions to a greater or lesser extent instrumentalize the role of the universities; in other words they consciously or unconsciously use the universities as tools for the accomplishment of their own objectives. In this way the university comes to be incorporated as an additional unit of an external system. Within the university system, each university, instead of striving for common objectives, is simply one branch serving different groups and functions and affected by pressure brought from without: the oldest state university desiring to maintain the traditional privileges it has received from the government; the Catholic universities whose structure of authority makes them inflexible and which are subject to the strictures of the ecclesiastical hierarchy; foreign universities or foundations anxious to export their own academic objectives through all these universities—state, Church, or private. Furthermore, all the benefactors have their own priorities or motives. It is of course true that all these benefactors—the state, the agencies of technical assistance, and the Church—coincide in requiring that the universities be active agents of social and economic development. Nevertheless, the government and, to a lesser extent, the technical assistance agencies impose their own short-term policies on the activities of institutions whose actions should be based on reflection and reason, and whose essential policy should be long-range.

International aid agencies, essentially multilateral in approach, have played a positive role; they have helped to change the center of gravity in the relations between state and private universities by inducing all the institutions of higher education to co-operate in the attainment of certain definite goals for which they make funds available.

A few universities appear to be introducing, by the action of extra-university forces, an unwelcome pattern into the emerging Latin American system. Conscious of their privileged position in each country but seeing their hegemony threatened, the national or state universities have united in those regions where there still persist the remnants of struggles between Church and state. Such a group is the Regional Inter-University Council bringing together the "national" universities of Argentina, Chile, Peru, and Uruguay. The Catholic universities, in their turn, set up almost ten years ago the Organization of Catholic Universities of Latin America. A third organization, the Latin American Association, or Union of Universities of Latin America, appears, on the other hand, to be promoting—although not very effectively—the unification of the Latin American university system with common objectives, excluding all ideological motives and respecting all positions compatible with democratic coexistence.

CENTRAL AMERICA

A type of association differing at the outset from those previously mentioned is that of the five national universities of the Central American countries.

The Council of Rectors, or Supreme University Council of Central America, as it is called, relying upon international technical and financial aid, has laid down a plan for the regional integration of higher education.[27] This Council, in the words of one of its numerous chroniclers in the United States, appears to be acting as a "Common Market for higher education in Central America." [28]

The plan is developing without difficulty insofar as the universities involved are concerned. Each participating university, most of them in the *static* phase at the beginning of the plan, is aware of having the same institutional status as the others, understands the advantages of unity, and realizes that without it international co-operation would not amount to very much. Owing to the receptivity of its representatives to the suggestions of advisers, it has not been necessary to make any amendments or adjustments in the objectives of the plan or the evaluation of its implications. In this way, following the educational model of the United States, a functional integration of the Central American universities has been set up, under which each one has undertaken to carry out a specific task at the undergraduate or postgraduate level, thus avoiding duplication of effort. Great importance is given to general studies and, in particular, to the "basic sciences." The Supreme University Council co-ordinates the awarding of funds and irons out any conflicts which arise as to the assignment of funds to research activities and to instruction for professional careers. By means of this co-ordination, dissension between departments or faculties is reduced to a minimum and, by assigning the same academic status to each university or department of a university, all struggles for hegemony or for the obtaining of undue percentages of economic resources are eliminated.

This process of integration has of course encountered some obstacles along the way. The change of orientation of the universities was marked by transitory tensions among them and between certain colleges or departments in the liberal professions.[29] Also, certain groups of students (especially Communist-inspired groups) looked upon this integrational plan as a manifestation of "Yankee imperialism."

The chief source of tension and latent conflict which is now beginning to appear derives from a phenomenon which has been developing during the last five years, and is related to the expansion of the university system beyond the original nucleus. Together with the increased interest in higher education in general, a movement has begun for founding new Catholic universities.[30] In this way, the problem of the formation and integration of a university system, now of greater amplitude and heterogeneity, threatens to reappear—although at another level.

In a broad sense, therefore, the university system in Central America actually consists of two sub-systems: the "official" system of the five national universities, which appear to be recognized by large numbers of international aid agencies, and the "marginal" sub-system constituting a trio of small Catholic universities, recognized by certain international bodies connected in some way with the Church. The "official" sub-system, due above all to the position of its component universities in each of the member countries, either ignores the existence of the Catholic universities or assumes a belligerent position toward them and asks the government for authority to control them.[31] The "marginal" sub-system, still weak in structure and of lesser academic standing, is attempting to shield itself from the "official" sub-system's vigilant attitude and desire for control. It is trying at the same time to obtain a portion of public funds to finance its activities, while simultaneously clamoring for recognition and incorporation into the "official" sub-system.[32] These efforts and aspirations are accompanied by conflicts and tensions between the two sub-systems, especially at the national level, which may have a profound effect upon the possible integration of both sub-systems into a single, overall system. As we have indicated, the relationship between these two groups of universities is to some extent analogous to that of the public and private universities during the *static* phase and early stages of the *critical* phase. In this case, however, the official nucleus appears to be dominated by an *ethos* which emphasizes dynamics, co-ordination, and co-operation. In any event, the Supreme University Council of Central America has put priority on the promotion of a broader and more fully representative university system in its area.

It remains for us to examine what measures will bring about the consolidation of effective social powers in the university system so that proper elites can be formed.

Some Lines of University Policy

In order to establish criteria for university policy in regard to different types of co-operation, we must clarify certain basic concepts.

If we ask the question "Does effective co-operation exist between public and private universities?" we must consider our answer carefully. Co-operation means joint action toward the attainment of a mutual objective. People co-operate because they have a common goal. The co-operation established between the public and private universities is, in the best of cases, tense, due to the superior legal and financial position the state universities have compared to the private ones. Hence we cannot strictly speak of a co-ordination of effort, but rather of a moderated subordination of the private universities to the official ones. Co-ordination means an alignment and adjustment of the activities of the one with those of the others in order to obtain common objectives, an action characteristic of groups having similar powers. For that reason, between the state and an isolated university only a subordination of the latter to the former is possible, unless the university is a privileged state unit endowed with special prerequisites. Between a state and a well-integrated university system, on the other hand, it is possible to have a discussion between equals and eventually a co-ordination of effort through which each will contribute in its own way to the good of the national community.[33]

Co-ordination both of the internal activities of each university and of inter-university affairs must be carried forward, and rational rules and operating decisions established which will lead to the accomplishment of common objectives and to the increasing integration of the entire university system. The moulding of an integrated system, not only of a national but also of a supra-national Latin American character, can be greatly accelerated by intelligent planning and action. In addition, the measures taken as a result of such planning should have the strong and authoritative backing of the component institutions. In other words, the associated universities should confer upon the Council of Rectors all necessary executive powers, and should throw their full support behind the policies which their representatives agree upon.

There is no instantaneous solution which will bring about optimum co-operation between public and private universities. We can, however, suggest some modest measures which will facilitate that achievement.

In the first place, the universities, whatever their respective character may be, should clearly state their views and realize that they have more points in common than they have differences concerning their objectives. This examination of objectives is a matter of intelligence which could be accelerated by intellectual contacts and discussion between universities who are willing to find the best way to alter their structures and answer the social challenges which we have indicated.

This first step—the clarifying of objectives—should precede any detailed proposals for the alteration or conversion of their structures. We believe, however—and this is our second suggestion—that one method of structural reform could be carried out in advance, namely a reorganization of the Councils of Rectors to give them greater executive powers, better representation, and fuller autonomy.

These two methods, critical discussion and structural reform of the Councils of Rectors, create efficient channels and instruments to accomplish an improvement in the relationships between the universities. Such relationships, established in an atmosphere of untrammeled co-operation, allow the universities involved to exercise without hindrance their vital function in the integration of the Latin American university system and, consequently, in its attainment of power and autonomy.

The process of integrating effectively the system of higher education will advance along with the creation of the new type of university of which we have spoken. The values and conceptual visions of both are identical. The elimination of the gaps between universities of different ideological tinge and legal status will mark the dawn of the new university, and with it will also emerge the new man, capable of directing social changes along paths propitious not only for the social and economic improvement of the continent but also for its cultural integration.

The danger still persists, however, that the universities may be nationalized or, because of their financial dependency, converted into instruments for attaining objectives alien to their real aims. Or the universities may be used as channels for brainwashing, or intellectual colonialism, stemming from more highly developed countries.

Finally, we are convinced that the harmonization of a part of Latin American university relationships should have a notable effect upon the rest of the continent. What is necessary, therefore, is for the Latin American universities to press forward to consolidate their individual units so that the closest possible co-operation can be established between them. These in turn can serve as models for other universities and systems until the whole fabric is transformed into a homogeneous group of autonomous units co-operating among themselves. This is the road leading to the cultural integration of all Latin America.

APPENDIX
State Grants to the Universities of Chile

	1963 ESCUDOS	1964 ESCUDOS
Budget of the Ministry of Education:	203,607,000	264,288,000
To the Universidad de Chile	31,876,000 (15.6%)	37,454,000 (14.17%)
To the Univ. Técnica del Estado	7,661,000 (3.73%)	10,415,000 (3.93%)
To the Univ. Católica de Chile	733,445 (0.36%)	733,445 (0.27%)
To the Univ. Católica de Valparaiso	263,154	263,154
To the Univ. del Norte	78,890	78,940
To the Univ. Técnica Federico Santa María	177,540	177,540
To the Univ. de Concepción	4,655,625 (2.26%)	4,697,113 (1.77%)
To the Universidad Austral	144,555	144,555
Treasury to individual universities:		
To the Univ. Católica de Chile	2,000,000	5,157,000
To the Univ. Católica de Valparaiso	665,000	1,324,200
To the Univ. del Norte	250,000	724,600
To the Univ. Técnica Federico Santa María	665,000	1,162,000
To the Univ. de Concepción		5,545,000
To the Univ. Austral	250,000	400,000
Ministry of Agriculture to individual universities:		
To the Univ. Católica de Chile		15,000
To the Univ. Católica de Valparaiso		5,000
To the Universidad de Concepción		10,000
To the Universidad Austral		5,000

Notes

1. Cf. Luis Scherz, *Una Nueva Universidad para América Latina* (Maracaibo: 1964), especially pp. 82–83. This work can be consulted for all aspects of the educational situation of Latin American universities.
2. This is the type of institution of higher education which came into existence in France, derived from the Imperial University established by Napoleon after the dissolution of the traditional universities. For further details concerning the original model, see the article by Marcel Bouchard, "Die französischen Universitäten," *Die Universitätszeitung,* 2 (1963), pp. 11–25.
3. The latter is the more common case. It can be stated in general that the three phases are currently found in developing countries, with gradual variations according to the intensity and scope attained by this process.
4. Other aspects and characteristics of universities in each of these phases will be pointed out in the course of our analysis.
5. Most of the students devote little time to their studies (being absorbed by ideological-political activities or by work outside of the university). The percentage of students who obtain their professional degrees is low (from 10 to 30 per cent of those who begin their studies for a professional career).
6. Because of the explosive population increase, the university is besieged by an unexpected number of applicants, many of whom are rejected.
7. There is also a high degree of integration of the respective students in the academic activities of these centralizing units of scientific instruction and research.
8. See Scherz, pp. 74–76.
9. At the Fourth Congress of Latin American University Students, held in 1961 at Caracas, the Marxist-inspired groups lost control of the Latin American Association of University Students which they had previously held. This and other facts reveal the increase of political power in university circles of the so-called "Democratic Left" (e.g. Christian Democracy).
10. Due to practical limitations, the role of the general socio-cultural systems of each country or region in inter-university relations will be considered in this study only in an indirect manner, through the university phases and the position of the government regarding them.
11. See details concerning some Latin American universities undergoing different phases in the article by Olga de Oliveira and María Leda Rodríguez de Almeida, "As Universidades Latinoamericanas e sua autonomía," *Boletim do Centro Latino Americano de Pesquisas em Ciências Sociais,* 4 (1961), pp. 212 ff.
12. Such was the case in Paraguay until very recently, and it is also true of the majority of the Central American countries including Panama.
13. Cf. records, addresses, and communications to the President of the

Republic, VIIIth National Conference of Rectors of Bolivian Universities held in La Paz from 7 to 10 October 1963 (published at Oruro, 1964). These records show the financial discriminations which the universities were subjected to by the government.

14. In Brazil, however, the military government which overthrew Goulart dissolved the National Students' Union and refused to allow university representatives to participate in the *Forum de Rectores* (a Conference or Council of Rectors).

15. That is very probably what has happened in Argentina and is gradually happening in all the Central American countries in the last few years. It should be pointed out that the union of Church and state in some countries does not mean an absence of conflict between the two institutions. Furthermore, in most cases the separation of Church and state has actually marked a decisive step in the mitigation of tension between them.

16. In Venezuela, the private universities receive no subsidy. In Peru, only the Catholic University of Lima receives assistance. In Colombia, all universities receive funds in a variable proportion, but always in a percentage lower than their budget of expenses. In Chile, the appropriation constitutes the principal part of the total financing of each university.

17. In Colombia, the 1964 tuition fees of the private universities amounted to approximately 2000 Colombian pesos per student (the annual per capita income in Colombia equals 3600 pesos, approximately). In Chile, however, the tuition fees charged by the private universities are comparatively low and are not very different from those charged by the state universities.

18. These universities are: the University of Chile, established in Santiago with a branch in Valparaiso and regional colleges at other places in the country (16,183 students, not counting the regional colleges); the State Technical University at Santiago with branches at other places in the country (3705 students); the Catholic University of Chile at Santiago (5309 students); the Catholic University of Valparaiso (2756 students); the University of the North, Catholic, at Antofagasta (568 students); the University of Concepción (3138 students); the Austral University at Valdivia (603 students); and the Federico Santa María Technical University at Valparaiso (360 students).

19. See text of Law 11,575 dated 14 August 1954, which provides that 0.5 per cent of all direct and indirect taxes of a fiscal nature and of all customs and export duties shall be devoted to the construction and equipment of research laboratories and institutions which will assist the improvement of productivity in agriculture, industry and mining, promote the inventory and rational utilization of national resources and effect a better organization of the various economic activities.

20. Cf. details in the table, p. 404.

21. The law provides for distribution of funds in the following proportions: 10/18ths for the University of Chile; 2/18ths for the University

of Concepción; 2/18ths for the Catholic University of Chile at Santiago; 1/18th for the Catholic University of Valparaiso; 1/18th for the Federico Santa María Technical University; 1/18th for the State Technical University; and 1/18th for the Austral University.

22. See communications on this subject sent to the Bellarmino Social Research and Action Center at the request of its Director, Hernán Larraín Acuña, S.J.

23. The Rector of the University of Chile is by statute Chairman of the Council.

24. See breakdown of budget in the appendix.

25. Cf. Werner Landecker, "Types of Integration and Their Measurement," in Paul F. Lazarsfeld and Morris Rosenberg (eds.), *The Language of Social Research* (Glencoe: The Free Press, 1955), pp. 19–27.

26. Cf. Pitirim Sorokin, *Social and Cultural Dynamics* (Boston: Sargent, 1957), pp. 638 ff.

27. As a result of this integration the appearance of a "Central American University" might be expected, with separate campuses in each country. See *Memoria de las actividades desarrolladas por la Secretaría permanente de la CSUCA* (Record of Activities of the Permanent Secretariat of the Central American Supreme University Council), Costa Rica, 1964, p. III, letter of the Secretary-General, Dr. Carlos Tunnermann B., to the Chairman of the Council, Dr. Arturo Quezada.

28. Cf. letter of J. L. Morrill, Director of the Ford Foundation, to Dr. Carlos Tunnermann, quoting the statement of Dr. Waggoner of the University of Kansas, in *Memoria de las actividades desarrolladas por la Secretaría permanente de la CSUCA* (1963), p. 153.

29. The UNESCO adviser, Dr. Jean Labbens, attaches great importance to the action of the collegiate professional bodies in Central America (see commentary on preliminary report of this study, presented in June 1965 at Montevideo).

30. The possibility of the foundation of Protestant universities is not excluded (e.g. in Guatemala).

31. See the opinion of San Carlos University of Guatemala in mimeograph report, *Opinión de la Universidad con respecto al proyecto del capítulo "Cultura" de la Constitución de la República preparado por la Comisión de los 25* (1965).

32. See *Boletín Informativo de la Universidad Centroamericana* (Managua, Nicaragua), Nos. 1, 2, 3, and 4, concerning the problem of legal status of the university and action undertaken by the authorities of that university with the Central American Supreme University Council and the National University of Nicaragua.

33. The university system potentially contains the elements which could lead it to assume in some cases almost as much social weight as the government itself in making changes.

I 2

Political Socialization in Universities

KENNETH N. WALKER

Surveys have consistently shown that education tends to increase people's acceptance of those values which sustain democratic processes and institutions. These values include the belief that involvement in the political process is incumbent upon the citizen and provides a means for influencing governmental decisions. Surveys have shown that such values, as well as political involvement itself, increase with the amount of education, even when the influences of socio-economic status are controlled. Many studies have shown that political tolerance, support for civil liberties, and opposition to authoritarian political leaders and groups tend to increase with education.[1] Studies conducted with university students have further shown that such values also increase with additional years of higher education. One such investigation showed that the proportion of students with civil libertarian values increased from entrance to graduation, and was highest among graduate students.[2]

These findings provide evidence that education is relatively successful in transmitting liberal democratic values, norms of political participation, and the knowledge and skills requisite to effective political action. But since most of the studies on which these generalizations are based were conducted largely in the more economically developed societies, and in societies which are predominantly democratic and politically stable, one may ask whether these findings may not be due in part to the fact that the political culture of these societies tends to sustain democratic beliefs and practices. In societies which have experienced the frequent breakdown of democratic processes, and the apparent ineffectiveness of democratic political activity and organization due to manipulation or nullification of the outcome of the electoral process, skepticism about the possibility of a democratic political culture may lead to skepticism about, if not withdrawal from, democratic values and procedures. This chapter will seek an answer to this question through an analysis of the responses of university students to questionnaires administered in three Latin American societies—Argentina, Colombia, and Puerto Rico.

The focus will be upon students' evaluation of political roles of incumbents and electoral processes; and on their evaluations of human nature. A democratic political culture would appear to require, among a large proportion of the population, a belief in the reliability and honesty of the incumbents of political roles, belief in and support for stable political institutions which are responsive to public demands but are also capable of resisting mass political pressure, and trust and confidence in the human environment.[3] Basic trust in human nature is an important if not necessary ingredient for democracy, in that it sustains the belief that men are both deserving and capable of choosing their own representatives wisely in open elections. Confidence in the reliability of incumbents in political roles appears to be necessary for responsible participation in the electoral process, since lack of confidence would lead to alienation from the political system and avoidance of participation. Finally, the maintenance of a stable democratic culture would appear to require a basic loyalty to political institutions, involving willingness to utilize legitimate means to bring about change in government leaders or their policies, and a willingness to comply with the acts of government when these may not be popular, on the assumption that in the long run legitimate means will prove effective.[4]

Since university students constitute the base from which the technical, professional, governmental, and business elites are recruited, this analysis will be suggestive of the political subcultures of the future elites of the societies from which the data have been drawn. Questionnaire surveys were conducted in the Universidad Nacional of Colombia in Bogotá, the Universidad Nacional in Buenos Aires, Argentina, and the University of Puerto Rico.[5] Each of these has the highest enrollment of any university in its respective society, is state-supported, and is generally considered the most important institution of higher education in its society. Their student bodies are probably more representative of the university student population of these societies than are the student bodies of other universities, with respect to socio-economic background as well as other characteristics. The Colombian and Argentine universities are typical of Latin American university struc-

ture, based on faculties or departments which are relatively autonomous and self-contained, and which direct the students' education
from entrance to graduation. The University of Puerto Rico is characteristic of North American higher education in having a two-year,
general studies program as a preparatory stage which seeks to give the
student a general education before career specialization in one of the
schools or faculties.

A more important difference for the present study is the participation of students in university government in Colombia and Argentina,
but not in Puerto Rico. In the former two universities, students elect
representatives to the directive councils of faculties or departments, and
of the central governing body of the university. But in Colombia student participation is minimal, with only one or two representatives on
each of these governing bodies, while in Argentina student participation is substantial, and students elect approximately one-third of the
delegates to these bodies. In Puerto Rico, students elect delegates to
student councils in a few departments but have no representation on
the governing body of the university. Participation in university politics is likely to have an important effect on general political socialization within the university, and it may be hypothesized that the more
significant this participation is for the governing of university affairs,
the greater the significance of such participation for political socialization.

Since universities do not exist in a social or political vacuum, but are
perhaps even more than other institutions responsive to politics in the
larger society, a brief discussion of significant political differences
among these societies is in order. In terms of Almond and Verba's discussion of political culture, most Latin American societies would be
considered mixed, lacking the congruency among the various role
orientations which these writers declare essential to the "civic" or
democratic culture.[6] Colombia especially is characterized by sharp discontinuities in political culture between the rural and urban areas, with
low political integration of large sectors of the population within the
political system. Colombia and Argentina, both with considerable political instability, have experienced a transition from dictatorships to
unstable democracies during the life-time of the students in our study.
The period since Perón's regime in Argentina has included several
crises of governmental authority and the persisting threat of military
intervention in the political process. Colombia has not experienced di-

rect military intervention in government since the overthrow of Rojas Pinilla (although there have been recurrent rumors of a military coup), but the governmental arrangement which alternates the presidency between the two traditional parties appears to lack wide popular support, to judge from the decline in voter participation since 1954 when this arrangement was institutionalized.[7] While both governments appear to lack a high degree of legitimacy among the population, Argentina probably provides a wider sense of political involvement for the populace than does Colombia. Argentina constitutes a "representative democracy with total participation," in terms of the typology put forth by Germani and Silvert.[8] Political power appears to be more widely distributed and diffuse in Argentina than in Colombia.[9] But perhaps more important for the formation of attitudes toward the electoral process is the difference between a system in which the winning party is predetermined in presidential elections, as in Colombia, and one in which majority rule has freer play, as in Argentina. While the outcome of elections is restricted in both countries, the belief by voters that their votes have meaningful consequences is perhaps more widely held in Argentina than in Colombia.

Puerto Rico presents a considerably different political culture from that of Colombia or Argentina. Puerto Rico has many of the same discontinuities between rural and urban areas found in other Latin American nations, including incongruent political orientations between traditional and more modern sectors of the society. But with respect to elections, there is probably a firmer basis for belief in the meaningfulness of the electoral process due to the lack of experience with military coups or dictatorships, or of a system which seriously restricts the outcome of elections. It is also true, of course, that one of the basic issues, perhaps most important, around which Puerto Rican parties are formed, that of the political status of the island, is determined in the final analysis by the United States Congress. This is most significant to supporters of Puerto Rican independence, who may doubt that an electoral victory would assure independence. In any event, only a very small minority of the population votes for the Independista party, so that alienation due to the feeling of a lack of governmental autonomy may not be widespread.[10] Figure 1 indicates the relative placement of the three societies with respect to the two major variables of the study.

If it is understood that no absolute meaning is assigned to the distance between the countries on these variables, but only their *relative* placement is indicated, the table will serve to suggest the hypotheses to be tested. The variable "level of democratic stability" indicates the larger political context, while the variable "student participation in university government" indicates the immediate university political context. Both variables refer to the extent to which a democratic culture obtains, in the society or the university. It is hypothesized that the

FIGURE I

		Level of stable democratic political culture	
		HIGH	LOW
Student participation in university government	HIGH	Increase	Decrease
	LOW	No effect	No effect

political culture of the larger society will determine the relative *level* of student responses to statements about the political culture. The higher the society is on the scale of stable democracy, the more likely students are to express confidence in the institutions and agents of the political system, and to increase in confidence with additional years in the university. This is based on the assumption that higher education should enhance the student's awareness of the value of democratic institutions, in a society in which these function with relative effectiveness.

A second hypothesis is that student participation in university politics should have an important socialization effect, to the extent that such participation is linked to student participation in self-government in the university, specifically through election of student representatives to faculty and university governing councils. But the consequence of such participation is also affected by the larger political culture. The more democratic the society, the more participation should enhance orientations supportive of democratic political institutions. Where the society is less democratic, the opportunity to participate in university government may simply increase dissatisfaction with the political culture of the larger society, leading to a withdrawal of support from political institutions of the society. The underlying assumption here is that active participants are likely to be those who aspire to play a significant role in the larger political culture of the society. Where there is congruence between the two cultures, criticism of the shortcomings of the political culture of the society is likely to be enhanced among political activists, who become aware that compliance with the norms of democratic university government has little or no relevance to the political roles they hope to play in the larger society.[11]

Finally, those who do not participate in university politics are less likely than those who do to change their political orientations over time. And similarly, where university student politics do not involve participation in university government, participants and non-participants are likely to reveal similar variations over time, since student politics is unlikely to be perceived as relevant for participation in the political culture of the larger society. The variation that does occur is likely to be largely the consequence of university education. The above hypotheses can be expressed in the following form:

FIGURE 2

Student participation in university government

	HIGH		LOW
HIGH			Puerto Rico
Argentina			
		Colombia	
LOW			

Level of stable political democracy

The above table describes ideal typical conditions which are unlikely to be found in reality. It would thus appear that Argentina approximates most closely to the upper left cell of the table, Colombia to the upper right cell, and Puerto Rico to the lower left cell, with no case approximating the lower right cell.

Analysis of the survey data will begin first with the influence of level in university upon political orientations, then turn to the joint effect of year in school and political participation on political orientations.

Belief in the Meaningfulness of the Electoral Process

The Colombian and Puerto Rican studies included only one statement referring to attitudes toward elections: respondents were asked to agree or disagree that "It makes little difference if people choose one or another candidate for political office, because nothing or very little will change." The Argentine study included three statements from which an index of "Confidence in the Electoral System" was formed. Disagreement with the first two statements was scored as "confident" on this index, while agreement with the third statement was scored as "confident":

(1) "Elections are nothing but the periodic replacement of groups who act solely in their own interests";

(2) "The electoral system changes the persons but not the fundamental political orientation of government";

(3) "The electoral system assures the representation of the people in government."

The following table presents the responses of students in all three universities to these statements; and it shows the variation in "confidence" by year of enrollment in the university career.

TABLE I

Confidence in the Electoral System by Year in University

	Per cent whose response indicated confidence in the electoral system				
	1ST YEAR	2ND YEAR	3RD YEAR	4TH YEAR	5TH YEAR OR MORE
Puerto Rico **	98	93	94	93	94
N *	(57)	(131)	(114)	(118)	(145)
Argentina ***	80	61	66	63	64
N	(30)	(100)	(163)	(119)	(145)
Colombia **	66	47	47	57	42
N	(121)	(106)	(68)	(48)	(41)

* In this and subsequent tables, N indicates the number of cases (in parentheses) over which the indicated response was percentaged. Those who failed to answer were not included.

** Those who disagreed with the statement quoted above were considered "confident."

*** The percentages refer to students with at least two out of three "confident" responses.

In the above and subsequent tables, the reader should avoid direct comparison between the figures for Argentina and those for Colombia and Puerto Rico, since, as indicated above, different statements were utilized. The *pattern* of response, however, can be directly compared, and the actual figures can be meaningfully compared between Puerto Rico and Colombia. The findings tend to reverse the hypothesis that education should enhance democratic orientations, since in Argentina and Colombia the overall trend is one of decline of confidence in the electoral process. In Puerto Rico, on the other hand, there is practically no variation over time, and the great majority of students indicate confidence in the electoral process. The findings do confirm, however, the hypothesis that students' orientations should reflect the national political culture. Thus students in Argentina and Colombia reveal skepticism about the value of elections, while in Puerto Rico students are almost unanimous in perceiving elections as significant.

One further observation is that in both Argentina and Colombia there is a sharp decrease in "confidence" between the first and second years in school, with less change thereafter, suggesting that family socialization in the predominantly middle- and upper middle-class homes from which most students come insulates them from an awareness of the nature of the political system. Entrance to the university, however, makes them aware of the discrepancy between political ideals and reality.

Confidence in the Incumbents of Political Roles

For the Puerto Rican and Colombian studies, the following two statements provided an index of "Confidence in Political Role Incumbents":

(1) "Despite what one hears, political corruption in this country has diminished in recent years"; and

(2) "In spite of what one hears, the majority of politicians are honest."

Those who agreed with either statement were scored as "confident." For Argentina, no statement on political corruption was included, but agreement with the following question will be considered an indicator of confidence in politicians:

"Of the following list of groups that exist in Argentina, which do you think have interests in common with your own, and which have contrary interests?"

Those who answered "interests in common with mine" with respect to "politicians" are considered to have confidence in political role incumbents.

Table 2 reveals a pattern of response rather similar to that for the previous table, with the exception that Puerto Rican students reveal a

falling-off of confidence during the middle years of their university career, but this is restored in later years. Argentina and Colombia reveal
a sharp decline in confidence between the first and second years, with
little variation in subsequent years in Argentina, but a slight increase in
confidence between the second and third years in Colombia. The pattern appears to correspond to the interpretation advanced above, that

TABLE 2

Confidence in Political Role Incumbents by Year in University

		Per cent who indicate confidence in politicians				
		1ST YEAR	2ND YEAR	3RD YEAR	4TH YEAR	5TH YEAR or MORE
Puerto Rico *		80	68	67	68	75
	N	(55)	(127)	(113)	(118)	(140)
Argentina		73	44	41	45	43
	N	(30)	(100)	(163)	(119)	(151)
Colombia *		47	28	37	35	32
	N	(123)	(104)	(68)	(48)	(41)

* The percentages refer to students whose answers to at least one statement of the
index were "confident."

political socialization in the university reflects the transition from the
insulation provided in middle-class families, to an exposure to the
larger political culture mediated through university experience. Such a
pattern is evident even in Puerto Rico, but overall the rank order of the
countries appears to correspond to that of the rank order of the level of
stable democracy among the three countries.

Populist Legitimation

The belief that government should be directly if not immediately responsive to the popular will may be defined as "populist legitimation."
Such a belief would tend to undermine the system of representative
democracy, which provides a political infrastructure standing between
public sentiment or demand and governmental response. There is general consensus in democratic societies in support of political institutions

which provide for a recognition of the demands of majority as well as of minority interests, in the context of basic societal values and goals, and which avoid immediate compliance with mass demands which might contravene these values and goals.

TABLE 3

Populist Legitimation by Year in University (Argentina only)

	Per cent who are low * on populist legitimation				
	1ST YEAR	2ND YEAR	3RD YEAR	4TH YEAR	5TH YEAR Or MORE
N	40 (30)	33 (100)	44 (163)	46 (119)	51 (151)

* Those who *disagreed* with statement (1) and *agreed* with (2) above.

Only the Argentine study provides statements touching on the bases of governmental legitimation. The following two were utilized to develop an index of "populist legitimation":
(1) "When people are not in accord with the government, they should not obey it";
(2) "A bad law should be changed, but meanwhile it should be complied with."
Table 3 shows the variation of populist legitimation with year in school.

In contrast to previous findings for Argentina, there is an increase over time in the proportion of students who express attitudes congruent with the civic culture, in this case, attitudes which imply allegiance to government and compliance with its laws, even when these are unpopular. There is, however, a decrease in the proportion who are low on populist legitimation, between the first and second year, similar to the pattern observed for previous tables, but followed by an increase to levels higher than that observed for the first year. This decline may also be due to the effect of the initial loss of confidence in politicians and the electoral system, expressed here as a withdrawal of legitimacy. But while confidence in the processes and the agents of the political system fail to increase with years in school, there does appear to be an increased awareness of the need for stable institutions, an attitude which the more advanced student is perhaps able to separate from his critical evaluation of the electoral process or of political role incumbents.

Confidence in the Human Environment

As stated earlier, the belief that other men are both deserving of the right to govern themselves through elected representatives, and the evaluation that they are capable of doing so in a responsible fashion, is a significant component of the orientations congruent with the civic culture. Underlying such beliefs is a basic faith in human nature, in the capacity of men to be generous, open, and reliable in their dealings with one another. Morris Rosenberg, in a study of American university students, found that attitudes indicating "faith in people" were related to democratic values and attitudes, and Almond and Verba, using Rosenberg's items, found that responses revealing trust in people were more frequent in those societies which approximate the civic culture model in their five-nation study.[12] The Argentine study provides three statements measuring faith in human nature, two identical to those used by Rosenberg and by Almond and Verba, and one which is similar, as follows:

(1) "These days a person does not know whom he can confide in, or whom he can count on";

(2) "Nobody much cares what happens to oneself";

(3) "If one isn't careful, people will take advantage of him."

The Colombia and Puerto Rican studies included the following three statements:

(1) "People should devote themselves to their friends and comrades and not pardon their enemies and adversaries";

(2) "A person can have confidence only in those people he knows well";

(3) "There are two kinds of people in the world: the strong and the weak."

Disagreement with each of these was scored as expressing confidence in the human environment. It is clear that statement (2) of the latter three is closest to the kinds of statements used in the Argentine study, while (1) and (3) reflect authoritarian or hostile attitudes toward others. It is nevertheless plausible that such attitudes would be inconsistent with an attitude of faith and confidence in others. In Table 4, the effect of year in university upon "confidence in the human environment" is shown.

Table 4 reveals a distinct pattern of growing confidence in the human environment with increased years in the university for Puerto Rico and Argentina, but almost no variation in this orientation for Colombia; only about one-third may be considered "confident" in

TABLE 4

Confidence in the Human Environment by Year in University

| | | Per cent who express confidence * in the human environment | | | | |
		1ST YEAR	2ND YEAR	3RD YEAR	4TH YEAR	5TH YEAR or MORE
Puerto Rico		43	45	56	58	67
	N	(54)	(130)	(112)	(119)	(144)
Argentina		33	49	53	59	56
	N	(30)	(100)	(163)	(119)	(150)
Colombia		33	32	30	30	32
	N	(119)	(106)	(67)	(49)	(40)

* Those who gave "confident" responses to at least two of the three used in the indexes.

terms of our index. This finding supports other studies which have shown that education tends to "humanize," to enhance the capacity for empathy, and thus to achieve an appreciation of the interests, aspirations, and values of men different from oneself. This is accomplished presumably through the increased self-understanding provided by education, as well as through a broader knowledge of the determinants of human action which education tends to provide. That education does not appear to have this effect in Colombia may be due not to a deficiency in the education process itself, but rather to characteristics of Colombian society. Colombia appears to manifest to a higher degree than either Puerto Rico or Argentina the characteristics of authoritarianism in social relations and the lack of multiple, cross-cutting social ties which would provide a secure basis for compromise and accommodation in political life, as well as in other spheres of society. The relatively recent history of political violence between the two traditional parties indicates the extent to which party allegiance in Colombia has been characterized by affect-laden primary bonds. The *Frente*

Nacional governmental arrangement, which was designed as an institutional means to prevent the recurrence of violent party rivalry, is an indication of the general anxiety among Colombians concerning their capacity to conduct a politics of accommodation.[18]

The most consistent trend of this data is that student orientations to the political culture reflect the degree to which each society has a stable democratic political culture. The effect of education on civic orientations is most apparent with respect to confidence in the human environment, but here the effect is evident only for Puerto Rico and Argentina. There is little variation by year in school for orientations to politicians or to the electoral process, except for a decline between the first and second years for Colombia and Argentina. Our findings, then, would suggest that higher education does not increase confidence in democratic political institutions in societies where these institutions lack stability. What the findings suggest is that in all three societies, higher education does not overcome skepticism about the political process, but in fact may enhance it. This may be a valuable consequence of higher education, if carried over into adult citizen life as a stimulus to correct undemocratic deficiencies in the political institutions of society. And the findings that confidence in the human environment is increased by higher education, in at least two of the societies in the study, suggest that the university educated, though critical of political institutions, are likely to be confident in men's capacity and right to govern themselves, a belief which is an essential component for participation in the democratic process. Furthermore, the finding that populist legitimation declines in later years of university education in Argentina suggests a growing awareness among students of the need for stable institutions of government, even at the expense of immediate responsiveness of government to popular demand. Rather than being less concerned with the responsiveness of government, students may become more concerned with the need for stable government as their education advances, and, in Almond and Verba's terms, more "allegiant," an orientation essential to the civic culture.

Political Activity, Ideological Orientation, and Confidence in Politicians

We now turn to an analysis of the influence of political activity upon general political orientations, beginning first with orientation toward political role incumbents. The procedure, in brief, is to compare activists and nonactivists in terms of changes in political orientations with increased years of university education. Because of the size of the samples, and for simplicity of presentation as well, the category years of university education is split, grouping those with one to three years in the "low" group, and those with four or more years in the "high" group, for both Argentina and Puerto Rico. Due to the smaller number of students in the more advanced years in the Colombia sample, it is necessary to divide them between the second and third years. Political activity will be measured in terms of two indicators, voting in student center elections (Argentina) or faculty student council elections (Colombia and Puerto Rico), and attending any university student meeting concerned with politics (Argentina), or a student council meeting (Colombia and Puerto Rico). Those who both voted and attended are considered "high" in participation, while those who did only one or neither of these are considered "low," in Colombia and Argentina. Since so few students both voted *and* attended in Puerto Rico, "high" participation includes all those who took part in either or both forms of participation.

Since political participation is most meaningful when ideological orientation is taken into account, students are also grouped into "left" and "center and right" categories, with full awareness of the ambiguity of these terms, but also with the awareness that sufficient consensus exists regarding their meaning for these terms to constitute useful indicators of general ideological orientation. For Argentina the definition of "left" is based on the student's response to the question, "What tendency did you prefer in the past election in which you participated?" Responses were categorized into left, center and right, with *Reformista* parties generally constituting the left and Centrist, Humanist, and other parties the center and right. For Puerto Rico and Colombia the students were asked to classify themselves with respect to "most other students in the university." The categories were: "much more left," "more left," "about the same," "more right," and "much more right." Leftists are of course those who chose one of the first two categories, with center and right constituting the rest. Self-identification in Colombia and Argentina, as well as party preference in Argentina, were found to be rather highly correlated with other measures of ideology, justifying the assumption that these categories have a fairly objective significance for crosscultural comparison among the samples.

The major concern here is to examine change, rather than simply compare the differences among the groups (defined in terms of ideology and participation) with respect to political orientations. The following tables provide the basis for both kinds of analysis; reading across the rows within each sample shows the proportions of each group who express a given orientation, while reading downward shows the amount and direction of change in the proportions of students expressing a given orientation. To briefly restate the hypotheses, it is expected that political participation is likely to increase orientations which are favorable to the civic culture in Argentina, to decrease such orientations in Colombia, and to have no significant effect, as compared to nonparticipation, in Puerto Rico. For Argentina and Colom-

TABLE 5

Confidence in Politicians, by Political Participation
and Ideological Orientation

YEAR IN UNIVERSITY		Per cent who indicate confidence in politicians **			
		High political activity ideological orientation		Low political activity ideological orientation	
		LEFT	CENTER RIGHT	LEFT	CENTER RIGHT
Argentina					
Low		29	47	47	49
	(N)	(45)	(36)	(70)	(142)
High		38	53	39	46
	(N)	(45)	(34)	(71)	(120)
Colombia					
Low		14	50	36	41
	(N)	(42)	(73)	(19)	(80)
High		21	40	(6) *	35
	(N)	(38)	(53)	(12)	(53)
Puerto Rico					
Low		45	64	69	75
	(N)	(22)	(58)	(23)	(180)
High		68	74	45	78
	(N)	(50)	(113)	(18)	(67)

* The number of students in this group are too few to compute reliable percentages, thus the actual number of students who indicated "confidence" is shown.
** In this and subsequent tables the measures of the dependent variable are the same as in earlier tables.

bia, it is hypothesized that whatever the direction of change in political orientations among nonparticipants, these changes will be less than that observed for participants.

By comparing students in the same category of activity and ideological orientation, between "low" and "high" categories of year in university, we find some confirmation for the hypotheses. Both left and right activists in Argentina increase their confidence in politicians, while nonparticipants decrease in confidence. In Colombia, both active and inactive center and right students decrease in confidence, while active leftists increase. In Puerto Rico, all groups except for inactive leftist increase in confidence. Perhaps the major finding of the table is that activists are most likely to increase in confidence whereas politically inactive students tend to show little change or else decrease in confidence. This suggests that political activity, regardless of the political culture of the university or the larger societal context, enhances an identification with the role of political incumbent, and the tendency to be less critical of politics and politicians. Political involvement presumably leads to a commitment to the rules of the political game, and to an awareness that what looks like corruption from the outside may often be the consequence of the necessary compromise, or give and take, which elected representatives must engage in if they are to represent constituencies composed of diverse interest groups, and reach the consensus necessary to political decisions.

Political Participation, Ideological Orientation, and Confidence in the Human Environment

In Table 6, the effects of political participation on confidence in the human environment is shown, again controlling for ideological orientation and measuring change by comparing students in earlier and later years of their university career. The categories of each of the variables —political activity, ideological orientation, and year in school— correspond to those discussed above and applied in Table 5.

The findings in Table 6 confirm rather well the hypotheses advanced above. In Argentina, both groups of activists increase notably in the proportion indicating confidence in the human environment, while among the nonactivists, there is either a decline in confidence, among inactive leftists, or a small increase, among inactive center and rightists. In Colombia, there is a marked decline in confidence among active leftists, an increase among active center and rightists, and relatively no change among inactives. Finally, in Puerto Rico, all groups increase in roughly similar proportions. It might be expected that leftists would express more confidence in the human environment than those with center or right political orientations, due to the populist strain in leftist ideology which tends to glorify the virtues of the common man. But since in Argentina activists of both center and right as well as left activists increase in confidence, while left nonactivists decrease, the argument is strengthened that political involvement as such is a highly significant factor in political socialization within the university. But in Colombia it is the active left, rather than the active center and right, which declines in confidence. Although it was predicted that both activist groups in Colombia would decline in orientations congruent with the democratic culture, the finding that this is true only for those

TABLE 6

Confidence in the Human Environment by Political Participation, Ideological Orientation, and Year in University

| | | Per cent confident in the human environment | | | |
| | | High political activity ideological orientation | | Low political activity ideological orientation | |
YEAR IN UNIVERSITY		LEFT	CENTER RIGHT	LEFT	CENTER RIGHT
Argentina					
Low		53	43	71	44
	(N)	(43)	(35)	(66)	(140)
High		80	59	59	47
	(N)	(44)	(34)	(70)	(118)
Colombia					
Low		51	19	42	31
	(N)	(43)	(71)	(19)	(80)
High		23	31	(5) *	35
	(N)	(38)	(52)	(12)	(52)
Puerto Rico					
Low		64	53	56	46
	(N)	(22)	(57)	(23)	(180)
High		70	63	68	59
	(N)	(51)	(114)	(19)	(68)

* Too few cases to compute reliable percentage.

on the left suggests an especially strong disillusionment among leftists in the Colombian context.

Political Participation, Ideological Orientation, and Confidence in the Electoral Process

In Table 7, the relationships among year in university, participation, ideological orientation, and confidence in the electoral process are examined.

Table 7 reveals some change, but primarily among those low in political participation. The less active center and right students in Colombia show a considerable decline in confidence, while inactive leftists in Puerto Rico show an increase. In general, however, the major conclusion which the table suggests is that there is relatively little change in

TABLE 7

Confidence in the Electoral Process, by Political Participation, Ideological Orientation, and Year in University

YEAR IN UNIVERSITY		Per cent confident in the electoral process			
		High political activity ideological orientation		Low political activity ideological orientation	
		LEFT	CENTER RIGHT	LEFT	CENTER RIGHT
Argentina					
Low		43	77	60	79
	(N)	(42)	(36)	(67)	(135)
High		45	78	55	76
	(N)	(44)	(33)	(67)	(112)
Colombia					
Low		48	66	58	56
	(N)	(44)	(71)	(19)	(80)
High		42	63	(6) *	40
	(N)	(38)	(52)	(12)	(53)
Puerto Rico					
Low		88	95	79	97
	(N)	(22)	(70)	(24)	(180)
High		85	96	100	93
	(N)	(51)	(114)	(19)	(69)

* Too few cases to compute a reliable percentage.

confidence between students in early and later years of the university. The few changes that are observed were not predicted by the hypotheses, except for the decline in confidence among active leftists in Colombia, from 48 to 42 per cent. To account for the overall lack of change, it is necessary to go outside the explanatory model advanced here, and focus instead on the possible meaning of the electoral process in the framework of political socialization. Since political participation appears to change attitudes toward the human environment and toward elected representatives, but not toward the process by which the latter are elected, it would appear that political involvement affects political socialization primarily in the realm of orientations toward the human agents of the political culture, but not toward its structural characteristics. Involvement in university political life is probably an important means for students to develop contacts which cut across the boundaries of career specialization, socio-economic and religious backgrounds, thus increasing the tendency to share common sentiments and interests among students of diverse backgrounds. At least this is likely to be the case in a more favorable political environment—one in which political activity implies direct involvement in university government, as in Argentina, and in which there is some congruence within a democratic political culture both in university and society. The evidence for Colombia suggests that active leftists there are likely to be isolated and alienated from opposing political groups, and to perceive opponents as hostile, presumably due to a less favorable democratic political environment in both university and society.

Since activity is measured here both by participation in elections as well as in political meetings, it might be expected that activists, at least in Argentina, should increase their confidence in the electoral process. That this is not the case suggests that university politics are not perceived as relevant for one's evaluation of the electoral process in society.

Political Participation, Ideological Orientation, and Populist Legitimation

The following table analyzes change in populist legitimacy for active and inactive Argentine students.

Table 8 reveals an increase in populist legitimation among left actives, and a decrease for all other groups, especially for left inactives. This finding tends to reverse the hypotheses concerning the groups within which change in political orientation is expected to occur. The difference in the proportions expressing a populist orientation toward legitimacy, between active and inactive leftists in later years of the university career, suggests that activity is probably related to ideological commitment, and that it is the *active* leftists who are most committed to the notion that the government should be directly responsive to the popular will, and should not be accorded legitimacy when it is not so responsive. Activity makes no such difference among students of the center and right, suggesting that it is less closely linked to ideological positions for them than is activity among students of the left.

TABLE 8

Populist Legitimation, by Political Participation, Ideological Orientation, and Year in University (Argentina only)

		Political participation			
		High ideological orientation		Low ideological orientation	
YEAR IN UNIVERSITY		LEFT	CENTER RIGHT	LEFT	CENTER RIGHT
			Per cent low in populist legitimation		
Low		28	50	22	49
	(N)	(43)	(36)	(65)	(136)
High		21	58	42	59
	(N)	(42)	(33)	(69)	(117)

Conclusions

This article has presented evidence of the effect of exposure to university education for political socialization, specifically for orientations toward the political culture, rather than for primarily ideological orientations. While the latter are obviously linked to more general political orientations, it has been shown that this linkage varies in different university and national contexts. One major finding is that university education tends to increase what has been termed elsewhere "faith in human nature," or, as stated here, "confidence in the human environment," while at the same time it tends to increase a critical orientation to the political system, the latter especially in those societies with a less stable democratic structure. The hypotheses concerning the interrelation between political activity and orientations to the political culture were substantiated to some extent, but primarily in the area of orientation toward the human environment and toward incumbents of political roles. In general, it may be asserted that students tend to reflect the political culture of their society, while active engagement in university politics plays an especially important role in the process of political socialization. But the consequences of political activity for political socialization depend upon characteristics of the environment, so that political activity appears to enhance acceptance of the norms and commitment to the values of a democratic culture only where such a culture exists both in the university and the larger society. These findings can be advanced only tentatively on the basis of the evidence presented here. Future research in other national and university contexts will permit further exploration of these relationships and provide an opportunity to substantiate or modify them.

To extrapolate from the results of research conducted with students, to their future political orientations and behavior, is hazardous. Nevertheless, the kind of socialization experience undergone by university students undoubtedly has a persisting effect on their future orientations, as a number of studies suggest, including some of those cited here. If this is so, political participation may have consequences for roles other than political ones, as in business or the professions, for the majority of student political activists who do not go into politics. Thus in a context such as that described for Argentina, political participation is likely to enhance respect for others and to increase the willingness to compromise in conflict situations, a valuable consequence for the conduct of political affairs as well as for activities in other spheres of society. In the context described for Colombia, political activity, at least for leftists, would appear to have a more pessimistic outcome, and in a context like that of Puerto Rico, political activity would appear to have little effect.

No one could justify drawing policy conclusions from these findings, except the obvious one that to raise the level of meaningful political participation, in both university and society, tends to enhance commitment to democratic norms and values. The evidence does appear to provide support for those who would argue in behalf of the benefits of student participation in university government in Argentina, although such participation may be detrimental to the conduct and character of university education on occasion.

To conclude, participation in university government is likely to have important consequences for the role performance of future elites, but the only way to determine these consequences would be to carry out a long-range study (over time) of the life careers of university student political activists, a study which would add considerably to our knowledge of elite formation.

Notes

1. V. O. Key, Jr., *Public Opinion and American Democracy* (New York: Alfred A. Knopf, 1961), pp. 315–343; Seymour M. Lipset, *Political Man* (Garden City, N.Y.: Doubleday & Co., 1960), pp. 55–60, 109, 184, and "Three Decades of the Radical Right: Coughlinites, McCarthyites, and Birchers (1962)," in Daniel Bell (ed.), *The Radical Right* (Garden City, N.Y.: Doubleday & Co., 1963), pp. 331, 343; Burton R. Clark, *Educating the Expert Society* (San Francisco: Chandler Publishing Co., 1962), pp. 30–36; Gabriel A. Almond and Sidney Verba, *The Civic Culture* (Princeton, N.J.: Princeton University Press, 1963), pp. 379–387; William Kornhauser, *The Politics of Mass Society* (London: Routledge and Kegan Paul, 1960), p. 69.

2. Hanan Selvin and Warren O. Hagstrom, "Determinants of Support for Civil Liberties," *British Journal of Sociology*, 11 (1960), pp. 51–73; Clark, p. 35.

3. See Almond and Verba, pp. 3–42.

4. See Lipset, *Political Man*, pp. 77–90; Kornhauser, pp. 119–128.

5. The Colombian and Puerto Rican surveys were conducted under the auspices of the Comparative National Development Study of the Institute of International Studies, the University of California, Berkeley. The Argentine survey was conducted by David Nasatir of the University of California at Los Angeles. The sampling procedures utilized in the two studies were somewhat different, but in all three surveys care was exercised to obtain systematic random samples of the student populations of these universities. See David Nasatir, "Estudio sobre la Juventud Argentina: Introducción," *Trabajos e Investigaciones del Instituto de Sociología*, Publicación Interna No. 69, Universidad de Buenos Aires.

6. This article is heavily influenced by the "civic culture" model in the five-country comparative study, *The Civic Culture*, of Almond and Verba. They are concerned with the social structures and processes that sustain the political culture of democracy, rather than with the primarily participant orientation stressed in American democratic civics texts. Understood in these terms, "democratic" and "civic" culture are interchangeable, and both will be used here, but with the broader implication of the concept "civic culture" as defined by Almond and Verba.

7. See Kenneth F. Johnson, "Political Radicalism in Colombia: Electoral Dynamics of 1962 and 1964," *Journal of Inter-American Studies,* 7 (1965), pp. 15–26; Orlando Fals-Borda, "Violence and the Break-up of Tradition in Colombia," in Claudio Veliz (ed.), *Obstacles to Change in Latin America* (London: Oxford University Press, 1965), pp. 188–205.

8. Gino Germani, *Política y Sociedad en una Época de Transición* (Buenos Aires: Editorial Paidos, 1962), pp. 147–162; Germani and Kalman Silvert, "Politics, Social Structure and Military Intervention in Latin America," *European Journal of Sociology,* 2 (1962), pp. 62–81.

9. See José Luis de Imaz, *Los Que Mandan* (Buenos Aires: Editorial Universitaria de Buenos Aires, 1964), pp. 236–50. No comparable study of Colombian elites is available, but the evidence suggests a higher concentration of power among a minority of political elites than prevails in Agentina. See, for example, John Martz, *Colombia: A Contemporary Political Survey* (Chapel Hill: University of North Carolina Press, 1962), pp. 11–14, 334–5; José Gutiérrez, *La Revolución contra el Miedo* (Bogotá: Ediciones Tercer Mundo, 1964), pp. 101–3.

10. See Gordon K. Lewis, *Puerto Rico: Freedom and Power in the Caribbean* (New York: Monthly Review Press, 1963), pp. 375–408.

11. Almond and Verba, pp. 327–8, make a similar assumption: "There are a number of reasons why one might expect the authority patterns to which the individual is exposed outside of the political realm to have some influence on his attitude toward politics. In the first place, the role that an individual plays within the family, the school, or the job may be considered training for the performance of political roles. He is likely to generalize from the former roles to the latter . . . [I]f outside the political sphere he has opportunities to participate in a wide range of social decisions, he will probably expect to be able to participate in political decisions as well." Their data suggest that participation in decision-making within the family, school, or job, tend to increase the individual's sense of civic competence. See pp. 330–74.

12. Morris Rosenberg, "Misanthropy and Political Ideology," *American Sociological Review,* 21 (1956), pp. 690–695; Almond and Verba, pp. 266–296.

13. See Martz, pp. 3–32, 249, 273, *passim;* Gutiérrez, pp. 67–124.

13
Intellectual Identity and Political Ideology among University Students

GLAUCIO ARY DILLON SOARES

Much of the discussion about the political instability in Latin America has pointed to the sharply alienative role of intellectuals and the overt student political activists as at least one reason, possibly a minor one, for the inability of most Latin American states to develop a stable political system, i.e. one which deals effectively and continuously with the very apparent needs for social and economic reform. To discuss adequately the values and activities of the intellectuals would obviously require a comprehensive study of this stratum. At the moment, no one has attempted such research, and the available secondary data are scanty, highly impressionistic, and seriously affected by ideological bias. The existence of questionnaire materials drawn from samples of university students in a number of countries, however, does permit a limited attack on the subject. In this chapter, I would like to examine the validity of the assumption that an identification with the role of the intellectual tends to be associated with a leftist political orientation, while conversely, involvement in a scientific or professional identity is more likely to be associated with more moderate political styles.

I. The Role of the Intellectual

Highly educated people generally identify themselves as scientists, as professionals, or as members of that ill-assorted subgroup—the intellectuals. The term intellectual often denotes creators of culture: scholars, artists, writers, scientists, rather than transmitters or practitioners,

The author is indebted to the Comparative National Development Project for financial and clerical support, and to Marguerite McIntyre and Carolyn D. de Romano for research assistance.

such as teachers, physicians, engineers. At other times, the only defining criterion is a high level of education.[1] The concept of intellectual (like the concept of social class) is used both as a determinate category for sociological analysis, and as a term of subjective identification.[2] Just as people identify with one or another class, regardless of where the researcher places them, those in the intelligentsia differ in seeing themselves as intellectuals or as professionals. Moreover, their identification is important for their political behavior. Those who consider themselves intellectuals are likely to think of their role as involving general competence on a wide spectrum of issues; those who see themselves primarily as professionals or scientists are more likely to see their role in highly specific terms, with expertise limited to one field. And as we shall discover, such a self-image of diffuse competence heightens one's commitment to politics, while perceiving one's role in narrow terms constrains political commitment.

Modern society requires increasing specialization in most positions. Industrialization involves a progressive division of labor and consequently a narrowing of professional and occupational roles. Those jobs which allow for diffuseness are likewise divided into more specific professions.[3] Thus, the medieval philosopher has been differentiated into sociologist, anthropologist, political scientist, economist, and psychologist, and within each of these sub-specialties are now developing. The result is fragmentation and compartmentalization of knowledge. People with broad interests are generally bothered by the limits imposed on them. Some become professionals rather than intellectuals and find themselves in roles which are incongruent with their psychological needs and ways of thought. Others seek to play a general intellectual role while holding down marginal jobs which are poorly paid and without prestige. In either case, alienation is the result. In the former situation, psychological alienation stems from the performance of daily tasks which are at variance with the individual's psychological needs and ways of thought; in the latter situation, social and economic alienation result. Although these varying types of alienation are expressed differently, both contribute to political radicalism of one type or another.[4]

II. Intellectual Identity and Diffuseness

The concepts of diffuseness and specificity may be considered on the cultural, societal, and personality levels.[5] On the personality level, they may be linked with general cognitive styles, particularly as these vary in attention deployment and focusing.[6] On one hand, there is the personality analogue to specificity, in the cognitive style which narrows, focuses, confines, concentrates, and the like; while the equivalent to diffuseness may be found in the style which includes, extends, and deploys.[7] One would anticipate from this that those attracted to diffuse roles such as that of the intellectual, and who reject occupational specialization, will be more likely to have personality characteristics which reflect a diffuse cognitive orientation. Furthermore, although the suggestion may seem far-fetched, I propose the possibility that a diffuse cognitive style may be linked to acceptance of broad diffuse ideologies, such as various radical or extremist doctrines.

The diffuseness-specificity dimension refers to the degree of structure and concreteness in the actor's role expectations. In terms of the purpose of this essay, those of professionals and intellectuals may be distinguished. Professionals and scientists have a fairly concrete idea of what they want from life and what their professional life consists of. Intellectuals, on the other hand, have a blurred picture and, indeed, find it very difficult to answer the question "What does an intellectual do?"

A professional identity is associated with a career within a recognized and accepted profession. An engineering student has a clear vision of what his future professional life will be and what his daily tasks are likely to be. He also has enough information to anticipate and pinpoint major alternative sources of employment. The humanistically oriented intellectual, on the other hand, is presented with fewer precise cues concerning his future situation.

Professional or scientific identity is linked directly to occupational position. For example, an engineer or a doctor would regard himself as a professional. A physicist thinks of himself as a scientist *because* he is a physicist. No parallels can be found in developing an intellectual identity. The intellectual must achieve the status in his own right, rather than by having it presented to him as an aspect of his occupational specialty. The academic specialties which carry a professional or a scientific identity are well-defined and institutionalized, while those more closely linked with an intellectual identity are not. As the attribute of being intellectual does not always stem from academic specialization, those who see themselves as such must find support for this image elsewhere, and they often base it on their cognitive styles and *Weltanschauung,* rather than on their academic fields or job titles.

Nevertheless, identity is not determined solely by academic field.

Within many academic specialties, some think of themselves as intellectuals, others as scientists or as professionals. Different identities imply varying ways of looking at the same profession, and these differences are not without consequence.

III. Industrialization, Role Specificity, and Alienation of the Intellectual

The alienation of the intellectual from specific roles must be placed in a historical and contextual perspective.[8] In the past centuries, an intellectual's status in society was well-recognized. It carried no pressure to demonstrate specific competence. Many areas of intellectual activity did not require any formal training and were open to anyone who wanted to pursue them. Today, these have become professionalized and are subject to increasingly stringent regulations and entrance qualifications. Sociology, political science, and psychology have undergone this transformation recently. These disciplines now require years of technical preparation, and almost all of the available jobs in universities, business, and government can only be obtained by those who hold advanced degrees in an appropriate field. Role interchangeability among these fields is dwindling, particularly in industrial societies.

Accordingly, one might infer that the intellectuals would be more alienated, and, therefore, more radical, in developed than in underdeveloped countries. However, this is not so, as the educational systems are also more modern in these countries. One indicator of educational modernization is the proportion of technical students in the total academic enrollment. Comparative data show that this proportion is greater in developed countries than in underdeveloped ones. When we consider changes both in the economic and the educational structures, we notice that it is precisely when the modernization of the educational structure fails to keep pace with economic development that the highly educated, considered as a group, are more alienated and prone to radicalization. Furthermore, the larger proportion of university educated persons in developed countries makes each educated individual politically less important. Because of the larger number of peers, relatively fewer feel the need and/or the duty to be politically active. Finally, the "middle-classness" of the occupational structure of developed countries, as well as their higher standard of living, permits a relatively large number of persons to be occupied *professionally* in fields such as literature, painting, and music.[9]

Other changes have contributed to the frustration of the intellectuals. Some stem from alterations in the class structure and from the democratization of the educational system. In societies in which status was fixed and education a privilege of the wealthy, intellectuals did not have to be gainfully employed, since they either possessed inherited wealth or could secure support from relatives or patrons. Today, however, inherited wealth is more unstable, and achievement is valued higher than ascription, making prolonged dependency on one's parents a socially disapproved way of life. With the democratization of higher education, fewer graduates are able to engage in non-lucrative intellectual activites. But even among the few who enjoy economic security based on personal wealth, one finds lack of social approval and self-esteem. For they, too, must have a recognized job—a specialty. Again, the thrust is toward narrowness and concentration, frustrating those who like to deal broadly in ideas and artistic creativity. One response to this alienation is radicalism. And since World War II resulted in the total discredit of Nazism and Fascism, left-wing ideologies have provided the most common channels for expressing alienation.[10] The logic of this analysis suggests that intellectuals would be more inclined to endorse reformist or radical ideologies, than would professionals and scientists.

IV. The Empirical Study of Identity

To test these hypotheses, I have analyzed some of the data collected in Puerto Rico as part of a comparative study of university students.[11] In this study, an effort was made to deal with the problem of dominant identity: "If you had to define yourself, would you say that you are more of an intellectual, more of a scientist, or more of a professional? (Choose only one)."

For the Puerto Rican survey, the sample was stratified by the several Departments and Schools of the University of Puerto Rico. A total of 576 interviews were collected. The only school which fell ostensibly short of the designed sample was medicine, which will be dropped from the analysis whenever academic field is controlled or analyzed. (Within each school, a systematic random sample was drawn from the enrollment lists.) The data are used only for an internal analysis of the sample. No attempt has been made to weigh the results in accordance with the sampling weights. From Colombia, in the case of the University of Los Andes, we obtained a near census, thanks to the facilities given by the university. The self-administered questionnaires, as in the case of Puerto Rico, were stratified by school, and the sampling weights will be disregarded in the analysis. Thus, they will be used in internal analysis only.

By using a self-identification question, the study avoided any necessity to define an intellectual. In this case, our concern was with the way in which men see themselves, rather than with how scholars may think of what they do. Of course, men are not usually concerned with all the characteristics which have a bearing upon their behavior. We forced our respondents to choose one of three alternatives since we were fundamentally interested in eliciting their self-images.

Identity, of course, is not an all-or-nothing issue. Most men have a multiplicity of self-images, which they hold with different degrees of intensity. Although we assumed that the forced-choice question evoked the *dominant* identity, it cannot be assumed that subsidiary identities are irrelevant in determining various behaviors and attitudes. To find out how salient these identities are, the forced-choice question was coupled with three indicators of intensity, one related to each of the categories: intellectual, scientist, and professional. The wording of the question was as follows: "To what extent do you think that you belong to the following categories of persons? For instance, do you think of yourself as an (intellectual, scientist, professional) most of the time, often, seldom, or never?" [12] Nevertheless, the dominant identity question was more important for the analysis. Furthermore, it elicited a smaller percentage of "Don't knows" and "no answers" than did the other questions.

The forced-choice question on identification, in spite of its predictive and heuristic usefulness, is obviously an oversimplification. Many think of themselves as both an intellectual *and* a scientist. Interviews indicated that some respondents felt some discomfort when answering this forced-choice question. This feeling may have been especially acute in certain disciplines, such as the social sciences, which are still somewhere between "scientific" and "humanistic." These disciplines, which are now acquiring a "scientific" character, have little consensus concerning some fundamental issues in the philosophy of science. Although the possibility of multiple identities exists, one of them is ordinarily dominant. Subsidiary identities do, however, have an effect on, and are symptomatic of life situation and *Weltanschauung*. Given the possibility of multiple identification it is significant that our indicator of dominant identity, the forced-choice question, is related strongly to an indicator of diffuseness (preference for general education).

Table I shows that dominant identity is a predictor of a diffuse orientation toward education. Thus, intellectuals are more likely than scientists or professionals to support general education as opposed to specialized vocational and professional training.[13] Among student intel-

TABLE I

Identity (Forced-Choice) and Diffuseness, by Identity, Puerto Rico

	FAVORING GENERAL EDUCATION (PER CENT)		
	DOMINANT IDENTITY		
IDENTITY INTENSITY:			
(How often thinks of self as)	INTELLECTUALS	SCIENTISTS	PROFESSIONALS
Intellectual			
Most of time, often,	54 (125) *	45 (20)	44 (71)
seldom, or never	38 (29)	26 (38)	28 (160)
Professional			
Most of time, often,	62 (42)	24 (21)	25 (264)
seldom, or never	46 (63)	34 (35)	20 (46)

* Totals over which percentages were computed. Overall totals differ as the number of rejections is not the same for the two questions.

lectuals, as among scientists and professionals, those who think of themselves as intellectuals most of the time or often are more likely to favor a general education than those who seldom or never do so.

V. Identity and the Academic Structure

The problem of identity is not independent of the field of study. Intellectual identities do not "happen" randomly in the various academic disciplines: they tend to concentrate in some fields. There are many links connecting identity and academic structure. Disciplines differ in professionalization, role specificity, and academic traditions, selectively attracting students of diverse inclinations. Furthermore, if I am correct in suspecting that both the problem of identity and of field choice are connected with variations in cognitive styles, this would be another factor linking identity and academic field.

A few obvious common sense hypotheses may be formulated at this point: fields which are research oriented, such as physics, biology, etc., should have a high proportion of students with a scientific identity; fields with a tradition of professionalization, such as engineering and business administration, should foster professional identity, while such diffuse fields as the humanities should have a high proportion of students with an intellectual identity. The data in this regard are extremely suggestive:

TABLE II.
Academic Field and Identity, Puerto Rico

ACADEMIC FIELD	IDENTITY				
	INTELLECTUALS	SCIENTISTS	PROFESSIONALS	TOTALS	N *
Business Administration	15.6%	0.0%	84.4%	100.0%	(64)
Engineering	15.7%	15.7%	68.6%	100.0%	(70)
Education	16.1%	6.5%	77.4%	100.0%	(93)
Natural Sciences	28.0%	48.0%	24.0%	100.0%	(50)
Law	31.5%	6.5%	62.0%	100.0%	(92)
Social Sciences	33.8%	15.5%	50.7%	100.0%	(71)
Humanities and General Studies	49.5%	8.4%	42.1%	100.0%	(95)

* Totals may not equal 100 due to rounding.

As expected, business administration and engineering have an extremely large proportion of professionals, and education is also very high. This pattern seems to reflect the influence of North American universities on the University of Puerto Rico. This is specially true in the case of the law school, which is a professional school on the United States model rather than the extremely broad school characteristic of most of Latin America, where relatively few students actually intend to practice law. The relatively high proportion (by Latin American standards) of Puerto Rican social science students, who think of themselves as professionals or scientists, may also reflect North American influence. The natural sciences include an extremely high proportion of students who identify as scientists, as might be expected. Finally, as anticipated, self-identified intellectuals are dominant in the humanities and general studies. These are, of course, the least professionalized schools.

Data from Colombia follow much the same direction. Although within each academic field Colombian students are more likely to think of themselves as intellectuals by comparison with Puerto Rican students, the *internal* comparisons lead to the same conclusions as in Puerto Rico. Only among students of engineering, medicine, social sciences, and natural and exact sciences do the scientists exceed 10 per cent of the total—a result identical in *direction* to that of the Puerto Ri-

TABLE III

Academic Field and Identity, Colombia

ACADEMIC FIELD	INTELLECTUALS	SCIENTISTS	PROFESSIONALS	TOTALS	N *
		IDENTITY			
Engineering	34.9%	20.2%	44.9%	100.0%	(530)
Medicine	36.6%	17.6%	45.9%	100.1%	(205)
Social Sciences	41.4%	14.2%	44.4%	100.0%	(99)
Natural and Exact Sciences	41.6%	16.9%	41.6%	100.1%	(77)
Education	42.3%	8.2%	49.5%	100.0%	(97)
Economics	42.4%	3.2%	54.4%	100.0%	(125)
Architecture	45.0%	3.3%	51.7%	100.0%	(60)
Law	60.7%	2.6%	36.8%	100.1%	(234)
Humanities	73.4%	1.6%	25.0%	100.0%	(128)

* Totals may not equal 100 due to rounding.

can.[14] Colombian students of natural and exact sciences, however, are considerably less likely than their Puerto Rican counterparts to have a scientific identity; by contrast, Colombian engineering students are slightly more likely to do so.

Looking now at the frequency with which a professional identity occurs in the various academic fields, we see that, with the exception of law and humanities, the range of professional identity is relatively narrow, varying between 42 per cent in the natural and exact sciences area to 54 per cent in economics. It is also interesting that Colombian students are less likely than Puerto Ricans to have a professional identity. These differences are remarkable in some fields such as engineering, education, and law. The one clear exception is the natural and exact sciences, as in Puerto Rico many more shift from a professional to a scientific identity.

Finally, looking at the self-identified intellectuals, we see that, in Colombia, law and humanities clearly stand out as having an extremely high proportion of students who identify themselves as intellectuals (see Table III).

VI. Identity and Social Class

Studies carried out in various countries have shown that students from poorer homes are more likely to be vocationally inclined than students from higher socio-economic background. The results of our current research in various parts of the "third world" show similar results. Those from lower socio-economic origins need a profession that will ensure them a good job after university. They cannot rely upon their parents for prolonged support.

Students from varying socio-economic backgrounds go to the university with different expectations. In highly stratified societies, college education is one natural consequence of high status, along with good manners and cultured tastes; in open systems, education is also an instrument of considerable social mobility. With modernization, growing numbers of parents, who are poorly educated themselves, develop achievement values and project their unfulfilled ambitions on to their children.[15] A good education is the best means that they can provide for them, and they make painful sacrifices to achieve this objective. Their children are not unaware of this situation, and feel obliged to dedicate themselves to a well-paid profession. The sons of a wealthy family, by contrast, rarely experience such pressures and are free to indulge in any intellectual pursuit, no matter how dilettantish or impractical, while attending a university.

Of course, today even in the most underdeveloped countries, the extreme picture of a completely closed stratification system fits only certain isolated rural areas. Social change and mobility are present everywhere. In few countries today are most members of the elite able to experience the old feeling of unchallenged security. Our test case, Puerto Rico, has moved a long way from being a predominantly ascriptive society to one which now places more and more emphasis on achievement. Thus, one would not expect to find as strong a relationship between status and attitude toward university work in Puerto Rico as in less developed and more ascriptive cultures.

The factors related to intellectual identity are obviously not independent of these processes. In a way, as will be shown later on, intellectual self-identity and non-vocationalism are associated. The identity of the impoverished students should reflect the greater specificity of their educational goals. A specific and well-defined status is associated with a professional or scientific identity at the university level. Consequently a larger proportion of students from lower socio-economic origins should exhibit a professional identity as compared to those of higher socio-economic background, who should have a more *diffuse,* i.e. *intellectual,* identity (see Table IV).

TABLE IV

Father's Education and Student's Identity

IDENTITY	ELEMENTARY	SECONDARY	UNIVERSITY
Professionals	66.7%	53.9%	52.6%
Intellectuals	21.7%	27.5%	29.5%
Scientists	7.5%	13.6%	13.7%
Others ADK's, NA's	4.1%	5.0%	4.2%
TOTALS	100.0%	100.0%	100.0%
n	(120)	(258)	(190)

The data show clearly that the proportion of students with a professional identity decreases substantially as paternal educational background changes from the elementary to the secondary level, and only slightly from the secondary to the university level. The reverse is true in the case of intellectual identity. Interestingly enough, scientific identity seems to have similar correlates for intellectual identity. A scientific identification requires a set of very special values only found in modern value systems, which in turn are characteristic of subgroups within the middle and higher socio-economic strata.

VII. Identity and Diffuseness

If the assumption about the meaning of an intellectual identity is correct, the "intellectuals" among the students should favor diffuse and general educational goals, whereas the "professionals" should have specific, job-oriented objectives. Informal interviews with students indicate that while many complain about the narrow and practical character of academic training, others have opposite complaints. Many of the latter argue that courses are too theoretical and are of no practical use. The

Puerto Rican data show that intellectuals are more likely to believe that the university's most important function is to provide a general education, as opposed to training for a professional life (see Table V). The majority of intellectuals reject professional-oriented training, while most professionals and scientists endorse it.

TABLE V

Identity and Diffuseness of Educational Goals (Puerto Rico), by Father's Education

| | PER CENT IN FAVOR OF GENERAL EDUCATION ** | | |
| | FATHER'S EDUCATION | | |
IDENTITY	ELEMENTARY	SECONDARY	UNIVERSITY
Intellectuals	58 (26) *	42 (71)	57 (55)
Scientists	— (9)	17 (32)	38 (27)
Professionals	34 (73)	30 (132)	36 (91)

* Totals over which percentages were computed.
** Question: What is the *most* important function of the University? To give the students a general education (*una cultura general*) or to prepare the students for professional life?

Colombian data support these conclusions. However, the small percentage of the total sample favoring general education (11 per cent as opposed to 37 per cent in the Puerto Rican case) creates serious analytic problems (see Table VI).

TABLE VI

Identity and Diffuseness, by Father's Education, Colombia

| | PER CENT IN FAVOR OF GENERAL EDUCATION | | |
| | FATHER'S EDUCATION | | |
IDENTITY	ELEMENTARY	SECONDARY	UNIVERSITY
Intellectuals	15 (167) *	12 (268)	10 (197)
Scientists	11 (37)	14 (81)	11 (64)
Professionals	10 (149)	8 (291)	7 (208)

* Totals over which percentages were computed.

The data suggest that intellectuals and scientists have more diffuse orientations than professionals. The differences, however, are not impressive. Among the students from lower socio-economic backgrounds, intellectuals have a more diffuse outlook than scientists and professionals; whereas among students from a middle and lower socio-economic background, scientists are more in favor of a general education, closely followed by intellectuals, with professionals overwhelmingly in favor of a job-oriented education.

On the other hand, among Colombian student intellectuals and professionals, there is a slight tendency for diffuseness to decrease with parental status. This result is different from the Puerto Rican case, where there is a curvilinear relationship, with the middle strata clearly

TABLE VII

Identity and Diffuseness, by Academic Field, Puerto Rico

| ACADEMIC FIELDS | PER CENT FAVORING A GENERAL EDUCATION | | |
	INTELLECTUAL	SCIENTIST	PROFESSIONAL
Business, Engineering, Education	44 (36) *	41 (17)	25 (174)
Natural Sciences	43 (16)	25 (26)	17 (19)
Law	62 (29)	— (6)	51 (57)
Humanities, General Studies, and Social Sciences	48 (71)	26 (19)	36 (76)

* Totals over which percentages were computed.

in favor of a diffuse educational orientation. Had the two samples been drawn from the total number of youths of a given age group in the two countries, one might venture the conclusion that the relationship between class and diffuseness is different in Colombia and in Puerto Rico. However, the differential degree of educational selectivity along class lines (degree of inegalitarianism of higher education) introduces another uncontrolled factor; also we did not deal with all universities in both countries. Thus, it is impossible to ascertain whether the differential relationship between class and diffuseness is present in the social structure of the two countries, or whether it stems from the differences between the samples.

Given the intimate association between self-identity and academic field, it is important to ask whether identity has an effect on other variables *independently* of academic field. In other words, is the correlation between identity and diffuseness spurious and due solely to their common correlations with the academic field?

In order to examine this hypothesis, academic fields must be held constant. This is feasible, for *within* each field there is substantial variation in identity. Identity is far from determined by academic field alone. Different individuals concentrating in the same subject have completely different images of the profession and of their personal roles. And as Table VII shows, *within* each group of academic fields, intellectual identity is associated with a diffuse orientation.

In all four groupings, those who identify as intellectuals are more likely to favor a diffuse educational policy than specific vocational training. Those seeing themselves as professionals and scientists fail to present any systematic pattern that would distinguish one from the other.

TABLE VIII

Identity and Diffuseness, by Academic Field, Colombia

| ACADEMIC FIELDS | PER CENT FAVORING A GENERAL EDUCATION | | |
	INTELLECTUAL	SCIENTIST	PROFESSIONAL
Law	23 (129) *	— (6)	19 (85)
Medicine	11 (73)	8 (36)	2 (91)
Engineering	9 (176)	9 (105)	9 (238)

* Totals over which percentages were computed.

Colombian data resemble the Puerto Rican results. In the three schools with the largest number interviewed in our sample—law, medicine, and engineering—intellectuals are most likely to favor a diffuse orientation. However, as the percentage favoring a general education is very small in Colombia, we may ask the question the other way around: how many intellectuals do we find among those favoring a general education (diffuse) and those favoring professional training (specific)? Among engineering students, we find 45 per cent who are self-identified intellectuals among those favoring a diffuse educational orientation, compared to 33 per cent calling themselves intellectuals among those favoring professional training; among medical students, the difference points in the same direction, the percentages being 62 per cent and 35 per cent respectively, while among law students, the differences, though smaller, still persist—65 per cent against 59 per cent. Thus, identity and diffuseness are still related after academic field is controlled for.

VIII. Identity and Political Self-Assessment

To turn now to politics, we previously suggested that intellectualism would be correlated with political radicalism. Table IX shows that a dominant intellectual identity is positively associated with a leftist image.

TABLE IX

Identity and Ideological Self-Assessment, by Father's Education, Puerto Rico

| | PER CENT MORE TO THE LEFT (INCLUDING MUCH MORE AND A LITTLE MORE) | | |
| | | FATHER'S EDUCATION | |
IDENTITY	ELEMENTARY	SECONDARY	UNIVERSITY
Intellectual	35 (26) *	34 (71)	38 (55)
Scientist	— (9)	22 (32)	15 (27)
Professional	10 (73)	14 (132)	13 (91)

* Totals over which percentages were computed.

Question: By comparison with the majority of the university's students, would you say that your political position is much more to the left, a little more to the left, about the same, a little more conservative, or much more conservative than the others?

Intellectual students are most likely to think of themselves as leftists, followed by scientists, with professionals exhibiting the most conservative political self-image. At each family socio-economic level, the order going from left to right is the same: intellectuals, scientists, professionals. Thus, in addition to the hypothesized radicalism of the intellectuals, Table IX shows that scientists place themselves more to the left than do professionals.[16] Looking at the data from another angle, the proportion of students having an intellectual identity decreases steadily when one moves from the most left to the most conservative pole on the political self-assessment scale. The reverse is true for professional identity. Moreover, the proportion who identify as professionals is greatest among those who failed to answer the political self-assessment question, which suggests a close relationship between professionalization and political apathy among university students.[17]

Colombian data also show that identity and ideological self-assessment are correlated, controlling for socio-economic status (father's education), with the differences pointing to the same direction as in Puerto Rico. Intellectuals are again most likely to think of themselves as more to the left than the majority of students, followed by scientists and professionals. However, in Colombia differences are less striking

TABLE X

Identity and Ideological Self-Assessment, by Father's Education,
Colombia

| IDENTITY | FATHER'S EDUCATION | | |
	ELEMENTARY	SECONDARY	UNIVERSITY
Intellectuals	42 (172) *	33 (289)	33 (211)
Scientists	38 (41)	25 (82)	30 (66)
Professionals	31 (151)	20 (297)	20 (212)

* Totals over which percentages were computed.

than in Puerto Rico, as a larger percentage of Colombian than Puerto Rican scientists and professionals place themselves on the left as well.

It has previously been shown that identity and academic field are correlated. Although identity has an independent connection with diffuseness after academic field is controlled for, it is still possible that academic field accounts for all of the common variance between identity and ideological self-assessment. In order to test this possibility, the data were analyzed controlling for academic field.

As Table XI indicates, in all four academic fields, those who identify

TABLE XI

Identity and Ideological Self-Assessment, by Academic Field,
Puerto Rico

| ACADEMIC FIELD | PER CENT MORE TO THE LEFT THAN OTHER STUDENTS | | |
	INTELLECTUALS	SCIENTISTS	PROFESSIONALS
Business, Engineering, Education	25 (36) *	24 (17)	7 (174)
Natural Sciences	14 (14)	13 (24)	8 (12)
Law	58 (29)	— (6)	25 (57)
Humanities, General Studies, and Social Sciences	35 (71)	21 (19)	16 (76)

* Totals over which percentages were computed.

as intellectuals are more likely to see themselves on the left than the majority of other students. Scientists follow in this respect: although differences between scientists and professionals are based on small totals, the variations are consistent. Professionals remain the most conservative group.

On the other hand, students of law and humanities, general studies, and the social sciences, are more likely to perceive themselves as leftists than those in other fields even after identity is controlled for. Thus, both identity and academic field have independent effects on ideological self-assessment.

Specific orientation and conservatism seem to go together, as can be inferred from their common relationships with identity and academic field. Scientists despite their tendency toward specificity appear fairly likely to be on the left, if one judges from this very insufficient number of cases.

IX. Identity and Party Preference

Although claims that "parties in this country don't mean a thing" or they represent a choice between "tweedledee" and "tweedledum" can be heard just about everywhere, public opinion surveys carried out in many countries have repeatedly shown that identification with a given party is associated with outlook on a series of issues.

Major political parties tend to have a differential appeal to the various socio-economic strata,[18] although the correlation between the socio-economic status and politics varies from one country to another, and over different periods.[19] In Puerto Rico attitudes toward political status for the island, i.e. independence, commonwealth, or statehood, differentiate the parties.[20]

Politics does not take place in a historical vacuum and cannot be understood outside of the concrete situation of the country at hand. For Puerto Ricans, political status is an important question and, within this perspective, the PIP (*Partido Independentista Puertorriqueño*) presents the most radical solution. It is backed by most leftists. There is general agreement that independence is leftist and even radical in this context, while the statehood proposal backed by the PER is the most right-wing alternative available. And as might be expected those Puerto Rican students who identify as intellectuals are found disproportionately among the supporters of *independentismo*.

As the data in Table XII indicate self-identified student intellectuals consistently are more likely to prefer the PIP. Scientists follow, although the differences between scientists and professionals are based on very modest totals. Once more it is apparent that an intellectual identity is associated with political radicalism.

Party identification is not a useful means of locating leftists in Colombia since the two major parties, the Conservatives and the Liberals, have an agreement to rotate the presidency between them and back the

TABLE XII

Identity and Per Cent Supporting the PIP, by Father's Education

IDENTITY	FATHER'S EDUCATION		
	ELEMENTARY	SECONDARY	UNIVERSITY
Intellectuals	35 (26) *	34 (71)	38 (55)
Scientists	— (9)	22 (32)	15 (27)
Professionals	10 (73)	14 (132)	13 (91)

* Totals over which percentages were computed.

same *Frente Nacional* candidate whose victory is guaranteed in the election.[21] Consequently, in Colombia I decided to use an attitudinal question, dealing with the Cuban revolution, rather than party preference as a measure of radicalism.

TABLE XIII

Identity and Per Cent Favorable to the Cuban Revolution, by Father's Education, Colombia

IDENTITY	FATHER'S EDUCATION		
	ELEMENTARY	SECONDARY	UNIVERSITY
Intellectuals	58 (172) *	33 (289)	25 (211)
Scientists	45 (41)	18 (82)	20 (66)
Professionals	52 (151)	24 (297)	21 (212)

* Totals over which percentages were computed.

The Colombia data presented in Table XIII show again the now familiar association between intellectual identity and radicalism. The percentage favorable to the Cuban revolution is systematically higher among intellectuals than among scientists or professionals. Interestingly, professionals are more likely than scientists to favor the Cuban revolution, thus reversing the Puerto Rican findings.

Looking at the influence of socio-economic status on political ideology, one finds that in all three identity groups, the proportion favorable to the Cuban revolution drops as father's education increases, with the major contrast between the lower and middle statuses.

Conclusions

The materials presented here point to some of the underlying sources for leftist orientations which seem to characterize most of the Latin American intellectual elite, and which form the dominant climate of political opinion on most university campuses. Although data from a variety of countries, including the United States, indicate that those involved in more humanistic as distinct from professional and scientific activities, are more likely to be leftist, the consequences are much more salient for Latin American than for the highly industrialized nations. In the latter, scientists and professionals predominate among the university educated strata. A large proportion, probably a majority of students, would prefer a scientific or a professional identity to an intellectual one. In most of Latin America, however, the majority group of those who identify as intellectuals are opponents of capitalism and traditionalism and advocate progressive or radical reforms.

The results suggest that as Latin American universities become more professionalized, as students and educated men become involved in scientific and professional roles—involvements which should be associated with greater industrialization and social modernization—the proportion of students and graduates who support diffuse radical politics concerned with global societal changes, rather than specific reforms, will probably decline. But observation of the behavior of intellectuals in developed countries suggests that such changes will not necessarily result in the incorporation of the intellectuals into the system, no matter how successful it becomes in improving the standards of income and levels of culture of the population. The alienation of the intellectuals from the predominant social institutions and their consequent political radicalism represent in all countries a reaction against the seeming weakness of intellectual values and activities in industrial society. With the processes of differentiation and the absorption of the masses into society which have occurred in highly developed nations, the creative intellectual is challenged in his right to comment on all activities. Role specificity, the rise of the technical expert, reduces the diffuse role of the intellectual. Also inherent in industrialization and modernization is the emergence of phenomena which have generally been described invidiously as "mass culture," which force many intellectuals to create for popular taste, a development which they often blame on capitalism rather than democratization. These processes work also to reduce the self-esteem of intellectuals, to make them feel rejected by and outside of the basic trends of modern industrial society. Consequently, even when economic development accomplishes many of the social objectives advocated by reformist intellectuals at an earlier stage, the intellectuals still remain outside as critics.

Notes

1. For a comparison of definitions, see J. Schumpeter, *Capitalism, Socialism and Democracy* (New York: Harper, 1950), pp. 146–147; S. M. Lipset, *Political Man* (New York: Doubleday, 1960), p. 311; E. Shils, "The Intellectuals in the Political Development of the New States," in J. Kautsky (ed.), *Political Change in Underdeveloped Countries* (New York: John Wiley, 1962), pp. 193 ff.; J. Galtung, "Development and Intellectual Styles," paper presented to the International Conference on Comparative Social Research in Developing Countries (Buenos Aires: 1964), pp. 3–7. The comparison of these attempts to define what is an intellectual reveals that we face a real conceptual and definitional problem. Other scholars, who analyzed intellectuals and politics, have avoided a clear-cut definition. See, for instance, R. Michels, *Political Parties* (New York: Dover, 1959), and M. Crozier, "The Cultural Revolution: Notes on the Changes in the Intellectual Climate of France," *Daedalus*, 93 (Winter, 1964), pp. 514–542. The impression one has from these is that we are dealing with a blurred concept which poses serious definitional problems at the conceptual level. In my opinion, few concepts would benefit more from an operational definition than that of the intellectual.

2. For a theoretical distinction of social class, as conceived along identification (or "subjective") lines, from socio-economic status, as conceived along occupational (or "objective") lines, see G. A. D. Soares, "Classes Sociais, Strata Sociais e as Eleições Presidenciais de 1960," *Sociologia*, XXIII (Sept., 1961), pp. 217–238.

3. See Talcott Parsons, *Essays in Sociological Theory* (Glencoe: The Free Press, 1954), Chapters II and XVIII, for a discussion of the relationship between professionalization and specificity. Parsons, however, fails to emphasize that the degree of specificity of different occupations is

not the same everywhere, and that industrialization tends to increase professional specificity.

4. One possible differential reaction among the social scientists is that the psychologically alienated would be primarily critical of the orientation of the social sciences, and only secondarily of society, whereas the reverse would be true of the socially and economically alienated.

5. T. Parsons and E. Shils (eds.), *Toward a General Theory of Action* (New York: Harper, 1962), Part II.

6. Schlesinger defined focusing as "not only the ability to take and maintain . . . [a given] set for accuracy when it is appropriate to do so, but *also* an underlying preference for experiencing the world in a narrowed, discriminating way even when the task does not demand such an approach." (italics ours) Schlesinger had two findings of relevance to this article. On the one hand, those who tend to greater inclusiveness made larger errors in a size-estimation test; on the other hand, focusers are less keen to affective experiences in a problem-solving situation. This can be related to the concept of affectivity and affective neutrality, provided one discards the Protestant ethic biases implicit in the definition of this variable along the hedonist-control dimension, and limits himself to the notion of a compartmentalization between cognition and affectivity. This, of course, would shift the focus of the question from a concern with hedonism versus postponement of rewards to a concern with affectivity (in the sense of emotionality). See H. J. Schlesinger, "Cognitive Attitudes in Relation to Susceptibility to Interference," *Journal of Personality*, 22 (1954), pp. 354–374, and T. Parsons and E. Shils, pp. 60 ff.

7. See in this respect, the work of J. Piaget, Vinh-Dang, and B. Matalon, "Note on the Law of Temporal Maximum of Some Optico-Geometric Illusions," *American Journal of Psychology*, 71 (1958), pp. 277–282, as well as the concurrent evidence presented by R. W. Gardner, "Cognitive Control Principles and Perceptual Behavior," *Bulletin of the Menninger Clinic*, 23 (1959), pp. 241–248. These studies have been interpreted in the sense that "Subjects who deploy attention extensively will tend toward relative underestimation [of the magnitude of an object of the center of the attentional field], whereas subjects who attend primarily to the obvious and interesting standard stimuli will tend toward relative overestimation."

8. Identity is not independent of the degree of modernization of the educational system, nor of the degree of economic development. Thus, comparing Puerto Rico (more modern and more developed) with Colombia (less modern and less developed), we see that in the University of Puerto Rico, 57 per cent of the respondents identified themselves as professionals, and only 27 per cent as intellectuals. In five Colombian universities (Javeriana, Libre, Los Andes, Nacional, and Popayan), the percentage with an intellectual identity varied between 35 per cent and 52 per cent and the percentage with a professional

identity varied between 27 per cent and 50 per cent. This suggests that the identity structure of a country's educated elite is responsive to the degree of modernization of the country's educational system and its economic development.

9. See Shils, "The Intellectuals in the Political Development of the New States," pp. 200 passim.

10. This does *not* mean that intellectuals do not venture into the radical right. It only means that, by comparison with the pre-World War II situation, there seem to be proportionately fewer intellectuals who adhere to rightist radicalism. Actually, there is abundant, however unsystematic, evidence that unattached and unemployed persons of high education provided a disproportionate percentage of the leadership of rightist, educated radical parties. On Nazi support and leadership among university students and the higher educated, see W. Kotschnig, *Unemployment in the Learned Professions* (London: Oxford University Press, 1937); K. Heiden, *Der Führer* (Boston: Houghton-Mifflin, 1944); W. Kornhauser, *The Politics of Mass Society* (Glencoe: The Free Press, 1951).

11. Puerto Rican data were collected during the summer of 1964 under the supervision of Brunhilda Velez Heilbron, as part of a comparative study of university students sponsored by the Institute of International Studies of the University of California, Berkeley. Several Puerto Rican educational authorities and scholars were most helpful in making student enrollment lists available, and suggesting adaptations of the standard questionnaire to Puerto Rican peculiarities.

    Colombian data were also collected in 1964, under the supervision of Jeanne Posada, to include various schools from five universities (Los Andes, Javeriana, Libre and Nacional in Bogotá, and the University of Popayan, Cauca). Colombian educational authorities and students were most helpful and suggested many adaptations of the questionnaire.

12. In Spanish, *La mayor parte del tiempo, a menudo, raramente, nunca.*

13. Taking those who think of themselves as intellectuals, two categories ("often" and "seldom") have large enough numbers to warrant further analysis. In the "often" category, 48 per cent of intellectuals favor a diffuse orientation, as opposed to 45 per cent of scientists and 44 per cent of professionals; in the "seldom" category, 40 per cent of intellectuals, 19 per cent of scientists, and 33 per cent of professionals exhibit a similar preference. Taking the question of intensity of a professional identity, the same categories, "often" and "seldom," have reasonable subtotals and will be analyzed separately. In the "often" category, intellectuals outrank scientists and professionals, percentages being 62 per cent, 25 per cent, and 34 per cent, respectively. In the "seldom" category, intellectuals once more are more likely to prefer general education, the percentages being 47 per cent, 32 per cent, and 17 per cent. Thus the results hold when more refined categories are used as controls.

14. Except for medicine, for there were too few students in the Puerto Rican sample to warrant analysis.

15. Kahl, in an interesting study, has shown that when parents' socioeconomic status and children's intelligence are controlled for, it is the frustrated parent with unfulfilled educational ambitions who is the most likely to push his children through college. See J. Kahl, "Educational and Occupational Aspirations of 'Common Man' Boys," *Harvard Educational Review*, XXIII (Summer, 1953), pp. 186–203.

16. Lipset, analyzing data from the *Time* College Graduate Study, has reached somewhat comparable conclusions: 60 per cent of those who checked "scientist" as their occupation voted Democratic, whereas no less than 80 per cent of those who checked "engineer" voted Republican. See Lipset, pp. 315–316.

17. A study of students in several universities located in different countries shows that radicalism and political participation are positively related. See G. A. D. Soares, "The Active Few: A Study of Ideology and Participation," *Comparative Education Review*, X (1966), pp. 205–220.

18. For a comparative analysis of abundant comparative data bearing on this problem, see Lipset, and S. M. Lipset and J. Linz, *The Social Basis of Political Diversity* (mimeographed, 1956).

19. See, in this respect, R. Alford, *Party and Society* (Chicago: Rand McNally, 1963); P. Converse, "The Shifting Role of Class in Political Attitudes and Behavior," in E. E. Maccoby, T. M. Newcomb, and E. L. Hartley (eds.), *Readings in Social Psychology* (New York: Holt, Rinehart and Winston, 1958, 3rd ed.), pp. 388–399.

20. This point has been emphasized by R. Anderson, *Party Politics in Puerto Rico* (Stanford: Stanford University Press, 1965), and by G. K. Lewis, *Puerto Rico: Freedom and Power in the Caribbean* (N.Y.: Monthly Review Press, 1963), pp. 375–408. The PIP, of course, favors independence, the PER favors statehood (Puerto Rico would become an American state), and the PPD favors the commonwealth solution, which is to maintain the *status quo*.

21. Only 44 per cent of the Colombian students disagreed strongly with the statement that "it makes little difference if people choose one or another candidate for political office because nothing or very little will change." By contrast, no less than 77 per cent of the Puerto Rican students disagreed strongly with the same statement. See, in this respect, Kenneth Walker, "La Socialisación Política en las Universidades Latinoamericanas," *Revista Latinoamericana de Sociología*, 2 (1965), pp. 200–219.

IV

Secondary Schools

14
Secondary Education and the Development of Elites

ALDO SOLARI

Secondary education, particularly academic education, has undergone significant changes in all countries and will most likely continue to do so in the near future. Even though these changes have varied widely throughout the world, certain phases of their development can be positively defined in distinct categories.

Educational possibilities in Latin America have been expanded at the secondary level with the creation of vocational and technical schools and the inclusion in academic schools of a wider proportion of the population. Until industrialization made it necessary to incorporate the lower strata into the educational system, traditional secondary education was the privilege of a few, most of whom were candidates for the university. At first the demands for more trained personnel were met by the establishment of vocational schools which prepared lower class students for certain occupations. Since these technical schools were considered to be of inferior status to the traditional secondary schools, their establishment often increased the separation among the classes by limiting the occupational mobility of the lower strata. Eventually, a series of factors resulted in the breakdown of these barriers in the educational system and in the development of universal secondary school education. At this point, it should be emphasized that the expansion of the educational system by the establishment of elite oriented academic schools is significantly different from the development of a universal or comprehensive school system: the former increases the separation between the classes, while the latter narrows the gap.

Academic education has generally assumed that it is by nature entirely different from elementary or primary education. This elitist view has been countered by the conception of secondary education as an extension of primary education, which must be available to the greatest number of school-age children. But the expansion of secondary education which results from the demands of an industrialized society cannot be accomplished without significant changes in the curriculum. In most countries these have involved a change in orientation from the classical humanistic approach to the more scientific or rational "learning by doing" of modern pedagogues.

An educational system has several functions: those of recruitment and distribution of talent, and those that involve the contents and the nature of the training. Secondary education may be considered as a terminal school which leads to immediate integration into an occupation, or it may be largely preparation for the university. We will attempt here to study secondary education in Latin America in order to determine its importance in the development of elites and political recruitment.[1]

Expansion of the System

In 1960 the enrollment in secondary schools in proportion to the population of school age varied from 3 per cent in Haiti to 32 per cent in Uruguay (Table 1). For analytic purposes Latin American countries may be classified into three groups: those with less than 13 per cent in school (Haiti, Guatemala, Nicaragua, Honduras, Mexico, Brazil, and the Dominican Republic); those with between 13 and 25 per cent (El Salvador, Colombia, Chile, Peru, Cuba, Venezuela, and Paraguay); and those with over 25 per cent (Panama, Argentina, Costa Rica, and Uruguay).

There are clearly significant differences among Latin American countries, from those in which secondary education is a privilege of a small minority to the group of countries where it is almost universal. In the latter the percentage of enrolled is comparable to those of many European countries. For example, in 1964 France had approximately the same percentage of students in academic school as Uruguay, while Spain has expanded its secondary school system less than Argentina or Uruguay has. Even though we are aware that in the last few years the increase in high school students has been greater in France than in Uruguay and Argentina, these comparative statistics enable us to assess the variations in secondary education in a worldwide context. One can

TABLE I

Matriculation in Secondary School and School-age Population (in thousands)

COUNTRY	1955			1960			Rate of growth of matriculation from 1957-62
	POPULATION	MATRICULATION	%	POPULATION	MATRICULATION	%	
Argentina	1810	484	27	1980	606	31	20
Bolivia	442	33	8	488	57	12	52
Brazil	9165	766	8	9825	1177	12	65
Colombia	1664	129	8	1937	286	15	50
Costa Rica	110	18	16	127	35	28	48
Cuba	660	76	12	737	122	17	137
Chile	878	166	19	982	230	23	53
Ecuador	481	43	9	579	67	12	59
El Salvador	242	21	9	264	34	13	52
Guatemala	396	19	5	446	27	6	76
Haiti	518	15	3	563	19	3	84
Honduras	176	9	5	198	15	8	71
Mexico	3405	179	5	3916	487[a]	12	89
Nicaragua	143	5[b]	4	165	10	6	116
Panama	111	25	23	130	39	30	54
Paraguay	195	16	8	215	28	13	33
Peru	1029	115	11	1177	202	17	93
Dominican Rep.	351	19	5	377	22	5	18
Uruguay	280	67	24	273	87	32	32
Venezuela	627	65	10	754	148	20	153
TOTAL	22683	2270	10	25133	3698	15	60

(a) Agricultural education not included   (b) Only the academic secondary education

Source: For 1955 and 1960, Document No. 49 presented by the General Secretary of UNESCO to the Conference on Education and Social and Economic Development in Latin America. (Santiago, Chile, 1962.) For 1957-62, UNESCO/AC–LAMP/VI/Add.1. (Meeting or Reunion of Brasilia, March 1964).

observe that the greatest development of secondary education in Latin American countries is found among those with higher levels of per capita income. It is important to note, however, that regional differences within countries are often greater than those between poor and rich nations. For example, secondary education is largely an urban phenomenon, closely linked to the process of urbanization. In these countries with only one large city—a characteristic of the majority of Latin American countries—academic secondary education has been almost entirely concentrated in the metropolis, especially in the early days of educational expansion. In addition to the discrepancies between urban and rural areas, there are also regional differences related to sharply different levels of development. The more developed areas have more secondary schools attended by a larger proportion of the age group than the less developed or poorer sections. The concentration of educational facilities in the more developed areas further increases the differences between the rural and the urban populations. For example, in Brazil we find a very high level of educational development in such cities as São Paulo and Rio de Janeiro, while in Northeastern Brazil, secondary education is as limited as in Haiti. Clearly the limited availability of secondary education serves in many Latin American countries to perpetuate an ascriptive elite system, while in other countries an extensive system of secondary education makes it possible to recruit new elements into the elites.

This rather static statistical view must take into account the enormous expansion in secondary schools all over the area. In the countries in the first group (under 13 per cent), enrollment increased 73 per cent between 1955 and 1960; for the second group (13 to 25 per cent) it rose 79 per cent, and in the third group (over 25), it grew 29 per cent in the same period. This pattern of growth throughout Latin America is very significant and corresponds to the general expansion which took place in developed countries several decades earlier. Based on current rates of growth, it may be assumed that by 1970 the majority of countries in Group I will reach 30 per cent of the age group in high school, those in Group II should attain a figure of 40 per cent enrolled, and those in Group III will be around 50 per cent. Whatever the influence in the widening of the sources of recruitment for elites exercised thus far by secondary education in Latin American countries, it may be safely predicted that these sources will grow considerably in the near future. But in order to judge accurately the significance of such growth measures two facts must be kept in mind: 1) Countries which have reached relatively high percentages of enrolled in high schools necessarily are less likely to reflect high rates of increase. A low rate of growth may simply reflect a high proportion already enrolled. 2) The meaning of the statistics is also affected by the fact that rates of population growth and of increase in school-age population are different from country to country. It is necessary, therefore, to differentiate countries depending on the relationships between changes in school attendance and the school-age population cohorts. On the basis of data the following classification can be made: a) countries in which school enrollment increases at the same rate as the population so that the proportion in secondary school remains the same, as in the case of Haiti and the Dominican Republic; b) countries in which the school enrollment figure increases very slightly more than the school-age population, and the ratio of those enrolled to school-age population increases very slowly—less than 1 per cent per year—as in the case of Argentina, Bolivia, Brazil, Chile, Ecuador, El Salvador, Guatemala, Honduras, and Nicaragua; c) countries in which enrollment is increasing considerably faster than the population resulting in an increase of those enrolled to age cohort of an average of between 1 and 1.5 per cent per year, as in Colombia (1.4), Cuba (1.0), Mexico (1.4), Panama (1.4), Paraguay (1.0), and Peru (1.2); and d) countries having the largest increase in the ratio of over 1.5 per cent as in Costa Rica (2.4), Venezuela (2.0), and Uruguay (1.6).

The problem is most serious in Haiti and Dominican Republic and in the countries in the second group, except for Argentina and Chile, which already have a high ratio enrolled. It should take El Salvador, Ecuador, and various other countries more than twenty years to reach the proportion of the age group in secondary school which existed in Uruguay and Argentina in 1960 if they increase their annual rate by 0.8 per cent. Nicaragua would need twenty-five years to do so.

Secondary school expansion is closely related to the urbanization process (see Table 2). Except for the special situations of Costa Rica and Panama, there is a strong connection between the extension of secondary education and urbanization. When the latter is defined by the proportion living in cities of 100,000 inhabitants or more, the correlation is even clearer. This is not surprising since the appropriate educational facilities and the occupations requiring secondary education exist mainly in the cities. Many Latin Americans see rural workers as be-

TABLE 2

Secondary Education and Urbanization

	Matriculation in secondary education in relation to school-age population (1)	Population in areas of 500 inhabitants or more (2)	Population in cities of 100,000 inhabitants or more (4)
Uruguay	32	71.7 (3)	41.2 (3)
Argentina	31	56.9	37.2
Panama	30	29.5	15.9
Costa Rica	28	26.1	17.5
Venezuela	20	42.0	16.6
Cuba	17	45.0	21.9
El Salvador	13	21.7	8.7
Paraguay	13	20.2	15.2
Mexico	12	34.7	15.1
Brazil	12	26.8	13.2
Ecuador	12	26.1	14.6
Honduras	8	11.9	0.0
Nicaragua	6	23.5	10.3
Guatemala	6	17.2	10.2
Dominican Rep.	5	18.5	8.5
Haiti	3	8.2	4.3

Sources: (1) Document No. 49, presented by the General Secretary of UNESCO to the Conference on Education and Development in Latin America, Santiago, 1962.
(2) Inter-American Institute of Statistics, *Characteristics of the Demographic Structure of American Countries* (Washington, 1964).
(3) Census of Uruguay, 1963. Almost all the countries correspond (or correlate) until 1950.
(4) UNESCO, *Urbanization in Latin America,* p. 96.

longing to an occupational world which does not require secondary education. In many countries the rural population not only lacks a secondary education, but relatively few are able to receive even primary education.

Another factor correlated with the expansion of secondary education is the percentage of people employed in tertiary (service) occupations. This correlation, however, is much weaker for reasons that will be developed later. Other factors associated with growth in secondary education are income level per capita, equalitarian distribution of income, and fewer marginal settlements (*villas misinas*). These factors are not always positively correlated with urbanization, since the latter is often accompanied by a regressive distribution of income and the formation of large marginal settlements.

In Latin American social structures, therefore, the interrelationship among these three factors tends to reduce the positive correlation between urbanization and expansion of secondary education. The growth of the tertiary economic sector correlates only partially with increases in per capita income. The tertiary sector includes many activities which are not related to the requirements or consequences of economic and social development. The internal composition of this sector may be quite different from that of more developed countries. The traditional tertiary section (domestic employees and petty shopkeepers) absorbs a very large proportion of the available manpower, and a large percentage does not need secondary education. Similarly, secondary sector occupations (manufacturing) include manpower employed in large-scale production units and those also in very traditional artisan units. Another source of statistical confusion may be found in the fact that urbanization in Latin America is often accompanied by a high level of unemployment or partial employment. In this context the existence of a clear-cut correlation between the development of secondary education and the relative size of the middle and upper classes is very significant (see Table 3). Those societies where urbanization is accompanied by a high level of income per capita and by a high percentage in middle-class occupations, e.g. as in Uruguay and Argentina, have developed a system of secondary education which approximates that of many European countries.

In Latin America most of the students who receive a secondary education are from middle-class families. The growth of the cities, the increase in the tertiary economy, and the growth in per capita income influence the expansion of secondary education mostly when accompanied by the growth of the middle class. In some countries a relatively high per capita income has not resulted in an expansion of the secondary level education at the same rate as other countries with a lower income level largely, because the middle class has not increased proportionately. However, in Latin America, as in Europe, academic secondary education is not only a status symbol for the middle class, but as countries develop economically it becomes also a *sine qua non* condition for maintaining one's social position or for upward mobility aspira-

TABLE 3

Matriculation in Secondary School, Distribution of the Active
Population, Social Classes, and Income Per Capita
in Latin America

	Matriculation in secondary schools in relation to population	Percentage of the secondary sector	Percentage of the tertiary sector	Percentage of the upper & middle classes	National income per person
	1	2	3	4	5
Uruguay	32	29.7	50.6	over 40	561
Argentina	31	29.0	43.7	36	799
Panama	30	9.7	25.7	15	371
Costa Rica	28	14.7	25.7	22	362
Venezuela	20	15.5	32.3	18	644
Cuba	17	18.3	36.6	22	516
El Salvador	13	13.9	18.5	10	267
Paraguay	13	17.5	20.8	14	193
Mexico	12	14.8	21.8	—	415
Brazil	12	16.7	21.2	15	375
Ecuador	12	25.3	19.1	10	223
Honduras	8	9.3	11.0	4	252
Nicaragua	6	13.2	16.2	—	288
Guatemala	6	10.3	11.6	8	258
Dominican Rep.	5	10.8	17.5	—	313
Haiti	3	7.4	11.5	3	149

Sources: Column 1: Document No. 49 presented by the General Secretary of
UNESCO to the Conference on Education and Development in Latin
America, Santiago, 1962.

Columns 2 & 3: ECLA percentile distribution of the labor force from census information of 1950. Bulletin, Vol. 11, No. 1, p. 22. For Uruguay the census
information has been taken from the 1963 census since none existed
earlier than 1908.

Column 4: Germani, "The Strategy of Fostering Social Mobility," as cited in note
9. For Uruguay estimates made by the author of this work based on the
information in the Survey on Social Stratification in Montevideo were
used.

Column 5: Indicates the national income per person in current dollars for 1961.
United Nations, *The Economic Development of Post-War Latin America,* 1963, Table 51.

tions. Only among the very poor can these functions be filled by technical or vocational instruction.

In a real sense, it may be said that the differences in the rates of expansion of secondary education among the various countries correspond quite closely to the differential rates of growth of the middle classes. Today in most of Latin America, secondary education, and especially academic secondary education, has become almost universal among the urban middle classes. The other socio-economic classes, however, have limited access to such education.

Types of Middle-Level Education

Most Latin American countries have two types of secondary education: the continuation and equivalent of classic academic education which leads to the university, and the various kinds of vocational and technical schools, aimed at preparing students for the industrial and agricultural areas as well as for various crafts.

The various forms of vocational training clearly belong to the secondary educational field. It should be pointed out, however, that this conclusion may misrepresent educational reality by being too optimistic. In a number of Latin American educational systems a pupil is not required to have completed elementary schooling in order to be admitted to vocational training. This fact, in addition to the very elementary character of the education provided in most vocational schools, casts doubt upon the extent to which much of vocational training should be considered as secondary level. On the other hand, in some countries a student must complete elementary school to qualify for vocational training. In such countries vocational education very often includes training analogous to that given in the classical secondary schools. Consequently, similar secondary school enrollment figures can have very different meanings. In general, however, the higher the level of economic development and consequent expansion of secondary education, the greater is the degree of genuine secondary education provided by vocational schools. In those poorer countries where there has been relatively little expansion of the educational system, technical and vocational education is usually inferior in content and in admission requirements to the academic high schools. It is often simply an extension of elementary education.

Table 4 indicates the proportion enrolled in the various types of secondary education in 1961. Given the problems of interpreting the meaning of vocational education, any analysis of this information is partly arbitrary. Nonetheless, one can still observe the relatively high percentages studying in the classic secondary education system. These percentages reflect very different situations. This observation is easier to understand if one considers that the lowest proportions are found both in the most developed country (Argentina) and in a very underdeveloped one (Nicaragua), while conversely, high percentages are to be found in countries as different as Uruguay and Haiti. In a country like Nicaragua, for example, only 11,000 of the 152,000 students in primary schools reach the secondary level, but one-fourth of these go to vocational schools. Academic high school education is clearly still a privi-

TABLE 4

Percentage of Secondary School Students to be Found in 1961

	General secondary school	Vocational schools	Training for school teaching
Argentina	25.3	50.5	24.2
Bolivia [1]	70.6	19.9	9.5
Brazil	73.4	18.9	7.7
Chile	70.1	27.3	2.6
Colombia	63.4	33.1	3.5
Costa Rica	80.2	15.3	4.5
Cuba	61.5	33.7	4.8
Dominican Rep	60.6	38.7	0.7
Ecuador	58.2	31.4	10.4
El Salvador	62.8	25.5	11.7
Guatemala	77.9	11.7	10.4
Haiti [1]	77.6	21.4	1.0
Honduras	78.7	14.0	7.3
Mexico [1]	54.3	32.7	13.0
Nicaragua [2]	53.5	27.4	19.1
Panama	67.4	30.4	2.2
Paraguay	55.9	15.5	28.6
Peru [1]	80.1	19.9	—
Uruguay	76.3	20.3	3.4
Venezuela	59.2	25.0	15.8

Source: From figures given by UNESCO. Statistical Yearbook 1963.
[1] 1960   [2] 1959

lege of the higher classes in that country, as is access to university. In Argentina, where the percentage of secondary students attending academic high schools is very high, the situation is quite different. With the exception of the *Colegio Nacional* and the *Liceo de Sennitas,* all the other secondary schools, including the vocational ones, grant a bachelor's degree or its equivalent which is accepted by the university. In other words, Argentina is at the other extreme in educational development. Argentina is a good example of a highly developed country which has a secondary level educational system composed of different types of schools whose curricula have many elements in common.

Haiti, on the other hand, is much more backward than Nicaragua. There are practically no industrial or vocational schools; the *liceo* still keeps all of its traditional prestige. No secondary education exists for the lower classes, all educational facilities are extremely limited. At another extreme, Uruguay, Argentina's neighbor, which is at a roughly comparable high economic level, presents a very particular case where the classic *liceo* has been expanded to such an extent that it actually performs the function of providing secondary education to all social classes. The greater access of middle and lower classes to secondary education has largely increased the enrollment of the traditional *liceo.* The enrollment in the vocational schools has increased very slowly; they are not considered the equivalents of academic high schools as they are in Argentina.

A study of the data bearing on the expansion of various types of secondary education suggests that the following phases of development are to be found in Latin America:

a. Countries where secondary education remains almost entirely of the classic type and is reserved for a very small minority (Haiti, Honduras, Guatemala). A "very small minority" does not necessarily mean the upper class, for it is often entirely composed of urban middle-class children who are the only ones with access to secondary education. What is significant, however, is not only that education is accessible to the urban middle class, but that this class is a small proportion of the population.

b. Countries where secondary education is reserved for a minority, meaning an "upper class," but where a type of vocational education, required by commerce and industry, is also slowly developing. In these countries (Dominican Republic, Nicaragua) the vocational education available increases the separation between classes.

c. Countries with a somewhat greater degree of educational development than the first two which includes a relatively large number of vocational and academic secondary schools (Ecuador, Mexico, Cuba, El Salvador, Paraguay).

d. Countries with a relatively high level of educational development, but predominantly academic secondary education (Brazil).

e. Countries with a considerable level of educational development in which secondary education enrollment reaches not only into the urban middle class, but also includes a small proportion of the working class given the large percentage attending technical and vocational schools (Venezuela, Chile, Panama).

f. Countries with higher percentages than those in the first five groups, but where academic education has been constantly expanding rather than vocational education, while the latter remains lower in status and achievement. Class distinctions between types of schools have largely lost their importance since lower-middle-class and working-class children are able to obtain academic schooling (Uruguay, Costa Rica).

g. Countries where secondary education is not only accessible to all the classes, but has also developed at the same rate in both types of schools. In such countries vocational schools are considered as valuable as the secondary schools and access to university is open to students from both institutions (Argentina).

With the exception of a few unusual cases, vocational education plays a very limited role in all of these groups, compared to its role in more developed countries, where secondary education is similarly differentiated. In fact, the data for vocational education overestimate the number of people who are receiving formal preparation for employment in the secondary (industrial) sector of the economy. These enrollment figures include not only students receiving training for industry and skilled crafts, but also those learning housekeeping and secretarial skills. In Uruguay, for example, not only is the registration in vocational schools low—only 20 per cent of those in high school—but only one-half of the registered vocational students are taking industrial training courses.

Furthermore, the statistics for vocational and technical education for almost all the Latin American countries include a rather large proportion studying what are commonly known as business training courses, consisting of preparation for bureaucratic office work such as typing, operating office machines, secretarial work, elementary principles of bookkeeping, etc. Business training and similar technical instruction have two characteristics in common: a short number of years of training and a very minimum prerequisites. Business instruction is, then, a kind of intermediate level between the classical and the technical vocational. In the less developed countries with secondary school systems, the students of business training schools are most likely to come from the lower ranks of the middle classes, while in the more developed countries a large number of such pupils belong to the upper ranks of the working classes. These business schools also serve as "second chance" schools to students from the middle classes, who have previously failed in an academic high school. A survey carried out in Montevideo (discussed later) indicates that a large percentage of the sons of lower level white-collar employees drop out of high school at the end of the first year because of bad grades. Since going to a vocational technical school involves preparing for a manual job with its consequent down-grading in social status, a large number of these lower-middle-class drop-outs go to business school where they are trained for a white-collar job. Thus, a business or commercial school education must be clearly distinguished from the technical school.

A second characteristic which strongly limits the significance of any general comparison between the enrollment figures of academic vocational schools is the difference in their rates of drop-outs. In Chile and Uruguay, for example, drop-outs are generally twice as numerous in vocational-technical or industrial schools as they are in academic schools. Since in almost all the countries, the drop-out percentage is greatest during the first year, a large part of the enrollment statistics is meaningless. Comparatively few students attend the technical schools long enough for this education to be of any significance. These are not academic considerations. Unless Latin American countries resign themselves to operate with very low levels of efficiency and productivity, they must begin to train their manpower to the highest possible degree in order to permit a fast absorption of modern technology. Such absorption implies much greater difficulties for contemporary developing countries than was encountered in the first stages of development of today's developed countries, when they were at a low technological level. The gap between the more and less advanced countries has grown over the centuries.

The problem, therefore, appears to be quite complex. The basic question appears to be as follows: everywhere the requirements of modern technology indicate the necessity of extending general, non-specialized education at the post-elementary level. One of Latin America's basic deficiencies consists not only in the fact that technical education has not developed sufficiently, but also in something more serious, that there has been little or no development of a general secondary education which could later be diversified.

In almost all of Latin America an analysis of the curricula of the technical schools would show that they train chiefly craftsmen or skilled laborers, rather than act as preparation for modern industry. Some European countries also face this problem. In general, we can observe that in countries in the process of development with a good level of absorption of modern technology and rapid growth, the traditional concept of technical occupations is changing. Schelsky says teaching how to handle technology generally is becoming almost more important than a specialized vocational training.[2]

This kind of training in flexibility should involve a common post-elementary level of two or three years to provide the intellectual attitudes necessary to adjust to changes in required skills. Two problems arise in this connection: a) practically none of the countries have reached the point of universal elementary education, and most of them still have large percentages of illiterates. In the face of these facts, it does not seem very realistic to insist upon a common curriculum for secondary schools; b) in those countries which have introduced courses with serious intellectual content in the curricula of the technical schools, a number of difficulties have arisen. Such work clashes with the expectations of the students or their parents. Some are looking for quick preparation for employment, either because they come from lower economic strata and are dependent on financial aid for their children. Others dislike the work because they have gone to technical schools after failing the requirements for regular high school. In addition, in view of the fact that the technical school instruction is planned for occupations considered suitable for the lower classes, the students are mostly from underprivileged backgrounds and seldom have the socio-cultural background which the intellectual content of the courses requires.

Thus, various arguments can be made against a broad general education for vocational school students. Despite the validity of these arguments, one cannot ignore the basic fact that this solution serves to keep the lower social groups in their place by limiting them to an education appropriate for lower-class life, and blocking them from any access to higher education. This point of view requires that society resign itself to preserving a traditional lower-class labor group incapable of improving its social position. Since economic development produces change in the occupational structure of society, persons educated in the traditional vocational school will lack the necessary flexibility to adapt themselves to the changes. It is thus no exaggeration to say that technical education, as it is generally known in Latin America, condemns the skilled laborer to unemployment, in the event of rapid economic growth. Conversely, it forces the new industry to train a labor-force within the factory, an expensive process. Basically we must recognize that a series of factors—concern for social prestige among the middle class, cultural backwardness in the lower class, etc.—intertwine to make vocational and technical education an inefficient type of secondary education, thereby reducing its possible contribution to the socioeconomic development of Latin America. And beyond the problem of content one must consider the fact that technical education reaches relatively few persons.

All of this means that the preparation of prospective modernizing elites remains in Latin America almost entirely in the realm of general academic education, which recruits its students from the middle and upper classes. It is important to understand that with the exception of Ecuador, Venezuela, and Chile, where the various branches of secondary education have been increasing in approximately the same proportion, in all the other countries the secondary educational system has expanded mainly through the academic schools (see Table 5). In addition, the proportion of students enrolled in vocational and technical schools is decreasing, while secondary education in general is expanding rather rapidly. Whether vocational and technical schools are being converted to give secondary education of a general type, or whether they simply fail to receive students attracted by the latter, the result is the same. In order to understand the significance of these changes, a more detailed analysis of secondary education is necessary.

The Curriculum in Academic High Schools

Although a thorough analysis of academic education is beyond the scope of this study, a brief discussion of the curriculum should consider the place of the sciences. Table 6 shows the percentages of course hours as compared to the total number of class hours by country. These data can be very misleading. For example, the introduction of science, often the result of imitating other countries, may not be accompanied by the necessary laboratories and equipment for effective training. However, even though the available information is rough and merely approximate, it is a valuable indicator of the concerns of different school systems.

Although there are considerable differences among the countries, classical education is clearly still of considerable importance as Table 6 indicates. This does not simply reflect the orientations of the schools; in Latin America the extra-curricular socialization processes

TABLE 5

Indices of the Growth of Secondary Education and
Its Various Divisions. Base 100 for the First
Year Indicated for Each Country

COUNTRIES	TOTAL SECONDARY EDUCATION	GENERAL SECONDARY EDUCATION	VOCATIONAL SECONDARY EDUCATION	SCHOOL TEACHERS
Argentina (1955–61)	123	130	112	143
Brazil (1955–61)	174	174	173	170
Chile (1955–61)	146	148	151	96
Colombia (1955–61)	187	202	192	75
Costa Rica (1955–61)	177	176	187	157
Cuba (1955–61)	231	230	280	105
Dominican Rep. (1954–61)	265	321	212	103
Ecuador (1955–61)	183	173	206	180
El Salvador (1955–61)	182	184	152	298
Guatemala (1954–61)	152	238	45	153
Haiti (1955–60)	127	128	127	91
Honduras (1956–61)	156	607	42	41
Mexico (1955–60)	174	194	138	220
Nicaragua (1950–59)	145	162	85	531
Panama (1955–61)	167	181	161	58
Paraguay (1955–61)	170	310	54	236
Peru (1955–61)	177	173	196	—
Uruguay (1955–61)	118	130	109	81
Venezuela (1955–61)	320	275	375	516

Sources: From UNESCO figures. *Statistical Yearbook 1963.*

also tend to be much more favorable to literature and other traditional studies. In any case as a study of students in various university colleges and departments also demonstrates, in the academic secondary schools the sciences play a very small part in the instruction of the students.[*] The additional difficulties posed by unqualified science teachers and use of poor teaching techniques mean that the prospective elites of Latin America are poorly prepared to accept a rigorous scientific outlook in university.

TABLE 6

Percentage of Time (Hours) Devoted to the Sciences
as Compared to the Total of General Secondary School Time
for Several Latin American Countries

COUNTRIES	PERCENTAGE
Bolivia	25.9
Brazil	18.9
Chile	30.4
Colombia	28
Costa Rica	23.4
Ecuador	36.9–32.9
Honduras	28.2
Mexico	35.1
Nicaragua	35.7
Paraguay	37.2
Peru	21.8
Uruguay	43.1

Sources: World Survey of Education. Secondary Education. Schedules sent by each country. In the case of Ecuador, the first percentage corresponds to secondary modern, the second, to classical.

Academic Education, Social Stratification, and Values

It is very easy to understand that in countries where secondary education reaches less than 20 per cent of the school-age population, it is most likely to benefit the upper class and the higher and middle sections of the middle class. Those in the lower middle class and upper lower class are rarely affected, and then only the urban dwellers. When the secondary school percentage falls below 10 per cent, only those from the highest urban strata receive secondary education as a matter of course. Enrollment figures must reach at least 30 per cent of the age cohort before many in the lower middle and the upper lower class reach the secondary schools.

These statistical differences result in a great variety of situations. The more limited the development of secondary education, the more likely that enrollment in academic education is made up of upper- and upper-middle-class children. For the rest of the middle class, technical or vocational education where it exists represents the maximum formal education available, and facilitates some social mobility.

The expansion of secondary education does not take place in a linear manner. There is a relative distribution of growth among academic, technical, and commercial education on a variety of non-economic factors, which inhibit the relative growth of needed vocational education. The most important of these is the difference in the social prestige attached to the various types of secondary education. Academic education, which permits university entrance, has of course greater traditional prestige; however, since it opens the door to higher occupational and social roles than the others, mobility aspirations reinforce tradition.

When the secondary educational system reaches an enrollment level of around 25 per cent of the group old enough to attend, those in charge of the educational system often seek to redefine the relations among the different systems of education. There seems to be a tendency for teachers in the countries with large high school systems to believe: that all forms of secondary education should be equal; that each system should have a terminal objective in the sense that each should provide a complete training which enables the graduate to find his place, rather than viewing it as a gateway to the university (expressed in a different way, secondary education should not be conceived of as an instrument *for*, but, to a certain extent, as an instrument in *itself*); that congruently with these principles all occupations should be considered of equal dignity. Intellectuals in such countries have written eloquently about the worth of manual labor. On the other hand, the great majority of parents and students continue to believe that the best form of secondary education is the general or classical high school, because it takes one to the threshold of the university. Not all can cross that threshold; many, considering their socio-economic situation, have little possibility of doing so. However, almost all behave as if they entertain the hope that, in spite of all obstacles, they will attain their goal. In actual fact, high school education is terminal for the great majority. But even if the high expectations are not fulfilled, the academic school fulfills a lesser, though socially acceptable, function of opening the doors to bureaucratic positions. Either way, it is identified with non-manual work. Technical education continues to be viewed as an inferior form of secondary school, because it has been linked to manual labor. The business school is looked upon as an intermediate form, because it is a path to lower white-collar work. The accent is on status. Parents seem to care little about the quality of the education which their children may receive, but they know and feel very deeply about the status correlates of different school systems.

For the upper-middle-class sectors, high grade civil servants, members of the liberal professions, etc., a minimum requirement for maintenance of family status is completion of academic high school (general secondary school), generally universal among them. On the other hand, those in lower white-collar positions can rarely afford to give their sons many years of schooling without heavy sacrifices, only justified for those who are particularly brilliant. Those sons who fail or show only mediocre scholastic propensities are taken out of high school often at the end of the first year and put in a school where they will be prepared for specific employment. This usually means courses in public or private schools of the type which are generally grouped under the term "business schools." Thus, they can expect to hold business jobs similar to those of their fathers. There is another factor which helps in this objective: the petty employee, in Latin American countries where personal relations are very important, usually has what may be called a small capital investment in such relations. This fact, together with the business preparatory courses taken by his son, enables him to place his offspring satisfactorily.

This latter particularistic factor may explain certain paradoxical differences between the school behavior of the children of manual and lower white-collar workers. In a survey of the academic secondary students in Montevideo,[4] the percentage of laborers' sons who dropped out between the first and second years was less than among the sons of lower white-collar workers. Although further study is necessary, it would appear that workmen who have succeeded in getting their sons to the secondary academic level try to keep them there as long as possible even if their scholastic record is low. In other words, the laboring class parents resist accepting the scholastic failure of their sons more than the office employee parents do. The difference may be related to the fact that employee fathers have personal relationships which enable them to nourish well-founded hopes of finding a place for their sons, even if the latter have not been very successful in their studies, while laboring fathers generally have no influential connections. Completion of high school is, therefore, the only way in which the barrier of manual labor can be broken. For most working-class parents, allowing their son to drop out of secondary school means giving up all hope of mobility. The more developed a country the greater the possibility that failure to complete academic education will lead to downward mobility even among the upper ranks of the middle classes.

There are two major points of great frustration in the secondary educational system. One occurs at the end of high school education for those who get that far but cannot for various reasons go on to university. Unfortunately, there are no studies indicating the reactions of this group. The other major frustration occurs when the student fails in the first or second year of academic high school. For the better situated part of the middle classes, failure at this point is met by as many repetitions of courses as necessary in order to continue. Conversely, as we have seen, the lower ranks of the middle classes will rely on business training and the personal relationships which they may have in order to maintain the status of their sons.

What occurs in the case of ambitious working-class fathers and their children, particularly in the more developed countries with larger secondary systems? It might be expected that serious conflicts and social tensions would arise among them, that they would perceive the higher rate of failure of their children as a result of systematic discrimination. This, however, does not occur. The few surveys which are available show that working-class parents accept the failure of their children as individual cases, not as a consequence of the social system. They say that their children failed in the academic school because they were just not smart or did not study hard enough. The fact that some laborers' children are able to carry on with their schooling is pointed to as a confirmation of that fact.

How can we explain this acceptance of failure as being individual, not a result of the system? Existing surveys do not enable us to answer this question with any assurance. One possible hypothesis is that the working classes internalize the values and expectations of the middle classes. Another hypothesis, which does not exclude the former, is that the fact that working-class children even succeed in reaching high school is appreciated greatly by their parents; and once this occurs, the rest is perceived as the individual's merit or lack of merit. Admission to academic high school is probably conceived of as a chance offered by the social system, and it is the student's own fault if he does not profit by it. Further studies would be necessary in order to answer these questions.

If Latin American countries continue to develop economically, the wealthier ones will be confronted with the dilemma that many European countries have already encountered or are now facing: how to have several branches of secondary education which do not have sharply different prestige ratings. If it is desired that all branches develop the same prestige, the differences between them must be consistently reduced,[5] or a Uruguayan situation will develop elsewhere; i.e. where the entire middle class conceives of academic education as being their children's normal future, and where the working class has increasingly similar aspirations. Increasingly, the Uruguayan upper working class sends its children to academic education and looks upon technical and vocational education as being an inferior kind of medium-level education.[6]

Thus, at the secondary school level the Latin American countries encounter an overwhelming preference for traditional occupations and a very scanty inclination among students for scientific and technical careers. The terms of the problem are rather similar. A developing country needs to encourage vocational or technical training, just as at university level a greater percentage ought to prepare for scientific and technical careers. But insofar as the present economic structure is concerned, the market facts are quite different. Young people completing secondary technical education do not find employment opportunities; or if they do find them, they are not much better off than young people who have not received that form of education. A considerable number of graduates of Latin American agricultural schools, for example, end up working in other tasks because the stagnant system of agriculture, which is only very slowly being modernized, does not need their services. Opportunities being equal, it is logical that parents should decide on studies associated with the greater traditional prestige.

This leads us to stress the fact that the scale of values is deeply rooted in the real structure of occupational opportunities afforded in Latin America. It would be erroneous to think that it is nothing but the product of a tradition which maintains itself when the actual situation on which it was based has ceased to exist. On the contrary, the traditional scale of values encourages certain studies that lead to definite activities; experience shows that these are still the most open, the best compensated, and carry the greatest social prestige.

It is not, therefore, the mere inheritance of certain values that maintains the structure in almost unchanged form. To a great extent, it is the structure that supports the traditional system of values. The scale of values is actually not as static as it is sometimes thought to be. When there are structural changes favorable to certain activities, when these activities are in strong demand and their level of compensation rises, those activities, as is logical, rise rapidly in the scale of social prestige. A recent example in Latin America are the changes in the profession of accountancy. A number of factors, which cannot be analysed in detail, have very greatly increased the importance, the demand for, and the compensation of that profession. As a result, the economics departments of the universities have very greatly increased their enrollments, and the social prestige of the profession has come close to equaling that of the professions of law and medicine. It has clearly surpassed that of the veterinarian and the agronomist which were recently much more prestigious. This example, and many others which could be cited for other countries, shows that structural changes precede a change in the scale of values and end up by producing profound modifications in that system. This is true even in the case of gradual transformations such as those we are considering here. It is obvious that revolutionary changes have a greater and more rapid effect.

At the maximum level of development of secondary education so far reached in Latin America, selection takes place under conditions which increasingly approach those which seem to be implied in the functioning of a real democracy, one of the professed goals of the society. But if the question of selection then becomes less important, issues of distribution and its compatibility with the requirements for economic and social development take on considerable importance.

These considerations lead us into a complex problem. A very restricted selection implies a considerable waste of society's potential. All contemporary studies tend to demonstrate the importance of adequately utilizing human resources from the economic and social development point of view. A system of limited secondary education would thus appear economically disfunctional regardless of whether it is in contradiction with real democratic principles.

The selection of elites from within the limited circle of those few groups which can achieve an academic education obviously is very biased against the lower strata. Differential drop-out rates mean that the percentage of upper-class background is much greater among graduates than entrants. In a survey previously cited of a representative sample of public high school (*liceo*) pupils in Montevideo, the lower classes accounted for 27 per cent of the first year class and only 13 per cent in the fourth (and last) year. As in other countries, the grades measuring the student's performance show a strong correlation with socio-economic background.

This example is presented because such differences occur in the biggest city of a country where academic education has reached its maximum expansion in Latin America. It may be inferred that in countries where the percentage admitted are much lower, graduation from secondary school is much more strictly limited to the upper and upper-middle classes.

These considerations are linked with the question of social mobility. For the traditional upper classes of Latin America, whose power is based on the ownership of land, and even for other sectors of the upper class, passage through an academic school (usually a private school) is normal, but it does not constitute an indispensable prerequisite for maintaining their status or for exercising the roles which society reserves for them. On the other hand, development of secondary education is bound up in a very peculiar way to the expansion of the middle classes. In Uruguay and Argentina, more than 35 per cent of the population belongs to the upper and middle classes, as compared to only 3 per cent in Haiti and 4 per cent in Honduras. In Costa Rica, where there is a very high percentage of secondary pupils, more than 20 per cent of the population belongs to the middle classes.[7]

It would be wrong, therefore, to measure the adequacy of a national system of secondary education in the training of elites only by reference to its size and continued rate of growth. It is essential to study the relationships of the school system to social stratification.

Absorption and Training of Elites

It is difficult, in an essay of this kind, to summarize the variety of situations occurring in Latin America, to maintain the necessary balance between easy generalizations and excessive detail, and to keep the overall perspective in mind.

To understand the function of secondary education in the training of elites in Latin America, it must be emphasized that in many countries and over a long period of time, it has been the highest institutional stage of the educational system. In many countries, universities finally appeared to close a void which some elements of the upper classes had filled by sending their sons to study abroad. But even after they appeared, access to the universities was, and is, so limited in most countries that academic education must indeed be considered the maximum possible schooling, except for a very small minority. Strategic roles in society do not always require university training, nor could the universities, being so restricted, produce the necessary numbers to fill them. As a consequence, a good portion of leaders were, and are, being trained in the academic schools. It must be kept in mind that if traditional academic education is conceived of as the antechamber to the university, it is also an institution of general high culture. It has given generations of leaders a fairly homogeneous outlook on the world and has contributed to the establishment of a common elite ideology.

In the effort to transmit a general culture, superficiality of technical training may be compensated by an overall vision of key problems. This is probably functional to countries in the first stages of their development. A large proportion of Latin American political elites have little formal education other than the secondary education. The academic high school does possess the virtues of the classic humanistic training. The so-called classical education was sufficient to create adequate leaders for European society in the past, men who have a good general vision of problems and the possibility of converting ideologies into principles of effective action. It is doubtful, however, that such training remains adequate to meet Latin America's requirements in the world of today and the future.

As academic education is universalized, it is somehow linked with the democratization of society, and even in Latin America it is accompanied by greater pluralism and a wider division of power. Academic education gradually has ceased to be chiefly the means to enter a university. If in the past one of its main functions, apart from the latter, was to give the maximum available education to those in the highest social positions, it now fulfills the same function for those in secondary level positions and also provides the opportunity for ascending groups to reach the highest positions in society. As new groups emerge and acquire increasing importance in the power structure, their elites are recruited partly from the academically educated. Imaz shows that in Argentina only slightly more than one-third of the elites in general, and a little over one-fourth of the business executives have a university education. A fair portion of the others only have a secondary school education.[8]

The persistence of traditional education planning is an important indication of the influence that those elements of the middle classes who first benefited from academic education still exercise. By prolonging the life of a declining culture, they are not only trying to maintain, consciously or not, a system of stratification, but they also disseminate in other social groups values which help to conserve traditional structures. Since these values are often in conflict with the interests of the new emerging groups, they tend to produce a disparity of culture and ideology which is certainly socially dysfunctional given the fact that a drastic and accelerated break with tradition is wanted.

The expansion of education takes on the character of the increment in new groups attaining the ranks of the privileged. Each of them in turn "displays an ambiguous attitude toward further extension of educational opportunities."[9] One of the subtler aspects of this ambiguity is that this extension seems conditional on the new arrivals accepting the ideology and the values of the previous group. This continued dissemination explains a fact often noted in other countries, which can be verified in an analysis of the contents of academic books. Academic school textbooks persist in painting a picture of a society essentially dependent on the landowner and farmer, in Uruguay and Argentina, in spite of the fact that industry contributes much more to national income than agriculture and that the manpower involved is larger in numbers for the former than in the latter.

The functions of secondary education, especially that of regular academic high schools in the selection of elites, their patterns of training, and the rate of absorption of new elites vary considerably from country to country. Their main variations correspond to the various stages of development attained by Latin American societies. Each of them resolves the problem in a different way, but they seem to have some features in common: a) the selection is done on a very restricted basis, and although this characteristic is rapidly changing due to an accelerated expansion of the system, it is still very far from anything which may be called equalitarian; b) change of the educational content seems to be much slower than expansion of the system. In other words, even though new elites emerge from the secondary system, their training has changed but little in most countries.

It should be noted, however, that some important elites have neither university nor secondary education This is the case, for example, of large numbers of industrial executives in many Latin American countries. These or other groups lacking secondary education can be, and are in many cases, much more dynamic and innovative than the well-educated.

While it seems reasonable to believe that academic education has contributed in the past and still contributes in the present to the preparation of the key elites, nothing guarantees that it will continue this function in the near future. It has and undoubtedly will have an important role in social mobility. Still, one can wonder up to what point it will have a positive influence on the training of new elites. Latin American leaders find themselves confronted simultaneously with the tasks of organizing their countries, of creating, in many cases, certain minimum structures for social unity, of arranging conditions suitable for competition with highly developed countries, and of overcoming their condition of dependency. Their situation is totally different from that of leaders in already developed countries. Academic education as the main instrument for the training of elites tends to prepare them in a spirit that can scarcely be termed modern. The pace of change, therefore, whether measured in terms of increased enrollment percentages or in modernization of the total secondary system, is still much too slow.

Notes

1. It is to a great extent inspired by Chapters IV to VII in George Parkyn (ed.), *World Survey of Education, Secondary Education* (Paris: UNESCO, 1961).
2. H. Schelsky, "Technical Change and Educational Consequences," in A. H. Halsey, Jean Floud, and C. A. Anderson, *Education, Economy and Society* (New York: Free Press of Glencoe, 1965), p. 35.
3. See the excellent article by Steven Dedijer, "Underdeveloped Science in Underdeveloped Countries," *Minerva,* 2 (Autumn, 1963), pp. 61–81.
4. A. M. Grompone, Germán Rama, Aldo Solari, Elida Tuana, *Investigación Sobre Los Alumnos de Los Liceos de Montevideo* (unpublished.)
5. A classic example of this problem is analysed by Olive Banks, *Parity*

and *Prestige in English Secondary Education* (London: Routledge and Kegan Paul, 1955).

6. Germán Rama, *Grupos Sociales y Enseñanza secundaria* (Montevideo: Editorial Arca, 1964).

7. Gino Germani, "The Strategy of Fostering Social Mobility," in Egbert de Vries and José Medina Echavarría, *Social Aspects of Development in Latin America*, I (Paris: UNESCO, 1963), pp. 221–230.

8. José Luis de Imaz, *Los que Mandan* (Buenos Aires: Eudeba, 1964).

9. C. Arnold Anderson and Philip J. Foster, "Discrimination and Equality in Education," *Sociology of Education*, 38 (1964), pp. 1–18.

15

Education and Development:
Opinions of Secondary Schoolteachers

APARECIDA JOLY GOUVEIA

It may seem curious to report in detail on a study of the background and opinions of secondary schoolteachers in a book devoted to the characteristics of the Latin American elite. Secondary schoolteachers, although normally well-educated, are rarely thought of as members of the elite in economically developed societies. There, any consideration of the role of the educational system in forming a nation's elite is us-

This work is based on data obtained for the project "Secondary Education and the Socio-Economic Structure," which originated at the Center of Comparative Education of the University of Chicago, and is being carried out in Brazil with Carnegie Foundation funds under the auspices of the National Institute for Pedagogical Studies of the Ministry of Education and Culture in accordance with arrangements effected by Prof. Robert J. Havighurst, of the University of Chicago. The project covers the states of Rio Grande do Sul, São Paulo, Pernambuco, Ceará, and Pará. In this study, however, no data relating to Pernambuco are included.

Of inestimable value in conducting the survey was the assistance of the Professor Queiroz Filho Regional Educational Research Centre at São Paulo. The following institutions also co-operated, chiefly in collecting and processing data: The Department of School Administration and Comparative Education of the College of Philosophy of the University of São Paulo, the Regional Educational Research Centre of Rio Grande do Sul, the Department of Sociology of the University of Rio Grande do Sul, the Educational Research and Guidance Centre of the State Department of Education and Culture of Rio Grande do Sul, the Department of Education of the College of Philosophy of the University of Ceará, the College of Philosophy of the University of Pará and the State Department of Education and Culture of Pará.

The work in the individual states was supervised by Professors Ivan Dall'Igna Osorio, José Augusto Dias, Levy P. Cruz, Eduardo Diatay Bezerra de Menezes, and Ivone Vieira da Costa.

ually limited to an analysis of universities. The situation, however, is quite different in most underdeveloped nations. A relatively tiny proportion of those of university age actually attend such institutions, and a much smaller fraction receive degrees. University faculties constitute a virtual handful of persons, albeit extremely influential. In practice, therefore, the secondary school system plays some of the same role in preparing individuals to occupy middle-class positions that the university does in North America and Europe. Thus secondary schoolteachers are an extremely important stratum. Knowledge about their attitudes and values, about differences among them, should tell us much about prospects for social modernization in forthcoming generations of graduates.

Secondary schoolteachers constitute the largest professional group in Brazil who have attained a university level of education.[1] Recent statistics indicate that in 1962 the number of persons in Brazil engaged in teaching at the secondary level was approximately one hundred thousand.[2]

The numerical importance of secondary-level teachers should, however, be evaluated not merely in terms of its present quantitative aspect but most of all in relation to its potential growth. Figures showing an increase in school matriculation, which are generally high as a simple consequence of population growth and of changes in the rural and urban composition of the population, are found to be especially high in medium-level education. In the period from 1950 to 1960, while enrollments increased by 86 per cent in higher education and by 64 per cent in elementary education, secondary school enrollments more than doubled, showing an increase of 118 per cent.[3] This would seem to indicate that the economic activities now expanding in the secondary (industrial) and most of all in the tertiary (service) sectors, are already beginning to widen the demand for education at the secondary level.[4] It is therefore to be anticipated that increasing economic pressures for greater productivity and efficiency will make secondary education an indispensable requirement for a growing number of jobs. Everything thus indicates that enrollment in secondary schools will continue to expand even more, and, in consequence, the number of persons recruited to teach in them will also increase.

This leaves us to consider the type of individuals now teaching at the secondary level and to examine the characteristics which mark the expansion of their profession.

The material presented in this paper will supply some information concerning the composition of the secondary school teaching body in different parts of Brazil. The main object of this study is, however, to give a certain picture of the values and attitudes of the persons in the profession. The data used for that purpose are derived from a sample survey study conducted in four Brazilian states: São Paulo, Rio Grande do Sul, Ceará, and Pará. Not all of the Brazilian states are represented in this sampling, but those which are included are characterized by large variations in their economic development and in their school situation.

Although the poll covered teachers in all the various branches of Brazilian secondary education—academic, normal, commercial, industrial, and agricultural—we concentrate here on teachers of the academic secondary curricula. Since the study would have been excessively long if we dealt with all five branches, we will examine only the most numerous group. In fact, not only in the states included in our study but in Brazil as a whole, the teachers of academic courses represent almost two-thirds of all teachers in secondary schools.[5] Besides constituting the largest numerical group, the academic school instructors enjoy the greatest prestige among the various branches and will probably set the standards of development for the other types of secondary teachers.[6]

I. Some Characteristics of Academic Schoolteachers

Sex. In the states covered by our study, as for Brazil in general, statistics show that approximately one-half of the secondary schoolteachers are women. This proportion is larger than it was in 1943, when women teachers represented only one-third of the total number of persons engaged in secondary teaching.

Age. The data indicate that secondary schoolteachers constitute a comparatively young group of adults, about three-fourths of them being under 40 in the states of São Paulo, Rio Grande do Sul, and Ceará, with an even greater proportion under 40 in the state of Pará. With the exception of this latter state, where analysis shows a considerable incidence of teacher turnover,[7] the explanation of this age profile is to be found chiefly in the history of expansion of professional groups, as shown by the indicators given in Table I. The high rate of increase in secondary school enrollment in the last twenty years has brought in

TABLE I

Increase in Number of Secondary Schoolteachers

YEAR	Expressed in numerical indexes of increase STATE			
	RIO GRANDE DO SUL	SÃO PAULO	CEARÁ	PARÁ
1943	100	100	100	100
1953	232	196	204	262
1962	600	322	598	383

Sources: O Ensino no Brasil and Sinopse Estatística do Ensino Médio, published by the Statistical Service of the Ministry of Education and Culture, Rio de Janeiro.

many new teachers with a resulting younger group as shown in Table II.

Degree of Education. The rapid expansion in the number of teachers also explains, at least partly, the mediocre level of their formal education. In spite of the increased number of university courses available, especially in the colleges or faculties of philosophy (arts and sciences), the institutionalized channels of access to employment as a secondary schoolteacher, the proportion of teachers having university de-

TABLE II

Age Groupings of Secondary Schoolteachers

AGE	Percentage in each specified age group STATE			
	RIO GRANDE DO SUL	SÃO PAULO	CEARÁ	PARÁ
Under 30 years	33.5	33.1	33.8	53.1
30 to 39 years	38.5	37.7	36.9	31.8
40 or over	28.0	29.2	29.3	15.1
TOTALS:	100.0	100.0	100.0	100.0
	(556)	(321)	(222)	(132)

Note: In this table, as also in the following tables, the figures in parentheses represent the total number of teachers serving as the basis for respective percentages. The numbers of teachers not giving any answer—who were of course not the same in number for every question—are not included in these totals.

Source: Sample Survey Data for the project, *Secondary Education and the Socio-Economic Structure* (see p. 484).

grees or diplomas of a corresponding level has not increased significantly in the last twenty years. Of the entire group of secondary schoolteachers in 1963, approximately three-fourths in Rio Grande do Sul,
two-thirds in São Paulo, and barely half in the states of Ceará and
Pará, had completed studies at the university level.[8] The proportion
has actually decreased in the state of Ceará, as shown by the percentages in Table III where comparisons can be made among the three
generations included in the analysis, namely older, intermediate, and
younger, indicating respectively those who have taught in secondary
schools for twenty or more years, for from ten to nineteen years, and
for less than ten years.

Table III also offers information relating to the educational level of
teachers of both sexes. In the most developed states—São Paulo and
Rio Grande do Sul—there is no significant difference in the educational level of men and women teachers.[9] Yet if we compare different
generations, we find that this equality between the sexes does not exist

TABLE III

Education of Secondary Teachers and Length of Time Taught

STATE	Percentage having a university level education Length of time already spent in teaching			
	LESS THAN 10 YEARS	10 TO 19 YEARS	20 YEARS OR MORE	TOTAL
Rio Grande do Sul				
Men teachers	76.9 (139)	82.1 (62)	85.7 (42)	79.9 (243)
Women teachers	77.1 (205)	80.0 (50)	52.0 (25)	75.3 (280)
TOTAL:	77.1 (344)	81.3 (112)	73.0 (67)	77.4 (523)
São Paulo				
Men teachers	66.2 (71)	60.0 (45)	60.0 (25)	63.1 (141)
Women teachers	67.7 (99)	75.0 (40)	36.7 (11)	67.3 (150)
TOTAL:	67.0 (170)	67.3 (85)	52.8 (36)	65.4 (291)
Ceará				
Men teachers	62.7 (81)	88.8 (27)	95.7 (23)	73.2 (131)
Women teachers	21.1 (52)	47.0 (17)	* (6)	26.6 (75)
TOTAL:	45.9 (133)	72.6 (44)	79.4 (29)	56.3 (206)
Pará				
Men teachers	57.3 (56)	83.3 (12)	* (3)	60.6 (71)
Women teachers	44.5 (36)	* (8)	* (5)	40.8 (49)
TOTAL:	52.3 (92)	65.0 (20)	* (8)	52.5 (120)

* Percentage not calculated because the total number of teachers was less than ten.
Source: Sample Survey Data.

among the older teachers in the state of Rio Grande do Sul, where there are comparatively more men than women with a higher education. More than three-fourths of the men have a college degree as contrasted with only about one-half of the women. In the next generation, that of the teachers who began their work between 1944 and 1953, the proportion of women teachers holding college degrees rises to 80 per cent, and from then on there is no longer any educational difference between men and women teachers. A comparable situation, for similar periods of time, appears to prevail in the state of São Paulo.

Contrary to the pattern in the more developed southern states, women teachers have less education than men teachers in the northern states of Ceará and Pará. This would seem to indicate some direct correlation between the degree of economic development and the access of women to educational opportunities. Within a few years, however, women teachers will be just as highly educated as men teachers in these states as in the south.

II. Values

RELIGIOUS BEHAVIOR AND THE IMPORTANCE ATTRIBUTED TO RELIGION

Although religious affiliation and belief remain important in many highly developed countries, evidence drawn from various less industrialized societies suggests that commitment to traditional religion is a good indicator of the strength of traditionalism in the society. The more involved in religious belief and practice, the less likely is an individual to favor the orientations which are presumably conducive to, or part of, the process of social modernization. In general, the better educated tend to be more modern, and less religious. An examination of the religious commitments of the secondary teachers, therefore, should tell us much about social development in Brazil.

Only a very small proportion of teachers interviewed, less than 10 per cent, are irreligious. And, as was perhaps to be expected, that proportion is still small among women teachers (Table IV). A more accurate idea can be obtained, however, with regard to the religious behavior of secondary schoolteachers if we examine the information provided about their observance of religious practices. More than half of the teachers attend "regularly" or "always try to attend religious services or worship." Here again, the men teachers, Rio Grande do Sul excepted, reveal themselves as being less religious than the women teachers (Table V).

TABLE IV
Religious Belief

| STATE | Percentage not having any religious belief | |
	MEN TEACHERS	WOMEN TEACHERS
Rio Grande do Sul	5.9 (253)	2.6 (304)
São Paulo	6.7 (149)	2.0 (164)
Ceará	7.5 (133)	0.0 (80)
Pará	1.4 (72)	1.8 (55)

Source: Sample Survey Data.

There are no significant differences in church attendance of men teachers living in different states, but among women, on the other hand, those of Ceará and Pará, the two less developed states, attend church much more faithfully than those in São Paulo and Rio Grande do Sul.

TABLE V
Attendance at Religious Services

| STATE | Percentage of secondary school-teachers who attend religious services "regularly" or who "always try to attend." | |
	MEN TEACHERS	WOMEN TEACHERS
Rio Grande do Sul	61.3 (253)	65.1 (304)
São Paulo	55.7 (149)	66.5 (164)
Ceará	55.8 (133)	83.9 (80)
Pará	54.2 (72)	83.7 (55)

Source: Sample Survey Data.

These facts would seem to indicate that the women are less independent from the pressure of the local cultural patterns than are the men. This conclusion is reinforced by the data about teachers in the capital and the interior in Rio Grande do Sul (Table VI). There is no significant difference in church-going between the men teachers of the capital and those of the interior, but among women teachers those of the interior are much more faithful than those of the capital.

In spite of the fact that a great majority of the teachers profess a religious belief—with few exceptions, Catholic—and that a large propor-

TABLE VI

Attendance at Religious Services by Secondary Schoolteachers of the State Capital and in the Rest of the State (the Interior)

	STATE OF RIO GRANDE DO SUL Percentage who attend religious services "regularly" or who "always try to attend."	
PLACE	MEN TEACHERS	WOMEN TEACHERS
Capital	57.0 (100)	48.6 (101)
Interior	64.1 (153)	73.5 (203)

tion attend "regularly" or "always try to attend" religious service, less than half of them consider it "essential" that the teacher should have a religious faith in order to teach well (Table VII).[10]

Some of the most devout and faithful participants in religious practices are apparently able to separate religion from their work (cf. Tables V and VII). These findings may reflect a tendency toward secularization which has been one of the concomitants of industrialization.[11]

In none of the four states, however, does the completely secularized group constitute a substantial part of the secondary school teaching

TABLE VII

Secularization of Teaching

STATE	Percentage who attribute to religion the degree of importance as specified				
	INDISPENSABLE	HELPFUL	DOES NOT MATTER	MAKES DIFFICULT OR PREVENTS	TOTAL (100%)
	MEN TEACHERS				
Rio Grande do Sul	43.3	39.1	14.2	3.4	(233)
São Paulo	37.4	36.7	25.3	0.6	(150)
Ceará	38.9	37.4	21.4	2.3	(131)
Pará	45.3	35.7	10.7	—	(75)
	WOMEN TEACHERS				
Rio Grande do Sul	53.8	30.9	14.3	1.0	(288)
São Paulo	37.7	39.5	21.6	1.2	(167)
Ceará	43.8	38.7	15.0	2.5	(80)
Pará	53.6	35.7	10.7	—	(57)

Source: Sample Survey Data.

body. On the contrary, if we add those who consider religion indispensable in teaching to those who feel religious belief to be a help, we find that a great majority of the teachers, three-fourths of them or more, consider religion to be a source of inspiration for teaching.

The percentages of those who believe religion indispensable in the different categories or types of towns or cities—capital city, large city, medium, or small town—reveal that the attitudes of the men teachers do not depend on the size of the town (Table VIII). However, among women teachers the percentage of those who believe in the paramount importance of religion decreases significantly as we go from the interior of the country to the capital, and from small towns to medium size and large ones in the interior itself. This reinforces the previous conclusion about attendance at religious services, that is women teachers are more sensitive to local values while men (at least those engaged in secondary school teaching) are more oriented to the influences which radiate from large urban centers.

TABLE VIII

Size of Town or City and Importance Attributed to Religion

| | STATE OF RIO GRANDE DO SUL | |
| | Percentage who consider religious belief indispensable for good performance in secondary school teaching | |
PLACE	MEN TEACHERS	WOMEN TEACHERS
Capital	43.7 (96)	38.6 (101)
Large towns	47.6 (61)	53.9 (91)
Medium-sized towns	43.9 (82)	67.1 (91)
Small towns	63.6 (11)	80.9 (21)

Source: Sample Survey Data.

But however important they may consider religion, teachers in general do not attribute too much importance to a person's being of the type that "complies with religious duties." Whether this is because they consider such compliance of secondary significance or implicitly contained in the concept of being a "good citizen" (which is the quality considered most important by the majority), they do not give it priority on the scale of qualities which define a person's life and character, as reflected in the answers to the following question:

The list given here presents a series of qualities which can be said to define a person's life and character. Please indicate the relative importance of each of these qualities by numbering them from 1 to 5 in the parentheses so that the quality you consider most important will be number 1 and the least important number 5.

Being a good citizen ....( )
Being a good father (or mother) ....( )
Being competent in one's profession ....( )
Being faithful in compliance with religious
   duties ....( )
Being a person of culture ....( )

The most desirable quality in general is being a good citizen (Table IX). Curiously, however, being a good father (or mother) is reported much more favorably in the two more urbanized and economically developed states than in the others. One would have to be rash to give an interpretation of these differences, but it is possible that the

TABLE IX

Human Ideals

Percentage considering one of the attributes listed hereunder, respectively, as being the most important

ATTRIBUTE	STATE			
	RIO GRANDE DO SUL	SÃO PAULO	CEARÁ	PARÁ
	MEN TEACHERS			
Being a good citizen	29.6	38.7	51.6	47.9
Being a good father (or mother)	39.2	27.5	10.7	21.6
Fulfilling religious duties	22.3	14.3	14.6	14.9
Being competent in one's profession	9.7	13.4	22.1	16.2
Being a person of culture	1.8	7.6	4.1	3.0
TOTALS:	100.0	100.0	100.0	100.0
	(223)	(142)	(124)	(69)
	WOMEN TEACHERS			
Being a good citizen	40.5	36.2	46.2	43.5
Being a good father (or mother)	38.3	35.5	21.3	15.7
Fulfilling religious duties	15.7	15.0	23.0	23.9
Being competent in one's profession	6.1	9.4	9.5	20.4
Being a person of culture	1.8	6.6	2.7	6.1
TOTALS:	100.0	100.0	100.0	100.0
	(282)	(152)	(76)	(53)

Source: Sample Survey Data.

concern for being a good parent in the more advanced states reflects the greater tensions between parents and children in areas character-ized by rapid social change. Possibly, parent-child relations are less problematical in Ceará and Pará than in São Paulo, and teachers in the former are, therefore, less likely to focus on parental traits. These results illustrate the difficulty of using the same questionnaire items as indicators of specific societal attributes in sharply different contexts. But whatever the qualifications which should be imposed in interpreta-tions of these data, it remains true that the secondary teachers of Brazil are a very religious group.

OPINIONS CONCERNING SCHOOL OBJECTIVES

Those concerned with fostering economic development have generally suggested that the school systems of most underdeveloped nations are not well adapted to this objective, because they are more concerned with a general academic education than with vocational education. Presumably the emphasis in the educational systems of the United States, the Soviet Union, and Communist China, on preparing students for their occupational career is one which underdeveloped countries would do well to emulate. The results of this study indicate that Bra-zilian secondary schoolteachers are still to be counted among those who denigrate the vocational training role of schools. Less than 12 per cent of them accept preparation for an occupation as the principal ob-jective of secondary education (Table X).

The teachers of the highly developed state of São Paulo do not differ from those in other states in their view of the function which the sec-ondary school should fulfill in occupational training.[12]

In São Paulo, as in the other states, only a small proportion considers preparing for an occupation the most important objective of the school attended by young people aged from 12 to 18 years. Although the em-phasis on vocational training tends to be slightly greater on the part of male teachers than females, the differences between the sexes in this re-spect are not large enough to be statistically significant.

Conversely, *improvement of character* is the favored objective of more than 40 per cent of the women teachers in all four states. For the men teachers, this objective is somewhat less popular, though it re-ceived second place in the state of Ceará more support than any other objective.

This strong emphasis on improvement of character is consistent with

TABLE X

Principal Objective of Secondary Schooling

OBJECTIVE	Percentage selecting the objective specified			
		STATE		
	RIO GRANDE DO SUL	SÃO PAULO	CEARÁ	PARÁ
	MEN TEACHERS			
Improve character	37.7	20.0	17.6	35.8
Develop concept of civic responsibility	21.3	15.0	28.6	21.5
Give good general culture	16.0	28.6	22.7	18.6
Prepare for an occupation	12.9	12.1	16.8	11.4
Develop reasoning power	5.3	11.4	6.7	1.4
Prepare for university	6.7	12.9	7.6	11.4
TOTALS:	100.0	100.0	100.0	100.0
	(225)	(140)	(119)	(70)
	WOMEN TEACHERS			
Improve character	48.7	42.0	48.6	46.9
Develop concept of civic responsibility	13.6	12.7	21.8	8.5
Give good general culture	18.3	21.7	9.0	27.8
Prepare for an occupation	11.1	8.9	11.5	6.3
Develop reasoning power	5.0	8.9	6.4	2.1
Prepare for university	3.2	5.7	2.6	8.5
TOTALS:	100.0	100.0	100.0	100.0
	(279)	(157)	(78)	(47)

Source: Sample Survey Data.

the philosophy expressed by the great majority of the teachers with regard to the broader aims of scholastic education. These aims were secured by asking the teachers to choose between an education directed toward the fulfillment of national objectives, specifically economic development, and an education exclusively concerned with the individual. The issue was put to the teachers as follows:

"Education should try to counterbalance the evil consequences attending economic development for the individual and for society.

"Education should have as one of its principal aims meeting the necessities of the economic development of the country.

"Education should largely aim at the complete development of the individual, all other objectives being secondary."

As in the case of the secondary schoolteachers of Chile, to whom the same alternatives were submitted in another study, the Brazilian teachers were overwhelmingly in favor of the complete development of the individual.[13] Curiously, the teachers from the less developed northern parts of the country were more likely to be among the small minority who thought that education should "aim to meet the needs of the economic development of the nations," than were those from the more advanced south. However, women were, as might be expected, less interested in education fostering economic gains than men (Table XI).

TABLE XI

Education and Economic Development

Percentage selecting each of the formulas given below				
PURPOSE OF EDUCATION		STATE		
	RIO GRANDE DO SUL	SÃO PAULO	CEARÁ	PARÁ
	MEN TEACHERS			
Education should try to counterbalance the evil consequences accompanying economic development	2.6	4.6	5.8	5.6
Education should chiefly aim to meet the needs of the economic development of the nation	5.2	11.8	11.5	13.8
Education should strive, first and foremost, for the full development of the individual; any other objective will be secondary	92.2	83.6	82.7	80.6
TOTALS:	100.0	100.0	100.0	100.0
	(230)	(152)	(139)	(72)
	WOMEN TEACHERS			
Education should try to counterbalance the evil consequences accompanying economic development	3.8	7.1	4.9	7.5
Education should chiefly aim to meet the needs of the economic development of the nation	2.8	2.4	8.5	9.4
Education should strive, first and foremost, for the full development of the individual; any other objective will be secondary	93.4	90.4	86.6	83.1
TOTALS:	100.0	100.0	100.0	100.0
	(286)	(168)	(82)	(53)

Source: Sample Survey Data.

The principal conclusion to be drawn from these results is that interest in using the school system to further the objectives of economic growth is supported by only a tiny minority of teachers. As in the case of the importance attributed to religion, secondary schoolteachers con-

TABLE XII

Educational Level and Opinion as to Secondary School Objectives

WOMEN TEACHERS
Percentage giving priority to each of the objectives specified below
OBJECTIVE

HIGHEST LEVEL OF EDUCATION COMPLETED	Improve character	Develop concept of civic responsibility	Give good general culture	Prepare for an occupation	Develop reasoning power	Prepare for university	TOTALS 100%
Rio Grande do Sul							
Normal school	49.0	14.9	23.4	8.5	2.1	2.1	47
University	49.4	13.6	17.6	9.7	6.8	2.8	167
São Paulo							
Normal school	47.5	15.0	15.0	15.0	2.5	5.0	40
University	37.8	13.3	21.1	8.9	13.3	5.6	90
Ceará							
Normal school	51.0	20.4	6.1	14.3	4.1	4.1	49
University	43.8	25.0	12.5	6.2	12.5	—	16
Pará							
Normal school	47.3	5.3	36.8	5.3	5.3	5.3	19
University	50.0	14.3	28.6	—	—	7.1	14

Note: The sum of the two types of education completed do not make the totals which appear in other tables because women teachers who received their certificates or diplomas from institutions other than Normal school or University Faculties of Philosophy (Colleges of Arts and Sciences) are not included in this table.

Source: Sample Survey Data.

stitute a rather homogeneous group. Their points of view converge to a very decided extent, not only within the same state but also from state to state. In spite of the great distances which separate regions so different—both geographically and historically—as those of the north, northeast, and south of Brazil, the differences of opinion are negligible.

DETERMINANTS OF VALUE ORIENTATIONS—EDUCATION

The similarities in opinions among teachers from most varied parts of the country raise the possibility that the principal source of variations

TABLE XIII
Educational Level and Importance Attributed to Religion

		WOMEN TEACHERS Percentage attributing to religion the degree of importance specified below DEGREE OF IMPORTANCE				
STATE	HIGHEST LEVEL OF EDUCATION COMPLETED	Indispensable	Helpful	Does not matter	Makes difficult or prevents	TOTALS (100%)
Rio Grande do Sul	Normal school	58.0	32.0	10.0	—	50
	University	50.8	31.4	16.2	1.6	
São Paulo	Normal school	47.5	42.5	10.0	—	40
	University	34.0	39.3	24.5	2.2	94
Ceará	Normal school	38.8	42.9	16.3	2.0	49
	University	64.7	23.5	11.8	—	17
Pará	Normal school	68.2	27.3	4.5	—	22
	University	42.9	50.0	7.1	—	14

Note: The sum of the two types of education completed does not make the totals which appear in other tables because women teachers who received their certificates or diplomas from institutions other than Normal Schools or University Faculties of Philosophy (Colleges of Arts and Sciences) are not included in this table.
Source: Sample Survey Data.

in values among them may stem from their more immediate social backgrounds, e.g. level of education, social status of family, rather than macroscopic elements differentiating regions of the nation.

An examination of the relationships between educational attainment and their opinions, however, indicates no consistent pattern. As the data in Tables XII and XIII indicate, no significant differences exist between the less educated (normal school trained) and the better educated (university graduate) teachers with respect to their attitudes concerning the chief objectives which should be fostered by secondary schools or the importance which they would assign to religion in the background of a teacher.

These findings are clearly puzzling. It is possible, however, that these are attitudes so fundamental a part of a traditional society as to stem largely from deeply rooted values which are formed very early in life, and are, therefore, not likely to be much influenced by education. With this possibility in mind, I decided to shift the focus of investigation to issues which should be more subject to direct educational influences, e.g. opinions concerning specific secular factors which are presumed to be hindering progress in our country. These matters were covered by factors such as the following: [14]

> "The lack of a proper concept of civic responsibilities on the large part of much of the population.
> "The profits of merchants and manufacturers.
> "The lack of responsibility on the part of trade-union (labor union) leaders.
> "The failure of politicians to inform the public.
> "The way in which landowners retard the development of rural areas."

As can be seen in Table XIV, the variations of opinion among the states are not very large on these issues either. In all four states, about half of the teachers criticize the populace at large for lacking a proper concept of civic responsibility. The remaining responses are distributed in more or less equal proportions among those who attack merchants and manufacturers, political parties, trade-union leaders, and landowners.

In Rio Grande do Sul, criticism of the civic sense of the general population is more general among women teachers than men, while in the other states there is no sex-linked difference on this item. Some differences may be observed between men and women teachers on the other items. In three of the four states—São Paulo, Pará, and Rio Grande do Sul—the profits of merchants and manufacturers are attacked more frequently by male than by female teachers, and in the latter state some sex differences may also be noted in hostility to trade-union leaders and landowners; men are more critical of both than women.

But in spite of my expectations, opinions about the *factors hindering*

TABLE XIV

Opinions as to Factors Which Hinder Progress

Percentage of secondary schoolteachers considering as the most important
each of the factors listed below

FACTOR WHICH HINDERS PROGRESS	RIO GRANDE DO SUL	SÃO PAULO	CEARÁ	PARÁ
	MEN TEACHERS			
A large part of the population do not have a proper concept of civic responsibilities	45.2	59.6	63.0	52.9
The profits of merchants and manufacturers	17.4	17.0	13.4	22.9
The political parties do not guide the public well enough	12.9	12.0	13.4	18.6
The lack of responsibility on the part of trade-union (labor union) leaders	15.6	6.4	3.9	2.8
Landowners retard the development of rural areas	8.9	5.0	6.3	2.8
TOTALS:	100.0 (224)	100.0 (141)	100.0 (127)	100.0 (70)
	WOMEN TEACHERS			
A large part of the population do not have a proper concept of civic responsibilities	70.4	67.5	58.8	67.3
The profits of merchants and manufacturers	11.0	6.2	17.5	8.2
The political parties do not guide the public well enough	9.0	13.1	13.8	12.2
The lack of responsibility on the part of trade-union (labor union) leaders	5.9	9.4	8.8	8.2
Landowners retard the development of rural areas	3.7	3.8	1.1	4.1
TOTALS:	100.0 (290)	100.0 (160)	100.0 (80)	100.0 (49)

Source: Sample Survey Data.

TABLE XV

Educational Level and Opinion as to Factors
Which Hinder Progress

WOMEN TEACHERS

Percentage of women secondary schoolteachers considering
most important each of the factors listed below

HIGHEST LEVEL OF EDUCATION COMPLETED, BY STATES	A large part of the population do not have a proper concept of civic responsibility	Profits of merchants and manufacturers	Political parties do not guide the public well enough	Lack of responsibility on part of labor union leaders	Landowners retard development of rural areas	TOTALS (100%)
Rio Grande do Sul						
Normal school	67.3	6.1	12.3	12.3	2.0	49
University.	70.7	12.7	6.6	5.0	5.0	181
São Paulo						
Normal school	64.9	5.4	18.9	10.8	—	37
University.	74.4	5.6	4.4	10.0	—	90
Ceará						
Normal school	49.0	14.3	20.4	14.3	2.0	49
University.	81.3	12.5	6.2	—	—	16
Pará						
Normal school	90.4	4.8	—	—	4.8	21
University.	28.6	14.3	35.7	14.3	7.1	14

Note: The sum of the two types of education completed does not make the totals which appear in other tables because women teachers who received their certificates or diplomas from institutions other than Normal schools or University Faculties of Philosophy (Colleges of Arts and Sciences) are not included in this table.

Source: Sample Survey Data.

the progress of the country do not depend on relative level of education. There are no significant differences between teachers who have university degrees and those who hold no other diploma than their normal school certificate (Table XV). Thus the university level of instruction has no significance. As with attitudes concerned with morality and religion discussed earlier, level of education attained is not associated with beliefs among those engaged in secondary school teaching. It is

TABLE XVI

Socio-Economic Origin

SOCIAL STRATUM OF ORIGIN	Percentage of secondary schoolteachers coming from each social stratum			
	RIO GRANDE DO SUL	SÃO PAULO	CEARÁ	PARÁ
Upper-middle	21.5	23.2	13.5	15.9
Middle-middle	29.7	31.1	35.5	26.1
Lower-middle	29.5	26.3	39.8	40.2
Laboring	19.3	17.8	11.3	17.8
TOTALS:	100.0	100.0	100.0	100.0
	(502)	(289)	(186)	(107)

conceivable that those teachers who did not complete university courses may still have secured an intellectual outlook equivalent to those persons who received a university degree, that teaching itself is a major educational experience. It is possible, of course, that the lack of correlation reflects the weaknesses of Brazilian higher education, that our universities have little effect on students' beliefs on issues such as these.

There is, of course, still another possibility which may explain these puzzling lack of correlations, and that is variations in family background, particularly as related to social class. Fortunately, for the purposes of this analysis, the secondary school teaching body proved sufficiently diversified in social origins to permit a detailed investigation of the effects of such variations. More than half the fathers of the teachers are from the intermediate or lower ranks of the middle stratum, largely consisting of small businessmen, civil servants, office employees, and other personnel of an equivalent level. The remainder are distributed in more or less equal proportions between children of manual laborers, and the upper middle class, represented chiefly by members of the liberal professions, directors of public services, managers of large companies, and owners of large or fairly large industrial, commercial or agricultural enterprises (Table XVI).[15] To what extent

TABLE XVII

Socio-Economic Origin and Faithfulness in Religious Observance

SOCIAL STRATUM OF ORIGIN	Percentage attending religious services "regularly" or who "always try to attend"			
	RIO GRANDE DO SUL	SÃO PAULO	CEARÁ	PARÁ
	MEN TEACHERS			
Upper-middle	31.3 (16)	44.4 (9)	25.0 (12)	60.0 (10)
Middle-middle	61.9 (21)	55.5 (18)	57.6 (33)	61.5 (13)
Lower-middle	52.0 (25)	75.0 (16)	51.1 (47)	52.2 (23)
Laboring	73.0 (30)	81.9 (11)	50.0 (12)	25.0 (12)
	WOMEN TEACHERS			
Upper-middle	53.0 (34)	66.7 (21)	* (6)	* (5)
Middle-middle	47.0 (34)	43.5 (23)	87.5 (14)	60.0 (10)
Lower-middle	41.2 (17)	43.8 (16)	72.7 (8)	88.2 (17)
Laboring	50.0 (8)	* (2)	* (3)	* (5)

* Percentage not calculated because the total was too small.
Source: Sample Survey Data.

does the profile of social origin explain differences in attitude and in values?

Starting with the analysis of religious faith, we may note that among males religious devotion tends to be associated with lower social status. Among women teachers, however, no such differences exist among various classes. Females from medium and high social strata are as devout as those coming from families of manual laborers (Table XVII). These two phenomena—a relation between social origin and faithful attendance at religious services among men and an absence of any significant differences among women—may be observed primarily in the developed areas, Rio Grande do Sul and in São Paulo, but not in the two other states.

Differences due to variations in social origin are observable, then, only among the men, and even among them, these differences cannot be said to be equally pronounced in all four states.

Moreover, insofar as the degree of importance attributed to religion as a guiding principle of teaching is concerned, no reliable pattern of difference attributable to social origin can be distinguished, either in the case of men teachers or that of women (Tables XVIII and XIX). In Table XIX the data concerning men teachers are reported for the entire state of Rio Grande do Sul, since, as previously stated, the degree of religious faith among men does not vary with the size of the town. Nor are there significant variations between social classes with regard to ideal human qualities. As can be seen from Table XX, the number of times that the various attributes are mentioned is not related to the teacher's social background.

On the whole, while the teacher's religious behavior and beliefs, as well as his or her concept of the ideal qualities, do not depend on the social position of the family from which he or she came, it cannot necessarily be infered that the teacher's convictions about the objectives of schooling are unaffected by the education which he or she received prior to becoming a teacher. It is conceivable that schooling means different things to persons from different social backgrounds. Having

TABLE XVIII

Socio-Economic Origin and Importance Attributed to Religion
by Secondary Schoolteachers

Percentage who consider a religious belief important ("indispensable" or
"helpful") for fulfillment of the teacher's work

SOCIAL STRATUM OF ORIGIN	PORTO ALEGRE	SÃO PAULO	FORTALEZA	BELÉM
	MEN TEACHERS			
Upper-middle	56.3 (16)	77.7 (9)	25.0 (12)	50.0 (10)
Middle-middle	71.4 (21)	72.3 (18)	44.1 (34)	64.3 (14)
Lower-middle	80.0 (25)	81.3 (16)	32.0 (47)	30.5 (23)
Laboring	79.9 (30)	72.7 (11)	8.3 (12)	16.7 (12)
	WOMEN TEACHERS			
Upper-middle	64.7 (34)	81.9 (22)	* (6)	* (5)
Middle-middle	67.6 (34)	69.6 (23)	31.3 (16)	30.0 (10)
Lower-middle	82.3 (17)	68.8 (16)	45.5 (11)	41.2 (17)
Laboring	* (8)	* (2)	* (3)	* (5)

* Percentage not calculated because the total was too small.
Source: Sample Survey Data.

started from disparate origins, the various groups of teachers would probably have varying concepts of the ideal functions of the school. It is easy to imagine, for example, that vocational training would have much greater interest for teachers who are children of manual laborers

TABLE XIX

Socio-Economic Origin and Importance Attributed to Religion by Men Teachers in the State of Rio Grande do Sul

Percentage who consider a religious belief "indispensable" for good fulfillment of the teacher's work

SOCIAL STRATUM OF ORIGIN	MEN TEACHERS
Upper-middle	41.7 (36)
Middle-middle	27.9 (61)
Lower-middle	57.2 (75)
Laboring	42.2 (52)

Source: Sample Survey Data.

and who have risen in the social scale through their own vocational qualifications, than for teachers from higher strata. And, conversely, that the latter should think more frequently than the former of objectives such as *general culture* and *improvement of character*.

Nevertheless, these inferences are not confirmed by the statements of

TABLE XX

Socio-Economic Origin and Concept of Ideal Human Qualities on the Part of Men Teachers of the State of Rio Grande do Sul

SOCIAL STRATUM OF ORIGIN	IDEAL HUMAN QUALITIES					
	Good citizen	Good father or mother	Faithful in religious duties	Competent in profession	Cultured person	TOTALS (100%)
Upper-middle	21.0	21.0	21.0	16.0	21.0	19
Middle-middle	37.1	28.6	5.7	20.0	8.6	35
Lower-middle	50.0	21.9	15.7	9.4	3.0	32
Laboring	35.0	25.0	20.0	20.0	10.0	40

Source: Sample Survey Data.

the teachers questioned (Table XXI). There is no significant variation in attitudes toward vocational qualifications which are related to
differences in social origin.

In general, therefore, it would seem that differences in viewpoints on
various issues have nothing to do with the varying socio-economic origins or educational attainments of the teachers.

It is difficult to believe that attitudes regarding matters such as those
studied here should not be colored by the experiences to which the individual was exposed because of his or her family origin or by degree
of education.

TABLE XXI

Socio-Economic Origin and Opinion as to
the Objectives of Secondary Education

MEN TEACHERS

Percentage considering most important each of the objectives given below

SOCIAL STRATUM
OF ORIGIN
AND STATE   SECONDARY SCHOOL OBJECTIVES

	Improve character	Develop concept of civic responsi- bility	Give good general culture	Prepare for an occupa- tion	Develop reasoning power	Prepare for univer- sity	TOTALS 100%
Rio Grande do Sul							
Upper-middle	30.3	18.2	12.1	15.1	6.1	18.2	33
Middle-middle	25.0	25.0	17.3	15.4	13.5	3.8	52
Lower-middle	43.2	16.4	22.4	8.9	3.0	8.9	67
Laboring	47.9	20.8	12.5	12.5	2.1	4.2	48
São Paulo							
Upper-middle	27.8	5.6	50.0	5.6	—	11.1	18
Middle-middle	15.8	21.0	21.0	10.5	13.2	18.4	38
Lower-middle	27.6	24.0	20.7	6.9	10.4	10.3	29
Laboring	11.4	11.4	37.8	11.4	14.3	14.3	35

TABLE XXI (continued)
Socio-Economic Origin and Opinion as to
the Objectives of Secondary Education

SOCIAL STRATUM
OF ORIGIN
AND STATE   SECONDARY SCHOOL OBJECTIVES

	Improve character	Develop concept of civic responsi- bility	Give good general culture	Prepare for an occupa- tion	Develop reasoning power	Prepare for univer- sity	TOTALS 100%
Ceará							
Upper- middle	—	35.7	28.6	14.3	14.3	7.1	14
Middle- middle	16.1	32.3	19.4	9.7	6.4	16.1	31
Lower- middle	15.2	26.1	26.1	21.7	6.5	4.3	46
Laboring	27.3	36.4	9.1	—	—	9.1	11
Pará							
Upper- middle	70.0	20.0	—	—	—	10.0	10
Middle- middle	53.8	7.7	15.4	7.7	—	15.4	13
Lower- middle	27.3	13.7	27.3	22.7	—	9.1	22
Laboring	27.3	45.5	—	9.1	9.1	9.1	11

Source: Sample Survey Data.

It is possible that the absence of expected relationships may be a result of inadequate measuring instruments. The type of questions which
have been used as the dependent variables, those which deal with attitudes on various issues, have been shown to be correlated with variation in social background in studies which deal with total national or
community populations, i.e. from poor to rich, from illiterates to university graduates. On the independent variable side, one would certainly anticipate differences between those who went to university and
those who did not.

The method utilized for determining socio-economic origins is a sensitive one and the categories established thereby should be valid ones. The same method produced quite plausible results when used in a study based on student jobs within the various branches of secondary education.[16]

The source of the analytic difficulties may lie in the fact that we are dealing with relatively homogeneous occupational groups working for similar employers, receiving comparable pay, and having similar status. The similarities in their position are probably more exaggerated in a country like Brazil, where only two out of every 1000 attend university, than in other educationally more fortunate nations. Regardless of social origin, to attend university or even normal school in Brazil places those who do so in a very special position. They are among the educational elite of the country. Those of modest origin who have succeeded in the quest for higher education must constitute a very special group among those with similar backgrounds. Hence any effort to differentiate conventionally among teachers by the simple indicator of parental background seemingly fails. Further analysis of this group clearly requires use of a much more subtle set of variables.[17]

One approach which may be extremely useful in accounting for internal variations among these teachers is the *reference group* concept.[18] In the context of this analysis, it may be suggested that the status of the reference group of teachers of more modest origins, or of those who attended normal school rather than university, may be as high or higher as those from more privileged backgrounds.[19] Hence unless we know something about the varying reference groups or those with similar objective backgrounds, it may be impossible to distinguish the effects of such variations. The results of this study point up the need for detailed social psychological investigation in underdeveloped countries, like Brazil, of the differences between members of the elite who are upwardly mobile as contrasted with those from elite backgrounds. The very fact that the elite is so small proportionately may make the task of analysis and the results of investigations quite different from those in more industrialized and urbanized societies whose elite is much more numerous, absolutely and proportionately.

III. Conclusion

This essay has had two aims: first, to assemble data providing a general picture of the attitudes prevailing among the secondary school teaching body, as those most involved in training the elite; and, second, to discover differences of attitudes among them which might indicate changing orientations.

Some differences of attitude were indeed brought out in the course of our analysis. Of particular importance is the finding concerning the continued strength of religious belief among this highly educated stratum of secondary teachers, and the fact that those in the more developed parts of the country were somewhat more secularized than those in the less industrialized regions. And as might be expected, from results around the world, sex proved to be a more or less constant source of variations in opinions. Women were more concerned with religion and more likely to adhere to local cultural patterns. Sex differences apart, however, individual variations in background—social origin and level of education—did not differentiate opinions.

On the basis of these observations the following predictions can tentatively be made: (1) Merely increasing the level of education of secondary grade teachers will not be conducive to changing their attitudes significantly; (2) it is unlikely that any significant change will occur if the strata in society from which the teachers come are changed; [20] (3) significant changes, however, may result if more women enter the field of secondary school teaching. Women teachers themselves, however, change somewhat by becoming more like their male colleagues, as the data concerning the influence of city life in the state of Rio Grande do Sul would seem to indicate. Even at the present time, the differences between the sexes are not very pronounced and in the final analysis their similarities are more noticeable than their divergences.

Although the results of this investigation may seem disappointing to those who like to find neat and conclusive relationships between diverse "objective" factors and attitudes, they are important for their implications for the prospects for modernization in Brazil. Basically, if we think of the study as a portrait of a segment of the elite whose role in producing new generations of the elite is very important, the findings are pessimistic with regard to prospects for modernization. Clearly, the secondary schoolteachers of Brazil, as reflected by these data, are relatively traditionalist in outlook. They remain committed to the predominant influence of religion; they are not prepared to place a high value on economic development; they have a fairly traditional outlook of the function of education as a form of character building. These questions, however, only begin to skim the surface of the problem. What is clearly needed is a variety of surveys which tell us in much more detail what various other influential, or potentially influential, segments of the Latin American elite are really like. Thus it may be hoped that the limitations of this research will help others who seek to study other branches of the teaching profession, including university faculties, students in secondary schools and universities, professionals in other areas of life, businessmen, civil servants, politicians, and the like. To understand where Latin America is going, we need to know what the embryonic and actual members of the Latin American elites are thinking and doing in as reliable and scientific a fashion as possible.

Notes

1. Estimates for 1959 show the following numbers for the larger professional groups: 52,518 lawyers, 35,227 doctors, and 26,241 dentists. See Américo Barbosa de Oliveira and José Zacarías Sá Carvalho, *A Formação do Pessoal de Nível Superior* (The Training of Higher Level Personnel) (Rio de Janeiro: CAPES, 1960). In that year, according to the Statistical Service of the Ministry of Education and Culture in *Sinopse Estatística do Ensino Médio* (Statistical Synopsis of Secondary Education), 1959, the number of secondary schoolteachers in Brazil was 67,214.
2. *Sinopse Estatística do Ensino Médio,* 1962, published by the Statistical Service of the Ministry of Education and Culture, Rio de Janeiro.
3. Estimates of the part played by demographic growth are to be found in the *Plano Trienal de Desenvolvimento Econômico e Social 1963–1965,* published by the Office of the President of the Republic (December, 1962).
4. According to data collected in a survey conducted in 1961–62 in the city of Rio de Janeiro, which is probably the town having the highest educational average in Brazil, approximately one-half (48.8%) of all commercial office employees engaged as bill-clerks, adding-machine operators, secretaries, typists, bookkeepers' and accountants' assistants, file-clerks, etc., had not even completed the first level of secondary school (equivalent U.S. junior high school). See *Distribuição e Composição Ocupacional no Comércio Brasileiro* (Occupational Distribution and Components in Brazilian Business) (Rio de Janeiro: National Commercial Apprenticeship Service, 1963).
5. The following were the proportions that teachers of academic courses represented out of the total number of secondary-level teachers in 1962, according to the *Sinopse Estatística do Ensino Médio:*

Ceará	74.1%
Pará	4.2%
Rio Grande do Sul	61.6%
São Paulo	61.3%
Brazil	63.8%

6. This statement is based on the fact that academic schools have the best educated teachers and pupils of the highest social level. See Aparecida Joly Gouveia, "O Nivel de Instrução dos Professôres do Ensino Médio" (The Educational Level of Secondary Schoolteachers), in *Pesquisa e Planejamento,* No. 7 (December, 1963), São Paulo, Regional Educational Research Center.

7. See Aparecida Joly Gouveia, "Desenvolvimento Econômico e Mudanças na Composição do Magistério de Nivel Médio" (Economic Development and Changes in the Composition of the Secondary School Teaching Body), *Sociologia,* 26 (December, 1963).

8. On the basis of our data, at least 50 per cent of secondary schoolteachers have completed a university education, while official statistics show that barely 0.2 per cent of the total population of Brazil even reach the point of enrolling in an institution of university level. See *Plano Trienal,* p. 91.

9. In this essay, the term "significant" indicates that the X^2 Test suggested the rejection of the hypothesis voided with a probability of error of 5 per cent.

10. The teachers were asked the following question:
"In your opinion, what is the importance of religious belief for a good performance of the teaching profession?
Please Check one of the following:
Indispensable
Helpful
Does not matter
Makes more difficult
Prevents."
This question and others which provided material for this work were taken from a questionnaire used by K. H. Silvert and Frank Bonilla in a study conducted with Chilean teachers. We wish to express our thanks to those investigators for having allowed us to use their formulas.

11. See Wilbert E. Moore, "Industrialization and Social Change," in Bert F. Hoselitz and Wilbert E. Moore (eds.), *Industrialization and Society* (Paris: UNESCO—Mouton, 1963), pp. 352–353.

12. This matter was put to the teachers in the following manner: "In your opinion, what should be the principal aims of schools intended for pupils aged 12 to 18 years? Of course, these aims could be numerous. We therefore ask you to indicate in the list given below the two (TWO ONLY) aims which you consider the most important and around the number 2 to indicate the second in importance:

	Most important	Second in importance
Prepare for university	1	2
Develop the concept of civic responsibility	1	2
Improve the individual's character	1	2
Give a good general culture	1	2
Prepare for an occupation	1	2
Develop reasoning power	1	2
Any other aim? Which?"		

In this analysis, only the answers marked number 1 are considered.

13. The consensus on this point is even greater in Brazil than in Chile, where 70 per cent of the secondary schoolteachers questioned "chose alternative 'b,' that the educator's chief responsibility is to the individual rather than to national economic needs and responsibilities." See K. H. Silvert and Frank Bonilla, *Education and the Social Meaning of Development: A Preliminary Statement* (New York: American Universities Field Staff, 1961, mimeo), p. 79.

14. The teachers were asked for their views: "In your opinion, which of the following factors make the progress of our country more difficult? Please indicate two (ONLY TWO) factors which you believe are the most serious or harmful. Draw a circle around Number 1 to indicate the most serious of all, and around Number 2 to indicate the next most serious."

15. Socio-economic origin was determined by using a slightly modified version of the classification system utilized by Hutchinson and his collaborators in studies of social mobility in São Paulo. Bertram Hutchinson, *Mobilidade e Trabalho* (Rio de Janeiro: Educational Research Center of the Ministry of Education and Culture, 1960).

16. This study is a part of the project on Secondary Education and the Socio-Economic Structure mentioned in the initial footnote, p. 484.

17. The relationship between intellectual ability and socio-economic level has been recorded in studies performed in various countries, including Brazil. See, for example, Kenneth Eells *et al., Intelligence and Cultural Differences* (Chicago: University of Chicago Press, 1951); Jean Floud and A. H. Halsey, "Intelligence, Social Class and Selection for Secondary Schools," *British Journal of Sociology,* 8 (1957), pp. 33–39; Henry Clay Lindgren and Hilda de Almeida Guedes, "Social Status, Intelligence and Educational Achievement among Elementary and Secondary Students in Brazil," *Journal of Social Psychology,* 60 (1963), pp. 9–14.

18. The "reference group" theory has been studied by a number of sociologists and social psychologists. See, for example, Tamotsu Shibutani, "Reference Groups as Perspectives," *American Journal of Sociology,* 60 (1955), pp. 563 ff., and Robert K. Merton, "Contributions to the Theory of Reference Group Behavior" (especially the part entitled "Reference Group Theory and Social Mobility"), in *Social*

Theory and Social Structure (New York: The Free Press of Glencoe, 1963).

19. Joseph A. Kahl, "Educational and Occupational Aspirations of 'Common Man' Boys," *Harvard Educational Review,* 23 (Summer, 1953), pp. 186–203, shows that in the United States family pressures can make students of modest origin acquire educational and professional aspirations which are not common among students of their socio-economic level.

20. Indications of change in the social strata from which teachers are recruited are presented by this author in "Economic Development and Changes in the Composition of the Teaching Staff of Secondary Schools in Brazil," *Social and Economic Studies,* 14, No. 1 (March, 1965), pp. 118–130.

Notes on Contributors

Frank Bonilla, a sociologist, is Professor of Political and Social Science at M.I.T. He has recently completed a book (with Myron Glazer) on the Chilean student movement which will be published soon. He has also written (with Kalman Silvert) *Education and the Social Meaning of Development*.

Fernando H. Cardoso is currently doing research at the Latin American Institute of Economic and Social Planning in Santiago, Chile. Before leaving Brazil in 1964, he was Professor of Sociology at the University of São Paulo. His books include *Empresário Industrial e desenvolvimento econômico no Brasil* and *Escravidão e Capitalismo no Brasil Meridional*.

Aparecida Joly Gouveia is Professor of Educational Sociology at the University of São Paulo, Brazil. She has written widely on the sociology of education.

Irving Louis Horowitz is Professor of Sociology at Washington University at St. Louis. He is also co-editor of *Trans-action*. Among his various publications are: *Three Worlds of Development, Revolution in Brazil, The War Game,* and *Radicalism and the Revolt against Reason*.

Henry A. Landsberger is Professor of Sociology at the New York School of Labor and Industrial Relations of Cornell University. He has published *Hawthorne Revisited* and many articles on the labor movement in Latin America.

Seymour Martin Lipset is Professor of Government and Social Relations and a member of the Executive Committee of the Center for International Affairs at Harvard University. Among his publications are: *Agrarian Socialism, Union Democracy, Social Mobility in Industrial Society, Political Man*, and *The First New Nation*.

Aníbal Quijano Obregón is currently on leave in Santiago, Chile, from his Professorship of Sociology at the University of San Marcos in Lima, Peru. He has written widely on peasant movements in Latin America.

Luis Ratinoff, a Chilean sociologist, is Director of the Instituto de Ciencias para el Desarrollo of the National University in Bogotá, Colombia. He has written many articles on problems of development.

Darcy Ribeiro is currently teaching anthropology at the University of Montevideo in Uruguay. Prior to leaving Brazil in 1964, he was Rector of the University of Brasilia; he also served as Minister of Education for Brazil. Among his books are *A Universidade e a Nação* and *A Política Indigenista Brasileira*.

Luis Scherz-García is Professor of Sociology at the Catholic University, Santiago, Chile. He has published *Una nueva universidad para América Latina*.

Robert E. Scott is Professor of Political Science at the University of Illinois. He has recently completed a book on student movements in Peru and Mexico. He has also published *Mexican Government in Transition*.

Glaucio Ary Dillon Soares, a Brazilian sociologist, is Director of the Latin American School of Sociology (FLACSO) at Santiago, Chile. His book *Economic Development and Political Radicalism* will appear soon.

Aldo Solari, Professor of Sociology and Director of the Institute of Social Science, University of the Republic of Uruguay, is working at the Economic Commission for Latin America (CEPAL) in Santiago. He has written various books including *Sociología rural nacional, La sociedad uruguaya, Sociología rural latinoamericana, El tercerismo en el Uruguay.*

Ivan Vallier, formerly Associate Professor of Sociology at Columbia University, is currently Associate Director of the Institute of International Studies at the University of California, Berkeley. He is working on a book on religion in Latin America. He has written *Anglican Opportunities in Latin America.*

Kenneth Walker is Assistant Professor of Sociology at the University of Toronto. He has recently completed a monograph on the Colombian and Argentinian student movements.

Name Index

518

Subject Index